THE WHITE TRIBE

ROBIN MOORE

Affiliated Writers of America/Publishers

Encampment, Wyoming

Printed in the United States of America

Edited by Jay Fraser

This novel is a work of fiction.

THE WHITE TRIBE. Copyright © 1991 by Robin Moore. All rights reserved, including the right to reproduce this book or portions thereof without prior written permission from the editor. All inquiries should be addressed to Permissions Editor, Affiliated Writers of America, Box 343, Encampment, Wyoming 82325, U.S.A.

Published by

Affiliated Writers of America, Inc.
P.O. Box 343
Encampment, Wyoming 82325

ISBN: 1-879915-03-0
Library of Congress Catalog Number: 91-76713

To the Crippled Eagles killed in Rhodesia fighting,
each in their own way,
for a cause in which they totally believed.
Among them are:

Trooper Joe Byrne (New Jersey)
Trooper Gary Dwyer (Massachussetts)
Sergeant Hugh McCall (New York)
David Cordell (Rhodesian, attached to Crippled Eagles Club)
Major "Spike" Powell (Australian)
Major Andre Dennison (British)
Sergeant Clive Mason (British)
Lord Richard Cecil (British journalist)
Sarah Webb Barrell (American journalist)

Foreword

THE WHITE TRIBE is the historical and political sequel to THE GREEN BERETS. It is the story of the betrayal of pro-Western Rhodesia to the "stabilizing" communists in Africa. Ironically, these "stabilizers" came to power through the most inhumane terrorism—vividly portrayed in this story—and remain in power as a one-party totalitarian government.

Several hundred former Green Berets, Marines, and other American combat veterans joined the fight being waged by black and white Rhodesians for a democratic moderate black government instead of the dictator who rules today, twelve years after the Carter Administration insisted on—and finally installed—Robert Mugabe in Zimbabwe. These American fighting men, harrassed by the Carter State Department in thrall to the black vote so vital to Jimmy Carter's re-election, called themselves Crippled Eagles and are indeed heir to the traditions of The Green Berets whose motto they adopted—*De Oppresso Liber*—to free the oppressed.

THE WHITE TRIBE is a work of fiction based on events in Rhodesia, now Zimbabwe, from 1976 to 1979. A number of historical personalities who helped shape the destiny of Rhodesia appear in the following pages and play their own roles as accurately as the author has been able to recreate them. These true-life figures are Lieutenant

Colonel Ron Reid-Daley, U.S. Amabassador to the United Nations Andrew Young, British Foreign Secretary David Owen, U.S. Ambassador to Zambia Stephen Lowe, Brigadier General Derry MacIntyre, and among the Africans, Bishop Abel Muzorewa, Robert Mugabe, Joshua Nkomo, Rex Nhongo, General Joshiah Tongogara, Eddison Svobgo, and Callistus Ndlovu.

All other characters are fictional and the product of the author's imagination, although their creation was designed to present a holistic view of the four fateful years in which Rhodesia changed from a British colony that unilaterally declared independence from the mother country to the totalitarian state which it has become. And as I write this Foreword, I am painfully conscious that what happened in Rhodesia may be repeated in South Africa.

Some individuals closely acquainted with the setting and action of this novel will undoubtedly claim that many of these fictional characters are merely thinly disguised portraits of real people whom the author met in southern Africa, Britain and the United States during the four years it took to research and write this book. It may go some way toward preempting this criticism if I point out that after the publication of my earlier novel, *The Green Berets,* there were no fewer than five officers who claimed to be a single character in that fictional work.

Throughout I have tried assiduously to obey the dictum of France's greatest writer of realism, Honoré de Balzac: "A storyteller must never forget that it is his business to do justice to every party."

— ROBIN MOORE

Preface

It was a shocking, horrifying sight, staring up into the sky and watching the Iraqi helicopters swooping down on the fleeing Kurdish rebels. Each time they pulled up for another strafing run the choppers left rows of bloody, twisted, destroyed bodies of moments-before staunch freedom fighters and their women, children, and old people writhing in the sandy dirt beyond the city of Irbil. Fixed wing Iraqi fighter planes backed up the choppers, diving down and raining bombs and heavy machine-gun fire on the army of tribesmen futilely firing up at the rain of death from the sky.

Roger Masefield nodded to his three fellow journalists and the Kurdish smuggler they had hired as guide, interpreter, and driver of their rented car. The Kurds' movement to take back their ancient lands from the murderous regime of Iraqi dictator Saddam Hussein was fast withering. Discretion was clearly the better part of valor and getting out of the path of the advancing Iraqi Republican Guards the order of the day.

By sunset the reporters had worked their way out of the barren valley and up the humanity-clogged, muddy, all but impassable roads, into the mountains. Here the Kurdish strongholds had been impervious to government troop deployments until the arrival of the helicopter gunships.

The reporters and their guide paused up in the mountain fastness and looked down at the surviving Kurdish guerrilla fighters under constant air harassment struggling to reach the mountains before the government tanks and armored personnel carriers now protected by war planes could catch up and crush them. The gray bearded guide, wearing a turban and smock, his pantaloons thrust into aging and cracked leather boots, spoke English, the common language of the smugglers and traders along the gulf coast. "I wish your 'Boosh,'" as he pronounced the United States President's name, "could see this. He tells us throw out Saddam and does not even keep his promise to make the airplanes stay on the ground."

"Never trust an American political promise," Roger Masefield growled. "I saw what happened to the Hungarians in 1956 when they believed President Ike. The Cuban rebels believed Jack Kennedy in 1962 when he promised them air support at the Bay of Pigs. They were destroyed when the president reneged. How many times did the White House go back on promises to our own troops in Vietnam?"

"How the hell old are you, Roger?" a young reporter asked.

"Even older than Peter Arnett," Roger replied with a sad smile. His hair would have been gray-white were it not for the supply of Grecian Formula he carried with him and although he kept himself looking trim his legs weren't what they had been when he covered Vietnam and a decade later the Rhodesian war in Southern Africa.

"And you're tramping through the mountains with us?"

"I covered the Kurds for my book on the gulf back in 1970. I couldn't miss this latest episode."

Wearily Roger gestured toward Iran to the east. "The U.S. joined with the Shah to arm and train Barzini and his Kurds on the Iran-Iraq border. We were all interested in keeping the Iraqi government at that time off balance. Then when we found ourselves cozying up to Baghdad we cut the Kurds off and left Barzini twisting in the wind."

Roger shrugged and looked off towards the exploding artillery and bombs in the valley below. "So I can't say I'm surprised that 'Boosh,'" he imitated the accent, "invited them to have a go at Saddam and then left them naked again. But I had to see it for myself."

Roger stared down at the sporadic battle below. "I don't want to be an alarmist but our government doesn't have a very good record on getting hostages released. I suggest we get out of here and head north into Turkey."

"Damn, I wish there was some way I could file this story," another reporter muttered.

"If we don't get out of here about now you may never file another story again," Roger urged. "I never thought the Kurds would cave in. But then they were promised there would be no Iraqi airpower." He turned to their uneasy guide and repeated his sentiment concerning moving out quickly. The guide nodded his cloth bound head and stood up, the others wearily following suit.

All that night they forced their vehicle through the rain-sodden roads in the mountainous northern-most region of Iraq hoping to reach the Silopi township region on the Turkish border before daylight when the Iraqi gunships would once again hawk-like hunt them down and kill as many Kurds as possible on the ground before they could slip across the border to safety.

Countless times the journalists jumped out of their worn out car to push the vehicle out of the mud. It was a grueling trip for even a young man and Roger would never see sixty again. Still, he had managed to keep himself in good shape for just such journalistic and literary eventualities as this. They were in sight of Turkey when the sun rose that chill early April morning. The Kurds were huddled miserably in the cold and mud, an entire family sharing one blanket. With daylight came the chuffing sound of the Iraqi gunships on their death mission against the Kurdish refugees who had dared to contend Saddam Hussein for their freedom.

The exhausted reporters, their guide, and the swarm of Kurdish refugees ventured out into the open area that marked the desolate border region. To their horror the armed helicopters began blasting away indiscriminately at the refugees attempting to flee across the open space which had been hacked out of the foliage and trees giving the Turkish border guards an unobstructed view of all traffic approaching from Iraq.

To have hidden out waiting for another nightfall would have been suicide with the Republican Guards closing up on them from the rear. But venturing into the wide, cleared strip running along the border would present an inviting target to the Iraqi gunships. With time running out Roger Masefield suggested that the reporters move eastward, away from the surging mass of Kurdish refugees which was keeping the helicopters occupied and then make a dash for it to a Turkish border post.

For two hours they moved toward the three-way meeting point of the Iranian, Iraqi, and Turkish boundary lines and then, separated by several miles from the largest mass of Kurdish refugees, they dashed out from the tree line and across the cleared area. Roger and several other reporters carried American flags which they waved at the Turkish border guards impassively watching their progress.

An Iraqi gunship left the field of slaughter to the west and sped down the open swath of land running parallel to the border but by the time it came within firing range of the reporters they were too close to the border post for the Iraqis to chance an international incident by firing their weapons.

The Turks were amazed to see the American passports but formalities were soon observed and arrangements made for the writers to travel to their various embassies in Ankara. Then the eyewitness stories by the reporters of the fall of the Kurdish rebellion could be filed and the journalists would be off for their next destination.

At Ankara's Grand Bayuk Hotel Roger Masefield checked in and then made the rounds of the various news agencies to feed the press all the color he could add to the other reporters' accounts. By arranging for his name to be inserted into as many of the war dispatches as possible he was building an awareness of his next book in the press and thus with the book publishing community. The notoriety would be of help to his literary agent in negotiating contracts. Roger added his personal observations of American betrayal of the rebel movement against Saddam that the President of the United States had encouraged.

At the Associated Press bureau Roger gathered up a handful of world-wide news telexes and finding a fold-up chair he opened it and sat down to examine what had been happening in the world in the past week.

There were political killings taking place in Albania as the decommunizing process continued. Roger looked for some sign that the legal King of Albania, Zak, and his Australian-born Queen might be trying to return and rule his native land. Roger thought back to Rhodesia in 1979 where Zak had established residence on a large and remote farm and was reputed to be training a crew of mercenaries to invade Albania and restore the monarchy. Such was the stuff of which novels were made and Roger had spent many hours with His and Her Royal Highness at the Monomatopa Hotel in Salisbury.

What caught his eye as he sifted through the news reports were the accounts of bloody black-on-black fighting in the Republic of South Africa. As he briefed himself on the recent events of the world he became increasingly convinced that the book he had planned to write on the Gulf War and its aftermath would be redundant what with all the writers who had been out here and were busily telling their stories.

The more he read the AP dispatches from Johannesburg and Durban the more curious he became about the situation down there. A predictable three-way struggle was unfolding in RSA similar in some respects to what was going on in Iraq. The dominant white minority government, weakened by years of world-wide sanctions, was well into the process of sharing power with the blacks. The two main factions, Nelson Mandela's African National Congress made up predominately of the Xosha Tribe and Chief Buthelezi's Zulus were waging a power struggle, hacking each other to death with machetes and shooting each other in daily and nightly encounters. Each of the two black factions was positioning itself to take over power in the vacuum left when the whites either voluntarily or otherwise relinquished their dominance over the nation.

In many ways the situation in South Africa was a reflection of what was going on around him in Iraq. Now removed from the sounds and fury of the genocidal destruction of the Kurdish people desperately fleeing gunships, artillery, and rapacious Iraqi troops Roger took a more rational view of what he had seen.

It would have been so easy, so riskless, for the President of the United States to order the Iraqi gunships to stay on the ground. One death-spewing Iraqi aerial gun platform shot down by the constantly patrolling allied war planes would unmistakably make the point.

But in protecting the New World Order which the President advocated, was there merit in allowing the militant Kurds in the north and fractious Shiites in the south the opportunity to wage an unending three-way war? After all, the Shiites were the very sect that had installed the fanatical Ayatollahs in Tehran and overrun the American Embassy and the Shiites were still holding Western hostages captured in Lebanon.

In the vacuum created by the demise of the Iraqi central government, the Kurds and Shiites would be at each other's throats battling for ultimate power even as they both turned the tables on the minority

Iraqis which now controlled the government and liquidated great masses of Sunii in a pincer movement from the north and the south. This would surely have happened if the allies had totally destroyed the Iraqi military.

As Roger cogitated on the scene in the relative tranquility of Ankara he had to recognize the practical, if cynical, approach that the administration in Washington was taking to the situation as it now existed.

Eventually, if left to its own devices, the government of Iraq would stabilize and Saddam Hussein's elimination achieved. The Kurds and Shiites in the north and south respectively were currently being decimated, subdued for at least another generation. The massacre of rebel Shiites and Kurds would soon be forgotten and an Iraq that could be easily dealt with by the Western Bloc of nations was on the verge of emerging.

Roger Masefield decided to return to South Africa. The situation there clearly reflected the Gulf. Two tribal groupings were fighting each other for ultimate power with the ebbing minority government trying to maintain stability in the nation.

If wisdom had prevailed in the Carter Administration during the Rhodesian situation the bloody wars between the Zulus, the Shonas, and the White Tribe could have ended with a stable, democratic, black majority-ruled and white-advised government. Instead, Zimbabwe emerged as a one-party communist dictatorship employing a North Korean battalion to train the army in the ruthless suppression of all opposition. And even the occasional massacre of whites was tacitly condoned.

From Ankara Roger sent out cables to his key contacts and friends in Durban and Johannesburg. Then he went about the arduous process of booking flights to sanction-tangled South Africa from Ankara to Cairo to Nairobi and finally into Durban.

The trip required a one night layover in Nairobi but on a delightfully warm, early April day, he finally stepped off the Air India flight and took a cab to the Durban Beach Hotel where he regularly stayed. To his delight he found messages from several old friends. Mike Hoare, "Mad Mike" as he was sometimes called, the famous mercenary leader was out of prison and looking forward to meeting him. Most important was the message from Mack Hudson. He and Ron Reid-Daley would be by for drinks at five. And yes, Reid-Daley still had his chief of security job for "The Man" up in Swaziland. Mack and others of the old Rhodesian gang were working for Ron.

By the time Mack Hudson and Ron Reid-Daley arrived at his room Roger had brought out one of the bottles of Johnnie Walker Black Label he purchased in Nairobi and had ordered up soda, ice, and glasses to his beach-view room.

Ron Reid-Daley still wore the genial look on his face that had always characterized him, even when he was angry and frustrated, as Lt. Colonel Reid-Daley, commanding officer of the Selous Scouts in Rhodesia a dozen years before. Mack Hudson, Reid-Daley's American former battalion commander, at six feet three or four inches tall towered over the Rhodesian. Both were wearing safari suits that looked like uniforms when they arrived at the appointed time and greeted Roger warmly. Without a word they helped themselves to the scotch and once seated, glasses in hand, they looked at Roger expectantly.

"And what brings you back to Durban?" Reid-Daley asked. "From your cable I gather you were in the thick of things in Turkey. I suppose you were covering the Kurdish debacle."

"I was. But the die is cast. America has insured that the current government stay in power. The Kurds and the Shiites are finished." Roger poured himself a drink. "I got to reading about the tribal warfare here and figured this is where the story is. The Zulus and Mandela's ANC are hacking each other up as the white tribe gets closer to sharing power. It looks to me like a decisive battle between Mandela goon squads and Chief Buthelezi's Zulu Inkatha brigades is eminent."

"You want to see the scouts I train for the Chief in action?" Ron Reid-Daley asked.

"That's the idea. I want to do a major piece comparing the internal affairs in South Africa and Iraq."

"Don't forget Rhodesia," Mack Hudson urged.

"That would be impossible," Roger declared. "Rhodesia was the mother of factional wars where the outcome is finally decided by the U.S. And look what the Zimbabwe created by Jimmy Carter and Andrew Young did recently at the United Nations, voting alongside communist Cuba and Yemen against humanitarian aide to the Kurds."

Ron Reid-Daley nodded in agreement. "Well, I believe there is going to be a bit of a punch-up tomorrow when the Zulus go after a militant bunch of Mandela's people on the outskirts of Durban."

"I have never met Chief Buthelezi," Roger commented.

"I'll arrange it," Reid-Daley promised. "Meanwhile what ever happened to the book you wrote about all of us during the Rhodesia terrorist war? The war we lost thanks to English and American interference."

"I plan to rewrite and finally publish it," Roger replied. "What happened in Rhodesia was the microcosm of the world-wide revolutionary macrocosm. It presaged, on a smaller scale, what I just saw in Iraq and what we are seeing right here in South Africa. I thought of Rhodesia constantly when I was in Central America during the Iran-Contra fiasco and the Iraq scene also brought it back."

"Well, why don't you stay right here and write it," Ron Reid-Daley urged. "Most everybody from the Rhodesian war who is still alive can be found here. And we have direct ties to the terrorists"—Ron Reid-Daley laughed bitterly—"pardon me, the statesmen in Zimbabwe, who led the revolution. Our friend, Nyati whom we should have killed when we had the chance, would talk to you by phone from Harare, as they now call Salisbury, where he's Minister of Safety."

"That's right, Roger." Mack Hudson was getting excited. "Quite a few of the chaps from the Rhodesian Special Air Service are around."

"We can fix you up with a nice place to live and even a new IBM word processor," Ron Reid-Daley pursued. "Now is the time to tell the story of Rhodesia as only you can. While we still have most of the players available."

"Why not?" Roger felt himself swept up in the excitement of the concept. "I'll bring Jocelyn over and we'll settle down again in Africa. She was never happier than in our home in Salisbury."

"You two are still married?" Mack asked.

"That's right. How about you and Carla?"

"She hasn't left me yet," Mack replied.

"That book could go a long way toward explaining the situation in South Africa today."

"I'd like to think it tells the story of many third world countries including Iraq now that it has been bombed into a pre-industrial state."

"It's done then," Ron Reid-Daley declared. "I'll have a place available for you in a couple of days."

"And I'll round up MacKenzie and everybody else that's around," Mack promised. "It's about time we told the story."

And so it was that Roger Masefield settled down in Durban and in record time wrote the story of how Rhodesia became Zimbabwe.

Chapter 1

June 1976

As they reached the border, Group Leader Nyati held up a cautioning hand. His guerrillas paused behind him. A veteran of many crossings, Nyati was adept at sensing the presence of Rhodesian Security Forces patrols and avoiding them. It seemed to be a quiet night with none of the hated Boers out tracking down the Freedom Fighters of Comrade Mugabe's ZANU party.

They slipped over the border from Mozambique into the country they called Zimbabwe and under cover of darkness headed for their first destination, two nights away at Musami.

All night they traveled through the bush, westward across the midlands. At dawn they sought refuge at the Catholic mission of St. Bonaventure. Here the guerrilla group's political commissar, Samuel Jobolingo, took over leadership. He stole inside the mission while the others waited outside and soon returned to the gate with a white woman wearing a long denim skirt, a sweater and a veil-like cloth draped over her head, the only garment indicating she was a nun.

At Jobolingo's commanding gesture the band of men, twenty strong, marched through the mission gate and followed the white woman through the labyrinth of buildings to what appeared to be a schoolhouse. Inside Jobolingo helped the woman pull open a trapdoor and, in obedience to another hand signal, the guerrillas followed him down a ladder that led into an electrically lighted cellar.

Jobolingo motioned the men to each take one of the cots lined up in rows where they would rest until starting out again that night. Then the commissar and the white woman climbed back up the ladder and closed the trapdoor behind them.

It was dusk when Jobolingo came back for his men. They had been given a hot meal by some of the mission workers and were ready to continue on their way. Outside the mission Jobolingo surrendered his command to the group leader.

Having walked all night, the guerrillas found a rocky, bush-covered hill, a kopje, where they could hide from any roaming security forces when the sun came up. They remained hidden all day and at sunset once more set forth. By the next morning they could see the church and the surrounding buildings of the St. Paul's mission, tinged russet by the rising sun. They took cover in the heavy bush near the church and waited for the moment to strike.

Several small boys, *mujibas* or apprentice guerrillas, serving as intelligence carriers, came to Nyati and Jobolingo with information about the white priests and nuns who administered the mission.

Jobolingo kept the mission under surveillance all day, perfectly concealed by dense leafage. White men came and went, many of them in the tropical white robes of priests.

Here at St. Paul's, unlike St. Bonaventure, the Catholic missionaries had preached to the people against Comrade Mugabe, a former Catholic. They had criticized the people's revolution for killing the sellouts and the white men at Mugabe's command. So, Mugabe reasoned, they must themselves be executed. How else could Mugabe's boys in the bush teach the people the errors of collaborating with the white man? Now they would give the white men in Salisbury and the Africans who listened to these priests a terrible lesson.

As the sun was sinking toward the hills to the west, with an hour of daylight left, Nyati gave his men the order to strike. The *mujibas* had informed him that the priests and nuns took tea in the common room in the late afternoon and that all of them came together at that time.

Rising from the bushes, the triangular-bladed bayonets they called pigstickers folded under their Russian AK-47 assault rifles, the guerrillas moved with stealthy deliberation toward the mission buildings. Some black Rhodesians who saw them coming moaned softly but did nothing to warn the bishop and the other clerics of their impending doom.

Nyati burst open the door to the common room and charged in, followed by his Freedom Fighters, all their weapons pointing at the gentle, unarmed priests and nuns.

"What do you need?" the bishop asked calmly. "Can we help you?"

"Outside!" Nyati cried, excitement making the blood rush to his head. The guerrillas behind him motioned menacingly with their rifles. Wordlessly the priests and nuns followed the bishop out into the street that ran through the compound and, obeying the terrorist leader's order, lined up with their backs to the church.

"You tell the people that Comrade Mugabe and the revolution is bad," Nyati shouted.

"No, my son," the bishop replied. "We preach that change must come soon but that senseless killing and torture are wrong, sins against God."

Nyati could contain himself no longer. His head pounding, his hands shaking, he pressed the trigger of his rifle and the bullets ripped through the bishop's white robes. He stared in fascination at the widening red splotches on the fallen cleric's soutane.

Another Freedom Fighter aimed his weapon at a nun's head and, squeezing the trigger, blasted half her face away. The remaining missionaries regarded their murderers with an equanimity that came partly from shock until, only moments later, they too lay crumpled in death. In the heat of their blood lust the guerrillas continued riddling the corpses with their automatic rifles; then Nyati shouted at them to cease firing and move out before the security forces started tracking them.

The guerrillas split into small groups to make their way back to Mozambique where they would regroup and report directly to their leader, Comrade Mugabe, who had ordered these executions.

Jobolingo and three men struck out eastward, paralleling a main highway to Salisbury. It was still daylight when they took up positions on a bluff commanding the road. They did not have a long wait before a Land Rover came speeding toward them, driven by a white man with an African beside him. The vehicle had what looked like an official plate mounted on the front bumper. When it came abreast of them, Jobolingo's men opened up on full automatic and watched their bullets rip through the Land Rover's windows. The face of the driver suddenly streamed blood.

As the Land Rover careened into a ditch and slogged to a stop, the guerrillas ran from their position down to the road and surveyed their handiwork at close range. The white man was dying and the African wounded. Quickly the guerrillas killed the sellout and then dragged the white man from behind the wheel, blood gurgling from a throat wound.

Jobolingo pulled his long razor-sharp knife from its sheath and slashed the man's trousers from his body. "For Comrade Mugabe," he cried, slicing off the white man's penis and testicles which he then jammed in the man's writhing mouth. At the sound of another vehicle coming down the road Jobolingo and his guerrillas scampered back into the bush beside the road and headed for Mozambique.

Group leader Nyati and the three men with him pushed through the tangled scrub and jungle all night toward their sanctuary across the border. By daylight they saw a white man's farmhouse and veered off into the Tribal Trust Land which adjoined the farm property.

Menacing the tribesmen with their guns, they demanded food and shelter for that day, after which they would continue toward Mozambique. The terrified tribesmen gave the guerrillas as much food as they could eat and hid them in their round, thatched huts. At midday several eager mujibas came to the hut in which Nyati was resting and informed him that the neighboring farmer and his wife had gone out to buy supplies and have drinks with their friends in the town twenty miles away and would not be back until it was almost dark. They had a little girl, about two years old, being cared for by a nanny. The child's name was Natasha, the *mujibas* reported. Nyati thought about this for some minutes and then devised a plan of action.

At three-thirty in the afternoon the four guerrillas walked up to the farmhouse. The African nanny, who was sitting on the veranda in the sun with the small child, watching her play with some toys, saw the men coming and, gathering up Natasha in her arms, fled inside, slamming the door behind her and bolting it.

Laughing raucously the guerrillas stamped up to the front door. They paused briefly to look at the oblong wooden plaque that ran above the lintel. On it was carved the legend: "This house first built by

Timothy Drexyl, trekker, 1898. Rebuilt by his grandson, Dennis, 1940." Nyati fired a burst at the lock, then kicked the shattered door in. The nurse, holding the child in her arms, cowered in the kitchen where the African servants, eyeballs rolling, watched in terror as the guerrillas burst into the room. Nyati reached for the little girl who was sobbing and crying out piteously to her nurse. Vainly the nanny tried to protect Natasha by throwing her body around the child, but Nyati roughly jerked her away from her charge and threw her to the floor, whereupon he dragged the screaming child out of the house and onto the veranda.

Nyati threw the girl onto the veranda, banging her head on the floor, and turned to one of his followers, making a chopping gesture with his left hand.

The guerrilla pulled the folding pigsticker from under the barrel of his AK-47 and snapped it into place. Then he moved toward the weeping child who was semiconscious from the blow to her head. With a stabbing lunge the Freedom Fighter impaled Natasha's small body through the chest. Lifting her in the air like a farmer pitching hay, he brought his arms down in a rapid arc and her convulsed body flew from the triple-edged blade onto the ground below the veranda.

The child lay silent, blood welling from the jagged wound. Another ZANU warrior pulled his knife, walked to the little body and hacked off the twitching right hand.

"Show at camp. Many dollars!" he grinned triumphantly.

"Come!" Nyati cried. "Now the Boers know we are at war."

Chapter 2

June 1976

Civilian life had been pleasant while it lasted, he thought. Indeed, it could even have become addictive. But now the Company, which always hung over him like the sword of Damocles, had contacted him. It would be only a matter of time before he was active again. Considering all the work it had taken to establish his Washington cover, the new public relations firm of Capital Dome, Inc., he hoped the firm could stay alive.

Alvin Glenlord glanced at his watch. Twelve-thirty. He explained to his partners he was lunching with an old friend. They were pleased at the business Glenlord brought in and asked few questions. Of course they never suspected that the Central Intelligence Agency had recommended their firm to some of the corporations with which it worked closely.

"Enjoy your lunch, Al," Bill Townsend called out as Glenlord walked to the door of their offices in the National Press building.

"See you all later," Al called back. "Be sure somebody gives Senator Akroyd a jingle this afternoon. We need his intervention at the Pentagon to make our big pitch."

"Will do, Al," his partner promised.

It was a beautiful June day in Washington. The heat hadn't settled in yet and the girls were wearing their sheerest summer dresses. Alvin decided to walk the six blocks to the second-rate restaurant where he was to be met. He had no idea who at the Agency would be making the contact. His case officer had merely told him on the phone two hours ago that he should go to the Easton Hotel Grille where he would be contacted.

Entering the cool interior of the lobby he dabbed away the sweatline along his upper lip and entered the grille. Over in a dark corner he saw a man in a seersucker suit and yellow tie stand up and tentatively raise a hand. Alvin Glenlord nodded, walked through the clusters of tables and approached the man at a conveniently seques- tered table for two.

He sat down in the empty chair across from the man he had come to meet.

"Hello, Glenlord. Call me Fred, Okay?"

"Okay, Fred."

Al did not prod his contact on the reason for this meeting. They ordered Cokes and tuna fish salads and then Fred began to explain.

"You've done a good job building your cover—"

"I thought you guys were going to leave me alone."

Fred smiled knowingly. "And now your expertise can serve a more important mission."

"I don't know, Fred. I like regular hours, getting home to my wife at night, watching the children grow up. Public relations is not easy to manipulate. If I leave . . ."

"Don't worry about it, Alvin. I think you're gonna like what we have in mind for you."

"Does it matter whether I like it or not?" He was thinking of the pay and allowances of bird colonel, the pension. "What's it all about?"

"Do you know anything about Africa?"

"What part of Africa?"

"Southern Africa. Specifically Rhodesia."

"Yes, I've been reading about Rhodesia. The white supremacist government holding down the Africans. They also happen to be hold- ing down the Communists. As far as I know we have no representation there whatsoever. I suppose there's one or two agents in place but it seemed to me that Rhodesia is the world's long lost kingdom as far as the State Department is concerned."

8

"You're right. That's exactly what it is. To tell you the truth we don't have effective coverage there. We've tried to insert a few agents into the Rhodesian Security Forces but they seem to get spotted and shunted off where they can't collect any hard intelligence. Our government is trying so desperately to prove that we will have nothing to do with a racist government that we haven't bothered to monitor in any meaningful way what goes on in the country. We need a high-level agent, a man above the military level. That's why you're here."

"You want me to penetrate Rhodesia?"

"Let me explain what's happening. All of a sudden over at the State Department the big Kraut has decided he's got to do something about Africa. Henry Kissinger may know the Middle East, he may know Europe, but he has no useful information on southern Africa. Politically, things are getting bad there."

The CIA contact leaned intently across the table, ignoring his meager lunch. "There *is* a war going on in Rhodesia. Atrocities are being committed every day. Atrocities of the worst kind. The Soviets are trying to subvert and take over Rhodesia by fanning the racism which effectively blocks the USA, and South Africa will be next. Without the sea-lanes around the Cape of Good Hope and the strategic minerals we can only get from South Africa and Rhodesia, the industrial development and defense capability of our country will be considerably threatened."

The solution seemed simple to Glenlord at first thought. "Then why don't we support the Rhodesian government? There must be some smart Africans working with Ian Smith, with political abilities and ambition."

Fred shrugged hopelessly. "Soviet propaganda spread by black socialists here has convinced most American blacks that only the two radical Marxist black leaders, Robert Mugabe out of Mozambique and Joshua Nkomo supported by Zambia, are true nationalist leaders. All the others, the moderates, the black caucus in Congress tells its people, are Uncle Toms, sellouts to the white man who has oppressed them all these years."

"Screw them," Al growled. "We've got to do what's best for all Americans. What the hell, we *are* observing the economic and diplomatic sanctions the United Nations imposed against Rhodesia. The racism must be opposed, unfair white supremacy must also be opposed, but they won't know what supremacy is until a brutal Marxist dictator gets power. Black or white, it will be *more* suppressive. That's always been the result of violent revolution in the Third World."

"You might say so. Of course when the Byrd Amendment passed, the United States started buying chromium again from Rhodesia so we could continue our manufacture of high-grade, weapons-quality steel. And what happens? Our black brethren in the Congress of the Marxist persuasion started clamoring for the repeal of the Byrd Act. This is an election year, don't forget. The Democrats with this Jimmy Carter running are going to use the racial issue. At the Company, however, we are not supposed to be political, we merely serve the administration. Right now the administration wants a sharp set of eyes and ears in Rhodesia."

"How do I establish cover?"

"They say you are one of our most resourceful operatives."

"I'll have to give it some thought, Fred. This will be a tough one to get started."

"There isn't much time, Al. The Kraut plans to go to Johannesburg no later than September. He's afraid the whole area will blow apart and the Communists take over. We've got to provide him an analysis of the economic and military situation."

"And that's my mission?" Al asked.

Fred nodded. "We're putting another man into the Rhodesian Army this week but I don't think it's going to do us any good. I don't know how they spot us. We've tried the officer class. They are compromised almost immediately. Usually it's other Americans over there who figure out who our agents are. Now we're trying an agent who has all the appearance of a real Georgia red-neck cracker."

Fred signaled the waitress to bring their check. "Just between the two of us, our good Secretary of State thinks that if he can get Ian Smith to accept the notion of black majority rule in Rhodesia a few weeks before the elections in November, it will help to make his boss president again and keep the Soviets out of southern Africa."

The CIA man took the check from the waitress, paid it and stood up. "When you get a lead on good cover, call us, Glenlord."

Chapter 3

June 1976

On Friday morning, two weeks after the meeting with his CIA contact, Alvin Glenlord was seated before the desk of Kenneth Towsey, head of the Rhodesian Information Office in Washington, D.C. Also in the meeting was a high-level representative of Rhodesia's Foreign Office, a youthful, early-fortyish Oxbridge type whom Towsey introduced as Dennis Barton, special assistant to the Foreign Minister.

Alvin, on behalf of his public relations agency, was unfolding his plan for improving Rhodesia's image in Washington, D.C. and the nation as a whole. "What we need is something to rally around," he explained. "We need a vehicle to generate favorable publicity for Rhodesia."

"And I assume, Mr. Glenlord, that you are here today to discuss this vehicle," Barton said smoothly.

"Affirmative," Al replied. "I think that at my agency, Capital Dome, we have evolved just the lead item to carry a favorable information program for Rhodesia to the public. We suspect that most news reports from there are biased."

Al flashed an owlish look at Towsey and Barton. "This is a very critical time to launch a campaign to impress upon Americans, the

11

Western world for that matter, that the terrorist leaders, Mugabe and Nkomo, are less than saints—indeed they are brutal, amoral Marxists and certainly are not champions of any democratic ideals."

Dennis Barton looked across the desk at Towsey for a moment and then turned back to Glenlord. "You understand that at the moment we have no way of funding a project in the United States. Our foreign exchange is drastically limited due to the economic sanctions against us."

"Except you can still sell us chrome under the Byrd Act," Al put in.

"Yes, that's true. It's our only source of U.S. dollars, but we have to conserve every penny. Besides, I'm told that there is a possibility that the Byrd Act will be repealed by the Congress."

"Not if the Republicans stay in."

"We have no way of knowing that the gentleman from Georgia, the farmer, Jimmy Carter I believe his name is, will not be elected president. We are aware of some of the people around him, for instance a black congressman, Andrew Young, who is bitterly opposed to the government of Rhodesia."

"In any case, we at Capital Dome are not concerned with funding at the moment," Al declared magnanimously. "We are information specialists and we are convinced that U.S. Foreign Policy in regard to the Third World is frequently based on inaccurate reporting—indeed, disinformation, if you will."

He paused to let the impact of his statement take effect. "We feel that with the right information, the United States would recognize the government of Rhodesia and lift economic sanctions altogether. If we are successful and you achieve free trade with the Western world, we feel certain that you would suitably compensate us for our efforts. Until then we will work at no expense to you."

"You may be certain, Mr. Glenlord, that if you are instrumental in bringing about an end to economic sanctions against the government of Rhodesia, we will be most generous in dealing with your company," Dennis Barton affirmed.

"Now what is your plan?" Towsey asked. "Being a sort of amateur public relations man, I am always interested in how you real professionals work."

"The difficulty is getting information to the public which affects U.S. Foreign Policy. The key to our program is to secure a well-known author to write a book about Rhodesia, preferably a novel which could be made into a big adventure movie. Such a book would give us the opportunity to publicize the positive aspects of Rhodesia and its government all over the United States. If we get the right author he'll be making appearances on television shows and radio in all the major markets of our country to sell his book, and of course to sell Rhodesia. We can see that copies of the book are given to every member of Congress and in general build an entire Rhodesian promotion campaign around it."

Barton and Ken Towsey looked at each other and smiled. Towsey brought up the important question. "What author do you have in mind?"

"Or authoress," Dennis Barton amended with a smirk.

"I know a man," Al said. "To tell you the truth I haven't approached him yet. I wanted your reaction first."

"It sounds like a masterful idea to me, Mr. Glenlord," Barton said boyishly.

"Would we know this author's name?" Towsey queried.

"I'm thinking of a friend of mine. I haven't seen him for quite a few years but I'm sure he'll remember me. His name is Roger Masefield."

"Of course," Towsey said. "I've read several of his books. He did the big one on Vietnam."

"That's where I knew him," Al affirmed.

"I believe I've heard of Masefield," Barton said thoughtfully, "I'm not sure what I've read by him. Is he one of those writing chaps that does a lot of research?"

Alvin Glenlord snapped open his briefcase, took out a stack of file folders, some bound in red, some in blue, and slapped them on the edge of Towsey's desk. "Here's a complete dossier on everything Masefield has done in the past twenty years," he pronounced triumphantly.

"To answer your question, Mr. Barton"—Al took a red folder from the top of the file—"here's the file on him from the day he approached the Department of Defense with the idea of going to Vietnam and writing a book about the United States Army Special Forces in action there."

Al opened the file. "You'll see he was given a special invitation to attend the army paratrooper school at Fort Benning. After becoming

13

jump-qualified, he went to the guerrilla school at Fort Bragg where he went through six months of intense training before pitching up in Vietnam."

"Why did the government give him those privileges?" Barton wanted to know.

"It appears that President Kennedy wanted a book written that would glorify the role of American guerrilla and counter-insurgency forces around the world. Also, Masefield had written a virtual textbook on Castro's guerrilla campaign in Cuba." Al placed a hand on the folder. "It's all in here, including the comments about him by officers and noncoms with whom he served both in training and in combat. He was an outstanding trooper even though he always retained civilian status. In World War II he was a nose gunner on B-17's in combat over Germany. I can tell you from personal experience that he never lost his touch with heavy machine guns."

Alvin Glenlord opened the file and leafed through the pages. "Yes, he researched the Vietnam book thoroughly. When he arrived in Vietnam he personally knew almost all of the officers and many of the sergeants from training days and he had what amounted to a presidential commission to go anywhere, do anything, see anybody, to write his book."

"Did it have the desired effect?" Dennis Barton asked.

"He did what President Kennedy, who was dead by then, had wanted him to do. He made the Special Forces world famous, and such a unique fighting force that the Department of Defense has not dared try to weed it out of the army since."

"What makes you think you can get him to do the Rhodesia book? Particularly since we can't offer him any money?"

"Roger Masefield is a cause man. If I give him the right information he will undoubtedly feel as badly as I do, as badly as most aware Americans, about the way the United States and Great Britain are treating Rhodesia. If you give me the go-ahead I'll try to get him interested."

"Oh I think it's a fantastically conceived idea," Barton enthused. "I'm just wondering what cooperation we can offer Roger Masefield to get him to take on the job and assure success."

"In the first place you'll have to give him total cooperation. You'll have to trust him. If you don't let him get out with the troops he will not be interested. You can even hand him a gun and he'll add one more member to your security forces. In Vietnam we Americans were always undermanned in the field. He was one of us. I can remember when we were attacked at a camp called Plai Mi: he handled the corner machine gun for two days and nights."

Dennis Barton frowned slightly. "We've tried to keep writers and journalists out of the sharp end—that's our term for combat zones. They tend to write stories which make the Communist terror war a racial issue. Racial against us."

"In order to get Roger Masefield to do this job," Al said quickly, boring in on the most vital question now that he had Barton absorbed in the concept, "in order for him to give his all to this project, you'll have to give all to him. That means the Prime Minister will have to see him, your Ministers of Foreign Affairs and Defense will have to be at his disposal. You'll have to let him see the whole ball game and be part of it. He's too smart to be buffaloed."

"What other books has he done?" Barton quizzed.

Al picked out the blue file and opened it. "He spent two years with the Special Narcotics Unit of the New York Police Department in order to write his book on dope smuggling. This file describes a shoot-out with a bunch of Corsican drug smugglers and another gunfight with a black dope gang up in Harlem. He takes his research very seriously." Al knew instinctively this was the time to close in. "But if he gets to Rhodesia and finds himself prevented from seeing everything"—he raised his eyebrows dramatically—"he'll leave, convinced that your government is covering up the real issues. Then he'll write against you."

Dennis Barton was intently thumbing through a file folder. Alvin Glenlord saw his own cover as a clandestine agent fast emerging and pressed onward. "He also spent a year in the Middle East and wrote a novel which has had some effect on our oil policy."

Barton and Towsey pored through the clippings on Masefield's books. "You'll see his books are invariably mentioned as being objective and unbiased," Al hammered. "He's developed widespread credibility. If you are not afraid of the truth, he's your man. If we can get Masefield, we may have won half the battle in getting the Congress and the administration to lift economic sanctions against you."

"How old is he?" Barton interjected suddenly. "It's pretty rugged out in our bush, you know. I go out with the troopies a lot myself, but even I find it pretty strenuous."

15

"Here's his biography. Roger Masefield is fifty years old but I'm sure that you don't have to worry about his physical fitness. I'm equally certain that you can trust him insofar as security is concerned. Just remember one thing: if you want to proceed with this plan you will have to give Masefield and his research team total freedom of movement."

"That could pose a problem of course," Barton mused. "The Rhodesian Security Forces have a cordial dislike of journalists. And what about this research team you are talking about? Who will be on it and how do we know we can trust them? We are already discussing an author who couldn't be controlled."

"That's precisely why his book would be so valuable in the USA. And if Roger Masefield decides to take on this project, I will personally take a leave of absence and go with him as his number one researcher. Masefield and I would thus be the two people you would have to trust totally. I'm sure even Roger wouldn't ask you to include anyone else in his security clearance."

"Very interesting, Mr. Glenlord. Your personal participation eases my reservations." He paused, as if in thought. "I feel certain my minister will like this plan. He knows the United States very well. As a matter of fact, he went to graduate school at Harvard University."

"Harvard! That's Roger Masefield's college," Al cried, as though that clinched the matter.

"Is he married?" Towsey asked.

"Yes, for five years to a girl named Jocelyn, about twenty years younger. She's an adventurous sort herself. She went with him to Turkey and the Middle East, and was helpful to him on a number of his other research projects. However, from what I've been able to learn since we've been studying this case, she spends a lot of time in New York while he's working out at his studio in Connecticut. I don't think there's any split up or anything like that, it's just that they each have their own lives to lead."

"You've certainly produced a lot of information about him," Towsey said approvingly. "And you haven't even approached him yet?"

Alvin Glenlord smiled, thinking of the concentrated effort the Agency had expended to build this protrait of Roger Masefield. "I'll make contact with him when you decide that you want to go along with this plan."

Dennis Barton's eyes met Towsey's and then the man from the Ministry of Foreign Affairs turned back to Al. "I can say with confidence that my minister will approve the project on the basis we have discussed, Mr. Glenlord. In order to expedite matters I would suggest you contact Mr. Masefield and determine whether he is amenable to this scheme. If he requires some persuasion we might as well get on with it. The sooner this book is published the better from our standpoint."

"I'll call Roger as soon as I get back to my office, and I'll let you know what he says," Al promised.

"Can you leave us this rather extensive dossier you have prepared?" Barton asked.

"Certainly, it's for you. Keep it in your files; it will be useful when you deal with Roger." Glenlord stood up. "I'll be back to you soon."

On the way to the office Al turned over in his mind the approach pattern he would follow during his first contact with Roger Masefield in almost a decade.

He had personally placed Roger in the most action-prone Special Forces camps in the Vietnam border areas. Back in Washington they had wanted a book glorifying Green Berets so Roger was given what he wanted.

Al had been forced to accept Masefield, even though he didn't really like him, but he didn't have to approve of the project. Alvin Glenlord was a soldier who did not believe in accepting outsiders into what was essentially a closed society of men who silently served their country, preferring anonymity to public acclaim. He also resented Roger's dilettante approach to the war.

He recalled that during the Viet Cong siege of Plai Mi, Roger had taken to mixing medical alcohol with the field rations fruit juice, leisurely sipping his way through a civilized cocktail hour, as he termed it. Roger had been aware that Al was attached to the CIA and was conducting cross-border missions, and Al felt that the writer had a way of learning too much too fast about clandestine operations and the people who ran them. No, he hadn't developed affection for Roger Masefield then and he doubted that he ever would. But he needed the famous author now so he would manage to establish a cordial relationship with him.

17

Roger Masefield's eyes followed the minute hand of the kitchen clock as it approached noon. The ingredients were laid out on the kitchen counter: the Beefeater gin, a lemon, a knife to cut the peel and the Martini and Rossi vermouth. Ice was in the silver bucket and a cocktail glass was chilling in the freezer.

At two minutes before noon he could start making the martini. It would be ready for sipping just as the minute hand comfortably ticked off the end of the morning, legitimizing the first drink of the day.

Drinks at lunch were self-imposed *verboten* when he was in the midst of the creative process, but it was Friday and a week ago he had delivered the manuscript of his newest book to the publishers. Now he was enjoying the interim period before plunging headlong into the next work.

All morning he had been reviewing the projects piled up for his attention. Two movie scripting jobs paying top dollar, a nonfiction book on narcotics smuggling in Florida and an exposé to be written in collaboration with a woman who had made love to two presidents of the United States in the White House.

With elaborate care he mixed the martini, stirring it carefully so as not to bruise the gin. Then, taking the knife, he cut two slivers of lemon peel and was ready for the final stage. He took an iced stem-glass from the deep freeze and poured a perfect five-to-one martini into it, then twisted in the lemon peel.

Roger carried the drink into his large studio where all his prospective literary projects were laid out for study. None of them was really what he was looking for; they were at best stopgaps until the next "big one" came along.

These days he wasn't quite as keen on risking life and limb in pursuit of an exciting story as he had been five or ten years ago. He glanced at his certificate of graduation from the Army Infantry Airborne School at Fort Benning, Georgia. That had been the beginning of the most notable writing experience of his life. Beside it was the diploma from the Army Guerrilla Warfare School and on the same wall the picture which so revolted the liberal intellectuals who on occasion gained admission to his sanctuary.

Ernest Hemingway was proud of the pictures taken of him with the animals he had killed. Roger didn't believe in killing animals. But there is nothing more ruthless, more brutal, than a communist guerrilla. The Marxist denouncement of religion, family, and traditional values produces men and women capable of total immorality and heinous crimes against humanity. And when in a firefight along a creek near Buon Mi Ga, in Vietnam, he had killed a Viet Cong guerrilla advancing through the water, he was proud to have his picture taken holding the dead Communist out of the stream by the head and shoulders.

He walked over to his bookshelf and looked at the row of the books he was most proud of, displayed full face on a prominent shelf, before glancing at the less inspiring works with only the spines showing in a lower case. Together they represented twenty-five years of writing. He had given his best to even these latter efforts, but now he wanted an idea for another major-impact work.

Roger sipped his martini contemplatively. He was off smoking, as he wanted to keep in the best possible shape for that next adventure that was out there waiting to be savored, catalogued and put between the pages of a book—like his other adventures in the Middle East, Latin America and Southeast Asia's Golden Triangle where the opium wars never ceased. His pursuit of perilous projects amounted to a craving for them.

Roger recalled with relish the surprise a famous network TV talk show host had evinced on first seeing him. "You? You are Roger Masefield, the big action writer?"

The interviewer had drawn a laugh from the studio audience with his long, incredulous stare. "You look like somebody's family doctor!"

People frequently expressed surprise at Roger's average size, graying and slightly balding head of hair, and benign expression. They expected a tall, thick-haired, hawk-beaked, glinty-eyed stud who matched the characters in his books.

"Don't judge a book by its cover," was his standard if hackneyed rejoinder.

Idly Roger wondered who Jocelyn was lunching with in New York City today. Her life revolved on the periphery of the worlds of the theater, museum functions and music. He thought she would be coming home for dinner tonight although he wasn't sure. More and more Jocelyn stayed at the small duplex apartment overlooking Central Park, while he preferred being at home in the Connecticut countryside, particularly now that it was summer.

The buzzer in the studio sounded and he picked up the intercom. His secretary, who had been with him for seven years, announced in a puzzled tone, "Alvin Glenlord on the phone. He says you knew him as Lieutenant Colonel Glenlord in Vietnam. We don't have him on the Roladex."

"I'll talk to him," Roger said, pressing the blinking button on the phone.

It had been a long time since he had seen or talked to Al. The familiar voice boomed over the line. "Roger, remember me, Alvin Glenlord?"

"Of course, Al." Now here was a man who looked the image people expected of Roger: square of jaw, piercing of eye, over six feet of solid muscle, with sandy hair cut military short and a stance that suggested he was ready at a moment's notice to take out an enemy bare-handed. He was just a bit too much the strong silent Green Beret officer, Roger remembered. Glenlord had always given him an uneasy feeling, but he had been an integral cog in the mechanism of getting his book research so Roger had learned to get along with him.

"Where have you been? Or shouldn't I ask?" Roger asked genially.

"I'm a civilian now; in the public relations business in Washington."

"What can I do for you? Endorse a product?" Roger bantered.

"Something like that, I suppose," Glenlord chuckled. "I got out of the army and went into civilian life so I could do and say what I believe in. I got interested in Rhodesia recently and thought I'd give you a call. You could do an outstanding book on Rhodesia."

Before Roger could get in a word, Glenlord plunged on. "You probably don't realize it but there is a war going on there of about the same intensity as the war in Vietnam when we first met. Incidentally, a few of our old friends from the Nam have joined the Rhodesian Army." He paused to let his words take hold, then shot into the silence: "How would you like to have a look at the situation with me?"

Whatever subliminal mistrust Roger Masefield might have felt for Glenlord, his imagination now popped like a flashbulb. "You say there are Americans over there fighting?"

"That's right. Why don't you come along?"

"You might have something, Al." Roger reflected for a moment or two. "When do you plan on leaving?"

"They tell me July and August are good months. It's their wintertime and even in the jungles you don't get that steamy heat this time of year."

"You think we could get some cooperation from the Rhodesian government? Would they let us get out with the troops?" Roger felt the adrenalin rising, like an old warhorse responding to the bugle call. "I should think that their military might be reluctant to let a couple of American civilians see what they're doing. The U.S. is treating them like they were the enemy."

"That's where you come in, Roger." Glenlord's voice brimmed with assurance. "As a public relations man I figure the Rhodesians badly need somebody like you to go over and write a book that would straighten the world out about them. I've made contact with the Rhodesian Information Office in Washington. They'd really appreciate it if you went over and saw the true picture there."

"I once thought about doing a novel on Rhodesia," Roger mused. "I figured it would make a colorful subject."

"It's even more colorful now with the war going on," Al was quick to add. "All that horseshit and gunsmoke you write about so well. What do you say, Roger?"

All Masefield's old reservations about Glenlord suddenly took a back seat in his mind. A surge of excitement coursed through him. "Let's do it! What's the next step?"

"I'll get back to you," Alvin said, with a smile Roger couldn't see. "I just wanted to know how you reacted to the idea."

"I'll start the research file right away."

"Any chance of you coming down to Washington?"

"Is next week soon enough?"

Chapter 4

July 1976

"I may sound like an American, but I'm a Rhodesian." Captain Mack Hudson thought about his statement a moment and then added, "At least until the end of my contract."

"Yes, sir," the heavy-set, ruddy-faced young man agreed.

Hudson looked sternly across the desk at this, the third American he had screened today. And there were two more to go. It had been a big day at Salisbury Airport for arriving Yanks. "Why do you want to join the Rhodesian Army?"

"Well, sir, I want to pop me a bunch of niggers. And since these niggers are commies it's like getting two birds with one stone, if you see what I mean."

Mack frowned at this familiar answer to his standard query. The newly arrived applicant looked up at his interrogator anxiously. "Hope I didn't say the wrong thing, sir. I mean I'm not prejudiced or anything, it's just . . ."

Mack stopped him with an upraised hand. "The chances are that you'll go to the RLI, that's the Rhodesian Light Infantry. It's an all-white outfit. But over here we fight shoulder to shoulder with black troops against the Communist terrorists. 'Terrs' as we call them. Call the Africans what you want. They're not playing language games; they're damn good fighting men and they hate the terrs as much as we do. Most every black Rhodesian in the army has had relatives murdered and tortured by the terrs. If it weren't for the Africans in the army, and I might add they're all volunteers, Rhodesia wouldn't be alive today. You'll learn to respect them."

"Yes, sir."

"You did two tours in Nam, I see." Mack looked up from the file he had been studying. "Bronze Star, Air Medal."

"I killed my share of gooks."

"How did you get your leg wound? Says fragments here."

"I was too close to the Lieutenant when a nigger fragged him."

Mack Hudson winced. During his own extensive experience as a Special Forces officer in Vietnam there had been no fragging incidents in his outfit. But everybody was aware of the racial tension in army units that led to grenades being tossed at officers by black soldiers. It was the greatest disgrace of the war, a situation that few army men ever discussed.

"Let me tell you, Sheehy"—Mack glanced down at the file folder—"there has never been a fragging incident or anything like that in the history of the Rhodesian Security Forces. Our Africans and whites fight together with mutual respect. The war in Rhodesia is not a racial conflict. It is political. We are fighting Communist terrorists."

"I know that, sir. I done my homework. It's like Vietnam. We got our gooks, the commies got theirs. And in Vietnam, ours lost."

"That's about right. But in this case our Africans are the better fighters."

Captain Hudson stood up and tapped the map behind him. "They come in, kill, torture, rape and steal and then slide back across the border into Mozambique or Zambia or Botswana. And now the enemy is putting trained, disciplined and well-equipped forces against us."

He turned from the map and sat down again behind his desk. "We're getting into Phase Two of the Communist insurgency. You know what that is?"

"Yes, sir. Phase One, random terror. Phase Two, guerrilla units coming in, hitting soft targets. And finally Phase Three, when we have battalion- and regimental-size battles. I studied Vietnam. The minute we started to move out the Communists moved into advanced Phase Three. And we lost."

24

"Yes, Sheehy, that about sums it up. Where are you from in the States? It says here Kearny, New Jersey, but you don't sound as though you were from any part of the Northeast."

"I've lived all over the United States, sir. I was brought up in Georgia and South Carolina but never went back there from the time I joined the army in 1963. My old lady's from New Jersey so I put that down as my home even though we're separated right now."

"Any children?"

"Yes, sir. I've got a girl four years old."

"How are you going to support the wife and kid while you're over here? You know you can't send any money back. Even if you save some Rhodesian dollars, with the United Nations sanctions against Rhodesia, they're useless anywhere else in the world."

"I left her with some money, sir. And she's got a job. I won't be worrying on duty."

"Your contract will be for three years. And Sheehy," Hudson said, his voice like steel, "I don't want any man I passed on taking the gap."

"Taking the gap, sir?"

"That's what they call deserting here in Rhodesia. It comes from their game of rugby. When a running back gets the ball he looks for the gap in the line and heads for it. It makes us all look bad when a Yank takes the gap. You know what I mean?"

"Yes, sir. I won't be taking the gap, sir."

"I see you were honorably discharged from the army as a tech sergeant, Sheehy. It would be my recommendation to the Rhodesian Army recruiting office that you be given a contract. I can't help you as far as rank is concerned—that's up to them. They'll probably start you as a trooper. If you're any good you'll work yourself up to sergeant again in a year. Is that good enough for you?"

"Yes, sir."

"The Rhodesian Army is a lot different from what you're used to, Sheehy. You'll find much firmer discipline here and they won't hesitate to throw you in the box down in Bulawayo if you fuck up. It's not a nice place so keep your nose clean. They may not make you go through the entire recruit training program. Judging from your record it would be a waste of time."

"That's what I think sir. Just give me a week's familiarization with these Belgium weapons they use here and you can send me out to the bush. No point in wasting my time or the Rhodesian Army's time. There's a lot of niggers out there need killing."

"When you get in the TTLs—those are the Tribal Trust Lands where the fighting is going on—just remember what I said: this is not a racial war. It just happens that most of the Communists are black. Maybe you'll get lucky and kill some Cubans or East Germans or even Russians. That's when you really feel you've accomplished something."

"I understand, sir. What do I do now?"

Hudson handed the file across the desk to Sheehy. "Go back to the recruiting office. By the time you get there I'll have talked to them on the phone. And by the way, they don't call Africans niggers here; maybe Kaffirs or houtes or munts. But the best advice I can give you is to call the ones on our side brother. You understand me?"

"Yes, sir."

Hudson watched Sheehy stand up, his file tightly clutched in his left hand. "Thank you for your time, sir. I can promise you you'll never be ashamed of giving the Rhodesians a green light on me."

"Sheehy, what went wrong those years between the time you got out of the army after Vietnam and the time you came here?"

There was a not unkindly tone to Hudson's voice. Indeed there was a glint of discernible sympathy in his eyes. No longer was it the screening officer checking out the recruit. It was one American asking another American a simple question.

"I wish I was smart enough to answer that question for myself. I just couldn't hack it after the war. Too many memories maybe. You never forget, you know that, sir." Hudson nodded but made no comment.

"Unless you were there a couple of times, 'specially the last days of Nam," Sheehy continued, "I guess you can't understand. Watching everybody die and everything going to hell, I began to understand for the first time what it must have meant to the Kraut soldiers when they lost World War II. And I guess I understood what it meant to General MacArthur when they wouldn't let him win the Korean War. I began to understand a lot of things. I'm not saying I'm over here as a big patriot. There's a lot of reasons I'm here. Maybe I don't even understand them all myself. But I'll give everything I've got for the Rhodesians."

Captain Hudson looked at him closely. "The Rhodesians don't always understand Americans, you know. It's particularly tough on guys like you coming in as a trooper. You'll have Rhodesian and South African corporals and sergeants that will walk all over you. You've got to remember, however, that these guys for the most part have never been outside of this part of Africa. There are a few American sergeants, a few Brits and Aussies and a few Germans that will give you more understanding. It's not that Rhodesians aren't happy to have us here. It's just they don't know how to treat us. We're different. We're foreigners. And for thirteen years the Rhodesians have not been allowed to leave their country except to visit South Africa. They just don't know the outside world. So be patient, eat a little shit if you have to."

Hudson stood up. "Whatever your motives, you're doing the right thing joining us here. But don't go into this army thinking you're doing them a favor. And if you ever think of taking the gap, come and see me first. You're a Crippled Eagle now. That's an American fighting in Rhodesia even though his own country threatens to take his citizenship away and harasses his family back home. You said you did your homework. You must know what the U.S. government thinks of us Yanks fighting over here." Sheehy nodded. "One guy here from Pittsburgh was trying to bring his wife over and the State Department froze his savings account so she couldn't get the money out to buy a ticket. You'll get plenty of harassment from Washington. So will your old lady. You'd better know what you're doing if you really want to sign a three-year contract."

"After seeing my government let the commies take over Southeast Asia it will be hard for me to totally respect it again. I didn't like the fighting, the killing, the dying. But what I hated was our government wouldn't let us win the war."

Mack Hudson smiled somberly. "Good luck to you, Sheehy. Keep your head down once you get out there at the sharp end, as they call the operational area. Like I said, the terrs are getting better all the time. Fortunately for us they have a ways to go. We still have the K factor working for us."

"Educate me a little more, sir."

"The K factor? The Kaffir factor. The African, no matter how much we try to train and discipline him, is never completely able to understand modern weaponry and machinery. For instance, in the department stores they sell electric irons for Kaffirs to use and abuse and electric irons for the whites. You have to buy three electric irons for the Kaffirs to every one for the whites, so they're priced accordingly. You'll learn all about the K factor, but take one more piece of advice from me. Don't count on it. It'll save your life a lot of times but once in a while you'll find a terr who is really good. And when you do, God help you if you make a mistake. Again, good luck, Sheehy. You'll need it."

Sheehy snapped a smart American-style salute, turned on his heel and walked out of Captain Hudson's office in the Special Air Service section of Cranborne Barracks.

Hudson watched him go. There was, he thought, something too goddamn pat about this particular recruit. Then he shouted over the partition that created his office, "Send in the next one, Sergeant Major!"

Chapter 5

July 1976

At Alvin Glenlord's second meeting with Fred, they were joined by his case officer, an aloof, aristocratic Bostonian. Alvin was well aware that this supervisor was mainly concerned about the inevitable bi-monthly polygraph tests. Most middle-level Agency personnel were required to undergo this humiliating experience designed to ensure that they were involved in nothing disloyal or against regulations.

"It was a very tough sell, I'll tell you that," Glenlord punched out. "Roger Masefield did not want to go to Rhodesia or anywhere else. He's a successful writer. He doesn't have to get his ass shot at like he did in Vietnam just for a story. I told him that he'd be doing the free world a great service and make as much money as he did on his big Vietnam book. I think I convinced him I could take a lot of the load off his shoulders, and of course he knows from experience I'm a good man to have on your flank. I'll have to say one thing for him: he's cool in a firefight. Anyway, Fred, it looks like I've got my cover. Roger has himself an invitiation to go to Rhodesia from Prime Minister Ian Smith, endorsed by General of the Army Peter Walls and the Foreign Minister. I'm going ahead of him by about ten days to check out the contacts he's made. It seems there's a woman lawyer there named

Beryl Stoffel. She's supposed to know more about Rhodesia and have more contacts than anybody over there. I'll try and convert her into an asset for us before she ever meets Roger."

"You've done a good job, Glenlord," the case officer approved grudgingly. "I didn't think you'd be able to establish cover that fast."

"That's how I made full colonel on the clandestine list at age forty-two, my friend," Glenlord replied. A military commander, superior to himself in rank, he would have called sir, but not a CIA case officer. For fifteen years his army career had been closely intertwined with the Agency but somehow he could never muster respect for the civilians, the college boys, the old-school-tie types that had sunk their roots securely in the rich soil of the Agency in the days of Allen Dulles and his successors. The case officer, he knew, had gone to Amherst. Glenlord had earned his college degree via Operation Bootstrap, the educational benefit given to army officers so they could get the equivalent of a college education.

"When are you and Roger Masefield leaving for Rhodesia?" Fred asked.

"I have to leave the initiative to Roger now. If I push him too hard he might say screw the whole thing. I've seen him do it before. We're just lucky that everything came together."

Alvin Glenlord stood up and began pacing the living room of the large apartment overlooking the Potomac River in Crystal City, one of the big apartment complexes in the Washington, D.C. area. This place was a safe house. Friends and targets of the CIA were brought up here to drink, indulge in sexual orgies with CIA-paid girls, and also to be interrogated. Interrogated under the influence of liquor, not the more drastic type, which was carried out in the backwoods of Virginia.

"In short, *compadres*," Glenlord boasted, "I've got this best-selling author eating out of my hand. So let's not drop the ball. I don't want any surveillance on me. Understand? You guys blew one deal for me that way. Remember? Just let me operate. And I could use five Ks cash. I've got to pay my own way the first time."

"You know money is no obstacle," Fred said.

"Right, but no accountability. Understand? I don't want some dickhead two years from now to use something against me. The way the Agency leaks its secrets to a bunch of left-wing liberal senators and congressmen, I'm beginning to think we are the most productive branch of the KGB."

The case officer grimaced sourly. Fred shrugged and stared at his drink.

"From the time I leave for Rhodesia until I get back, there will be no contact, okay?" Al pounded on. "And if you did plant a man in the Rhodesian Army I don't want him to know about me."

Fred and the case officer signified their assent.

"Well, that's about it then. I'll be in Rhodesia by the end of July and back in plenty of time to give the Kraut a complete briefing on what's going on."

"Glenlord," the case officer said tonelessly, "at some point you may have to stop this Roger Masefield from doing whatever book he has in mind or making whatever statements to the press he may plan. If Masefield becomes a rallying cry, as he has before to a large segment of Americans, forcing the administration to make a move that might hurt the President politically in the coming elections, it will be your job to turn him off. Do you understand?"

This announcement came as a surprise. Alvin had a high regard for Roger's talent and yes, he even felt a certain regard for him. The thought of taking him out was sobering. "I understand," he said quietly. "I don't think it will be necessary to terminate Roger Masefield with extreme prejudice. But you can be sure that as soon as I get my supports in place I'll be in a position to do whatever is necessary." He reached across the glass table toward Fred, his fingers making a beckoning motion. "Our next meeting will take place when I get back from this first trip to Rhodesia."

Fred slapped a brown letter-sized envelope into his hand. "Five thousand dollars. That should see you through the next couple of months."

Alvin took the envelope, opened it and extracted the sheaf of green treasury notes. He counted them and put them back into the envelope. "Anything else on your minds?"

The case officer and Fred shook their heads.

"Then I'm going home. See you when I see you. By the way, any of our people over there now I should know about?"

"Just got word that our man went up for Rhodesian Army screening in Salisbury today," the case officer replied evenly. "He won't know about you—and let's keep the converse true as well."

The meeting was clearly over. Alvin Glenlord stood up and walked to the door. The suggestion that he might some day have to terminate

Roger weighed on him. Yes, he belonged to the Agency. No, he did not always like it.

Chapter 6

July 1976

Glenlord stretched his long legs out in front of him and for the final time reviewed the dossiers he had been studying all the way over. In two hours the South African Airways jumbo jet would be landing at Jan Smuts Airport, Johannesburg. There he would just have time to make the Rhodesian Airways flight to Salisbury. Since Roger Masefield had finally decided to treat him as a temporary research employee, Al used some of the expense money the case officer had given him to upgrade the ticket Roger had purchased for him from tourist to first class. He was well acquainted with the structure of the Rhodesian Security Forces and now, using Roger Masefield, he must get cleared for visits to the operational areas so he could actually go out on combat patrols.

The business community would be more difficult to penetrate. One of his most important assignments was to identify the convoluted trading channels through which the Rhodesian government purchased and imported its weaponry and equipment. Despite the trade sanctions against Ian Smith's government by the United Nations, the war was being successfully prosecuted. Glenlord had been briefed on the work of the so-called sanctions busters, but although the Agency had some suspicions as to who they were and how they worked, nobody at Langley or the U.S. Department of State had a clear-cut picture of how French helicopters, American weaponry and British heavy machinery were reaching Rhodesia. Of course, thanks to the Byrd Amendment, the United States was buying Rhodesian chrome which accounted for a substantial portion of the foreign exchange Rhodesia used to keep the war against the terrorists going.

Al caught himself in mid-thought: the terrorists . . . He wasn't supposed to call them Communists. He wasn't even supposed to think of them as terrorists. The State Department said they were black nationalists who were merely supplied by the Communists.

Roger Masefield had really been an inspiration, Al Glenlord complimented himself smugly. If the Agency were run like a military outfit he would have been awarded at least another Bronze Star for that one.

He reached into the briefcase on his lap for the glossy photograph of Beryl and smiled at what he saw. How could such a beautiful woman be a lawyer? Roger, who had developed her as a contact through his South African connections, presented him with this thorough dossier on Beryl just before his departure. Forty years old, she was married to a wing commander in the Rhodesian Air Force, by whom she had two children, a daughter sixteen and a son fifteen. Beryl and Wing Commander Stoffel, originally from a prominent South African family, were married in name only according to Roger's notes. They shared a beautiful home in Salisbury but the Wing Commander was seldom there. They had agreed to stay married until the children were grown up. They saw little of each other but were respectful and friendly when together. Beryl Stoffel, it seemed, had one of the best entrees to the circles of power of any woman in Rhodesia. It would be Alvin Glenlord's goal to encourage her to share her contacts with himself and Roger Masefield, and as soon as possible to cut Roger out altogether.

At the moment, however, it was the famed author that had Beryl excited, not his research assistant. Beryl, sophisticated in the ways of the world and much traveled compared to most Rhodesian women, knew the value of having a big popular novel written about Rhodesia.

Looking at the photograph of the blonde woman with the haughty chiseled features of an English aristocrat, Al thought of his rather plain wife back home in Virginia. Lorraine was a good wife, took care of the children and didn't ask him questions. He didn't know whether she believed his story about being in the public relations business and retired from government service, but it didn't make any difference.

The flight had been a long one, sixteen hours, but Al had dozed off from time to time in the plush comfort of his first class cabin and he didn't feel the least tired. The hostess came by offering a final drink before the bar closed. Al declined and began to put his papers, the dossiers he had built up, and the Roger Masefield novel he had been reading back into his attaché case. It would be good to get on the ground again, he reflected.

The 747 jumbo jet landed at Jan Smuts Airport right on time. Alvin Glenlord was almost the first person off the plane and he headed for the line in front of the immigration office. He did not want to miss the Rhodesian Airways flight to Salisbury. Beryl Stoffel had cabled him that she would be there to meet him. He had hardly gone through the immigration proceedings when he heard himself paged. As he walked over to the information desk a burly, genial-looking man wearing a brown uniform greeted him.

"Mr. Glenlord? I'm Eric Klein with Rhodesian Airways. I will see that you get aboard our Salisbury flight and make sure that your luggage is with you." The official escorted Al up the escalator to the lounge, sat him down and promised to return with his ticket processed through to Salisbury. Al wandered to the glass windows that gave onto the huge airport. Aware of American voices he turned and saw three young men, drinks in their hands, also gazing out the windows. Undoubtedly more Americans on their way to join the Rhodesian Army, he thought. The war in Rhodesia was attracting men from all over the free world, the adventurers, the misfits and the cold professionals who only felt happy and fulfilled in a war situation. Al nodded to them and then asked pleasantly, "Are you men heading north?"

"We sure are. How 'bout you?"

"I'm going up to Salisbury too."

"Have you already got your offer?" one of the Americans asked.

"No, I'm just going up to look around."

"Were you in Nam?" the same man asked.

"Four tours," Al replied.

"You shouldn't have any problem, then," another American observed. "That's what they want, experienced combat soldiers."

"I've had my share of that," Al allowed. The three Americans introduced themselves and when they learned he had come out of the army a lieutenant colonel, they whistled. "Maybe we'll get to serve under you, sir," one of them said respectfully. "We're all going in as troopers, although I was a sergeant when I got out."

"I guess it won't take you long to get your stripes in the Rhodesian Army then," Al said.

The Rhodesian Airways executive returned and handed Al his ticket and boarding pass. "You're all set to board. Should be about twenty minutes from now."

"Thank you, Mr. Klein. I sure appreciate it."

"When Beryl Stoffel calls, we try to oblige." Klein gave Al an up-and-down look of approval, smiling as though amused by some inner thought. "Have you actually met Beryl yet?"

"No, I haven't. I'm certainly looking forward to it, though."

"Oh, you'll enjoy knowing Beryl. Yes, you certainly will. Well, if there's anything else I can do for you, let me know, Mr. Glenlord."

"Thank you." Al watched Klein walk away, then went over to the duty-free counter and bought two bottles of Scotch in accordance with the instructions he had received. Because of sanctions, good liquor was scarce in Rhodesia and had become a valuable trading commodity.

When Alvin boarded the Rhodesian Airways plane he found himself sitting next to one of the Americans. During the hour-and-a-half trip to Salisbury he and his fellow Yank talked at length about the Rhodesian military and the reasons why Americans were flocking to Salisbury to join up.

"I'm not very important in this world, but I want to do something important. Those goddamn politicians made us lose in Korea and again in Vietnam." He paused reflectively. "These Rhodesians got a lot of guts. I'm looking forward to fighting with them."

The flight went smoothly and it was just getting dark when they arrived at Salisbury Airport. Al was again one of the first off the plane. As he walked down the steps he saw her. Yes, it certainly was Beryl Stoffel standing with airline officials and a stewardess, looking up at the passengers disembarking. She was even more maturely beautiful than he had anticipated. Al walked straight up to her.

"I never expected you'd be right out here to meet me," he said cheerfully.

"Come on, Mr. Glenlord, follow me. We'll wait in the VIP Lounge until all the baggage is off the plane." As they walked she glanced at him. "How was the flight? No problems?"

"No problems. It was nice of you to have that Mr. Klein meet me. He was very helpful in Joburg."

"Oh Eric is a good chap, very helpful. I've known him a long time."

"It seems like you know everybody," Al remarked.

They walked across the concrete to the terminal and an official opened a door for them into the comfortable VIP Lounge. "When the baggage is off they'll let us know. Would you like a drink or a cup of tea?"

"No, I don't need anything now. Later maybe."

"When is Roger Masefield coming?" Beryl asked.

"A week from today. He's stopping off for a few days in London."

"He's not bringing his wife, then?"

"He figured there might be shooting in the streets and terrorist activities, all of which fascinate him but not his wife."

Beryl laughed aloud. It was a gay, melodious laugh. Al liked it. "He'll find it very peaceful here, I'm afraid. No excitement in Salisbury. But we'll get him out to the sharp end and he'll see all the war he wants."

"We're both very interested in getting out on operations." No point in wasting time, Al thought.

"We'll get you cleared at ComOps, that's Combined Operations, as soon as possible so that you can see some action. It takes a little while. We've had some rather nasty experiences with journalists. The English are the worst. They tell the most blatant lies about us. Three months ago two writers—actually one was a photographer from the London Express—threw silver coins in the garbage pails and the little black kids on the street jumped in after them. They took pictures of the children going after the coins and the newspaper printed them, saying that starving African children wait outside the white man's hotels for the garbage to be brought out and then eat out of the pails."

Her voice became indignant. "Another English photographer took pictures of Africans sleeping on the grass in Cecil Park at high noon. Those pictures came out in the newspapers above a caption saying that the white police had just shot them. It's shocking, shocking what the world press does to us. We all feel Mr. Masefield will be on our side. I don't think you and he will have any trouble getting whatever you want here. It's my job to see that you are well taken care of."

"We're certainly appreciative of your interest, Mrs. Stoffel."

Beryl laughed. "Now come on, call me Beryl. You're Alvin, right?"

"Sure, just call me Al, Beryl."

"Al is so American."

An airline executive came across the VIP Lounge to them.

"I guess your luggage is ready," Beryl said. "All you have to do is identify it and it will be carried out to my car."

By the time Glenlord's two suitcases had been stowed in the trunk of Beryl Stoffel's four-door Mercedes sedan and they were leaving the airport, darkness had fallen. "You must be tired after this long trip," Beryl commented.

"That's what everybody says. Actually I'm not tired at all."

"I'll just take you around to the cottage we've arranged for you and Mr. Masefield to use while you're in Rhodesia. Compliments of the Friends of Rhodesia Trust. If you feel like some dinner I'll wait while you get unpacked and freshened up and then we can go down to the Meikels Hotel for dinner."

"Outstanding," Al exclaimed. "I certainly didn't expect to be met by a beautiful woman like you and taken to dinner my first evening here."

"We have a lot of plans for you when Mr. Masefield gets here."

Twenty minutes later Beryl Stoffel drove her Mercedes into the driveway of a one-story cottage nestled in a clump of trees. "Here we are. On the grounds of Jenny Huggins's estate. Jenny is one of our biggest supporters at the Friends of Rhodesia Trust."

While Beryl went to the door and unlocked it, Alvin retrieved his two suitcases from the trunk of the car, then followed her into the living room of the cozy, well-appointed cottage. There was a fire burning in the fireplace.

"It looks so nice it's almost a shame to go out," he commented.

"Isn't it, though," Beryl agreed. "But if you want to go downtown to dinner, get ready. I'll make a few phone calls here."

Over dinner in the Bagatelle Room of the Meikels Hotel, Alvin learned more about the woman who had met him at the airport and was apparently in charge of his and Roger's visit to Rhodesia. Beryl Stoffel made no bones about her fortieth birthday having fallen just two months before. She talked about her two teenage children and

38

briefly about her husband. "Christian Stoffel decided to stay in the air force permanently. We pretty much lead our own lives. Sometimes he's home, sometimes he's out in the bush. I never know. A nice enough chap. You'll like him. A patriotic Rhodesian. We both, in our own way, serve our country."

After dinner and a brandy and coffee, Beryl drove Al back to the cottage. He invited her to come in for a drink but she demurred. "We've got a big day ahead of us tomorrow, Alvin. And midweek I'm having sundowners, a cocktail reception you'd say, for people I think you'd be interested in meeting. Mr. Masefield said he particularly wanted to meet Americans in our security forces. I've had a call out for some of the American officers, but it's hard to contact them. Most of them don't even like to be known as Americans. They even try to change their accent," she laughed. "It's so funny to hear them try to talk the way we do. Anyway, I thought that tomorrow I'd start introducing you to the people that can be most helpful to you and Mr. Masefield."

"That's just fine, Beryl. But right now, even before he gets here, you'd better get used to calling him Roger. When anyone calls him Mr. Masefield he always says, 'Mr. Masefield is my father and very much alive. I'm Roger.'"

"Sort of the informal type then, you might say."

"Yes, you might say," Al grinned.

"You have your key now?"

"Right in my pocket."

"Be sure, be absolutely certain that you lock up at night. We have never had any terrorism within the city but you never know when it will start."

Alvin gestured his understanding. He had noticed the small nickel-plated automatic in Beryl's pocketbook when she opened it after dinner to take out her compact.

Beryl sat in her car watching until Al had opened the door to the cottage. He turned and waved. She backed out of the driveway, tooted her horn twice and drove off.

Alvin walked into the cottage and gave it a quick surveillance. Sometime in the next two or three days he would have to check it out for bugs. But until Roger arrived and they began having conversations, there was no need.

Once again Al congratulated himself on securing Masefield for cover. The author would totally insulate him from any Rhodesian government suspicion of being an American intelligence officer.

Chapter 7

July 1976

For the last hour of the flight from New York to London, Roger Masefield had one major thought in mind. Sarah Chase. Sarah Cobb Chase to be exact. Sarah's mother always felt that the Cobb family had distinguished itself far more than her husband's people and insisted that Sarah use her middle name as well as her father's name.

Roger tried to recapture an image of her in a filmy summer dress, her long shapely legs silhouetted behind the gossamer material. Even in Saigon, when the other American women, particularly the journalists, wore jodhpurs and camouflage jackets, Sarah sported a bright summer dress, her long auburn hair loose and blown by the wind instead of tucked up into a fatigue cap as was the prevailing style. The ubiquitous Nikon camera hung over her shoulder, the strap clearly delineating the cleavage between her firm breasts.

Older and more experienced newshens sniffed at the very sight of Sarah Cobb Chase. Although a mere stringer taking what assignments she could get, she frequently filed exclusive controversial stories as a result of the instant rapport she generated with American officers hungry for the sight of a little round-eyed femininity.

Roger was not at all disturbed that his wife Jocelyn had chosen to stay in New York rather than join him in London. It would give him more opportunity to become reacquainted with his new leg-girl. There would still be plenty of evening-on-the-town left ahead of them when the plane landed. He savored the glass of wine; he had refrained from indulging in more than two cocktails since he wanted to be ready for anything and everything in London. Finally the announcement came that the 747 was descending into London's Heathrow Airport. The local time was announced as 8:30 P.M.

Clothing bag over one arm, briefcase in hand, Roger strode down the long corridor toward the main terminal well ahead of the other passengers who streamed out of the plane behind him. Actually there was no reason for him to hurry; the baggage would be a long time coming off the plane. But he didn't know how to walk slowly, a trait which caused Jocelyn to frequently complain.

He thought about Jocelyn during the interminable wait for the baggage. She was a good wife to him, reasonably undemanding of his time. Looking back he wondered why he had wanted to get married again. But meeting Jocelyn at the celebrity-studded party, a beautiful young woman who seemed unaware of her own allurement in the midst of all the Hollywood, Broadway, literary, society and financial luminaries, Roger had been immediately smitten with her unassuming charm. He managed to separate her from the man-about-town who had brought three young women with him to the party and took her away to finish the evening at a table for two in a dark bistro near her apartment.

It was the classic case of a somewhat jaded sophisticate falling in love with a much younger woman who was refreshingly different from the worldly, man-wise ladies to be met at the parties around town.

However, now, five years after the marriage, Jocelyn herself had become as worldly, as canny, as much a part of the haute monde as the other women on the Manhattan scene. Childless going into their sixth year of marriage, they had given up on progeny, immersing themselves more deeply in their other interests.

Perhaps sometime Jocelyn would join him in Rhodesia if he deemed it safe and productive, Roger thought. If not, well, while he was in the midst of this literary mission she would find much to occupy her in her own world.

Finally the familiar brown leather suitcase, which he had decorated with red and green tape so nobody would take it by error, appeared on the luggage carousel. After going through customs, Roger pushed through the swinging doors into the main terminal. And there she was, waiting for him. Just the way he had envisaged her. The long auburn hair hanging loosely almost to her shoulders, the slightly freckled face, totally devoid of makeup, breaking into a smile as he appeared. The long legs below the hem of the skirt of her lightweight dress were spread slightly apart in a position that suggested she'd been waiting for some time.

Sarah Cobb Chase gracefully walked to him and raised her cheek to be kissed, which he accommodated warmly.

"Let's get out of here. I've got a super bash lined up for you. I took the liberty of using some of the expense money you gave me to hire a car and driver for the night. We've got a lot to do."

Within minutes they were being sedately chauffeured toward London.

"Okay, tell me what you got done last week, miss charming assistant," Roger began.

"I've made the most delicious contacts, Roger. You should be very pleased. Everybody that can be helpful to you in Rhodesia and happens to be in London at the moment I have been to see. We'll drop by the hotel, get rid of your luggage and go over to Lord Johnny Cravenlow's flat. Lord Johnny is very interested in Rhodesia, you know. He's been there several times, strong family ties. His grandfather was the British commissioner there right after World War I."

"Forgive my ignorance, Sarah, but I'm not sure I know who Lord Cravenlow is."

"He's a super guy. You'll like him. He was in the British Special Air Service, did a year and a half of duty in Belfast and now is out of the army and working as a journalist. He's made a good connection with Time magazine and he strings for the London Telegraph. I was very lucky to get to know him."

"How did you manage it? Or shouldn't I ask."

"I found out where he lived, went up and rang his doorbell," she giggled. "My, was he surprised. He had a lady in his apartment. Boy, if looks could kill I wouldn't be here to meet you."

"What did you say?"

"I told him I worked for you and that you were on your way to Rhodesia to write a novel and wanted to meet him."

"He'd heard of me?" Roger asked.

"Of course, darling. You're a celebrity, you know. I've seen your books all over London. Anyway Lord Johnny invited me in and gave me a drink, introduced me to his girl friend, Lady something. I really wasn't too impressed, and he took us both out to dinner."

"Lady 'something' must have been delighted."

"Oh she was. She finally got up at the restaurant and told Johnny he could have his little colonial intruder if that's what he wanted, and with that walked out." Again Sarah gave her musical giggle. "Johnny has been a big help in getting me to meet people that can be of use to you."

"And to you also, I'll bet," Roger said with the barest hint of jealousy.

"For both of us," Sarah came back promptly. "Remember you said that even though I was working for you I could take on other assignments."

"Well, I may have something for you. The foreign editor at the *New York News World,* that newspaper that just started up, said if you have any pictures or stories they could use to send them along. Also, I met with an old friend at ABC News and they might be able to use some stories from you. Did you have any luck contacting any of the African characters? I understand Bishop Muzorewa is in London now."

"I'm way ahead of you, boss. I've already called on Muzorewa and his number one man, Godfrey Chakarama. The bishop's a sweetheart, Chakarama is the evilist looking S.O.B. I ever saw outside of Vietnam. They've agreed to have you come up and talk to them at their hotel."

"You're marvelous, Sarah. I'm surprised the AP or UPI didn't hire you long ago."

Sarah looked piqued for a moment. "I just can't seem to land a job in the big leagues. Sure they all like to have me string for them in places they don't have correspondents, but a real full-time job?"

"Working for me isn't in the big leagues?" Roger asked slyly.

Impulsively she put her hand out and took his. "That isn't what I meant, Roger."

"I know. Someday you'll end up with just the job you want."

"Do you think so?" she asked hopefully.

"I know so." He regarded her searchingly. She could be so self-assured, so confident, so clever one moment and then become so vulnerable, so in need of a strong friend to help her the next.

"You know I'll be thirty on my next birthday. I've spent nine years free-lancing, stringing, sending in my pictures, and still no real job."

Roger leaned toward her and kissed her tenderly. "For what it's worth, you've got me. I promised you a credit on the acknowledgment page of my book. Now tell me what else you've done over here."

Instantly Sarah brightened, the cheerful, self-possessed aura once again taking over. "You'll see. I've set up briefings for you at the Foreign Office, I have arranged for you to go to the House of Commons and talk to a group of MPs who are in favor of lifting economic sanctions against Rhodesia, and you'll have tea with the bishop who represents the World Council of Churches in London. The WCC is supporting the Communist terrorists in Rhodesia."

"Doesn't the WCC know these rebels are communists?" Roger asked.

Sarah sighed. "The racial aspect of the conflict is more important to them."

Roger shook his head. "But a racial war is even more vicious than a religious war. And war has never helped either cause in the long run. But then the world has never been able to learn that. Look at the Middle East."

Roger and Sarah sat silently for some moments, her hand still on his. When the driver pulled up in front of the Westbury Hotel Sarah asked him to wait and she went into the lobby with Roger.

"We're all checked in," she said brightly, handing the porter a room key and gesturing at Roger's suitcase. "Do you want to freshen up a bit before we go out?"

"I'd like to see our digs," Roger said cheerily.

"It's a good thing all this is tax-deductible. My God, a two-bedroom suite costs a small fortune here in London. I've been putting it to good use though. You'll probably scream at the room service bill but I had to entertain in order to make the contacts you wanted."

"Don't worry about it, sweetheart. It sounds as though you've done a hell of a good job." Upstairs in the suite Roger Masefield surveyed the scene approvingly. The flowers, liquor, ice and glasses gave the parlor a lived-in look.

"Your room is over there, mine is here," Sarah explained. She tipped the porter and he left them alone.

"Looks so nice here I hate to go out," Roger commented.

"Lord Johnny is expecting us," Sarah remonstrated.

"Well, we'll enjoy our suite later on."

"Johnny thinks he has a date with me tonight," Sarah remarked offhandedly.

"Does he in fact?"

Quizzical parentheses appeared at the corners of her lips. "You're the boss."

"I think we've got a lot to go over, Sarah Cobb Chase. You'll still be in London after I'm gone."

"You're not taking me on to Rhodesia?" she asked quickly, surprised.

"As I told you, I want to go alone the first time around. I'll arrange for you to get there at the appropriate time."

"The time seems to be getting more appropriate every day," Sarah observed coquettishly. "And it would be appropriate for us to make our way over to Lord Johnny's flat ASAP."

Lord Johnny Cravenlow was a tall, sandy-haired, pleasant-faced young hereditary peer of the realm; in his early thirties, Roger guessed as he shook hands with his host at his spacious flat in London's fashionable Belgravia.

It was a lively party and Roger judged that at fifty he was probably the oldest person present. Not that he looked his age. Some biological quirk kept Roger Masefield looking far younger than his years, abetted by luck, he thought, and well-aged liquor and the company of young women. Nevertheless, since the remark about his looking like somebody's family doctor, he had kept his thinning hair darkened.

Lord Johnny greeted Roger warmly and sputtered some profuse praise of his books. Taking him by the arm, he then shepherded him around the party introducing him to his friends.

"And this little mucked-up bugger, this bloody left-wing, national give-away artist is Lord Banglish." Roger noted the dark skin and fine-boned features of the peer. Sarah's briefing came back to him. Lord Banglish was an Indian whose family had performed services for the British before and after independence and the labor government had created him a lifetime peer. Roger and Banglish shook hands.

"And this is his current bird. What's your name, darling?"

"Her name is Cynthia, Johnny," Lord Banglish informed his host, not at all offended.

"She's beautiful, Bangie." Cravenlow turned from the girl to Roger. "We're great friends, you know. Some day maybe I'll bring enlightenment to his dim skull. He hates Rhodesians. He'd like to see us string up old Ian Smith by the thumbs and scourge him in the old-fashioned way. Lord Banglish, unfortunately, has no conception of what we English did for darkest and most backward Africa."

Lord Banglish blinked his eyes in assent and turned to Roger. "So you are the famous writer? And now you are on your way to Africa." He spoke with a high-pitched voice that seemed consistent with his puny stature and small pointed features. There was a gnomish air about him.

"I am looking forward to seeing Rhodesia," Roger acknowledged. "Just what I'll find I don't know. But that's one of the most exciting things about the early days of a new project. You come up with a conception, then you go out in the field and test that conception against reality and determine if you have a valid subject for a book." Suddenly Roger felt self-conscious. There was no reason for him to be revealing himself this way. However, Lord Banglish, Johnny and others crowded about him to hear what he was saying.

"You're pretty proud of glorifying the American invasion of Vietnam, aren't you?" Banglish taunted rhetorically.

"Did you happen to read my book?" Roger asked.

"No, I can't be bothered to read American radical right propaganda."

"Then you don't really know that it was propaganda," Roger retorted. "As I've always said, criticism from whatever source and of whatever hue is always valuable if the critic knows what he's talking about."

Johnny and the others burst out laughing. Undaunted, the Indian peer pushed on.

"Did you ever find a preconceived notion invalid?"

"Yes, once or twice."

"And what were those circumstances?"

"I went to Turkey convinced that the Turks had been totally wronged in the Cyprus situation. While I came back agreeing with that notion, I was unable to write a novel about heroic Turks and dastardly Greeks. It was an interesting trip though."

47

"And what is your preconceived notion about Rhodesia?"

"I expect that I'll find what I have always believed to be the truth. That Rhodesia is the most sophisticated country in all of Africa despite ten years of economic sanctions against it. I expect I will come to the conclusion all over again that the Rhodesians did no more than we Americans did two hundred years ago when we declared unilateral independence from Britain.

"At that time the founders of our country believed in a limited voting franchise," Roger continued, noting that no one else at the party was talking. "Most of them kept slaves. I've never heard of slavery in Rhodesia."

"The whole country is one great slave state, six million Africans owned by 250,000 whites," Banglish shrilled.

"The Indians in Rhodesia don't own any blacks then, I take it?" Roger asked sarcastically. "They pay their black employees more than the whites do?"

"The Asiatics are as much in thrall to the whites as the Africans," Banglish snapped.

"Since the Asiatics are shopkeepers and run their own small businesses and are a wealthy segment of the population, I would hardly say they are oppressed," Roger observed drily. "Where the blacks in Africa have taken power the Asiatics have been stripped of their businesses and possessions. Uganda is a good example. Certainly this isn't true of Rhodesia and South Africa."

For a moment Lord Banglish seemed nonplussed. Laughing, Lord Cravenlow broke in with, "Be careful, Roger. Bangie is a herpetologist. You upset him, he might turn his cobras loose on you."

Banglish chuckled. "One thing about cobras, they're not prejudiced. They'll poison anyone in range." Then to Roger he went on, "You'll find a more subtle method than confiscation used by the whites in Rhodesia to make the Asiatics feel inferior and to limit their opportunities. For instance, they can not move from Asian neighborhoods to white residential areas. Most of the best hotels and restaurants refuse admission to Asians as well as blacks. You have a lot to learn before you start writing."

"I'm sure," Roger replied. "And I suspect that one thing I'll learn is that you also have a lot to learn. I know statistically that Africans from all over the central part of the continent go to Rhodesia for a better standard of living." He paused but nobody interrupted him. Banglish was edgy yet attentive.

"I know that the arms being employed against the Rhodesians, both African and European, are totally Soviet and Red Chinese supplied and that the tactics of the terrorists are precisely those of the Viet Cong in Vietnam. I don't believe that the war in Rhodesia is based on racial considerations. That's merely the Marxist line for getting free world support for the Mugabe and Nkomo terrorists. I think that African moderate majority rule is the answer, not rule by fanatics like Mugabe and Nkomo who proclaim they will wipe out the white man and all his ways." Roger smiled blandly at Banglish. "Those are the notions I'll be testing."

"Total balls! I've never heard such idiocy mouthed by an American before, not that this isn't what we expect from Americans."

"Have you been to Rhodesia?" Roger asked.

"I wouldn't go near that fascist, racist, police state!"

"Well at least I will be able to test my notions against what I can observe," Roger said. "Which is precisely why people who read my books believe what I say."

A short round of applause and laughter greeted Roger's statement. The volatile Indian seemed no whit abashed. He merely turned to his host and displayed an empty champagne glass. "I'll give you one thing, Johnny: your salon certainly exhibits the pick of reactionary Tory thinking still available in this country of ours. As empty as this glass."

"Bangie, your empty glass we can do something about right now." Cravenlow plucked a champagne bottle out of the ice bucket and filled his guest's glass. "About your head, I don't know what we're going to do, dear chap."

He turned to Roger. "You never would know it, of course, but we really are good friends. I would be quite lost without Bangie around to bang ideas against. And while you might find this difficult to credit, he's actually changed my mind on occasion. Not very often, but it's been known to happen. Right, Bangie?"

"You do have your moments of rationality, Johnny."

Sarah came up to Roger and handed him a glass of champagne. "Johnny," she said, "you haven't introduced Roger to Mike Cleary yet."

"What a happy couple they should make," Banglish said spitefully.

"By all means," Cravenlow agreed. "You'll never find Mike in the proximity of Bangie, that's for sure."

At the other end of the room was an archway into a study through which Lord Cravenlow led Roger and Sarah. Standing beside a small bar was a trim, businesslike Englishman holding a drink and talking to an attractive young woman. The party was liberally laced with attractive young women, as Roger had noticed the moment he entered. This Lord Johnny was obviously a good man to know in London.

"Mike, I want you to meet Roger Masefield. He just flew in from New York, your old stomping ground." Mike looked up with interest. He exchanged greetings with Roger and kissed Sarah lightly on the cheek. "So you finally got around to joining us tonight, did you, Sarah?"

"I can't help but be amazed at how fast Sarah has got herself into such interesting circles," Roger said.

"Quite right. A week ago I never knew Sarah Cobb Chase existed. Now I feel as though we've known her forever."

"She has that gift," Roger agreed.

"Roger's on his way to Rhodesia," Sarah announced.

"So you told me, so you told me, Sarah," Mike murmered. "Another book, I presume?"

"I hope so," Roger replied. He vaguely wondered how many of the attractive men at this party Sarah Cobb Chase had already been intimate with, not that he allowed his mind to dwell on that aspect of her research.

Mike Cleary was one of those middlemen in business who specialized in the Rhodesian economy. Since the world had placed economic sanctions against Rhodesia, people like Mike Cleary were unofficially known as "sanctions busters." Mike, like the others at Lord Johnny's party, seemed to be in the thirty-five to forty age group, a man in his prime.

"I reckon I'll be in Salisbury in about ten days," Mike said. "Look up my associate there, Jack Cornwell. He'll tell you when and where to find me."

"Thanks, I will. You might even be disposed to give me some insight into the Rhodesian economy."

"I'll do the best I can, Roger."

"I might say that no sensitive activities fictionalized in my books have ever been compromised," Roger added with a smile.

Cleary reached for Roger's empty glass. "Here, let me fill you up. By the way, I suppose you've been told this before, but when you go to Rhodesia bring all the Scotch you can get into your bags. The troopies don't have much trouble getting pissed on cane liquor or the gin and vodka they make in Rhodesia but at the officers' mess and at the gentlemen's clubs good Scotch is preferred."

"I'll remember," Roger promised.

He was surprised, but not displeased, when Mike began discussing some of his books. Evidently Mike found them excellent reading on airplanes.

By one A.M. Sarah extricated Roger from the party, which was still in boisterous progress, and took him back to the suite at the Westbury Hotel.

"Are you tired, Roger? Ready for bed?" she asked sympathetically.

Roger couldn't restrain a yawn. "That was a very illuminating party you took me to. I learned a lot from the people there. Thanks, Sarah."

"The Wog Lord, as Johnny sometimes refers to Banglish, was as acid-mouthed as ever," Sarah noted.

"He expressed what is unfortunately a widely held view, a view I hope to challenge in the book." Roger leaned back in an overstuffed chair and smiled peacefully at Sarah. "You sure make a lot of strong contacts fast. I'm impressed."

"Wait till I get to Rhodesia," she promised.

"I hope you've got a double bed in your room, Sarah Cobb Chase. Those two cots they call beds in my room are hardly big enough for one."

"You're taking a lot for granted, Mr. Masefield," she scolded impishly.

"Oh, I don't know. Remember the Caravelle Hotel in Saigon? Your first visit just before the Tet nonsense? How old were you, all of twenty-two?"

Sarah nodded. "But you were the most famous writer over there. Of course I wanted to know you. Everyone did."

"Well you sure did," Roger chuckled. "And then we went up to Da Nang and I let that Marine colonel take you away from me."

"And me, just a stringer, I hit the front pages all over the world with my stories and pictures of the relief of Hue," she chortled.

"I can't forget our little episode after the Vietnam War in New York. Started at Costello's Bar. Lasted three whole days and nights. Counted 'em—three."

Suddenly the smile faded from Sarah's face. "Why did you marry Jocelyn?"

There was a long pause. "You were stringing in the Middle East. Anyway, you weren't ready for marriage." He paused again, his own grin failing. "And neither was I."

"I think I am now, if the right man came along," Sarah said seriously.

"Meantime, you're a damn good, dangerous-living newswoman. Let's enjoy while we can. The grave's a fine and private place, but none I think do there embrace."

"Anything you say, boss." The direct stare and expressive parentheses lines at the corners of her lips teased him into action. He stood up, walked over to her, put his arms around her, and kissed her. She responded. Finally, she pulled away. "You have a nine o'clock breakfast date downstairs with a feature writer from the Daily Telegraph. Nothing wrong with getting a little publicity on this book, is there?"

"So you're not only a researcher and a writer but a press agent too. But yes, you're right. Maybe it will help me to get a good advance sale with a London publisher. This is going to be one expensive project, I can see that. It should be worth it though." Casually, he turned off the lights in the living room and led Sarah into her own bedroom.

"I may seem to be taking it lightly, Sarah, but I've been thinking about this all the way over on the plane," Roger breathed hoarsely. "I didn't know we'd have to get through a party first."

"I've kind of been looking forward to our own private party too, boss," she whispered back.

Chapter 8

Group Leader Nyati kept his Freedom Fighters moving even after the sky had become tinted with light from the rising sun. Then, in sight of the kopje where they would hide until darkness returned, he halted the column. They were following an indistinct cattle path which made walking through the bush easier as the barrels of their rifles encountered less foliage.

Suddenly, terrifyingly, a huge tortoise appeared on the path in front of them. In this area of the Rhodesian borderland with Mozambique, where rivers, ponds, and dams abounded, there was always the fear of finding a tortoise in the way. Nyati pointed out the slow-moving shelled creature to his men and sat down on the ground, placing his RPD machine gun beside him. They followed his example and stared in awe at the tortoise. There was no worse *muti*, "medicine," than a tortoise in your path. For half an hour Nyati and his men sat watching the ponderous amphibian, praying it would turn and go back whence it had come.

Samual Jobolingo, too, had been brought up to fear the *muti* of a tortoise crossing his path. In his five years as a ZANU Freedom Fighter he had only twice had this happen, and in both cases, with security forces pressing him, he had chosen to brave the terrible tortoise *muti* rather than the guns of the Boers. Since he had slipped back to his

ZANU camp in Mozambique alive and unwounded each time, he decided that the tortoise spirits had understood his dilemma and forgiven him. Group Leader Nyati obviously had no such faith in the tortoise spirits' willingness to forego the veneration that was their due in deference to the exigencies of freedom fighting. This was a situation that Jobolingo, as political commissar, had to think out carefully.

Soon the sun would be up and the likelihood of being discovered by enemy aircraft or even patrols increased. Yet Jobo was well aware of the fact that every man in this group was terrified of offering insult to the tortoise. Forcing them, against their deepest beliefs, to traverse the tortoise's path could conceivably cause a mutiny. Well trained in Tanzania as these men were, the ancient beliefs were strong within them.

Although even Jobo watched the tortoise with some trepidation, he knew he must lead the group to the protection of the fortresslike stone kopje ahead which was concealed by thick bush. He would allow Nyati fifteen minutes more, and then if the leader would not move ahead, he, as political commissar, would have to use his authority to place himself in command.

Jobolingo mused on the fact that he was only two days walking from his birthplace in the Mt. Darwin area. He had gone through his standard six years of schooling, could read and write and was considered above average in intelligence. He had been brought to the attention of the white district commissioner as a young man deserving further government-paid education. Indeed he was about to be sent to a Catholic mission high school when his kraal was attacked. He and his wife were sleeping when the rocket-propelled grenades were fired into the group of huts. Thirty-two guerrillas, divided into two sections, had entered the kraal and abducted Jobolingo, his wife and the rest of the young men and women, threatening to kill them and their parents if they did not go with the gunmen.

Ninety young men and women had been taken from their villages that night and marched out of their Tribal Trust Land homes. They were going to cross the Zambezi River by boat. A bus would be waiting to take them to Tanzania where they would be trained in guerrilla tactics. They would also be taught how to drive an automobile or a truck, a cherished skill. And they were promised that later, when Rhodesia was taken over by Robert Mugabe's ZANU Freedom Fighters, they would be privileged men.

Their first stop was Mozambique. The security forces had quickly picked up their spoor but were unable to catch up with them. And so Samual Jobolingo became part of the ZANU movement.

In Mozambique there had been no food and no transport. All the young men and women from the kraal were hungry and tired. But when they lagged behind their abductors they were beaten and threatened, so they kept going. Inside Mozambique they continued walking north and finally reached the Zambezi River. At last they were given clothing, a meager food ration and taken across the river in boats. In the town of Mapapa they met a group of FRELIMO soldiers, the Mozambique guerrillas fighting the white Portuguese colonial government.

Instead of welcoming the Rhodesian Freedom Fighters, the FRELIMO took what little they had. In addition the FRELIMOS took all the women who had come out of the villages, including Jobolingo's wife, and marched the men north to a training center in the town of Chuifumbi inside Zambia.

That was the last Jobolingo ever saw of his wife. Later he learned she had been murdered because she refused to become the concubine of the FRELIMO commander. They had called her a sellout and shot her. Of the ninety villagers who had been abducted, twenty-four were women, the rest young men. The youngest male was thirteen, the oldest thirty-two. The group had been assembled from raiding all the kraals in the Tribal Trust area much in the manner of the old slave-trading days which Jobolingo had studied at school.

Separated from their women, the young men began their training. From five-thirty until eight-thirty every morning they took physical training, which included long runs. Then until one P.M., when they were given lunch, they were lectured on the goals of Robert Mugabe, leader of the Zimbabwe African National Union, ZANU, and indoctrinated in Marxism. After lunch political indoctrination continued on into the night. Soon Jobolingo learned the truth about his native country and oppression he and all of his fellow Zimbabweans were suffering at the hands of the white man. Despite what FRELIMO had done to his wife, he learned to understand that their actions were correct. They were fighting to rid their country of the hated Portuguese exploiters.

Jobolingo and his comrades were indeed fortunate that they had been brought into Robert Mugabe's ZANU army. When they won the war in Zimbabwe and the white man was exterminated they would take their rightful place in important ruling positions. The great houses that the white man had built with cheap African labor would go to the Africans who had fought for their freedom. Jobolingo would become an important man in his native country when the war was over. He learned to become thankful that he had been taken from the sellouts who ruled his kraal and given the opportunity to become part of the new order.

Jobolingo and the other male abductees could hardly wait to be given guns. They would have the privilege of killing the sellouts back in Rhodesia, and the daughters of the sellout chiefs were eligible for rape in the presence of their families. Once they were given their guns they could attack the security forces easily and soon they could win the war.

How proud Jobolingo and his fellow trainees had been when, after a month of intensive political indoctrination, they were taught how to handle the Russian AK-47 assault rifles. Jobolingo had been the star pupil, the first to be able to assemble and disassemble his weapon. He quickly learned how to fire from the prone position and standing up. He learned how to run with his rifle, how to shoot it and how to use the three-sided bayonet which they called a pigsticker. Like the others, he was also taught how to handle explosives.

After two months Jobolingo's group was divided into sections and taught other specialties. One section learned how to plant land mines and booby traps. Another section became specialists in the mortar. Yet another learned the heavy machine gun and several others how to run through the bush firing assault rifles. Jobolingo's section specialized in land mines and booby traps. He received his training from Chinese instructors and some Africans. He became proficient in carrying the mines and in burying them and placing the detonator.

At first Jobo missed his wife, and his bitterness against FRELIMO was slow in subsiding, but finally, imbued with the greater principles in which he had been so fortunate as to be indoctrinated, the only desire that gripped him was to kill the Boers and African sellouts in his homeland.

As his training moved closer to the day when he would go back to Rhodesia and kill Boers and sellouts, he and his comrades were puzzled to find themselves in the middle of a quarrel between Joshua Nkomo's Zambian-supported Rhodesian guerrillas, known as ZAPU

(Zimbabwe African Peoples Union), and Robert Mugabe's ZANU faction. This hostility was furthered by the mutual hatred that had always existed between black Rhodesians and Zambians. Although they were training in Zambia, Jobolingo and his comrades in the revolution used to say, "We don't eat off the same plates as the Zambians."

Jobolingo was well aware that the President of Zambia, Kenneth Kaunda, had long championed the Zulu tribesman Joshua Nkomo. Nevertheless, Jobolingo and his group were indoctrinated to be loyal to Robert Mugabe's ZANU, just the same.

This stage of their political and military training completed, they were sent back to Mozambique, which they found to be in chaos.

It was explained to Jobolingo that back in Europe, in Portugal, there had been a Communist coup d'etat and the Portuguese were being pulled out of the colony. The FRELIMOS were beginning to take over under their Marxist leader Samora Machel. This was a great time for the Rhodesian Freedom Fighters, to whom Machel gave protection and supplies.

In Mozambique Samuel Jobolingo met Russians, Chinese and Cubans who came to visit the ZANU training centers. By now he was a promising Freedom Fighter and had been earmarked for leadership. As a result, his training became more extensive. Besides weapon instruction he learned first aid and more advanced skills such as laying out ambushes. Of course he was privileged to participate in constant political indoctrination.

Finally, eight months after his abduction from Rhodesia, his training was over. What at the time appeared to be the catastrophe of his lifetime had opened up his future. He would never forget the excitement of his first foray back into Rhodesia.

It was in 1974 that he crossed the border with ninety other ZANU Freedom Fighters. Once in Rhodesia they separated into sections of about twenty each. Their orders were to indoctrinate the local people into the Marxist socialist doctrine. Robert Mugabe himself had come to see them before they left. His orders were clear. If the local people did not accept the thinking of the Freedom Fighters then they were to be taught what happens to Africans who sell out to the whites, who oppress them and use them for slave labor.

Mugabe had left it to the discretion of the individual Freedom Fighters to decide what coercion was necessary to make the tribal villagers turn from the white district commissioners, the African assistant district commissioners, the school teachers and all others who represented the central government in Salisbury. And so, well armed, Jobolingo and his comrades set about their mission.

At first it puzzled, annoyed and frustrated Jobo and his fellow ZANU-trained Freedom Fighters that the people could not understand what he meant when he talked about the struggle for freedom. But Jobo and the members of his section persevered. Soon they found that the Communist doctrine of terrorism with which they had been imbued paid off. They used their pigstickers to good effect. If the people could not understand their political speeches, at least they understood what it meant to have a bayonet pushed through their bellies.

By torturing and assassinating the representatives of the Salisbury government, they soon intimidated the people into at least listening to their political lectures and promising not to cooperate with the government. Jobolingo quickly discovered how to cure inattention at these political sessions: he merely shot the first person that did not seem to be absorbing his words. After that the others listened carefully.

The men of Jobo's section took great enjoyment in their task of torturing. Heady with power, they walked into a village, raping the daughters and wives of the headman and kraal chiefs and often burning their whole families alive in their huts. At first Jobolingo had little stomach for this sort of cruelty but he came to realize that this was the only way that the white man, who had subjected his people to slavery, could be defeated. He and his section were so successful in alienating the people from their government that he was made a provincial intelligence officer under the operational commander of the ZANU forces in the First or Northern Province of Rhodesia. As an intelligence secretary he was equivalent to a political commissar and had the right to challenge any section commander in the province.

Food was always on the minds of the Freedom Fighters and sometimes made then incautious. Once, when Jobolingo was out with a section commander named Mobu on a food foraging expedition, an aircraft flew over them. Jobolingo didn't know about spotter planes then and failed to realize that it was radioing their position to the security forces.

Since it was a hot day Mobu allowed all his men to have a swim, and it was while they were in the water that four helicopters flew over.

The last helicopter spotted Mobu, Jobolingo and their group, then turned and came back firing. Mobu shouted orders for his men to run, but Jobolingo, who had quickly assessed the situation in his role as commissar, challenged the authority of Mobu. He ordered the men not to run but to stay and fight. The area was clear and even if they did bombshell, running off in all directions, they would easily be picked off by either security forces in the area or the helicopters. By now two sticks of security forces had been landed by the other helicopters and were closing in on them. Mobu ran for a rocky hill where he hoped to find cover but was immediately killed by the security forces, who were rapidly moving in.

Jobolingo fought back, firing bursts from his AK-47 which held off the government troops long enough so he could gather nine of his Freedom Fighters and escape from the contact. Later he picked up three more of his men. The rest, he was sure, were dead. He led the men to a kopje atop which they watched as the helicopters landed and picked up the troopers who had been pursuing them.

That was three years ago. Since then Jobolingo had been in many contacts with the security forces. He had risen to the rank of full political commissar and was responsible for several hundred Freedom Fighters whose military leaders he had frequently been obliged to relieve of their commands, taking these over himself. His name by now was well known to the ZANU hierarchy, and to the Rhodesian Special Branch. For the past year, when Jobolingo reported to ZANU Head-quarters in Maputo, Mozambique, he frequently stayed in the same house with Robert Mugabe. Also occupying the house was Mugabe's chief political officer, Rex Nhongo, and his chief of staff, General Tongogara.

Tongogara had a fearsome reputation for murdering ZANU func-tionaries considered on the verge of disloyalty to Mugabe and himself. Indeed it was Tongogara who had blown up the internationally known lawyer and leader, Herbert Chitepo, in Zambia. Chitepo, who had won a measure of international respect for the ZANU cause, had become a threat to Tongogara's standing in the movement as military commander and number two man. It was well known that Tongogara aspired to take over Mugabe's position when ZANU finally came to power.

When Samuel Jobolingo first started moving up in the ZANU organization he wondered why Robert Mugabe had expressly ordered that the genitals of any captured white man be cut off and stuffed into his mouth while he was still alive. On those rare occasions that a white man was taken alive after an attack on a farm or a contact with the security forces, Jobo's men vied with each other for the pleasure of complying with Mugabe's order.

The reason for these instructions, Jobolingo learned when he became a full commissar, was that Mugabe himself was a man without genitals. Since no African would ever allow himself to be ruled by a man who was not wholly a man, Jobolingo believed that Robert Mugabe could never become the ultimate leader of Zimbabwe—or at least not for long.

In the revolutionary stages of the ZANU movement Mugabe's worldwide recognition as a nationalist leader made him valuable. But at the appropriate moment one of his closest followers would assassinate and supplant him. General Josiah Tongogara was the likeliest to do so.

Mugabe, suffering from a long unarrested case of syphilis, had developed cancer of the penis and testicles and while he was in prison for subversive activities, in order to save his life, a white surgeon had excised the diseased parts. It would have been better for Mugabe to die of the cancer rather than suffer the drastic cure. He was doomed now, his followers were convinced, never to take secure hold of the reins of true power in Zimbabwe.

As Jobolingo impatiently sat with his group staring at the tortoise and waiting for it to move, he thought of the discussions he'd had with Mugabe, Nhongo and Tongogara. They had talked with him at length about the conduct of the liberation war and the political structure that ZANU would bring to Zimbabwe when it took power. The white man would either flee or be massacred. A total Marxist socialist system would be put into effect, patterned after the Mozambique system of Samora Machel. Jobo felt his first twinges of concern at this. He had traveled throughout Mozambique. He had seen the murder of twenty-seven tribal chiefs and the destruction of tribal society, a necessity, he realized, if a true Marxist state were to be achieved. The old ways had to go. But it worried him that the population of Mozambique was starving and only the commissars and military officers of high rank had enough food to eat. To be sure, his concern was somewhat muted by the fact that he himself would be a high-ranking commissar in the new Zimbabwe.

When Mugabe talked to you directly you were inspired, you were certain that all his promises were going to come about, Jobo thought. But once you got to the front—he looked around at his men patiently waiting for the tortoise to move and then up at the sky, searching for spotter planes—yes, once you were fighting security forces, your friends died and you looked at their bodies and you suffered. Also, you had nowhere to sleep and no blankets. At times like this, when they were in danger of death at the hands of the Rhodesian Army, Jobo couldn't help comparing himself with the local tribesmen who lived in a kraal and led a better life than any Freedom Fighter, always on the run, always looking for food: at moments like this everything was different from what Mugabe told him.

Jobolingo glanced at his watch, then up at the sky again. Suddenly he made his decision. He stood up and shouted commands at his men, ordering Nyati to the rear. He started toward the kopje ahead, making straight for the tortoise. Turning around, he saw his men standing fast.

"*Chimaranga!*" he cried. "Follow me." The group leader stood as though rooted to the spot. The men were hesitant whether to follow Jobolingo into the path of the evil *muti* before them or stay with Nyati.

Jobolingo considered shooting the group leader but decided that the noise of the rifle shot might attract attention. Also the group leader was a skillful fighting man and ZANU needed every such man it could get. Once more he shouted his orders, his hot eyes fixing on each man separately. He then turned and walked forward, making a wide arc around the tortoise. One by one the men tremulously followed, their eyes wide with fear as they passed the giant tortoise. Finally the last of them had maneuvered beyond the sinister humpbacked form and now they moved forward rapidly toward the protection of the kopje.

Just as Jobolingo's men were entering the heavy foliage around the kopje and the first of them had begun climbing its craggy sides, one of the airplanes that Jobolingo had come to be particularly wary of, the kind with two engines, one at the front pulling and the other at the back pushing, appeared in the sky above them. He shouted an order and the men quickly blended into the bush and foliage or found protective fissures in the steep walls of the kopje. Jobolingo wondered if they'd been seen. The whole mission since they left Mozambique had, in his opinion, been unduly sloppy. Perhaps this group leader would improve with experience; he hoped so. He would return command to Nyati once they started out again that night. His evaluation of the group leader's overall performance and the performance of the assistant commissar he was training would decide the speed at which these two advanced within the ZANU organization.

Chapter 9

Mack Hudson knew he should go home to Carla who would be waiting for him in their apartment in the Avenue. Instead, after his last interview he marched purposefully to the SAS officers' mess and went inside. There were the usual group of Rhodesian officers at the bar, some in civilian clothes, others wearing the camouflage fatigues that was their regular uniform.

"Is Major Atkinson around?" he asked.

"No sir," a young lieutenant replied. "He went home about an hour ago."

Mack felt himself relaxing. Another American officer, Captain Hugh McKnight, sidled up to him, "Buy you one?"

"Thanks, Hugh. A Castle." McKnight ordered the bottle of ale from the African doing bar duty.

"Any action?" Mack asked.

"Intelligence just came in that a large group of terrs crossed over from Mozambique up in the Mrewa Tribal Trust Land."

"Anybody going after them?" Mack asked.

"The RLI strike force at Mtoko will take care of them if they surface."

A light came into Mack Hudson's eyes. "Maybe we should go out and help them," he suggested.

"Didn't you get into enough trouble with Major Atkinson last time you ran off on your own?"

"Sure. And we killed eighteen terrs." He took a long pull on the mug of ale. "The Rhodesians pay me to kill terrs. I don't feel like I'm earning my money in garrison."

"There's a chopper standing by on the pad," McKnight said suggestively.

Mack straightened. "Where's Sergeant LeClair?"

"Probably in the sergeants' mess."

"And the Kraut?"

"Houk? He's with LeClair."

"Then we've got a fire force."

Nervously McKnight downed his drink. "If you're thinking what I think you're thinking, we ought to at least have one Rhodie officer with us."

"Sure, if we can find one who doesn't plan to make the military a career."

McKnight looked up and down the bar and then around at the tables. "We'll find someone."

"Get the latest intelligence report on those terrs," Mack ordered.

He was into his second Castle when McKnight returned. "They've got the terrs pinpointed now. An RLI fire force will go in at first light."

"At first light? By that time they will have tortured and murdered half the villagers in the area. We've got to stop them tonight."

"Well then, you better call your friend Major Bruce Atkinson. As commander of SAS he'll have to request permission from ComOps to make a strike before daylight."

A sergeant stamped into the officers' mess, walked up to Captain Hudson and saluted. "Sir, we just got a signal from ComOps. They want Major Atkinson to call them back. Now-now."

Mack looked about the bar. "Seems like I'm the ranking officer here. I'll call ComOps."

"You could get the major at home, Mack," McKnight suggested uneasily.

"Wouldn't want to bother the poor chap. He gets little enough home life as it is." Hudson strode from the bar, out of the mess and across to the Operations Room. The sergeant followed behind him.

Inside Mack picked up the direct line to Combined Operations and identified himself. "Captain Hudson, SAS, replying to the request for Major Atkinson," he reported. In moments he was talking to the deputy commander.

"Where is Major Atkinson?" Colonel Vey asked sharply.

"Not here, sir. I felt I should call directly."

"Yes, quite. You're the American." It was a flat statement of fact.

"One of them, yes sir."

"We've got a report of large-scale terr activity along the border near Mrewa. I don't like to request a night jump but there is an area up there an SAS force could jump into."

Hudson glanced at the map behind him. "Yes, sir. Drop Zone Red Seven."

"Can you drop a stick in there and move through the TTL and try to make contact?"

"Yes, sir," Hudson replied eagerly. "That's what we're here for."

"I'll send a briefing officer right down. Be prepared to take your stick out to the air force Operations Room at New Sarum. There'll be a plane ready to fly you to your mission site."

Mack Hudson stalked into the sergeants' mess. "LeClair!" he shouted.

"*Mon capitaine,*" the sergeant replied, springing to attention beside the bar.

"Get your stick together, kit up for a jump. Draw two hundred rounds a man. We'll be heading for New Sarum in fifteen minutes."

Mack could picture Major Atkinson now, sitting at home trying to tack together the remnants of his marriage. Bruce was a short, stocky, ruddy-faced Rhodesian in his mid-thirties who had become insufferably arrogant since he made major. Even his wife found him hard to take. He had never been outside Rhodesia except for a training tour in South Africa and it was difficult for him to understand the aggressive Americans who came in to the unit. Many of them, indeed, were anathema to him.

Maybe if Atkinson had been taller or he shorter they would have worked better together, Mack thought. But the difference in height, added to Mack's delight in jumping into combat with his men instead of staying in a helicopter or at a safe command post coordinating signals as ordered by Major Atkinson, had produced a decided antipathy between the two men. Atkinson himself, though once enterprising and belligerent in cross-border operations, now preferred to organize his unit's forays against the terrorists from the rear.

There would be hell to pay, Mack knew, when Atkinson discovered that the bloody Yank had gone and done it again.

Thirty minutes later two truckloads of SAS troopers, combat ready, FN rifles and machine guns slung over their shoulders, pulled up in front of the Operations Building. Mack Hudson jumped out of the cab of the lead truck and strode into the briefing room. A group of air force and army officers were gathered around the map of Rhodesia looking at the northeast corner of the country. They turned as Mack Hudson walked in.

"You chaps ready?" a lieutenant colonel asked.

"Yes, sir," Mack replied.

"Get your men aboard the Dakota out there. When word comes in from ComOps to go, you'll be on your way. There'll be trucks to pick you up in the morning. Good hunting!" he added cheerfully.

Mack turned from the Operations Room, walked outside and addressed the two ranks of twelve men each. Sergeant LeClair stood in front of them. All were now strapped into their parachutes.

"*Nous sommes prets!*"

"Come on, Sergeant, you're not in the Foreign Legion now."

White teeth grinned in the grease-blackened face of the sergeant.

"OK, Captain. What are zee orders?"

"Get your men into the Dakota."

"I'm coming with you, Sergeant."

White eyes widened in the shadowy face of Sergeant LeClair. "But sir, I understand you do not go on combat jump. Major Atkinson posted eet on the board."

"Sergeant, I'll be leading this stick. You can take it up with Major Atkinson when, as and if we get back."

"Yes, sir." The Frenchman saluted and turned to his troops.

"*Allez-vous-en!*" he shouted. "Board zee plane!"

The SAS paratroopers needed no further urging and in single file clambered into the Dakota.

As Mack Hudson was about to step up he heard a familiar American voice call out, "Hey, Mack, you jumping?" Mack looked at the tall grinning pilot, Hubert Kirkendale, the waxed ends of his moustache curling fiercely upwards.

"Kirk, I didn't know they put you on drop flights. I thought your job was ferrying gold bullion down to Joburg."

Kirkendale laughed. "That's where I thought I was going tonight. I really had me something nice waiting down there too. Now I've got to fly you guys out to the bush instead."

"Can you find it all right, Kirk?" Mack asked anxiously.

"No sweat. I've been there before." He clapped a hand on Hudson's shoulder. "Get in, Mack. I'm going to warm up the engines."

Mack pulled himself up the steps into the rear end of the Dakota and buckled himself into the seat beside the door. The worst part of a jump was the waiting. Waiting to take off. Waiting to get over the drop zone. Waiting for the paratroopers to hook up. Waiting for the light to turn green above the door. Then it was out into the slipstream, and from then on everything was automatic.

As he sat staring ahead, the engines roared into life and for a moment he thought about Carla. In all the haste he had forgotten to call and let her know he wouldn't be back tonight. Not that this didn't happen frequently. She had been an exemplary wife to him, he thought. Here she was in a strange country just to be with her husband, and here he was . . .

Suddenly the Dakota vibrated violently as the engines were run up and down by the Yank pilot. Mack wondered what Carla was doing now. Probably reading and expecting him to come home any minute. He felt guilty that he had not gone directly back to the apartment from the Special Branch meeting. Well, when Bruce Atkinson discovered that the Yank captain had taken over virtual command of SAS and led a stick in an operation, he'd be wild. Then he'd confine Mack to garrison duty for sure and Carla would see plenty of him.

Chapter 10

All day Jobolingo and his men had hidden in the kopje watching for any sign of security force activity. There had been none, and as the protective blanket of darkness settled over the land his fears about the push-pull airplane they had seen that morning subsided. Now they were ready to move out again and go into the village which was their objective.

The men were excited. They looked forward to teaching the sellouts a lesson. Although they were hungry and had no food with them, they would soon gorge themselves on the supplies in the village. And also on the young women of the sellout headman's family.

Group Leader Nyati, having been restored to command, led the Freedom Fighters out of the kopje and across the scattered bush toward the Tribal Trust Land and the villages within. It was a three-hour trek but finally they reached their target.

Before them were a hundred huts, comprising one of the largest villages in this Tribal Trust Land. Without formalities the guerrillas marched into the village shouting for the people to come out of their huts and assemble in front of the headman's thatched home. Then they demanded food which was immediately provided. Maize and meat were distributed, the latter left over from a steer that had been slaugh-

69

tered to commemorate the engagement of the headman's daughter to a member of the tribe.

After they had eaten, the Freedom Fighters made all the villagers stand and listen to a two-hour indoctrination speech on the new political order that Robert Mugabe and ZANU would bring to Zimbabwe. It was the first big speech of Jobolingo's new assistant political commissar but if he were overzealous and spoke too long, thus endangering the Freedom Fighters' security, he would seal his own fate.

Jobolingo had been given special orders that came from Tongogara himself. He was not to take any more chances than necessary. He was not to be captured. He was to avoid personal contact with the security forces. This mission was more of a training and assessment expedition. The ZANU leaders did not want to lose so valuable a man as Jobolingo. He would at all times guard his safety and if necessary abandon the rest of the Freedom Fighters to make good his escape. He had been told of the location of a certain Catholic mission which would feed him and hide him if he had to flee alone. Now, therefore, Jobolingo stood apart from the others and watched as the assistant commissar harangued the populace and the group leader menaced them with his AK-47. It wouldn't be long, Jobolingo knew, before the boys, their blood lust up, would start teaching the sellouts a lesson.

At New Sarum the Dakota taxied across the runway. The mission was on. Mack looked at the men of his stick, gave them a thumbs-up and settled back in his bucket seat.

Ninety minutes later, from his seat beside the door, he saw the light blinking above the pilot's compartment. They were getting close. He stood.

The dispatcher—jump master, Mack would have called him in a U.S. air-borne operation—was standing at the back of the plane facing the cockpit. Securely belted to the bulkhead behind him, he stood swaying with the motion of the plane.

"Stand up! Hook up! Check equipment!" The dispatcher shouted the commands.

The troopers struggled to their feet and, reaching up, hooked their static lines onto the cable which ran down the fuselage.

The twenty-four men stood facing each other in equal lines and carried out the familiar drill. The man at the head of one line shouted out his number, rapidly followed by the man next to him, and so on down the row. "Twelve OK, eleven OK . . ." In moments came: "One OK. Starboard stick OK!"

The men on the other side rattled through the same procedure. ". . . One OK. Port stick OK!"

With the command, "Action stations," the men turned to the rear of the plane and stomped forward several paces in unison. Mack was now two feet from the exit, his left hand over the door taking his weight. He glanced quickly at the air force dispatcher, an old friend from many jumps. They engaged in a few words of banter, a ritual with them.

"Hey Mike, you coming with us?" Mack shouted above the roar of the engines and the whoosh of the slipstream outside the open door.

"Crikey, mate, not bloody likely!"

Both men grinned at each other. Then the dispatcher shouted, "Stand in the door!"

Mack, followed by his stick, stomped forward one pace. His left foot was firmly planted at the edge of the exit. Now he was ready to leap, on command, into the cool beckoning darkness. He leaned out and looked down, trying to identify Drop Zone Red Seven.

The stream of rushing air made his cheeks distend and ripple. This was not the kind of jump he liked. Usually there was a reception committee below to light the drop zone. Tonight they would drop blind. However, every member of his stick had been here before.

He looked down and spotted the familiar contour of the river which ran through the center of the Mrewa TTL. They would jump into the clear areas at the edge of the TTL where there were no houses. Strict curfew regulations were in force and the tribespeople would all be in their homes. Any tribesman who ventured more than twenty meters from his house or store was subject to being shot on the grounds that he was either a curfew violator or a terrorist. A number of curfew violators *had* been shot, but there was no other way the terrorist movement could be controlled.

They were now about two minutes from the drop zone, Mack estimated. He had great faith in Hubert. The Texan pilot had dropped many airborne assault teams before, both in Vietnam and in Rhodesia.

The dispatcher's eyes were riveted on the light above the door. Suddenly it changed from red to green. "Go!" he shouted.

Mack thrust himself forward and out into the rushing air currents. Elbows tight to his sides, hands cradling the auxiliary chute, head down, legs stiff and outstretched, he fell through the air only a few seconds before the parachute suddenly jerked open and floated him toward the ground four hundred feet below.

He looked up, checked his chute and peered around for the rest of his team. They were all floating, a neat line of enormous mushrooms. This was a low combat jump in which the men stayed in the air no more than thirty to forty seconds before hitting the ground and rolling over in a parachute landing fall.

Quickly Mack was back on his feet disengaging the chute from his shoulder harness and pulling it in. He stuffed it into the bag that had been tucked into his combat webbing and left it on the ground for future retrieval. The twenty-four-man stick of SAS paratroopers quickly packed up their chutes and, weapons at the ready, followed Mack from the drop zone toward the village. Using hand signals, Mack deployed them into a fan and they silently advanced on the TTL.

Soon they reached the outskirts of the village they were aiming for, a large group of round mud dwellings with conical straw roofs. They walked soundlessly past the houses toward the village center, the area where the chief would be living with his wives and children— and where the terrorists would be heading. The Rhodesian authorities had been trying for six months to get the tribesmen from this TTL to move into protected villages so that they would not be molested by the terrorists. However, local resistance to this kind of evacuation, even if temporary, was so strong that the Internal Affairs branch of the government had decided against it.

As the SAS stick moved toward their destination, they heard a voice shouting in the distance. Mack motioned to a corporal to move up beside him. The corporal spoke virtually perfect Shona, the tribal language of the Mashona tribal group, which comprised more than sixty percent of Rhodesia's African population.

As they stole closer to the open space at the center of the village, whence the harangue was coming, the corporal held up his hand and the men halted.

"It's a political commissar, sir. He's giving them the party line straight from Mugabe over in Mozambique. These people are being told they must have nothing to do with Bishop Muzorewa or his representatives."

"How many terrs do you think there are?"

"I can't tell you, sir."

The team continued their catlike advance. By now the words of the commissar were distinctly audible. Muffled cries and wails of women could be picked out, mingling oddly with the commissar's strident sloganeering. Despite the near-darkness, Mack could see the silhouettes of forty to fifty armed terrorists. They formed a ring around the assembled villagers who, some sitting, some standing, all seemed to be staring at the ground.

"He's telling them that their headman has been dipping his cattle in the white man's cattle dip," the corporal went on. "It's better to let the cattle die of the flea disease, he says, than use anything given by the government. Therefore, before they kill the headman, they will force the assistant district commissioner to rape his daughter. He says any African that works for the government will be assassinated."

Suddenly the scene became illuminated as several terrorists torched the dry thatched roofs of the native rondavels.

"They're burning up the headman's house!" the corporal cried excitedly. "I think they shot one of his sons before but he is still alive inside."

Mack could make out the village headman now, sitting slightly apart. He seemed too numbed with horror and grief to react.

A group of terrorists gleefully pulled a young girl out of the house next to the one that had been set ablaze. She screamed and tried to resist. As the commissar went on with his harangue the terrorists threw the girl on her back in front of the burning building. Three of them held her down and then, despite her kicking and squirming, a fourth man fell on top of her and raped her quickly, savagely.

Another of the headman's daughters was pulled out of the house, this one even younger than the last. The African assistant district commissioner, still wearing his khaki uniform, his shorts crisply pressed, his knee-high stockings immaculate, was prodded forward at the end of a bayonet.

The assistant district commissioner is the primary connection between the central authority of the Rhodesian government and the people out in the Tribal Trust Lands. He works directly under the district commissioner, a white Rhodesian with long training in caring for the people of the TTL. Everything from agricultural needs to education is supervised by the district commissioner through his native ADCs, and the latter take great pride in their role.

There was a hopeless, bewildered look on the ADC's face as he was pushed forward, the bayonet biting into the flesh of his back. The intention of the terrorists was obvious. The ADC would be forced to rape this young daughter of the headman. She would not only be rendered unmarriageable as a result, but the people would see she had been raped by a representative of the government. The fact that he was forced to do so would be of little consequence either to her or to them. The ADC—he would die soon anyway. But the girl would be worthless now: any man that wanted her could take her without paying lobola to her father.

Suddenly there was a shout as other terrorists dragged a pregnant woman from a house beside the headman's burning hut.

"That's the headman's newest and youngest wife!" The corporal was almost beside himself. "Are we going to shoot them, sir?"

"I'm worried about the crossfire, Corporal," Mack said grimly. "We could wipe the terrs out easily enough, but what about the villagers?"

There was an anguished look on the corporal's face. "There must be some way we can stop this, sir."

The pregnant woman was now dragged out and thrown on her back. The commissar pointed at her and continued shouting at the top of his lungs. A hundred or so villagers, all standing now, moaned softly.

Mack looked at the corporal. "Sir, he says that the wife of the sellout headman does not deserve to have a baby. He says that in the name of ZANU and their leader Robert Mugabe this sellout baby must not be born."

Mack heard the pitiful scream. One of the terrorists had placed a bayonet to the pregnant woman's belly and was slowly pressing it through her.

"Let me shoot the bastard, sir," a Rhodesian trooper said.

"The entire village could die if we start a firefight now." The sweat stood out on Mack's brow. "You can be sure the terrs will shoot everybody and claim it was government forces that did it. We'll kill every one of them when they leave here though," he gritted.

74

"But sir, how can we let this bestial activity continue?" another SAS trooper asked plaintively.

"All right. Pass the word," Mack ordered. "I want every man to have a bead on one terrorist and have his second target picked out. When I fire, everybody shoot. If we can kill twenty instantly and get another ten on our second volley, we can probably take care of the rest with minimal casualties to the villagers."

A last, thin, strangled scream was wrung from the pregnant woman as the terrorist leaned on his rifle butt. Then, slowly, he pulled the three-sided blade of the bayonet, dripping with blood, out of her belly. At that moment the headman's hut erupted in flames, and shortly after there was an acrid smell of burning human flesh. Now the terrorists turned their attention to the assistant district commissioner.

With two bayonets pressing deeper in his side, the eyes of the ADC rolled helplessly in his head, their whites flashing. He flinched first from the pigsticker menacing his right side, then from the one that was drawing blood from his left. Finally, reluctantly, he dropped his pants and although his malehood was badly wilted, knelt in front of the girl and whispered a few words to her. She stopped her kicking and screaming.

"I guess he told her it was this or they'd both die," the corporal commented. "Of course what they do is kill him once he's deflowered her." Vainly the ADC tried to hand-pump some life into his flaccid organ. The bayonets were now drawing blood from both his sides. "They just told him they wouldn't torture him to death but would make it fast if he succeeded," the corporal intoned.

"Is everybody ready?" Mack whispered. The twenty-four SAS paratroopers were now fully deployed and their weapons raised. Mack raised his FN rifle and took aim at the commissar. Slowly he squeezed the trigger and a shot rang out. The commissar, shot squarely in the gut, sprawled backwards against the flaming house, his stomach a mass of red. The FN has the most powerful shock effect of any rifle used in Rhodesia.

Before the surprised terrorists could make a move, there was concerted volley from the encircling troopers. At least twenty of the terrorists fell dead or wounded, followed by others hit by the second burst of fire. Still, the remaining terrorists recovered from their shock more quickly and to better effect than Mack had anticipated and there began the crossfire which he had dreaded.

In compliance with General Tongogara's orders, Jobolingo had been watching his Freedom Fighters administer their lesson to the sellouts from beside the wall of a hut some fifty feet away. Now, horrified, he saw almost half his men suddenly blown to pieces, the rest prone on the ground or sheltering behind villagers but likely to die shortly. He had no choice. Turning from the fight, he ran through the darkness toward the rear of the village. He must escape this contact and get back to Mozambique. He had suspected that the group leader's carelessness might compromise this operation. He should have relieved Nyati much sooner, he castigated himself. But it was too late now. His only salvation lay in getting to the St. Bonaventure Mission where he would be hidden and fed before proceeding back to Mozambique.

He threw down his AK-47 as he ran, and stripped off his camouflage jacket. A weapon would be no good to him now. The security forces would mow down anyone they saw carrying an AK-47 or any other Communist weapon. St. Bonaventure was forty miles from this village and Jobo should be able to get close enough to it before daylight so that, if he hid all day, he would reach it the following night.

The firing behind him was intense. The boys that were left alive were at least going down fighting, he thought with grim satisfaction. Although Jobo had confided his own escape plan to no one in his group, Nyati and the assistant commissar well knew that one of the Catholic missions in this area was hospitable to the boys when they needed help. From what he had seen and could hear, however, it was doubtful if any of the Freedom Fighters would live to tell the story.

Jobolingo loped through the bush in a desperate effort to get out of the area before security forces started combing it.

For some minutes, heedless of the villagers in the way, the Mugabe terrorists kept up a withering return fire against Mack's stick. Then, as if at a signal, those still alive threw down their weapons and ran, stripping off their outer layer of clothing as they went. The terrorists frequently wore three and even four sets of shirts and pants so that if they were identified in one set of clothing they could quickly discard it for another.

The SAS troopers chased after the ten or so fugitives who, realizing their chances of getting out of the village undetected were slim, began throwing themselves inside the native huts. The many villagers now cowering there were threatened with instant death if they did not conceal the terrorists from the "Boers."

Systematically, the SAS men went through each hut with flashlights and, predictably, more civilian casualties ensued. As SAS troopers entered a hut in which a terrorist was hiding, the family inside begged them to leave, insisting no *gadangas* were there. When a terrorist knew he was going to be found, he opened up with his AK and in the resulting crossfire innocent tribesmen were killed or wounded.

When the shooting stopped, Mack checked his troopers and found that three of his men had been wounded though none had been killed. Sergeant LeClair let out a shout from the other side of the camp and Mack ran toward him. LeClair was standing over a wounded terrorist, a pistol in his hand pointing at the man's head.

"Keep him alive, Sergeant," Mack ordered. "Let me get our interpreter. Maybe he can tell us something."

Once the Shona-speaking SAS trooper arrived and the terrorist had been given a cigarette, which he gratefully inhaled, it did not take long to elicit the information that this captive was a guerrilla under Group Leader Nyati. Further questioning, intermingled with threats and promises of mercy, yielded the information that one of the highest-ranking ZANU political commissars in the area had been with them. The name Samuel Jobolingo was revealed. So was the fact that somewhere in this northeast area of Rhodesia there was a church mission hospitable to the Freedom Fighters.

Mack Hudson had to restrain LeClair from aiming a kick at the terrorist's head when the interpreter said the words "Freedom Fighters."

"There must be half a dozen missions in the area up here," Mack said, "Can you get any more out of him? Is it a Catholic mission, a Methodist mission? What religion is involved?"

After some rapid exchanges with the guerrilla in Shona, the corporal declared that he felt the man did not know.

"Can I shoot heem now, sir?" LeClair asked.

"It may be that Special Branch can extract more useful information from this man," Mack replied. "He'll hang anyway."

By daylight the operation had been concluded. Mack and his troopers lined up the bodies of all the terrorists they'd killed. The only wounded terrorist left alive was the man being taken back for further interrogation. The SAS had seen too much that night. Saving these men for the judge and the hangman seemed like a waste of time. And they weren't in the mood for small mercies anyway.

The sun came up over thirty-eight terrorist bodies, neatly laid out for photographing and inspection. The ADC, who introduced himself as Jeremiah Luthu, was busy making arrangements for funeral services for the dead villagers and hospitalization for the wounded ones.

"Seventeen dead in the crossfire, Captain," he reported after making a complete inspection tour.

"It could have been worse, much worse," Mack said. "But even having to report seventeen dead in a crossfire will bring all kinds of flak in on us. I can see what the foreign press will make out of this one. They'll report the terrorists were peaceful villagers and we came in and gunned them all down. Thank God we have a Communist weapon for each one of them. How's the headman?"

"In shock, sir," Luthu replied.

"Can't you get these people into protected villages?" Mack asked.

"Up until now, no. Maybe this will help."

Mack expected the BSAP (British South African Police) to be there shortly. "We'll leave it in the capable hands of the cops," he told Luthu.

"You saved me, all of us, from a very bad death. These terrorists, these ZANU criminals led by the mad Mugabe, will do anything. I never knew such animals walked around on two legs."

"Don't let yourself get caught by them again, Luthu." Mack advised. "Looks like it's open season on ADCs."

"If Mugabe ever comes to power he will kill every African who ever worked for the government," Luthu proclaimed. "He's trying to do it now. We must fight to prevent that from happening. I will die to keep the murderers out of my country."

"That's why I came here from America to fight with you," Mack said warmly.

"Captain Hudson, maybe you will meet my brother, Sergeant Charles Luthu. He's in the Rhodesian African Rifles for ten years now."

"Perhaps I will, Luthu. I might even end up in the RAR myself." He thought about his commander, Major Bruce Atkinson.

"I will write to my brother and tell him about you. A few years ago our father and mother were murdered by Nkomo's ZAPU terrorists. I don't know who is the worst, Nkomo or Mugabe. When our parents were killed, my brother and I both took an oath to fight the ZAPU and ZANU terrorists, each in our own way."

Mack Hudson bid goodbye to the ADC, reassembled his men and led them back to the drop zone where they collected their parachutes. Radio instructions had been received to wait in the drop zone for the trucks which had already been dispatched.

It was late in the day when the trucks finally rumbled across the dirt roads to pick up Mack's stick. Thus it wouldn't be till the following morning that he called Carla to tell her why she hadn't seen him for two days. Well, that's the way war works, he thought philosophically.

Well, Mack sighed, he might as well get the recrimination and disciplinary threats over with.

Mack was chagrined, though not surprised, to see Major Bruce Atkinson, the SAS commander sitting beside the driver of the lead truck.

Atkinson jumped to the ground and, hands on hips, watched the men of his command climb into the trucks with their parachute bags and weapons. Mack tried to evade the inevitable confrontation and slink into one of the trucks in the midst of the men, but the major's bawl carried across the drop zone.

"Captain Hudson! Report to the lead lorry!"

The return to SAS barracks in Salisbury was a torturous affair for Mack. Fortunately, Atkinson was enough of a commander not to berate a subordinate officer in front of an enlisted man but the comments he did make were biting.

"Seventeen civilians killed in crossfire," he remarked scathingly. "How's that going to look in the press? You know how the jackals will report it."

"Yes, sir."

"Thirty-eight terrs killed. They'll say the terrs were innocent civilians too."

"So what do you propose, Major? Leaving them to pillage freely?"

"Of course not," Atkinson snapped. He was silent for two or three dusty miles, then suddenly announced, "We'll discuss the entire matter back at headquarters. By the way, Hudson, you are going out to sundowners tomorrow evening."

"I had no such plans, sir," Mack retorted.

"You have now. Beryl Stoffel ordered up one Yank officer for her reception tomorrow night. I volunteered you."

"Oh, that's just super, sir," Mack rejoined with heavy irony.

"Your wife will enjoy it. Constance and I will be there. And I understand M.M. De Vries is coming. Also General St. John."

"Why me?" Mack asked helplessly.

"Beryl's doing this for some important American who just arrived. He's interested in Yanks fighting with us."

Mack would have preferred almost any disciplinary action to a VIP party. He worked at keeping a low profile and disliked being singled out as an American. But this, he recognized, was to be a command performance. Oh well—he resigned himself to a long, boring trip punctuated by Major Bruce Atkinson's caustic observations on the role of foreigners in general and Yanks in particular in the Rhodesian Security Forces.

Chapter 11

Beryl led Alvin Glenlord through her rambling house of white wood and red brick. All the rooms looked out over a gracious lawn and a large shimmering swimming pool. She glanced at her watch and shook her head.

"Oh dear. Five o'clock already. Everyone will be here in half an hour. Could you help me with the bar, Alvin?"

"Of course."

"MM will be a bit late."

Mentally Alvin ran through his dossier on important Rhodesians he should get to know well. M.M. De Vries was at the top of the list. He let Beryl repeat her briefing on the Minister. "Remember, MM is called the Minister Plenipotentiary or Minister at Large but he's really the deputy prime minister, even though there is another minister with that title. Actually, MM has the power to meddle in all the other ministers' business. Futhermore, he does it. And whenever a minister gets sick, dies or is asked to step down, MM goes in and takes his place until a new one can be found. For a while MM was Minister of Defense. He has also served as Foreign Minister, Minister of Law and Order, the lot. He comes from an old South African family with connections in London, to say nothing of Amsterdam, Paris, Madrid and the highest circles in Germany and Austria. He's also a bachelor," Beryl added as an afterthought.

Alvin thought he detected a sly smile on her lips as she said that. "If you're close to MM, you're laughing," concluded Beryl gaily. "Now I'll get changed. Fix yourself a drink."

"Where's the Coke?" Alvin asked.

"My African will give you some. Here's the key to the liquor cabinet. Christian does keep a good liquor supply. He's down at Bitebridge every week and buys liquor over the border in South Africa for the officers' mess, some of the ministers, and of course for us. You'll find that we have a fairly decent supply of Scotch."

"That reminds me, I notice they didn't inspect my baggage. Will Roger get the same treatment when he comes in?"

"Oh certainly."

"Then I'm going to cable him in London to put a dozen bottles of Scotch into his baggage. It's better than currency here. What could I ask him to bring for you, Beryl?"

Beryl thought a few moments. "My favorite perfume is Shalimar."

"He'll bring the biggest bottle of Shalimar on the market."

Alvin Glenlord watched Beryl walk away from him through the large, heavily furnished living room. She had a regal, almost haughty carriage. She was a real *grande dame,* but a beautiful one. And what a figure.

After putting out the liquor, Alvin found the ice bucket and made his way to the kitchen. There an African couple were putting the finishing touches on an elaborate buffet. The manservant immediately went to the refrigerator and took two pans of frozen water from the freezer compartment and began to break up the ice with a pick. Another item almost impossible to find in Rhodesia was American-style ice-cube trays.

Alvin carried the filled ice bucket back to the patio and put it down with the glasses and bottles. As he turned from his task he saw a tall, muscular-looking man with close-cropped hair and bright blue eyes coming across the lawn toward him. The newcomer, who was wearing a well-decorated Rhodesian Air Force uniform, walked up and greeted him cheerfully. "Hello there. You must be Roger Masefield. You know, I've read two of your books."

Alvin shook his head. "Roger will be around in a few days. I'm Alvin Glenlord, his researcher."

The Rhodesian officer reached out a huge hand which Alvin shook. "I'm Christian Stoffel. Beryl was not expecting me, but it turned out I could get away and she does put on good cocktail parties."

Alvin concealed a twinge of displeasure. "I'm happy to meet you, Wing Commander. This will be a nice surprise for Beryl."

Stoffel chuckled. "Let's just say it will be a surprise." He looked approvingly at the bar Alvin had set up. "I see you've done my job for me. By the way, call me Chris. Alvin, is it?"

"Try Al."

"From what I hear, Beryl's got quite a bash lined up for sundowners. Even has M.M. De Vries coming over. Did she tell you he's the godfather of our son?"

Al was surprised. "No, she didn't mention that."

"Oh yes. She and MM have been very close friends since before he got into politics here. As a matter of fact, she knew him before the two of us met," Stoffel went on casually. "Fortunately, or so it seemed at the time, MM was engaged in a rather flamboyant affair with a certain young Spanish duchess. Undoubtedly that's the reason Beryl and I found ourselves before the bishop being joined in holy matrimony." His eyes twinkled, but without irony.

Christian Stoffel made himself a Scotch and soda and Alvin, mindful of the whiskey shortage, concocted a weak gin and tonic despite Stoffel's good-natured protests. "That gin we make is all right but it takes a while to get used to it. Besides, I know where a couple more bottles of Johnnie Walker Black are stashed away."

Alvin tasted the gin and tonic and couldn't check a grimace. Stoffel laughed aloud, took the glass out of his hands, threw its contents onto the lawn and proceeded to make his wife's guest a proper Scotch and soda which he handed over to him. "You'll thank me before the evening's over," he said.

"Ah, the early birds are arriving," Stoffel observed, looking out over the lawn. "Here comes Jack Cornwell. Fascinating chap. You'll really like him. He's one of the businessmen that keeps Rhodesia and the war going." Stoffel turned to Cornwell and his wife. "Jack, Melinda, meet Alvin Glenlord. He's the advance party for Roger Masefield."

The businessman, whom Alvin judged to be in his mid-forties, shook his hand. Relinquishing his assignment as bartender to the real host, Al now gave his full attention to Cornwell, reputedly one of the most effective of the so-called sanctions busters. Somehow he would have to penetrate the manner in which these people operated. The guns, helicopters, equipment and ammunition were certainly flowing into Rhodesia, that was obvious.

Just as Alvin, Jack Cornwell, and his wife, Melinda, were getting into conversation, Beryl emerged in a clinging white gown, its deep cleavage revealing the flawless bosom which had heretofore been shrouded in the jackets and high-necked blouses she customarily wore.

"Chris,"she exclaimed. "What a nice surprise. I really didn't think you'd be able to make it."

"I was scheduled to go down to Fort Vic but managed to evade that assignment. What can I make for you, my dear?"

"The usual. Light."

As the guests arrived and were introduced to Alvin they questioned him about the famous American author who was coming. The covert CIA man recalled Roger telling him about his research assistants and co-authors who were unable to cope with their apparent insignificance in the public's perception. He reflected that if he himself were not on an assignment that transcended his role as a mere writing assistant, he might feel more like an errand boy than the author's equal and associate.

Just then the Minister at Large, M.M. De Vries, strode across the lawn. A flutter of excitement rippled through the gathering. In Rhodesia everybody had to go to MM at one time or another to get what they wanted from government. This was as true of businessmen and the military as it was of the politicians.

De Vries was tall, aesthetic looking, the picture of an aristocrat. His black suit was flawlessly pressed, his striped regimental tie pinned to his spotless white shirt with what looked like a military decoration. His long hair, parted in the middle, gave him a somewhat Oscar Wildean appearance. His face was lean, pale, almost gaunt and when he smiled his large teeth gleamed.

There was no mistaking the proprietary air with which Beryl at once took him over. She ran her hand through his left arm and led him over to where Alvin Glenlord was standing. He had not missed De Vries's dramatic stride across the lawn from the driveway beyond.

The first thought that came into Alvin's mind was that Count Dracula had appeared a little too soon before sunset. He half expected to see MM turn to dust. Beryl introduced them. M.M De Vries had a very delicate handshake, Alvin noticed.

"It's so good to meet you, Mr. Glenlord," MM greeted Alvin in a cultured drawl. "I hope you will find your visit to Rhodesia both interesting and productive. Beryl tells me I must take good care of you, and of Mr. Masefield when he finally arrives."

"We'll certainly appreciate any cooperation you're able to give us, Mr. Minister," Alvin replied. There was an aura of condescension about the Minister at Large that he didn't much like.

Faint smiles and exchanged glances among the cognoscenti betrayed the fact that the relationship between the Minister and Beryl Stoffel was more than that of long-standing family friendship.

"MM, I've been waiting to ask you," Beryl began in a torrent of unsuppressed excitement. "What is the story on the latest terr contact, was it yesterday or the day before?"

"Two nights ago, I believe." He gave her a mock stern look. "We haven't released anything on it, you know."

"No, of course. But what really happened? I heard, strictly unofficially of course, that we killed thirty-eight terrs and seventeen more people running with them."

MM looked briefly at Alvin. "Be careful, Beryl. We haven't decided just how to release the story to these damned hyenas that call themselves journalists."

"You can be certain that I'm not a journalist, Mr. Minister," Alvin asserted.

"I know, Mr. Glenlord. In any event the word has come out of the Tribal Trust Lands that there was a big contact so we're working on the story to give out in the morning. An SAS stick killed thirty-eight terrs in the Mrewa area. Unfortunately seventeen villagers were killed in the crossfire. It couldn't be helped, of course, but you know how the foreign press dotes on that sort of thing."

"We had the same problem in Vietnam," Alvin said sympathetically. "No matter what happened, the Green Berets were committing some sort of a massacre."

"The press is the same everywhere. Too bad we can't just ban them out of existence here. That's what I tried to do, but my lord and master in Government House says we are a civilized nation and a free press or some semblance thereof is a necessity."

"Well, now *that's* settled in my mind I'm going to leave you two alone to talk," Beryl said, moving off toward a new guest.

Scotch and soda in hand, the Minister began questioning Alvin about U.S. strategy in the war against the Communists in Vietnam, displaying a surprising knowledge about the subject himself.

Alvin wondered whether the Minister had any suspicion that he was talking to an agent of the United States Central Intelligence Agency. Several times during the conversation Alvin mentioned that Roger Masefield was even more knowledgeable about the Vietnam War than he was. He also made sure that the Minister was apprised of how bitterly the State Department and Department of Defense had resented Masefield's several books on Vietnam.

Al smiled self-deprecatingly. "Probably they'll take my pension away when they find I'm working for Roger Masefield."

The minister gave him an almost disturbingly knowing look and drawled, "Oh no Mr. Glenlord. I really don't think that is likely. After all, it would only draw further international attention to the work you and Mr. Masefield will be doing over here. It would cause controversy which, I understand, is what makes best-sellers."

Beryl Stoffel, who had returned to the Minister's side, exclaimed, "Oh good, here's the Yank we were expecting. It's Captain Mack Hudson. He's with his commander, Major Bruce Atkinson, and I see his wife, Carla, is with him." She turned to the Minister. "MM, have you met Mack Hudson, one of the Yanks with SAS?"

"Yes, I believe I met him once or twice when I took the salute over there."

Beryl greeted Mack Hudson and brought him over to the Minister and Alvin Glenlord.

The eyes of the two Americans met in instant recognition. Alvin was shaken. There was no way he could have anticipated that Hudson, of all the people he had been associated with in Vietnam, would be in Rhodesia, much less at a party being given by Beryl Stoffel.

"You two Yanks should get to know each other," Beryl said brightly. "Mack Hudson, meet Alvin Glenlord."

"Good to see you, sir." Hudson's wide grin was mocking.

"Likewise, Hudson," Alvin managed. Both of them were obviously thinking of Laos. Mack Hudson had been in charge of a CIA-controlled Special Forces base specializing in ambushing the North Vietnamese regulars coming down the Ho Chi Minh trail.

Alvin Glenlord, then lieutenant colonel, had been one of the most respected Special Forces officers assigned to the Agency and the overall commander of half a dozen clandestine units including Hudson's team.

"I believe you will find the situation here most interesting, sir," Hudson said. "May I present my wife, Carla." Alvin took the hand of Carla Hudson in his for a moment, noting that she was outstandingly attractive with something of a Latin cast to her.

Mack Hudson shook hands with the Minister and presented his wife. De Vries smiled graciously and took Carla's hand. "It's such a pleasure to meet you, Mrs. Hudson. I have visited the SAS officers' mess and met your husband but never realized he had so charming a wife." After a short conversation the Minister was deluged with guests who wanted to talk to him and subtly plead some cause or other, knowing what a word from him could do in the right quarters.

"What's this business about a book?" Mack asked Glenlord when the two of them were apart from the other guests.

"Oh, yes. You know Roger Masefield, of course." Mack nodded. "He's ready to write a book on Rhodesia."

"You're working for him now?"

"Affirmative. I retired from the army."

"As I recall it, sir, you were an upper five-percenter. I'm surprised you didn't stay in and become a general."

"Sometimes it isn't worth being a prisoner of the policies of the United States Government."

"I understand, sir," Mack Hudson replied, obviously unconvinced.

"I hope so," Alvin said. "And for chrissake will you stop sirring me, Mack. I'm a civilian. You know my name."

"Yes, sir—Al."

"Did you ever meet Roger over in the Nam?"

"You may recall that where I was we didn't see writers, not even Roger Masefield. The only outsiders we saw were the Agency control officers, like you."

Alvin winced inwardly. His mission could be doomed before it ever got off the ground. It would take him at least two months to get himself so firmly in place that chance remarks by Americans like Mack Hudson could not compromise him.

"Does Roger think he'll get the same access to troops here that he had in Vietnam?" Mack asked.

"He wouldn't be here unless his book was considered an integral part of Rhodesian government objectives," Alvin replied.

"If they let the wrong man get out in the operational area, let him see how we're operating, let him see the weaponry we've got, it could certainly hurt the Rhodesian war effort," Mack observed.

"I know what you're saying," Al shot back. "You think I'm still with the Agency? Hell, you were a Company man. Do they know that?"

Mack Hudson nodded uncomfortably. "They know my background. They also know Special Forces always worked closely with the Agency."

"OK, Mack, if that's your answer, why isn't it mine?"

"I guess you've got a point there, sir—Al," he amended hastily.

Out of the corner of his eye Mack saw General Ashley St. John talking with Carla. To Alvin he said, "There's a gent you want to meet. Among other things, he gives the clearances for visits to the operational areas. I'll take you over."

Carla was just saying, "Oh General, what a good suggestion. I'll call around at the hospital about volunteer work tomorrow," when Mack and Alvin came up.

"I'm over there at least three afternoons a week visiting our chaps who've been wounded," General St. John beamed. "Ah, Captain Hudson. Splendid piece of work you did two nights ago."

"Thank you, sir. I wish my commander shared your enthusiasm. Have you met Colonel Glenlord? We served in Nam together."

"Beryl was telling me about you, Glenlord," St. John said affably. "I expect I'll be seeing you in my office in a few days. From what I'm hearing there should be no trouble getting you cleared for whatever you want, within reason."

"Thank you, General," Al said. He had heard that the lean, handsome St. John was a notorious womanizer, and he could see why. A movie producer would sign him to play a Rhodesian officer if a cinema version of the war were ever made.

"When does Roger Masefield come?" Carla asked. "I think I've read everything he's ever written."

Al grinned. "His answer to that would be 'I hope not.' We expect him in from London next Monday. I'll see that he meets you and Mack."

M.M. De Vries was taking his leave and Beryl walked with him across the lawn to the driveway.

An hour later, the sundowners having turned to nightcaps and the guests departed, Alvin and Beryl sat in her living room. "Well, you've met some of the people in Salibury I wanted you to get to know," Beryl said in her cooly amiable manner. "Now I think we owe it to ourselves to get away alone. I can show you a very nice restaurant nearby. They even have music after eight."

"What about Chris? Will he join us?"

"Oh no. Chris will stay here. The children will be back shortly. I sent them off to their friends for supper. A pity really. MM always likes to see them. He's their godfather, you know."

"Chris told me."

Later that evening, over dinner, Beryl Stoffel recapitulated the high points of the party while Alvin inwardly chomped at the bit in his anxiety to get away long enough to dictate all his impressions into the tiny tape recorder he always carried with him. He was afraid he might forget something significant if he didn't get everything down while it was fresh in his mind.

Then Beryl brought up the subject of Mack Hudson. "Yes, Hudson is a good soldier. He served under me in Vietnam," Al said quickly.

Beryl looked up surprised. "You knew him before? What sort of operations were you both in?"

"The same sort of things he's probably doing here. Cross border stuff. We used to go after the Communists and kill them where they thought they were safe. Of course, it was strictly top secret. Our politicians claimed we didn't go across borders. If we hadn't, South Vietnam would have been wiped out sooner than it actually was. That's the sort of operation Roger Masefield and I are interested in observing here."

"I'll try to help. I'm sure the SAS is getting good value from Mack Hudson's Vietnam experience."

"They should. We were both working for the Central Intelligence Agency, the CIA, on temporary assignment from Special Forces."

"So you were what they call a spook, were you?" Beryl asked, smiling.

"Not really. We weren't spies. We merely ran secret operations against the Communists where they lived. I guess Mack and I both suffer from the same stigma. Once you've been with the Company, people seem to think you never get out."

"Is that true, Al?"

"No. People like Mack and I were regular U.S. Army before and after the CIA assignment. We weren't career spooks."

Dinner over, Al suggested they have nightcaps in the cottage. Beryl thought that was a fine idea.

In front of the fire as they sipped their drinks, Beryl said languidly, "You know, Al, before Roger does get here maybe you'd like to see Victoria Falls."

"I'd love it, Beryl. Are you going to show it to me?"

"Certainly. We could fly up tomorrow night, spend the weekend and get back to meet Roger on Monday. A change of scene before you and Roger get down to your real work would do us both a lot of good. I'll make the arrangements tomorrow."

Beryl stood up, yawning delicately. "Big day tomorrow, but I'll be ready to leave at three. Come by the office first thing in the morning. I want to get you over to Ashley St. John while he's still mellow from the party. And from Carla Hudson," she added. "Mack had better watch his wife. I know how that lounge lizard works."

Alvin walked her to her car and watched her take the .38 magnum from the box under her seat and place it beside her. "Good night, Al," she said sweetly.

He leaned his head in the open window and kissed her. "Good night, doll." He withdrew his head and gazed after her as she drove away. What a woman, what a total woman she was, he thought. And Victoria Falls. What an idea!

Chapter 12

For a week Roger Masefield's loyal leg-girl expertly steered him to and from the many appointments she had made for him in London. She also made his life pleasant and exciting. It was a good relationship, he thought. And she made him feel twenty years younger.

Lord Johnny Cravenlow had secured for himself several free-lance assignments in Rhodesia. He and Roger made arrangements to meet in Salisbury at the home of the Duke of Ainsworth, a prominent resident of Rhodesia and a member of the government. The duke, Johnny chuckled, was forbidden to come back to Britain as a result of his participation in the Salisbury government.

Perhaps the most significant of all his meetings, Roger thought, was the one with Bishop Abel Muzorewa, the most likely candidate to become the first black prime minister of Rhodesia should majority rule come about. The bishop's top political aide, Godfrey Chakarama, opened the door of a spacious suite at the Grosvenor House Hotel, introduced himself and brought Roger into the parlor. The bishop was sitting behind a leather-top desk.

The bishop stared at his visitor, rather vacantly, Roger thought. He was in formal attire: white clerical collar, purple vest and black mourning coat.

On the desk in front of him was the London *Express*. Roger had wondered before coming to this meeting whether the bishop had seen the headlines: FIFTY-SEVEN BLACK RHODESIANS KILLED AT PO-LITICAL MEETING. Below came the information that forty African nationalist guerrillas were killed when Rhodesian Security Forces opened fire on a political orientation rally organized by Robert Mugabe's ZANU party, and that seventeen civilians died in the crossfire. Roger decided against questioning Muzorewa on the story at the beginning of the interview.

After a brief exchange of amenities Roger moved directly to the point. "Bishop, I'm on my way to your country. I plan to write a book that will make the Western world understand Rhodesia, which it certainly does not at the moment. Can you give me some advice and tell me what to look for?"

Bishop Muzorewa waited some moments, presumably in con-templation, before answering. "I think you will see the situation when you get there. There's nothing I can tell you that you won't see for yourself."

"What about Nkomo?" Roger asked.

"Nkomo? He does not represent the people of Zimbabwe."

"But, Bishop, it appears to me that Rhodesia, Zimbabwe, whatever the name of the country will be, is indeed headed for a majority rule government. If you become the first African prime minister, how will you deal with Nkomo and the other terrorist leader, Robert Mugabe, in Mozambique?"

The bishop allowed himself a wintry smile. "We will know how to deal with that problem at the right time."

"How about the president of your neighbor to the north, Kaunda of Zambia? He seems to favor Nkomo. It seems as though the coun-tries around Rhodesia are helping the terrorists and condemning a leader like yourself who is known to be a moderate. Even if majority rule comes about, how will you cope with Nkomo, his Russian equip-ment and advisers and the fact that he's being given sanctuary by Kaunda?"

Muzorewa shot an eloquent glance at Chakarama. To Roger he said, "You say you're not a journalist? Yet you are a writer."

"I'm not a journalist in the sense that I write a column or report hard news for daily newspapers. I expect my book will be out in about two years from now, six months after I've finished my manuscript."

"Very interesting," remarked the bishop. "As a matter of fact I have written a book myself and am hoping to do another. Unfortunately my book was not published in the United States. Perhaps you might know a publisher who would be interested in it."

Good, Roger thought, he wants my help. "I'll get a copy of your book here in London and see what I can do."

The bishop turned to his aide. "Would you give Mr. Masefield a copy of the book before he leaves?"

At last, this shy little man was warming up. Roger glanced at the newspaper and the bishop also looked down; then his eyes met Roger's. "Those were my people that were killed. Not the guerrillas, the Trust Land people."

"Do you feel bitter about the tribesmen killed in the crossfire?"

"I know what happened. It has happened before and unfortunately will again," he said enigmatically.

"Then you don't blame the security forces?"

The bishop seemed on the verge of replying and then his strangely thin lips compressed.

Seeing no answer was forthcoming, Roger continued. "To get back to the problem of Nkomo and Kaunda: traditionally, host countries are not keen on having guerrillas use them as a base for operations against a country next door. It has happened more than once that the host country was itself overthrown by the guerrillas."

Muzorewa nodded appreciatively. "Yes, I believe that President Kaunda is full of doubts, fears even, regarding the presence of Nkomo's well-armed and well-trained army. We know, of course, that only a small part of Nkomo's best trained troops are being committed to the terror war in Rhodesia. He's holding them back for a civil war with Mugabe. We feel certain that at the appropriate time, it may be possible to enter into some arrangement with Mr. Kaunda that would neutralize Nkomo's threat against a new legitimate majority rule government of Zimbabwe. Zambia cannot survive economically without us."

"What about the chances of bringing Nkomo and Mugabe into any new government you may form?" Roger asked.

"That is unlikely to the point of being absurd," the bishop said tartly. "Nkomo knows he could never be elected by a popular majority. Mugabe knows he'd have even more trouble. Both Nkomo and Mugabe plan on taking over Zimbabwe by force of arms. They believe in Mao Tse Tung's political axiom that political power comes from the barrel of a gun. They could not beat me in an election. In fact if a free election were held in Rhodesia today I am the only candidate that could command enough votes to form a government."

"Assuming that the terrorists don't cut you off at the polls via the barrels of guns," Roger put in.

"That's the most difficult single problem we face. How can fair, impartial elections be carried out with Communist guerrillas roaming the countryside? It is going to be a difficult struggle to achieve elected majority government." The bishop sighed. "But it will come, mark you it will come. When it does we will deal with Mr. Nkomo. And with the help of President Kaunda."

Godfrey Chakarama had gone out of the room and returned with a copy of Bishop Muzorewa's book which he handed to Roger.

"Thank you, Bishop. I'll read this book with great interest on the airplane back to Rhodesia."

"I shall be returning to Salisbury in a week, Mr. Masefield. If we can help you with your book you can always find me at the First Methodist Church of Salisbury."

Seeing the interview was over, Roger stood up and thanked the bishop and his aide for their time.

Sarah Cobb Chase was waiting for him in the lobby. She glanced at her wristwatch. "Well, that didn't take long. Was it useful?"

"I think so. All these little pieces will fit into each other and hopefully produce a finished literary mosaic."

"What a poetic concept," Sarah chirped.

"Looks like I've about wrapped it up in London. Salisbury, next stop."

"I think you're mean not to take me with you, Roger," Sarah wheedled. "You'll miss me when you have to do all your own re-search. And, I understand it really is chilly in August," she added disingenuously.

"You know I'd like to take you with me. But I've got to make it alone my first trip. Even Jocelyn must stay behind."

"Well, boss, am I still on the payroll? What do you want me to do for you now?" Despite the question, she sounded a little crestfallen.

"We have a pub lunch on Fleet Street with Johnny," Roger said. "Then we'll see."

They found Lord Johnny Cravenlow waiting for them, conversing with Lord Banglish. The little dark brown peer's blond girl friend, Margot, was sitting close to him, listening to his words in silent admiration.

"Well Roger, so you're leaving us tomorrow?" There was no mistaking the cheerful note in Johnny's voice as he glanced roguishly at Sarah and said, "We'll miss you."

"You'll soon be in Salisbury, too," Roger replied.

"I hope you mean 'you' plural," Sarah shot in.

"Of course," Roger assured her. "Just let me get settled. My chief of staff, as I like to call him, Colonel Glenlord, should have everything fixed. I want to get started right away on the book."

"Obviously, your proclivities are to defend the Fascist Ian Smith," Banglish piped bitterly.

"What I see, what I believe to be true, will be the basis of the book," Roger parried.

"Was your meeting with the bishop productive?" Johnny asked.

"He seems to take a moderate view on the political situation in his country," Roger answered.

"Did he say anything about the army massacring fifty-seven Africans listening to a black nationalist political speech?" Banglish cried in a high-pitched wheeze.

"Not really." There was no point in getting into a verbal feud with the nasty gnome, Roger thought. "The bishop seemed to be of the opinion that the guerrillas were terrorizing the people when the army caught up with them, and that the civilian casualties were an unfortunate but inevitable circumstance of war."

Moving away from provocative subjects, the two lords and their American guests ordered lunch and conversed about Britain's economy and recurring labor troubles.

While they were having coffee, a newsboy walked in with the afternoon paper. Johnny called him over and bought a paper which he immediately studied. Then he let out a whistle.

"What did you say the bishop's attitude was towards the killings?" he asked Roger. "Listen to this—"

Roger craned his neck to look over Lord Johnny's shoulder as he read aloud.

Bishop Abel Muzorewa condemned the brutal murder of fifty-seven Africans by Rhodesian Security Forces in an interview today at his hotel. He expressed the opinion that white soldiers needlessly fire upon Rhodesian tribesmen and burn their homes in the name of antiterrorist actions. "Until the Smith regime is replaced by a majority government these shootings of innocent Africans will continue," the bishop declared.

"Why the hypocritical little munt!" Lord Johnny exclaimed. Banglish flashed him a sharp look on the word *munt*.

"You can say that again, Johnny," Roger agreed. "He as much as told me he could understand that such things happen and the security forces were trying to save the villagers from a terror raid."

"That's Africa," Lord Johnny sighed. "I guess an African politician reckons he can't ever miss an opportunity to rubbish the whites." He looked back into the paper again and cried: "Look at what this editorial says! 'Britain should come to the aid of the African nationalists fighting for freedom in their Rhodesian homeland.' My God, that's not cricket. I've got to get over there again and start setting the people here straight."

"One can make a valid case for both the nationalists who come in from outside Rhodesia, the terrorists you call them, and the others in Salisbury," Lord Banglish commented magisterially. "I heard something last night when I was with Dr. Owen."

He turned to Sarah. "Our Foreign Secretary."

"I may be an American but I'm not ignorant," Sarah came back.

"It's just that until now he's been quite low-key," the peer murmured. "A lot of foreigners don't know him."

"Bloody left-wing university liberal," Johnny growled.

"Anyway, be that as it may, David says that he's trying to organize an all-party conference in Geneva among all the Rhodesian leaders, black and white, and try to settle the problem once and for all. He wants to do it before the end of the year."

"That should be a sight to behold," Lord Johnny said sarcastically. "Half those Afs don't know what plumbing is. It will be like Castro and his *barbudos* coming to New York with their live poultry and trying to cook them over an open fire in a hotel lobby."

Banglish looked at his colleague disapprovingly. "It might be productive to see how the arguments of the various parties to the dispute measure up in parliamentary proceedings." The Indian stood up. "I'll see all you good people presently. Sorry we have to run off. Important appointment." He helped his silent girl friend to her feet and they left the restaurant.

"So you leave at the weekend?" Johnny asked.

"I promised to be in Salisbury on Monday."

Johnny cocked a meaningful look at Sarah. "I'll look after her when you leave, Roger."

"I'm sure you will."

"Sarah can look after herself. She's been doing it for going on ten years now," Sarah Cobb Chase blazed. "Just get me to Rhodesia before it's all over."

"It's hardly started, I'm afraid," Lord Cravenlow said soberly. He glanced at the luncheon check and pulled out his wallet. "Don't forget, my place for drinks at six. I've got the *Time* magazine bureau chief coming around. I hope to be their chief contributor from Salisbury."

"We'll be there, Johnny," Sarah promised as they walked out of the restaurant.

"What do you want to do now, boss?" she asked.

"Someplace I've got to find Shalimar perfume. Will you help? I received a cable from my chief of staff in Salisbury. I wonder what he wants with that?"

"Guess he's scored, Roger," Sarah replied. "Or wants to. Let's try Harrod's first. It's on the way home."

Chapter 13

Alvin Glenlord leaned across Beryl to look out the window of the Air Rhodesia Viscount. His right arm unobtrusively brushed against firm breasts straining against the open, holiday-style blouse she wore. This was to be a carefree weekend; there'd be none of the severe dresses and suits so characteristic of the Salisbury lady lawyer. She had changed after a Friday morning at the office, taking the afternoon off so they could reach Victoria Falls well before dusk, traditionally ambush time in Rhodesia.

"Can you see it now, Alvin?" she asked.

"Wow! You bet I can," he replied. A great thunderhead of white steam boiled up from the thick green bush a few miles ahead of the plane. "One of the seven natural wonders of the world," he pronounced.

The pilot announced they were coming in for a landing. Beryl pinched the nostrils of her high-bridged nose and blew, clearing her ears as the jet lost altitude.

The incomparable Jimmy Michaels greeted them at the airport.

"When you see Jimmy you know you're on holiday," Beryl laughed as Michaels helped them put their baggage in the trunk of his Mercedes. She directed Alvin to sit in the front. Al climbed in beside Jimmy who now snapped open his attaché case and assembled the three parts of his Sten gun. Thrusting a magazine into the breech, he placed it on the seat beside him and started up the car.

"Are you having much trouble with the terrs?" Beryl asked.

The good-natured smile faded momentarily from Jimmy's face. "They hit the motel last night. Threw in a couple of RPD rounds, let go with automatic rifle fire and killed one bar patron. The rest of the bar went charging out, their guns blazing, and the terrorists ran off. Security forces are out in the bush looking for them."

"Wasn't in the paper when we left this morning," Al said.

"No, it wouldn't be yet," Michaels replied. "Happened about midnight and of course the tourist department tries to downplay these things." He caught Beryl's eye in the driving mirror. "Would it have changed your plans, old girl?"

"Of course not. Maybe we'll get a few shots at the bloody houtie Communists ourselves while we're here."

The main item in Beryl's smart makeup box was her trusty magnum. Alvin had packed his own revolver in his suitcase. Traveling in Rhodesia was unlike traveling anywhere else in the civilized world, he reflected.

Jimmy Michaels swung his car onto the main road toward the town of Victoria Falls and stepped on the accelerator. Alvin watched bemused as the speedometer registered seventy, eighty, ninety, and then one hundred miles per hour, at which point Jimmy leveled out.

"Ever been ambushed around here?" Al asked.

"No. But there's always the first time," Jimmy replied cheerfully.

The trees on either side went by in a blur. Nervously Al's fingers gripped the edge of his seat as Jimmy took his eyes off the road to look at Beryl in the mirror. "Hear any new jokes?" he asked.

"That's your department, Jimmy," Beryl laughed. "Jimmy is the chief entertainment here when he isn't running the tourist department."

"Or my auxiliary police stick," he added. He turned to Alvin.

"What's the latest laugh from Yank land?"

Alvin had been ignoring the scenery flashing by outside his window even though he was supposed to be some sort of a semi-tourist and Beryl had briefed him on Jimmy Michaels. Besides being an apparently lighthearted tourist director, he was also one of the shrewdest Special Branch officers in the country. Victoria Falls was not only a tourist haven, but a hotbed of communist spy activity.

The stores in Zambia offered woefully limited stocks, and whites from Britian and Iron Curtain countries on contract to Kaunda's Zambia came into Victoria Falls to shop. They also came to gamble in the casino and drink in the lively bars, and some of them came to gather intelligence on Rhodesian military matters.

Alvin decided this was the moment to establish himself as a fun-loving Yank with more than a passing interest in the beautiful woman who had brought him to the famous resort. He was supposed to be looking forward to a dirty weekend, as the Rhodesians called an adulterous weekend tryst. Obviously Jimmy Michaels would be sending an evaluation of him to Special Branch headquarters in Salisbury. Alvin Glenlord had to avoid even the slightest hint that he might be a member of the United States intelligence community.

"I remember jokes a lot better over my quota of beers at the bar than I do knocking off one hundred miles an hour on a country road," he chuckled.

"You get used to it," Jimmy laughed. "A good joke helps."

"I don't know if I can tell any in front of Beryl," Al hedged.

"Try me," Beryl invited.

"We'll be at the bar of the Vic Falls Hotel in thirty minutes. Pretend you're there now," Michaels urged.

"Well, let's see," Al began. He had heard enough of the ubiquitous Van der Merwe jokes in the last few days, especially the evening he'd spent at the SAS officers' mess at Mack Hudson's invitation, to be able to retell one with an American twist.

"Well, you probably heard about old Van der Merwe, the famous veterinarian down in Bulawayo," he began tentatively.

"Van der Merwe, the veterinarian in Bulawayo?" Jimmy took up. "I'll stop you if I've heard it, and you buy the first round."

"Fair enough, Jimmy. Seems the prize cows of a farmer down there were going cross-eyed."

Jimmy Michaels grinned. "Going cross-eyed? What did old Van do?"

"The farmer led Van der Merwe and his African assistant to five cows, all of them cross-eyed as hell. The farmer wanted to sell them but he knew he wouldn't get the right price if they were cross-eyed. Old Van knows just what to do. He takes a one-inch pipe out of his kit, hands it to his African and points at the first cow. The African takes the pipe, shoves it up the cow's"—Al paused delicately—"rear end. Then the African gives one mighty blow down the pipe and the cow gives a grunt and her eyes straighten right out. Well the farmer lets out a shout of joy and the African pulls the pipe out of the first cow's rear end and repeats the process with the second cow. Same thing happens. The second cow's eyes straighten right out and the farmer again cheers. The African goes through four cows, straightens them all out and then he comes to the fifth cow, shoves the pipe up its rear again and blows. But this time the cow's eyes cross even worse. Now the farmer is upset. It's his prize cow. 'I'll give you double, Van, if you can straighten this one's eyes out,' the farmer cries.

"Well the African gives another blow up the prize cow's rear end but it doesn't do any good. 'Triple price for this one, Van,' the farmer shouts, reaching into his pocket.

"Old Van is pretty disgusted with his African and shoves the munt out of the way. He grabs the pipe, pulls it out of the cow's ass, turns it around and starts taking deep breaths until he gets his lungs full of air. Then he puts his mouth on the pipe and lets out the mightiest blast of air he's ever blown. Son-of-a-bitch if the cow doesn't let out one great thundering moo and her eyes straighten right out.

"Now Van der Merwe turns to the farmer and holds his hand out for the money. The farmer happily pays him and then says, 'Tell me one thing, Van. Why did you turn the pipe around?'

"'I couldn't put my mouth on the same end of the pipe my Kaffir was blowing on.'"

Jimmy Michaels burst into a roar of laughter and kept sputtering and chuckling for the next mile. Beryl giggled in the back seat. "I'll get a lot of mileage out of that one," Michaels cried merrily. "First two rounds at the hotel are definitely on me."

Now that he had established himself as being "regular" in his attitude toward Africans, Alvin hoped Michaels would regard him as just another Yank tourist up in Victoria Falls for a good time. He turned in his seat and caught Beryl's eye. They grinned at each other.

Al and Beryl checked into their separate rooms at the hotel, Al on the first floor, Beryl on the second. The very fact that she had gone to such lengths to preserve appearances gave Al hope that after dinner they would end up together in her room. After several drinks on the large terrace of the sprawling old Victorian colonial hotel, and just as it had turned dark, Jimmy Michaels took his leave, saying he had tourist board duties to perform and still had to get his auxiliary police in place.

After Jimmy left, Beryl put her hand on Al's. "I'm ready for a shower and dinner," she said. Al took her upstairs to her room. She unlocked the door and turned to him. "Come back in forty-five minutes, Al. I'll be ready."

In the formal dining room of the Victoria Falls Hotel the most casual observer would have had no difficulty discerning which ladies were Rhodesians and which tourists. Rhodesian women wore floor-length dresses, the visitors sweaters or blouses and skirts; some even wore slacks against the cool African winter night. Unlike the open-necked, shirt-sleeved male tourists, Alvin Glenlord was wearing a dark suit, white shirt and striped tie to complement Beryl's white, figure-revealing gown. Beryl's figure, Al noted, was well worth revealing.

Al and Beryl grinned conspiratorially across the table at each other as they sipped South African wine with the *coq au vin*. The occasion was too important for a local wine from the recently developed Rhodesian vineyards. Until now, although they felt a strong attraction for each other, they had gone no further toward releasing their physical urges than warm kisses goodnight. Tonight, their instincts told them, would be different.

"A cognac with coffee?" Al asked after the flaming dessert had been served and consumed.

"Why not?" she responded gaily.

At ten o'clock they stood up from the table and walked out on the wide veranda into the night breeze coming off the Zambezi River just below the hotel grounds. Neither could come up with an appropriate comment so they were silent. Then Beryl put her bare arm through one of Al's and drew close to him. "You'll enjoy it here, Al," she said softly.

"I know I will if you do," he replied.

Snappy small-talk had never been Alvin's forte. Basically he was not a ladies' man. He had married Lorraine the day he graduated from Officers Candidate School as a second lieutenant. The difference between himself and most of the other graduates was that he had a year of heavy combat duty in Korea behind him. He had never had the opportunity or the inclination to absorb the social graces of some of his more urbane fellow officers, and once married to good old Lorraine, who promptly bore him three sons and a daughter, there was no need for further refinement.

He was a soldier, the best. That was enough. Glenlord's lack of elegance had not prevented him from being a top five-percenter, nor would it prevent his name appearing on the clandestine promotion list to brigadier general at some point in the future.

But when it came to seducing an elegant lady so as to make her a secure Agency asset, he might come up short. He resolved to let Beryl set the pace and follow her lead.

"Is there anything you'd like to do tonight?" Beryl asked.

When Al hesitated she laughed. "I mean like dropping by the Casino Hotel for some roulette or dancing?"

"Whatever you want," he said.

"Well, it has been a long day and we want to be up early and do things tomorrow . . ." Her voice trailed off.

"So let's have an early night."

"Yes, I think so." Beryl turned them from the veranda and they strolled back through the hotel's inner lobby, past the people drinking and talking at tables. Wordlessly, they proceeded to the west wing and up the stairs to Beryl's room. She had given him the key to her room when he called for her earlier and now he took it from his pocket, unlocked her door, and pushed it open.

He closed the door behind him. That didn't seem too overt a move, but he had to be careful not to do something clumsy, he thought uneasily. With the initial stage of his infiltration so close to accomplishment, he couldn't afford to botch the mission now.

"I brought a bottle of Scotch with me," Beryl said. "Would you like a nightcap?"

She walked across the spacious, high-ceilinged room to a table just below the wide double windows. Standing on it was the bottle of Johnnie Walker Black Label beside a thermos pitcher. "There's ice water to go with it."

"Sure. I could handle a drink," Al replied, moving close to her. She turned from the window and was in his arms. If their kisses had been warm those nights they had lingered at the cottage, they were torrid now. Her lithe figure and generous bosom pressed against his body, her lips moved passionately.

It's OK, he told himself. You can let off the brakes. Beryl pulled away slightly. "Why don't you take off your coat and tie and be comfortable," she suggested huskily. "Make me a light drink. I'll be right back." She slid out of his embrace and walked hurriedly to the bathroom.

Al hung his coat and tie neatly over the back of a chair and opened the three top buttons of his shirt. He glanced at the king-sized double bed and grinned. His own room had two single beds. Beryl must have specially requested this room.

By the time she emerged from the bathroom he had made the two drinks and also braced himself with several clandestine draughts from the bottle. Beryl was wearing a diaphanous peignoir. Silently he handed her the glass. She took it, held it up and smiled invitingly. "Cheers."

They sipped their drinks. Then Beryl sat on the bed, suggestively patting the space next to her. Al sat down, the drink still in his hand. He put an arm around her shoulders, his fingers playing idly with the gossamer material covering her body.

"Do you want the loo?" she asked. "Why don't you make yourself comfortable?"

"Good idea, doll. Sorry I don't have a bathrobe or anything."

"You won't need it."

A real take-charge woman, he thought. And he liked it. "Won't be a minute."

"Take your time. I'll still be here."

When Al returned to the room the lights were off but enough illumination filtered in from the window for him to see that her thin nightgown had been laid over his coat. She was in bed, sitting up against the pillows, holding the sheet so it just covered her nipples.

Words seemed unnecessary. He slid into bed beside her nude body. Beryl let go of the sheet and Al shivered at the sight of her full white breasts and the upturned nipples. She rolled against him, her arms going around him, one hand on his buttock, her nails lightly scratching. Al reached for her, pulling her tightly to him, feeling her breasts against him.

Hungrily they mouthed each other, their week of suppressed desire flooding them with savage intensity as the instant of fulfillment approached. Beryl's hand moved and found what she wanted so desperately now. He felt her shudder as she ran her fingers up and down his scepter of male strength.

"Oh God, Al. I can't wait. Now, darling. Now!"

She twisted from her side onto her back, pulling him on top of her, her knees up and apart. To himself Al said, *Yes ma'am.* Without recourse to finesse he plunged into the primed and demanding sheath, eliciting uninhibited cries of rapture. He felt Beryl's fingernails digging into his buttocks as with feral intensity she worked her loins against him.

In seconds orgasm seized them and Beryl's wild exhortation subsided into low throaty moans. Alvin felt the rigidity leave her body, which fell limp and spent, away from him. For many moments she lay panting, her eyes staring glassily at the ceiling.

"Oh my God, Al. I needed that," she breathed.

Al had no reply except a smile. And a smile came over her face, too.

"Next time we'll make it last," he promised.

Both fell into a deep drowse, neither asleep nor awake, which was shattered by the harsh ringing of the telephone beside the bed. It rang a second time and a third before Beryl reluctantly turned over, propped herself up on an elbow, and reached for the instrument. "Good timing," she whispered over her shoulder. "It could have happened just at the wrong moment."

She pulled the receiver from its cradle and fell back on the bed. "MM," she cried, "what are you doing up so late?" A pause. "You say it's not late?" She winked at Al. "Of course I'm all right." She listened a few moments. "Oh that. Just a hit-and-run terr attack. They won't be back. Security forces are out in the bush after them." Again she listened and Al could hear the Minister's British drawl, threaded with earnestness now.

"Yes of course, MM. I'll be careful. Jimmy Michaels is looking after us. I'm going to show the American around tomorrow and be back Sunday night. Dinner? Of course, MM. See you then." She replaced the phone.

"He calls me almost every night," she replied to Al's quizzical look. "After all, you must realize MM and I have been very close since I made my debut over twenty years ago in Johannesburg and Salisbury." Beryl gave him an enigmatic smile which nonetheless told him that he was sharing this magnificent woman with the most distinguished and eligible bachelor in Rhodesia. Come to think of it, he was lucky, Al mused.

"Now that the so-called massacre of fifty-seven Africans has been publicized around the world," Beryl went on, "MM is worried that we'll have increased terrorist attacks like the one on the motel last night." She faced Al with an impish twinkle in her eye. "Well, now that we're awake . . ."

Chapter 14

Over a hearty breakfast on the terrace next morning Beryl outlined their plans for the day. She was wearing a violet, open-necked silk shirt and white cord jodhpurs tucked into ankle boots. "We're not going to do anything constructive, just have fun. When Roger Masefield gets here we'll plan a trip for him and his wife."

"I don't know whether Jocelyn will be coming or not," Al said. "Certainly not the first trip, anyway."

"What sort of a marriage do Roger and his wife have?"

"It seems to be happy enough. She's a beautiful girl and she and Roger seem content to go their own way much of the time, and to be pretty compatible when they are together."

"Do you think Roger will want some feminine companionship when he's here alone?" Beryl asked. "We want him to be happy, don't we?"

"Let's play that by ear. Roger's a funny guy. He appears to be easygoing but I think basically he's serious. So what's the first item on our schedule today?"

Out at the crocodile ranch, Al and Beryl looked at the sinister reptiles for an hour. They went all the way from babies just coming out of the eggs to full-grown monsters. One fearsome creature had been darted and put to sleep on the Zambezi River before being carried to the ranch. It was known to have devoured at least six tribesmen.

"Mack Hudson tells me that he uses crocs for expedient devices," Al chuckled.

"Expedient devices?"

"Yes, a weapon fashioned out of the materials at hand."

"I wish we could train them to eat terrorists," Beryl remarked.

"Selling crocodile skin must bring in a lot of foreign exchange," Al said.

"Yes, and we could bring a lot more foreign money into Rhodesia if we weren't so bloody conservation-minded. MM tells me that one crocodile's skin brings in the equivalent of several FN rifles and a thousand rounds of ammunition."

"I should think you could finance a large part of the war just on elephant tusks and animal skins," Al observed.

"We're going to have to have to give up something. Even if it means shooting and selling ninety percent of the wildlife in this country."

"How do you sell what you do dispose of?" Al risked.

"Well, officially we take what we have to South Africa and sell it to foreigners. But of course if you go to Salisbury Airport any night after dark you'll see the big cargo jets taking off loaded with tobacco, tea, farm produce and I suppose animal skins to be sold in the European markets. I have to laugh at those sanctimonious Brits, Frenchmen and West Germans who say that Rhodesia is a racist country and not to be dealt with. Our produce is all that's kept London and Paris eating during this last food shortage they've been having in Europe. You met that chap Jack Cornwell at my party. He works with another chap in London, Mike Cleary, and together they account for a rather largish percentage of the buying and selling Rhodesia does on the foreign market."

"What else do you sell overseas?" Al asked.

"It's no secret we have emeralds and gold bullion, and of course our mainstay is chromium. Thanks to your Senator Harry Byrd, we can at least sell our chromium in the United States. Without that I don't know that we could survive economically."

"Well I've seen enough crocs. Where do we go next?"

"Do you want to buy some curios? Some African relics to take home to your wife and children? I'm sure Lorraine would appreciate some mementos from Rhodesia."

Al realized he hadn't thought of his wife for several days. And last night had pushed her even further back in his memory than usual.

The Victoria Falls market area was indeed fascinating. Al found himself poking through the native handicrafts and studying antique trading beads. The latter were even more valuable today than in the days when they had been used as barter for slaves. Al made a few token purchases, Beryl advising him on what was good, what was merely for the tourists.

"Are you going to bring Lorraine out here?"

"I doubt it. I don't know where the money would come from and I certainly wouldn't ask Roger for it. Besides, she's got the kids to take care of. We still have two at home. And I'm going to be so busy I wouldn't have a chance to do anything for her if she did come."

"Good point, Glenlord." Beryl continued down the sidewalk of the native shopping center. "I'm going to take you with me to see a very remarkable man," she went on seriously. "You don't know Africa. It's probably hard for you to comprehend the fact that I'm an African. Oh, I belong to the white tribe. But that doesn't mean I'm not just as much an African as any tribesman out in the bush. If you're born in Africa, if your parents were born here, then you're African, despite all the trappings of European civilization that you see in places like Salisbury and Joburg. Most of us, whether we admit it or not, deeply believe in certain things that you, an American, would laugh at and call superstition. I know better. And so will you if you stay here long enough."

"What are you talking about?" Alvin was perplexed.

"When you meet my witch doctor you'll understand."

"Witch doctor!? You don't really believe in that sort of thing?"

"There's good *mutie* and bad *mutie*. Both can be summoned to influence people, events, and even whole nations."

Al saw that her seriousness approached religious conviction. He turned his most sincere look upon her. "Give me a chance to see it your way."

"All right, follow me." She led him down to the end of the shopping center and turned into an alley behind the row of shops. They continued walking till she reached a small hole in the wall of what looked like a dirty, native curio shop, the type tourists would never venture into even if they found their way into this back alley, which was not likely. A grass or reed curtain hung over the hole. Beryl parted the curtain and stepped through, followed by Alvin. The interior was so dark it was some moments before they could see anything at all.

Seated cross-legged at the back of the shop was a gnarled old African wearing a grass skirt, bright beads around his neck and ankles, and a knitted cap on his head. His torso was bare. He looked up as Beryl and Al walked in and smiled at Beryl. He greeted her in some native language, a greeting she returned. Then she turned to Al, a strange light in her eyes. "He says he has been waiting for me."

"What did you do, make an appointment?" Alvin wanted to chuckle, but refrained.

"Yes, but not the way you think. I knew I would come here this morning. He knew it too. You can stay if you want to, but stand over by the entrance."

Al did as he was told and watched the scene before him with rapt attention. Beryl squatted down in front of the witch doctor, her pants stretched tight over shapely buttocks.

Beryl and her witch doctor conversed in some African dialect with great intensity. Then he reached behind him and brought forth a handful of bones of various sizes and shapes. Beryl reached out both hands and placed them firmly around the sinewy claw which held the fortune-telling relics, tightly closing her eyes in deep concentration. When she let go, the fortune-teller shook the relics in his hands, then threw them on the floor in front of him, like a crapshooter, Al thought.

For some moments the witch doctor stared in silence at the pattern the bones made. Then, closing his eyes, he tilted his head backwards. Beryl kept her eyes fixed on the bones. There was almost a full minute of total silence before the witch doctor began talking. Al watched Beryl's head as it repeatedly wagged assent to the old man's words.

The words came slowly and deliberately, as if the witch doctor weren't sure of Beryl's grasp of his language. Al felt a prickling sensation in his scalp and at the back of his neck as he watched the performance. Instinctively, he knew the witch doctor was talking about him. He had the frightening feeling that this ignorant half-naked African had penetrated his cover. There *was* more to Africa than most white men could understand.

112

Al's eyes went from the witch doctor to Beryl, trying to read in her expression the impact of the words. More and more Al felt as though his inmost thoughts had been bared for scrutiny, even though the old man's eyes were closed, his face toward the ceiling. The witch doctor and Beryl seemed to be in a world outside time.

Finally the session ended. The witch doctor opened his eyes and gave Beryl a snaggle-tooth smile. Beryl rocked back on her heels, stood up, and reached into her pocket to bring out a handful of Rhodesian dollars. The seer shook his head, indicating he did not want money. She tried to press him but he intoned a few words and she put the money away. Reaching forward she shook the ancient native's hand, then turned and walked toward Al. He pushed the grass curtain aside and they suddenly found themselves blinking in the glaring sunlight of the alley.

"What was that all about?" he asked, unable to keep the apprehension from his tone.

Beryl glanced at her watch. "Twelve noon. Shall we have a spot of tea?"

"Sure. I want to hear what just happened."

Beryl led the way to a small teahouse in the shopping center where they sat down and ordered tea. Beryl looked at Al intently. "For the first time he wouldn't let me pay him. He makes his living telling fortunes."

"So why didn't he take the money?" Al asked, instinctively sensing the answer.

"He said what he told me was so important that he didn't want any money for fear I might not take it seriously."

"Do you take it seriously?"

"Yes. Although I'm not sure what he actually meant. He's like an oracle. When you understand the answer, it makes sense."

"What language is that you talk to him in?"

"It's a dialect of the Shona language. I speak Shona. We all speak Shona or Matabele, an off shoot of Zulu, and many of us speak both languages. His dialect is a strange one, though. For you, the equivalent would be talking to an Irishman with a heavy Dublin brogue."

"OK, doll. Now what did he say?"

"I'll tell you what he said. You tell me what it means. First he told me the usual things about my husband, Christian, and myself. Even though we share a common house, he said, we were living in two different countries separated by a wide, deep river. He told me a few other things about myself, mostly things I knew. Then he started to talk about you. He said that the man with me had made me very happy and could make me even happier. He also said the man could hurt me very much."

"Isn't that true of any man-woman relationship?" Al interrupted.

"My witch doctor went on to say that the man with me is from a far-off country. He said that the man's country will make my country suffer. He said the man that was with me must help his country do what his country leaders tell him. The man is here in Rhodesia serving his own country."

Beryl paused and looked questioningly at Al. Once again he experienced a prickling sensation as of live electrodes being passed over the back of his neck and up his scalp. He said nothing and Beryl went on. "'This man with you brings another man from his country to you,' the witch doctor told me. 'Someday the man with you will have to hurt the man he is bringing to you.'"

Beryl was silent for several moments. "What could he have meant by that, Al?" For the first time since he had known Beryl, she seemed bewildered.

"I don't know, Beryl. It doesn't make sense to me at all." But to himself he thought, *score one for the Africans.* "Neither of us wants to hurt the other," he continued. "Our making love didn't hurt you, did it?"

"Of course not, Al. I don't think he was referring to our love life. We don't have any secrets from each other. At least not about our personal lives."

"Or about anything else as far as I'm aware." Al made his voice sound as positive as possible.

Beryl looked at him doubtfully for a moment, then gave a nervous laugh. "I just wish he'd taken my money. I always feel heavy after I've talked to him, but when he didn't take the money—that made it worse."

She sipped some tea and laughed again, this time light-heartedly. "You know? I didn't want tea. Let's go to the hotel and have a drink. We're on a holiday, aren't we? After lunch we'll go around to see the Falls."

Outside, Al spotted the car that Jimmy Michaels had assigned to them and waved to the driver to pick them up.

Chapter 15

September 1976

Alvin Glenlord's control at CIA headquarters in Langley, Virginia re-read the transcript of his operative's oral assessment of the situation in Rhodesia. This was raw intelligence but the case officer seriously considered passing it along to the Director just as it was. The Director knew Glenlord personally from Vietnam where he had been Operations Supervisor of all Southeast Asia and Glenlord had reported to him on a regular basis.

Glenlord's observations, made over a two-month period, were so perceptive, so salty, and yet so full of innuedo that to reduce them to the bare bones of fact would rob them of some of their value. Much better to let the Director read the report in its unvarnished state. The Director would himself be reporting to the Secretary of State and was best able to cull the intelligence that was pertinent to Kissinger's mission to Africa scheduled for a week hence.

The case officer clucked his tongue. Few if any agents could get away with such a freewheeling oral account of their missions, but Glenlord had always been a maverick and perhaps that was where his value lay.

Since Glenlord did not want to go near the headquarters in Langley, the case officer and two other African specialists had debriefed him in the safe house in Crystal City. It had been an absorbing session. Al had taken a bourbon and water to loosen himself up and then begun.

"The most important single accomplishment of my first mission to Rhodesia was to find this beautiful and well-informed woman, Beryl Stoffel, and make her into a valuable unsuspecting asset. By the time my other asset, the novelist Roger Masefield, arrived in Salisbury I had Stoffel firmly in place. She is a highly patriotic Rhodesian woman, a lawyer, and has access to the most sensitive information coming out of the government and the military.

"Stoffel has been sleeping with the Minister Plenipotentiary, Mr. M.M. De Vries, since she first met him in her early twenties. She is forty now. The Minister talks to her almost every day wherever she is. After I had been in Salisbury for a week, she took me to Victoria Falls for a weekend and we made love. Since then she has told me everything she knows. After satisfying the Minister's sexual needs she comes back to me with all the latest news from cabinet meetings. De Vries has close access to the military and gave Stoffel a detailed account of that cross-border raid into Mozambique. Piecing the dope I got from her together with what I've been able to pick up at the SAS officers' mess and elsewhere, I can give the attached account of how the highly successful raid into Mozambique was pulled off."

Glenlord had finished one drink before starting the account, the case officer recalled disapprovingly, and by this time was well into a second.

"The finest, most elite fighting unit in Rhodesia is the Selous Scouts. Their commander, Lieutenant Colonel Ron Reid-Daley, was troop sergeant for the present commander of Combined Operations, General Peter Walls, when they were both young men serving in Malaya during the emergency there which Britain handled with troops from all over the empire. Reid-Daley again served the general, as his sergeant major, when the Rhodesian Light Infantry was formed and Walls was a battalion commander. Reid-Daley was called out of retirement by Walls to form the Selous Scouts. The Scouts are comparable to our Special Forces. Their berets are fawn colored.

"There is probably no officer in the Rhodesian Army closer to the commanding general, Peter Walls, than Reid-Daley. Were this not the case, Selous Scouts could not survive. The other generals in the Rhodesian forces resent Reid-Daley and feel about the Selous Scouts the same way our conventional generals feel about the Green Berets: they'd like to see the unit disbanded.

"When Roger Masefield and I went to Inkomo Barracks to visit the Selous Scouts and Colonel Reid-Daley, the total force in the Selous Scouts was about four to five hundred men, some sixty of them white. The training is magnificent and any man that gets through it is a topnotch bush fighter.

"The Selous Scouts, along with other units recently mounted an incursion into Mozambique, driving across the border and continuing deep inside in captured FRELIMO trucks. The supplies to the guerrilla camps are brought in by FRELIMO truck convoys. The Rhodesian military had received intelligence that a camp of twelve hundred terrorists was situated about forty miles from the Rhodesian border just north of Umtali, the Rhodesian city that used to be the center of commerce between Rhodesia and Mozambique.

"The plan was daring and very simple. The Rhodesians were dressed in FRELIMO uniforms and crossed the border at night, heading for the terrorists' camp. The white troops all had their faces blackened with camouflage grease. They were close to the terrorist camp at daylight and drove along singing FRELIMO songs. Rhodesian intelligence was really sharp. They knew that the day of the raid was the one scheduled for a supply run. They also knew that a new African commander recently arrived from Moscow and Tanzania had recently taken over the camp and was trying to instill some discipline into the men. Every morning a reveille parade was held at seven A.M.

"The terrorists were lined up in ranks as the trucks drove up and pulled to a halt in a line along the parade ground. Thinking this was their FRELIMO-supplied rations for the week, the terrorists began to cheer. The cheering didn't last long. The Rhodesians dropped the sides of their trucks and opened up on the guerrillas with heavy machine guns.

"My source told me that they killed about a thousand in a matter of three minutes. Apparently a few got away, including the camp commander. The Rhodesians spent the next few hours collecting weapons and all the camp records and stacking them into the trucks. Then they headed back to the border.

"But they had a problem. One of the Rhodesian armored personnel carriers ran into a ditch and broke down. A decision had to be made whether to try to tow it back to Rhodesia or leave it. They were reluctant to leave the APC since it was obviously a Rhodesian army vehicle and they had planned to deny the raid had ever been made if the Mozambique government should complain. Finally they decided to destroy the APC with explosives and continue to Rhodesia. By now the FRELIMO knew that units of the Rhodesian Army were in Mozambique and heading home; however they had no stomach to engage them in combat and the Rhodesians returned without a single casualty. It was only when the still identifiable armored personnel carrier was found that the Rhodesians took responsibility for the raid, which had been a great success from their point of view and a tremendous morale booster in Salisbury.

"There will be many more of these raids as terrorist activity increases. It is the only way the Rhodesians can slow down the brutal attacks against farmers, whites and Africans alike. I have personally seen scenes of torture and murder where the terrorists systematically wiped out whole families, burned people alive and raped the women. In one case the terrorists put gunpowder up the vaginas of two young daughters of a village chief accused of cooperating with the central government in Salisbury. These brave Freedom Fighters who, tacitly at least, have the support of our government, then lit the powder. You can imagine the results. Both girls were alive when I saw them a while later. This sort of thing goes on day in and day out.

"The Americans—I estimate there are at least three hundred U.S. citizens with the security forces—are extremely bitter about the harassment they and their families back home suffer because they are fighting what they regard as an extension of the Vietnam War. They honestly believe they are fighting for American interests in a just cause. They call themselves Crippled Eagles—patriotic Americans crippled by their own government.

"I met a captain who said that his wife's savings account had been frozen by the State Department so that she would not have the money to come over and join him. Others say that their families back home have been questioned and told that their sons would lose their American citizenships unless they left Rhodesia.

"I saw reports from the Rhodesian Medical Association showing that American doctors practicing in hospitals and missions in Rhodesia had been sent standard forms asking them to give three fortnightly periods of medical assistance a year to the Rhodesian Security Forces. All the American doctors refused. In each case they said they were in fear of jeopardizing their American citizenship and would not be prepared to serve at any time.

"I know the Agency is required to deal in facts and actualities and not form opinions. However, since our work is used to create opinions in the administration, I will pass mine along, based as they are on what I've seen in the last six weeks in Rhodesia. The United States should lift trade sanctions against Rhodesia and recognize Rhodesia as a nation. If it doesn't it will only be a matter of time before this country goes the way of Vietnam. I know there is some talk of repealing the Byrd Amendment and thus no longer buying Rhodesian chrome. This would be madness and the Secretary of State should know it. Not only do we need the chrome, but we need a strong Rhodesia to prevent the Communists, through their cat's paws Robert Mugabe and Joshua Nkomo, from overrunning the country and eventually South Africa.

"I get a feeling of déjà vu here. The similarity to our Vietnam fiasco is frightening. Even the same kinds of torture are used by the Communists to intimidate the people in the Tribal Trust Lands. If the Communists take over, there will be slaughter of some whites and all blacks who have worked with the government. You will have an Idi Amin-type dictator in Nkomo or Mugabe, whichever one knocks the other off first.

"Through Beryl Stoffel, who as I said gets the most sensitive information from the Minister at Large, M.M. De Vries, I can tell you that there is deep concern at the highest levels of the Rhodesian government over its ability to keep the war going effectively. The figure De Vries gave Stoffel as the cost of the war was a million four hundred thousand dollars a day. It is a tribute to the ingenuity of the industrious Rhodesians that with the world against them their economy is this strong. But they can't go on forever. It is my opinon, based on what Stoffel tells me, that De Vries, Prime Minister Ian Smith and some of the other powerful ministers are ready, if pushed hard enough, to compromise on the question of majority rule. The Rhodesian Front, which is the ruling party, keeps saying it will never allow black majority rule in Rhodesia, but it is prepared to arrive at a formula that would produce just such a result.

119

"Black African rule is against everything the two, three, four and five generation Rhodesians believe in. But De Vries is a realistic man and so is Ian Smith. Our Secretary of State will be able to get this concession from the Prime Minister if he pushes hard enough. As I said, the plans are already on the drawing board.

"As to my own operations, I think my cover will hold. A former Special Forces officer whom I controlled when I was with the Agency in Vietnam and Laos, named Mack Hudson, recognized me immediately. I think I convinced him I'm no longer a Company man although I'm not sure. In any case he has been a source of some information to me, particularly after Roger Masefield arrived. Working as a researcher for Masefield has been of enormous advantage. I do not believe I could otherwise have achieved penetration—"

Glenlord's case officer remembered the agent's laughter when he had uttered that last word. The laughter, like Alvin's second drink, was noted on the transcript. The case officer also added the comment that Glenlord, while dutifully reporting everything from Rhodesia, appeared to feel some remorse for the necessity of deceiving Stoffel, Masefield and the Rhodesians, with whom he had seemingly formed close attachments. He went back to reading the transcript, continuing to make periodic notations in the margins.

"—penetration of all sectors of the Rhodesian business, government and military communities. Stoffel and I met Roger Masefield at the airport when he came in from London. Apparently he made a lot of good contacts there including an important one with Bishop Abel Muzorewa who is a weak man but strongly supported by the Africans. One thing about blacks everywhere: all one of them has to do is put his collar on backwards and the others believe every word he tells them. The mail order licensed-preaching business must be the most profitable industry in Africa."

The agent was just finishing his second bourbon and water at this point, the case officer noted.

"Stoffel was impressed with Masefield and it was a good thing that I made her a solid asset before his arrival.

"Before Masefield actually arrived on the scene I was never able, even with Stoffel's help, to get out into the sharp end. The first week Masefield was in Rhodesia he ingratiated himself with Prime Minister Ian Smith, M.M. De Vries, the Minister of Information, the Minister of Defense, General Peter Wall, Colonel Ron Reid-Daley and every other trusted confidant of the establishment here. Of course they'd all read his Vietnam books and seen his movies and he became an instant celebrity.

"For three days the local newspaper, the *Rhodesia Herald*, had articles about him. Stoffel arranged for him to go to Umtali to visit with General Derry MacIntyre who commands the military in the area known as Thrasher. We went down to Umtali and in two days you would have thought Derry MacIntyre was Masefield's oldest and dearest friend.

"At the SAS mess in Salisbury, Mack Hudson, the other Americans in the SAS (a list of whom is enclosed) and the commander of the SAS, Major Bruce Atkinson, became his best buddies. They invited him to go on an actual parachute raid with them. As you know, Masefield made fifteen operational parachute jumps in Vietnam, the result of his having graduated from both Paratrooper School and Special Warfare School in Fort Bragg. General Wall would have let him go but the government is so worried about his safety that the jump was not approved. They don't want to lose him until he's done the job for Rhodesia he came here to do.

"In Umtali General MacIntyre let us both go out into the operational area with Lieutenant Colonel Peter White who is the main combat commander in the Thrasher area. We interviewed a couple of captured terrorists and were in actual contact with terrorists in the Honde Valley. Much of the detailed military information which will follow was acquired as a result of Masefield's instant acceptance, which of course transferred itself to me.

"Masefield has come up with some elaborate planning as a result of the six weeks he spent in Rhodesia and is now in New York City implementing that planning before his return. His book project is being almost superseded by his desire to promote the Rhodesian cause actively. Masefield could be extremely dangerous to the implementation of United States foreign policy in southern Africa unless that policy coincides with his perception of what it *should* be. You will recall he almost singlehandedly forced the Pentagon to abandon its scheduled phasing out of the U.S. Army Special Forces as a unit.

"With Stoffel's help, and of course my own, Masefield bought a house in a convenient part of Salisbury across from the Andrew Fleming Hospital. This location he picked for two reasons. One was that again with Stoffel's help, he could get a telex installed in this location, an impossibility for anyone else over here. The other was that he wanted to be near the hospital so he could easily visit the wounded Americans.

"After meeting Yanks all over Rhodesia, Masefield discovered that foreigners serving with the Rhodesian Security Forces have no offical representation of any kind. Since the United States has no diplomatic ties with Rhodesia, he plans to call himself the 'Ambassador' and his house the 'Embassy.' He has already set up plans to make his 'Embassy,' as he is already calling it, into a meeting place for Americans fighting in Rhodesia. This of course will be of inestimable value to my operations. I should be able to get the name of every American in Rhodesia for your files.

"When I go back to Rhodesia with Roger Masefield I'll maintain a neutral stance until after the elections. I assume President Ford will win, Kissinger will remain as Secretary of State, and hopefully a policy more favorable to a democratically elected majority rule government in Rhodesia will be adopted. It is imperative that we do not allow either of the terrorist regimes to exert coercion at the polls. It is a brave and innovative little nation, and the only country in Africa that has proved to be self-sufficient despite no foreign aid and severe restrictions on trade. Every time I hear its national anthem played—they adopted Beethoven's *Ode to Joy* from the Ninth Symphony—I feel great admiration for what they're doing over there."

The case officer signed his name, attesting to the fact that this was a true transcript of the oral debriefing of Special Operative Alvin Glenlord, Colonel U.S. Army. Below his signature he scrawled a note of warning. Glenlord was becoming too involved in the fortunes of Rhodesia and might find his loyalty wavering if administration policy ran strongly counter to his personal beliefs.

The case officer put the Glenlord transcript into a red envelope addressed to the Director and left his office to deliver it into the Director's hand personally.

Chapter 16

July 1977

Carla DePlata Hudson glanced at the clock ticking away in the corner of the living room of the flat on North Street in the Avenues. Ten o'clock and no word from Mack. Carla sighed and put down the copy of *Illustrated Rhodesian Life*. She'd picked through the magazine three times and still had not absorbed any of its content. Typical of Mack, she thought. Her pride wouldn't let her pick up the phone and call the SAS officers' mess to ask for him. Mack had been furious the last time she did that. "The old lady wants you home, Mack," the men had laughed derisively, according to her husband.

She stood up, paced the floor, went to the refrigerator, took out the bottle of Castle that was left and poured herself another beer. She didn't really like to drink alone. There was plenty of South African and even Rhodesian liquor around the house but Carla had always been frightened of acquiring a drinking habit out of boredom.

The phone rang. She let it ring two more times, her hand on the instrument, before taking it from its cradle.

"Yes, I'm here," she said, without attempting to keep the annoyance from her voice.

"It's not who you think. It's Ashley."

"Ashley?" Her voice softened. "I thought . . ."

"I know what you thought, Carla. I'm just around the corner from you. Why don't I pick you up and we'll go over to Giamo's for a late drink?"

"I can't, Ashley. Mack should be here any minute."

There was a wry laugh on the other end. "I doubt it. We just reached his commander who approved his leading an operation tonight. Hoping he'll get killed, I'm told. But don't worry. Captain Hudson won't even make contact with the terrs although I doubt if he'll be back within two or three days. What about it, Carla? Now come on, old girl, there's no point sitting there staring at bare walls."

Carla looked about the small living room. Suddenly, impetuously she breathed into the telephone, "All right, Ashley, I'll stand outside. I feel like some air anyway."

"That's a girl. I'll be by in five minutes."

Carla hung up, her pulse quickening as she thought about General Ashley St. John, that handsome, obviously wealthy and at times maddeningly arrogant Englishman who had renounced his inherited title of Sir Ashley when Rhodesia announced its unilateral declaration of independence from Britain.

She felt a twinge of shame, along with a rush of excitement, at the thought of a late-night rendezvous with this reputed Don Juan. Once she had started her job as a volunteer at Andrew Fleming Hospital, she began seeing him two or three days a week. As deputy to the C-in-C of the Rhodesian Army, General St. John made frequent visits to the hospital to visit the wounded, and no soldier left the hospital without at least one personal visit from him.

Ashley's interest in Carla soon became unmistakable. It was her quaint accent, he said, that had first caught his attention. The Rhodesians all thought that Americans had a quaint way of talking. But it wasn't just her accent, Carla realized.

When she worked at the Defense Language Institute in Monterey, California she had attracted far more attention than she could handle. Her raven tresses falling to her shoulders, her sultry Latin look and her firm full bosom and tall slender figure had always made her an immediate center of male interest. Indeed, it was the apparently insatiable desire she aroused in almost every man she met that had probably caused her to become engaged before she was quite ready for it.

Mack Hudson had clearly been the most attractive officer in the language school. His six feet two inches of lean masculinity, his angular face and craggy features, his thick curly sandy-brown hair and the quizzical sparkle in his eyes when he was with her, had made him as attractive to her as she knew she was to men in general. Mack was well educated and their topics of conversation ranged from world events and the declining curricula at universities to politics and the latest books.

Carla had immediately recognized that Mack was well-bred and from a good family. Even though he had been talking about making the military a career, she felt certain he would do more with his life than soldiering. In this assumption she had been wrong. And now she was undeniably attracted to another soldier from another nation. Ashley was at least ten years older than Mack, his aristocratic demeanor, his rather haughty attitude toward officers of lower rank, unless they happened to be wounded, and a particular disdain for foreign officers which he never tried to camouflage, for Mack Hudson in particular, was all too evident. Yet they all combined to make him interesting, and certainly very different from any man she had known before.

Twice, sometimes as often as three times a week, the general met Carla for afternoon tea after her hospital hours. General St. John was a consummate ladies' man, she quickly realized. But with Mack away so often and only the rather drab apartment to look forward to, she gratefully absorbed as much of his time as he could give her. She learned about his upbringing in one of England's old and respected families, his distinguished record at Sandhurst. He had come out to Rhodesia to visit family landholdings and immediately commenced a love affair with the robust young country. Ashley had joined the Rhodesian Army and stayed with it when it became the Federation army of Northern and Southern Rhodesia and Nyasaland. When Northern Rhodesia became black-ruled Zambia and Nyasaland became Malawi, another black dictatorship, he gave his allegiance to Southern Rhodesia, now Rhodesia, the only country remaining out of the one-time federation that offered a viable way of life for white farmers, businesmen and soldiers.

Feeling excitingly naughty, Carla changed from her loose-fitting blouse to a snug black bodice, threw a white knitted shawl around her shoulders and let herself out the apartment door. She walked down two flights of steps to the ground floor and then out into the cool winter air. As she stood on the sidewalk waiting for Ashley to come and pick her up, she thought of the first time she'd mentioned General St. John to Mack. He had snorted with a disdain that matched Ashley's. The general had never heard a shot fired in anger in his entire military career, Mack declared. Opportunities for combat assignments had presented themselves but he had managed to avoid going to Malaya with the Rhodesian detachment to fight the Communist terrorists there and had somehow missed the border skirmishes in Africa during the days of the Federation Army.

Ashley's lack of fighting experience was almost a joke among the officers who had seen, and were daily engaged in, combat operations.

"He has more stomach for garrison intrigue than incoming mortar bombs," Mack summed up. To Carla this seemed quite natural. She would have preferred Mack to be the same way. In fact she would have preferred it if Mack had stayed in Virginia and worked his way up the corporate hierarchy of IBM.

Down North Street she saw headlights approaching. She watched them loom larger and brighter, then saw the familiar Mercedes pull up and Ashley St. John spring out and hold open the door for her. She slid onto the front seat beside him and pulled the door shut. Ashley stared hungrily at her a few moments, put the car in gear and sped away.

"Do you know where Mack is?" she asked. The question sounded foolish to her even as she asked it. Ashley hadn't invited her for drinks to talk about Mack.

"An operation began tonight. Nothing of consequence. Not much more than an SAS training exercise, really. He'll be back in a few days. Meantime . . ."

Carla looked at him questioningly as he left the sentence unfinished. "Where is it we're going?" she asked. "It wouldn't be wise to run into any of Mack's friends."

"Don't worry, nobody your husband knows would be at Giamo's. His clientele is strictly made up of the biggest government officials, leading businessmen and the larger landholders when they are in town. You'll enjoy it, Carla."

Ashley St. John had been quite correct when he told Carla that none of her husband's military friends would be at Giamo's; in fact they had probably never even heard of it. But the general had not counted on the self-appointed American Ambassador to Rhodesia,

Roger Masefield, who was indeed there entertaining a Pittsburgh industrialist interested in one of Rhodesia's chief export items, chrome.

"You said we wouldn't run into anybody that knew me," Carla expostulated. "And who do we see first but one of Mack's best friends, Roger Masefield, and his wife, too."

"Now, dear Carla," Ashley answered patronizingly, "there's certainly nothing wrong with us having a little drink. Besides, Masefield is not going to go running to Mack and say something like 'Hey, buddy,' or whatever one Yank calls another, 'what do you think? I just saw your wife out with General Ashley St. John.'" Ashley looked over at the table. "I see he's got Arthur Anderson with him. We gave the bloke a bit of a briefing yesterday on how the war is going. It's strange, you know, hard to understand: so many prominent Americans come here and are totally with us, yet they can't change their government's attitude toward us."

Carla, looking across the room at the table where Masefield and his wife were sitting with the Pittsburgh businessman, caught Roger's eye. They smiled at each other and waved. Then she turned to St. John. "He's been out in the bush with Mack two or three times, you know."

"Yes, I know. I have to give him clearance when he goes out." The general laughed. "Now he wants to go on our external missions into Mozambique. I'm afraid we had to put our foot down on that one." He waved to a waiter who came over with a menu. "Are you hungry, my girl?"

"Now that I think about it, I never did get around to having dinner. I expected Mack home early today." Carla studied the menu. "Oh look, they have fish. Sea fish. I do love saltwater fish. That's the only trouble here in Rhodesia, it's so hard to get fish."

"Well, we are landlocked, you know, with enemy between us and the ocean on all sides, except for South Africa. It takes some doing to get fresh sea fish into Salisbury."

"You all eat much too much meat," Carla said. "But then of course: that's what you have the most of."

"Yes, we have the highest meat ration per man of any army in the world. Now go ahead and order your fish. A bottle of wine?"

"Thank you, Ashley. This is really a big treat for me."

When they'd finished eating Ashley poured the last of the Chablis into the two wine glasses and sat back on the banquette beside Carla, his right hand slyly reaching for and taking her left. Carla smiled and returned the squeeze.

"Would you like a pony of cognac with coffee, my dear?"

"That would be nice, Ashley," she replied.

The general summoned a waiter and gave the order. "We should really do this more often. You know, I hate to think of such a beautiful woman"—he pressed her hand again—"a lady so appreciative of life's amenities, sitting alone in some dreadful little flat when she could be out savoring life. It's a short one, after all."

"Our apartment isn't so bad," Carla replied defensively. "And we aren't going to be here forever, you know."

"Well, while you are I'm going to make it my business to see that you enjoy our country to the utmost."

"It's certainly been delightful tonight."

Ashley lifted his small glass of cognac. "It's not over yet, my dear," he smiled.

By now the guilty feeling of being out with another man while Mack was in the bush had disappeared.

They sipped their cognac and Carla asked, "Why did you leave England to come out here, Ashley?"

The general smiled as though at some inward thought her question had provoked. "This is a beautiful country."

"But, to use a real Americanism, you had it made in England."

"My father, Sir Robert, was a very wise man and saw what must inevitably come in England. He could see creeping socialism getting a stranglehold on British life as he had known it when he was growing up. 'One is going to have to be extraordinarily rich to enjoy our country by the 1950s, and it will get worse,' he told me after the war. So, with his help, I researched the colonies and we decided that Rhodesia had the most to offer. And, of course, we had connections out here."

Ashley finished off his brandy. "So I quite merrily accepted a down payment on my inheritance from Father and took my hereditary title and Sandhurst education to Salisbury and have lived here most happily ever after. Sending me out to Africa was my father's finest bequest to a potentially errant son who didn't really know what he wanted to do with his life."

"This is a happy country—for Africans and Europeans alike," Carla agreed. "Even with the war."

"It's not such a bad war really," Ashley said. "As wars go. If we can only keep Rhodesia safe from Soviet Marxism we can realize a dream society here."

"It's worth fighting for," Carla said simply.

"Someday the free world will come to Rhodesia for chrome and tungsten and tea, tobacco, coffee, yes and gold and farm produce. We could feed all the starving Communist dictatorships around us. And there's plenty of time for polo, golf, gaming, eating, drinking and loving, the truly important things in life. No?" Ashley's ingratiating smile prompted a titter from Carla.

"Oh, but yes, Ashley," she enthused. "I hope you get this war over and we can all concentrate on enjoying life again." Then, thinking of Mack who would surely find the next war, wherever it was, she frowned.

"Quite." Ashley's fingers tightened on hers. "There's a fair amount of living and loving left in this very night. What?" His eyebrows lifted and his smile broadened.

Carla suddenly recalled Mack's comment about General St. John's natural aversion to the combat aspects of war. But in every army in the world it was the same, she knew. You became a general much quicker by sitting at a desk and showing up for luncheon and dinner at the officers' mess than you did by going out into the field and shooting at the enemy.

Roger Masfield, his wife Jocelyn, and the Pittsburgh businessman briefly stopped by the table to pay their respects on the way out. "It's been a while since I've seen you, Ashley," Masefield said genially after introducing Carla Hudson to the visiting American. "Very fine briefing you gave us yesterday, General," Anderson added. "I'm on my way to South Africa tomorrow and then back to the States. You can be sure that every bit of influence at my command, all the influence that Pittsburgh can bring to bear, will be used to pressure the Senate of the United States into dropping sanctions against Rhodesia.

"God, how that, that"—Anderson's voice shook and his jowls quivered—"President Carter's black racist, Andrew Young, who purports to represent America in the United Nations . . . The way that traitor to the free world is allowed to destroy everything Americans believe in over here in Rhodesia is nothing short of treason at the highest level."

He let out a deep sigh that ended in a sheepish grin. "I didn't mean to become so agitated, General. I just feel I have to go around apologizing for the appalling mess the government of my country is causing here."

"We appreciate your sentiments, Mr. Anderson."

Ashley and Carla watched the three Americans leave Giamo's and Ashley took her hand in his again. "It's my own country, I should say my former country, that's really causing the mess over here. Britain is the real culprit. My father was right. No wonder we're called Perfidious Albion. When she places another Idi Amin, a Robert Mugabe, here in Salisbury, and the country goes completely Communist, and Pittsburgh is no longer able to get chrome from us but has to buy it from Russia at three times the price for half the quality, then perhaps the British government will be happy."

Ashley gave a little snorting laugh. "But why are we talking about such dismal topics when we are together? Let's go over to my flat for another spot of cognac. I have some real French Napoleon spirited in to me from Johannesburg."

"As long as you take me home at a reasonable hour, Ashley," Carla warned, but with a impish emphasis on *reasonable.*

"I promise. But only for this night. There will be others . . ." He signaled the waiter to bring the bill.

Chapter 17

Saturday morning in Salisbury, even among the military, was very much like Saturday morning in most other towns. Although the war didn't actually pause so that everybody could enjoy their weekend, it certainly geared downwards.

On this particular Saturday Mack Hudson indulged himself in the luxury of sleeping late. Then slightly hungover from drinking the evening before with other Americans and their girl friends or wives, he percolated a pot of coffee and brought it to the bedroom.

"What are we going to do today, honey?" Carla asked, reaching from the bed for a steaming cup of coffee.

"I'm in the mood for some laughs. Let's go over to Roger Masefield's American Embassy of Good Will. I really get a lot of fun out of hearing those guys bullshitting each other and Roger."

Carla put the cup down on the bedside table and looked up at Mack. "Oh don't let's go over there. You know what a zoo it turns out to be."

"Well, that's what I'm in the mood for, the zoo. The Saturday afternoon bunfight, as Colonel Glenlord calls it. The animal house."

"I don't know how Jocelyn stands it," Carla sighed. "But honestly, Mack, do you really want to go over there today?"

131

"I can't think of anything else to do. Except maybe go over to the mess at SAS. But if I do that I'll run into my esteemed commander, Bruce Atkinson. Besides, I haven't seen Roger for a couple of weeks now. Colin Adderley will be there with his American girl friend. And I want to find out who's taken the gap. I hope none of the guys I approved has run out on his contract."

Carla decided she'd better prepare herself and Mack for the possibility that someone might mention her and Ashley St. John having been at Giamo's together the other evening. She even suspected that Ashley might carry out his threat to go around to the Embassy just to see her. She rolled out of bed and walked nude into the bathroom, Mack's eyes following her. She was as beautiful, perhaps even more beautiful than when he'd married her, he thought. Her breasts were still taut despite their ample size, her long legs and well formed buttocks and torso still excited him after six years of marriage.

Carla emerged from the bathroom in a robe, her hair hanging loosely about her shoulders. "You know, a funny thing happened the other night when you were out on an operation." She left the sentence hanging. Finally Mack looked at her questioningly.

"What?"

"While I was sitting here wondering where you were the phone rang. I thought it was you. But it wasn't."

"Of course it wasn't," Mack said irritably. "I was getting ready to go on an airborne operation."

"It was General St. John."

"Was he trying to locate me? Why didn't you tell me he called? He's another one of those general staff officers that think I'm too aggressive." Mack laughed disparagingly. "The Rhodesian Army is aggressive, General St. John once told a group of us Americans, but not *too* aggressive. When is aggressive *too* aggressive?"

"He wasn't looking for you, Mack," Carla replied. "He wanted to talk to me."

"You!"

"I've told you that I see him at the hospital two or three times a week. He's always very nice to me. I guess he knew you were out on an operation because he asked me if I'd like to have a nightcap with him at Giamo's. I was bored and accepted. General St. John is really a very interesting gentleman."

"I'll bet."

"Well, it did a lot for my morale not having to sit around the house all evening wondering where you were. And there's nothing wrong with having a little chat with an interesting person, is there?"

"No, no, I guess there isn't," Mack replied. "As long as it's just a chat."

"Oh, Mack, you don't think I'd get myself involved, do you?"

"Over here, in this situation, a war going on, men going away from their wives for weeks on end, anything can happen and usually does."

"You don't suspect that Ashley and I . . ."

"Ashley, is it," Mack chuckled mirthlessly. "I know all about that English gentleman. He goes after every beautiful woman he sees, married or single. That's the big difference between a British-oriented army and an American army. We don't approve of our officers being womanizers. To the British and the Rhodesians that doesn't seem to make any difference."

"Mack, Mack," Carla laughed, "you sound such a prude. I know where your eyes, and probably a lot more than your eyes, have been from time to time. Now let's not talk about General St. John any further. I enjoyed dinner with him and that's it. You want some breakfast?"

Mack looked at the clock in the living room. "It's more like luncheon, I'd say."

"Well, we can get hamburgers over at the Embassy."

"Yeah, that'll be good enough for me. We'll go somewhere for dinner tonight, a quiet dinner."

"That would be nice," Carla concurred. She felt better now that she had told Mack about her evening with General St. John. She didn't really think that Roger or Jocelyn would have said anything but you never knew what might come out in conversation. Better to be prepared.

It was not a long drive from their apartment to the imposing house that Roger Masefield had bought and turned into an "embassy." Three flags flying—the Rhodesian flag, the American flag, and the flag depicting an eagle with a bandaged right wing. Even though the U.S. government was harassing Americans for being in Rhodesia these days, it gave Mack a feeling of pride to see the Stars and Stripes flying here in Salisbury. Roger had created an American presence and all the Americans fighting in the Rhodesian Army appreciated it.

They parked their car and went up to the door, on either side of which was the seal of the unofficial American embassy. Nobody, least of all Roger, called it the U.S. Embassy. The seal depicted the trademark wounded eagle perched on the red-and-white-striped shield with blue bar across the top. Beneath the eagle's talons was an FN rifle crossed by a quill pen signifying, as Masefield put it, the truth in writing. Mack was wearing the Crippled Eagle pin he had been presented by Roger Masefield. Every American had one of these pins which they wore on Saturday when they came to the club. In fact they wore them whenever they were off duty just to identify themselves to each other.

The front door was unlocked and they walked in. There were several Americans with their foreign guests sitting around the large living room and in the bar beer and Rhodesian-made gin and vodka were being served. The parlor had French windows opening onto the front yard. A wide arch in the far wall led into the bar, and beyond that, through another pair of French windows, could be glimpsed the back lawn with its swimming pool and tennis court.

Mack spotted Jacques LeClair standing with a group of Frenchmen and Belgians and one West German. No animosities left over from World War II, he noted. He and Carla walked over to the Frenchman. "Jacques," Mack greeted him.

Jacques turned and grinned. "What's 'appening with you, *mon capitaine.*"

"Same old thing. Major Bruce Atkinson hates me as much as ever," Mack answered cheerfully.

Jacques took Carla's hand, bent down gallantly and kissed it.

"Always the Frenchman," Mack chuckled. "Where's the Ambassador?"

"He's outside putting in the flags." Followed by Carla, Mack walked through the living room and bar to the rear of the Embassy. He paused for a minute at the glass doors which were swung open. Scotch-taped to them were the baseball scores from the United States which had come in over the Embassy telex.

Roger was sticking a fourth cardboard flag into a board against the wall. It indicated the nationality of his latest visitor that day. On these informal Saturday afternoons Roger wore his Crippled Eagles T-shirt and slacks. He had 300 of these T-shirts made up in the U.S. and sent over to Rhodesia so that every American could wear the colorful Crippled Eagle insignia. They had gone so fast he'd had to order another batch, and now a third order was in the works.

"Good to see you Mack, Carla," Roger greeted them. "Jocelyn was just asking for you, Carla."

"Where is she? I'll go say hello." Carla looked around. There was Jocelyn standing by the tennis court watching a lively game of doubles between two Americans in Crippled Eagles T-shirts and two Rhodesians.

"I hear you and Bruce Atkinson have somewhat widened the breech between your points of view," Roger said with a grin.

"How did you know that?" Roger had a keen intelligence network, Mack knew, which penetrated the military, civilian, business and even the game-hunting and tourist industry.

Masefield ignored the question. "Three guys took the gap this week. I tried to talk them out of it. Hendrixon, Hank the Yank and old Will. Hank couldn't hack the training over there at RLI. He went through three-quarters of it, the hardest three-quarters, and then quit because he didn't like that South African sergeant major that kicks ass and takes names all over Cranborne. You know the one I mean? Botha."

"I know Botha," Mack sighed. "He's hard. But he's a good NCO. He's the kind of man you need to make an army work. Hank should have been able to take whatever Botha had to give out. What the hell did he think he was getting into over here?"

"Hank and the others were not Special Forces like you, Mack."

Mack nodded. "You don't see any ex-Marines, any ex-Green Berets, or any other combat men from the Nam wilting at the discipline here. We need a little more of it in the United States Army. We'd be better off. The Rhodesian Army would cut an American division to pieces, go through them like a dose of salts through a constipated goose." Mack Hudson glanced about the swimming pool area. "I see my latest recruits have all found your embassy," he observed.

"They all pitch up here."

"That's the trouble, Roger. A lot of the good guys don't come because of the bums that show up."

Roger's face showed concern. "I know. I've heard that before. But at least on Saturday afternoons there's got to be some place where foreigners, Americans in particular, can feel welcome and get a touch of home. Those of you who are really established here, doing the job out in the bush, fighting the terrs regularly, you're the men I like to have here. But after all, we do have six other days in the week when the place isn't wide open to every American and his friends."

Roger looked around the Embassy backyard. At least fifty men, many with their girl friends were swimming in the pool, watching tennis or eating the hamburgers which he and Jocelyn had spent many patient hours teaching the two Embassy housemen to cook. "I tried to get a McDonald's arch to put over the hamburger grill, but no luck." Then he said earnestly, "This place means a great deal to these guys. The Americans, yes of course, but also to the Brits, the French, the Belgians, the West Germans, the South Africans and the Canadians. Today we also have two Israelis and one young Swede. Even the Rhodies seem to enjoy coming around. I feel like it's the least I can do for everybody, this one afternoon a week."

"I see two very attractive young ladies sitting under the umbrella over there with a group of our chaps." Mack gestured at them. "Somehow they look familiar, I just can't place them."

"The brunette is a sergeant, the blonde is a corporal. They work in the recruiting office."

"Oh yes, now I remember them. Do they come around to make sure the recruits they've signed up are happy?"

"On the surface, that's what you might think. SB sources say the girls are here as monitors. ComOps is nervous about so many foreigners and even Rhodesians sitting around, relaxing, drinking and talking to each other. I discourage talk about operations. But someone at ComOps got testy about the conversations that might be going on around my good will embassy. I'm glad they sent attractive girls over rather than cop types."

"Quite a club you've got here, quite a club," Mack murmured approvingly. "I'm sorry if I called the place a zoo."

"Well, I guess it is on Saturday afternoons, but at least everybody is happy. How about a drink?"

"I'll go find myself a Castle."

As Mack headed for the bar a young man sporting a Fu Manchu moustache appeared from around the corner of the house. He was short and carried a large canvas camera bag over one shoulder. The youth walked over to Roger Masefield and put out his right hand. "Mr. Masefield, Hans Foss told me to look you up. I'm Jeff Brigham."

Pleased, Roger Masefield put his hand out. "How is Hans these days? I understand he's a big shot at World Press now."

"He's my boss. I'm stringing for WP. When Hans sent me here he said that if I mentioned his name you'd talk to me."

"Any friend of Hans Foss has got to be a friend of mine," Roger said warmly. "Old Hans and I had a lot of hairy experiences together in Vietnam. Matter of fact it was Hans that got me an invitation to the execution of Madame Nhu's brother-in-law."

Masefield's eyes fixed on the bag of photo equipment. "You're stringing for WP, huh? Well, one thing. No photographs without the express permission of everybody in any shot you take. There are people here who don't want the world to know where they are. People from a lot of countries who are fighting under a nom de guerre. I don't want to be responsible for blowing their cover."

"I understand, sir. But I would like to meet some of the Americans. Who's that fellow with no legs sitting in the wheelchair with the group over there?"

"That is a real live American hero. His name is Keith Nelson from DeKalb, Illinois. He's been a medic in the RLI for a year and a half. About six months ago he was on an operation into Mozambique in hot pursuit of terrorists fleeing across the border. A couple of the guys were wounded and Keith went across to take care of them and bring them back. Somehow he managed to step on a land mine. He's doing fine now. We're all very proud of him."

"Do you think he'd object if I took his photograph?"

"He's been photographed before. I'll ask him for you."

Jeff Brigham followed Roger Masefield over to the group of Americans sitting around the legless young man in the wheelchair. Beside him was a girl who was watching him attentively.

"Gentlemen," Roger addressed the group of Americans, "this is Jeff Brigham, a reporter, a photographer for World Press. I've told him the ground rules here—no photographs unless everybody in range of the camera is warned. Jeff wants to talk to Americans in the security forces. Just remember he is a newspaperman." Roger smiled at Jeff. "OK, you're on your own. Just don't unlimber that camera without permission."

"I won't," Jeff promised. "Is there anything I can do for you? I'll be glad to take any pictures you want and make you prints. Also, if you ever do want worldwide publicity I could get it for you through

WP. Just let me know how I can help you and the Embassy." The diminutive photographer gave Roger an anxious smile. "I'll keep checking to see if there's anything I or WP can do for you, Mr. Masefield."

"Thanks, Jeff. And call me Roger. Everybody else does." Roger turned from the group and walked to the bar to mix with his guests. A volunteer bartender, a Canadian who had been in the French Foreign Legion for three years, handed his host a gin and tonic.

"Roger!" He spun round to see the young man he considered his protégé. Cary Donnelly, wearing his Crippled Eagles T-shirt, walked into the bar from the parlor.

"Cary! Where've you been? We've been in action here an hour. The hamburgers are damned near eaten up."

"If I don't write home Saturday morning I don't get it done at all," Cary explained cheerfully.

"And what do you hear from New Rochelle?"

"Same old thing. When Mom and Dad tell people where I am, they ask where? and why? and shake their heads."

"Has your mother forgiven me for bringing you over here?"

"Oh sure. She knows I would have made it even if you hadn't lent me the money for the ticket." He looked around at the throng to the rear of the house, splashing in the pool, watching tennis, munching hamburgers and guzzling beer. "Hell of a party as always, I see. There's quite a few guys here who'll be in the bush next Monday with me."

"Yes, I heard that One Commando is moving out."

"The bush is where it's at, as they say. We killed fifteen terrs confirmed last time. Now we're going for thirty. This skirmishing is becoming a war." His eyes darted around. "Where's Jocelyn? I want to be sure to see her before I get away. I heard you two were going back to the States for a while and I thought maybe she'd give my mother a call and tell her Cary is fine." A shadow crossed his face. "We'll miss you while you're away. Don't stay too long."

"We won't. And Al Glenlord will carry on in our absence."

Cary reached for the beer the Canadian behind the bar held out to him, then looked Roger in the eye with visible effort. "Hey, Roger," he began huskily, "the guys think the world of you and Jocelyn . . ." He paused as though reluctant to continue.

"Go on, Cary," Roger urged. "If you have something to tell me, forge ahead."

Cary looked around and, satisfied that nobody could overhear him, blurted, "All the Americans here think Colonel Glenlord is still CIA. We don't feel too comfortable around him. If it wasn't for you nobody would come around. We all signed the guest book for you but we're worried what Colonel Glenlord might do with those names. There's a lot of Crippled Eagles who don't want it known back in the States they're here."

"I know that, Cary. But Al is not a CIA operative now. Sure, he was in Vietnam. But that's finished."

"Maybe you're right, Roger," Cary replied dubiously. Then, after a long consultation with the neck of his beer bottle, he said jauntily, "Any chance of you getting out and joining us in the bush?"

"I plan to be with you for an operation out of Grand Reef. As a matter of fact General St. John is dropping in on us this afternoon to discuss my clearance. Just an excuse," Roger chuckled. "What he really wants is to check the female action."

"That's great, Roger. You'll get to meet my girl friend in Umtali. Serious, man."

"Already?" Roger asked.

"Wait till you see her. I'm not leaving Rhodesia single. Maybe I'm not leaving Rhodesia, except to check in at home and introduce her."

"Jesus. Now your folks will really hate me. I'll bet she's not even a Catholic. Bad enough this Protestant got you into the war, but now he's steering you away from the faith."

Cary grinned. "But they'll love Jessica, and so will you."

"I can hardly wait. I suspect that you'll want me and Jocelyn to break the news in New Rochelle that their son is not going to be a political science professor at Fordham after all, and is marrying a Rhodie."

"Something like that," Cary agreed. "Hey, there's Hughie McCall. I'm going over to have a drink with him. Back on post I have to call him Sergeant and practically salute."

As Roger mingled with the Saturday afternoon Embassy visitors he felt a satisfaction that even a successful book no longer gave him. He was doing more than writing a book; he was helping to fight Marxist domination in a vital area of the globe.

It was a good turnout despite the warning just served on him by Cary Donnelly. He noticed that Al Glenlord seemed in deep conversation with one of the regulars, Earl Sheehy.

Glenlord did not see Roger heading his way. He was in the midst of insisting that he was not a CIA agent, and Sheehy was regarding him with a cunning smile. "I understand, Colonel. I just want you to understand and pass it on that I can't do the job I was sent here to do. It's not worth the Company's money to keep me here. It's almost as though ComOps knows who I am and deliberately keeps me in low-grade but damned dangerous jobs. I want permission to take the gap and report back for another assignment."

Glenlord shook his head. "I'm just working for Roger Masefield as a research assistant, Sheehy. You're dead-ass wrong thinking what you are."

"Look, I'm a Company man. I recognize another one of us when I see him. And if you don't mind my telling you, so does damned near every other American that's seen this setup here. Masefield is just your asset."

Imperiously Glenlord held up a hand. "We don't allow talk like that at this club. Roger is on the way over," he added sharply.

"Sorry, Colonel. I'll be careful." To Al's relief Roger suddenly halted before reaching Sheehy and himself.

Roger had heard his name called by a familiar female voice and turned to see Sarah Cobb Chase coming toward him. She was accompanied by a truly stunning blonde. He wondered how they had ever made it through that house full of woman-hungry combat men, most of whom had nothing to look forward to but long weeks in the bush tracking terr spoor.

Jacques LeClair and the Englishman, Captain Colin Adderley, were right behind the two beauties.

Roger walked across the terrace to meet the women. Sarah threw her arms around him exuberantly and kissed him on the lips, hardly forward or unseemly considering their former relationship.

"How you doing, sweetheart?" Roger whispered in her ear, a broad grin mocking his confidential tone. "How about coming to Umtali with me next week for a few days and nights? We're about overdue, you and I."

"Roger," Sarah exclaimed in elaborate affront, "you know that part of our relationship is over."

"Pity," Roger said with a hint of real regret.

With his assistance, Sarah was stringing for both an American broadcasting network and an international newspaper, scoring enviable scoops with information he suspected a number of knowledgeable officers and government officials whispered into her ear in the privacy of the bedroom.

"Let me introduce you to Veronica Montgomery." Sarah gestured the beauty forward.

"Go ahead." Roger took the girl's outstretched hand, looking into wide blue eyes that searched his face frankly. She was, for all the world, a younger and fresher Beryl Stoffel, he thought. The same chiseled Anglo features.

"Veronica contacted me from Joburg," Sarah explained. "She's up here writing stories for South African magazines and wants to interview you and write a story about the Americans who call themselves Crippled Eagles."

"I expect that can be arranged," Roger smiled. "Get you a drink and I'll introduce Veronica to some of the more colorful hoods here today."

"How exciting," Veronica gushed. "I'm thrilled, Mr. Masefield."

"Mr. Masefield is my father. My God, I must seem as old as Noah."

"I told you, Veronica," Sarah said reprovingly.

"Anyway, I should seriously doubt that you will be half as excited and thrilled as the men who meet you." Roger winked at Captain Adderley. "Right, Colin?"

"Too right, old chap. I'm for keeping these birds away from all the lecherous buggers crawling around this place."

Sarah turned to the black-haired, ruggedly handsome Englishman and kissed his cheek. "Don't be selfish, lovey. I'm having dinner with you tonight."

"And don't you forget it, Sarah Cobb Chase," Adderley said with pretended severity. "Next week it's the bush for me, blowing up munts." Possessively he put an arm around her shoulder and she looked up at him with bright responsive eyes.

"I want to hear all about it, Colin. I'm all yours—later." Flashing a warm smile at the officer, Sarah turned and took Veronica by the arm. They followed Roger who led them toward a bluff, older man with rusty-colored hair, his lined, weathered face a beacon of joy as they approached.

"First, meet the ranking American in the Rhodesian forces, Major Mike Wyatt. He's second-in-command of Grey's Scouts, the cavalry unit," Roger explained.

At fifty Mike Wyatt lifted weights every day and kept himself in top physical condition. He had made an outstanding name for himself in the Scouts brandishing a flamboyant trademark, a cavalry saber which he always carried in action. He was known for riding down terrorists and slashing them with his sword rather than shooting them. Mike was one of the legendary Americans in Rhodesia. He felt, rightly, that publicity could not help his career in the Rhodesian Army and shunned reporters at all times. Veronica was one journalist, Roger was certain, that Mike would take to his bosom.

"I love horses," Veronica breathed as she and the major shook hands.

"They're the dumbest goddamned animals the Lord ever created," Mike said gruffly.

Veronica was taken aback but Major Mike, as he was known to everyone present, quickly put her at ease. "If you really love them, maybe I'll put you on one and we'll go for a ride."

"Oh, I'd love that, Major. When?"

Wyatt looked around at the envious glances darting his way. "Why not right now? My car's outside and I have to go up to Borrowdale, only a couple of miles from here, and look at some new mounts we've been offered."

"This minute?" Veronica asked in surprise.

"No," Roger interjected. "There's a lot of people you should meet first."

"And I thought we were old-time buddies from three wars," Mike grumbled.

"Later," Roger soothed. "By the way, Veronica is a news reporter. She wants to do a story on the Americans in the Rhodesian Security Force. I know how you feel about journalists."

Mike's lips parted in a sensual grin. "No sweat. By now they know all about me at the CIA and U.S. State Department. I'm another American mercenary in their eyes fighting for the white supremacist rule of Ian Smith against the poor downtrodden terrorists. Shocking what we're doing here, isn't it? Killing off the killers."

"Articulate for a mercenary, isn't he?" Veronica quipped.

"I'm not even a mercenary. You know what my take-home pay is? And I can't even save it and take it home."

"I know, Mike," Veronica said sympathetically.

He put an arm around her shoulder. "I can give her all the story she needs. All we have to do is get Veronica a clearance from General St. John, who I see has just arrived, and I'll take her out on a real horse patrol."

"I thought you had promised that to me, Mike," Sarah scolded.

"You get Colin Adderley to take you out with the SAS, if he can arrange it," Mike said, keeping his eyes on Veronica.

Roger started toward Ashley St. John. "If you'll excuse me, I'd better attend to the General. It's not often we get that kind of brass over here on Saturday afternoons."

"I'll watch out for the young lady who loves horses," Mike called after him happily.

General St. John and Roger almost collided, the former on a direct course for Carla Hudson, his only reason for coming to the party. She was chatting with Jocelyn.

Carla looked up and greeted the general shyly. "What a surprise, Ashley," she murmured, her eyes darting about in search of her husband.

"Glad you could make it, Ashley," Roger welcomed him. "I've got a bottle of VIP Scotch hidden away when you're ready."

"In due course, Roger," St. John replied pleasantly.

"We were just discussing where you can get a good fish dinner in town," Jocelyn remarked wickedly.

"And you came to the conclusion that Giamo's is best," Ashley picked up. He beamed at Carla.

For the fist time that afternoon Alvin Glenlord joined Roger—and it was to shake hands with General St. John. "To what does the Embassy"—he said the word with the trace of a sneer—"owe the honor of a visit by such a high-ranking member of ComOps?"

"Good afternoon, Colonel Glenlord. Where is Beryl? She's often here, I understand."

"She went to a garden party at the P.M.'s residence with M.M. De Vries."

"Oh, of course. I expect I'll soon drop by."

"We're doubly honored," Jocelyn bantered, "that you would take the time to visit us first."

Ashley St. John and Carla looked meaningfully at each other, and then Ashley said, "I promised Roger I'd look in. These Saturday afternoon receptions at this Embassy of yours, Jocelyn, are becoming quite famous, you know."

"Thank you for calling it a reception, Ashley." Out of the corner of her eye Jocelyn saw that several of the male guests were lunching drunkenly and that two Crippled Eagles beside the swimming pool were vying with each other to cover the greatest amount of a girl's near nude body with their hands.

"Roger, you know there are several journalists here," Glenlord said ponderously, obviously for St. John's benefit. "I thought we had agreed with ComOps not to let reporters get close to the men in off-duty circumstances."

"And I thought you were a public relations man," Roger returned airily. Then to Ashley: "Although we don't actually invite journalists, they sometimes drop by, especially American ones." A crafty smile tugged at his lips. "We do have a South African journalist here, a young woman. She came with Sarah Chase. They're over there."

For the first time since he had arrived, Ashley St. John's attention was diverted from Carla as he followed Roger's glance. He virtually sprang to attention when he saw Veronica who was laughing gaily at something Mike Wyatt was saying.

"That girl, the blonde, is a journalist?"

"Yes, she is," Al answered abruptly. "And so is Sarah Chase, as you know, and now we have one Jeff Brigham, a photographer-reporter from World Press also here. And a couple of others, too. It's difficult to keep them out, and seems kind of ornery."

"I understand," Ashley muttered, his gaze riveted on Veronica. "Of course you do your best." For a moment he looked away from the blonde South African. "Roger, since I have a certain amount of responsibility for press coverage of security forces perhaps you had better introduce me to the new reporter from South Africa."

"Of course, Ashley. Let's walk over there." Roger led the general across the lawn. On the way to their objective he said, "Ashley, I'm planning to get out to the bush next week. I'm visiting Lieutenant Colonel Peter White and Brigadier MacIntyre, also Grand Reef and One Commando of RLI. Is my blanket permit good enough or do I need something else?"

"Oh, everyone knows you; it's all right. I'll send MacIntyre a signal on Monday."

"Anything I can look into for you?" Roger asked.

"No, nothing I can think of." He stopped a moment. "Yes, there is one thing."

General St. John lowered his voice conspiratorially. "There's a Sister Anne Marie McFarland, Catholic missionary, who seems to travel pretty much at will around the country. Some of our chaps have spotted her out in the TTL missions along the Mozambique border and we know she's in contact with the terrorists. Of course she also has an office in Salisbury—at the Catholic Commission on Justice." His voice reflected disgust. "Unlike most nuns, she has her own flat as well."

"I think I know who you mean, Ashley. Sort of pudding face, about twenty-eight or thirty."

"That's the one. There's no doubt she's trafficking with the Communists. We hear she's getting it on with the African boys." The general grimaced. "I've known foreign white women who've come here and gotten involved that way. But this is the first nun we've had reason to believe is totally enamored with African-style equipment. If you know what I mean."

"Well, I knew about a couple of the mission priests that were making some of the black girls into nuns and then making the nuns," Roger said. "Out in the bush anything can happen, I guess."

"Whatever you can find out will be appreciated," St. John suggested. "We've been losing men in ambushes in several Tribal Trust Lands that have Catholic missions nearby. And in almost every case this Sister McFarland has been at the mission when the ambush took place."

"That old scoundrel that calls himself a priest over in Weya," Roger added, "I know he tried to set up an ambush on Major Wyatt when his Grey's Scouts squadron was down there. If it hadn't been for the K factor Mike would probably have been one more American casualty. Ask him about it. He's talking to the girl you want to meet."

St. John looked across at the blonde talking and laughing with Mike Wyatt. "He seems to be taking an inordinate interest in her," he noted peevishly. They approached the small group of animated men around Sarah Chase and Veronica Montgomery. Roger made the introductions and the general wasted no time intruding himself into conversation with the blonde reporter. Mike Wyatt was pushed aside, midway through requesting a clearance for Veronica so she could come out and do a story on Grey's Scouts. Jeff Brigham asked for a clearance to go into the operational areas. The general cut him off with a succinct "Come to my office in the Milton Building Monday afternoon."

Mike turned to Roger angrily. "What is this? Fuck your buddy week?"

"Beyond my control, *compadre,*" Roger apologized.

With a reassuring smile to Veronica, General St. John explained that among his myriad assignments at Combined Operations he was charged with approving clearances for journalists. He would be happy to assist her in whatever manner possible to carry out her journalistic endeavors.

Veronica was clearly willing to use the face and figure which had given her runner-up status in the Miss South Africa contest the previous year to further her career. So when, after a bare five minutes of persiflage with Ashley St. John, the latter let drop, "I'm afraid I must leave now for the Prime Minister's garden party at Government House. Would you like to go with me?" she instantly answered in the affirmative.

A disappointed Mike Wyatt and the other equally chagrined Crippled Eagles watched the general escort the gorgeous neophyte journalist from the party. St. John did not bother to take his leave of either Jocelyn Masefield or Carla Hudson. He merely maneuvered Veronica through the obstacle course of drinking, staring foreign nationals, then led her around the corner of the red-brick house to the front gate, beyond which his Mercedes awaited.

"How 'bout that?" Roger asked Sarah.

"She'll be very successful here," Sarah said with conviction. "I'm glad I was able to help her. By Monday morning she'll be able to do some powerful favors for her friends."

"Sure you won't come to Umtali with me for a dirty midweek?" Roger teased.

"In the first place you don't mean it," Sarah chuckled. "In the second place you really do love your wife—when she's around. And in the third place I love Colin."

"I can get you to the sharp end," Roger persisted with a laugh that nullified the implied proposition.

146

"It's damned unfair that ComOps won't let any of us see what goes on in the operational area," Sarah complained. "Only you and Johnny Cravenlow, Francois Darquennes and one or two other favorites."

"The government knows we are not going to write a lot of rubbish about the racist regime of Ian Smith."

"But the outside world wants to read about how badly the whites treat Kaffirs over here," Sarah countered.

"So you have to file spurious stories to fill that need? Why can't you tell it like it really is. The Africans live better in Rhodesia, with less discrimination and a higher standard of living, than anywhere in Africa."

"You know what the editors do when they get that kind of stuff?"

"Then don't feel sorry for yourselves that you can't get out into the sharp end with the troops," Roger admonished. "I'll bring you back some stories and pictures from Umtali you can use, and you don't have to reward me."

"You bastard," she laughed. "But thank you, Roger. I just wish I could get them myself."

"Maybe Veronica can do something for you after she's done something for General St. John. So it's you and Colin Adderley getting it on these days. I thought Lord Johnny was the man in your life."

"Johnny is too elusive. He can have any woman he wants, in Rhodesia or anywhere else. And you're here *en famille*, so to speak." She shot a look at Jocelyn. "Colin is a fascinating guy. I could write a great story on him if he'd let me. Explosives expert in Ireland before he quit the Brits and came here." She winked and smiled smugly at Roger. "He's already asked me to marry him and maybe, when the war is over, I will."

"Well good, Sarah Cobb Chase. Colin is a lucky man. Used to be a man had to be able to do you some real good to get close to you."

"You cynical bastard. Colin makes me feel like a real woman, not a girl who'll do anything for a story."

"God bless, Sarah," he laughed. "You are some woman."

Roger Masefield walked away across the lawn, and looking at his happy, chattering guests he felt a warm glow of accomplishment.

Chapter 18

August 1978

Masefield sipped the coffee that had been put beside his raised stretcher on the cement floor of the old one-story farmhouse being used as operations center by the Fourth Battalion of the Third Rhodesia Regiment. On a stretcher beside him reclined Lieutenant Colonel Peter White, commander of the regiment, looking as fresh and ruddy-faced as ever.

"Lots of activity last night," Colonel White remarked happily. "We had eight ambush parties out in this part of the Honde Valley. Four reported contact. We killed six terrs and wounded more that are still being tracked. We'll go look at the bodies," he added with relish. Then: "Jesus, Roger, you snore like a warthog."

"Sorry, Peter." Roger pulled himself out of his sleeping bag, drew a pair of camouflage fatigue pants over his shorts, slipped his feet into his boots and walked outside to watch the sun rise over Mozambique. They were only half a mile from the border.

He stood beside a jawless human skull stuck on the end of along stick whose eye sockets "gazed" over the scene. White came up beside him and patted the bleached skull. "Last year he was a terr group leader specializing in burning alive kraal chiefs and their families in

149

their huts. Some of our African lads finally caught up with him and gave him a piece of his own medicine."

Beyond the skull for several hundred meters were tents and bunkers housing the battalion's territorials, civilians who did this form of National Service when their turn came up.

"How about some graze?" the colonel asked.

"Good idea. Damn but you have a good cook out here."

Peter White came from five generations of Rhodesian farmers, his forefathers having come in as trekkers with Cecil Rhodes and cleared the land that the family still worked profitably. Peter had finally decided he would have to leave the family farm for his wife to manage while he stayed in the army fighting off the Communist terrorists until the war ended.

Over breakfast with Colonel White and his officers and NCOs, Masefield announced his reason for being with them in one of the most terrorist-infested areas of Rhodesia. "If anybody can spare a little time today, I'd sure appreciate it if he'd take me up to the St. Bonaventure Mission. I want to have a word with that scallawag priest from the fine city of Boston, Massachusetts. Through my sources I have learned that America's contribution to the mission nuns in this part of the world, Sister Anne Marie McFarland, is out there with him."

The Rhodesians let out groans and mock cries of pain. "I've got a good contribution to make to that mission," White remarked, "about ten mortar bombs right in the middle of it."

"What are you waiting for?" Roger asked. "Public opinion is against you anyway. When the terrs kill missionaries the world is led to believe that the deed was done by Rhodesian Security Forces."

"We Rhodesians believe in liberty and justice for all," the colonel said with a bitter laugh.

"That's right, sir," a lieutenant chimed in. "We can't even kill the odd houtie breaking curfew without a British South African Police investigation." He gave the BSAP's formal designation in a derisive sing-song.

"That reminds me, a cop's coming over to interview me today," Colonel White's sergeant major said.

"What did you do, Sergeant Major?" Roger Masefield asked curiously.

"Oh, I was driving up from Umtali yesterday about noon and this Kaffir's walking along the side of the road. He's got a pet monkey spidering along behind him with a collar around its neck and a chain attached to it. You know how gentle these people are with their animals. He's jerking the monkey along. So the monkey falls down and the Kaffir drags him screeching."

The sergeant major polished off the last of his scrambled eggs. "Every so often he gives a real jerk on the chain and the monkey lets out a scream. I stop my vehicle, get out and ask the Kaffir what the hell he thinks he's doing. Then I take the collar off the monkey's neck, give the poor scrawny creature a goodie from my ratpack and he takes off into the trees. The Kaffir goes to the cops and says that I mistreated him, took his pet monkey away from him, and he wants to prefer charges against me. Can you imagine, with the terrorists murdering and torturing every night, the cops are worried about a pet monkey getting away?"

The sergeant major looked at Masefield with mock incredulity. The officers had a laugh at the BSAP, a frequent butt of their jokes. Then the chuffing sound of a helicopter overhead brought all the men to their feet. "That'll be Brigadier MacIntyre," the colonel said. "We got a signal he was on his way."

Peter White was wearing a greenish-brown camouflage T-shirt, a pair of shorts and tennis shoes over heavy socks. He reached for his beret on the front of which was pinned a three-inch ostrich feather under the unit insignia. He marched out of the battalion field headquarters to meet the helicopter. Roger got to his feet and followed him. It was a short walk down the road to the helicopter landing pad, and the chopper was already settling. Brigadier MacIntyre leaped out and, keeping his head down, ran out from under the revolving blades. The colonel greeted the commander of this area of operations known as Thrasher.

"How's it going down in Umtali?" White asked.

"Oh, about the same. No mortar attacks for a week, if that's what you mean." Brigadier Derry MacIntyre, a youthful-looking forty-six, had a slightly high-pitched voice and a Scots burr. A professional soldier all his life, he'd originally been an officer in a Scottish Highland regiment; then, in the mid-1950s, he had accepted a commission in the burgeoning Rhodesian Army.

MacIntyre had fought with the Rhodesian contingent in Malaya and seen more action than any other officer of his rank in the Rhodesian Army. A veteran of the skirmishes involving the now defunct

Federal Army, he was a past commander of the illustrious Rhodesian Light Infantry. He prided himself on having learned two African languages, which was a great help in the present war. Frequently he personally interrogated prisoners who pretended not to speak English.

The three men walked back to the battalion headquarters and sat down at the table.

"I don't know what the buggers are up to," MacIntyre growled, pointing vaguely toward Mozambique. "They seem to be forming up into battalion-size units over there. The last terr I talked to, a pretty high-ranking political commissar, told me, not without some resistance at first"—he smiled grimly—"that a lot of white men were with them. I guess that means our Cuban friends are coming out in force. Probably they've got East Germans with them too. I'm trying to get permission to send a combined air and ground strike against them. Break them up, you know. Our big problem, of course, is that there are so many people in Salisbury who are afraid of world opinion. And it's always tough to get government to make up its mind on something like this anyway. In the meantime, you'd better exercise double precautions, Peter. They could come over any time."

"We're as ready as we'll ever be, sir," White said. "The Honde Valley area is as secure as it's possible to make it."

"We've got to keep those tea estates functioning. I don't have to tell you how much of the foreign exchange that pays for this war comes from our tea exports. Isn't it wonderful that all these countries of the world that piously follow United Nations sanctions against us must have their tea?" The brigadier turned to Roger Masefield. "Can I give you a lift somewhere, Roger?"

"No thank you, Derry. I'm going to take a run out to the St. Bonaventure Mission. Just pay a friendly call, you know. I want to see what's going on. It really blights me when Americans aid and abet the terrorists, and it doesn't make it any better if they are Catholic missionaries."

"Oh, 'the boys' get a lot of comfort from the St. Bonaventure Mission, I can tell you that. They have to be certifiable lunatics, those missionaries. Particularly that woman, Sister McFarland. Some of the 'boys' are gooning her, I can tell you that," he laughed.

"I've heard about her from captured terrorists," Peter agreed. "She's a real Kaffir kisser that one. And bloody stupid. A bunch of

Mugabe's terrorists could come in fresh from training in Tanzania and murder every white missionary they come across, including Sister McFarland. We can't seem to make the missionaries realize that helping the terrs, giving them medical supplies, feeding them, hiding them, doesn't score any points in the long run. The next bunch, crazed on kill lust, will line them up and shoot them like they did at St. Paul's, just because they're white."

The brigadier snorted in disgust. "The dear sister can be getting it on with one of her African boyfriends one night and get her tits cut off the next day by his pal. As long as Mugabe over there in Mozambique and Nkomo in Zambia preach their doctrine of rape, torture and murder, these munts will continue to be craven animals. And of course the bounty on hacked-off parts of white bodies does not exactly discourage the mutilation of terr victims."

"I'll pass that information along to Sister McFarland if I see her," Roger promised dryly.

"Be careful going to the mission. There are a dozen or so terrorists hiding out there at any given time. My God, I'd love to get permission to really raze the place. But no, we must always respect the church, the missions." He laughed shrilly. "If Mugabe or Nkomo or any of their cutthroats ever do take over their Zimbabwe, wait and see what happens to the missionaries. They won't even get a chance to be deported. They'll be murdered on the spot."

The brigadier sighed wrathfully and finished his coffee. "So much for my theories on missionaries." He stood up. "OK, Peter. I'm on my way north. I want to warn every battalion commander in Thrasher personally about the build-ups. Put out extra security watches at night. They're up to something."

White's sergeant major strode into the room, snapped to attention before the brigadier and then turned to his commander. "Sir, a truck just came in with the terr bodies from last night. It's down by the helicopter landing."

"Good. Thank you, Sergeant Major." He turned to MacIntyre. "You'll get a chance to inspect last night's bag."

"How many did you get?"

"Radio report said six. We'll soon see."

Masefield followed Derry MacIntyre and Peter White to the helicopter pad. Nearby was parked a truck, behind it six terrorist bodies laid out in a neat row. Several enlisted men of the ambush party stood proudly beside the results of their previous night's work. The brigadier and White looked down in satisfaction at the corpses. Next to them were their weapons, the Russian-made AK-47 assault rifles.

"Shot the shit out of them," Masefield commented. One corpse had most of the torso and head blown away.

"That one had a grenade on his webbing, sir," a trooper explained. "A lucky shot detonated it."

"How many got away?" the brigadier asked.

"Hard to tell, sir," a corporal replied.

"We've got four sparrows out after them," White said. "Best trackers I've got. They got one terr unwounded. He threw down his weapon." White laughed. "The radio signal said this terr claimed he'd picked up the AK on the ground and was taking it into the BSAP to collect a reward."

"I fear the white man will never learn to lie as ingeniously and consistently as the African," MacIntyre said without smiling. He strode toward the helicopter.

"I'll see you at the mess in Umtali tomorrow, Derry," Roger called after him.

"I hope you've bloody well improved your dart game," MacIntyre threw back.

The drive to St. Bonaventure was a slow one. Roger, escorted by a four-man patrol in a Leopard, an anti-mine vehicle, kept a sharp eye on the surrounding countryside. Ambushes were frequent and deadly in this part of Rhodesia. The Leopard was a small cylindrical vehicle with a V-shaped steel bottom which would deflect the blast of a land mine. Its double-width tires turned on the ends of extra-long axles. In the event that one of the wheels did detonate a land mine the blast would occur away from the center of the Leopard.

Roger knew that a patrol went up to the St. Bonaventure Mission area from Peter White's battalion headquarters in the Honde Valley every day as a matter of routine. Thus he was not asking the military to make a special trip on his behalf. He sat beside a young lieutenant, a deputy company commander from the battalion. Lieutenant Arnold explained the type of terrorist action they had experienced in the last month. He also gave Roger some of the latest information on the St. Bonaventure Mission.

The police had reported that in the last year 350 terrorists had been recruited from among the African students attending the mission school. They had all gone voluntarily.

Roger's previous experience with the Catholic mission system in Rhodesia had not made him admire it. Donal Lamont, formerly the bishop of Umtali, had been arrested and charged with violating sections of the Law and Order Maintenance Act for aiding and abetting terrorists.

Bishop Lamont had made no attempt to deny that he had assisted terrorists and encouraged the priests and nuns of his mission to do the same thing. After much investigation Lamont was spared a trial in which he would have been found guilty by his own admissions. He was banished from Rhodesia as a PI (prohibited immigrant) and returned to his native Ireland.

Numerous deaths of white and black civilians were directly attributable to Bishop Lamont's assistance of terrorists. Indeed the grimly efficient BSAP had tracked the murderers of seven Catholic missionaries, both priests and nuns, to a large unit of terrs who had been hidden, fed and given medical supplies by the missions administered by Bishop Lamont. It could be effectively argued that the assistance Lamont gave to the Robert Mugabe terrorists was directly responsible for the murder of the missionaries at St. Paul's Mission north of Salisbury.

Yet, to the dismay of the majority of educated Rhodesians, Bishop Lamont was lionized in his native Ireland, in Britain, and in the United States where he was presented an award at Notre Dame University. Although Lamont had been deported from Rhodesia, many of his followers were still in the country carrying on his good work, as the growing number of murder victims testified.

The Leopard drove into the grounds of the St. Bonaventure Mission and came to a stop. Lieutenant Arnold opened the door in the round bulkhead at the end of the cylindrical body and stepped down, followed by Roger Masefield.

Roger didn't notice anything unusual about the activities within the mission complex. The usual number of African nuns dressed in white robes strode back and forth between the chapel block, the classrooms, and other buildings.

The appearance of Masefield and the lieutenant caused excitement among the Africans. Roger stopped a nun and asked where the priest could be found. Open-mouthed she pointed to a red-brick building next to the chapel.

"If you want to look around, Lieutenant, see what you can spot, go ahead. I don't think I'll be more than an hour here."

"Take your time. We're going to give this place a good going over. I'll be around if you need me."

St. Bonaventure was a large mission. It had a small clinic, several dining halls and even an electrical generating plant.

Roger strode to the rectory and knocked vigorously on the door. As he stood waiting he realized that with his camouflage pants and dark green T-shirt he was probably being taken for a member of the security forces. A group of young girls walked by and suddenly stopped to stare at him. When he stared back they immediately stuck their right index fingers up their nostrils, their eyes widening at the same time, characteristic indications of alarm. Then they turned and hurried off in the opposite direction.

Several young African nuns passed by. There was certainly no Christian fellowship in the looks they gave Roger. He had seen that look in other eyes—those of terrorist suspects in the Tribal Trust Lands. He was about to knock again when the door opened. A medium-sized, redheaded, bespectacled man in a sport shirt, tan pants and open-toe sandals peered out. Behind him was a young and attractive African nun in a flimsy white habit which looked as though it had been hastily pulled on. The man nodded coolly to Roger and turned to the girl. "Thank you for the report, Sister. You can go now. We'll talk again this afternoon about the instruction program for the new students."

The nun rustled by Masefield and went out into the bright sunlight. He looked after her, then realizing that the man in civilian clothes before him was indeed the priest, he recalled having heard rumors about Father Leary's proclivities toward his charges, both male and female. He felt inclined to believe them.

"Father Leary?"

The priest nodded. "Yes, I'm Father Leary. This is my mission. What is it that brings you out here?"

"I'm Roger Masefield, an American writer working on a book about Rhodesia. I also try to smooth relations between Americans and the Rhodesian government and business community."

"Oh, do you now? And what can I do for you?"

"Perhaps you can tell me about American missionaries here in Rhodesia. It might help me in writing my book."

"Well, why don't you come in. It's almost time for luncheon. I'll find us something to eat." Now the priest seemed almost affable.

"I don't want to trouble you, Father Leary."

"Oh, it's no bother, no bother at all." The good father smiled and motioned his guest to follow. He opened a door from the chapel onto a veranda outside and they continued toward a cafeteria reserved for the mission staff. As they walked along Father Leary pointed out various buildings. They stopped in front of a large wooden signpost on which was painted a schematic diagram of the mission.

Masefield noticed that there were several large structures which must once have been used as classrooms but were now empty, the area next to them overgrown with heavy bush. Long unpainted, the windows broken, they stood apart from the other, surprisingly well-kept buildings. Roger made a mental note to the effect that Arnold or a patrol from the battalion might do well to inspect these apparently deserted schoolrooms.

The sight of a white man in camouflage uniform and with a large automatic handgun protruding from a holster on his belt seemed to considerably upset the Africans they passed. Inside the cafeteria a young African woman directed a long, intense gaze at the priest. Masefield wondered whether she was another member of the harem.

"Mr. Masefield, make yourself at home," Father Leary said, pulling out a chair. Before them was a long table covered with a cloth of Irish linen and impressive silverware. The priest asked what Masefield would like for luncheon.

"I don't suppose you'd have such a thing as an omelet?"

Father Leary turned and called into the kitchen. A black cook emerged and Leary put in the order, requesting a sandwich for himself. Despite the priest's relaxed manner, Roger could feel hostility in the stares he was receiving from all corners of the room. From the kitchen came a sudden loud clash of utensils, and other noises. Unobtrusively he slipped the Smith and Wesson 15-shot automatic pistol from his holster and laid it in his lap, hiding the weapon with the tablecloth. One never knew when these terrorist sympathizers might do something foolish, and it didn't seem unlikely that there were terrorists in the cafeteria.

"I understand you're from Boston, Father," Roger began. There was in fact no mistaking the priest's Boston Irish twang. "That's my hometown too. Where did you go, Boston College?"

"Indeed I did," Father Leary said with apparent bonhomie.

"And after that to the seminary, I suppose, right there in Brighton?"

"Of course."

"In all my travels through the underdeveloped countries of the world it seems like three-quarters of the missionary priests come from Boston," Roger remarked.

"I guess that's a fact now," Leary replied.

"I have been told that three hundred and fifty students from this mission school have gone over to Mozambique in the last year to join Robert Mugabe's ZANU forces," Roger shot out, trying to get the priest off balance.

"Indeed you're right, Mr. Masefield," Leary said, his tone perceptibly cooler. "I guess some of the boys do steal in here at night and talk to them. Then the next thing I know a few more students are missing."

"The terrorists don't have to kidnap them from this mission, I take it," Roger observed dryly.

"We can't stop the students from doing what they want to do," the priest replied, a glint of anger in his eye.

"It seems to me you have a fine opportunity here to tell students about communism. Explain to them what really happens in Mozambique. Tell them how many tribal chiefs have been murdered since the Communists took over and how the tribal structure has been destroyed. You could tell them that the population of Mozambique now lives in communes where they are subjected to slave labor. That the entire family life within the African tribal system is being systematically destroyed. That all individual initiative is being discouraged."

Roger paused and Father Leary asked with thin-lipped sarcasm, "Well now, will that be all, Mr. Masefield?"

"No," Roger went on. "There's a lot you could do that would prevent the students from joining the terrorists. And as you probably know, once some of the brighter ones have seen what the life of a terrorist is and what conditions are really like in Mozambique, conditions which Robert Mugabe wants to duplicate in Rhodesia, they get angry at the people like you who didn't give them proper guidance.

158

More than one missionary has been killed by former students angry at not being told the truth—that their life as terrorists would mean hunger, confusion, the strong likelihood of being killed by the security forces and the near certainty of being killed by their comrades if they tried to defect."

Patiently, and with a hint of what might have been self-pity, Father Leary replied, "You don't know what the conditions are really like out here, Mr. Masefield. I do my best to keep the mission open and operating. There are things we can't do, instructions we cannot give if we want to keep functioning."

"Have you submitted the names of the students that have disappeared to the police?"

Leary shook his head. "Have you visited any of the other missions since you've been out here in Rhodesia?"

"Yes, quite a few." Roger decided it was time to get down to the point of his visit. "Tell me, Father, is that nun here with you, also from Boston, Sister McFarland?"

"Oh, she's around here someplace. She visits all the missions in this area of Rhodesia."

"This area meaning along the Mozambique border where the terrorists are most active. Do you suppose I could have a word with her? I do try to keep track of all the Americans here whether they be in the security forces, in business, or even in the clergy."

"Do you now? And why?" the priest asked in prickly defensiveness. It was obvious that as far as he was concerned, the less his activities were observed by outsiders the better.

"Since the United States government doesn't see fit to have any sort of official presence here, I try to fill the job. I've tried to be as helpful as I can to the government and to Americans. And let me tell you right now, Father Leary"—he paused—"when, notice I say *when* not if, Sister McFarland is apprehended in the act of assisting terrorists she's going to need all the help she can get."

"Oh, so it's assisting terrorists now?"

"Assisting them and giving them comfort, if you want to use that euphemism," Masefield grinned.

The priest suddenly stood up, pushing his chair back. "And what does that mean?"

"Take it as you will, Father Leary. Rhodesia is fighting for its very life, whites and blacks together. I fully realize that your mission out here is a sitting target for the terrorists. I understand that you may have to compromise with them at times. But I can also tell you that both the blacks and the whites in the Salisbury government are pretty fed up with the way missionaries are helping terrorists. I can assure you that the Catholic Commission on Justice is going to be of no help to you if Sister McFarland or you should be brought up on charges of assisting terrorists. *I* might be able to help at that time. If I know who I'm helping."

The priest turned away abruptly, as though he could hear no more, and sped off, calling over his shoulder, "Wait right here, finish your luncheon. I'll be back." Roger watched Father Leary leave the cafeteria. Then he finished the omelet, which was delicious. Deciding that no hostile action would occur, he slipped his M-59 back into the holster.

He did not have to wait long before Father Leary returned with Sister Anne Marie McFarland. She was sensibly dressed in jeans, heavy shoes and a loose blue work-shirt. Her only concession to her clerical status was the short gray veil over her head, which could well have been a bandana had it been red. Sister McFarland had a round face and small incandescent eyes which at the moment expressed pure hostility and mistrust. To say she was plain would be putting it kindly. But she did have one thing going for her, Roger thought, at least so far as "the boys" were concerned: she was white.

"Well, Mr. Masefield," she spat out, "to what do I owe the pleasure? You can always find me in Salisbury, you know. It's much safer and easier to see me in my office there."

"When you're there," Roger said coolly. "Which isn't that often. Besides, I haven't been out in the Honde Valley for some time."

"No doubt you're staying with the security forces. Maybe you didn't hear that they shot six young men last night." Her eyes flashed.

"Six terrorists," Roger amended.

"They were six boys who got caught out after curfew and didn't know where to go. Another boy was arrested and is probably being tortured right now."

"Why was it he carried an AK-47 assault rifle?" Roger asked blandly.

"He picked it up and was bringing it in to the police," Sister McFarland retorted.

"Do you believe that?"

"What business is it of yours anyway? Father Leary said you wanted to see me. Here I am. You're seeing me. What do you want?"

"It disturbs me to see Americans, even missionaries, doing things that make them suspected of helping terrorists. You may laugh at me, many people do, but I take pride in the fact that I've established some sort of central American presence here in Rhodesia where so many Americans are living and working—and fighting the Communists."

"You and your Communists," the nun cried in exasperation. "These people are fighting for their freedom, they aren't Communists; they are poor oppressed black people, oppressed by the white Fascist regime in Salisbury."

"Then why did so many Africans come from all over central Africa to Rhodesia to find jobs and to live? You know as well as I do they're more oppressed by their own people in their own countries than they ever were in Rhodesia."

"It is dangerous to be with white people too much," she said, suddenly thoughtful. "You begin to get confused and see too many sides to the issues. And you lose track of what the boys are fighting for."

"Sister McFarland, I will talk to you back in Salisbury. But I did want to see you out in the bush. You have unique access to the operational areas and you can pretty much travel at will between them and Salisbury. It really is a serious error for you to become involved in assisting the terrorists."

"What makes you think I'm actively assisting the Freedom Fighters of the Patriotic Front?" she blazed. "I try to be a liaison between the Catholic Commission for Justice and Peace in Rhodesia and the missions in the countryside. Your dear friends in the secret police put you up to coming out here." Her eyes darted accusation.

"There are no secret police in Rhodesia," Roger said quietly. "Counterintelligence, of course. But no night arrests, no police torture or star-chamber proceedings. I came out here because I'm writing a book about Rhodesia and because I'm trying in my own way to assist a country that is basically fighting what should be an American war against Communist expansion."

Sister McFarland threw her head back and laughed in a raucous, most uncclesiastical way. "Brainwashed you are, like the other white Americans over here, committing treason, fighting in a foreign army against American interests. Fighting against poor Africans giving their lives for the freedom of their people."

"I hope your attitude does not reflect that of the entire Catholic church here in Rhodesia," Masefield said coldly with a quick glance at Father Leary. "Actually I don't believe it does. I came out here to tell you that if you continue to help the terrorists you will surely be caught. I also want to tell you that you are a disgrace to the Catholic church and an impediment to the cause of political and social stability in the whole of southern Africa."

Sister McFarland let out a strangled groan. "At the risk of slipping down to your level," she cried, "may I use a phrase you will understand?" She stared at him and then shouted, "Bullshit!"

Father Leary gave her a startled look, but recovered his composure and smiled.

"Well, nobody can say that Catholic missionaries in Africa are conventional," Roger said caustically.

"If there's nothing more you want from me, I'll get back to my work," Sister McFarland snapped.

"What do you do out here?" Roger asked, sincerely curious. "I mean what communicating or liaising are you doing?"

"We have a school here and we have a hospital. Due to the constant harassment by the security forces neither is very effective, but we do our best."

"Security forces? I would say if anyone is harassing you it's the terrorists coming over from Mozambique. And even they don't seem to be giving you much trouble."

"Do me a favor, Mr. Masefield?" She paused for effect. "Get lost!"

"Good day, Sister. I'm afraid there won't be much that I will be able to do for you when the time comes."

Sister McFarland did not reply but turned on her heel and strode from the room, more like a general than a nun. Father Leary and Masefield looked after her.

"She's unusual," Father Leary remarked.

"What is her background?"

"She comes from a good Catholic family in South Boston. She went to Catholic schools, decided to become a nun and was apparently somewhat troublesome to the other sisters during her novitiate. I'll confess there was a sigh of relief in Boston when Sister McFarland decided to go into foreign missionary work." Father Leary's tone had lost some of its asperity, and by comparison with the term agent who had just left he seemed positively friendly.

"Well, let me say it one more time and then I'll go. She's going to get all of you, all of us Americans, in real trouble if she continues to actively help 'the boys.' "

"I'm afraid you're right. We do what we have to do out here, I won't deny that. I never agreed with Bishop Lamont when he told us to go out of our way to help the terrorists. I've just tried to keep the mission alive and well."

"It is sort of your little domain, your tiny empire, isn't it?" Masefield probed.

"I don't really think of it that way, no I don't. I've been happy here doing God's work; I won't deny the great satisfaction I get as I walk around the mission each day. But St. Bonaventure as a personal fiefdom? No."

"Well, Father Leary, I'll leave you. Good luck out here. And be careful. How you run your mission is, I suppose, nobody's business except God's. But how you relate to the terrorists is very definitely the business of the Ministry of Justice in Salisbury. And I can tell you the Africans and Europeans are going to be equally draconian in the way they treat anyone accused of harboring or otherwise aiding the enemy."

"I hear what you're saying," Leary said soberly.

Roger Masefield thanked the priest for lunch and found his way to the center of the mission compound where Lieutenant Arnold was standing beside the Leopard munching a sandwich.

"Ready to go?" Arnold asked.

"Yes. There's nothing more I can do here."

"Climb aboard then. We'll report back to battalion headquarters."

Chapter 19

August 1978

Sister McFarland, still angry at the intrusion by the American, strode swiftly along the mission walkways, finally reaching a deserted classroom at the back of the building complex. She pulled up a trapdoor partly concealed by the teacher's rostrum and climbed down a ladder to the basement below, easing the trapdoor down over her head.

The large cement-floored basement was lit by a string of naked light bulbs. She walked between the row of cots on which men were sleeping until she came to a second basement. The door was closed. She opened it and walked inside. There sat an African in his late twenties, his left arm bandaged and in a sling. He was sitting in a comfortable chair and across from him a wide bed with a coverlet on it gave the room a homey look. Sister McFarland closed the door behind her.

"How does the arm feel, Jobo?" she asked cheerfully. "Do you need anything?"

"Just my AK-47 so I can go out and kill white men," he replied bitterly. "My arm's almost healed. I could go out tonight."

"There were security forces here just now. I think they're leaving but you never know."

"It won't be long before they'll be hiding from *us*. How many were there?"

"I only saw four soldiers. They came with an American, Masefield, who works with the Smith regime."

"We know all about him. He and his pretty wife are numbers one and two on our kill list. I wish we could get them alive."

Sister McFarland's eyes sparkled. Jobolingo was one of the top political commissars in the Robert Mugabe branch of the Patriotic Front. His violent nature, his stories of the whites he had killed, had a disturbing but strangely exciting effect on her. The anger and frustration which had consumed her during the meeting with Masefield began to ebb away.

"Jobo, there's a lot of fighting ahead of us. Stay here until you're well. You're too badly needed to sacrifice yourself now. The security forces and the secret police in Salisbury know that I'm helping the Patriotic Front. They don't know how, they certainly don't know how much, but we must be careful. It was nice of Masefield to come out and warn me of that at least."

She laughed sourly. "He thought he could frighten me into abandoning you boys. God, how I wanted to scream at that racist pig. He walks arm-in-arm with the Fascist Ian Smith and his own group of criminals."

Jobolingo grinned approvingly. "You sound more like us every day."

"I felt like this before I met you, Jobo." She looked at her watch. "I have to go to Salisbury soon, but I'll be back."

"Why must you go? I thought you were going to stay with us?"

"I can help you more in Salisbury. I am getting information which will be useful to you and help them back in Mozambique. I believe I can get you the radio frequencies the security forces are using as well as an adapter for your radios which will help you monitor the security forces' signals."

"How can you do that?" Jobo asked. "No, don't tell me, Anne. I must know nothing. If they capture me they will make me tell what I know. When must you leave?"

"I must drive to Umtali. I'll spend the night there. It is important I get back. I didn't realize how strongly suspected I was until the American came out here." Sister McFarland and Jobolingo exchanged longing looks. His eyes darted to the bed and then back to her.

"I don't have to leave for another hour or more," Sister McFarland said softly.

"Ah, you are beautiful," Jobolingo breathed.

Even though Sister McFarland was well aware of her limitations in the field of feminine allure, it thrilled her, made her pulse quicken, to hear Jobolingo say this to her. "I just want to help the boys, Jobo," she said demurely.

"That is what makes you beautiful." Jobo's deep resonant voice, the acrid odor from his body, and lust now burning in his eyes made Sister McFarland's knees weaken. She sat down on the bed across from him. "Would you like a drink of Father Leary's Irish whiskey?" Jobo asked.

Sister McFarland nodded. Jobo reached behind his chair and pulled out a bottle of Old Bushmill's. He took the top off the bottle and lifted it to his thick lips, seeming to swallow the neck of the bottle as he tilted it, and drank deeply. Then, letting out a sigh of pleasure, he handed the bottle to Sister McFarland who held it in both hands and put her dainty mouth to the neck where that much larger and more sensuous mouth had just been. The burning liquid running down her throat and into her stomach braced her. She handed the bottle back to Jobo, a confident smile on her face. Jobolingo took another swallow, replaced the cap on the bottle and put it behind him.

"It will be hard to go back to the bush," he said. "Sometimes I wonder how Mugabe would put up with the hardships, the fear of death we all know." He rose from his chair, went over to the bed and sat down beside Sister McFarland, putting his good arm around her shoulders and drawing her to him. "This time we have at the mission will give me strength to go back and fight," he muttered huskily.

It never ceased to astound and confuse Sister McFarland when she found herself in a situation like this. At the convent school she had been taught that sex was the most evil act that an unmarried woman could indulge in. Even thinking about it was evil. But like so many of the other girls at the school she had found it impossible not to fanta-size what it would be like to have a man use her body. And then, in Boston, with the influx of Negroes into the areas around South Boston and Roxbury, she had imbibed the spirit of liberalism as an antidote to the hatred her parents' generation expressed for "the niggers." Why should the blacks be discriminated against? she asked herself.

She met many liberal priests while going to Boston College. She had always wanted to be a nun but she felt, in deference to her family, that she should go through college first. For a year or two before college all her outside activities had been devoted to anticapitalist, antibourgeois causes. One of her girl friends had even been involved in robbing a bank as an act of defiance against the establishment.

The Catholic church must change, she had heard from the young Catholics with whom she associated. It must truly be a church for the masses. She had been among those who actively sought out the black Catholics, there were not many of them, and tried to help them. Just how she had helped them she never really understood. But she believed that her very presence, a white woman among the poor Boston blacks, did something to improve their lot. She avoided debates. Facts tended to confuse her.

Somehow in her mind, although sexual relations with white boys was a sin, it seemed to her that she might be doing God's work if she became intimate with blacks. She would be helping to uplift them, to give them new confidence, to make them realize they were as good as whites. Surely this was God's work.

Her first affair had been with a young black intellectual who claimed to be striving for the freedom of his people against white oppression. She had been shaken to her very core by the total sensual pleasure she had received from the ebony body which had held her, filled her, brought her to a new understanding of life. This was no sin. It troubled her that she received such an ecstatic thrill from the brief affair but, she rationalized, it was God's way of showing her that she was not committing a sin. Indeed God was showing her the enormous joy that came from doing his work and helping the black people.

Sexual relations with frustrated, psychologically confused black men became a calling. Even during the two years of her novitiate, despite the rigid discipline and constant surveillance, she was still able to justify the social work she was doing in the black neighborhoods to the Mother Superior. It never occurred to the pious lady that this zealous young Irish Catholic girl would even fantasize any sort of intimacy with the Negroes, much less indulge in it.

Although Anne Marie had only the faintest knowledge of contraception methods, she had enough sense to realize that if she was going to perform God's work, she needed to be protected from the dangers of conceiving a child. Fortunately her first black lover had provided her with a supply of birth control pills, told her how to take them and given her instructions for purchasing more. He had also convinced her to study communications at college and learn all she could about the technology of radio operations. This training would best prepare her to work for a revolution against the white capitalist oppressors of the black man.

At the convent where she pursued her studies toward becoming a nun, her greatest terror had been that the Mother Superior or some of the other novitiates would discover her secret cache of birth control pills which she kept in a big bottle clearly marked Unicap Vitamins. Once, in confession, she had revealed to a priest how she was serving her God. She could hear him gasping on the other side of the confession booth and realized that all her ambitions to be a missionary nun freeing the exploited blacks would be blasted if the priest was so horrified that he violated his vows and reported what she was doing. She never again confessed these activities. Certainly it was better not to reveal everything in the confessional if that would interfere with her life's work.

No sooner had she been accorded the status of a missionary nun than she received the coveted assignment to Africa. The skills she had acquired at college, such as typing and being able to communicate by radio, were of great value to the missionary movement. Kenya, where she'd first been sent, did not appeal to her. There was no war of liberation going on. Revolutionary zeal surged in her unfulfilled. Finally she had succeeded in getting herself transferred to Salisbury. Now everything she had dreamed of seemed about to come true. Here was a true black revolution against the Fascist, racist white oppressors. Here at last was a cause for her to throw her entire life and energy into. Never had she been more blissful in her work for God.

Some of her colleagues called her a fanatic and she found it convenient to keep from them the full extent of their endeavors on behalf of the oppressed Africans.

Father Leary, whom she immediately recognized as a corrupt and even depraved priest, became her greatest ally. She was well aware of his own sexual activities. Somehow it seemed sinful to her that Father Leary was enjoying sex with black girls, whereas what she did for "the boys" was to give them the psychological stamina they needed to face up to the white security troops. Of course they were fighting black security troops more often than white ones, but these blacks, she rationalized, were no more than pawns of the white man. They were a disgrace to their race.

Father Leary was Sister McFarland's only Rhodesian colleague aware of the extent of the comfort she offered certain of "the boys" beyond binding their wounds, feeding them, giving them a place to rest and hiding them from the security forces. Father Leary's alliance with Sister Anne was a natural one since each was serving God according to his or her rather special precepts.

Jobo's lust rose as his hands found Sister McFarland's breasts beneath her loose-fitting denim shirt. His fingers trembled with the desire that coursed through his veins. Never in his wildest imaginings had he thought he would have this kind of relationship with a white woman.

Sister McFarland felt tremors of heaven-sent joy as she responded to Jobo's uncontrollable needs. How inspiring it was to be able to give love and strength to this boy, this creature of God fighting for his rightful place on earth. Benignly she watched as Jobo pulled her shirt open and buried his face and black wool between her breasts. Gently she patted his neck.

The muffled exclamations which he now groaned out in his native Shona language thrilled her as she unbuckled the belt about her waist and opened her heavy dungarees, revealing her simple cotton shorts. Jobo's arm was obviously improving rapidly, she reflected. Although he favored that arm, the wound did not interfere with his single-minded purpose. Still, she had to help him get her dungarees and shorts over her hips and down her legs.

"Wait, wait, wait, Jobo. We don't want you injuring that arm again. Let me."

Jobo pulled away from her long enough so that she could get her heavy shoes and socks off and then wriggle out of her jeans and underpants. Now she was nude except for the shirt which hung from her shoulders, exposing her large breasts.

Jobo sat on the bed and Sister McFarland eased his pants off and then unbuttoned his shirt so that the two of them would be skin to skin. As Sister McFarland lay back Jobo plunged deep inside her and let out a deep grunt of pleasure. She cried out in happiness as he moved within her.

"Oh God, thank you, God. Thank you, God, for letting me do your work." The spirit of the Lord suffused her as she experienced the ecstatic pleasure of giving herself over to His will.

Jobo's pent-up venal appetite was now in full spate. His mind was aflame as he approached consummation with the white woman. Sister McFarland, reaching a climax that she knew would be perfectly timed with his, cried out in religio-erotic rapture. Then Jobo filled her with what seemed to be the very essence of his being.

Sister McFarland and Jobo lay spent and gasping for many minutes. Finally Jobo rolled off her. Hastily Sister McFarland reveled in the penetrating odor that came from his body. She wondered idly if white men smelled like this in the throes of sexual expression, and then castigated herself for the sinful thought.

She was a nun, dedicated to God's work on earth. Even thinking about sex with a white man, just sex for its own sake, was a blasphemy before the Lord, her religion, her mission in life, her deepest beliefs.

Chapter 20

August 1978

In Rhodesia's border town of Umtali, which in happier days had been a rail and oil pipeline link between Salisbury and the Mozambique port of Maputo, Roger checked into the new Cecil Hotel where he'd left a suitcase full of clean clothes and his car in the parking lot. After being assigned a room he walked next door to the old Cecil Hotel, which was now the headquarters of the Third Brigade of the Rhodesian Regiment.

It was six o'clock in the evening when he stopped at the entrance and presented his pass to the American M.P. on duty. Roger and Corporal Walker had become good friends, and Walker had taken him out to the training field where he taught his squad of black and white Rhodesians the M.P. tactics used in the United States Army. Wayne Walker, as was the case with a number of Americans who had been in the Rhodesian Security Forces for a year or more, had worked hard at losing his American accent. As a result, although he didn't sound like a Yank, he didn't talk any other recognizable dialect of the English language. Rhodesians who did not know him thought he might be from Northern Ireland or perhaps was speaking some tortured strain of Australian English.

"Is the Brig in?" Roger asked.

"Yes, sir. He's shooting darts in the Officers Club."

"I'll just go in and give him a game then. Might as well let him win his next Castle from me as from anyone else."

Roger walked down the hallway past what used to be the hotel ballroom but was now partitioned off into offices and turned right into what had been the hotel bar and was now the officers bar. Inside, Brigadier MacIntyre was pitching darts in his own special style. At each throw he rose up on his toes and bent forward almost to the point where gravity captured him before releasing the dart directly along his line of sight.

Derry MacIntyre was wearing a brown-knit army sweater and camouflage pants neatly tucked into his boots. Roger watched him beat his opponent handily. The loser went off to the bar to get a beer for his commander. The brigadier looked up at Roger standing nearby and invited him to play a game. In anticipation of the brigadier's zest for darts, Roger had procured a dart board and tried to practice at home. However, MacIntyre's skill had developed over many years of playing in Scottish and British pubs and at officers mess evenings. After Derry had resoundingly defeated Roger, they walked over to the bar and Roger bought the drinks. The brigadier was especially interested in his observations regarding the St. Bonaventure Mission.

"There's no doubt they're harboring terrorists," Roger said. "I'll bet if you tore the place down you'd find a nest of them hidden away."

"Yes, I'm sure of that. We pitched Bishop Lamont out of his cathedral around the corner here in Umtali and he became a hero in Ireland and the United States. We should have had the bugger up against the wall. He's the one that made it fashionable for mission priests to hide the terrs. A lot of good men are getting killed because of that. Every time I see missionaries in Umtali I want to pick them up. They watch everything, every movement of our troops. Sister McFarland visits the missions in Thrasher every month. She's bloody well not discussing the Apostles' Creed either. She's collecting information on what we're doing and then getting it out to the bush. More than once intelligence has caught her out near Grand Reef trying to see what's going on and claiming to be salvaging souls when apprehended and questioned."

"Speaking of Grand Reef, Derry, I'd like to get out there myself tomorrow with the First Commando, RLI."

"I'm going out first thing in the morning. We've got some brass coming down from Salisbury. I've got to give them a conducted air tour of the operational area here."

"Well, nothing like arriving with the commander of Thrasher." Roger replied.

After the drinks Roger and the brigadier went into the mess and had dinner together. Then MacIntyre went to his quarters to study the latest situation reports coming in from all over his command.

Early the following morning Roger rode with the brigadier in his staff car out to Grand Reef Air Base fifteen miles outside Umtali. It was one of the main bases for the RLI strike force sticks which were always on instant alert to be helicoptered to the site of reported terrorist activity.

The pair walked into the wooden shed that was the office of the RAR commander at the base, Lieutenant Colonel MacVay. He snapped a salute at the brigadier and remarked cheerfully, "Looks like your chaps from Salisbury might get to see a bit of a show today. A lot of terr activity coming across the border. I'm sure they have in mind kicking up a fuss around election time at the end of the month."

MacVay turned to Roger. "What brings you to Grand Reef? You have your ComOps clearance with you?"

"Sure, John." Roger reached into the pocket of his bush jacket and pulled out the blanket clearance he had been given in Salisbury, a rare mark of confidence. Colonel MacVay went through the formality of examining the credential and handed it back to Roger. "OK, what are you interested in today?"

"I want to go over and visit One Commando of the RLI. They're on strike force duty. I'd like to sit around with them while they're waiting for a chopper to take them into a contact. Matter of fact, I'd like to go out with them if that could be arranged."

"We'd have to give you an FN rifle and let you do the job of the man whose place you'd be taking," Derry MacIntyre declared.

"It wouldn't be the first time," Roger said. "I was a gun-carrying, terr shooting member of Colonel Peter White's territorials up in the Honde Valley."

"I'll have a word with the RLI commander here at Grand Reef," the brigadier promised.

"It's Captain Parker, sir," Colonel MacVay said helpfully. Then to Roger: "Why don't you go find One Commando? They're down at the end of the field where the helicopters are standing."

Roger tossed an American salute at Colonel MacVay and Brigadier MacIntyre and paced out of the office. It took him about ten minutes to walk down to where the helicopters were perched on their pads. Nearby were four-man groups with their weapons and ammunition handy. Each stick of four men had one radio, one light bazooka-type grenade launcher and one machine gun. Three of the men carried the standard FN Belgian rifle. An officer was walking among the sticks talking to his men.

The rather casual attitude toward uniforms that pervaded the Rhodesian Security Forces always amused Roger. It made him think of World War II when the British flair for unique uniforms was a constant irritant to General Patton and many other American field commanders. The RLI troopers waiting to go out on strike force duty were dressed in green fatigue shorts, green or camouflage T-shirts and Bata tennis shoes, some of them not even wearing socks. The tennis shoes were smooth-soled so as to avoid leaving recognizable tracks and had laced upper parts that climbed six inches above the ankle.

RLI troopers were given wide latitude in the combat webbing they wore. A few of the men here were strapped into the regulation issue equipment—pistol belt, ammunition pouches, yoke harness and pack, but no two were kitted out identically, though they all sported the wide-brim floppy hats so popular among the white troops in the RLI and the SAS. Some of the men waiting to be called on a strike force mission wore their hats inside out, displaying a six-inch by six-inch red fluorescent panel that could be easily seen from above by friendly aircraft.

Roger had started to walk among the men when he heard his name called and looked up. It was Cary Donnelly. Roger went over to him and they shook hands. Although Roger was impartially fond of all the Americans in Rhodesia, Cary Donnelly was a particular source of satisfaction to him. As he looked at him in his combat gear waiting for the call to mount up and be helicoptered to some scene of terrorist activity, he thought back to the time he first met Cary, only eight months ago in New York. Roger had been invited to talk on the Barry Farber show about Rhodesia. The session had lasted from midnight till two in the morning and Roger had given a vivid account of how the Soviets and Red Chinese were using the black terrorists as their surrogates to destroy the Western-oriented black moderates.

When the phone calls started coming in, one of the first was from Cary Donnelly who asked if he could talk further with Roger if he came to New York City. Roger took Cary's phone number and promised to call him the next day, and this resulted in their luncheon.

Cary Donnelly was from a large Irish family in New Rochelle, New York. The youngest son, he had just received his Master's in political science and hoped to start a career in teaching. At their first meeting Cary expressed a desire to supplement his theoretical learning with some practical foreign experience. Roger agreed to sponsor his enlistment in the Rhodesian Security Forces. He loaned Cary the money to buy a one-way ticket to Salisbury and personally shepherded him from New York to Salisbury via Johannesburg.

Cary spent a week at the Embassy while he investigated the possibilities of joining the Rhodesian Army. He had no military experience behind him, which the Rhodesians counted an asset. They liked to teach their troopers from scratch. He was assigned to the RLI and Roger had followed with keen interest his extremely tough four months of training. Frequently, Roger had driven out to the RLI barracks and discussed with the training commanders the performance of foreigners in the security forces. By and large, the foreigners, highly motivated, had done very well in their training period, but occasionally, the Americans in particular, complained about not just being given guns and sent out to shoot terrorists. The training officers admitted that some of their sergeants were hostile toward non-Rhodesian trainees, didn't understand them and did not entirely trust them. This made it that much harder for them to get through the course.

Finally, when Cary Donnelly had finished his course and received his colors, he had been cited by his training officer as one of the three most outstanding recruits. He had been assigned to One Commando in a group headed by Corporal Hugh McCall, a former New York actor who had become one of the most experienced combat troopers in the RLI. Returning from forays into the field, Cary would come over to see Roger and give him enthusiastic reports about the contacts and how fortunate he was to have Corporal McCall leading his group of sticks. Roger had known Hugh McCall since a few days after he arrived in Rhodesia on his first trip. Mack Hudson and Hugh McCall,

177

along with Major Mike Wyatt, second-in-command of Grey's Scouts, had been among Roger's first American friends in the country.

Hugh McCall, who had only recently been promoted to sergeant, ambled up to Roger and Cary. "What brings you out here, Roger?"

"I thought you might need the help of an old vet of three wars. How about it?"

"That's the trouble. About three wars too many," Hugh grinned.

"You got pretty well shot up in Vietnam," Roger countered. "I guess I could keep up with you."

"Don't bet on it. I'm in better shape now than I was before I picked up that gook grenade fragment."

"How's that pretty girl you've been bringing around on Saturday?" Roger asked.

"Josie? She's fine. We're thinking of getting married."

"You're kidding," Roger exclaimed.

"She understands why I'm over here. Sure, we all want to fight the Communists, but there's a real thrill you can't get anywhere else when you're out in the bush tracking down the terrs."

Hugh looked at the men of his stick, all waiting for the action to start. Then he turned back to Roger. "It's hard to explain but when you're out after them, man to man, and maybe they'll get you but more likely you'll get them, there's nothing else like it."

The Yank sergeant's eyes glistened. "And when you're in the contact, and someone's got to die and then you let the terr have it and you drop him, it's the most exhilarating sensation a man can know. No kind of sex or winning a million dollars in a crap game comes near it."

"I know what you mean, Hughie," Roger answered. "How's my man here doing?"

"He'll be all right. He's got him one terr now. After he's slain four or five more he'll be a first-class soldier." He turned to Cary and clapped a hand on his shoulder. "Just for chrissake learn to keep your head down. I know you got your first terr by popping up and letting off half a magazine but once in a while you find a terr that knows how to shoot back.

"The terrs," he said to Roger, "are sending in Tanzanian officers trained in the Canadian Army. They're pretty good. We killed one on our last contact and on the body found a bunch of addresses in Toronto. The Canadians don't do anything about civilizing the gooks they train. The men this Tanzanian was commanding had just hacked up their quota of kraal chiefs, headman and ADC's, raped whatever nannies they found and bayoneted two pregnant women."

A Land Rover rumbled toward them down the dirt road paralleling the runway. It pulled to a halt beside Roger and Colonel MacVay jumped out. "The brigadier got you cleared to ride in the K car with Captain Parker on the next alert. I'm afraid we can't put you on the ground but you'll get a good look at your fellow Yanks in action." MacVay bestowed a friendly smile on Sergeant Hugh McCall and Trooper Cary Donnelly. Both saluted smartly. MacVay returned the salute and then jumped into his Land Rover and raced back to his headquarters, trailing a cloud of dust behind him.

"Hey, that's great, Roger," Sergeant McCall congratulated him. "You'll be able to hear our radio signals and you'll actually see the action better with the captain from the K car than you would on the ground. You'd better go over and report in to Captain Parker now. When we get an alert we're into the air in less than two minutes."

"I can see why the terrs don't come out by daylight very much," Roger smiled.

Cary looked at Roger hopefully. "If you're going to be in Umtali a couple more days maybe you could meet my girl friend. They're going to let us go into town on Saturday."

"Tell me about her," Roger said. Then he looked across the field. "Later, that is."

Roger went across the runway to the helicopter beside which the command element of One Commando was standing. Suddenly the radio in the helicopter started to crackle and then the message came in loud and clear: "Sun Ray Two, this is Sun Ray. Terrs spotted in Vumba, about fifty of them. The Lynx spotter plane will guide you when you get there. Report back when you're over the enemy."

Instantly the helicopter pilots climbed into their seats and started the turbines of their prized French Alouette helicopters. The sticks mounted their choppers and within two minutes from the time the signal crackled, five helicopters were in the air and heading south along the Mozambique border toward the Vumba Mountains and the Vumba wildlife park beyond. This was a favorite place for the guerrillas to hide since there was heavy foliage to give them cover. Also, there was abundant game to be snared for food.

In Mozambique the wildlife was almost extinct. Starvation had driven the slothful Mozambicans, hopeless at farming without their Portuguese overseers, to the wholesale slaughter of wild animals, though a few survivors had crossed the border into Rhodesia where conservation policies were still strict.

Roger, sitting beside Captain Parker in the K car, observed the operation with sharp interest.

Ten minutes after takeoff they spotted the push-pull two-engine Lynx circling over heavy bush ahead. During this, the dry winter season, movement on the ground was far more visible than during the lush rainy season when the undergrowth became dense and the snarled and twisted trees sprouted thick leaves.

Captain Parker was talking into his radio headsets. Roger could not hear what was being said, but as he watched, the four helicopters abruptly plopped down into a clearing in the bush and discharged sixteen troopers. From the air, Roger watched them fan out and surround a small, rocky hill from the side of which orange smoke was streaming. This was the marker signal dropped by the Lynx pilot and indicated where the terrorists had last been seen.

The four helicopters headed back to Grand Reef, leaving the K Car hovering over the contact area. Captain Parker was peering down intently, talking again into the radio, picking up signals from Sergeant McCall who was leading the sixteen-man assault on the terrorist invaders.

A helicopter crewman was crouched over the 20mm cannon that protruded through the left door of the Alouette, ready to give supporting fire to the small assault team below. Roger could see the muzzle flashes of the RLI troopers closing in on the enemy. Behind the rocky hill was flat, open terrain. If the troopers could force the terrorists to retreat from the hill onto the plain, the latter would be vulnerable from the air.

Now Roger spotted the muzzle flashes from the terrorists as they fired back on the men of One Commando from the top of the hill. There followed two bright explosions, one close to the hilltop (some rookie terrorist would get it in the neck for that), then a larger one among the troopers. The RPGs (rocket-propelled grenades) were a favorite weapon of the guerrillas. They delighted in the loud explosion the weapon made and it increased their self-confidence.

The K Car gunner opened up on the area from which the muzzle flashes had come. The heavy explosive projectiles from the fast-firing 20mm cannon spattered into the terrorist positions as the RLI troopers climbed the hillside after the enemy.

If the figure of fifty terrorists given back at Grand Reef was correct, here were sixteen men assaulting a decidedly superior force, Roger mused. Superior in numbers only, of course. Inexorably, the RLI troopers pushed their way up the hill toward the terrorists, who were firing furiously. As Roger's helicopter moved in close over the contact, its door gunner directing a withering spray of fire at the hilltop, Roger looked down apprehensively. He had been in helicopters in Vietnam that had been shot up by the same AK rifles as those used by the terrorists coming out of Mozambique and Zambia.

Fortunately, the bursts from the 20mm cannon were keeping the guerrillas pinned down so they couldn't fire up at the chopper.

The door gunner ceased firing. Peering down, Roger could see the RLI men on the attack, the red panels on their hats turned upwards, clearly distinguishing friend from foe. Individual guerrillas, wearing blue denim pants and jackets, could be spotted from the air as they retreated down the other side of the hill away from the lethal lines of fire moving up on them. Clearly they had made an irreparable error in allowing themselves to be spotted by the Lynx. Had it been night-time, they might have stood a chance of getting away.

The difference in fighting caliber among the guerrillas was clearly discernible from the K car. Though outnumbering their attackers better than three to one, only a handful stood their ground, firing back, throwing grenades and laying mortar bombs and RPG rounds into the troopers attempting to dislodge them. These would be the hard-core fighters with perhaps as much as a year of Marxist indoctrination and tough physical training behind them. The remainder were fleeing pell-mell down the hill, casting their blue denims and their weapons into the bush as they went.

With the RLI troopers almost in the midst of the terrorist rearguard, the door gunner addressed himself to picking off the terrorists scampering down the hill and onto the plain.

One after another fell to the gunner's fire. Suddenly Captain Parker leaned forward, patted the pilot on the shoulder and pointed below. All shooting seemed to have stopped. The pilot slowly descended on the top of the hill and gingerly set the chopper down on a flat spot.

Parker pulled the earphones from his ears, jumped out, and met Sergeant McCall and his men. Roger too hit the ground, anxious to assist. Several troopers had been wounded and it appeared one was dead. Blood-spattered bodies of terrorists lay about the crest of the hill.

Hugh McCall gave Roger a grin and then reported to the captain. "Sir, I'm afraid Hartley is dead. We have three wounded, one man seriously, I think. If you'll casevac my casualties we'll chase the rest of the terrs down and slay them. They can't get away from us in that open area below." With the aid of his comrades, a wounded trooper was lifted aboard the helicopter, his left arm hanging shattered. Then another, unconscious casualty was lifted aboard followed by the less seriously wounded man who was able to climb into the chopper on his own. Finally the dead man, blood soaking through his T-shirt from the three bullet holes in his chest, was hauled aboard. McCall grouped his men together and discovered that one man was missing. "Who last saw Halloran?" he asked.

"I was beside him, Sergeant," Cary Donnelly reported. "We were crawling up, shooting, taking heavy return fire. They must have had an RPD light machine gun up there somewhere."

"Go back and see if you can find him," McCall ordered. As Cary scrambled down the slope they had just ascended to look for his comrade, McCall ordered the rest of his men to charge down the forward slope of the hill and kill whatever fleeing terrorists they could catch.

Captain Parker walked around the contact area searching the bodies of the dead guerrillas for documents that would be useful to intelligence.

Without being asked, Roger started to police up the enemy weapons strewn about and put them into the helicopter beside the wounded soldiers and the dead man. Using his handkerchief, he gathered as many of the spent shell casings as he could see for the police ballistics laboratory. The experts there would analyze them, identify them, identify the individual weapon that had fired them and match them up with casings that had been previously recovered. Roger handed the casings to the door gunner and turned to Captain

Parker. "You'll need all the room in the chopper you can get. I'll stay with Sergeant McCall."

Parker hesitated. This was a situation he hadn't anticipated. But Masefield was right, especially if Donnelly returned with a wounded or dead trooper. "OK, Mr. Masefield, go ahead. Do you want an FN?"

Roger shook his head and patted the M-59 9mm automatic on his belt. "I'm supposed to be a noncombatant but if we run into trouble this will be enough for me." He turned to McCall. "Let's go, Hughie."

McCall and the rest of his men proceeded down the steep rocky incline toward the open area below, sliding, holding on to protruding pieces of rock. They came across several broken terrorist bodies, the victims of the eagle-eyed door gunner. A 20mm round shatters the human form when it makes contact.

At the bottom of the hill the troopers, spent though they were from their hard upward climb under fire and their blazing contact with the hard-core guerrillas, who had stood their ground to the end, started to trot across the plain after the terrorists. Obviously the enemy had bombshelled, run in all directions, but they weren't so far ahead of the One Commando troopers that they couldn't be caught. Ahead, the troopers saw an African wearing an orange shirt and blue shorts running barefoot through the bush. Hugh McCall dropped to one knee, aimed carefully and squeezed the trigger. The man went down. "Goddamn stupid gook. Thought he could fool us into thinking he was a civilian."

"How do you know he wasn't?" Roger asked.

"The chances are he stripped off his clothes down to that sort of typical civilian gear," McCall replied. "Maybe I made a mistake but I doubt it. If he really was a civilian he wouldn't have run—or shouldn't have."

The troopers continued through the open bush toward the village of round huts in the Tribal Trust Land beyond. Three more Africans of questionable identity but probably terrorists, were shot down as they ran for the huts, whose occupants would hide them. It was not that the tribesmen liked the terrorists, or were unwilling to give them up, but they knew the fate that would be in store for them some night soon if they betrayed them.

Pushing into the village, the Rhodesians, who all had a working knowledge of the Shona language, began questioning the tribesmen. Naturally, everyone questioned denied that anybody from outside the village had come in. Nevertheless each hut was searched and all males from thirteen years old to middle age were hauled out and questioned. Suspicious cases were sent under escort to the nearest police post for interrogation.

Corporal McCall radioed the Lynx still cruising above the area that he was ready to be evacuated. Trooper Donnelly rejoined his stick with the news that he had found Trooper Halloran, wounded, and had carried him back up to the top of the hill where he had been casevaced in the K car.

"Five casualties," McCall lamented. "Final confirmed killed is eleven. Not bad, but one of ours dead to twenty dead terrorists is a more acceptable ratio. Well, it's been a good day's hunting. By wiping out that group we probably saved two or three of the big farms out this way from being attacked and at least three of the tribal villages from having their headmen tortured to death. We probably should have wasted those suspicious villagers we sent to the police. That way, if they really were terrorists, they'd never kill again."

The welcome sound of the helicopters alerted McCall and his men to get into the clearing outside the village.

"Don't forget, Roger, we've got a free weekend in Umtali," Cary reminded his friend.

"I'm looking forward to meeting your young lady, Cary."

Soon the Alouettes settled down, picked up the One Commando troopers and Roger Masefield, and flew them back to Grand Reef.

Chapter 21

August 1978

It had been somewhat of a sacrifice for Roger Masefield to stay over in Umtali Friday night since he tried to be in Salisbury on Saturdays for the Crippled Eagles meetings, and he knew the American troopers were disappointed when he wasn't there. However, Cary Donnelly had been so anxious to have Roger meet his girl that he felt it was justified, and Jocelyn, Alvin Glenlord and Beryl Stoffel would between them at least ensure that the party took place. He was increasingly concerned, though, about the implications of so many Americans believing Al was still a CIA agent.

Roger walked into the canteen where the local women were serving tea, soft drinks, cookies and much cheer and hospitality. They reminded him of the Red Cross girls, the doughnut dollies, in Vietnam who were on hand to provide "wholesome recreation" for the men when they came in from the field. He was sure that what the Rhodesian troopers were looking for, what all soldiers sought when they finally got a few days respite from a forward combat area, was a type of entertainment not quite classifiable as "wholesome." Nevertheless, all the men in the canteen seemed to be enjoying the attention being lavished on them by the women, who ranged from teenagers to matrons in their sixties.

He spotted Cary Donnelly who was waving furiously at him from a corner. Roger changed course, headed over to the table and sat down with Cary and a beautiful girl, no more than eighteen, Roger estimated, but remarkably well-developed for her age. He looked into a pair of solemn blue eyes that regarded him intently from a fine-boned face surrounded by a cascade of blonde hair.

"Roger, this is Jessica Richardson. Jessica, meet Roger Masefield," Cary announced proudly.

Jessica reached out and shook hands firmly with Roger. "I've read some of your books, Roger. It's really exciting to meet you. And here in little Umtali. I don't believe it. Nobody comes to Umtali except soldiers."

"It's one of my favorite towns," Roger replied. "You're at the Umtali Girls High School, aren't you? Where are you really from?"

"We have a farm down south of here in Melsetter," she said. "It's basically a coffee property but we also have cattle and we grow a lot of maize."

"Jessica has invited me to visit her family whenever I can get a leave during her holidays," Cary said eagerly. "She's written to them about me. I guess they're not too happy that Jessica's taking up with a Yank. But maybe if I meet them they'll feel differently."

"Of course they will," Jessica said confidently. "You came all the way from America to help us fight the Communists. They should not only like you but be grateful to you."

Jessica stood up. "Let me get you some tea or a soft drink, Roger."

"Tea would be about right," Roger said. He looked after Jessica as she walked over to the counter where tea and soft drinks were being dispensed. "A beautiful girl, Cary. The epitome of Rhodesian womanhood."

"We're going to be married as soon as we can work it," Cary blurted. "These women over here are facing the destruction of their way of life, even death; yet their courage is incredible. I wish the girls in the United States could see them. Do you know that three girls at the Umtali Girls High School have been killed this year alone by terrorists, and one girl last year had both her legs blown off in a mine accident when she was visiting home. They've suffered attacks from the FRELIMO across the border, mortars have fallen right into the school. Yet they keep going. In all my life I've never met a woman like Jessica."

"If you get married, how will she feel about going back to the United States with you?" Roger asked.

"As I told you before, I don't know whether I'll go back. To tell you the truth I feel more like a Rhodesian than an American, whatever an American is these days. I just might stay here. There'll be plenty of opportunity once this war is over and the country settles down. Black majority rule is inevitable. But if they get the right blacks this can be a great country, everybody working side by side to build it. Look how they've kept going economically with the world against them."

"You may have something there, Cary." Roger watched Jessica walk gracefully back, holding a tray. "I'm sure you will figure some way to ingratiate yourself with her mother and father."

"Yeah. Jessica has two younger sisters but no brother. I could help out on the farm."

Roger chuckled. "That's along way from teaching political science at some college in the United States."

Jessica set the tea down in front of Roger and then sat with them. "Would you like to meet some of the girls from UGHS?" she asked blithely.

"Sure, but later. As I recall it, the last time I was in Umtali, I guess it was about five months ago, none of you girls were allowed to leave the school grounds and come downtown. What happened?"

"Well, the headmistress finally realized there was no point in making rules none of the girls were going to live with. So she said that any girl who got permission from her parents could come down here to the canteen and cheer up the boys. Of course we're pretty carefully watched. You might notice there are two teachers keeping an eye on me right now. But we manage to have some fun for ourselves." She smiled mischievously at Cary.

"I guess the war has liberalized things somewhat," Cary remarked.

"Well, one girl got pregnant and is going to have a baby in about a month," Jessica said, her eyes sparkling. "When she has the baby, they're going to let her come back and finish school and have the baby with her."

"Keep that up and your classes will sound like a Catholic Mass," Cary laughed.

"I don't believe the baby will be in class with her," Jessica said, laughing too.

"Cary tells me you two have some fairly serious plans for the future," Roger probed.

Jessica reached under the table and took Cary's hand. "That's right. We're going to get married as soon as we can. I will graduate at the end of the year and we'll get an apartment in Salisbury. When the war is over and Cary gets out of the RLI, we'll visit America so that I can get to know his mother and father and his brothers. Then if Cary still wants to we'll come back to Rhodesia and either we'll farm or Cary can teach at Salisbury University."

"You got it all figured out, haven't you," Roger smiled. "I hope everything works out the way you want it."

"How are we going to get you out of the canteen today?" Cary asked Jessica.

"I think I have it fixed with Miss Farnsworth. She's not supposed to let us out of her sight, but I told her that Mr. Masefield had come to Umtali especially to see us and that Mr. Masefield is an old friend of your family's in New Rochelle, wherever that is. I told her that Mr. Masefield wanted to take us to tea where we could really talk and not be in the middle of a bunch of troopies. So she agreed that we could have tea with Mr. Masefield and then get back here just in time to go back to school with our chaperones for supper."

"Well I'm glad I can be of some use then," Roger said. "Point out Miss Farnsworth to me. I'll go up and have a word with her."

Jessica nodded toward an attractive young woman who didn't look much older than Jessica herself. "Her name is Diane," Jessica said. "She's really very nice. She understands us much better than the older women at school do."

Roger went over and introduced himself to the teacher. She gestured toward an empty table and they sat down together. "If Jessica doesn't get back here to the canteen before we are due at school, I'm in real trouble, Mr. Masefield. You understand that?"

"Yes, but please call me Roger. Mr. Masefield is my father," he recited.

"All right then, Roger. Maybe you don't understand the strange effect this war is having on the girls at Umtali Girls High School, in fact, all the girls in the country. They seem to have developed a sort of *live for today, tomorrow we may die* attitude. They're well aware that

Rhodesia's civilized way of life is threatened and may even disappear. And the girls do in fact live in physical danger, particularly the ones on farms. Thank God we've had only one girl hurt on school grounds—that was during a mortar attack—but when they go home to their farms there's always the danger of land mines and ambushes. One of our girls lost both her legs and several of her friends were killed when a farm truck they were riding in drove over a terr mine. It's funny, Shirley Wickstead, that was her name, had some sort of premonition that this might happen. She had even told all her friends which of her possessions they could have. Now the girls have all drawn up little informal wills leaving their record player or whatever to special friends. They've become very fatalistic, and as a result, discipline is difficult to maintain. The girls just don't care." Diane Farnsworth looked searchingly at Roger. "I suppose I shouldn't talk about such things but I wish we were permitted to give the girls more information on birth control. For instance, I know what is going to happen this afternoon between the Yank troopie and Jessica. She thinks she's very much in love with him."

"I assure you, Diane, that I will be a very good chaperon and—"

Diane Farnsworth held up her hand. "Come on, Roger, I know what the score is, as you Americans say. Personally, I don't blame either of them. I just prefer to keep myself out of trouble. So all I ask is you get them back here. I'd say that at least three-quarters of the senior girls are having affairs. When they sneak out at night at least they're on their own and it's not my responsibility. Even our stern headmistress, who would be more at home running a convent, has resigned herself to the disciplinary breakdown. My sympathies are with the girls." She smiled disarmingly. "I guess we teachers are doing the same thing."

"Say, I don't have to go back to Salisbury this weekend. Can you get out tonight after you put your children to bed?"

In mock alarm at the proposition, Diane Farnsworth shook her head. "Mr. Masefield, what a suggestion."

"What's wrong with it?" Roger asked, grinning widely.

"You know exactly what's wrong with it."

"I'm too old for you?"

Again, Diane Farnsworth shook her head. "Not at all. I guess this spirit of *live for today, tomorrow we may die* has infected all of us. But one thing I do put my foot down about is going out with married men.

189

I've seen pictures in the *Rhodesia Herald* of you and your wife. You're both quite famous in Rhodesia, you know. It's bad enough that we do what we do, without getting involved in some international scandal."

Roger laughed. "I don't believe I'm capable of stirring up a scandal. Anyway, Diane, I can promise you I'll get Jessica back by the appointed hour. "

"I would appreciate that Mr. Masefield." Then she smiled teasingly. "If the time comes that your wife deserts you and Rhodesia and goes home, give me a call. Actually, I like older men."

Roger took her hand. "Diane, you can count on it."

At two-thirty in the afternoon, Roger, Cary and Jessica crossed the intersection of the two main streets of Umtali and walked past Third Brigade Headquarters to the new Cecil Hotel. "If it's all the same to you, Roger, Jessica and I will just go in the back door and up the elevator to my room where we can talk."

"Just don't fail to meet me downstairs at five-thirty." Roger ordered. "I must make a show of escorting you back to Miss Farnsworth and the other girls."

"Don't worry, Roger, I won't let you down." Cary promised.

"It'll be yourself and Jessica you're letting down if you aren't in the lobby on time." Roger watched the two lovers as they went into the back door of the Cecil Hotel. Then he walked back to Third Brigade Headquarters. The officers' bar was empty except for Major Harper, the Australian operations officer. He was drinking a beer and standing by in case any sitreps on terrorist activity came in.

"What's happening out there?" Roger asked after buying a beer. "What are the terrs doing?"

"We don't really know. But we hear they plan some kind of attack to protest the white elections on 31 August."

"I was fortunate enough to be in the middle of a good punch-up yesterday."

"I heard." Harper frowned. "If those journalists ever knew you were in a K car over a contact, they'd bloody well demand equal treatment."

"But I'm not a journalist, I write books," Roger reminded the major. "I've only been out here a year now but what I saw made me think we were seeing just the advance party, with unusually brave leadership, I might say."

Harper looked into his beer. "This sector is in for big contacts in the next two weeks. You'll have some fun if you stay with us. The terrs have to do something dramatic before we all go to the polls and vote for old Smithy to negotiate black majority rule. Just what Mugabe over there"—he gestured toward the Mozambique border less than a mile from where they stood—"doesn't want. The worst part of this war will come when the Communist gooks start to fight whatever black leader finally becomes prime minister of what they call Zimbabwe. That's when the white-led army gets caught in the middle. Know what Zimbabwe means?" he added parenthetically. "It's Shona for 'revered house.' That's a laugh—or it will be."

"I'll be back again before the elections," Roger said, suddenly feeling rather depressed, "but I've got to be in Salisbury tomorrow." The two drank beer and Roger listened to a familiar story as the Australian described why he had left his native land to come to Rhodesia. The labor unions, the British Communists undermining the country, the workers blindly following their Marxist leaders . . . Someday, Roger resolved, he would have to visit Australia to see for himself.

At five-fifteen, Roger returned to the Cecil Hotel and waited in the lobby anxiously. At five-twenty-five Cary and Jessica appeared. "You cut things pretty damned close," Roger growled.

"We'll make it on time," Cary said calmly.

At exactly five-thirty Roger delivered Jessica to Diane Farnsworth, who had been getting nervous.

"Diane, don't forget me," Roger called to her as she bundled the girls from UGHS into the Land Rover. "I'll phone you if things change in Salisbury."

Back in the bar of the Cecil Hotel Roger bought beers for Cary and himself. "Well, what are you doing for the rest of the night? Going back to Grand Reef?"

"Hell no. This afternoon was just the appetizer. At nine o'clock I'm going out to the school, Jessica is letting me into the kitchen door and we're going up to her room for the night."

Roger sputtered into his beer, foam splashing on his eyebrows. "You're crazy. You can't do that. If you're caught the cops will put you away."

"I won't get caught. It seems several of the girls have boyfriends who come and sleep with them over the weekends, when there isn't

191

any surveillance to speak of. They take turns so the place doesn't get overrun with guys."

"But, my God, how could a girl face her family if she was kicked out of school for having a man stay overnight in her room?"

"They don't give a damn, Roger. As Jessica says, and I quote her, 'We never know when we may be seeing each other for the last time. A mortar bomb could land on the top of the school any day or night and kill us.'"

"Well, have a good night then. Be careful. I'd hate to have to come down here to get you out of jail."

"We'll have a hell of a night. The only trouble is we have to be so quiet, and that's hard for Jessica." He downed his beer with a roguish grin. "I'm as hungry as a bear in March. How about we get some graze."

"You're on," Roger agreed. "My treat."

Chapter 22

August 1978

By mid 1977 President Jimmy Carter had consolidated his grip on presidential power. He had also totally capitulated to his black Chief Delegate to the United Nations, Andrew Young, on the matter of foreign policy in Southern Africa. It was Young, a popular U.S. Congressman, who had delivered the black vote to Carter, no easy task after the candidate had made some ill advised ambiguous remarks about preserving ethnic purity. In the close election of 1976 it was the black vote that barely squeezed Jimmy Carter into the White House.

It was the policy of the White House that in Rhodesia everything possible would be done to create a new government giving total power to the true black nationalists, Joshua Nkomo and Robert Mugabe. The other candidates were summarily dismissed as Uncle Toms. In the Republic of South Africa every opportunity would be taken to tighten sanctions against the white government and once Rhodesia became Zimbabwe further punitive actions would be applied against RSA by the United States using the United Nations as the administration's cat's paw.

Alvin Glenlord used the embassy supply run to South Africa as his excuse to meet his CIA control officer for the debriefing he had been postponing for several months. He disliked any contact with the CIA in South Africa where the Rhodesian Special Branch operated hand in glove with South Africa's secret police, BOSS, to spy on anyone known to travel between Johannesburg and Salisbury. But the Agency was nagging at him through coded telex messages and one passing agent posing as a journalist actually ordered him to meet with a control officer for debriefing. The new head of the Agency, Jimmy Carter's old Naval Academy pal, Adm. Stansfield Turner, was being pressured to start taking steps toward hastening the process of deposing the white government in Salisbury.

Glenlord did not want to leave his post for a Washington visit at this crucial time in Rhodesia's changing political scene and finally an elaborate scheme was hatched so that Alvin could surreptitiously meet and be debriefed by an agent in Johannesburg.

Alvin knew that despite the cordial relations he had established with Special Branch through Beryl's auspices, the top man, Ken Flowers, was a very thorough type. SB probably would have him followed and his hotel room wired as a matter of course. But there was no other course open to him. He would have to go south immediately if not sooner. The Company had summoned him in its own unorthodox manner. Now he must respond. Fortunately, it was time for a normal Embassy resupply mission to the well-stocked stores and larders of Johannesburg, and SB, which knew everything about the Embassy, would be aware that this was normal procedure on his part.

Eric Klein, supervisor of the Air Rhodesia staff at Johannesburg's Ian Smuts International Airport was at the gate to greet Alvin Glenlord and escort him through customs and immigration. "How's Beryl?" he asked.

"Good. She told me to give you her best."

"Down for a bit of shopping, are you?"

"That's right. We've got to keep the Embassy respectably stocked. You won't believe this but one of the big items on my list is ice-cube trays.

"And the stuff to put the cubes in, I'm sure you're not forgetting," Eric chuckled.

"Oh, I'll buy the airport out of Scotch when I go back tomorrow. I'm set on the two-thirty flight, I assume."

"You're on it all right. I had to put you ahead of everybody on the wait list but you're confirmed."

Al waited for his two empty suitcases to come through the baggage counter and then followed Eric Klein to the airport entrance. A cab moved up to him and the driver put the suitcases into the trunk. "You travel light, sah," the driver commented."

"If you bring me back to the airport tomorrow you'll hardly be able to lift them," Al replied. "See you tomorrow, Eric. And mind you don't let them weigh my bags. I don't want to be paying for overweight."

"Don't worry, Al. Anything you and Beryl need. You staying at the Landdrost as usual?"

"Right. If the flight's delayed, call me there."

The cab brought Alvin to the front of the Landdrost Hotel where the doorman greeted him by name and asked about the lovely lady from the north who was usually with him. Al checked into his room and immediately put through the phone call. A young woman's voice answered.

"Hello, Donna, this is Al. I'm in town alone and I thought maybe I could buy you dinner."

"Al, you took me by surprise. Actually I have a date tonight, but for you I guess I've got to break it."

"That's the spirit. I kind of miss talking to American girls. Hurry on over, you hear?"

"Be there in less than an hour."

"I'll wait in the bar." Al hung up the phone and went into the bathroom to shave, shower and put on a clean shirt.

He slipped the headwaiter five rands to give him the most private table in the popular bar. "I've got a dream girl for a date tonight, Louis," he explained. "I need privacy." Louis grinned knowingly.

Al had almost finished his beer when he looked up and saw Louis approaching the corner table leading an exceptionally pretty young blonde.

"It's been a long time, Donna. I'm really glad you could make it on such short notice," Al said as the girl slipped onto the banquette beside him. "What can I order for you?"

"A glass of sherry, I think."

"Another beer for you, sir?" Louis asked.

"I'll have a Scotch and soda now," Al replied. As Louis walked away from the table he looked at the woman beside him.

"I can see the Company is recruiting some pretty girls for a change."

"Thank you, Al," the girl smiled. "I've heard a lot about you back at Langley. It's good to meet you."

Alvin waited until the drinks were served before continuing their conversation. Then: "Are you wired?"

The girl put her hand on his. "Of course. My memory's good, but they like exact transcriptions."

"Well, to begin with, I hope we can find more excuses to work together," Al said. "You sure beat the hell out of some of the hoods they send me. And that's on the record." He grinned at the girl.

"Do you really have to be so careful?" she asked.

"If you knew Special Branch the way I know Special Branch, you'd be damn certain we have to be careful. They work hand in glove with BOSS down here. I assume your cover is secure. They'll sure check out the phone number I called from my room."

"And they'll find a studious girl working for a Ph.D. on African studies."

"I don't think it'll come to an interrogation, but the Rhodesians and even the South Africans are fighting for their lives. They're not careless people. Now, I'll just spiel off to you, smiling, holding your hand a little, everything that I've got and then maybe we can enjoy the evening."

"I wasn't kidding about my date tonight, Al," Donna reminded him.

"Look, if we just talk for a while, if we don't have a real evening together, if you don't come up to my room for one drink, they're going to be suspicious."

"If you say so. But I think you're dramatizing this whole security thing."

"You're new at this game, Donna. You won't last long if you aren't thinking security first, last and always."

"Maybe I *am* thinking security." She smiled coyly. "They didn't tell us at Langley about going up to hotel rooms."

"Someone's going to get a big charge out of reading this dialogue," Al muttered. "OK, here it is.

"Roger Masefield has made deep inroads into the press corps, both permanent and transient, in Salisbury. Knowing the administration's spin on South Africa I have tried to discourage his journalistic contacts and I have intercepted many requests for interviews with Roger and turned them down. I have convinced Beryl Stoffel to head off as much personal publicity for Roger as possible. She couldn't understand this, but I made her think that the government in Rhodesia will figure him for a publicity hound and not serious about writing the book that will promote their objectives and lead to a lifting of sanctions.

"Although Roger listens to me and Stoffel I know that he is sneaking down to the Quill Club and introducing himself to the local press. At least I've convinced him to keep them out of his so-called Embassy. His thought, and you must remember he is an expert on public relations, is to marshall the press in favor of a biracial government which includes Ian Smith and the moderate black leaders. Basically the press is hostile to the government and that's the reason it gets so little hard news. I am convinced that Masefield will be able to devise ways of using the press to his own advantage, which is to say to the advantage of the Rhodesian government. He has no reason to think I am anything but his stout number two. However, I feel that he does not confide all of his intentions to me. He has the money, the charisma and the expertise to turn public opinion on Rhodesia in almost any direction he sees fit.

"Now that the new administration in Washington has developed a clear foreign policy toward Southern Africa, I am constantly devising means of discrediting Masefield with the Rhodesian government. On his last return from the USA Masefield brought in a briefcase full of *Playboy* and other sex magazines which are banned in Rhodesia. Needless to say, these books are enormously popular with the troops. Even a couple of Rhodesian generals were happy to get them.

"I arranged for Masefield to be observed by my SB contact passing out this forbidden literature. He's keeping a dossier on Masefield. When this is built up sufficiently it may be damaging enough for the Rhodesian government to withdraw its support of him and perhaps even P.I. him, that's what they call deporting an individual as a prohibited immigrant.

"About a week before we were to come back to the States, I caused Masefield's Smith and Wesson M-59, 9mm automatic to disappear. When he couldn't find his gat, Stoffel and I told him he had to report it missing. He didn't want to. He was certain that an American of unsavory reputation who had been in his house had taken the weapon and that he'd get it back.

"We prevailed upon him to report it missing. The police questioned him and a second black mark was entered against him in the SB file. The fact that I caused the pistol to reappear did not halt the dossier being built up against him. I have exacerbated the inevitable incidents that occur when men are drinking at his house. Many opportunities will arise to accumulate points against him.

"Masefield has set up an office in New York that will be in constant telex communication with him and distribute the articles he is writing for publications worldwide. He also established a Washington contact with an old friend of his, one Bucky Simon, who acts as his listening post in the capital. I have arranged to put one of our agents into Roger's net. When all this is in place I will be able to send brief signals to control through a cutout using my wife, Lorraine's, name.

"I am doing everything I can to disrupt Roger's plans to put on a big show at what he calls the 'embassy.' Too bad he's smart enough to keep calling it the "American" embassy of good will, and never, under any circumstances to indicate a United States of America connection.

"The press is in Salisbury en masse for the white elections which Ian Smith will probably win even though he is now advocating a democratically elected black rule government. I am well aware that the administration is backing Mugabe and Nkomo because those are the people Andrew Young wants to see in power. Roger Masefield will probably succeed in putting on a demonstration of international unity against the two terrorist leaders by dramatizing the international make-up of the Rhodesian Security Forces.

"So get set for a propaganda blitz in favor of black democracy instead of black communist terror which the president is unwittingly supporting because of what I consider to be prejudiced advice. The press in Salisbury have little else to cover until the election so there will be a total turnout of every cameraman and reporter from the press of the world presently in Rhodesia. Nevertheless, I am carrying out the assignment thrust upon me to the best of my ability. I hope I will not be ordered to conduct a wet operation to get rid of Masefield, but if I am, so be it. Despite my own opinions, I will continue to carry out orders."

For thirty or forty minutes, Glenlord continued to recite the salient items of interest he had gathered since his last debriefing, accompanying the information with grins, light caresses and occasional laughter whenever waiters or bar patrons came near the table. Finally, there was nothing of importance left to communicate. "OK, why don't you turn off the bug?"

Donna winked, reached into a pocket in her skirt and shut off the tiny tape recorder. "We're clean now, Al."

"Let's go into the dining room for dinner. Roger Masefield pays all the bills at the hotel, but I'd have a problem justifying a glamorous nightclub."

Donna laughed. "Glamorous nightclub in Johannesburg? How much time do you spend here? Besides, the food at the Landdrost is as good as it is anywhere in the city."

Al signed the check, stood up and pulled the table out for Donna. "We've been under constant observation by a gentleman at the bar, undoubtedly from BOSS or SB, so if you can manage it, appear to be enjoying my company and looking forward to seeing me again—in case we need another face to face debriefing."

Donna winked at him. "I'll try. But I am standing up a very nice young man who will probably never invite me out again."

Al grinned for the benefit of anyone who might be watching. "In our business there is no room for a personal life unless it compliments our mission."

"Like with you and Beryl?"

Al nodded. "As long as she is useful."

Chapter 23

At six A.M. Roger Masefield walked down the stairs of his house in Salisbury, unlocked the telex room, gathered up the long strip of telex paper that had rolled through the machine the night before and read the messages, along with the *Rhodesia Herald*, over breakfast.

In this morning's *Herald* the news of the August 31 election was overshadowed by a story from Washington, D.C. Andrew Young was coming to visit Africa again. He announced that he and his British counterpart, Dr. David Owen, would be in Salisbury the day after the Rhodesian whites had cast their votes for either Ian Smith or his opposition, the Rhodesian Action Party. Young would stop off in Lusaka for talks with President Kaunda after meeting with white and black leaders in Salisbury, and then proceed to meet with other frontline state leaders.

The telex messages had more interesting information to offer. Bucky Simon in Washington, D.C. related that his sources indicated Andrew Young was paving the way for a visit by the President of the United States to Nigeria and other African states later in the year.

There was another message addressed to Alvin Glenlord and signed Lorraine. Al's wife frequently sent him cryptic little messages which only Al understood. Roger would have thought they were in code, certainly deliberately garbled, had they been from anyone but

Lorraine. In fact Roger was beginning to wonder whether these arcane bits information that came over the telex signed Lorraine really were from Al's wife. Occasionally he speculated on who else might be contacting Alvin.

Roger was well aware that Al and Beryl, both on his payroll now, had their own operation going, one that had nothing to do with the goals he had set for the Embassy. They had converted the garage below Roger and Jocelyn's bedroom into an office for their own enterprises. Beryl, he knew, was withholding much information that would be useful to him both as a writer and as self-appointed American ambassador. His Embassy was getting out of hand, but what could he do? Roger was anxious to get his first book on Rhodesia completed. Until then, internal complications were to be avoided.

The African moderate leaders, the Reverend Sithole, Chief Chirau and Bishop Muzorewa were getting closer to settlement with Prime Minister Ian Smith. After the whites had reaffirmed their confidence in Smith in the elections now only a week away, and a new constitution for majority rule had been agreed upon, the Communists and Andrew Young would be doing everything possible to denigrate the remarkable joint achievement of the black and white leaders. Roger wanted his book out by then.

By seven o'clock he had finished breakfast and put the telexes back on the desk in the telex room, having scribbled a large question mark on the message from Lorraine. He went up to his private office on the second floor of the Embassy. Jocelyn would be up shortly to get ready for her nine-fifteen meeting at the American Women's Club.

Roger noted on the calendar that he had an appointment with General Ashley St. John to discuss his next sharp end visit. He took a cup of coffee with him and walked up the imposing circular staircase to his office.

At six-thirty in the morning, after a little light lovemaking with Beryl, Alvin crept out of her bed and left her room through a side entrance that gave onto a backyard separated by a vine-covered lattice from the kitchen complex and servants' prying eyes. He walked around to the outside entrance of his own small room and soon, dressed in his bush jacket, shorts and knee-length knitted socks, presented himself in the dining room where he called for the cook to bring him his breakfast.

Christian Stoffel was now stationed at the big air force base of Thornhill, 150 miles southwest of Salisbury, and was only occasionally able to get home. This worked out very nicely, Alvin thought. When Chris was there the three of them got along admirably and Chris was a gold mine of information about air force activities. When he wasn't— that was even better.

Something big was in the works. Undoubtedly a major external operation was being planned against terrorist bases in either Mozambique or Zambia. Alvin was fairly certain from piecing together the information Beryl brought back from ComOps, and from his own observations and what he heard at the Saturday afternoon "Embassy" open house, that the most likely target was in Zambia.

He slowly read the *Rhodesia Herald* over breakfast and noted the item about Andrew Young's prospective trip. He was anxious to get to the Embassy and read the overnight telex messages. There would be something from Washington for him regarding the Young visit.

Just before eight o'clock Al arrived at the Embassy and marched into the telex room. As usual Roger had been there first. Eagerly he looked through the telexes and snatched up the one signed Lorraine. Another CIA operative would be coming to Salisbury. This annoyed him. He was supposed to be left alone. By now he had developed an intense respect for the Rhodesian Special Branch and its intelligence gathering capability, even as it extended to Europe and the United States. In Salisbury, it was infallible. He hoped Jack Fredericks, whoever he was, had unimpeachable cover.

Glenlord had given a great deal of consideration to how telex messages should come to him from his CIA control. His first choice had been no communications at all. The telexes were monitored by Special Branch so code was out. Messages should appear to be aboveboard. Therefore, if they were signed by his wife Lorraine, suspicion would be minimal.

He and Beryl had formed their own company recently to work with outside business interests attempting to gain a foothold in Rhodesia. When the settlement came and economic sanctions were lifted, the lucrative business opportunities here could be exploited. Alvin and Beryl were also engaged in a certain amount of sanctions busting which lent authenticity with the Rhodesian Foreign Office to their travels outside Rhodesia. On these trips, Al was able to contact representatives of the Agency directly.

Someday Rhodesia would be welcomed into the international community, and then Beryl, with her law practice and her business entrepreneurship, would thrive. Of course just about that time the Agency would have a new assignment for Al.

In repayment for Beryl's unwitting help, he would at least be leaving her with a corporate entity which could make her a wealthy woman. He might even be able to share in her wealth. He hoped to convince the Agency that it should leave him in Rhodesia, under deep cover. Certainly the company they were forming, Beryl Stoffel, (Pvt) Ltd., would provide that for him and give him cover to travel all over Africa, in fact everywhere in the world, on behalf of her corporation.

One good thing about the Agency—it didn't mind you making money in private business. He thought of his old friend in Bangkok, Jim Thompson, the Agency's most valuable man in Southeast Asia. Jim had made a fortune for himself in Thai silk. Of course to this day the mystery of his disappearance had never been solved.

It was with regret, an emotion he seldom experienced, that Alvin realized he'd be expected to pass on to the operative under *Washington Herald* cover all the military intelligence he had gathered in Rhodesia. It would be reported to his own control, who in turn would undoubtedly spill it all to Andrew Young, President Carter's black representative at the United Nations, who would pass it on to the terrorist leaders.

For the first time in the sixteen years that he had been associated with the CIA, Al considered holding back information from a case officer. He felt so strongly about the Rhodesian cause, and the heroic manner in which these people were defending their country from radical Marxist Africans, that he hated to be party to anything that would harm it. Wasn't this perhaps the time to retire and give fully of his loyalty to the business he and Beryl had founded?

He smiled ruefully to himself. Nobody leaves the Agency. Glenlord's thoughts were interrupted by the whining of Jocelyn's tape recorder upstairs. She was up and about. That song that he and Beryl hated and had never heard played elsewhere in Rhodesia permeated the house. He hurried to the private office in the garage. Fortunately he and Beryl had had the foresight to spend a little more money and have it soundproofed.

The refrain of "Daytime Friends and Nighttime Lovers," sobbed out by some country western singer, followed him from the telex room, down the hall past the formal dining room on one side and the kitchen on the other to the door into the garage sanctuary.

He just managed to escape another of the choruses that all too eloquently evoked his relationship with Beryl. Next, he knew, would come Tom Carvel in his ice-creamy voice. Jocelyn had taped several commercials on her last trip to the States to remind her of home.

Neither Beryl nor he could suffer Jocelyn's company for more than the minimum time courtesy required. And he was tired of acting the role of Roger's chief of staff. His cover was now sufficiently secure so that he could remove Roger from the scene by whatever means was most expedient. The new director of the CIA, an old Navy comrade of President Jimmy Carter's, was already complaining that Roger was causing the President and his top black official, U.N. Ambassador Andrew Young, considerable embarrassment. Termination, though he hoped not of the extreme kind, was just a matter of time. It wouldn't be long, he thought with satisfaction. Citing Roger's frequent stateside trips, he had persuaded the author to give him a total power of attorney to act for him in his absence. At the right moment, he would deed the Embassy, as Roger insisted on calling his house, over to Beryl Stoffel.

Inside the office he and Beryl referred to as the Hermitage, Al sat at his desk and once again reviewed the telexes.

He had arranged on his last trip to Washington to infiltrate a domestic CIA agent into Roger's telex facility. Roger's old friend, Bucky Simon, allowed the agent to carry out many of the research assignments Roger telexed to him.

Al grinned at the message the agent had given Bucky to send Roger. "Free-lance photographer and writer now working for World Press in Salisbury, Jeff Brigham, is reputed to be trustworthy and objective. Past performance indicates his pictures and stories will be oriented in favor of the Rhodesian government rather than the Marxist guerrillas." In short, Al interpreted, Brigham is a left-wing activist not to be trusted by the Rhodesian government, a reporter who will certainly take the opportunity to find at least one sensational story that will heighten public perception of the Ian Smith government as Fascist, racist and condoning brutality toward Africans.

By now, Alvin knew, Special Branch would have read and digested the contents of this telex. Perhaps he would not have to make

205

any overt move whatsoever to get Roger in such trouble with ComOps and the Rhodesian Ministry of Information that they PI'd him.

Pushing aside the telexes, Al looked through the file of correspondence and memos on his desk relating to Roger Masefield's latest project to draw attention to himself and the book he was finishing, and to the iniquitous manner in which the United States and Britain were treating Rhodesia. Iniquitous had been Roger's word.

In as subtle a manner as possible Al had tried to resist all Roger's planning. Unfortunately, Roger had personally, without even consulting Beryl and himself, gone to the Rhodesian Foreign Office and even the Prime Minister. He had sold them on the enormous worldwide public relations value of a scheme to manipulate the foreign press converging on Rhodesia to cover the elections. Roger's plan was clever, Al had to admit. He would stage a major ceremony at the Embassy. Every branch of the Rhodesian Security Forces would be represented by foreign uniformed troopers, men who believed in the Rhodesian anti-Communist cause sufficiently to risk their lives for it.

As Roger, step by step, had choreographed his scenario, Glenlord had tried to nullify it. Yet Grey's Scouts had agreed to have two Americans and an Australian from the unit mounted on horseback at the ceremony. The air force would assign one of its star American pilots to be present and was contributing American dog handlers whose guard mastiffs patrolled the perimeters of the crucial air bases.

Ron Reid-Daley would represent the foreigners in the Selous Scouts. Nobody in Selous Scouts was ever photographed except for the colonel himself who was a well-known figure.

From the RLI, representatives of eight different nations would be present. Roger had contracted with a Salisbury seamstress to make a flag for every country that had a national serving in Rhodesia. There were fourteen of them.

An American doctor who had served the Africans out in the bush at his medical mission would be awarded a check from the Embassy for one thousand dollars to purchase new surgical supplies in the Western World.

African buglers from the Rhodesian African Rifles would play "The Last Post" ("Taps" in the United States Army) in honor of foreigners killed fighting the Soviet-backed Marxist guerrillas of the Patriotic Front.

Alvin had quietly tried to persuade M.M. De Vries of the inadvisability of allowing such a ceremony to take place. For the first time, De Vries, whom Al had always recognized as the most astute and internationally aware minister in the Rhodesian government, had shown a flicker of suspicion. Why did Glenlord, Roger Masefield's chief of staff, feel that such a show for the international press could possibly do anything but help the Rhodesian image worldwide? Here would be a veritable United Nations that recognized the justice of the Rhodesian battle against communism.

At that point Al had judiciously ceased his campaign. He was well aware of the new CIA director's support of the Carter administration's African policy to force the Mugabe-Nkomo faction on Rhodesia; but he had reached the conclusion that he could do nothing but assist Masefield's display of international public relations if he wanted to maintain his cover.

There was a knock on the door to the "Hermitage" and Roger walked in.

"I thought you'd be working all morning on the book, Roger." Al remarked.

"I thought so too. But there's so much to do for Saturday, only three days away, that I thought I'd better check with you that everything is operative."

"I have no heartburn," Al said with a smile. "I don't know about you."

"I got a call last night from Mike Wyatt. They're having trouble getting horses from Inkomo Barracks for us. We've got to display horses."

"Why?" Al asked. "You seem to forget they've got a war going here. Maybe the horses are needed out in the field."

"This battle we're fighting on Saturday is going to do Rhodesia more good than killing a hundred terrorists." Roger snapped. "We're trying to get some horses from the Borrowdale Riding Club. Will you check on it?"

"Sure. What other problem is there?"

"I heard from an RLI source that now the army doesn't want men appearing in uniform. I can't see what the objection is."

Glenlord smiled to himself. Maybe his behind-the-scenes efforts to knock some of the glitter off Roger's exhibition were paying off. "I'll check on it and let you know."

"For chrissake, Al, it's Thursday. If we are not assured of having everything I need to make this the biggest pre-Rhodesian propaganda blast that's ever been set off, I'm going up to see the P.M. himself, this afternoon. When I got back from Umtali on Sunday, I thought everything was set. And suddenly, Monday, Tuesday, Wednesday, one goddamn thing after another keeps coming up. It almost seems as though somebody is sabotaging this show. I know Rhodesians don't understand public relations, that's been their trouble for the past five years, but this can be the most significant international message in their favor ever sent out. The fifteen most important Western block nations are all represented here by men who are being paid a pittance to fight for the principles that America and Australia and South Korea fought for in Vietnam, and the world doesn't know it. But they will after this Saturday. Sometimes I think you don't like what I'm doing here, Al."

"Hey, Roger, you're getting all uptight about this thing." Alvin flashed his wide reassuring grin. "We'll make it work. That's what I'm here for. I'll get Beryl to talk to MM and I'll go over to ComOps this morning and see what the problem is."

"Good. Meantime I'm making an appointment with the P.M. just to make sure. The last time I talked to him he was all in favor of this."

"I think your problem is with Ashley St. John," Al replied. "He doesn't like any part of this whole scheme of yours."

"What does a soldier who's spent his career as a staff officer craftily avoiding any possibility of hearing shots fired in anger know about international psychological warfare? He knows only one thing; cover your ass at all times."

"Well, his ass would certainly be hanging out if this production of yours somehow backfired," Al retorted.

"Maybe I ought to give Ashley a call myself."

"I wouldn't advise it, Roger. Let's see what happens."

The phone rang and Al answered it, repeating the last four digits of their number. He listened and then cocked an interrogative eye at Roger. He handed him the phone. "It's Ashley St. John."

"What do you know?" Roger took the phone. "Masefield here."

"General St. John calling you," the crisp woman's voice on the other end announced, and then Ashley was on the line.

"Hello there, Roger. I'm afraid I have some bad news for you."

Through his mind ran the argument he would advance when the general told him he couldn't have uniformed men at his ceremony on

Saturday. "You're not going to let me do this Rhodesia rally on Saturday in style, eh?"

"I'm afraid it doesn't concern that, Roger." There was something in Ashley's tone that made Roger suddenly alert, and a knot of dread formed in his stomach.

"Go ahead, General," he said.

"You're listed as next of kin to be notified in case of death or injury, by Trooper Cary Donnelly of New Rochelle, New York."

"What happened?" Roger rasped hollowly.

"Trooper Donnelly was killed in action yesterday evening at five o'clock in the operation area. He died of gunshot wounds."

"Where did it happen?"

"I'm afraid we can't answer that."

"What were the circumstances, Ashley?"

"We have no details. I'm sorry."

"Where is Trooper Donnelly's body?"

"It was brought in at first light this morning to the RLI morgue."

A wave of nausea swept over Roger. It seemed impossible. Not Cary. "I have his parents' address in New Rochelle, Ashley. If I give it to you, will you inform them?"

There was a hesitation on the line and then General St. John replied, "Since you're listed as next of kin, our responsibility actually ends with you. However, of course, we will officially notify the parents if you'll give us their names and addresses and phone numbers."

"I'll call Mr. and Mrs. Donnelly. Right now it's," he glanced at his watch, "ten o'clock here. That's three A.M. Daylight Savings Time in New York. I'll call them about nine o'clock their time. A lousy way to start off their day."

"We'll wait an hour after you've called and then make the notification."

"Is there anything more you want to tell me?"

"No. Oh, about the uniformed appearances. It seems that higher authority than mine has cleared it. Your uniformed ceremony has been approved by the Ministry of Defense."

"Thanks, General." Roger hung up. Al Glenlord looked at him. "Cary?"

"Yes. I have to break the news to his parents. Jesus. I'm the one who brought him over here. I wish I could get a little more information. Al, see if you can get all the details on how Cary died. Beryl can usually pry things out of De Vries if necessary. I really want to know what happened and where."

"Roger, don't even ask. As Beryl puts it, haven't you blotted your copybook enough already?"

Roger stared at his chief of staff incredulously. "Whose side are you on anyway? We're supposed to be concentrating on helping Rhodesia, not arguing among ourselves."

"You aren't helping Rhodesia when you keep doing things the government doesn't like. You bring in banned magazines—like *Playboy* and all the rest of that dirty literature."

"I bring them because the guys like them."

"Any time the police come here with a search warrant and find your little collection of gash shots, you could be PI'd. Everywhere Beryl and I turn we find something else you're doing to embarrass us. Even the taxi company has been complaining about coming here because troopies who have been your guests get drunk at your house and then abuse the driver or don't pay him. All these things are recorded. And then you lost your gun," he added wickedly.

"And found it the next day and paid an eighty-dollar fine," Roger retorted. "They should have been delighted with the eighty dollars."

"Then every Saturday afternoon you've got a bunch of loose-lipped soldiers over here. God knows what they're saying and to whom they're saying it. The press comes too. You let anybody in on Saturday afternoon."

"That's what we're here for. We've got to provide some club for Americans."

"Now you've gotten yourself all involved with the black leaders. Meddling in internal politics is one thing that you can be sure will get you in big trouble. You got Sithole and his mob together with Chief Chirau, and now you and your friend Neville Romain are trying to put them together with Bishop Muzorewa and create some kind of black caucus, your unity program."

"It's not my program. I've merely tried to keep myself informed about what's going on."

"And now you're pushing the government to have all the troops here in uniform on Saturday. They know you want it because the press of the world is going to be in Salisbury. The government knows you're pushing yourself and your books. You should be keeping a low profile."

"A low profile is just what the hell I don't want!" Roger cried. "I want to focus the attention of the world on what we're doing, the fact that Rhodesia is not fighting blacks, it's fighting Communists." He flashed a fierce look at Al. "You know what we're going to do on Saturday? We're going to have a special memorial service for Cary Donnelly."

Glenlord was staring at him, a look of stunned bewilderment on his face. Roger could not understand why Al seemed to take delight in frustrating everything he wanted to do. He was sick of this supposed friend who was constantly denigrating him and, it seemed, deliberately trying to frustrate his efforts to establish an internationally recognized American presence in Rhodesia.

"Why don't you go out to the RLI?" Al finally suggested. "Probably someone from One Commando brought the body back. They've been out at Grand Reef now for two weeks. It's about time they were being rotated home."

"You keep pretty good track of the security forces' movements, don't you," Roger said angrily.

"That's one of my chores on your behalf, Roger. I try to give you colorful and accurate information on the war which you can put in your book."

Dismayed, heartsick, Roger walked out of Glenlord's office to the driveway beyond and stepped into his car. It was a twenty-minute drive to the RLI barracks on the airport road. He parked close to the headquarters of One Commando and found Captain Parker inside. Parker saw by Roger's expression that he had been told. "I'm sorry, Roger. I know you were quite close with Trooper Donnelly."

"I brought him here," Roger said sorrowfully.

"Yes, the trooper told me that. He thought very highly of you."

"At least the last time I saw him he was about to enjoy a most delightful occasion."

"I'm glad to hear that, although I can't imagine what it would have been at Grand Reef."

Roger let the remark go. "Can you tell me how it happened?"

"I'm afraid I can only tell you that four sticks led by Sergeant McCall were caught in an ambush just at sunset. Cary was the only one killed. Two other wounded were casevaced back to Fleming Hospital."

"Can I view the body?"

"If you want to. You're officially next of kin. McCall came in this morning with Trooper Donnelly's body. He should be in One Commando Barracks if you want to talk to him."

"Thank you, Ian."

Roger found Hugh McCall on the second floor of the barracks in the private room assigned to him as sergeant.

"I figured you'd be here, Roger," McCall said.

"Where is he, Hugh? In the morgue?"

McCall nodded. "I'll take you over if you want to go."

"I guess I'd better. It's my job now to notify his mother and father."

Roger followed Hugh to the dispensary. A medical officer ushered them into an antiseptic, bare-walled room. The body was in a green plastic bag. The medical office zipped it open and suddenly Roger was staring down at Cary Donnelly's body. There was a round, black hole below his left eye. The back of his head had been blown away.

"Can you tell me how it happened, Hughie?"

"We were caught in an ambush. Cary did the right thing, just like in the immediate action drills. He took a grenade off his harness and stuck it on the rifle grenade launcher and fired. Then he reached for a second grenade and as he fitted it over the barrel his head came up a little too high, I guess. You can see he got it right in the face."

"Was that the only wound?"

"That was enough."

Roger turned from the body. "I guess that will do it." He and McCall left the dispensary and walked down the road.

"Yesterday was our last day on duty. We were scheduled to come back today anyway. Cary was looking forward to being at your party on Saturday. I think his girlfriend had some deal worked out so she could spend the weekend in Salisbury with a friend. You know, he told me that his girl's parents had come around and invited him to the farm any weekend he could make it with her."

"Does she know?"

"Not yet. I flew in with the body this morning."

"That means I'm going to have to break the news to her too. Hughie, do you want to come over to my place for a drink?"

Hugh shook his head. "Thanks, Roger, I can't come over now. But I'll see you Saturday."

"In uniform," Roger reminded him.

"We've got permission?"

"Yes. General St. John told me uniforms were approved when he gave me the message about Cary. Where exactly did the ambush take place?"

Hugh looked at Roger a moment. "I'm not supposed to say, but of course I'll tell you. That group of terrs we caught on the hill the other day when you were in the K car was only part of a large group, maybe a hundred and fifty or more, who were in Tanzania a week ago. They took the usual route, overnight boat trip to Maputo from Dar es Salaam and then a few hours on the railroad from the dock to our border.

"We'd been tracking them for a couple of days and caught up with them close to the border. They ran back into Mozambique figuring they'd be safe and we got clearance to follow them. We must have been about five miles inside Mozambique when we got into a godawful firefight, with FRELIMOS and terrs fighting together. The first time I ever saw that happen. The Freddies were good. We had a helluva time fighting our way out and Cary was killed. We must have slain about twenty of the gooks on our way back. The amazing thing is that Cary was the only KIA. Like I said, he got off the first grenade and that shook them up enough so we could fight our way back into Rhodesia. ComOps wouldn't be so happy if the story leaked that we were in Mozambique at the time."

"You can be sure I won't let it out," Roger promised.

Chapter 24

The scene at the American Embassy of Goodwill in Salisbury was even more resplendent with color and excitement than Roger had dared hope. This would be the climax of his first year in Rhodesia. Never before had the press of the world sent so many reporters to Rhodesia at one time. Comprising perhaps the smallest electorate of any country on the globe, about 80,000 eligible voters out of the 280,000 whites in the country, the Rhodesian elections had captured the attention of the world.

Ian Smith, campaigning on a platform dedicated to negotiating with black leaders to form a moderate, pro-Western, majority-rule government was being opposed by the RAP (Rhodesia Action Party) which denounced compromise or negotiations with any black leaders. Ian Smith, the man who had said never in his lifetime, never in a thousand years would black rule come to Rhodesia, was now putting his political reputation and personal charisma on the line to bring about just what he had most stringently opposed.

By four o'clock on Saturday afternoon, when the Embassy ceremony was scheduled to commence, eight television crews from nations around the world were set up to record the proceedings. With three days to go before the elections, this drama provided by Roger Masefield was a godsend to the media which had nothing substantial or colorful to report until election day. An American and an Australian were mounted on horseback, the horses standing just behind the fifteen flag poles from which flapped the flags of the various nationalities represented in the Rhodesian Security Forces. In front of each flag stood a foreign national in the uniform of his unit. An honor guard composed of foreigners in the security forces stood twenty strong behind the podium, which was to the left of the flagpoles as the audience faced them. Behind the podium flew the flag of the Crippled Eagles.

Over one hundred and fifty invited guests watched the proceedings, from the Embassy's front lawn where they stood or sat. Roger Masefield, wearing a blue-black suit and a black tie to signify respect for the dead American in whose honor he was about to conduct a memorial service, mounted the podium and placed his hands palms down on the lectern. He looked out over the assembled spectators and media representatives.

When the crowd was hushed and the only noises that could be heard were the clicking of cameras and the electric whir of the cinecameras, Roger turned to Major Mike Wyatt beside him. "As the ranking American in the Rhodesian Security Forces, lower the flag to half-mast, Major Wyatt." Mike Wyatt marched smartly to the flagpole and lowered the American flag to half-mast. Then he recleated the cords. He repeated the process with the Crippled Eagles flag and marched back to the podium.

"We planned to have a memorial for all the foreign soldiers who have died in the service of the Rhodesian Security Forces," Roger began. "Now, sadly, we open these proceedings with a short memorial service for RLI trooper Cary Donnelly of New Rochelle, New York, who was killed in action earlier this week. It so happens that I myself brought Cary to Rhodesia. On a trip back to the United States to enlist public support among Americans for the cause we're all fighting for today, I appeared on Barry Farber's phone-in radio broadcast in New York and described the struggle this small nation is waging to protect its multiracial population from the Marxist terrorists who threaten to destroy it.

"One of the listeners who telephoned me was Cary Donnelly. One week later he was flying to Salisbury with me to join the Rhodesian Light Infantry. Cary had been working on his Master's degree in political science and this would be his first military service. He had performed only five months of that service when he was killed, cour-ageously fighting the enemy that is the enemy of all of us here.

"Cary had planned to marry a Rhodesian girl and perhaps settle here and throw in his lot with the new nation that will evolve from the internal accords reached by Prime Minister Ian Smith and such moderate and enlightened African leaders as Senator Chief Jeremiah Chirau, the Reverend Ndabaningi Sithole and Bishop Abel Muzorewa. It is a sadness that will live with me forever that Cary Donnelly will not be here to share in the exciting development of the new, free, Western nation that we trust Zimbabwe-Rhodesia will become.

"As an American, I will always be proud of Cary Donnelly, and of the other Americans and foreign nationals who, understanding the true situation in the southern part of this vitally important continent, gave their lives in a struggle that the entire Western world should be joining, not repudiating. Cary Donnelly, at age twenty-five, had a far deeper perception of what southern Africa is all about than most members of the United States Department of State and the United States Mission to the United Nations.

"I wish I could hold out more hope to Rhodesians that America will expeditiously come to the realization that such Americans as our Ambassador to the United Nations, who arrives here on September 1, are doing incalculable harm to the entire Western world's chances of survival. If Ambassador Young succeeds in putting Robert Mugabe's Marxist terrorists in power, this nation is lost, to its own people and to the west. However, we can only pray that the holding action in which Cary Donnelly died can be sustained until those of us in the sometimes misnamed Free World who do know the situation here can convince our fellow citizens to demand that their governments recog-nize Rhodesia diplomatically and lift the economic sanctions that are crippling it."

Roger turned from the audience. "Will the bugles now sound 'The Last Post,' which we in American know as 'Taps.'" Two African bu-glers from the Rhodesian African Rifles' band, wearing red sashes over their shoulders, marched to the American flag at half-staff beside the green and white Rhodesian flag and placed the trumpets to their lips.

The haunting strains of "Taps" sounded forth. Except for the photographers and the television crews, who were busily recording the moment, there was hardly a dry eye in the crowd. Roger caught the glance of Jessica Richardson who had arrived with several classmates from her school in Umtali. He smiled sadly at her. Cary was mature enough to have made this wartime love affair into a durable marriage. Jessica held her head up proudly, from time to time dabbing away a tear.

Roger noted with satisfaction that Jeff Brigham, like some of the other cameramen, was sending rolls of film back to his office by runner. This meant his pictures would make the Monday newspapers in America. When the last melancholy strains of "Taps" drifted away, Roger once again addressed those present. "Later on this afternoon, the RLI will congregate at the bar on the rear lawn and sing the traditional 'Tracking the Spoor' in honor of Cary Donnelly.

"We now come to a happier part of this ceremony. For twelve years, one of America's most dedicated medical missionaries, Dr. Harold Comstock, has been treating the hundreds of thousands of people in the tribal areas north of here for every manner of disease and accident. Dr. Comstock and the missionaries who built the medical mission have given themselves selflessly to the task of alleviating human suffering. They have provided hope where there was none before."

To a prolonged round of applause Roger then handed the doctor a check for one thousand dollars to buy much needed medical supplies for the mission. Although most of the military men despised missionaries, they made an exception for Comstock and some few like him. For one thing, they knew Comstock had saved the lives of many wounded security forces men.

The next presentation was of five Crippled Eagles plaques to the five branches of the Rhodesian Security Forces. In all but one case, an American serving with each branch came forward to receive the plaque, which would end up over the bar in either the officers' or the sergeants' mess. Colonel Ron Reid-Daley accepted the plaque for the Selous Scouts.

Roger smiled at his audience. "Now, with the formal aspects of this ceremony completed, the bar and refreshment area to the rear is open. Sergeant Jim Tebble of the air force will give you a demonstration of how his guard dogs operate. We have several officers from the Rhodesian Information Service available to assist the press in interviews with those Rhodesian and foreign officers and men who don't mind being interviewed. And, I'm sure Sergeant Ed Wandell, seated on his Grey's Scouts mount over there, will be happy to talk about the

Scouts and perhaps put on a little display of military horsemanship in the field across the street. I would again remind the press that sometime in the next half hour or so Cary Donnelly's comrades in the RLI will sing the traditional 'Tracking the Spoor' in his honor. This usually takes place after drinks have been hoisted."

Over the next hour, Roger estimated, at least a mile of film must have run through the myriad of cameras peeking about the Embassy grounds. In the tennis court gazebo a crew was interviewing an American officer in the RLI. A man from *The Wall Street Journal* was talking to Hugh McCall, and the *Rhodesia Herald*'s defense reporter seemed, as always, to be having difficulty getting fresh news from General Ashley St. John.

He noted that Alvin Glenlord seemed to be in deep conversation with an American journalist to whom Roger had not been introduced. He suspected it was the man from the *Washington Herald* referred to in the recent telex. Glenlord clearly was not pleased with the journalist's presence, Roger could see.

"This is quite a bear-baiting your asset is putting on, Al," Fredericks observed.

"I just hope to hell your cover is good," Glenlord said between clinched teeth. "I thought it was understood that nobody would contact me."

The CIA man ignored the rebuke. "When all this hits the press in the United States you can be damn sure you'll hear from the Department of State, and of course Andy Young will stomp the shit out of us all."

"What could I do? At least I persuaded M.M. De Vries and other ministers not to come. Maybe that will give the party more of a renegade look."

"Not with all those uniforms," the CIA journalist snapped.

"If I had done anything to sabotage this party, even my best asset, Beryl Stoffel, would have become suspicious."

"As a result of this melee the State Department is bound to take a lot of flack from senators and congressmen for not presenting the Rhodesian side of the question."

"That's exactly what Roger had in mind."

"You'd better terminate him as quickly as possible," Jack Fredericks ordered.

"He'll hang himself, but I'll help in every way I can." Al looked around uneasily. "This place is crawling with Special Branch."

"You're getting jumpy, Glenlord. I've been writing for the *Washington Herald* foreign affairs section three years now and everything I've done on Rhodesia has been favorable. Don't worry about my cover." The agent's voice became urgent. "I'll be flying from here to Lusaka on the plane with Andrew Young and David Owen. They're going to call me up front during the flight, ostensibly so I can interview them. Actually I'm going to brief them on everything I find out from you. I want to know all about the chances of Smith bringing about an internal settlement with the three black leaders."

"Roger Masefield has been in the middle of all that," Al replied. "Some of the meetings have been held right here at the Embassy. As a matter of fact, that's one of the ways we're going to sink him. The government doesn't like outsiders meddling in black politics."

"I need all the military information you can give me. That's particularly important. We're trying to make an assessment of how long the Rhodesian government can hold out against the Patriotic Front."

"I can give you all that," Glenlord replied. "I've got a pretty good idea how, when and where the next external mission is going to take place. What bothers me is that if I give this to you, you'll give it to Young and he'll give it to Mugabe and Nkomo, and the Rhodesians will be jeopardized."

"If we don't come up with some good information your mission is going to be jeopardized, I can tell you that. Our job is to provide hard intelligence. How it's used is none of our business. I'm going to drift away from you now, Glenlord. Meet me tomorrow morning for breakfast at the Monomatopa. You can give me a little sightseeing trip around Salisbury and we'll be able to talk. And stop looking so goddamn fidgety, will you? I'll file a story to the *Herald* which will make Rhodesia and the American *heroes*"—he accentuated the word derisively—"fighting here on their own initiative come out great. You can take credit for the story. So don't worry about being seen with me."

"All right Jack, no more heartburn. I'll give you a full briefing tomorrow."

The agent looked about at the party in progress with distaste, then turned to Al. "You might also brief me on your plans for ending this sort of thing."

"I have constructive ideas on that." Al Glenlord glanced across the back lawn to the bar. Roger had ensured that a good supply of Scotch would be on hand and the RLI troopers were taking advantage of a largess that seldom came their way. To Fredericks he said, "You're about to see and hear something that will make even hardened spooks like us feel a little lumpy in the throat. They're going to sing 'Tracking the Spoor.' "

"What's that?"

"Tracking the spoor is what they do—follow the trail of the terrorists until they make contact."

A Rhodesian sergeant lifted a glass of whiskey and the others followed suit. "Here's to Cary Donnelly," the sergeant toasted.

"To Cary Donnelly!" the others chorused. Then, as the television cameras zoomed in on the group at the bar, they began the song, at once mournful and rousing, that was saved for such special occasions.

"Tracking the Spoor, tracking the spoor,

Cary won't be tracking it no more."

As the voices swelled, a hushed silence fell over the hundred or more people on the Embassy grounds. There were several more lines, then came the climax of the song which was enough to send shivers up the stiffest spine.

"Raise a drink to the dead already,

Hurrah for the next man that dies!"

The RLI troopers, thoroughly warmed-up now, sang the song through a second time. Jack Fredericks glanced at Al and shook his head slightly. "Wait until that hits the tubes of America."

"The recruiting office here will be busy," Al agreed.

Roger was trying to be everywhere at once monitoring all aspects of the party but it was impossible; too much was going on. As he was refreshing himself with a Scotch on the rocks, General Ashley St. John came up to him with the startlingly beautiful blonde South African girl, Veronica Montgomery, a Nikon camera over her shoulder.

"Roger," Ashley greeted him. "Remember Veronica Montgomery from Johannesburg?"

Roger shook hands. "It seems to me I introduced you two. Are you finding all this interesting, Veronica?"

"It's marvelous, Roger."

"I hope you're getting a good story for the press down in Johannesburg."

"That's what we wanted to talk to you about a moment if you don't mind, Roger," St. John said.

"The problem is, Roger," Veronica took up, "I really can't stay in Salisbury without a job. My free-lancing just won't keep me going here."

"How can I help?" Roger asked.

"You send your Embassy newsletter every month," St. John prompted. "You must need research assistance. I must say we all admire and appreciate your syndicated articles in the American and European press. What Veronica needs is a job as what you Americans call a leg-girl." The general's eyes dropped below the hem of Veronica's short skirt. "You'll have to admit the description is apt."

Roger chuckled at this rare display of near-humor on St. John's part.

"Quite right, Ashley. Well, let me figure what I might be able to do." He looked across the lawn to where Sarah Cobb Chase, also armed with a Nikon, was holding on to Colin Adderley, her British captain in the RLI. If he were going to hire anybody it would be Sarah Cobb Chase, of course. But she was picking up enough free-lance assignments, obviously, so that she could stay in Salisbury where the excitement and the big man in her life were.

Roger spotted Jeff Brigham taking photographs of the RLI troopers singing "Tracking the Spoor." He caught Jeff's attention and beckoned him over. As Jeff approached, Roger explained to St. John: "Jeff Brigham with World Press is coming up with some constructive reporting and I have a feeling he might be in a position to ask WP to give him another hired hand. We could talk to him about it."

"Fine," the general acceded. "Checking him out for a security clearance, we found some good reports on him."

"We got the same from our own sources," Roger said. He was a little taken aback at St. John's congeniality, though he knew its cause: getting a job for Veronica meant keeping her in Rhodesia.

Brigham came up to them and Ashley St. John shook his hand warmly. Roger noticed the photographer's eyes open wide with excitement as St. John outlined what he had in mind for Veronica.

"That's interesting, General St. John," Jeff said, his drooping mustache twitching. "Just yesterday I came to the conclusion we needed another reporter in the WP offices here. Things are really popping now. I'll telex my boss in New York with a request to hire an outstanding South African newswoman who would be a valuable addition to our staff here."

Ashley St. John beamed. "That's most encouraging."

"Yes, as a matter of fact I'm trying to get out in the field more myself and that means somebody has got to cover for me here in Salisbury."

"That would be a fine job for Veronica," Ashley encouraged. "And of course she has excellent sources both in government and the military." There was no denying that statement, Roger thought, as he saw St. John fix the beautiful young woman with a lascivious stare.

"Do you know when you might get an answer to your query, Jeff?" Veronica asked.

"I suppose in a few days. If I don't hear promptly I'll telephone New York."

Ashley St. John and Veronica smiled at each other and then Ashley turned to Brigham. "By the way, Jeff, I believe a request from you came across my desk a week ago. You wanted to visit our cavalry unit, Grey's Scouts, out in the field. Is that correct?"

"Yessir. I thought some good pictures of Grey's Scouts riding through the bush on their horses would make good copy around the world and demonstrate that the Rhodesian Security Forces are a full service shop, so to speak, complete with cavalry."

"I see the 2-IC of Grey's Scouts, the American, Major Wyatt is here. Have you talked to him about it?"

"Yessir, I certainly have. Major Wyatt said it would have to be approved by ComOps and that was why I made the request."

"Well, Jeff," Ashley said heartily, fixing the diminutive reporter with a compelling eye, "let's each of us expedite the other's request, what?"

Roger grinned to himself. Certainly this was an interesting bit of horse-trading. He excused himself and walked over to where his friend Mike Wyatt was having a drink with Mack Hudson and Carla.

"Christ, I spent half the party dodging newspaper photographers," Mack greeted him.

"If there's one thing I've learned in four wars," Mike Wyatt declared, "it's to keep away from journalists. They're always bad news for soldiers." He paused, looking over at Veronica. "Unless they look like her."

Boisterously Mack rejoined, "About half the men here would be in trouble with estranged wives, not to mention the law and their governments, if their photographs were ever published."

"True," Roger acknowledged, "but those that don't mind being photographed are sure adding a lot of color to this occasion. By the way, Mike, it looks as though you're going to have a journalist for a traveling companion in the near future."

Mike cocked a hungry eye at Veronica Montgomery. "You don't say."

"Sorry, not that one. It looks as though Jeff Brigham is going to get clearance from ComOps to go out in the bush with you."

"Oh, horseshit!" Mike exclaimed. "No reporter has ever been given clearance to come out in the bush with us except Lord Cravenlow, yourself and that French photographer, Francois Darquennes."

"Well, you can add a fourth to the list now. Jeff Brigham rides again."

"How do you know?" Mike looked both displeased and alarmed.

"I just heard a conversation between General St. John and Brigham."

"I'm going to get hold of my boss and warn him. If there's one thing we don't need it's some dickhead newspaperman following us around."

"Jeff seems to check out pretty well," Roger said. "Though personally I'm beginning to have my doubts. Just instinct."

"Well, if I can block it you can be damn sure I will," Mike declared.

Roger shrugged and turned to Mack Hudson. "You wanted to meet the Commander of Selous Scouts to put in your pitch for yourself, Colin and the rest of your team. This is your chance." He drew Mack's attention to Colin Adderley standing beside Sarah Cobb Chase, her arm entwined through his. "If the Colonel goes along you're going to make one American newsgirl very unhappy."

"My wife won't be seeing so much of me either if this works," Mack allowed.

"I'll bring the colonel over and you're on your own."

Although only a lieutenant colonel, Ron Reid-Daley's reputation and power within the hierarchy of the Rhodesian government and the military were such that even generals were fearful of crossing him. No man in the Rhodesian military was closer to its ultimate commander than Reid-Daley, and there was no chain of command between General Peter Walls and Prime Minister Ian Smith.

Roger walked over to Reid-Daley. "Ron, there's a Yank who would like to talk to you, Captain Mack Hudson."

"Oh yes, SAS chap. I've heard a lot about him. What does he want?"

"I'll let him tell you." Roger guided the Selous Scouts commander over to Mack. "If you gentlemen want a quieter place you can use my office inside," he said as he left the two alone.

"Would you ask Colin Adderley to join us?" Mack called after him.

"I'll send him right over."

"And Sergeant LeClair and our Kraut friend Horst Houk too," Mack shouted.

Reid-Daley gave Mack a suspicious look. "Sounds as though you plan to pack my squad, Captain."

"Quite, sir. With the best of what you don't already have." Reid-Daley chuckled. "I might add, sir," Mack got in quickly, "Colin Adderley is the best demolitions man in the SAS."

The colonel merely said "Hmm." But there was a glint in his eye.

As darkness fell over Salisbury the Embassy reception waned; the press and guests departed. Other than the odd brawl between inebriated troopers, which helped to decorate the affair for the cameramen, it ended peacefully.

Reid-Daley, holding the plaque of the Crippled Eagles under his arm, stopped to take his leave of Roger. "Thanks for the party, Roger. A great bash. And I appreciate your introducing me to Hudson and the rest of his chaps. I hope they make it through the selection course. We're going to need them more than ever as we move toward majority rule. The Communists aren't going to allow a moderate black government to take over in Salisbury. They want their own men in power, those tree-swingers, Mugabe and Nkomo." He looked around the dwindling throng. "I'll say hello to one or two more blokes and then be on my way."

People were saying goodbye to Jocelyn who had, throughout, been as gracious a hostess as any genuine ambassador's wife. No American embassy party anywhere could have been more significant diplomatically or better covered by the International Press than this one, Roger thought. It had been expensive. Only the best-grade roast beef, seafood flown in from South Africa for the occasion and all the Scotch anybody could drink. That had been the big problem, but he, Al and a number of others had made the liquor run down to South Africa and Chris Stoffel had been particularly helpful. Roger found Jocelyn, took her hand, kissed her and said, "Someday maybe we'll be real ambassadors." Then he laughed at himself and finished off the Scotch in his glass.

"Ashley St. John was funny," Jocelyn chuckled. "There he was with Veronica on one side and Carla on the other, trying to court both of them."

"By next week we should have made the TV and newspapers in every major city in the world," Roger exulted.

Mack appeared on the front lawn where Roger and Jocelyn were saying goodbye and receiving congratulations on the party. Carla retrieved her husband. "Shall we go home, Mack?"

"Sure, via the Oasis Bar. I promised a couple of guys I'd stop by."

Finally there was just Beryl and Al standing with Roger and Joceyln.

"What say we go inside, have a nightcap and eat some of the best leftovers," Roger suggested. Thanks to the caterers and the servants, the lawn and the house itself were immaculate.

Al and Beryl exchanged looks. "No thanks," Al said. "We'll leave you two alone. It's been a long, tough day."

"Roger," Beryl said, her eyes shining, "this was really a great moment for Rhodesia. I can hardly wait to see what comes out in the foreign press. The memorial service was a master stroke."

"I didn't mean it that way, Beryl," Roger replied sadly.

"It was brilliant, I assure you," Beryl said. "Everybody was wiping tears from their eyes."

"I'm afraid a lot more good men, Rhodesians, Americans, Australians, Frenchmen, Germans, Brits, men from all over the free world will die before this situation is resolved." Roger glanced at the row of national flags flying in the evening breeze. "You can be sure that Andrew Young's visit with David Owen next week is going to be the signal for a whole new wave of fighting when they try to tell Bishop Muzorewa and the other moderate Africans to give Rhodesia to the terrorists."

"We'll make it, we'll hold out," Beryl proclaimed stoutly. Al Glenlord took her arm and led her to her Mercedes.

"Is the coast clear at home?" Al asked her.

"I am planning to be with MM tonight," she replied, a bit haughtily Al thought. Now what? he asked himself.

"I was hoping we might be together," he said mildly.

"Well, maybe you'd like to catch the evening flight to Joburg and see your American girl friend."

"What are you talking about, Doll?" Al asked.

"I heard from a friend that you and a very attractive young graduate student named Donna Guest had quite an evening together recently at the Landdrost Hotel."

"Oh?" Al asked nonchalantly although his stomach knotted up at the possibility he had been compromised. "How did this friend of yours know her name and that she's a student?"

"He has his ways. Who is she, Al?"

"A friend of my wife Lorraine's family actually. She was told to call me if she wanted to see Rhodesia and get a guided tour of the ancient city of Zimbabwe."

"For a friend of your wife's you certainly enjoyed her company." There was no mistaking the sarcasm in Beryl's tone.

"She's an interesting lady," Al allowed casually. "But come on Beryl, there's nothing whatsoever between Donna and I. Who is this friend who saw us in the cocktail lounge of the Landdrost?"

"Nobody you know," she replied sullenly.

"Well, I can promise that you're the only love interest in my life. Donna is a friend. Nothing more."

"Do you plan on seeing her again?"

"I might. But there's nothing for you to be jealous about. After all I don't complain about you dividing your favors between MM and me."

"That's different."

"Hey, no problem. You're the only one for me."

As they reached her car she put both hands on his arm. "I'm sorry, Al. I didn't mean to sound like a jealous bitch. It's just that it was a shock when I heard about this girl for the first time from Ken Flowers." She put her hand over her mouth. "Oops, I wasn't supposed to say that."

"I don't mind Special Branch watching me," Al replied. "I've got nothing to hide."

Beryl smiled up at him. "Come on home with me, Al. I'm not really going to see MM tonight. I was looking forward to being with you this weekend. And then Monday, the elections."

Without another word Al walked around the Mercedes and climbed into the passenger seat beside Beryl. But he was worried and wondering how to contact Donna and tell her to make certain her cover was secure.

Roger and Jocelyn were perplexed as they watched the tiff between Al and Beryl. After the two had apparently made up and driven off together, Roger took Jocelyn's hand and they surveyed the empty grounds of their home. "Would you believe it? We're alone."

On the front lawn an African member of Gray's Scouts was taking a broom and shovel to the evidence of the horses' recent presence which had added color to the ceremony. A pungent odor of the stables still lingered. The flags were being taken down and neatly folded by a servant. Roger conducted Jocelyn inside, closing the door and locking it after them.

"Madam Ambassador, you are a consummate diplomat as well as a beautiful young woman. I'm proud of you."

It was the most gracious compliment Roger had paid her in a long time. "I love you, Roger," she said simply, turning her face up to be kissed.

Chapter 25

September 1, 1978

Andrew Young and his entourage, along with the British Foreign Secretary, David Owen, arrived in Salisbury aboard a British Royal Air Force VC-10. Landing about nine A.M., they were whisked off in a fleet of cars, Owen's limousine having been brought up from the British Embassy in South Africa, to Miranda House, the former official British residency in Salisbury. From there they were taken to meet with Prime Minister Ian Smith with whom they held a long and inconclusive meeting. The Prime Minister had just been reelected by a more than ninety percent majority of the white voters and given a clear mandate to negotiate a black majority rule government for the new nation, which would be known as Zimbabwe-Rhodesia.

In the United Nations Andrew Young had been lavish in his praise of Robert Mugabe and Joshua Nkomo. He actually referred to moderate black leaders such as the Reverend Ndabaningi Sithole, Senator Chief Chirau and Bishop Abel Muzorewa as "Uncle Toms."

Andrew Young and David Owen listened sullenly as Ian Smith pointed out that he had agreed a year ago to black majority rule but wanted the people of Zimbabwe-Rhodesia to choose their leaders through free elections with no terrorist coercion. When Young realized he would be unable to pressure the Prime Minister into handing the Rhodesian government to the Patriotic Front on a plate, he became uncommunicative, leaving the discussion to Owen and Smith.

Later that day at Miranda House, Young and Owen conducted meetings with Sithole, Chirau and Muzorewa. Throughout the meetings Andrew Young sat in stony-faced silence. He had obviously made up his mind long since that power must be given to the violent revolutionaries who, under the political leadership of Nkomo and his ZAPU faction and Mugabe and his ZANU faction, made up the Patriotic Front. He had no interest in alternatives. When, on the night of September 1, 1977, Andrew Young and David Owen left in their VC-10 along with the press and junior diplomats for Lusaka, little had been accomplished in Rhodesia. But now came the meetings for which Andrew Young had primed himself.

President Kenneth Kaunda, leader of the one-party Marxist state of Zambia, greeted Young and Owen, and the following day Young met with Robert Mugabe and Joshua Nkomo. They immediately addressed themselves to the business at hand, namely how to deliver the nation and people of Rhodesia into the hands of the Soviet-backed Patriotic Front leaders. As Young had said on previous occasions, the Cubans were a stabilizing influence in Africa and he had no problem with Marxist governments.

The American Ambassador to Zambia, Stephen Lowe, provided the venue for the talks between Young and Owen and the Patriotic Front leaders. Until now Young had deferred conversational initiative to Foreign Secretary Owen; but in the more congenial company of the militant radical activists who were actually engaged in the day-to-day prosecution of the war against the Rhodesian population, he warmed to the meeting. There was, of course, a very discernible hostility between Mugabe and Nkomo. They sat on opposite sides of the room with Young and Owen between them.

"You will be interested to hear the non-results of our meetings in Salisbury," Young said with a wan smile. "At this moment I expect that Smith is meeting with Muzorewa whom we talked to yesterday."

"The little bishop," Nkomo said scornfully. "Smith thinks he's talking to the real Zimbabwe when he sees that weak little man? No. It is we who are entitled to take power. It is our revolution that has put the pressure on Smith so that he will have to negotiate with us. It is our Freedom Fighters, and"—he let a condescending glance fall on

Foreign Secretary Owen—"your economic sanctions that will force Smith to give us our country. It is not the bishop, it is not Sithole, who has deserted the armed struggle and run back to Salisbury to lick Smith's boots, it is not that pitiful, ignorant tribal chief, Chirau, who can make Smith come to heel. It is our Freedom Fighters, our attacks on the security forces, our work with the people in the villages to make them realize how they are being oppressed, how they are being kept in slavery by Smith and his government that will prevail. So do not come here asking us to stop the fighting while everybody talks. Talking without the liberation war being waged every day, every night, is useless."

The British Foreign Secretary interjected: "You wouldn't be willing to stand for election on a one-man-one-vote basis?" His defeated tone betrayed the fact that he had only asked the question so that later he could report an effort at conciliation.

The fiery-eyed Mugabe, his arms and hands shaking in agitation, cried out in his high-pitched voice, "We must be given the power. We must be given the government in Salisbury. Our Patriotic Front Freedom Fighters must take the place of the security forces, who must be disbanded. Only then will Zimbabwe have true majority rule government."

"We felt after our meetings with Smith that there was room for compromise—" Dr. Owen began.

Shrilly Mugabe interrupted him. "There is no room for compromise anymore. Smith and all of his people must go."

"I find it difficult to disagree with that last statement," Owen replied woodenly. "However, everything we are trying to achieve can be accomplished much more quickly if somewhere between your position, that total power be given you outright and that your Patriotic Front Freedom Fighters replace the security forces, and Smith's position, which is that a new constitution be drawn up which gives enough protection to the whites so that they will stay—"

"The whites must go!" Mugabe shrieked.

"I understand your position, Mr. Mugabe. But please let me continue," Owen pleaded. "Smith's position is that there should be some safeguards for whites in the form of a meaningful white representation in Parliament. After the constitution has been drawn up, elections will be held and all the black leaders who wish to stand for election to Parliament will go out in the countryside and ask their constituencies to vote for them. The leader of the party that gets into Parliament with the most number of members becomes prime minister."

"You don't have to give us a lesson in British parliamentary procedure," Nkomo cried scathingly. "Once we are given power, once we control the security forces and the police, we will hold elections on a one-man-one-vote basis. But elections cannot come about until we are in power."

"Don't you think it would be destructive to drive the whites out?" Owen asked.

"We want the whites to stay, all right," Nkomo said. "But they will not have any political power. They will be paid as technicians, as they are here in Zambia."

"What about the land owned by the whites now?"

"The lands will be redivided among the people," Mugabe snapped.

"Oh, you may argue that dividing up the land reduces productivity," Nkomo conceded. "That may be true, but in the long run the people will be better off."

The American Ambassador to Zambia and the other delegates sitting in on the meeting remained silent.

"I have often said," Dr. Owen observed, "that the people of Zimbabwe and in fact all the countries that are working toward liberation from colonial-type rule should be happy to accept a lower standard of living if it means being ruled by their own people."

Nkomo, the great elephant of African politics, shifted his huge bulk in the confining chair and produced a long, indecorous, ripping fart. Smiling slyly, he continued. "We fight the war of liberation in Zimbabwe. Either the power will be given to us or we will take it through the barrel of a gun as we are doing now."

"What makes it difficult for us to place you in power, Mr. Nkomo," Owen said, "is the critics in America and Britain who keep reminding their representatives in Congress and Parliament that the Patriotic Front is financed and equipped by the Soviet Union and the Chinese Communists. Although we know better, our opposition shouts that when you take over Rhodesia you will be a one party communist satellite—that the strategic minerals such as chromium and lithium and tungsten will go to the Soviet Union. In other words, the Western world will be giving up to the Communist block one of the most strategically vital countries in Africa and—"

"I will take arms from the devil himself if it's necessary in order to drive the white oppressors out of Zimbabwe!" Nkomo yelled.

"Because the Russians give us arms does not mean that when the war is over, when we are in power, we will show them any special favor," Nkomo continued. "The Russian Ambassador here in Lusaka, Comrade Vassily Solodovnikov, truly wants to help us throw off the yoke of oppression our people have borne since the white man came to Zimbabwe in 1890."

Finally the U.S. Ambassador to Zambia could no longer restrain himself. "It is the policy of the current administration in Washington to bring about majority rule in Zimbabwe-Rhodesia with the Patriotic Front in the dominant position, but the atrocities which are reported in the world press are counter-productive. Nevertheless, you will notice that even when the Woolworth store was bombed in Salisbury and so many people were killed or maimed, neither the United States nor Her Majesty's Government made comment. It was your ZANU party that claimed responsibility for the bombing, Mr. Mugabe, as I recall."

"That's right!" Mugabe confirmed. "That is the only language that Smith and the whites can understand. These reminders that the liberation movement continues and will win in the end can be counted upon to continue, and to become more forceful."

"And, Mr. Ambassador," Nkomo addressed himself to Lowe, "it is Smith's own security forces, the Selous Scouts in particular, who commit these atrocities and then try to blame them on us."

"Yes," Mugabe took up. "I was brought up a Catholic. I have studied at Catholic missions. I would not order my men to murder missionaries."

"I know that, we all know that in this room," Owen remarked. "But with people like that American writer Masefield now living in Salisbury spreading a blanket of subversive propaganda, taking thin facts and twisting them into false conclusions, it becomes increasingly difficult for us at home to continue our support of the Patriotic Front over that of other African leaders in Zimbabwe-Rhodesia."

"Don't you think that extreme terror tactics hurt you internationally?" the U.S. ambassador asked.

"We are not interested in international thinking. We are interested in taking back our country, Zimbabwe," Mugabe shrilled.

"In our talks with Smith yesterday," Dr. Owen began reasonably, "he indicated that he would be willing to meet with both of you along with other internal African leaders and try to reach some compromise."

Mugabe's voice reached a strident soprano. "We will sit down with Smith, we will even sit down with the funny little bishop, provided it is first agreed that the Patriotic Front Freedom Fighters will replace the security forces in Zimbabwe and that we will be the controlling factor in the new government!"

"Smith was willing to go into the conference with no preconditions," Owen replied.

Finally Ambassador Young entered the debate. "May I suggest that Joshua, Robert and I discuss this matter among just we three brothers?"

Ambassador Lowe and the Foreign Secretary looked at each other in surprise. Although Owen, the equivalent of the Secretary of State in the United States, outranked Young in the matter of African affairs, everybody deferred to the American black who carried the direct mandate of President Carter. The meeting having taken on a suddenly more informal note, Ambassador Lowe merely agreed. "Of course, Andy. We'll wait for you here."

Mugabe, Nkomo and Young stood up and Young led the way out of the embassy conference room down a hall to a smaller office where he sat behind a desk whose only adornment was an archaic telephone. He gestured to the armchairs on either side of his desk and the guerrilla leaders took seats. At last Young felt he could speak freely. "Talking with all those white diplomats back there is going to get us nowhere, right?"

Mugabe and Nkomo chorused, "Right!"

"Very well. You know I support your position. But I have to be careful. I am the target of more abuse than any member of the President's immediate political family. Everything said in that meeting will be reported back to Washington and eventually will appear in the press. You, the true revolutionaries, the men with the guns, the men who have been killing the whites and their sellouts, to you the power will eventually go. But, we have to be careful. It is true that the reported atrocities attributed to you, and those for which you have taken credit, make my job in the United States and the U.N. more difficult. Every day our side is losing support among congressmen and senators—"

Young held up a restraining hand. "No, don't interrupt me. If I'm going to hand you power, without going through elections which you cannot win except with guns, you will play the game with me."

He fixed the two fiery-eyed Africans with a commanding stare. "Every time I'm away from New York and Washington for more than a week the President starts to waver under congressional pressure on the subject of Rhodesia. It is only when I go back there, sit with him, talk to him as I'm talking to you now that I bring him back to our side.

"'The true revolutionaries will prevail,' I tell him. 'And we had better be on their side.' Now here is what I want you to do. In the first place, accept a meeting. Go to it. You don't have to change your stand, only seem to be open-minded. Do you understand me?"

Mugabe and Nkomo nodded.

"Good." The U.S. Ambassador to the UN leaned forward intently. "Senator Chief Chirau, who seems to be the most credible of the African moderate leaders, has applied to come to the United States the middle of the month. He discussed this with me just yesterday. I assured him that at the United Nations I would do everything I could to be of assistance to him. However, this morning I sent a cable to Richard Moose, Assistant Secretary of African Affairs at the State Department in Washington, ordering him to deny Chirau entrance to the United States. This may be difficult since he has already given Chirau verbal approval. However, what has been done can be undone."

Young focused his attention on Nkomo. "Joshua, you make application here to Ambassador Lowe for a visit to the United States. I will see to it that you and you alone of all the African leaders involved in the Zimbabwe question speak before the United Nations. Muzorewa asked me yesterday if he could speak before the United Nations, and Sithole, who plans to come to the United States later this year, has asked to address the Security Council. I may find it difficult to block their visits since they've been to the United States so many times before, but I can certainly keep them from speaking in the United Nations."

"What about me, as leader of ZANU?" Mugabe asked querulously.

"Joshua can speak for the Patriotic Front. But I have in mind something else for both of you. Nobody knows that I have convinced President Carter to come to Africa. He will visit Nigeria among other countries. When he gets to Nigeria I will arrange for the two of you to have a secret meeting with him. You Robert, you Joshua, myself and the President of the United States. You'll be the first Zimbabwe leaders that he talks to and the only ones. The bishop, Chief Chirau and Sithole all asked me to arrange talks with the President. I told them he only sees heads of state. In Washington that is true. But in Nigeria—that's another matter."

"The President of America will see us?" Nkomo asked incredulously.

"I elected the President of the United States and I own him," Young snapped. "He will do exactly what I ask of him. We will put you in power. But you've got to help me to help you. One way to help would be to stop bombing department stores in Salisbury. America is a racist country, never forget it. My own Freedom Fighters in the South went through the same struggle you are going through now. Secretly every white American sympathizes with the Smith regime."

Young paused, fixing the two Marxist leaders with a stare of mesmeric intensity. Then he went on. "It is easy for propagandists such as Roger Masefield, the writer now living in Salisbury, to exploit atrocities and make you look like killers and murderers. A cable came in this morning from Washington expressing concern over the propaganda this writer has generated in America in the last few days. Throughout the nation there are rich racists fighting what I am trying to do, even trying to get me fired."

The ambassador laughed mirthlessly. "You don't have to worry about that and neither do I. I have this job or any other job in the United States government I want so long as Jimmy Carter is President."

"What will I do about expenses coming to New York?" Nkomo asked.

"I'll see that the United Nations or the U.S. Mission takes care of all your costs including airfare."

"My people have tried to kill Masefield but we have been unable to get near enough to him," Mugabe complained. "Since you are so close to the President, couldn't you arrange to have him neutralized?"

"It is very difficult to restrain the opposition in the United States," Young replied patiently.

"It is very difficult to get Freedom Fighters into Salisbury," Mugabe shot back. "However, we have Cuban and Russian and East

German advisors. Perhaps I could send a team of them into Salisbury to get him. We know where he lives; his house is always watched by our people."

"Assassinations tend to backfire," Young observed. "They create martyrs and every word the martyr ever said becomes gospel. Forget Masefield. He'll be taken care of in another way that will not make him an oracle. Now for a more important matter. I was given an intelligence briefing on the plane between Salisbury and Lusaka. The Rhodesian Air Force is planning a major strike into Zambia against your nationalist camps up here. I was also told that Selous Scouts are contemplating new cross-border operations against your staging areas. I can't give you anything more specific than that—yet."

"I'll tell President Kaunda to be alert," Nkomo cried excitedly.

"I suggest we go back now and join the diplomats. I take it we're all in agreement that you have decided to attend an all-parties conference with no preconditions."

"That's right," Nkomo confirmed.

"Good, then this diplomatic mission to Lusaka has been a success. When the British proposals for a settlement are published, the Patriotic Front will attend the meetings to discuss them."

"We will come," Mugabe said dourly. "But we come because you tell us to. Because you tell us that the only way you can give us the power in Zimbabwe is if we play the game, as you put it."

"You don't have to worry on that score. And if anything happens to me, my assistant ambassador will take over my post and continue our work." Ambassador Young stood up and his two guests followed his example.

"Play the game, play the game," Nkomo echoed wonderingly as they walked into the hall to join the other diplomats in the embassy conference room. "We are not game players. We kill the whites and sellouts."

Chapter 26

The commanding officer of Grey's Scouts, Major John Hingham, was examining the large map of Rhodesia in his Operations Room. With the point of a pencil Major Mike Wyatt tapped the large Lupane Tribal Trust Land region. This was Matabeleland north, home of the Ndebeli tribesmen, descendants of the Zulus and reputedly the best fighting men in Rhodesia. Matabeleland was Joshua Nkomo's home base in Rhodesia and provided him with some of his best guerrillas.

Terrorist incidents were climbing in the Lupane Tribal Trust Land and it was here that a German woman missionary doctor had been murdered by terrorists while she was operating on a local tribesman. The Nkomo terrorists had rampaged through the maternity ward, bayoneting the "sellout" women in their beds. One pregnant woman ran from the maternity ward and delivered her baby safely in the bush outside the mission.

Orders finally came down from ComOps for Grey's Scouts to send a squadron into Lupane to halt the terrorist attacks.

"If they weren't so candy ass in Salisbury, John," Mike said to his commander, "we could do a lot more to discourage the terrs. Why don't you let me burn down every house in every kraal that gives food and information to them? They'd get the idea. That's what we did in Vietnam. Any village harboring the Cong we destroyed. Let one shot come out of a village at us and we mortared it. We weren't supposed to but when you saw a few of your buddies dead it wasn't hard to rationalize bending the rules."

"My dear Yank, we just don't do that sort of thing over here."

"You better damn soon get on with that sort of thing. Those gooks don't understand anything else."

As Mike Wyatt was discussing strategy for tracking down and killing terrorists in Lupane, his telephone rang. He picked it up.

A woman's voice on the other end said, "Sir, it's Major Richard Banner, the PRO from Army. He says it's urgent."

Mike looked at his commander darkly. "Army Public Relations calling me. You know what that means? Some VIP or visiting fireman wants to get a good look a Inkomo Barracks and our horses. I've got to get out with the squadron to Lupane, not spend the day squiring idiots around showing them piles of horseshit!"

The Rhodesian commander smiled indulgently. His American number two was refreshingly outspoken.

"OK, put him through," Mike said grudgingly, picking up a ballpoint pen and a pad.

Over the phone Mike heard the familiar voice of the Army PRO. "Mike, this is Dick Banner."

"OK, Dick, what do you want?"

"A journalist, Jeff Brigham, has been approved by ComOps. He's at Roger Masefield's place and I want you to take him to Lupane and show him how you operate."

"Dick," Mike bleated, "that guy's bad news. You may have gotten all the good reports in the world on him but I'm an American and I know a bad American when I see one. He's it. We're going to be into some sensitive stuff in Lupane; the last thing I need is a newspaper man with me."

"Don't worry, Mike. He's been cleared and HQ is happy with him. Send a driver to town, you can pick him up at the American Embassy. Cheers!"

Mike heard the click and hung up in disgust. He turned to the Grey's Scouts commander who shrugged back at him. "I don't even know if he can ride a horse," Mike growled. "He claims he's pretty good, but we'll find out in the bush. I'll take Corporal Mandell and we'll go get him."

At noontime Mike Wyatt, sitting beside Corporal Mandell, who was driving the Grey's Scouts Land Rover, pulled up in front of Masefield's house. Roger had a sheaf of news clippings spread out on the dining room table as Mike walked in.

He looked up exultantly as the two men entered. "Look at the stuff that's coming in. All over the world they carried stories about the Crippled Eagles. You should see the mail we're getting." He handed Mike a photograph from the front page of an American newspaper. "This was taken by Jeff Brigham here." He motioned toward the diminutive figure beside him. "It was carried everywhere, showing Jocelyn and me standing in front of the American flag with the Embassy in the background."

"I'll get some good shots of Grey's Scouts in action for you, Mike," Brigham promised.

That's what I'm afraid of, Mike thought to himself, but he said, "How did you manage to get cleared to go out with us?"

"I just applied," Jeff replied innocently. Roger caught Mike's eye and nodded his head toward the door. Mike followed him out and to the back of the house.

"How about a cold beer?" Roger invited.

"Why not," Mike accepted as Roger pulled two bottles of beer from the small icebox below the bar. He opened them and handed one to Mike.

Then, leaning across the bar, Roger said, "I'll tell you how he got cleared. He got a job for General St. John's girl friend. She started yesterday. Jeff didn't have clearance to hire her but he paid her one week's salary out of his own pocket until authorization comes through. He wasn't getting any ComOps clearance until Veronica was hired," Roger laughed. "I may be wrong, Mike, but to tell you the truth I've come to think he's OK. Of course, I keep going back to the Vietnam War when his boss, Hans Foss, and I were out in the boonies chasing Green Berets who were chasing Viet Cong. I can't believe Hans would have anybody working for him that wasn't reliable."

"Well, there's nothing I can do about it anyway," Mike sighed. He took a long gulp of beer.

"Can I give you some lunch before you leave?"

Mike shook his head. "No, let me get this dickhead out of here and we'll be on our way to Lupane."

"How long are you going to be out there?"

241

"I guess I'll be there three weeks. I'll see you when I get back."

"I wouldn't mind joining you myself," Roger said.

"Why don't you come with us? You've got clearance, and maybe you could neutralize the little bastard. I'm going to tell him I can't detach any of my people to wet-nurse him while he's with us. If the army wants him to take combat pictures, he'll damn well have to pull his own weight. I can't see how the little creep is going to get those skinny shanks of his across the back of one of our horses and keep up with a call sign at a canter. I suppose he could always wiggle his mustache and go airborne." Mike Wyatt knocked back the rest of his beer and then walked back to collect his charge.

"OK Brigham, next stop Bulawayo. I've got kit for you in the back of the Land Rover." Eagerly the photographer, equipment bags hanging from both shoulders, followed Mike Wyatt and Ned Mandell out of the Embassy and across the lawn to the waiting vehicle. Wyatt put Brigham in the back and sat up front beside Mandell.

Wyatt's concern about the WP photographer had infected Roger and made him recall his earliest distrust of the man. Wyatt had been a combat commander in three wars and had risen to the rank of lieutenant colonel before he retired from the U.S. Army after two long tours in Vietnam. He was famous for the accuracy of his instincts, his hunches. Mike's intuition had kept him and the men who served under him alive on many occasions. Hans Foss could be wrong about Brigham. And it was, after all, sensationalism that made the big wire service breaks around the world.

He knocked on the door to the Hermitage. It was locked and some moments went by before Alvin Glenlord opened up. Roger went in and guessed that Al and Beryl were in the midst of some deep discussion. "Sorry to disturb you but there's something bothering me I'd like to talk over with you two," Roger said.

"What is it, Roger?" Beryl asked solicitously.

"This Jeff Brigham. I know we got a telex clearing him but I wonder how good the information was. Who exactly was it that ran the check on him for us?"

"Bucky Simon sent the telex," Glenlord replied.

"You have a guy sending telexes too. Are you sure it wasn't him?" Roger asked.

"Simon is your man, Roger. If you don't trust him, don't come to me with your doubts. Why don't you go back to the States and get your Washington act together?" Alvin Glenlord was getting more surly every day.

"Why do you ask now?" Beryl was curious.

"Brigham just left with Mike Wyatt to go out into the bush with Grey's Scouts. Ashley St. John cleared it for him but Mike is damned worried. He dislikes journalists in general and Jeff Brigham in particular."

"He's gone out with Mike, eh?" Glenlord's self-satisfied grin and sudden interest further alerted Roger. "Well, I hope Jeff and the WP appreciate what you've done for them if he comes back with a good picture story."

"What do you mean?" Roger asked.

"If it wasn't for you, Jeff never would have met Mike and the other Crippled Eagles. You were the one who got him to Ashley St. John. It all happened here at your house." Glenlord was driving home a point whose truth Roger had to recognize. It was a point that would be made abundantly clear to such as M.M. De Vries if anything went wrong on Brigham's trip.

Roger stood up. "I understand what you're saying, Al."

"Cup of coffee?" Beryl invited, obviously hoping he would refuse. He did. Leaving the plotters' inner sanctum, he walked to the teletype room.

"Get out the telexes for the month," he told Mona, the secretary Beryl had hired.

"Did Mrs. Stoffel ask for them?"

"No, I want them, Mona."

"I'd better ask Mrs. Stoffel." Mona was a short, plump young lady who face seemed permanently on the verge of breaking out. She had one cardinal virtue—loyalty. To Beryl and Al.

Roger strode to the file cabinet and tried to pull open the telex drawer. It was locked. He turned. "Give me the key to the filing cabinet, Mona."

Mona sprang from her desk and fled from the office. In moments she came back with Al. "Now what's going on, Roger? What do you want?" He was making no attempt to conceal his annoyance with the man who was supposed to be his boss.

"I want to look at my telex file. Since when do we keep it locked away from me?"

"Security has been pretty damn lax around here," Al scolded. "Why do you want to look at the telexes?"

"I want to analyze them for a month. Perhaps I'm missing something when I'm reading the traffic."

Al hesitated, then nodded at Mona and handed her the key. She unlocked the cabinet and pulled the telex file out. "Do you want to keep the key until we lock it, Mr. Glenlord?" she asked.

He started to reach for it. "Hold it," Roger barked. "I'd like to keep the key. After all, in theory I'm supposed to be the commanding officer around here."

Glenlord held his hand out for the key another couple of seconds, then withdrew it. No need for a confrontation yet. "Whatever you want, Roger. If you can't understand something, call me and I'll try to explain."

Roger pulled the telex file marked August and took it back upstairs to his office. Until late in the afternoon he studied the cables and the frequently obscure messages from Lorraine to Al. He reflected on Glenlord's obturated behavior, which had become increasingly pronounced over the past two months, and actually obstructionist in the past two weeks. Roger had never been paranoid but he couldn't help feeling that all he was trying to accomplish in Rhodesia was coming increasingly under threat from Alvin Glenlord.

The drive from Salisbury to Bulawayo was a long one and by the time the Grey's Scouts Land Rover reached the Holiday Inn just outside the city, it was dark.

As Mike swung himself out of the vehicle, pack over his back, he turned to Mandell. "Give our guest VIP treatment, Corporal. Get him drunk, get him laid, whatever. I don't want Army on my ass. He seems to be real cozy with them," Mike glanced at Brigham sitting in the back of the vehicle. "And for God's sake, don't let him blow his foot off with the Uzi."

"Don't worry, sir. He'll be fucked flat come tomorrow," Mandell laughed, shifted gears and screeched off.

The pretty, buxom, blonde Rhodesian Mike had telephoned from Salisbury before leaving was waiting for him in the bar. He went up to Marilyn and kissed her. "Mike," she cried. "I've been waiting almost an hour."

"We had to pick up some excess baggage on the way out of Salisbury and that delayed us a little," Mike said.

"Where's your horse, cowboy?"

Mike laughed. "The horses are waiting for us in Lupane. We don't go from Salisbury to Bulawayo on horseback. Are you ready for some dinner?"

"Anything you say, Mike."

Mike enjoyed a good dinner and good night's lack of sleep with Marilyn. The next morning at seven o'clock Corporal Mandell arrived. Slumped in the back seat was a bleary-eyed Jeff Brigham, his Fu Manchu mustache at half-mast, his hound-dog eyes peering groggily ahead through thick glasses.

"He's puked twice on the way over," Ned Mandell announced triumphantly.

"Marvelous. Just magnificent." Mike settled into his seat for the long ride north to Lupane. About forty kilometers outside Bulawayo a BSAP roadblock stopped them. They identified themselves and a constable warned Mike that there had been four terrorist incidents the previous night. Corporal Mandell started up the Land Rover again.

Mike turned to the limp form in the back seat. "From here on we're in terr country," Mike yelled. He tapped the Uzi submachine gun which he'd issued to Brigham. "If we get zapped, for shit's sake don't shoot through the cab. Try to get the thing pointing at the side of the road. OK?"

Jeff Brigham shook his head and began trying to focus his eyes on the scrub brush to either side of the road. Despite the danger, he dozed most of the trip, but occasionally he came away and waxed talkative. He asked Mike his opinion on the political situation in the country now that Ian Smith was negotiating with black leaders to form a new government.

Bluffly Mike replied, "I'm a professional soldier. We go to great lengths to avoid getting involved in politics." He gave Brigham a cool stare. "Or with people involved in politics."

Just under two hours out of Bulawayo they arrived at the mission of Lupane and drove on to a collection of wooden shacks beyond which were tethered two dozen or so horses. After they'd climbed out of the Land Rover Mike took Corporal Mandell aside. "Stick with this little fart and don't let him out of your sight. Show him anything he wants to see but don't let him in the Operations Room or around the situation map."

"Roger, sir." Corporal Mandell double-timed after Brigham who was headed for the horses milling around a temporary paddock next to the headquarters' shack. Mike Wyatt strode into One Squadron's Operations Room and glanced at the acetate overlay on the situation map. All suspected terrorist nests were marked with red circles. Three Troop of One Squadron was at the town of Sipepa about sixty kilometers to the southeast. Its nineteen-year-old troop commander, Lieutenant Walter Gore, was waiting in the Situation Room for his squadron commander.

Mike was very fond of young Gore who was tall and thin with hair like bleached straw. He had taken him on patrols along the Botswana border for several months, helping him get used to horse operations. And now, youthful though Gore was and inexperienced in the ways of the world, Mike considered him to be one of his best troop commanders. He was tough, confident and popular with his men. Most important, Mike had never known him to avoid a fight.

"Walter, I'm sending this journalist that's been shoved onto us by Army and ComOps, Jeff Brigham, out with you. I can tell you I don't like it. I think he'll screw us if he can. Don't risk anybody by letting them wet-nurse him," Mike said emphatically. "If he can't keep up on patrol, make him wait back at your CP. Check?"

"Dead right, I'll take care of him. Not to worry, sir."

Mike couldn't explain it to himself but he did worry about Walter Gore taking the photographer out with him. Somehow he felt that the young Rhodesian officer might not be able to cope with the ambitious and slippery photographer.

Mike Wyatt went outside, found Brigham, brought him back into headquarters and introduced him to Walter Gore.

"OK, Jeff, you'll ride in the Land Rover with Lieutenant Gore up to Sipepa. You'll be right in the middle of a lot of terr activity. I'll see you in about ten days. Keep your head down."

Chapter 27

Roger Masefield was worried. The growing rift between himself on one side and Alvin Glenlord and Beryl Stoffel on the other was disturbing. It was something he sensed rather than was able to substantiate. The very fact that Glenlord seemed so pleased about Jeff Brigham being out in the field with Mike Wyatt's One Squadron made him uneasy. He had long since come to the conclusion that his interests and those of Alvin Glenlord were no longer joined. Alvin had been hard put to conceal his displeasure over the enormous amount of worldwide publicity Roger had received from the ceremony at the Embassy. Just why Al should be annoyed was something Roger couldn't understand. And there had been the picture of Roger and Jocelyn in *Time* magazine with a story about them both that had triggered an inexplicable rage in Glenlord.

For whatever reasons, Alvin Glenlord was seeking to compromise him; and with his first book on Rhodesia virtually completed, he had more time in which to notice the fact. Jocelyn too sensed the restlessness and muzzled hostility of both Glenlord and Beryl Stoffel. Roger was seriously considering taking both Beryl and Alvin off the payroll and reducing the Embassy to a mere home.

The fact that he had signed a contract with Beryl and Al to pay them five thousand dollars a month to cover salaries, expenses and mortgage payments on the house disturbed him more and more. One question that had journalists and in fact all visitors to the Embassy puzzled was where the financing was coming from.

Roger had signed the contract because Alvin and Beryl had shown him a contract they had with a private Salisbury group which specialized in furthering worldwide Rhodesian interests and sanctions busting. The contract called for matching funds in Rhodesia for the money Roger was to put up stateside. For every five thousand dollars he put into their U.S. publicity operation, the group in Salisbury put up another five thousand dollars in Rhodesian currency to maintain the Embassy. On top of that there was the extra thousand a month he gave Glenlord to pass on to his wife Lorraine so she would ignore the affair between her husband and the haughty beauty, Beryl Stoffel, being conducted eight thousand miles away.

The contract, Alvin Glenlord had assured him, although it had a three-year life, could be broken at any time Roger wanted to break it, without penalty. But the contract was necessary in order to get the matching funds.

The more Roger thought about Jeff Brigham being out in the bush with Mike Wyatt, the more concerned he became. He had invested in a phone call to the United States and found out from Bucky Simon that it was a friend of Alvin Glenlord's who had passed him the information that Brigham was reliable. Bucky himself had made no check on it.

Much as he disliked leaving Jocelyn alone in the Embassy, Roger decided to visit Mike at One Squadron Headquarters in Lupane. Impulsively, he strode out of his own office on the second floor and found Jocelyn on the rear patio reading in the sun. Already sensitive to the vibrations of discord at the Embassy, she was upset at the news.

"I wish you wouldn't go and leave me alone here, Roger," she pleaded.

"I'm afraid I have to. You could always stay at Beryl's house while I'm away if you don't like it here."

"No!" she replied decisively. "I'll stay here. Just don't be away too long."

"No longer than I have to," Roger promised.

That afternoon he drove out to Inkomo and found Major John Hingham. He made arrangements with the Grey's Scouts commander to get a ride on the BSAP aircraft that ferried the Scouts around the country.

Mike Wyatt was flabbergasted to see Roger Masefield walk into his bush headquarters at Lupane. He was transferring information from the latest sitrep to the acetate overlay when he heard Roger's voice behind him ask, "Need another gun around here?"

"For chrissake, Roger, where in hell did you come from? This isn't just the bush, this is deep bush. We're averaging six terr contacts a day."

"Anything going on that would be interesting in the book?"

"We seem to be having a whole raft of bus robberies here in the Lupane TTL. The cops should be handling it but the poor buggers have damn little manpower to work with, so the monkey is on my back."

"What are you doing about them?"

"I posted some of my African troopers on the buses. So far they haven't killed any of the terrs who were pulling these holdups. It didn't take me long to find out I'm too old to ride on top of a goddamn African bus carrying a shotgun and trying to find some crazy Kaffir playing Jesse James."

"Where's our favorite newspaperman?"

"I haven't seen him in a week, thank God. He's out galloping around with Three Troop."

"Have you any objections if I go out and see what he's doing?"

"No, I wish you would. I can't get over the feeling that the little bugger is big trouble."

"I think you've got trouble too, Mike. That's why I came out here. How do I get to where he is?"

"It's too late to go out today. First light I'll have someone drive you out there. I'll send a signal to Lieutenant Gore that you're coming."

"Tell him not to tell Brigham."

That evening Mike Wyatt had a batman fix a stretcher for Roger and they talked about home, the United Nations, and what the United States was doing to Rhodesia, before finally turning in.

At first light Mike Wyatt commandeered a Land Rover, a driver and a machine gunner and sent Roger out into the bush. The drive through obscure trails and dirt roads took about two and a half hours and by ten o'clock they had reached their destination.

Lieutenant Gore was waiting for Roger at his command post which consisted of a canvas shelter, a cot and a radio. Roger had met Gore once or twice before when he visited the headquarters of Grey's Scouts in Inkomo, their home base. "How does it feel to have not one but two Yank journalists out here?"

"Well, sir, it may serve to relieve the boredom."

"I thought you were having contacts," Roger said.

"A few. You picked a day when at least something is happening. We got word that a terrorist suspect, a schoolteacher named Nehondo has revisited his old school about two miles from here. Probably he's trying to recruit students to become terrs. I sent out a call sign under Sergeant Milton to look for him."

"I suppose Brigham is with them, right?"

"Right, sir. I thought I'd wait for you, and now that you're here we'll see if they found Nehondo. The BSAP have him number one on their list of terr suspects in the area."

Roger mounted the horse that had been saddled for him and he and Lieutenant Gore rode for two miles through the bush until they came into a large clearing. There was an L-shaped schoolhouse and a typical African store to one side of it. For once in his life, Roger thought, he had arrived on the scene at the propitious moment.

As he and Gore silently watched, sitting on their mounts, four Grey's Scouts troopers dragged an African out of the schoolhouse and into the schoolyard. The African was protesting, struggling and kicking at his captors.

"That's Nehondo, I take it," Roger said.

"I hope so," Gore replied. "I've never seen him. I hope it isn't some innocent schoolmaster who belongs here."

"I don't think an innocent schoolmaster would be giving them that much trouble," Roger observed.

"Yes, sir, I agree with you. And there we have Mr. Brigham in action," the lieutenant commented dryly.

Brigham was snapping pictures as the Grey's Scouts dragged the suspect to the flagpole, pushed him to the ground, tied his wrists together at the base of the flagpole and then tied his legs together.

With the suspect thus restrained, his shirt almost torn off his back, his bare chest heaving, Brigham strode over to him, drew back his booted foot and kicked him in the head several times until his cries subsided.

"He gets right into the spirit of things, doesn't he?" the lieutenant commented acidly.

"Oh he's a pistol all right, I can see that," Roger agreed.

"At least they can't say *my* men abused the suspect."

A Grey's Scout who had been watching the proceedings while finishing off a bottle of Castle beer ambled up to Brigham who was standing over the terrorist.

Brigham looked from the African on the ground to the trooper, then snatched the latter's empty beer bottle. He poured the last few drops out on the ground, took a large Zippo lighter from his pocket and flicked it into a flame which he held underneath the bottle.

When the bottom was well seared, Brigham plunged it against the bare chest of the African, holding it there as the victim shrieked and writhed.

"We learn something from you Americans every day," the lieutenant remarked impassively.

"Are you going to let him get away with it?" Roger asked.

"I wouldn't let one of my men do it. I don't know whether I have any authority over a Yank civilian," the youthful officer replied. Roger dismounted and handing the reins of his horse to the lieutenant, went across the schoolyard to Brigham. The little photographer looked up, his eyes alight, a freakish, twisted smile on his face.

"You're supposed to be a noncombatant, Jeff," Roger reminded him. He looked down at the red second-degree burns on the suspect's chest. "Was that necessary?"

Brigham looked about in surprise as though he had just become aware of Roger's presence. "What are you doing here?"

"Looking for a story, just like you, and it seems I found it."

A tall Rhodesian sergeant walked up. "Welcome to Sipepa, Mr. Masefield."

"I see you have an interrogator along with you," Roger remarked disgustedly.

"Oh, Mr. Brigham? You should have seen him lay a bat on the arse of the suspect we picked up yesterday. Had him telling us everything we wanted to know in about one minute. That's how we knew that Nehondo here was coming in last night."

"Has he been getting many photographs?" Roger asked, as though Brigham were not standing right next to him.

"Oh, right sir, he's been snapping that shutter for a whole week now. You'd think he'd run out of film."

"I wish I had a picture of his performance just now," Roger said.

"Well, Mr. Brigham's got plenty of pictures. Two days ago,when nothing had been happening, he got our Kaffir cook to pose with a rope around his neck. He said he'd send him the pictures when they came out. He had a helluva time stopping the houtie from laughing long enough to get the picture. And then he got one of me with my bat. After that he got a really funny one. We were all doing our exercises one morning and he got Corporal Titche to pull out his handgun and point it at our black troopers doing their push-ups. Fierce picture that one." The sergeant laughed.

Roger looked at him incredulously. Then he turned to Brigham. "What were all those pictures about, Jeff?"

"Oh, nothing much was happening so I thought I'd shoot something that might be useful some day."

Roger turned to Sergeant Milton. "Sergeant, do yourself and Major Wyatt a big favor. Don't let this man fake any more photographs which might be used against you, if you know what I mean."

"I'm not sure I do know what you mean, sir," the sergeant said, perplexed.

"Aside from the fact the little bastard is a sadist and enjoying himself, he just may be planning to get himself some kind of a prize for war pictures in Africa. Let's go back to your CP. I want to get Major Wyatt on the radio." By noontime they were back at the command post and Lieutenant Gore sent a radio signal to One Squadron Headquarters in Lupane that Masefield was on his way back by Land Rover.

Late that afternoon Roger explained to Mike Wyatt that his worst fears had been realized. "Can't you call him in?" Roger asked.

"I got strict orders from ComOps to give this photographer everything he wants, within reason."

"I would advise you to figure some way to neutralize him," Roger said.

"What am I going to do?"

A hard-bitten French sergeant, a veteran of the Foreign Legion and French paratroopers, had a suggestion. "Why you do not let me take him on a patrol, Major? That will solve all our problems."

"One dead WP journalist who was tight with General St. John would give me more problems than I've ever had," Mike said hastily.

"Oh, I don't know," Roger argued. "He'd get his name up on the Overseas Press Club honor roll of reporters killed in action. That's quite a distinction." When he saw that Mike Wyatt was having second thoughts, he laughed and shook his head. "I was just kidding, Mike. But watch him. If there's any way you can get his film I think that would be a good idea."

"And have General St. John all over my ass? He never lets me forget I'm a major in this army on the sufferance of the general staff. I like it here," Wyatt continued. "I found a home in Rhodesia. I don't want to muck it up by mistreating a friend of the general's."

"If you can flag down a passing airplane and get me back to Salisbury, I'll see what I can do from that end," Roger said.

"Sorry to see you go, Roger," Mike said, "but I guess you're right. I'll take you down to the airstrip. There's always some traffic between here and Salisbury."

Roger and Mike Wyatt sat in the Land Rover drinking beer for an hour before a light plane came through and picked Roger up.

"I'll do the best I can to head off some media disaster, Mike. Take it easy. A couple of grizzled old guys like us have to stick together."

Chapter 28

August 1978

The training of a Selous Scout was the most arduous military training in the world. Selous Scouts were all volunteers and prospective members were well aware of the rigors they would have to undergo to gain acceptance into Rhodesia's most effective counterinsurgency unit. The Selous Scouts were totally integrated, with blacks and whites fighting side-by-side under the most hazardous conditions imaginable. They were the best and they had to be. The guerrilla terrorists of Robert Mugabe and Joshua Nkomo hated the Selous Scouts more than any other branch of the Rhodesian Security Forces, and whenever a terrorist leader found it inexpedient to take credit for a massacre or an atrocity, he blamed the Scouts.

On Saturday, August 6, 1977, when the Woolworth store in Salisbury was bombed, Nkomo was unable to claim credit for the deed since he was in the Caribbean at the time negotiating with Castro for arms and troops. However, he blamed the bombing on the Selous Scouts rather than let his Marxist arch rival Mugabe claim responsibility for what was one of the most brutal acts of urban insurgency committed in Rhodesia up to that time. Hundreds of innocent shoppers were killed or wounded in the attack.

Because of the intense respect the black and white members of the Selous Scouts had for each other, this unit was able to accomplish missions other units would not even attempt.

The bush training camp for the Scouts, with the curious name of Wafa Wafa, was in the country's largest game preserve on the shore of Lake Kariba, the second largest man-made lake in the world. It is surrounded by dense undergrowth where temperatures can rise to over 110 degrees Fahrenheit in the summer months of December, January and February and frequently sink to below freezing in the winter months of July and August.

There was no shortage of volunteers for a place in the Selous Scouts. Named after Frederick Selous, a famous hunter and scout who explored Rhodesia in the 1890s, it had become a legend in less than four years. The Selous Scouts were as much at home in the steaming heat of the Zambezi Valley or in the mountains of the Eastern Highlands as in their base camp, André Rabie Barracks, twenty miles from Salisbury. Frequently, when they were given an opportunity to take a furlough, the men opted to remain in the bush to fight terrorists. They had learned to exist in the bush almost indefinitely and were known to follow groups of terrorists for weeks, living off the land and pursuing tracks which to anyone else would be invisible.

As many as 400 trained soldiers from the Rhodesian Security Forces were screened in any given month in order to select 100 candidates suitable for the Selous training course. Of these 100, only one-sixth survived the first six weeks of bush training.

The selection course that finished at the time Captains Mack Hudson and Colin Adderley, and Sergeants Jacques LeClair and Horst Houk presented themselves for their trial by torture had begun with 126 volunteers. It ended with only 15.

Mack and his three companions arrived at the Selous Scouts training base on Lake Kariba two days before their course would begin. Officers and enlisted men were treated alike, and slept in the same barracks with the Africans.

"Damned if this is like anything in the British Army I ever saw," Adderley commented sourly.

"Ja ja," Houk echoed.

"But, *mon dieu*, we are right in with the Africans," LeClair protested. "In the Foreign Legion, in every operation I ever knew about in Africa, white men were separated from the Africans."

"We asked for it," Mack responded sharply. "Now let's get on with it!" He studied the list that had been appended to his orders. Looking down the names, it was apparent that of the 115 men starting the course, only 28 were white. "I have a hunch we'll be calling these houtes *brother* for real, and damn fast," Mack exclaimed. The African names were indecipherable to him although he resolved to try and remember as many as possible. They would be out in the bush together for six weeks and survival might well depend on good white-black relations.

As he ran his eye down the list he came to the name, Luthu, Sergeant Charles, a volunteer from the first battalion of the RAR. To be a sergeant in the RAR a man would be about thirty, Mack knew. The name Luthu somehow struck a responsive chord. Who was this Luthu? he asked himself. Suddenly he remembered—the assistant district commissioner whom his SAS stick had saved from having to rape the headman's daughter before being killed himself. Jeremiah Luthu. He'd mentioned that his brother was in the RAR.

Mack knew he would need every friend he could make in this situation. Obviously the training officers and sergeants would not be their friends during this six-week period since it was their job to eliminate everybody they could. He resolved that before the training exercise started he would find this Charles Luthu and introduce himself. Maybe his brother had already told him about the American who saved his life.

Suddenly the door to the mixed barracks was thrown open. A full-bearded sergeant major, a plume in his campaign hat and a swagger stick under his right arm, stomped in. At the top of his voice he bellowed, "Attention! I am Sergeant Major Princeloo, command sergeant major of Selous Scouts," he glared around. "You will all come to hate me in the coming weeks. That's as it should be. It is my duty to see that only the best get through this selection. You will think you are in hell and I'm the devil. Well, gentlemen, let me assure you I am a devil and this selection course is certainly going to be hell on earth for you. You have the rest of the weekend to get acquainted with each other.

"Monday morning at 0400 hours we will start the course off with a twenty-mile run. And I'm not talking about an RLI trot around those fields at Cranbourne Barracks. This is a run through the bush. Along half-cleared paths through the jungle. My advice to you is don't try to get in shape by tomorrow. If you're not fit now, it's too late and you might just as well leave before you waste our time here.

"Beginning Monday morning you will need every ounce of energy you can store up. Understand?"

"Understood, Sergeant Major!" Mack Hudson came back lustily.

Princeloo thwacked his thigh with his swagger stick and marched down the aisle between the double-decker bunks to where Mack Hudson was standing at attention. With the tip of the stick he probed at the three pips on one of Hudson's shoulders. "Oh, you're Captain Hudson, the Yank."

"Correct, Sergeant Major."

"I expect you think you're going to get off easy because you're a captain."

"I have been thoroughly disabused of that notion, Sergeant Major," Mack replied steadily.

"You're the Vietnam ace. I've heard about you over at SAS."

"And I've heard about you, Sergeant Major," Mack shot back.

"I don't know what you Yanks think you're doing over here. You lost your war in Vietnam; now you're coming over here to make us lose ours."

"I didn't come here to lose," Mack said, staring the Sergeant Major in the eye.

"I don't know what in hell the bloody recruiting department thinks they're doing bringing Yanks into the Rhodesian Army. And I certainly don't know what the colonel is thinking about bringing you people into Selous Scouts."

"Because every American has been a failure?"

For an instant the eyes of the sergeant major flickered and he looked away. Then he returned his steady gaze. "No!"

"I'll be around in four weeks, Sergeant Major. Any American who can make it in Special Forces can make it in the Rhodesian Army. And that goes for the Selous Scouts as well."

"Just don't think you're any different from any other man, African or European, in this barrack—Captain," Princeloo sneered.

Mack Hudson, who had thought he was doing the right thing by responding to the sergeant major in the first place, realized he had made a mistake. This was going to be a tough one. Tougher than Special Forces, he knew.

"I'll be watching you, Captain Hudson," the sergeant major bawled out. Then he turned to Jacques LeClair. "We've got a frog in here with us too, I see." Then to Houk. "And a Kraut. What are you doing outside of Kraut land?"

"Fighting for Rhodesia, Sergeant Major," Houk replied imperturbably. C.S.M. Princeloo said nothing and turned to Adderley. "And we've got a bleeding Brit. How do you like the way your Queen is treating us?"

"The fact that I'm here should answer that question, Sergeant Major," Adderley snapped. Princeloo let out a grunt, pivoted on his heel and strode out of the barrack. The four men watched him leave.

"Reid-Daley was not exaggerating, I see," Mack grunted. "If this is the beginning I can imagine what it will be like about the middle of next week."

"It's better than trying to go back to SAS," LeClair observed.

"You can say that again, Jacques. Here it's Saturday night at beautiful Lake Kariba. Though I rather doubt we're going to get us a pass to visit the Kariba gambling casinos and nightclubs."

"I wouldn't make the request, my friend," Adderley said.

"Neither would I," Mack returned grimly.

As they were talking an African walked up and saluted Captain Hudson.

"Hey, brother, you just got me ten lashes from the sergeant major. Don't salute me until this exercise is over."

"Captain Hudson, I am Charles Luthu. Does this name have meaning to you?"

Hudson looked into the black face with the ivory smile. "Yes, you must be the ADC's brother."

"Oh, that right, suh. I never think I be in this selection course with you."

"It doesn't look like it's going to be easy."

"Nothing good come easy, suh," Luthu replied.

"Until this course is over call me brother, call me anything you want but not sir, and not captain, OK?"

"Oh yes, bass."

"And for chrissake don't call me or any other white man *boss*. We're all the same in here. And that's what Rhodesia is all about even though a bunch of my ignorant, liberal countrymen led by Brer Andy Young have no understanding of the fact."

"Yes, Brother Hudson. We owe you much. You save my brother. It was you who make SAS save him that night. I stay close by you. Maybe I help you like you help my family."

"Charles, my friend, I feel that you and I are going to get to know each other very well in the coming few weeks."

Chapter 29

Mack Hudson sat comfortably, he knew, for the last time until the selection course was over, in the office of a Selous Scout combat commander, Captain Herbert Spence.

"Cup of tea, Captain?" Spence asked, a man in his early thirties sporting the almost obligatory full beard.

"Thank you, Captain." Mack accepted the tea.

"The colonel suggested I have a word with you before we get underway tomorrow. This will be tough testing. I well remember when I transferred from RLI to the Scouts and had to go through it. We thought that at least we could help you to the extent of explaining a little more about the course. Ordinarily we take the recruits, throw them in and let them sink or swim. Most of them sink."

The officer's bright eyes gave Mack a piercing look. "There isn't a man giving this course that hasn't been through it and passed it himself. I want to take the opportunity of telling you that the colonel, myself and all of us wish you the best of luck and hope you come through."

"Thank you, Captain," Mack said with a tight grin. "I don't give up easily."

"You've got to realize that it is not capricious, but with good reason, that the men in the selection course are deprived of food, denied sleep and forced every day through the most grueling training exercises and the most forbidding assault course ever devised.

"A former British commando helped the colonel design this course. If you get through you will realize that although few people in our country know it, it's the Scouts, and only the Scouts, that stand between the terrorists and our borders. You will do much of your fighting against the Communists across the border. The purpose of this course is to prepare you for that. During this training period you men will be given one ration package every three days, one ratpack to be shared between two men. You will have to supplement this meager diet with pieces of the odd baboon you can kill or raw sections of any animal you may have an opportunity to slaughter."

"Sounds appetizing."

"The training sergeants will go all out to break you. They'll keep at you all the time, picking on you, pressuring you, never letting up. The real battle here is psychological. You'll have to fight yourself not to give up, prove to yourself you can make it."

Spence smiled almost apologetically. "There are readily recognizable phases. To begin with you'll find the recruits around you are sullen and despondent. The pressure quickly tells on them. Then, hopefully, they'll start to team up and fight back. They'll become determined. Once that determination sets in they'll be all right. You'll go through the same thing yourself."

"I'm already determined, Captain," Mack said.

"Yes, I can believe it. I don't know why a Yank wants to go through this anyway. I came up from South Africa. My family owns a cattle property here. We're fighting for our homes, our farms, the land our grandfathers and *their* fathers carved out of this wilderness. They were the trekkers, some of whom came here with Cecil Rhodes and his chief scout, Frederick Selous. They helped subdue the Zulus. They brought peace between the warring tribes here. It's that heritage that keeps us going. For the life of me I can't see why a contract soldier would want anything to do with us."

"I'm a professional soldier, Captain. A professional likes to be with the best in any army to which he may be offering his services."

"Well, the final phase of this little exercise, after you've been with us for four weeks, is the worst of all. Those recruits still remaining will be sent out on a four-day, ninety-mile forced march. You'll be carrying more than seventy-five pounds of weight on your back. This is the hardest test of all, and it weeds out many of the men who have survived everything else. This is where determination and endurance tell."

Captain Spence picked up his fawn-colored beret and pointed to the silver device on it. "And when you win this, the osprey, our symbol of excellence, you'll immediately go into combat operations. The best fighters the terrorists have trained are being thrown at us now as we get close to elections. I've studied the Korean War. The North Koreans launched their most savage attacks while the peace talks were taking place at Panmunjom. We expect the same kind of situation here."

Spence sat back in his seat and regarded Mack Hudson amiably. "Captain Hudson, I hope you will be with us. I know your military experience. I'd like to have you out in Mozambique and Zambia fucking up the terrorists with me. And we badly need Colin Adderley's demolition experience." A regretful look crossed his face. "And those, I'm afraid, are the last encouraging words you'll hear from any of us here at this infernal training camp until the course is over. Good luck!"

"Thank you, Spence." Mack said, standing up. He was grateful for some sign of encouragement from Colonel Reid-Daley, and he recognized the captain's short lecture as just that, a steadying word from the top before he was plunged into the breach of the selection course.

Chapter 30

M.M. De Vries escorted Beryl Stoffel from the dining room of his elegant Salisbury home, a townhouse eminently suited to the ministerial rank of its owner. Alvin Glenlord followed them from the scene of a sumptuous though intimate dinner for three into a richly furnished parlor. He took a seat opposite the Minister Plenipotentiary and the coldly beautiful blonde lady, whose favors tonight, in the interest of diplomacy and expediency, he was constrained to defer in favor of his host.

A white-jacketed black servant wearing a red fez and a scarlet sash from shoulder to waist appeared carrying a silver coffee service which he placed on the table in front of his master. De Vries said a few words in Portuguese and the servant went over to a walnut sideboard and brought back to the table a bottle of cognac and another of Drambouie.

Curtly De Vries dismissed the functionary. Al knew the Minister set great store by the fact that his servants were from Mozambique and could not understand English. Personally, Al had his doubts. The sensitive information discussed in this room on an almost nightly basis seemed to his trained instincts sufficient reasons for far tighter security.

De Vries poured a cognac for Al and Drambouie for Beryl and himself. Beryl served the coffee. Conversation over dinner had been inconsequential. MM had described his most recent hunting trip to a location which he referred to vaguely as "up north." From Beryl, Al knew that these trips were actually visits paid to a magnificently appointed hunting lodge in Zambia where vain talks were sporadically held with Joshua Nkomo and emissaries of President Kaunda. MM had merely said of his last shooting trip that he had bagged nothing worth mentioning. Now, over coffee and a cordial, the real conversation would take place. And at the proper moment Al would make some convenient excuse to leave Beryl and MM alone.

"How are the negotiations with the internal African leaders coming along, MM?"

Beryl asked after taking a sip of her Drambouie. "It must really drive you all around the bend trying to sort out the silly buggers."

De Vries smiled wearily. "Oh, they want it all laid on for them, everything. Much as they hate us, they are fortunately even more afraid of Nkomo and Mugabe and their terrorists. Basically, I think we're making progress. If the bishop weren't such an intransigent little twerp and if Reverend Sithole could just forget the years he was in detention and concentrate on what the future could hold for his people, we might make more progress. Only the chief of chiefs, our friend Senator Chirau, makes any sense at all and displays some moderation in his negotiations."

MM took a thoughtful sip of his Drambouie. Then he pursued his reflections, seemingly addressing himself to Al who had an uneasy feeling that this high-level minister was trying to project a message through him to Washington. "We've had the whole world against us for eleven years just because we wanted to preserve a stable society here. Look at the chaos in the countries surrounding us. Until now we were able to go our own way and create the highest standard of living for the African on the continent. But we can't go on forever; in fact I don't see how we can go on for more than another year, two at the most, without trading normally with the world. We just can't keep paying thirty-five to fifty percent to middlemen for everything that comes into this country and the same for what our products are sold for on the outside." He paused, a pained expression on his face.

"But we can't let the Africans take over everything we've built before they're trained and ready. It will take them less than two years to destroy eighty years of our efforts to build a modern country here. Look at Zambia, Tanzania, Mozambique. The Africans are starving because they've taken the white man's land and divided it up into little two-acre lots which are impossible to farm efficiently.

"In all of Africa there is not one successful black government. They're all dependent upon the big powers doling out aid to them. Only here in Rhodesia, where the so-called free world has tried to strangle us economically, do we have law, order, and peace among the tribesmen and a ratio between salaries and purchasing power that makes it possible for every African to live decently."

MM laughed sardonically. "And that hopeless excuse for a foreign minister from Britain, dear Dr. Owen, tells these people that they should be willing to forego their standard of living, to starve if that's what it takes, in order to be ruled by their own people. Well, we'll see how they like being exploited by their own. We should be able to have elections for the new African government in three or four months' time."

"And that will be the end of Rhodesia," Beryl stated flatly.

"Not necessarily, my dear," MM rejoined. "If our strategy works we'll hold on here, helping the Africans to govern themselves, and in effect ensuring that economically and politically the new Zimbabwe"—he nearly choked on the word—"prospers as a result of a whole new economy built on foreign trade. Of course, even with black majority rule in Salisbury the Communists will keep the people stirred up. Whoever is elected will be called a puppet, a tool of the white man. But with world trade we can buy helicopters and jets and modern weaponry to wipe out those insurgents that stay in the bush. In short, we can prevail."

"When the United States and Britain do lift sanctions, business sure will be good here, MM," Glenlord remarked.

"Yes, you can bet on that. The carpetbaggers are already arriving. By the way, your boss, the author-ambassador seems to be taking quite an interest in this African unity movement."

Al shot a look at Beryl and shrugged his shoulders. "MM, I don't know what to do about Roger. He always seems to be in places he shouldn't."

MM appeared surprised by the remark, but chose to let it lie. "Oddly enough, only a spirit of unity among the moderate African leaders in Rhodesian can save us now. And when we have the elections the Afs that don't get in must support the ones that do. That, of course, is the hardest thing to accomplish in Africa. It seems they only understand one thing."

MM pitched his voice high imitating an aroused African. "'Me de boss. No me de boss!' How else have the white people, outnumbered twenty to one, survived here? Sometimes I think you are a little hard on your boss or whatever your relationship is with Roger," MM concluded pointedly.

For a moment Al felt an apprehensive chill. Did De Vries know he was with the Agency? Al was well aware that back in Washington eight separate congressional committees were overseeing clandestine operations and being briefed on the missions of operatives such as himself. There was a considerable risk that his cover might be blown. At least in this pro-Western, civilized nation he wasn't in fear for his life. He might be declared a prohibited immigrant. Or perhaps he'd be allowed to stay but carefully insulated from all contacts that could provide him vital information.

"Tell me, Al," MM said curiously. "If Roger Masefield is so upsetting to you, why do you continue working for him? Neither you nor Beryl are really dependent upon his largess, are you?"

"Beryl and I formed a company, you know, MM. Alberl Associates. Our offices are in the Embassy and all our contacts have been coming through the Embassy. The publicity that Roger has been getting has brought in a lot of mail from business people in the United States who want to get into the Rhodesian economic boom when it comes. We provide the funnel for them to get in and naturally a certain amount of the action sticks to the side."

"Once sanctions are lifted after the elections your company should be making money hand over fist," MM observed.

"Can we really pull off the elections with all this terrorist activity?" Beryl asked.

"The Selous Scouts will be very busy," MM responded.

"I hope you're not worried about world opinion at this point," Al interjected. "You've got to continue to knock off the terrorist staging areas in Zambia and Mozambique."

"We're planning a job soon in Zambia," MM countered darkly.

"Those terr staging areas on Lake Kariba should be bombed out of existence," Al prompted.

268

"That would be the easiest way to achieve our objective, of course. However, ground operations may cause less of a storm in the American and European press."

"MM, why do we worry about world opinion?" Beryl asked in exasperation. "The world is trying to force communism on us."

"We'll contain the terrorists, Beryl. Camp Nkomo, as they call it after their leader, is their biggest staging area in Zambia at the moment. It's on the Choma River where it enters Lake Kariba. I'd say that's our next target. We'll send the Scouts up the river after them. Then we'll hit the Mozambique camps. We'll have elections just as soon as we can be sure the terrorists are controllable."

MM finished the last of his Drambouie and looked across the table at Al. "Another brandy, Al?"

"No, no thank you, MM." It was time to leave the Minister alone with Beryl. "I'll push along back to the Embassy. There should be a lot of telex traffic to handle. If you'll see Beryl home, I'll take off now."

Al Glenlord walked happily out into the chilly July night. This had been a valuable evening for him, he thought, as he folded his large form into the Toyota automobile that he had bought in South Africa for the Embassy. It wasn't often that he stayed over at the Embassy, but if MM himself did eventually take Beryl home that night, it wouldn't do for Al's car to be parked in her driveway. With Christian nearly always away, it didn't really make much difference if Beryl got back before daylight or not. The two children got themselves off to school without awakening their mother anyway.

As Al drove up to Roger's Embassy he felt the old ambivalence coming over him. Now he knew the target of a forthcoming strike by Rhodesian Security Forces. First thing in the morning he'd get out his maps and pinpoint the location of the Choma River. If he could just determine the approximate time of the attack he could send vital intelligence back to his control.

What distressed him, of course, was the near-certainty that when the Director proudly passed on the information to the President, Carter would pass it on to Young who would pass it on to the Zambia comrades.

Roger and Jocelyn were already in bed, Al surmised as he poured himself a nightcap in the Embassy bar. When he was not in the bush, Roger liked to get up at five in the morning, a good time to read the telexes and work on his book.

Al Glenlord paced the living room, sipping a bourbon and water as he contemplated the position he was in. He was irritated with himself for entertaining the futile thought that he might be able to resign from the Agency. Yes, it was ineffective now, its covert capabilities all but destroyed by publicity-mongering congressmen who wanted credit in their Vietnam-weary constituencies for cutting the CIA down to size. It was crippled, but it could still bite. The lack of security in Washington made Al nervous. Members of those congressional overseeing committees were known to blow off their mouths just to make themselves look important.

M.M. De Vries was beyond question the most sophisticated and intelligent man in Rhodesian politics. He undoubtedly had access to intelligence networks outside the ordinary Rhodesian facilities. Even now MM might be toying with him, Al thought, knowing perfectly well that he was an operative. Maybe MM had deliberately fed him the wrong information tonight. Maybe there was not even such a place as Camp Nkomo, although Al had picked up references to it at the SAS officers' mess.

It was a curious situation. Here were he and Beryl counting on sanctions to be lifted in order that their business could thrive, but here was Al having to support an administration policy that might destroy what they were working for.

The only way an operative could stay totally sane in this world was to remember what he was—an operative, pure and simple. Anything else was extraneous. In that context Al knew he had to destroy Roger Masefield before the author gained enough credibility to embarrass the administration, or even force the President to change whatever Rhodesian policy he wished to maintain.

Chapter 31

Four o'clock pounced on the men in the barracks. Sergeant Major Princeloo walked through shouting at the selection course volunteers. "This is it, men. We're going for a bracing run in the jungle. Everybody up."

Mack Hudson fell out of the lower bunk, got to his feet, quickly pulled on his shorts, shirt and tennis shoes and socks, the required uniform for the day. So this was it, the endurance run. Well, he had been running an average of five miles a day for the last two years so he was not worried about this feature of the training program. He and Jacques LeClair had teamed up, as had Houk and Adderley.

"I'll get the ratpack," Mack volunteered. The men formed up outside the barracks and Mack went to the supply truck and took the precious box of rations that would have to last him and Jacques for three days. In preparation for the coming ordeal they had all eaten as much food as they could get into themselves the previous night.

Mack put the ration package into a canvas bag attached to his belt and he and the others were ready for the run. Their nemesis, Sergeant Major Princeloo, herded them into a clearing and pointed to the beginning of the course, a wide trail, almost a road, through the jungle. Then, with Selous Scouts instructors leading, the hundred-odd volunteers started their run.

Instructors ran in the midst of the group and others at the rear. The only thing they had going for them, Mack thought, was the weather. Yes, it was chilly, conducive to brisk exercise.

At first the run was invigorating, even pleasant. Mack drew in great gulps of air, smiling from time to time at the others running with him. But as the miles fell behind and the roadway through the bush seemed to grow rougher and narrower, the men began to feel the strain. Lifting their legs and putting them down was becoming an effort. Surely they'd stop and walk, Mack began to tell himself. A man can't run through this kind of terrain steadily without breaking stride and walking. No halt to the running was called, however.

As the sun came up, the air temperature rose. Mack could feel the sweat pouring off him. Still he kept going. He tried to estimate how far they had run. Surely six or seven miles. Now it was agony to even turn his head to see how the others around him were doing. He just kept pumping his legs, propelling himself forward, and the pain began to wrack his chest, his throat, his sides. How long could they expect any man to go? he asked himself angrily. Did they want to kill them all without even giving them a chance at the rest of the course? Vaguely he was aware of the gasps of the others around him. He noted with a touch of chagrin that the Africans seemed to be gliding along as if they could do it all day. But damn it, a white man's lifestyle just didn't give him the stamina for this kind of thing.

Somehow he kept going. But he sensed collapse was imminent. Looking ahead, he picked out a tree at eye level. He would make it as far as that tree. He would think of nothing beyond making it to that strange-looking tree. Panting, his breath whistling through bone-dry tubes, he concentrated on reaching the tree. It was getting closer. Could he get there? Mentally he reached down inside himself and got two handfuls of guts and pulled them up. Yes, he'd make it to the tree.

Already the casualties were falling to the side of the trail. Three Europeans, one African. The tree came closer. He had to make it. Just get to the tree, don't think beyond that. Keep going. The tree was coming closer. He felt his legs trembling but he kept going. Now he was almost there. At last! He passed the tree. He'd done it. His eyes misting over, the world a haze around him, Mack picked another tree fifty to seventy meters ahead. He focused on the tree. Just make it to the tree.

The world seemed to slip away from him. The box of rations on his belt weighed a ton, pulling him toward the ground. If he had had the strength to raise his arms and undo his belt he would have dropped the precious rations. But all he could do was to keep loping drunkenly toward that tree.

And then he felt himself blacking out. He couldn't control it now. The misty wavering blackness kept hovering about him, threatening to engulf him. He felt himself stumbling. No, no, he told himself, just get to that tree. Yes, make it to that tree and then the next one and the next one. If only he knew exactly how far he had to go it would help.

He heard himself letting out what seemed a distant moan. He struggled to keep his balance and then knew he was falling. Suddenly, from nowhere, he felt a source of new strength. His arm had been seized and draped over the shoulders of another man running beside him. Then from the other side, another wave of strength. He was being half-carried by two Africans, one on either side of him. His legs seemed to belong to some sozzled marionette. He wanted to laugh, but it was too painful.

Now a surge of energy came into him. He was willing himself forward, his legs pushing the ground back. His mind was giving the orders and his body, somehow, obeyed.

Then it was over. The survivors were dead on their feet. On their feet because they were forbidden to collapse on the ground.

Slowly Mack recovered full consciousness. He was still being held erect by his ministering spirits. Supporting his right arm was Charles Luthu, his left arm one of Luthu's friends.

"Quite a nice run," Luthu grinned.

Mack Hudson tried to reply but only rasps came from his throat. He wagged his head gratefully. The two Africans helped him to a truck, then Luthu went over to a canteen and got him water in a paper cup.

Now Mack was back in the present. "Thanks," he gasped. He realized that the run had taken them in a wide circle through the jungle. He was ready to stumble into the barracks, throw himself on his cot and spend the rest of the day recovering. However, that was not to be.

After a rest, which was only long enough for the men to regain their wind, Sergeant Major Princeloo was shouting orders again. They would proceed to the rifle range and begin a familiarization course in captured Communist weapons. At least no more running.

The men were formed up and marched to the range. Luthu hovered beside Mack, making sure he could make it.

Chapter 32

September 1978

In the north wing of Andrew Fleming Hospital where the battle casualties were treated, Carla tried to concentrate on her job as nurse's aid. There were three American patients which was unusual. The fighting was getting worse out in the sharp end. One of the Americans, a sergeant, a Marine veteran of Vietnam, had been seriously wounded in both legs from a land mine.

Carla knew she would never get used to the wounded men who came in every day. The American lieutenant, Hardie Clifton, had been shot three times and somehow survived. Although very weak, he could converse with Carla and enjoy talking to a beautiful American woman way out here in Rhodesia. The Americans seemed to draw some comfort from hearing each other talk after long stretches with Europeans and Africans.

Carla glanced at her watch. Three-thirty. Visiting hours were just beginning. She was not surprised to see that the first visitor was Roger Masefield. He was carrying the familiar leather attaché case in which, undoubtedly, he would have stashed away two or three of the forbidden *Playboy* or *Penthouse* magazines. Any magazine with even a hint of prurient content was confiscated at the airport. However, Masefield,

275

who came in and out of Salisbury frequently, was well known to all the customs officers and his baggage was never searched. It was almost as though he had the diplomatic immunity accorded a real ambassador.

"Hello, Carla, how are our Yanks doing?"

"Lieutenant Clifton is feeling better. Sergeant Cannon over there seems to be in good spirits."

Masefield walked over to the sergeant. "How's it going?"

"My legs are still attached to me. Thank God for small favors." His eyes lit on the attaché case. "Got anything worth reading in there, Roger?"

"The new *Life* magazine from the States, Bill." Masefield grinned at the look of disappointment that come over Cannon's face.

"You can wrap it around the *Playboy* I brought. Just don't let that centerfold get you too excited. They tell me you're supposed to lie quiet."

Carla tittered at the wide grin that lit up Sergeant Cannon's face.

"I'm next," the lieutenant said weakly.

"How come I always suck hind tit?" the third American asked plaintively.

"Hang on till you see what else I've got in here," Roger replied. "They're going to PI me out of Rhodesia one of these days for bringing these in but what the hell." Masefield reached into his attaché case and handed a copy of *Rhodesian Illustrated Life* to the other American.

"You expect me to read this, Mr. Masefield?"

"Take a look inside," Roger advised. The Yank did. Then he grinned and let out a whistle. "That's more like it. *Hustler.*"

The unmistakable chopping noise of a helicopter interrupted the banter. Everybody looked out the window, but no comment was necessary. Another casevac was coming in. Carla knew there would soon be more work for her.

Leaving Roger with the wounded Americans, she walked down the hallway to the receiving point for new patients. The sadness she felt each time a casualty was brought in took her mind off the disappointment and resentment she felt that Mack had just disappeared into the bush and she had heard nothing of him in almost three weeks.

The elevator door slid open and a nurse and hospital attendant pushed a cot on wheels out into the hall. Above the cot was suspended a bottle of blood plasma from which a tube led down to the arm of the man who had just been flown in. Carla looked at him as the cot was wheeled by her. So young, she thought. He didn't look seventeen.

Everything she heard about the war indicated that it was getting worse every day. Certainly the casualties were rising alarmingly. When she had first started working at the hospital only half the wing had been required for battlefield casualties. Now the entire north wing was full. She watched the young casualty being wheeled down to the operating room and through the metal doors.

"Carla, I hoped I'd find you here." She recognized Ashley's voice and turned round.

"Hello, Ashley. I haven't seen you for awhile."

"I've been down at Fort Vic. I've missed seeing you here at the hospital."

"Oh?" Carla asked coquettishly. "And what about that lovely girl from South Africa you've been seeing? The journalist."

"Veronica? She isn't an intelligent, mature woman like a certain American lady I know."

"And," Carla mocked, "she doesn't seem to be around anymore."

"When the job at WP never materialized I could have arranged for her to stay," General St. John replied petulantly.

"Why didn't you, Ashley?"

"She's too young. She just isn't . . . as I said, mature enough to cope with the wartime situation here."

Carla pretended to deliberate over this. "I see," she replied gravely. "What happened to her job?"

"That bloody Yank reporter never did have a job for her. He just wanted me to—" Ashley stopped himself. "I suppose he wanted to look like the bureau chief. But he's left Salisbury himself. Nobody knows what he's up to."

"Well, it's good to see you again, Ashley. I guess I'd better get back to the wards."

"Carla, I just had an inspiring thought. Why don't you come out to the polo matches with me next Sunday. I'll be playing, and after-wards we'll have dinner."

"It's a lovely idea, Ashley. I appreciate your thinking of me. But I'd better stay home in case Mack calls."

St. John laughed. "Mack won't be calling. He'll be totally occupied with Reid-Daley's little dirties. Take my advice, forget Mack for a good long time and try to get some enjoyment out of life. Now what do you say, Carla? A Sunday afternoon and evening away from sitting around the flat?"

"I suppose I could leave word where I am at the Embassy. That's where Mack would call if he didn't reach me at home."

"Now that's good thinking. You can always be reached at the Polo Club."

"It does sound like fun," Carla murmured wistfully. "I've never seen a polo game."

"I'll be around to fetch you at twelve noon sharp, my dear," St. John said in an authoritative tone that put an end to the matter. "And now, darling, if you'll excuse me, I'll do my rounds. Shall we have drinks afterwards?"

"All right, Ashley. I'll see you when my shift is over at five." She watched him walk down the long hallway and turn into the first ward.

Chapter 33

September 1978

"You can give me the combat, always. But this is, what you call? you Yanks, *merde de poulet*, cheekin sheet." Jacques LeClair was squatting over a fire where a tin can of water was heating. Sergeant Luthu dropped in two eyeballs and some entrails, all that was left of the tiny dik-dik he had caught in a snare.

Nothing that could be eaten was wasted. It had been three days since the small baboon had been trapped and devoured by the ravenous Scouts. After the animals they trapped had been chewed up, the bones were split to get at the nourishing marrow.

"In the combat you have a gun, you can control what 'appen. Here?" LeClair shrugged expressively.

They had endured two and a half weeks of near starvation, illness from eating rotten meat, minor injuries and an endless stream of insults from the instructors. The African sergeants seemed to delight in harassing the Europeans in the selection course. At night there was one blanket to two men to ward off the chill.

The would-be Scouts had been ordered on twenty-five-mile forced marches through the bush with seventy pounds on their back and given rendezvous times which they could miss by no more than thirty minutes. If, after the grueling hike, a Scout arrived even a minute late he received no rations or water. They sometimes had to bore into the thick baobab tree for water, and although they carried their weapons because bands of terrorists marauded through the training area, they were not allowed to shoot game.

Survival became a group effort in which black and white trainees gave each other help and encouragement.

"Jesus, two more of this," a hollow-eyed Mack Hudson muttered. He peeled back the leather flap over the face of his watch. "Five hours to rendezvous. Let's eat Jacques' haute cuisine and push forward."

The starving men reached into the simmering tin of water and offal and pulled out unappetizing morsels which they gobbled down. The dik-dik's eyeballs were cut up and distributed. Then, painfully, miserably, the men slowly pulled themselves to their feet and started off through the bush.

At the unexpected chuffing of a helicopter overhead Mack looked up and spotted an Alouette, its blade whirling, gliding across the sky in front of them.

"Bloody low level. I wonder what they're looking for," Adderley said.

"Do you reckon there are terrs out here?" Mack asked. "Maybe we'll get a little action," he added hopefully.

"We won't see terrs, they're afraid of the jumbos herding in this area."

"*Ja*, the elephant scare them away. *Und* scare me too, those big beasts. Six today already." Houk grunted and looked about as though to see whether any elephants were on their trail.

Jacques was watching the French-made helicopter through squinting eyes. It seemed to be circling around a point a mile ahead of them. Then it dipped out of sight behind the tree line and they heard a series of distant rifle shots. The pops reverberated above the chopping noise of the engine and spinning rotor blades. Moments later the chopper hove into view again, but only briefly.

"What you think this is all about?" Jacques asked, looking at the others.

"I think we'll find out pretty quick," Mack replied. "Let's head over to where the chopper was circling."

They changed direction slightly and pushed through the dense bush. An hour later they came across an open area surrounding one of the many rivers that flowed into Lake Kariba. Stunned at the sight before them, they halted and stared.

"I count fifteen," Mack said in a subdued voice.

"Everybody keep their weapons handy," Adderley cautioned. "There'll be others still alive around here. And they won't be happy with mankind."

The dead elephants lay in a circle, and as the Selous Scouts recruits walked up to them, keeping an eye out for enraged survivors, they admired the huge, gleaming, eighty- to ninety-pound ivory tusks worth forty dollars a pound on the foreign market.

Houk looked from the massacred elephants to his watch. "Captain, we have three hours to reach the ration truck."

Mack nodded. "I'm hungry too, Horst. Let's move. And when we get back don't anybody mention what we saw. This is something we shouldn't know about. Understand?"

Without warning, Luthu and several of the other Africans leaped at the head of one of the dead elephants and pushing apart its huge jaws, proceeded to cut the tongue out. Luthu turned to Mack, displaying the piece of meat as the Africans went after another elephant corpse. "We can eat this on the march." He began cutting the tongue into strips and handing them out. Ravenously the aspiring Scouts tore at the tough, pulpy strips as they resumed their hike back to the camp and their first regular rations in nearly three weeks.

It was exactly five P.M. when Mack led the exhausted contingent into the clearing outside the camp at Wafa Wafa. Wearily they looked for the ration truck. Horst Houk shook his great shaggy head when he saw there was no ration truck waiting for them.

"*Ja, und* now what do they do to us?"

"Oh those bleeding bugger-begotten bastards," Adderley moaned. "Not even ratpacks. I say let 'em have their war and let us be shut of it."

"Hang in there, Adderley. You can stand it another two weeks," Mack encouraged. "Don't give up now. Can't disappoint the colonel after he pulled his relationship with General Walls to get us in."

"Yes, Mack, you're right," Adderley agreed. "But we're not going to be much use if they starve us to death."

The sound of trucks could be heard down the dirt road and soon two big lorries appeared. Captain Herbert Spence jumped from the cab of the lead vehicle.

Although he ached in every bone and could only think of ratpacks and rest, Mack pulled himself to attention. "How goes the course, Captain Hudson?" Spence asked, his beard framing a cheerful grin.

"Just fine, Captain Spence," Mack responded. "We're all enjoying this outstanding exercise and looking forward to the last two weeks."

"Oh? Then I'm afraid I have some bad news for you."

Despite his state of near collapse, Mack held himself erect and allowed his face to betray no hint of his feelings. What now? he asked himself. Silently he prayed that his thirty-four-year-old body could endure whatever new piece of fiendishness had been devised for it. Mentally he could take anything, he had discovered, even the African course instructors' calculated persecution.

Spence savored the suspense for a few moments, then said, "This course is over for you."

This was too much, Mack thought. He had put up with every physical and mental indignity the test had to offer. Now his face did betray him.

Spence saw the look of disbelief and shock. "Oh you've passed the course, all of you here. You'll receive your belts and berets from the colonel personally, tomorrow."

Mack looked around at the German, the Briton and the Frenchman, and then at Sergeant Luthu and the other Africans in the group. Suddenly wide smiles spread across their faces, and horse whoops leaped from their throats.

"You'll pile into these two trucks and be driven back to barracks where you can shower, have some real graze and get a night's sleep. Tomorrow's Monday. You'll be flown back to André Rabie barracks at Inkomo. For the first time in damn near two years, the entire Selous Scouts force will be in from the field at the same time."

More shouts from parched throats greeted this news. "That's about the finest gift I ever had given to me," Mack declared.

Captain Spence gave him a wink. "You Yanks have an expression it might serve you to recall," he said. "You don't get something for nothing."

Mack thought about it for a moment. "Oh shit," he muttered. "What now?"

Chapter 34

Polo had never been part of the lifestyle Carla and Mack Hudson led. But now the excitement of the game gripped her. Even though she didn't really understand what went on during a chucker, she could see that Ashley St. John was the star player out there on the polo field. As he galloped his pony up and down, thwacking the ball with his mallet, driving it steadily toward the opposition's goalposts, she could feel an irresistible attraction to this dashing general. She didn't stop to consider at this point whether this implied disloyalty to Mack.

Carla had been wondering more frequently these last few days whether perhaps she had made a mistake in her marriage. She despised herself for the thought; but surely there was more to life than waiting night after night, sometimes even a week or two at a stretch for her husband to come back. And in a strange country too. The other wives of Americans over here reacted differently. Those with children almost invariably gave up and went home, leaving their husbands to do their thing alone. Other wives retreated sullenly into a lonely shell. Still others tried to enjoy such life as was available to them in Rhodesia.

Sure, she thought bitterly, it was all very exciting and thrilling for the men. And the idealists among the Americans, including Mack, found great satisfaction in re-fighting the war America lost in Vietnam, even though their country neither understood nor appreciated their effort.

The last chucker of the day was underway. Carla watched as Ashley galloped toward the goal, slapping the ball ahead of his pony's head. An opponent was making a determined effort to cut him off. Carla wasn't sure who was ahead although she thought Ashley's four-man team was perhaps one goal up. She gasped as the opposing pony collided with Ashley's and the latter fell to the ground.

Ashley appeared to be pinned under his mount. Carla let out a cry of dismay. The spectators close by smiled at her as Ashley extricated himself and stood up, patting his horse, getting the animal to its feet, and then remounting and charging back into the fray. There was sustained applause from the grandstand and cries of "Good show" and "Get after them, Ashley." Carla blushed at her display of emotion. A number of men and women gave her knowing glances. Moments later the chucker ended and Ashley and his team rode from the field. He dismounted in front of her and a groom ran up to take his pony and lead it away.

"Well, Carla, how do you like polo?"

"It's exciting, Ashley. Are you all right?"

"Oh certainly. You take these falls as they come. The main thing is to get back up and continue riding. Come along with me now. We'll say hello to a few friends and then you can have a pink gin while I shower and change in the clubhouse. Is that all right?"

"Oh yes, quite all right, Ashley," Carla replied, smiling.

St. John introduced her to a few friends, all of whom gave her that same speculative smile. All right, she thought, I know. Another one of Ashley's conquests. Well, maybe he was one of *her* conquests, even though they didn't look at it that way.

Carla didn't really like pink gin but it seemed to be what everybody was drinking; Scotch was hard to get in Rhodesia. The Rhodesians had learned to make their own gin and vodka, and foreign exchange was too precious to spend it on liquor. It was not long before Ashley met her on the veranda of the clubhouse. He sat beside her and with sundown not far away, ordered a drink for himself.

"So I've introduced you to something new. Well, you'll have to come out here with me every Sunday until I am permanently posted to Fort Victoria." He noticed the slight frown coming across Carla's face and chuckled. "Fort Vic is an easy airflight from here. Now do you feel more cheerful?"

"Don't people get hurt playing polo?" she asked wide-eyed.

"Yes, of course. It happens. Part of the game, you know," he added cheerfully. "Where would you like to go for a bite of supper tonight?"

"Anywhere you say, Ashley."

"We'll find something suitable."

Later, after a light supper at an intimate restaurant in the avenues not far from Ashley's apartment, they returned for a brandy and coffee at his place. She asked the question that had been on her mind for several days now. "Ashley, isn't there a Mrs. St. John someplace?"

He dismissed the questions airily. "Oh yes, my love; you have your Mack, I have my Edna. We're more or less separated at the moment. She's visiting in Capetown with her family. She's actually South African, not Rhodesian. Now that we're getting a spot of urban terrorism in Salisbury, she's somewhat lost her taste for life here. I doubt if our marriage will last much longer, actually. But then, why do we talk about such depressing subjects?"

They were sitting beside each other on the wide sofa in his expensively furnished living room. Without more ado St. John put his arms around here and pulled her to him. She willingly allowed her lips to met his. It was a long, disturbing kiss, disturbing in the sense that it almost shook the last vestiges of resistance from her.

Then the thought of Mack, out in the bush, struggling to get through his selection course infused Carla with new resolve. She gently pushed Ashley away and stood up. "Please take me home, Ashley. Actually, why don't you let me call Rixi Taxi."

There was no mistaking the disappointment on the general's face as he stood too. "Oh Ashley, I'm sorry, I shouldn't have let myself go like that. I guess I'm confused. Forgive me if I let you think something that can't happen."

Ashley stood up beside her, a brave smile on his face. "I understand, my dear. But don't think I'm giving up. I'll take you home now. And tomorrow I'll see you when I come around to the hospital. Maybe we can have sundowners at five."

"Thank you, Ashley. Thank you for understanding."

"And you're not taking a taxi. My car is parked out in front."

Chapter 35

Mack Hudson arrived at the first gate leading into Inkomo Barracks, his small car groaning with its load of men, and announced himself to the African guard. The African peered into the window of the car, saw the captain's pips on Mack's shoulder and snapped a smart salute. Mack was wearing his SAS uniform since it wouldn't be until today that he would be awarded the forest green Selous Scouts belt, with its round silver buckle, and the coveted fawn beret with the pinned-on osprey device.

Still, LeClair, Houk, Adderley and Luthu were now all chattering and laughing and the rich stew of accents had the guard bewildered. Finally Mack snapped, "Tell this fucker who we are, Luthu."

"Luthu and the guard conversed in Shona, then the latter went back to the guardhouse and got on the line to Selous Scouts Headquarters. Suddenly Luthu burst out laughing.

"What's so funny?" Mack asked.

"He say car full of white men who all talk very funny waiting at the gate, sir," Luthu answered.

Mack turned to the others and grinned. "I though it was only you chaps who talked funny."

The guard returned to the car and in slow, precise, and polite English informed Mack that a Land Rover would soon be there to meet them and escort them to headquarters.

Moments later a Land Rover pulled to a halt in front of Mack's car and a bearded European color sergeant jumped out and approached Mack.

The soldier saluted. "Colonel Reid-Daley's compliments, sir. I'm Color Sergeant Marley. The colonel asked me to escort you to headquarters. Just follow me and please try to keep close as all strange vehicles are stopped by our roving patrols."

"I'll be right on your tail, Sergeant," Mack replied.

It was a three-mile drive through the military reserve to Selous Scouts Headquarters. Twice they passed recruits in work parties along the side of the road and each time the workmen came to attention and saluted smartly as they saw Mack's pips. At a second gate, which guarded the perimeter of the HQ, Mack signed in his group and gave the registration number of the Toyota.

Finally the color sergeant was leading them through the door to the long headquarters building and down a hall. He stopped at the entrance to an office. "This is the RSM's office, sir. He will take over." The regimental sergeant major, a big, burly man with a neatly trimmed brown beard, stood up behind his desk, on which lay his silver-trimmed ebony pace-stick. He crashed his heels on the floor and gave a copybook salute. Mack saluted back.

"Colonel Reid-Daley always welcomes each man into the unit personally. If you will follow me I'll take you into his office." The RSM walked briskly to a closed door, rapped on it, opened it and stepped inside.

"The new men are here, sir," he announced portentously.

Mack and his party walked in and saluted Colonel Reid-Daley. The colonel, one of the few Scouts officers to be clean-shaven, returned the salute and said, "Stand easy, gentlemen. I'm glad to have you in Selous Scouts." He smiled ironically. "Sorry to have interrupted your course but we are in the midst of a rather historic occasion here. We have brought all the Scouts in from the field, five hundred strong, for a Regimental Day and retraining. Only twice before have we done this. I felt it would be helpful for you to meet the men of your regiment here at our home barracks. You will receive your Selous Scouts colors in front of the entire regiment. The RSM will see about assigning you quarters. Again, welcome to Selous Scouts." He gave Mack a warm glance. "There will be a special meeting of officers tomorrow morning. The RSM will notify you."

On their way to assigned quarters the RSM gave Mack and his companions a brief tour of the Selous Scouts home base known as André Rabie Barracks, named after a founder of the Scouts who was killed in action. It contained all the headquarters offices, a parade ground, and the round bar where the Africans drank native beer by the tanker truck full and sang their songs. On occasion the European Scouts joined them, though drinking their own beer, the African variety being very much an acquired taste.

Outside the bottom gate were cool thatched-roof family houses which the Africans preferred, and also housing facilities for the European Scouts.

A large swimming pool had been built and every Selous Scout was required to be a proficient swimmer. Few Africans know how to swim since the water available to them is dangerous. Crocodiles take several hundred African lives a year.

"If any of you men have families, quarters will be made available," the RSM said as he pointed out the housing facilities. "I believe, Sergeant Luthu, that you are planning to bring your wife and children into the compound."

Luthu nodded. "Yes, RSM. Down at Zaka where they live the terrorists come into the kraals almost every night."

"No place for the family of a Selous Scout to live," the RSM commented. He turned to Mack. "Once the terrs find the name of a man in the Scouts they try to track down his family and kill them."

After the brief tour they were assigned to temporary quarters in the headquarters compound and Mack and Captain Adderley went to the officers' mess for lunch. The others went to the sergeants' mess where African and European noncoms ate together.

Captain Herbert Spence and Major Conrad Van Roolyan, the two group commanders, invited Mack and Colin Adderley to sit with them and explained to the new officers a little of what was ahead. The third group commander had been killed on a Scouts mission into Mozambique. Spence, a Rhodesian, and Van Rooyan, a South African, hinted broadly that a Yank might become the new commander of Three Group. Mack hardly dared let himself hope that this command would indeed be given him. He was a newcomer, although he had two years of heavy combat duty in Rhodesia behind him, to say nothing of his last three tours of duty with Special Forces in Vietnam.

"Well," Spence said, "this afternoon you new chaps are going to be the stars of the parade. When I got my belt and beret there weren't enough Scouts in camp to form up, we were so busy. Strange that now, at the height of the war and with the infiltration getting worse every night, the colonel should bring us all in."

"Ours is not to question why," Major Van Roolyan answered.

Chapter 36

September 1978

Just before four P.M., at the upper parade ground near the entrance to Inkomo Barracks, the parade to welcome the new men into Selous Scouts was about to be held. Families and friends of Selous Scouts were on hand to watch the colorful ceremony.

The spectator stands were filled and a large group of Rhodesians, black and white, were standing at the edge of the parade ground. Carla Hudson, accompanied by Roger Masefield, Alvin Glenlord and Beryl Stoffel, was present to watch her husband receive his beret and belt from Colonel Reid-Daley.

"You must be happy that they cut Mack's selection course in half," Al observed. "I never heard of the Scouts giving their trainees a break before."

"I don't know whether it is a break or not," Carla replied.

"Well, I think it's a break," Sarah Cobb Chase interjected. "I haven't had so much as a glimpse of Colin since this whole thing started."

"From what little I could get from Mack, you're not going to see much of him anyway," Carla said. "Something's about to happen and they need every man they can get."

"So I gather," Glenlord mused, looking out across the parade ground.

"I don't care what they're up to, they damn well better give Colin a few days off," Sarah declared roundly. "We've got a lot of catching up to do."

At exactly four P.M. a lusty chorus of singing voices burst out from one side of the woods surrounding the parade ground. Although every regiment in the Rhodesian Army had its own marching band, Colonel Reid-Daley had never accepted one for the Selous Scouts. The Scouts distinguished themselves by their singing. The as yet unseen chorus, rendering the first African song of the day, brought goose pimples to the skin of the spectators.

Suddenly the Scouts emerged from the trees. Five hundred Africans and less than one hundred bearded European Scouts, in five ranks, marched slowly onto the parade ground, their voices rising to a mighty crescendo in front of the seated spectators. The battalion came to a halt exactly as the song finished.

It was a highly charged moment as the twenty-eight survivors of the selection course, led by Mack, marched proudly out onto the parade ground and formed up between the battalion of Scouts and the audience.

The Selous Scouts presented arms as their new comrades appeared before them, ready to join the ranks of this, the elite unit of the Rhodesian Security Forces. Stiffly erect, hatless, and in the camouflage fatigues of the security forces, the newcomers awaited the arrival of their commander.

Colonel Reid-Daley strode out onto the parade ground with his adjutant and RSM. They were followed by two African Scouts carrying a table piled high with fawn berets and green belts which was placed before the colonel.

"Stand easy, men," Reid-Daley commanded. He paused to cast his eye swiftly over the new recruits.

"Men, welcome to the Selous Scouts. You have passed through the most rigorous training any army has ever devised. Tomorrow you will be out in the operational areas fighting with the Selous Scouts groups to which you have been assigned. There is no more I need to say." He turned to his adjutant who handed him a list of the new men's names.

"Captain Mack Hudson!" Reid-Daley shouted. Mack came to attention, walked to the colonel and saluted. Then he took the colonel's outstretched hand and shook it.

"Glad to have you with us, Mack," Reid-Daley said. A sergeant came up to him. The colonel took the fawn beret and belt from the sergeant and handed them to Mack. Mack clapped the beret on his head and held the belt in his left hand. He saluted the Colonel, turned smartly and walked back to the formation.

"Captain Colin Adderley," Reid-Daley announced. Adderley came forward and in the same manner as Mack received his fawn beret with the treasured osprey on it and his green belt. The entire presentation took twenty minutes. After applause from the spectators, the Selous Scouts battalion then launched into another of its African songs.

By quarter to five the ceremony was over. Mack, followed by Adderley, walked to the spectator stands. Sarah Cobb Chase threw herself into her lover's arms, but Carla was more restrained.

"Congratulations, Mack. I'm really happy for you, darling," she said. "Is it all right to kiss you here?"

"Of course. Even Selous Scouts can kiss their wives. I think." He grinned. "I forgot to get the protocol on that from the adjutant." Carla put her arms around her husband's neck, pulled herself close to him and they kissed, to the applause of the men who had shared the weeks of hardship with him.

"Are you coming home with me tonight?" Carla asked.

Mack made a grimace. "I can't, darling. The colonel wants to see me first thing in the morning. The adjutant tells me that first thing in the morning for Colonel Reid-Daley is six A.M. "

"Oh Mack, I'm so disappointed." She sounded stricken. "I miss you, Mack." He was wrenched by her plaintive tone.

"I'll be in tomorrow after the meeting with the colonel, I promise you, Carla. And what's more, we're going to have ourselves a nice house out here in the officers' section."

"Out here?" It was almost a wail.

"Selous Scouts are a family of their own, Carla," Mack lectured. "All the families are out here. The Africans, of course, have to bring their families in. If it ever becomes known that they're Selous Scouts, their families are automatic targets of the terrorists." He put his hands on her shoulders. "And I can tell you from what I've seen you won't be disappointed in our quarters."

"What about my job at the hospital?"

"We'll find something for you to do here, Carla. Just let me get adjusted and see what the situation is."

Carla looked up at him and smiled bravely. "Of course, Mack. It's just—"

"I know, I know, Carla. It's been a long time since we've been together. And now this tease. It's hard on both of us." He thought about what he'd said and smiled shyly. "You can be sure it is on me."

Carla chuckled. "Couldn't we get away now for at least a few hours. You can drive back here in time to get some sleep before you see the colonel tomorrow."

"Carla, I've got to go to a Scouts beer drink tonight. It's expected of me. I couldn't miss it and still have the Scouts think of me as one of them."

"A beer drink?" she repeated, shocked.

"I know it sounds stupid to you, Carla. But there's a lot of tradition here and I'm part of it. First we put in an appearance at the African beer hall. I can't have my Africans think I'm not with them all the way. Then at the officers' mess the colonel is expecting us all for dinner."

He felt uncomfortable as he looked at his exotic wife. Mack was well aware that Carla had given up her way of life, her interests, her friends, everything to come out here to Rhodesia just to be with him. He was torn between all that he knew he owed Carla and his need to be an integral part of his new unit.

"So I guess I'd better get on back to the apartment," she said, her eyes downcast.

Mack looked at her miserably. "Not right this minute, Carla. We can go to the mess and have a drink together. Some of the other wives will be there and of course girl friends, like Sarah." He glanced over at his British comrade-in-arms who was trying to explain to Sarah why they were being denied the night together. "But then we'll have to go over to the African Club for a sing."

"How do the other wives and girl friends take it?" Carla asked.

"I don't know, Carla. I guess it's hard on all of them. I'm sure Sarah Chase is the most unhappy girl out here."

Roger Masefield, closely followed by Al Glenlord and Beryl Stoffel, approached them. "Congratulations, Mack," Roger said, shaking hands.

"Good to have the Embassy turn out for me," Mack smiled.

"I'm sure you're sorry to miss the second half of the selection course," Al chuckled. "From what I hear you really got a good break."

"Maybe," Mack conceded.

"I guess they've got something in mind more important than running you guys through the bush," Al probed.

"Seems that way," Mack replied noncommittally.

Sarah Cobb Chase and Captain Adderley walked up arm in arm. Sarah looked at Carla brightly. "Well, I guess the two of us will be celebrating our men's graduation without them. Maybe we can get Roger and Alvin and Beryl to join us."

"Not even one night off?" Al asked.

"Looks that way, Al," Mack replied. "They didn't bring us back early for fun and games with our ladies." He looked down longingly at his wife.

"During the Vietnam War we always said the war won't last forever," Carla said reproachfully. "But with you Mack, the war *will* last forever. If it isn't this one it will be another." There was no anger, not even resentment in her face. Just resignation. "Let's go over to the mess," Mack suggested. "You girls will find a few other women going through the same problem with their men."

"Sure, but their men, the Rhodesians, are here fighting for their country." Carla's face clouded. "And for them, some day the war *will* be over."

"I feel I'm fighting for my country too." Mack sighed as he repeated the old rationale. "This is a war the United States should be supporting. If the Rhodesians lose and the Marxists take over, it's only a matter of time before we'll feel it in the United States. Now come on, you and Sarah meet the men of my unit."

There was a festive atmosphere in the Scouts officers' mess as Mack and Adderley walked in with their ladies, Roger, Al and Beryl close on their heels. The colonel came across the room and Mack and Colin Adderley presented their women.

"We are proud to have your men in Selous Scouts," Reid-Daley said warmly. "I hope you'll be able to understand the sacrifices we must make. With the elections coming up in a few months and the terrorists promising to wreck them, our work is cut out for us. You'll have plenty of time together. It's just that right now we need every man we've got. This country is depending on us."

"If you need a special volunteer, I'm available, Ron," Al Glenlord put in ingratiatingly. "Four tours with Special Forces in the Nam, mostly cross-border work, I might be of some use to you. I'm sure Roger can spare me."

"I appreciate your concern, Colonel Glenlord," Reid-Daley replied with more coolness than might have been expected.

"I'll be standing by if I can be of use. Looks like something's in the works right now," Al observed conversationally.

"Could be," Reid-Daley said curtly. "By the way, Mack, here's a couple of your Yanks you didn't know were in the Scouts, I'll bet." He gestured toward two sergeants drinking beer.

"For God's sake, Joe Late and Eddie Wilson. When did they go through the selection course?"

"Eddie Wilson came aboard just three weeks ago. He's been with Grey's Scouts next door to us here at Inkomo. We have so much work ahead I decided not to waste his time with the course."

"But you could waste mine," Mack answered with a grin.

"Well now, Mack, I just felt I owed it to you to let you see what the Scouts are really about," Reid-Daley laughed. "Tomorrow morning you'll understand better."

"What about Late, sir?"

"Well, we needed an expert parachutist and a man with jungle experience."

"I can tell you Joe Late has that. He organized our halo missions in Vietnam."

"Yes, I know. He has also been leading innovative parachute missions with both SAS and RLI. I had a hard time persuading our air force to let us have him and I couldn't take a chance on losing him in the selection course."

"Sir," Mack said forthrightly, "There were a few times you damn near lost *me*."

"I don't think so, Mack. I kept a pretty close watch on how you were doing."

A short, swarthy, overweight captain wearing the Selous Scout belt and beret came up to Reid-Daley. "Sir, I'm sorry to disturb you but there's a telephone call in the Operations Room for you. It's from ComOps. General St. John."

Carla felt her face flush slightly as Mack gave her an inquiring look. The colonel turned to them. "Meet Captain Paul Karl. You'll see Paul around here quite a bit. He's in charge of the Operations Room when he's out here with us. A territorial, you know, but nowadays with territorials serving one hundred eighty days in the military each year, there's very little difference between them and the regulars."

Carla stared at the captain. "Haven't I seen you before, Captain Karl?"

"Yes, I believe you have, Mrs. Hudson. When I'm not serving out here I run the family antique and curio business in Salisbury. I believe you've been in the store." He gave a slight bow.

"Of course, I bought two ivory bracelets from you. I had planned to send them back to my sister but I grew so attached to them I kept them for myself."

"I will see to it you get another pair for your sister, Mrs. Hudson," the antique dealer-Selous Scouts officer said gallantly. Then he addressed Mack. "It's a great pleasure to have you with us, Captain Hudson. I know about some of your exploits with SAS and RLI."

"I didn't know I was that well known," Mack said with genuine modesty.

"Well, I supposed I'll have to go over to the Ops Room and talk to the bugger," Reid-Daley excused himself. "Always when we're in the midst of something important like an external or a beer drink, dear General St. John absolutely has to talk to me." Still grumbling, he left the mess to take his call.

"You deal in ivory?" Mack asked Karl.

"All commodities that have a sales value, Captain Hudson," Karl replied.

To Mack, prudence seemed in order at this point. He had a vivid mental image of the dead elephants out in the Wafa Wafa preserve, their tusks gleaming in the sun, but he decided that the precise functions of this physically unfit though undoubtedly mentally agile soldier-merchant might best be left unpursued. He was a valuable man to the colonel and probably accounted for much of the foreign exchange which the Selous Scouts needed for their own unconventional and expensive weaponry.

Sergeants Joe Late and Eddie Wilson drifted over to Mack. They said hello to Carla and promised Roger and Al Glenlord they'd try to make it to the next Embassy party. They greeted Mack enviously. "I heard a rumor that you may take command of Three Group, Captain," Late said.

Mack shrugged. "I don't know. I'd sure take it if they gave it to me, Joe." He approved of the sergeant not addressing him by his first name even though in Vietnam they had both been officers together. Joe had received a battlefield commission after a particularly dangerous cross-border jump into Cambodia.

The Rhodesian Army, like the British Army, did not give out battlefield commissions and did not recognize an officer who received his commission in that manner from another army. To the Rhodesians Joe was still a sergeant.

Eddie Wilson paid his respects to Carla in the elaborate manner he had cultivated over the years. Eddie, a New Englander from New Hampshire whose freshman year at college had been interrupted in 1965 by the Vietnam War, voluntarily on his part, had served in the Special Forces until 1972. By that time he didn't exactly hold civilians in contempt, but he spent as little time around them as possible.

"So you fuckers got out of the selection course, did you?" Mack shot at them.

"That we did, Mack. And glad we are of it," Wilson replied. "I am led to believe that it's a strenuous exercise. Since I'm already in better shape than any mother around this camp, and keep myself that way, it would be a shame to let the sands of time run uselessly as I hastened through the jungle in pursuit of exactly nothing when I could be out slaying terrorists. The colonel saw it my way," he added.

"What do you know about that Captain Karl?" Mack asked.

"Other than that he is the richest man in the Selous Scouts, probably one of the richest men in the army including the general, not very much."

"Can you get that rich running an antique shop?"

"Well, now," Eddie replied thoughtfully, "it depends upon the antiques you sell and where you sell them. Captain Karl used to come over to Grey's Scouts next door to here, where I was a ferrier. The ivory we were able to bag on a good day, and the occasional zebra and lion skins, translated into new saddles from the States via our friend Captain Karl. He has a plethora of passports."

"Say no more. I understand. How about getting us all some of that good Castle Ale?"

Eddie Wilson headed over to the bar, picked up a handful of bottles of lager and brought them back to the group around Carla and Mack. They all drank from the bottle, Carla and Sarah gracefully curving their lips around the neck and eliciting stares and gulps from the Scouts in the room who had been eying them keenly from the moment they entered.

The RSM finished his own beer, ordered another and turned to the European Scouts who had gravitated to one end of the room, "Gentlemen, let us join our African members at their club. They're expecting us." There were a number of African sergeants at the European mess, old Selous Scouts who were so at home with their white counterparts that there was no feeling of separateness between them. Two of the black officers who had graduated from the first African officers' course the year before were also in the mess with their wives.

At the RSM's announcement the men bid goodbye to their ladies, who would return to Salisbury, and headed off for an all-male evening.

Sara and Colin Adderley walked outside for a last private kiss.

Mack turned to Carla. "Here's the key to the car. Drive it back to Salisbury. I'll get a ride in tomorrow."

Carla's lips quivered but she said, "It's been so long already I guess I can wait one more day for us to be together."

"Thank you, Carla. Goddamn, I appreciate your understanding." He looked into her face. "Oh shit! I'm sorry. Come on, I'll walk you out to the car."

Chapter 37

September 1978

At six-thirty the next morning Mack Hudson met Captain Herbert Spence and Major Conrad Van Roolyan in the adjutant's office. They saluted the tall young adjutant, Captain Turneville. It was customary for officers to salute the adjutant the first time they saw him in the day.

"The colonel is waiting for you in the Ops Room. I'll take you in," Turneville said. The two group commanders and Mack Hudson were led into the Operations Room. Their attention was immediately captured by a bearded man in a wheelchair beside Colonel Reid-Daley, who was standing beside a large situation map of Rhodesia. This, Mack knew, was the legendary young South African captain Derryk Bullard, who had been paralyzed by a gunshot wound in the spine. He had been one of the first Scouts and his combat exploits were legion. Beside Colonel Reid-Daley and his crippled operations' officer stood the rotund Captain Paul Karl. They were all intently staring at the lines Reid-Daley was drawing on the map's acetate overlay. Reid-Daley turned as the officers walked in and returned their salute.

"Good morning, gentlemen."

301

He introduced Hudson to the man in the wheelchair. "Captain Hudson, this is Captain Bullard, our operations officer." Mack shook hands.

"We've been looking forward to meeting you, Captain Hudson," Bullard said pleasantly. "Welcome to Selous Scouts."

Reid-Daley motioned the newcomers to chairs. "Gentlemen, for the last week General Walls and I have been meeting to plan the role for Selous Scouts in the coming months as we prepare for the first one-man-one-vote elections in Rhodesia. Ours is a key mission in the overall military planning to protect the population from the Communist Terrorists, who have promised to turn the balloting boxes into bloodbaths. It is the job of the Selous Scouts to make sure they don't."

He turned to Captain Hudson. "Mack, I'm sure you wondered why the selection course ended early, but it was necessary to get every man we could out in the operational areas. Before we go any further, let me tell you you'll be commander of Three Group, Selous Scouts. Congratulations."

Mack felt a thrill of pride greater than any he had experienced in his entire life. "Thank you, sir. I assure you you will never regret appointing me to the command."

"I'm well aware of your record in Vietnam and, more important, here in Rhodesia these last two years. It is obvious that your previous unit commander could not cope with you. The mission of Selous Scouts today, however, is such that only the most aggressive leaders can carry it out."

Reid-Daley turned to the map. "Now, to get to the heart of the matter, let's take a look at the methods of executing the mission which the commander of ComOps, General Peter Walls, has approved. He has told us what to do and we will do it without burdening him unnecessarily with specifics."

He laid his finger on the spout of the teakettle-shaped country of Rhodesia. "Right here is Lake Kariba." The colonel's index finger traced the northern border of Rhodesia from Victoria Falls all the way across the Mozambique border. Then he ran the finger from north to south down the Mozambique border to where it joined with South Africa at the Limpopo River.

"All along this Mozambique border are camps of terrorists just waiting to disgorge their murderers into Rhodesia."

At the northernmost point along the border he ran his finger deeply into Mozambique. "Here, fifty kilometers inside the border, is the largest terrorist staging area. We call it Camp Mugabe after their leader. At the moment there are about twenty-five hundred terrorists in the camp. We have our people inside posing as terrorists and giving us information on what's happening. It appears that this camp, like several others along the border, is preparing to receive as many as ten thousand terrorists. Here they will be armed, briefed, provisioned and sent into Rhodesia during the week before elections.

"The air force had deliberately refrained from overflying the camp which is well concealed in heavy jungle. We want the terrorists to think we don't know about this staging area, and no missions of any sort are being launched across the border against it. We are doing everything in our power to make the terrs think they have a secure campsite here." He stabbed a finger into the area in question.

Reid-Daley turned from the map to face Mack Hudson and the other two group commanders. "Our strategy, gentlemen, put in the simplest terms, is to raid, harass and destroy the terrorist camps inside the borders of Mozambique and Zambia while ignoring Camp Mugabe. It is our objective to make the enemy concentrate all his available men up in that one camp."

The colonel turned back to the map. "Our first target in Zambia will be this camp on Lake Kariba, a main terrorist staging area. We will call it Camp Nkomo after their fat leader, Joshua Nkomo. I'm just sorry the name sounds like our base here, Inkomo. There are probably five hundred men there right now and their number is growing. Ordinarily for an operation of this sort we would take three weeks, even a month to rehearse the assault. But, gentlemen, I'm afraid we do not have that luxury. We are getting close to the time the Prime Minister promised for elections. Six days from now I want that camp taken out and as many terrorists killed as you can manage."

Reid-Daley looked directly at Mack Hudson. "Mack, now you see why we decided not to waste any more of your time in the selection course. I know that you have actually been on several externals into that part of Zambia."

"Yes, sir. I have been on the ground near Camp Nkomo."

"Right. Mack, your Three Group will be given the job of taking out Camp Nkomo." He turned to his other two group commanders. "While Mack is executing the Zambian operation, your two groups will concentrate on Mozambique. We will be operating against targets from the Limpopo River all the way up to the region opposite the Gona-Re-Zhou game reservation and north to the Inyanga area. We stay south of Inyanga since we want them to believe Camp Mugabe is safe. If it were only the Kaffirs we had to worry about our strategy would work. However, we know they have Cuban, Russian, East German and Chinese technicians and strategists. It is possible that these advisers might sense our tactical plan. However, we trust the K factor will work in our favor. The terr leaders will opt as they always do for what seems the easiest and safest way. They will most likely ignore their white advisers and use Camp Mugabe as the main staging area. Mugabe hates *every* white man, even the ones that are trying to help him. He has promised to execute *every* white man he finds in Rhodesia once his Patriotic Front takes over."

There was silence for a few moments in the Operations Room, interrupted when a batman came in with tea for the colonel and coffee for the others.

"There's one other point of strategic importance which you should be apprised of," the colonel went on. "It has been decided to hold elections over a five-day period. Each day, one-fifth of the country will vote, giving the security forces a chance to cover that one-fifth in force."

He paused and Mack asked, "When do we start getting ready for the operation in Zambia, sir?"

Reid-Daley gave him a bleak smile. "As soon as you've finished your coffee, Captain."

"Yes, sir," Mack replied. His thoughts went to Carla. He wouldn't see her today, in fact maybe not even until after the operation in Zambia.

"Mack, you work out the plan with Derryk Bullard and his Ops group and Intelligence. Between all of you I think you'll come up with a plan of action that you can immediately start to execute. We'll use the airstrip at Bumi, right there on Kariba for a staging area. We'll have to restrict civilian aircraft from landing at Bumi the day you come in with your men."

The colonel glanced at his crippled officer who smiled back. "When you return from the mission in Zambia, all of you, including your wives and girl friends, are invited to a three-day wedding bash at the Kariba resort. Derryk is getting married. So you'll have something to look forward to. Until then, naturally, we've got to make this a very secure operation so I'm afraid you can't tell your wives much until you get back from the mission."

"That sounds reasonable, sir," Hudson said.

"Then, after the wedding in Kariba, you Mack will be going down to Mozambique and backing up the other two groups. Never has a small army like ours had to do so much in so short a time. But if we succeed, if the elections come off, there's no reason why Rhodesia should not be recognized by the entire Western world."

Reid-Daley looked around his group of officers owlishly. "At that point it will be up to the African gentleman who becomes prime minister to decide what he wants to do. Naturally, we all pray that the United States and Britain will give this little country the recognition it deserves, trade with us and let the white man and the African live and work side by side which is the way we do things in the Selous Scouts."

He rose. "Well, gentlemen, your work is cut out for you. I have a breakfast appointment in Salisbury with General Walls." Turning to Mack, he said, "Good luck, Mack. I'll be watching your progress. I'll be at Bumi to meet you when you get back from Camp Nkomo."

"I'll get the job done sir. It's a great honor to be given this operation. I have wanted to wipe them out for a year, but SAS never could get permission to go in force."

"I'm afraid your force will be a small one. We can only spare Three Group."

"That's almost a hundred men, sir," Mack replied. "More than enough to take out five or six hundred terrs."

"I agree," Reid-Daley said. He faced the other two commanders. "Spence, you and Van Roolyan will concentrate along the Mozambique border here."

The colonel stepped over to the map and ran his finger along the border. "FRELIMO troops are guarding this railhead here in Mozambique which is only five hundred meters from the Rhodesian border in the area of Gona-Re-Zhou. Troopships have been bringing trained terrorists from Dar es Salaam in Tanzania down the coast to Maputo."

The colonel pointed to Maputo, the large port city of Mozambique. "From there the terrorists go across Mozambique by train and arrive at the railhead thoroughly rested. It's then an easy matter for them to cross our border at night and murder helpless civilians. One of our missions is to wipe out this railhead and the tracks and roads leading to it. There are two other railheads along the border serving the same purpose. These must be put out of action as well."

Reid-Daley tapped several points deep in Mozambique. "All bridges that afford communications to the terrorists inside Mozambique must be blown up. We want to give the FRELIMO a taste of the sort of terrorism we are subjected to here. Perhaps they won't be so happy about hosting their terrorist friends when they see what the results are to their own country. Gentlemen, you go into Mozambique with unrestricted authority to lay waste to any FRELIMO camp you come across. I think Samora Machel will get the message." The group commanders cheerfully voiced their agreement.

"And so, to sum up, our strategy is twofold. One, discourage FRELIMO and Machel from aiding and protecting the Communist terrorists. Two, make every area of Mozambique contiguous with Rhodesian territory south of Camp Mugabe a virtual death trap for the terrorists. We do this and we drive all the terrorists up to Camp Mugabe where the entire Rhodesian Security Forces will concentrate a surprise attack and wipe out ten thousand terrs. Then we can have safe elections that will be meaningful to the rest of the world." He looked at his officers one by one. "Any questions?"

"Just one, sir." Mack said. "Is it permitted to make a phone call from here? I'd like to tell my wife she won't be seeing me tonight."

"Call her, Mack. But no explanation. I suspect that a certain general in the army, who hates Selous Scouts because I go around him to General Walls, keeps our phones under surveillance. Nobody but General Walls himself, and of course the P.M., knows anything about this operation. Recently there was a little matter of extra foreign exchange which the Selous Scouts have been arranging." Reid-Daley winked at Captain Karl. "Somehow the rather unorthodox methods we have been using to get foreign currency to buy special equipment was discovered by General St. John. Were it not for my unique relationship with General Walls we would have been in deep trouble. You understand why telephone security must be tight, Captain Hudson?"

"Yes, sir," Mack replied. "I'll prepare my command for the Kariba mission."

"Captain Turneville will arrange the air transport to Bumi for your Three Group."

"Yes, sir. Can I have my pick of the men that went through the selection course with me?"

"Yes, Mack, you can. For the Kariba mission. After that we apportion them out among the other two groups. Wouldn't be fair for you to have them all, now would it?"

"I'll worry about that after we've wiped out Camp Nkomo, sir."

"Good luck, Mack." Reid-Daley nodded to the other group commanders. "All right, gentlemen, please return to your groups." They saluted, turned and walked smartly from the colonel's office.

Chapter 38

Carla Hudson tried to conceal her disappointment and hurt as she walked through the wards at Andrew Fleming Hospital talking to the sick and wounded troops who had been brought in from the bush. Mack had been so uncommunicative, so cold-sounding on the phone when he had waked her up with his call. All he said was he wouldn't be seeing her for a while but after that they would have a lovely holiday. She had been hearing about the holiday for months. Now she doubted if there would ever be one. But the troopies here at the hospital, the men with nothing more to look forward to than getting well enough so they could go back to combat, didn't want to see sad faces on the nurses and assistants that worked the wards.

Just as she glanced at her watch and noted it was about the time General St. John usually arrived at the hospital, she heard his familiar sonorous baritone. "Sundowners when you get off work, Carla?"

Carla agreed almost gratefully. She had no idea when, if ever, she would see Mack again. The thought of sitting alone in the apartment another night dismayed her.

Roger and Jocelyn Masefield had, of course, invited her to come to the Embassy anytime, indeed to stay there if she was lonely. But she preferred the familiar apartment where Mack could reach her, even though she knew he probably wouldn't be trying to call her for a while.

"I expect Mack will be out in the bush for some time," Carla mused out loud.

"Dead right, Carla. Now that he's become one of Reid-Daley's ruffians I'm afraid you're not going to see much of him. But it will give us a chance to get acquainted again."

"Now that gorgeous creature from South Africa has gone home," Carla couldn't resist.

"Veronica?" He breathed airily. "She was never very interesting." A frown appeared on Ashley St. John's face as he thought about the WP reporter and his spurious job offer to Veronica. He remembered the pictures and story he had later submitted to ComOps for censorship as being quite tepid. A smile replaced the frown as he looked down at the beautiful, generously proportioned American girl. "I'll pick you up at the parking lot entrance at five o'clock. We'll go over to the Polo Club for sundowners."

"I'll be waiting, Ashley. I think I'll be able to use a drink about then."

Shortly after making her date with St. John she was surprised to see Alvin Glenlord come into the military wing of Fleming Hospital. He had been walking about the wards looking for her. "Hello, Carla," he greeted her. "I was hoping I'd find you here."

"Where else would I be? There's nothing else in my life these days."

"Any new Americans here in the last forty-eight hours?"

"Not that I know of. Quite a few chaps have been casevaced here from RLI operations north of Umtali. It's all so frustrating and endless," Carla sighed.

"What do you hear from Mack?"

"He called me this morning. About seven-thirty. He had his meeting with the colonel and all he said was he wouldn't be seeing me for at least a week."

"He'll be back, Carla. So he's off to some operation now, is he?" Al asked chattily.

"Obviously something's up. They cut short the training exercise and sent him out to the real thing."

Glenlord touched her on the shoulder. "I'm going down to Joburg on the five o'clock plane to do some shopping for the Embassy. Anything you need?"

"No, thanks just the same."

"Let Roger know if any Yanks are brought in here. He'll want to visit them and see what we can do to help."

"I'll ring the Embassy if any come in, Al," Carla promised.

Al Glenlord hurried from the hospital back to the Embassy where he was packed and ready to catch the flight to South Africa. He had no desire to explain to either Beryl or Roger why he was leaving so precipitously. When he returned tomorrow with two cases of Scotch for Embassy entertaining and the other items that couldn't be procured in Salisbury, these would seem reason enough for his trip.

Arriving at the Embassy, Al glanced disparagingly at the three flags flying on staffs outside before going in and making his way to the telex room.

"Anything I can do for you, Mr. Glenlord?" Mona, the secretary Beryl had hired for Roger, asked.

"No thanks. I'm on my way to Joburg. If anybody is looking for me I'll be back tomorrow. I've been putting off this supply run too long already."

"Could you pick up some thirty-five color film for me?" Mona asked.

"Of course. Anything else?"

"Well, my boyfriend gets back from National Service next week. I would love to give him a bottle of whiskey."

"I'll see what I can do for you on our Embassy allowance."

Salisbury was delighted by the existence of even a spurious American embassy and was disposed to allow its emissaries to bring in quite generous entertainment rations. "Call down to Air Rhodesia in Joburg, Eric Klein, and make sure he gets a reservation for me on the plane back tomorrow afternoon. And now I'm off."

311

Chapter 39

Tiffeny's was undoubtedly the most posh discotheque in Johannesburg. While the rock music blasted through the eccentric dancers on the ballroom floor there was also a soundproof dining room looking out through wide scenic windows over the gyrating couples who flocked to spend their money here. It was in this relatively quiet room that Al Glenlord waited for Donna Guest to arrive. He surveyed the bar closely and identified two men, either one or both of whom could have been Special Branch or BOSS operatives.

On this trip he had told Beryl in advance that he was meeting Donna and even where the meeting would take place. He reiterated that she was a friend of Lorraine's family and there was no thought on either side—the truth he thought ruefully—of any intimacy between them. And now there was the unmistakable face and form of one of Ken Flowers' men at the bar.

Al stood up as he saw Donna arrive at the maitre d''s desk at the entrance to the restaurant section of Tiffeny's. Once again he mentally congratulated the Agency for hiring a woman this beautiful. Her conservative black suit which contrasted with the long blonde hair was tailored in such a way as to emphasize her physical charms. This was a young lady who definitely stood out in any company, the very last person anyone, including the two secret police agents at the bar, Al was certain, would ever suspect of being a covert operative.

A broad grin came over his face as he anticipated the report Beryl would receive about the physical appearance of the young woman who was a friend of Al's wife. Al took Donna's arm and led her to his corner table, seating her on the banquet and sliding in beside her.

"It's great to see you again, Donna," Al greeted her.

"Nice to see you, Al."

In lowered tones he said, "Beryl heard all about our last meeting. I expect that at least one SB guy is at the bar."

Donna smiled back at him. "I felt just the slightest breeze of interest in me but it quickly blew over. I have to assume my apartment in Hillbrow is bugged and handle company business accordingly."

"Oh you are fine and this surveillance is just routine. I have served Rhodesia well for a year, even getting into sanctions busting on their behalf but they're still suspicious of most foreigners."

"Was Beryl upset when she heard about me?"

"She had a jealous pique for a while. I told her your family and my wife Lorraine's were old friends and I promised to show you the ancient city of Zimbabwe." He chuckled. "She said she would come along with us to make sure you didn't miss anything."

They ordered drinks and Al's hand toyed with hers on the table, where the gesture could be seen.

"You're going to get quite a lecture from Beryl about," her voice was tinged with irony, "old family friends."

"Better that than an interrogation at SM about my contacts when I leave Rhodesia."

Donna nodded, a serious look coming over her face. "Sometimes I forget how dangerous all this really is."

"Just be careful—and alert."

The drinks were placed in front of them and when the waiter moved off, Al, openly affectionate, leaned closer to her. "Am I tuned in?"

"Go ahead, Al."

"OK love. Don't mind if I slightly paw you from time to time for the benefit of our tails at the bar."

"You mean you won't really mean it?" she mocked.

"As a matter of fact I will. But we can go into it later—and you can erase that little remark from the wire."

"Start," she commanded.

"About three weeks ago I was at the home of the Minister Pleni-potentiary, M.M. De Vries for dinner. There was just himself, Beryl Stoffel and me. During the conversation he told me that a prime, a priority external target was a guerrilla staging area which the Rhode-sians call Camp Nkomo, for obvious reasons, on the Zambia side of Lake Kariba. Actually it sits beside the Choma River."

Al picked up her hand and held it a moment. "With the interim biracial government headed by Ian Smith working toward elections for a black nationalist prime minister to take place late in the year, they've got to start taking out these terrorist camps. Apparently from Camp Nkomo hundreds, even thousands of terrorists will be trans-ported across Lake Kariba to the Rhodesian shore. According to MM there can be as many as a thousand of Nkomo's men there at any given time. At dinner MM said that this camp will be attacked from the Choma River by the Selous Scouts. I gather they will go up river by boat, stage a landing, and sweep through the camp. Personally I hope they obliterate it and kill every terrorist in Zambia."

"When is the attack going to take place?" Donna asked eagerly.

"The Selous Scouts just two days ago cancelled a training exercise in order to run a major operation. I estimate the attack will take place in a week, ten days at the most. It will take them that long to get their logistics in place."

"I'll go over to my control at the U.S. Embassy student visa de-partment and send this to Langley first thing in the morning." There was a gleam of excitement in Donna's eyes.

"Hell, they're six hours behind us. Sleep late and relax," Al ad-vised with a suggestive grin on his face. "You know how the Director likes to let the President know what's happening before it happens. Well, he's still got plenty of time on this one. There isn't anything that the administration is going to do about this situation anyway. The President will probably let his buddy Andy Young know about it so he won't be surprised."

Al placed a hand on hers. "You know, Donna, if we're going to be working together we should get to know each other better. I really think it is important for you to come up to Rhodesia and see the country—Zimbabwe; Bulawayo, original home of the Zulus; Victoria Falls—after all you are working for an advanced degree in African studies."

"And you and Beryl will show me around?" She looked at him with wide, innocent eyes.

"I think I can handle that sight seeing trip all by myself," Al chuckled.

Donna pushed a lock of lustrous blonde hair away from her eyes. "Will that be all, or is there anything else you want to say to the little microphone in the tip of my bra?"

Al became serious. "I've made the following observations and deductions. First, let me say that in view of the current administration policy toward Rhodesia and South Africa the sooner we arrange to get Roger Masefield out of Rhodesia the better. I see all the mail that comes in to him. He's building a large and influential following in many parts of the industrialized world. I have a number of contingency plans which I will outline, including his termination with extreme prejudice, which I am prepared to carry out if so ordered."

"You could do that? To your friend?" She seemed truly shocked. "I am under the impression that neither we nor any other agency or arm of the United States Government were permitted to order or carry out assassinations. We are what we call ourselves, an intelligence gathering organization."

Al decided against any form of advanced indoctrination in Donna Guest's case. She was well situated, operating under secure cover, in an area where Americans were rightly suspect and innovative U.S. agents needed. Let her continue to be a scholar at heart so long as she was useful. With delivery to control of his information on the pending Selous Scouts attack into Zambia, Al had accomplished his mission. Now he would concentrate on what he wanted his SB surveillance agents to think he was doing here, dating a pretty fellow American girl while on a purchasing trip for Roger Masefield.

They had a pleasant dinner and then joined the oscillating crowd on the floor in the next room for one blast of the disco. Here Al could talk to her without fear of being picked up on either her wire or by the SB or BOSS agents.

"We'll make it an early night and I'll take you home. Now I want you to invite me up for a nightcap when I take you home." She started to protest but he cut her off. "This is business, Doll. I'll just sit around for a decent interval and then leave but tonight's got to look social. The entire life style, even the very lives of these people in Rhodesia and South Africa are in jeopardy and we Americans, at least as long as

Jimmy Carter is the President, are part of the enemy. There may well be some suspicion of you and me already. We've got to head it off."

"By having a romantic fling together?" she asked sharply.

"By at least appearing to be doing something of the kind," he shot back in exasperation.

"Don't you see?" he went on. "If by any chance they discover that the Scouts' mission has been compromised I'm going to be suspect. And anybody I have been seeing that they can't unequivocally account for will be considered an accomplice. So we're going to sit around up in your place talking about your tour of Rhodesia with me—Boss has probably got you wired—"

"I've always assumed so," Donna agreed.

"And we're going to talk suggestively and when you finally kick me out it will be with the promise that next time maybe we'll have a more intimate relationship. Understand?"

"I suppose so."

"If you and I have convinced them, I'll know all right."

Donna laughed aloud. "Beryl will be informed and she'll give you hell."

"Right. And when that happens we're clear, you and I, of any subversive activities."

"OK, Al. That all registers top form with me. When do you want to take me home?"

"Are you enjoying the evening?" Al asked, holding her to him as he made a turn on the floor.

"I always feel a sense of satisfaction when I've done my job," she replied flatly.

"Right. Then we might as well go along now." He led her off the floor and out of the syncopated tumult. At their table he paid the check, noticing that the original pair watching him had been replaced by a fresh team.

"Yes, Al, I did enjoy my work tonight," Donna said as they waited for a cab outside Tiffeny's.

"I like hearing that." A cab pulled up and he helped her into the back seat and slid in beside her. "Tell him where to take us, Donna."

Donna gave the driver her address and sat back. "How long do you intend to stay at my place?" she asked with more curiosity than impatience.

"Let's play it by ear. Do you have a window that looks over the street?"

"As a matter of fact I do."

"Well, we'll give the boys a chance to wonder what we're doing and then I'll leave you and let them follow me back to the Landdrost Hotel."

"Anything you say. This kind of stuff they don't teach in any of the courses. You have to learn it by yourself."

Chapter 40

Carla was suffused with a sense of well-being as she sat back on the sofa beside Ashley. They had enjoyed sundowners on the veranda of the Polo Club, followed by a leisurely dinner, and now in Ashley's comfortable flat the record player was providing a soft curtain of semiclassical music. Ashley, who had his arm around her shoulders, drew her closer; she could feel her breasts against him and succumbed to another warm kiss. Then she sat up straighter and took some brandy from the snifter.

"Oh dear," she said. "It's almost midnight. I should be getting back, Ashley."

"Why? Tomorrow is not your day at the hospital. What else is there to do?"

Carla lifted her shoulders prettily. "I don't know. I just feel I should get home."

"Have you enjoyed the evening?"

"Of course. It's just that—"

"You feel you are being disloyal?"

"I suppose so. But I shouldn't. There's nothing else to do."

She thought of the cryptic phone call that morning. Mack would not be able to see her as planned. He would be incommunicado for an indefinite period. But soon they would have a nice holiday together.

Surely, she thought with sudden pique, if he had really wanted to he could have slipped away for a few hours.

Yes, of course, Mack and all of them were fighting for a cause they believed in. But their own country was against them. As far as Carla was concerned it was Rhodesia's war; for foreigners to participate in it was madness.

"And there won't be anything else to do," Ashley broke harshly into her thoughts, "as long as Captain Hudson is with that wretched outfit. I don't know why Peter Walls ever allowed it to be formed. Reid-Daley runs his own little military fiefdom out there at Inkomo Barracks. The rest of us at ComOps have nothing to say about Selous Scouts operations. Sometimes I wonder myself if they go out and commit some of these atrocities and blame them on the terrorists."

Carla gasped. "You can't believe that, Ashley."

"No, of course not. But there's something badly wrong when a lieutenant colonel can bypass a general and run his show precisely the way he wants to."

"Mack says that's why Selous Scouts are so effective."

Ashley St. John again allowed his arm to draw her close. She didn't resist. "Carla, we're in a war. The way Britain and the United States are treating us we could lose. The Communists could win power here. Let's live while we have the opportunity. God knows what the future will bring. And you can be sure you won't see much of Mack Hudson. They go out for a month or more at a time. What kind of a marriage do you call that?"

"Mack is a soldier. I married him for better or worse."

"Well, he didn't have to come here and get into our fight. But since he did, I think a beautiful woman like you should not let life pass her by."

It was true. At thirty Carla could not escape the feeling that life was somehow getting away from her, that she was not really living. She swallowed the last of her drink. Yes, she *would* enjoy her life. If Mack's pleasure was to be out in the bush killing guerrillas, let him have what he wanted. She had the right to live too. "Ashley, could I have one more drink please?"

A slow smile spread across Ashley's handsome face. "Of course, my darling." He took his arm from her shoulder and leaned forward, picking up the brandy bottle and pouring the dark aromatic liquid into the glass globes before them.

Later, after he had given her a kiss and she had returned it with equal pressure as his fingers idly caressed one of her breasts, she murmured without a great deal of conviction. "Ashley, I'm not staying with you. I hope you understand that."

"My dear, you'll do just what you want to do. Of course I'd love to have you stay over with me tonight and, as often as you can. But that has to be your decision."

"Thank you Ashley. I'm glad you understand." Once more, re-laxed, contented, she snuggled against this urbane and reassuring presence.

There was a tenderness about the way Ashley held and kissed her. He seemed to understand her feminine nature. Maybe it was wrong of her, but she was enjoying it. She acknowledged the truth of Ashley's words about living, too.

Just a few days ago she had just missed being on the corner of Rhodes Avenue and Fourth Street when a bomb had exploded, killing two people and wounding several more. Salisbury was becoming a risky place to live. She had thought of going home, but that would have been deserting Mack and she couldn't bring herself to do it. Yet what was she doing now?

Ashley was pulling her to him even more closely. She responded. Putting her arms around his neck and letting him caress her, kiss her neck, his tongue in that sensitive hollow where neck and shoulder joined, she felt sensual vibrations throughout her body.

Mack Hudson had always been a rugged, straightforward, sexu-ally satisfactory lover. But this was something new. Mack was the only man she had ever allowed to make love to her. She had given herself to him before they'd been married. But not to anyone else. It was the Latin influence, she guessed.

"Oh no, no, Ashley. I told you I can't." His hand was now nestled deep between her thighs. She'd hardly noticed it until suddenly he had almost reached a point of no return.

"Of course you can, my darling," Ashley breathed in her ear.

Carla struggled from his arms into a sitting position. "No, Ashley, I'm sorry. I didn't mean to let it go this far. But I can't. I can't do it to Mack. He's out there in those ghastly jungles somewhere and here I am doing this."

"Apparently he's where he wants to be, Carla," Ashley remarked dryly. "You went to the Selous Scouts passing out parade yesterday."

"Yes." She sighed. "I saw Mack for all of one and a half hours. Then he had to go to some beer drink with the Africans. He couldn't even come back into town with me. And this morning . . ." A betrayed look came into her eyes.

"What happened, Carla?"

"He called. He only said that he wouldn't be able to see me."

"Did he say any more than that?" General St. John asked curiously.

"No, that's all he said. Just that he would be in touch with me when he could."

"That will be quite a while, Carla."

"Why do you say that?"

"That bunch of renegades he belongs to will probably be engaged in unilateral external activities."

Carla wanted to cry.

"Don't look so tragic, my dear."

"There's no end to it, Ashley. Every day more boys wounded in the war. . . Oh, I don't know." She compressed her lips. "I'm sorry, Ashley. You must think me a terrible complainer. Compared to what you all are going through, I have no problems at all."

"Carla, what you need is to get away from here. Let me take you this weekend up to the Bumi Hills Lodge. It's a beautiful place. You can look at elephants, baboons playing, hippos; we'll take a boat ride out on Lake Kariba and relax a bit. We both need it. I can see you are about to go into a depression."

"I appreciate the thought, Ashley. But I guess I'd better stay at the apartment. Mack might call."

"Stay if you want to. But Mack won't be calling. Take my advice. I'll get us each a nice room and we'll have a long weekend and forget the war. I'm going anyway, Carla. Let me take you along. I'll book a room for you."

Carla looked around Ashley's warm, hospitable flat and thought of her own lonely apartment. For a moment she relived the brief meeting with her husband yesterday. He had seemed so preoccupied, so cool to her.

"I'll pay for my own room, Ashley," she uttered impulsively.

"As you like, my dear." A slow smile of anticipation spread across his face. "You'll love Bumi, Carla. I'll lay on a small plane to fly us up there."

"It sounds like fun, Ashley!" Her eyes were bright. She had made the commitment and was happy about it. Ashley of course was right: there was no telling when she might see Mack again. A nagging doubt gnawed at her. Supposing Mack did get a few days off and tried to reach her at the apartment? But no, as Ashley had said, Mack and his precious Scouts would be off on some wild mission.

"But Ashley, just let me work things out for myself, OK?" He nodded sagely and then bussed her on the lips. "I'm sure we'll have a beautiful time at Bumi," she managed to get out.

"Of course, darling. Do you want me to take you home now?"

"I think that would be best. I'm looking forward to Bumi already. I've heard so much about it. Mack and I were always planning a trip there."

"Don't wait for him. The Selousies don't see much of hearth and home." Ashley stood up. "Right then, love. I'll take you home." He held his almost empty glass aloft and toasted roguishly. *"A bientôt.."*

Chapter 41

The United States Ambassador to the United Nations stood in his eleventh floor office in the Mission Building and looked out over the stately, modern, architectural creation that was the UN. Beyond it flowed the East River where an endless procession of barges and tugboats plied to and fro. The ambassador, despite the aggressive bravado that was his trademark in public never ceased to marvel inwardly that he, a black man from the deep South, bearing all the scars of the Civil Rights movement in which he had fought so bitterly, could be the master of this mighty international assembly. For indeed, like it or not, the U.S. Chief of Mission was the hidden force that made the UN work. Without America's funding the UN would collapse.

"He's waiting outside, Andy," a prompting voice came from behind the ambassador.

"Are we secure, Stoney?" Ambassador Young asked.

"Swept the office just an hour ago."

"This is the only room I trust. I sure don't say anything of any consequence over at that fine suite in the Waldorf."

"Are you ready for Professor Zvobgo?"

"Sure, send him in."

The ambassador's assistant stepped outside and led the tall black into the office. "Professor Eddison Zvobgo," he announced.

"We're old friends," the ambassador said, reaching out to shake his visitor's hand. "You never been up here before?"

"No, until now I have never been to your office." Zvobgo looked around wonderingly at the collection of African artifacts that festooned the ambassador's office. "Place looks like a museum for black studies," he chuckled. "Doesn't leave much doubt where your spirit is."

The ambassador gestured toward a chair and facing sofa. "Sit down, Eddison. We can talk openly here. To tell you the truth, except for my office right after it's been swept for bugs, I don't know a place in the UN where you can talk without being taped. You've heard the expression 'walls have ears'? They do here, and so does the glass in the windows. Something to do with vibrations. Anyway, we're OK for a while. What do you hear from Zimbabwe?"

"We are proceeding on schedule. When they finally have the elections we will wreck them. As our leaders say, we'll turn the balloting places into bloodbaths. Just don't let the Fascists in the United States pressure you into lifting sanctions against whatever white man's puppet government follows the Smith regime."

"That may be difficult, but we'll prevail. A lot of powerful senators, some in the President's own party, are giving him hell to lift sanctions."

An alarmed look crossed the pockmarked black face. "You can't let them do it. If Zimbabwe can trade with the world before Nkomo and Mugabe take power, the Patriotic Front will lose."

The ambassador lifted a stilling hand. "Peace, brother Zvobgo. The President will not do anything in Africa without my personal approval. I don't care if the Senate passes a resolution or even a bill, the President will not lift sanctions."

"I heard that a book written by some American is having too much influence in Washington."

The ambassador screwed up his face. "The Fascists found their mouthpiece in this Roger Masefield. But your people are helping him. He got a lot of mileage out of the atrocities, and when comrade Mugabe tells the world he plans to create a one-party Marxist state in Zimbabwe and massacre all the whites, it makes it difficult for us to continue supporting the Patriotic Front."

"Robert does get his blood up," Zvobgo conceded.

"Even worse politically, Mugabe and to an extent Nkomo give the impression that they will nationalize industry and mining and the Soviets will take over the strategic minerals the United States needs to stay equal with Russia in defense capabilities." the ambassador complained. "Fortunately for us, most Americans miss this, and even at the Department of Defense they're accustomed to say to industry, 'This is what we need, build it.' Until now industry has always had the materials to produce. Masefield keeps reminding people—every member of Congress was sent his book—that if the United States does not lift sanctions and support a moderate government, the Marxists will come in and America will be helpless to compete with Russia in any future arms race."

"What can you do about him?" Zvobgo asked, his eyes flashing fiercely. "Can't you take care of him?"

"Yes, and we will. In our own way. I have tried to make Robert and Joshua understand how important it is for them to use more restraint in the rhetoric that finds its way back to America. I wish you would impress that on them. If I didn't own the President, he would have found it convenient to give in to congressional pressure, and it's growing every day, to lift sanctions against Rhodesia even before it becomes Zimbabwe."

"I've seen this racist writer Masefield on the TV and read newspaper interviews," Zvobgo ranted. "I saw the advertisement, a full page on the back of the *New York Times*, for his book. He took a picture of Nkomo in his damned field marshal uniform that makes him look like Idi Amin, and he splashes the question, 'Why does Andy Young support this terrorist for the new leadership in Rhodesia?'!" Foam specked the professor's mouth as he railed on. "How can you let him do this? You must stop this Fascist. He is like Hitler!"

Again the ambassador held up a restraining hand. "We have him in our sights. He's doing a lot of damage, but even though *he* doesn't know it he's also helping us mightily."

"And how does that happen?"

The ambassador chose not to answer the question directly.

"I'm going to give you some information the President passed on to me last night. I am not supposed to repeat it but I think you will be discreet."

"Of course, of course." Zvobgo leaned forward attentively.

"In about five days the Rhodesian Selous Scouts are going to attack one of your staging areas in Zambia."

"Do you know which one?" The African asked eagerly.

"The Rhodesians call it Camp Nkomo."

"That could be any one of a dozen camps," Zvobgo snapped.

"It's on Lake Kariba at a point where a river called the Choma joins it. They plan to go up the river in boats, according to my intelligence sources. Does that narrow it down for you?"

"A little." The long slow smile that spread across the gnarled black features told the ambassador that his visitor knew exactly the location to which he was referring.

"I haven't told my colleague from Zambia," the ambassador continued, "because it would soon get back to my people in Washington that I had let loose a secret. But you, I think, have plenty of time to warn Joshua what's coming."

"I wish there was a way to thank you adequately, Mr. Ambassador."

"There is. Wipe out every red-neck in Rhodesia and take over your country. I can keep the President behind you. I tell him what to do in Africa."

"I'll have this information on the way to Lusaka in an hour." Zvobgo stood up to leave.

"You forgot something, Professor," the ambassador said. He walked around to his desk and picked up a note. "Give this to the receptionist downstairs and she'll issue six tickets to the Security Council meeting for you and your top students. That's why you came to see me, remember?"

Zvobgo took the note and smirked. The ambassador, a hand on the professor's shoulder, walked him to the door of his office. "Good luck, Eddison!"

Chapter 42

Samuel Jobolingo's arrival in Lusaka on a Mozambique Airways plane lent credence to his mission to form a tighter military liaison between the two squabbling factions of the Patriotic Front, Mugabe's ZANU party and Nkomo's ZAPU party. He was exhilarated at the honor bestowed upon him which, when the war was over, would assure him of one of the better white man's homes in Salisbury.

General Tongogara and Rex Nhongo had both supported Jobo for this assignment and Mugabe himself had approved it. Jobo had no affection for Nkomo or his Zulus of the Matabele tribe. Like all the ZANU Freedom Fighters, Jobo was Shona. But tribal and party differences had to be put aside now. Somehow the white man's elections to install a puppet African prime minister in Salisbury had to be disrupted.

Only a coordinated effort by the rival factions of the Patriotic Front could accomplish this. Mugabe, the wily tactician, had been the first to send one of his officers to Nkomo's camp. Now Nkomo would be obliged to do likewise and hopefully, instead of fighting each other, ZANU and ZAPU, Shona and Matabele would fight together.

Jobolingo had been escorted from the airport in a ZAPU automobile straight to Nkomo's headquarters in Lusaka. It was the first time he had been in Zambia's capital and he was impressed with the large concrete and glass buildings. It was not the city Salisbury was and there was an air of decay about it, but still it was far superior to any city he had seen in Mozambique.

The ZAPU leader kept Jobo waiting for almost two hours as black men and some whites walked through the waiting room in the direction of Nkomo's office. Although it had affronted Mugabe's delegate to be kept waiting while others were ushered into the presence ahead of him, Jobo sat quietly until his name was called.

Two uniformed men led him from the drab anteroom through a parlor in which a group of men, all speaking the Matabele language which he did not speak well, seemed to be holding a meeting. Then his escorts opened a set of double doors and Jobo found himself in the presence of the ZAPU leader. He instantly recognized the "great elephant," as Nkomo was sometimes known. He was incredibly fat and wearing the field marshal uniform that had been tailored for him in London. Around him were a number of his functionaries, standing or sitting.

Nkomo addressed Jobolingo in English, language of the hated white man but the only language that cut across tribal dialects. For the first twenty minutes Nkomo lectured the rival guerrilla leader's emissary about the strength of ZAPU's army, known as ZIPRA (Zimbabwe People's Revolutionary Army), and its ultimate invincibility, and then asked Jobo how ZANU's army, ZANLA (Zimbabwe African National Liberation Army), was preparing to disrupt the coming elections.

Jobo began by boasting of ZANLA's military prowess. "We will have three hundred tanks at our disposal when we are ready to invade. And we have SAM missiles and are trained to fire them at aircraft."

This last interested Nkomo. "Are you able to fire the Russian-made SAM?"

"Yes. And I have trained many men, too."

"Now how does Comrade Mugabe propose that we work together efficiently to wreck the elections?"

From his plastic briefcase Jobo pulled out a document and laid it on Nkomo's desk. "This is General Tongogara's plan for sectoring Zimbabwe into battle zones which we will divide up between us. As you will see, there are three basic operational designations, Northern Province, Central Province and Southern Province. We will fight in the eastern sections of the provinces nearest to Mozambique and you will fight in the western sections along the Zambia and Botswana borders where you are strongest."

Nkomo studied the maps laid before him. "Comrade Mugabe has it all worked out, I see," he commented dryly.

"He suggests that we be careful not to enter each other's battle areas in Gaza, the Southern Province."

Neither man had to comment on the reason for the suggestion. Both were well aware of the pitched battles between ZANU and ZAPU forces in the South where the Rhodesian Security Forces had stood aside and watched their enemies take a fearful toll of each other. The ultimate war, of course, would be civil in nature as Nkomo and Mugabe battled for the leadership of Zimbabwe.

"Are you empowered to negotiate the exact sectors of responsibility?" Nkomo asked sharply.

"Yes, unless some sectors are in dispute."

"Temporarily then, let's agree now on the sectors in the Northern and Central Province. I have a thousand men ready to send across Lake Kariba sometime in the next two weeks. Comrade Mugabe and I will personally negotiate on Gaza."

"That is good." Jobo well knew that the Gaza Province was the seat of Matabele Zulu strength. Nkomo's birthplace near Bulawayo, Zimbabwe's second largest city, was in this Southern Province.

As Nkomo's men drew around the desk, he inked out the sectors of responsibility that Zanu would terrorize during the elections. "I wish we knew when the election will really be held," Nkomo commented. "Smith and his puppets in Salisbury say before the end of this year. He's announced it to the world. It will be embarrassing for him to wait until 1979."

When the sectors had been meticulously defined Nkomo made a suggestion. "You take a copy of this map down to my staging area on the Choma River and make sure that our commanders there understand where they can go and where they must leave it to your people. I pass on to you the responsibility for making certain that my people know they must not trespass on Comrade Mugabe's sector. So, Comrade Jobolingo, as they say in London, the ball is squarely in your court."

Nkomo laughed and poured himself a tumbler full of brandy from the bottle on his desk. He drank deeply, not offering any of his refreshment to the others in the office.

Jobolingo froze his facial muscles so as not to show the revulsion that gripped him in the presence of this monstrously fat Zulu. It would only be a matter of time before Mugabe wiped out Nkomo and his forces. For the time being cooperation against the white man's puppets was the only way to ultimate victory in Zimbabwe.

"Now, to demonstrate how good our intelligence is," Nkomo chortled, "you are being sent to our main staging area at an exciting moment, Comrade. We know that in the next few days the Selous Scouts are going to attack us. They will come up the Choma River in boats and land at the base. But we are waiting for them and will wipe them out to a man. I wish I could be there myself," he added with relish. "What a great moment. We will send the heads of the white officers on poles back to their friends."

Jobolingo, for the first time since entering Nkomo's office, felt a surge of joy. What sweet satisfaction it would be to shoot or preferably bayonet some Selous Scouts. On the other hand, he thought, his orders had been strict and clear. He was not to get into any fighting if he went across into Zimbabwe. He was too valuable alive. But in a defensive battle?

"And now, Comrade, we will have our map here copied and you will be driven down to the staging area before nightfall," Nkomo concluded.

"Yes, Comrade Leader," Jobolingo replied with a wide smile. "I am grateful for this opportunity."

"By the way, Comrade, don't tell anyone at all about this," Nkomo cautioned. "We wouldn't want our Zambian friends to find out. President Kaunda is becoming nervous about Rhodesian raids into Zambia and I'm afraid will soon ask us to stop using his country for launching attacks on Rhodesia. This Selous Scouts matter is one we can handle ourselves."

Chapter 43

Just before last light, three Dakotas landed at the Bumi airstrip and taxied down to the far end next to the waters of Lake Kariba. Mack Hudson and seventy-five other Selous Scouts picked from Three Group disembarked and walked into the deep bush. Each man was carrying a weapons bag. Because they frequently carried AK-47s and other Communist-manufactured weapons, the colonel had decreed that the Scouts carry such armament concealed in these special bags which he had designed himself. The Communist weapons, in many cases better than those available to the Rhodesian Security Forces, were associated by the locals throughout the country with terrorists. Either the Scouts would be mistaken for terrorists if they carried these weapons openly, or the people would conclude the terrorists had better weapons than the security forces if the Scouts carried them in preference to their own.

The AK-47 was lighter than the FN carried by the Rhodesians and a combat load of 210 of its rounds weighed half a similar load of FN ammunition.

Of particular value to the Scouts was the Russian-designed RPD light machine gun which weighed 15 pounds as compared to the 25-pound machine gun that was standard in the security forces. Also the RPD delivered more firepower and one man could carry 500 rounds, rounds which could also be fired from the AK-47. Altogether it was the finest light machine gun made in the world, Mack Hudson was convinced.

Mack led his men past the Selous Scouts security guards and into the maximum security staging area used by the Scouts for some of their missions on Lake Kariba.

By the time they reached the briefing hut darkness had fallen. Inside the structure, which was invisible at night and difficult to see even in the daylight, the men of Three Group sat on benches looking at the charts and diagrams that had been affixed to easels. Captain Turneville, six feet five inches tall, stood facing Mack's group. On one side of him was Captain Karl, on the other an African dressed in camouflage fatigues. Also present were the pilots whose aircraft would support the raid. Derryk Bullard had not been able to come on account of his wheelchair.

Turneville wasted no time getting into the briefing. "Captain Hudson, men of Three Group, in one hour you will be taking the booze cruise. Without the booze though, I regret to inform you." He gave them a tight smile. "The cruise boats will pick you up at the dock just beyond this position. You will cruise five miles along the lakeshore to our marina where you'll pick up ten Zodiacs, inflatable rubber boats that hold eight operational personnel and two other crewmen. Each Zodiac has two 40 h.p. outboard engines. The cruise boats will tow the Zodiacs across Lake Kariba until they reach this point here"—he tapped the chart with a pointer—"which is two miles from the point you will land inside Zambia."

He turned to another chart, a large-scale blowup of the immediate area where they would be conducting their operation. "You will land your boats here at the mouth of the Choma River where Camp Nkomo has been constructed. Pull your boats up onto high ground and set up the big means TR-48 HF radio relay point close by.

"Our original plan had been to take the boats two miles up the river and land on the beach just below the camp. However, the river is apt to amplify any sounds the boats make; moreover, we just learned the river is alive with crocodiles. These crocs are so vicious they will turn over the native boats to get at the people inside. All in all it seemed that a two or three mile jungle stroll to Camp Nkomo would be preferable to tangling with the crocs."

"Here, here!" a number of the Scouts agreed.

"This information, and the fact that there could be one thousand terrs at the camp at the moment, comes to us courtesy of a young man who will be your chief asset on the raid. One week ago a radar patrol boat intercepted a terr craft and managed to take one prisoner alive. He has been most cooperative since," he added with dour humor, "thanking us for saving him from his former Chimuranga comrades."

Turneville turned to the skinny, sallow-faced African beside him. "Cancer here was in Camp Nkomo just a week ago. He will be with you and guide you through the bush to the camp. He's decided he prefers our side to the terrorists' I'm happy to say. But I would advise you, Mack, to have one of your men keep him under close surveillance. If he shows any sign of ratting, shoot him."

Cancer listened to these instructions without batting an eye. Turneville went on: "I will stay in touch with you through the HF radio relay when you form your assault lines behind Camp Nkomo. Because commo up here is so bad, an air force Lynx will be hovering above the operation at all times and can relay signals back to us here."Mack listened intently, Jacques LeClair on one side of him and Horst Houk on the other. The Englishman, Adderley, sat with his stick on another bench.

Mack stood up and scanned the grease-blackened faces of his seventeen stick leaders. "OK, you know what the score is," he began. "I want to make damn sure we get in amongst those bastards before we open fire. We want a few prisoners. But only a few," he added somberly. "Before I issue my five-paragraph order I want you to re-check the following items."

Seventeen heads bent intently over their pocket-size notebooks, pencils held at the ready. "Each stick will carry the following weaponry." Mack began to read.

"One RPD light machine gun with 400 rounds.

"One FN grenade launcher with 6 fragmentation rifle grenades and one WP rifle grenade. Also 180 rounds of FN ammo.

"The other two men will carry either AK-47s or AKMs with 300 rounds each.

"Every man will carry 2 fragmentation hand grenades.

Mack looked up from his notebook. "You stick leaders will carry the requisite signaling equipment to back up your small means A-63 radios: air panels, pencil flares, grenades, heliographs, and whistles. Each stick will have a basic combat medic pack and the more technical stuff will be with Doc McCracken who will be located with my head-quarters stick at the center of the assault line. Now for fuck's sake, caution your people about target identification. We don't want to shoot each other. Remember, a green pencil flare followed by red means cease fire. Stick leaders will also blow their whistles for cease fire."

He then launched into his five-paragraph attack order. Each phase of the operation was clearly and concisely explained: situation, mission, execution, administration, logistics and finally signals. To the untrained ear some of what he said might have sounded needlessly repetitive, but to the battle-hardened professional it was all consistent with the 6 "P" principle: Prior Planning Prevents Piss-Poor Performance.

When the briefing was over the Scouts filed outside and drew from the ordnance building the additional weapons and equipment they would use on the mission. Every other man in the eighty-man strike force carried an AK-47. The others carried an assortment of grenade launchers, FN rifles and rocket-propelled grenade launchers. They all had grenades attached to their webbing.

The two cruise ships commonly used for sightseeing along the Kariba River were waiting at the dock and the heavily armed band made its way on board, splitting into two detachments of forty each.

It was eight o'clock at night when the cruise ships pulled out of Bumi and headed along the coast to where the Zodiac rubber boats were waiting five miles away. The Zodiac boats were tied to the stem of a larger vessel which would ferry the men across Lake Kariba at high speed until it dropped anchor at a point close to shore. Then the Scouts would pile into the Zodiacs and head for the target area.

Chapter 44

The more he saw of Nkomo's ZIPRA, the more confident Jobolingo became in the ability of Comrade Mugabe's ZANLA forces to win the final war and take over power in Zimbabwe.

Driving south toward Lake Kariba with two of Nkomo's officers was a tedious business, particularly since the latter talked to each other in Matabele. In English the driver of the car informed him that they were just passing the Pemba Zambian Army garrison. It was fifteen miles down the road to the ZIPRA staging area.

"In Mozambique the FRELIMO help to protect us," Jobo said, looking at the army installation as they passed by. "If we knew an attack was coming we would ask them for help. These Zambians are different."

One of the ZIPRA officers, who spoke excellent English, laughed. "Zambia's army is a joke. If they knew when an attack was coming they would be far away when the shooting started. They are out of their minds with fear of the Rhodesians and they accuse us of making the Rhodesians attack them."

The other ZIPRA officer growled, "The Zamboos always say they at war with Rhodesia, but the best they do till now is shoot up tourist women at Victoria Falls. They are stupid, cowardly and dirty, including their president."

Halfway from the army garrison to the camp the pavement came to an end and they jolted along rough dirt roads the remaining distance to the staging area. It was just getting dark when Jobo spotted the first ZIPRA soldiers. They were standing guard at the side of the road, dressed in Russian-supplied camouflage suits and carrying AK-47 assault rifles. The driver pulled to a halt and the officers identified themselves, after which the car was allowed to proceed.

It was another mile to the litter of thatched huts, wood buildings and tents which housed the ZIPRA guerrillas and marked the last stage of their journey to the Rhodesian border.

Even before the car came to a halt at what appeared to be command headquarters, Jobo could tell by the dreadful smell that the sanitation discipline maintained at this camp was execrable. "Don't your Russian and Cuban advisers tell the camp commanders anything about slit trenches or latrines?"

"The camp commander tell white advisers to teach how to use guns, not tell us how we live," the second officer guffawed.

As in the ZANLA camps in Mozambique, Jobo noticed the presence of many women. They were bringing food and water to the flimsy barracks, but of course they would tend to the Freedom Fighters' sexual needs as well.

"Come, you meet camp commander, Comrade Nohondo. To he you must explain the map and the province sectors." The officers stepped out of the car and escorted Jobolingo into headquarters. Nohondo was waiting for the emissaries from Lusaka in his bare office, a map of the Lake Kariba area on the wall behind the rude table that served as his desk. Nohondo shook hands, turning his palm up and milking the thumb of each visitor in turn in the traditional African nationalist grip, then focused his interest on Jobolingo.

Until now his only contact with Mugabe men had been at a Tanzania training camp when a bitter, pitched battle had raged between Nkomo's ZIPRA trainees and Mugabe's ZANLA recruits. ZIPRA had decisively won the encounter, its leaders having taken the precaution of arming themselves and locking the ZANLA men's armory. Nohondo still remembered with satisfaction the thirty-one ZANLA bodies they had buried under the football field.

After a brief exchange of amenities, Nohondo invited Jobolingo to convey his message. But before Jobo could bring out his briefcase and maps the officers who had escorted him to the scene excused themselves, pleading meetings they must attend at Comrade Nkomo's headquarters.

"You do not want to stay and take part in the massacre of the Selous Scouts when they come?" Nohondo asked in disgust. "It might be tonight."

Their orders had been to deliver the ZANLA representative and then return, they insisted. Nohondo turned to Jobo. "Do you find that the headquarters people always have orders to return to the side of Comrade Mugabe when there's fighting to be done?" he asked contemptuously.

Not wishing to be involved in an internecine feud within the ZIPRA organization, Jobolingo muttered innocuous platitudes as he watched his escorts hastily make their exit from Nohondo's command post.

"Comrade Nohondo, before we look at my maps will you take me for an inspection of the defense positions against this coming attack?" Jobolingo requested. "If I am drawn into the fight I should know the order of battle."

Nohondo led his visitor out of the hut and through the camp. "Tomorrow, whether the attack comes tonight or not, we begin sending our men across to Zimbabwe. We do not know when the puppet election takes place but our men are needed to persuade the people not to vote."

Jobo was surprised at the unconcern shown by the men and women of the camp as he walked among them. An attack by the dread Selous Scouts was imminent, yet these ZIPRA troops seemed not to care. He expressed his thoughts to Nohondo who laughed.

"Come, I'll show you the reception party awaiting the enemy." At the top of a bank overlooking the river they came across a line of sandbag bunks in which were positioned light and heavy machine guns, rocket-propelled grenade tubes, mortars and even antitank weapons.

"No Selous Scout will leave this beach alive. The men that aren't shot out of their boats and eaten by the crocodiles will be blasted apart when they get to the sandbanks." He pointed out the positions of the flare guns. "We will light up the river and the beach like midday. It will be the greatest massacre of the Selous murderers ever."

Jobo stared at the deadly defenses for some moments and then looked back across the camp in the direction from which he had arrived. "Suppose the criminals come from behind?" he asked.

Nohondo stared at him in surprise, then shouted, as though shouting turned speculation into fact, "They will not! Direct from Comrade Nkomo we were told, they will come up the river and land. They can not come from behind."

"Why not?" Jobo asked.

"Too bad in the jungle back there. They could not find their way. Why would they go through the jungle many miles, making noises we hear, running into our sentries, when they can so easily come up the river and surprise us?" He laughed grimly.

"There's still time to set up defense positions behind the camp," Jobo argued.

"That would take guns away from the river where they're coming."

"Did your advisers give you officers military history?" Jobo asked. "We were taught by the Chinese many lessons from history. The British in Singapore had all their guns pointed south and east and west but the Japanese in 1942 came through the jungle from the north and killed or captured the British army in a few days."

Nohondo frowned deeply at the ZANLA emissary. "Me, me commander here!" he shrilled. "Don't need some Shona ZANU man to tell me how to run this camp."

There was no point in arguing, Jobo thought. Besides, it did make sense that the hated Selous Scouts would come by boat. He wondered how the ZAPU leader had received his information. Surely the missionaries couldn't have penetrated the Selous Scouts' secrecy. Somehow Nkomo must have put a spy into the special unit, though no African would have been privy to the time and target of an attack like this one week or more in advance.

Nohondo stared challengingly at Jobolingo for several moments, but the visitor made no comment. Finally the camp commander nodded. "Now, give me Comrade Nkomo's instructions."

Wordlessly, Jobo followed Nohondo back to his office. A kerosene lamp had been lighted and for an hour the two guerrilla leaders discussed the sectors that the ZIPRA troops would be responsible for.

After the briefing by Jobolingo, during which he had no more to say about his host's defensive strategy, Nohondo became less hostile toward this Shona tribesman who represented, after all, an ally, how-ever temporary, in the fight against the white man and the despised African puppets.

"Two hundred of my best-trained men are waiting for the white bandits to come up the river. We have been in our positions for three nights now. Meantime, the men who go across the lake tomorrow night are having a celebration. As our guest from our ZANU allies perhaps you would like to join in the party. There will be beer, and a truckload of young girls, who recently left their mission school in Zimbabwe to join their Chimaranga comrades, will be delivered here tonight."

"All this with an attack by the Selous Scouts on the way?" Jobo asked incredulously.

The frown returned to Nohondo's face. "We have waited three days. It may never come. But if it does, my defense cadres will destroy the enemy in a matter of minutes. Meantime, the morale of the men going across the lake to face very hard times—most of them will be killed before the war is over— is most important."

Jobolingo privately considered Nohondo to be virtually a suicidal idiot and his low opinion of Nkomo's ZIPRA was reinforced but there was obviously nothing to be gained from further argument about military strategy. He himself doubted that there was any way Nkomo could have accurate information on Selous Scouts operations. Sister McFarland, with the best intelligence gathering machinery, with her skilled radio technique and the entire Catholic Commission for Justice and Peace in Rhodesia contributing to her efforts, had never been able to produce any useful information on the Selous Scouts.

Whenever Jobo thought of the white nun his usually strict self-discipline eroded and the warmth of desire stirred in his groin. To have made love to this white woman, to have violently erupted deep inside her, his face between those large white breasts, had spoiled him for the concubines provided for the use of favored ZANLA cadres. The frightened girls abducted from the mission schools were merely un-willing childish receptacles for the pent-up juices of the men that used them. And when the women provided were loving and open, they were already evil-smelling, fat and flabby. He forced his thoughts away from the bountiful Sister and concentrated on the situation con-fronting him.

"Do you want my assistance in briefing your officers and men on the sectors they will infiltrate and those they will leave alone?" Jobo asked.

"I will give all instructions to my men," Nohondo answered peremptorily. "The truck that brings the nannies can take you back to the Zambian Army garrison and they can provide a way for you to reach Lusaka tomorrow."

Prudence would have dictated that Jobo accept the offer. His job was more diplomatic than combative, as Comrade Mugabe and Comrade Rex Nhongo had reiterated when they sent him to Lusaka. Moreover he found the company of the officious Matabele ZIPRA commander distasteful in the extreme. The possibility of killing Selous Scouts almost overrode good sense but there didn't really seem to be much likelihood of a raid. He totally mistrusted Nkomo's intelligence.

"I'll let you know when the truck gets here," Jobo replied.

Nondo shrugged. "Shona can never make up his mind."

Jobolingo ignored the barb. "I will go out and look around the camp."

Nohondo waved at the door. "Go. If you decide you want to sit in the ambush you are welcome. If not, watch for the truck."

Jobo raised his hand in assent and left the headquarters hut.

Chapter 45

For the uneventful hour and a half trip across Kariba, the second largest man-made lake in the world, Mack was thankful. He thought of the times when he had intercepted terrorists coming the other way and wiped them out with machine-gun fire. What he could do to the terrorists, they could do to him.

Slowly the scraggly, swampy Zambian shore of the lake came into view. The shoreline said much about the mentality of the African. Before this section of the Zambezi had been flooded by the huge Kariba Dam, which provided badly needed electric power for both Zambia and Rhodesia, the Rhodesians had cleared areas of jungle on their side that would be submerged and molded the contours of what would become a neat shoreline. As a result the fishing on their side of the lake was excellent.

On the Zambian side the snarled jungle floor of the lake made for poor fishing and defied the best efforts of the fishermen to land their boats. Zambia's president for life, Kenneth Kaunda, had opposed the dam and the creation of Lake Kariba. Despite the fact that Zambia was short of electric power, the superstitious black leader was convinced that constructing the dam would release evil spirits.

Two miles offshore the mother ship dropped anchor. The two-man crews of the ten Zodiacs pulled their rubber craft along-side and the

Selous Scouts swung over the rails of the ship and backed down ladders into them.

Mack rode in the lead Zodiac, beside him the mission's guide, Cancer. Cancer stared sullenly ahead, without any appearance of nervousness. If he had any regrets about the fate of his former comrades, whom he was about to betray, he did not show it.

As the boats approached the tangled shoreline, Mack thought of the briefing officer's admonition regarding the crocodiles and looked apprehensively into the murky water.

The crewmen guided their Zodiacs over and between the jagged tree stumps until the boats finally made it to relatively firm ground. The crew pulled the boats up on shore and began setting up the long-range HF radio.

"Adderley, you stay here with your stick and the boat crews. This won't be a big demo job, and I want you to man the radio. You're the only one of us that doesn't talk funny. We wouldn't want any of our chaps at headquarters to misinterpret what is said. We'll keep in touch with you on our A-63s and you can relay our progress back to headquarters through your TR-48.

"OK, Mack." The British captain looked disappointed at not being part of the action.

"When we signal you we're coming out, have those boats ready. We may be on the run."

"We'll be ready for you Mack, with the .50 caliber in place to cover your withdrawal."

"Be sure you have a chopper pad cleared and marked with lights, just in case."

"We'll be ready to receive a helicopter in one hour if it's necessary."

Moving off from the boats the seventy men adopted a single-file formation on account of the thick vegetation and the darkness of the night. "Not the safest formation but we've got to be in position by moonlight, 0100 hours," Mack muttered.

"LeClair, you take over the stick. I'm going up to the point with Luthu and Cancer. When we're in position, I'll rejoin you here in the middle of the assault line for the attack."

"Oui, mon capitaine."

The file moved silently forward like a giant reptile. Although there were frequent stops to listen for suspicious sounds and check bearings, the initial five thousand meters were covered without incident.

Cancer walked directly in front of Mack as point man. The Scouts were divided into three platoons of five sticks each. Mack, with Luthu at his shoulder led the first, Sergeant LeClair the second and Sergeant Houk the third. Proceeding through the dense bush, they looped away from the river on a track that would bring them into an assault line behind the camp. The terrorists, Mack expected, would be fighting with their backs to the river and thus be at a disadvantage, unable to disappear into the bush.

After an hour's stealthy march, Luthu turned and placed a cautioning hand on Mack's shoulder. Mack nodded and Luthu went on alone toward Camp Nkomo. As Mack and the others and the front of the file watched, a sentry appeared from the bush. Luthu, with the AK-47 that would identify him as a terrorist slung over his shoulder, held up a hand in greeting.

"*Chimaranga*," Luthu said softly. The terrorists used this word to mean liberation war, victory and death to the white man, in short all they were fighting for.

The sentry repeated the greeting and approached Luthu. As he came up close, Luthu, holding his AK-47 loosely in one hand, stabbed the long knife he'd been carrying concealed in his other hand swiftly and fatally into the guard's throat. With a muffled grunt the sentry collapsed to the bush floor. Two more knife thrusts assured Luthu that this sentry would never give another warning. Then he gestured the others to follow.

When the file caught up with him, Cancer once again took up the point position, just ahead of Luthu this time. Cancer had been well aware of Luthu's knife and had he entertained any notions about switching allegiance back to his old *Chimaranga* comrades, the ease with which Luthu had cut down the sentry must have convinced him that he was on the right side of this conflict now.

A few minutes later Luthu dropped back to whisper into Mack's ear. "Cancer say they only have one sentry behind the camp, or maybe two. They think if the Boers attack it will be from the river. But we will be watchful."

The seventy highly trained scouts, adept at silent bush marches, continued their careful progress. Suddenly, ahead of them, they saw the glow of campfires and heard sounds of singing. Cancer and Luthu conversed briefly, then Luthu turned to Mack. "They are having big beer drink, sir. Tomorrow night they go across the lake and start killing."

"So they're having a bit of a celebration, are they? Well, we can certainly add some fireworks to the show," Mack whispered grimly.

Halting his men at a dirt road running from the Zambian interior to the terrorist camp some one thousand meters away, Mack assembled the two special teams. "LeClair, you and your demo team have got ninety minutes to mine this road connecting the terrorist camp with the Zambian Army barracks at Pemba. I don't think the Zambians will be all that anxious to help their brothers, but leave them some surprises just in case. I want that TMH boosted so it will blow a tank, and also plenty of antipersonnels scattered around." The Frenchman nodded.

"Sergeant Houk, you will perform an initial area recce of the camp." Mack regarded the German's expressionless blackened face. Christ he's good, the best damn man in the bush during the selection course, he thought. "Synchronize watches. It's now 2200 hours. Return no later than 2330 hours." The two teams, LeClair with three men and Houk with just Luthu, silently left their comrades who were formed into a circular defensive perimeter.

Houk knew they were closer to the camp than the sounds from it suggested. He could smell the foul odor. Slowly as stalking cats, he and Luthu crept forward. A cigarette glowed not fifty feet to their left. They froze, listened and then carefully retraced their steps for a hundred meters.

Safely out of the sentry's hearing, Luthu whispered in Houk's ear. "That sentry is Kaffir, not soldier." Houk grinned and motioned his partner forward again.

Methodically they explored all approaches on the landward side of the terrorist camp, noting the positions and actions of the two sentries posted there. Often they were not more than twenty to thirty meters from the camp, but with their expert bush craft and the noisy merrymaking of the terrorists they went undetected.

LeClair's mission had not gone without incident. Having posted a sentry with an A-63 radio a hundred meters on each side of the spot he had selected in the middle of the dirt road, he began carefully placing the antitank mine, which he would boost with a second one. His third man, rifle in hand, listened on an A-63 radio for possible warnings from their own sentries.

Fifteen minutes into the mission, a whispered warning came over the radio. "This is Lima One. Get off the road. One man on a bicycle coming fast." LeClair and his sentry grabbed the big Russian TMH mine and quickly rolled into the brush. Seconds later the African on the bicycle came bouncing by. LeClair saw him glance down without stopping at the partially dug hole and made his decision.

"Lima Two, take them out," he ordered softly over the radio to his far sentry. Two clicks, the sign of acknowledgment, sounded in response. Seconds went by, then minutes. Finally the radio came to life. "Lima, this is Lima Two. The bicycle man won't be a problem, but I've got one," came the calm whisper.

"What's zee problem?" LeClair rasped back.

"I hit the fucker in the head with my AK. He'll never get up, but I broke the stock on my gat."

Stifling a laugh, LeClair whispered, "Your weapon will still fire from zee hip. We are fini in twenty minutes." Two clicks answered.

Finishing the placement of the two antitank mines, LeClair then carefully salted the area with AP mines, noting their locations on the map. That done, he ordered his sentries to remain in place until he could personally collect them.

He picked up the first sentry, then made a wide 180 degree arc toward the second. Finally all four men proceeded back to the main body of Scouts.

To avoid making contact with the other special team, they entered the friendly perimeter from the south, after alerting their comrades by radio that they were coming in. Simultaneously Houk and Luthu entered the perimeter from the north whereupon both teams made their reports to Mack.

After being assured by LeClair that the mines were correctly positioned and the body of the nocturnal cyclist hidden, Mack turned to the German. "How's it look, Horst?"

"We may have to take out two more sentries, but that's no problem."

Mack glanced at Luthu. "Can you get close enough?" The lithe African merely flashed his widest smile.

"Good enough." Mack knew there could be few better with a knife than Luthu.

For the next hour the Selous Scouts concentrated on forming an assault line behind the camp a hundred meters from the edge of the

347

cleared area in the middle of which squatted the decrepit one-story huts of wood and mud that housed the terrorists. It was midnight when Mack, over the HF radio strapped to the back of his radio man, contacted Adderley at the relay station. He reported their position and described the situation.

The night was unusually starless. About half of the camp were still up and drinking beer. The attack had to take place in time for the Selous Scouts to withdraw to their Zodiac boats, get back to the mother ship on Lake Kariba and be well across the lake before there was enough light for the Zambian jet fighters to come out and hit them. They would have to launch their attack on Camp Nkomo by one o'clock, an hour away.

Through the headsets now clamped firmly to his ears, Mack heard Adderley relay this information to the Selous Scouts staging area on the other side of Lake Kariba. Soon the answer came back. Attack at one o'clock or else withdraw altogether.

"We'll hit them at zero one hundred!" Mack rasped back over the HF radio. He looked back at Camp Nkomo, hoping that the terrorists would drink enough beer to put them soundly to sleep before one o'clock.

Luthu and Cancer stood beside him looking into the camp. In the distance they heard a truck rumbling along a dirt road that appeared to run parallel to the lake.

"Fuck's sake. We didn't mine one road," Mack cursed. "Too late now."

"Cancer say that road go to small civilian group. Not used by army," Luthu reassured his commander.

Soon a new late-model British Bedford truck drove into the clearing and stopped. There were shouts of glee from the terrorists as the occupants of the cab jumped out, ran around to the back, pulled the tailgate down and shouted orders. A group of terrified young African girls who looked to be between the ages of thirteen and fifteen were pulled out of the truck. About eighteen nannies stood in the illuminated area as the terrorists leered at them.

Cancer whispered to Luthu who whispered to Mack. "Those are the girls kidnapped by Nkomo terrorists from the mission school in Rhodesia near the Botswana border two weeks ago."

As they watched, Nkomo's men walked up to the girl children, huddled in fear, and looked them over. Each man took his pick and, half pushing, half dragging, led the girl toward the rows of huts.

"By morning, all the terrorists that want girl will have one of those." Luthu looked over the scene and ground his teeth. "That is the freedom these dogs are fighting for? I will enjoy this, sir."

"There's no way we can protect them from the crossfire," Mack observed grimly. "And we can't let these terrs get across Lake Kariba and fuck up the elections."

Luthu nodded bitterly. "This I am very mad to see. Those poor nannies. Now they never know anything but rape and death."

Besides the kidnapped schoolgirls there were many other females in the camp, concubines to the terrorists. They wandered from hut to hut, carrying the beer that had been brewed for the Freedom Fighters to celebrate their last night in camp.

Again Luthu whispered into Mack's ear. "Cancer say these nannies mostly Zambian girls. Zambian men very angry that Nkomo men take their women. After election in Rhodesia, Zambian men say all Nkomo people must stay in their new country, Zimbabwe, and not come back. This big problem to President Kaunda. He must help Nkomo but his people don't want Nkomo people here."

"Well, we're going to do Kaunda a big favor," Mack commented. "We're going to get rid of about five hundred of these gooks for him just about now."

Mack checked his watch and held a short whispered conference with LeClair and Houk, who had stolen through the bush to report his platoon was ready to attack.

Now that he could clearly see the objective, Mack cast his final attack plan. The quantities of beer the terrorists had consumed, the young girls they had gorged themselves upon and total surprise—these elements would make up for the difference in manpower.

Chapter 46

The Selous Scouts were not the only ones to be disgusted by this truckload of human "supplies."

As Mack's men were taking up their concealed positions, Jobo had been completing his inspection of the ambush fortifications above the river. Jobo was appalled at the ineptitude of the ZIPRA forces. At first he had asked each machine gunner how long it would take him to turn his weapons around if the attack came from the rear of the camp. None of the ZIPRA men had even considered such a maneuver. Jobo had just finished making one heavy machine gun crew go through the exercise—it took them over a minute—when Nohondo stalked across the camp to the gun positions and angrily ordered Jobolingo to stop interfering with his command.

"Find a position for yourself; I will give you whatever weapon you want from the armory, but do not confuse my men. They have their orders," Nohondo shouted.

"I will take an AK-47 with pigsticker," Jobo replied.

"Then follow me."

They walked to the cement blockhouse in the middle of the camp. "All our weapons and ammunitions are in here," he explained. "Some of my boys have been drinking beer and I don't want them to get their hands on these weapons until we send them off tomorrow." He reached for the key on his belt and started toward the two armed guards standing in front of the armory door.

Just at that moment a heavy rumbling could be heard. Nohondo turned to his visitor and motioned toward the big new lorry rolling up to the headquarters building. "Before I issue you your weapon there is an administrative detail I must see about," he said, trying to hide a smirk. Jobo followed the commander to the back of the truck where already the driver and a cheering group of half-drunken ZIPRA troops were pulling down the tailgate.

He saw terrified, shrieking girls being dragged out of the truck by the men who well knew this was their last night for such revels before they went into combat with the security forces on the other side of the lake.

"Nice young girls these," Nohondo laughed. "Right out of the mission school." He leered at Jobolingo. "As our honored ZANLA guest, would you like one for yourself before the men take them all?"

For a moment the long dormant thought of his wife entered Jobolingo's mind. It had been years since she had been stolen from her village along with him and then given to the FRELIMO officer when they crossed into Mozambique. With his elevation to high rank, Jobo had almost forgotten her. Those things happen in a war of liberation, he had come to realize. But now these girls, abducted from their own familiar surroundings and about to be fed to the lust-crazed Freedom Fighters, made him recall his hatred of the FRELIMO when his wife had been taken from him.

"We will get plenty of warning if the Boers come up the river," Nohondo chortled, misunderstanding Jobolingo's long hesitation.

"Thank you, Comrade Commander," Jobo replied, "but no, I will not share these poor nannies with you."

Annoyed at the look of disgust on his visitor's face, Nohono shouted: "It is their patriotic duty to give comfort to our brave Freedom Fighters before they go to battle the white man and his puppet soldiers. They should be happy to give our men a last night with a woman before they cross the lake."

Jobo stared at the terrified looks on the schoolgirls' faces as they shrank from the men surrounding them. "They are not women, just children," he muttered angrily. Then he said forcefully, "Comrade, I will not require the weapon. I will accept your offer to ride back in the truck."

"Suit yourself." With that Nohondo strode toward the cowering nannies, their forefingers now firmly implanted in their nostrils. Rather gently he took one trembling child by the arm and led her toward the headquarters building. This was the signal for the men who would be making the lake crossing the next night to lunge into the knot of shrieking young females, who were now clutching each other tightly, and start tugging them off one by one to their huts.

Jobo swung himself up into the cab of the truck with the driver. The guard who had ridden in with the driver had decided to stay at the camp and avail himself of the opportunity of taking one of the girls. Despite some regret that he might be missing a battle with the Selous Scouts, Jobo was happy to see the camp of Matabele ZIPRA savages disappear behind the truck as it ground its way out of the staging area.

Chapter 47

Mack Hudson and his attack line watched the Bedford leave the camp after depositing its human cargo.

"Fuck, wouldn't I like to blow that vehicle up," he moaned. They watched the truck drive into the darkness down the road, then turned their thoughts back to Camp Nkomo.

An important objective in the staging area would be its arms depot, a square cement building surrounded by barbed wire and guarded closely.

At five minutes to one A.M., Mack once more raised Adderley on the radio. "We hit in five minutes. I'll report back when it's over."

"You bloody lucky bastards!" Adderley replied enviously.

"Don't worry, Colin, there's only a hundred thousand or so more left to kill. You'll get your chance." Mack clicked off the radio and made a last visual surveillance of the camp. The activity had abated somewhat but there were still men walking around the various huts swilling beer from tin cups or even cruder vessels and looking for stray nannies whose sated temporary mates had gone to sleep.

At 0100 hours seventy men rose as one and slowly moved forward, a relentless wave of death. Jesus, our firepower will be unbelievable, Mack thought to himself. Seventeen machine guns plus seventeen rifle grenade launchers, backed up by three commando mortars and the rest of the rifles. He grinned reassuringly at the men of his headquarters stick in the center of the assault line. Behind them was Doc McCracken and his two-man medical team.

Each step they took toward the camp surprised Mack. He couldn't believe that the terrorists were so slothful that seventy men could come out of the brush into the clearing at the edge of the camp and continue toward the heart of the staging center without being seen and fired upon. The line moved forward, step by step, all weapons aimed into the camp. Finally, when they were well within killing range of their objective, the men stopped and silently brought their weapons into the firing position. On Mack's command, the rifle grenadiers let fly their deadly missiles and the entire force opened fire. The grenadiers had been ordered to aim for the far side of the encampment so as not to injure their own comrades with lethal shrapnel. Likewise, the mortar men had been instructed to place their bombs no closer then one hundred meters to the assault line.

Suddenly, it was as though daylight had broken over the river as the ambush party released their flares. Stunned, the guerrillas began firing at the river until they realized to their horror that the hail of fire was coming from behind them.

Mack and his Scouts stared in shocked amazement as the formidable river ambush was silhouetted for them by the flares.

"Oh Jesus," Mack cried. "They were waiting for us."

Every Scout was sickeningly aware of what would have happened to them had they indeed come up the river as originally planned. Only one machine gunner had the presence to whip his weapon around toward the attackers, but an accurately directed grenade blew gun and crew out of their bunker.

However, other ambushers now belatedly struggled to redirect their fire at the enemy hidden in darkness behind the camp. As a result, those ZIPRA troopers in the camp that hadn't been killed or wounded by the Scouts' opening fusillade found themselves in a deadly crossfire. For a while no human sounds could be heard above the stutter and crump of weaponry.

The Scouts sent furious salvos of mortar bombs and rifle grenades into the ambushers, whose positions were clearly pinpointed by their own fire. A relentless staccato of sustained automatic fire reaped a devastating toll of dead terrorists. The screams and death cries of

ZIPRA men and their women could be heard amid the crack of bullets and the detonation of bombs.

The Scouts too were taking incoming fire from the few ambush positions still in operation. One Scout beside Mack fell, dropping his weapon and clutching his chest.

By prearrangement eight Scouts quickly detached themselves from each end of the assault line and moved in outward-curving patterns sealing off each flank of the camp. The terrorists now had only one route of escape—the river.

On Mack's command, the assault line moved slowly, inexorably forward and entered the camp, each Scout firing from the shoulder at anything that moved, unless he could be sure it was a woman. Death was now being dealt at close quarters by both rifle and machine gun fire. Mack saw two more of his men fall before his mortars and grenades neutralized the last of the ambush bunkers. Fragments of enemy bone and flesh splattered the Scouts, making the fight seem suddenly personal, and more ugly.

"Goddamn, dress to the fucking center!"

"Keep the line straight!" Mack heard the stick leaders yelling between bursts of fire.

"Watch your front. Don't fire into the flanks, there are friendly forces out there!"

"Sullivan, if you don't keep up I'm going to kick your Irish ass."

As they moved across the camp dozens of terrorists appeared to be milling around the cement blockhouse. The concentrated fire of several RPDs cut them down where they stood. Mack's A-63 radio suddenly crackled to life.

"Sierra Fox One, this is Sierra Fox Three, over."

"This is Sierra Fox One. Go," Mack snapped back.

"Boss, looks like the concrete building is the weapons armory. Want to blow it?"

"That's a negative, we'll blow it on the way out. Post a stick to guard it."

"Roger D," answered the voice on the other end.

As the assault line reached the far side of the camp it halted. Glancing over his shoulder, Mack saw that his men had done their job well. Nothing moved, and only a few female sobs and wails were audible.

"All call signs, this is Sierra Fox One. Give me a sitrep. Over." The call signs checked in with situation reports and the two flank blocking forces informed their commander that three prisoners had been taken.

At that moment sporadic fire broke out from the riverbank, and groans and cries on his flanks told Mack he was taking more casualties than had been expected. He motioned his line of death forward again. The Scouts would try to help their own wounded later.

There was only one escape route left to the survivors of the initial phase of the attack and they took it, retreating toward the river, occasionally pausing to fire back at the advancing Scouts. Coming to the top of the riverbank, the Scouts fired flares so they could get a good look at the scene below. Mack signaled the RPD machine gunners to set up their weapons to rake the river's edge.

The guerrillas were frantically trying to launch some of their twenty brand-new fifteen-foot fiberglass boats, each with a gleaming unused Johnson outboard engine attached.

Mack pointed at the boats and turned to Luthu beside him. "There's how the World Council of Churches' money is spent. Twenty thousand dollars' worth of boats to ferry murderers across the lake so that they can kill innocent civilians," he growled.

They watched as several of the boats, crammed to the gunwhales with terrorists, put out into the river. Desperately the men in the boats tugged at the pullropes, trying to start the engines.

Mack laughed throatily. "They don't even know how to start the engines." He shouted the order to the RPD men and a hail of machine gun fire reached out into the river, blowing boats apart one by one. The agonized cries of wounded terrorists spilling into the river reached the grim-faced men on the bank.

When all the boats had been shot out of the water, the machine gunners turned their weapons on the boats still on the riverbank, heavy bullets smashing into engines and splintering the fiberglass hulls.

Terrorists still milling on the beach now became the target of the gunners, and many leaped into the river in a feverish attempt to escape the withering fire from above.

All of a sudden ghastly screams resounded from the river. They were interspersed with hissing, growling and thrashing sounds. The Scouts, now standing atop the ambush bunkers stared down in fascination. A churning, swirling mass of crocodiles was foraging among the terrorists who had jumped into the water.

More of the huge creatures were skimming toward the feast from all directions. Everywhere the Scouts looked they saw powerful jaws snapping into an arm, a leg, a torso and dragging some hapless terrorist, berserk with pain and fear, to the river bottom.

"*Sacre bleu*, even in zee Congo I never see such as this," whispered LeClair.

Dismembered bodies floated in the river. Pieces of human anatomy littered the riverbank. One terrorist, reaching the temporary safety of a sandbar jutting out from the shore, started to run. "Don't shoot him," a Scout shouted. Fire was held. As the men watched, an eight-foot crocodile emerged some twenty meters behind the bounding terrorist and overtook him with unbelievable speed. The crunching of the man's bones could be distinctly heard over his shrill death cries.

"Jesus K. Christ, I had no idea these crocs could move that fast," Mack breathed.

"Sir, those fuckers are faster than a horse over a short distance," volunteered one of the riflemen assigned to Mack's HQ stick.

Streams of blood running down the river attracted yet more of the primordial beasts. They shot through the water, their jagged-toothed jaws opening in wicked grins as they neared their prey.

Mack and the other Selous Scouts watched the scene in flesh-creeping elation. Here was vengeance indeed.

The attack had swept into the mop-up phase. The Scouts were determined that none of the terrorists would run away and live to kill another day.

Camp Nkomo was now totally destroyed. The dead and badly wounded lay all around. Down at the riverbank a squad of terrorists had emerged from the bush. They threw down their weapons and stood shivering, their arms high, begging their adversaries not to kill them. Mack turned to the French sergeant beside him.

"You've got two prisoners for sure, right?"

"Yes. Damaged but they can talk."

"That's all we need," Mack replied. "I want to know why they were expecting us." He watched pitilessly as the Africans among the Selous Scouts fired AK bursts into the terrorist squad.

"Mercy!" Mack spit in disgust. "Our chaps have seen the sort of mercy they show when they walk into the kraals and Tribal Trust Lands."

"Every African in Selous Scouts has seen at least one or two members of his family murdered by the Gadangas," Luthu pronounced as the last of the terrorists fell writhing to the river bank.

"Coquille of fresh live gook for zee crocs," LeClair observed with cynical relish.

Mack fired a green pencil flare, then a red one and began blowing his whistle. The shrill cry was taken up by others and the firing abruptly ceased.

After redistributing ammunition so that each man had an equal load, the assault line reversed its course through the terrorist camp. Moving slowly, looking for documents and weapons, anything that might be of value to military intelligence, they stopped to give a final coup de grace to any terrorist who showed signs of life. The remaining women, wounded or otherwise, had seemingly disappeared into the bush.

The medical detail led by Doc McCracken administered aid to the Scouts' wounded, mournfully identifying the dead and placing them on litters to be carried back for helicopter evacuation. Four Scouts, three Africans, and one European, had died in the assault. Ten had been wounded, of which six would walk out and four would have to be carried.

Mack searched through the splintered headquarters shack himself, stepping over the sprawled bodies of a terrorist, his camouflage pants down around his ankles, and a young girl whose clothes had been half torn off her.

Horst Houk, behind his commander, shook his head. "Very *nein shone* we are. Five more minutes and he would have died happy."

Mack looked through the scattered papers by the light of his torch and paused to study a map. "Looks like they've sort of divided up the country between them." He stuck the map in his pocket and turned to the German. "Police up all these papers. We'll take them back with us. Now let's get ready to move out smartly. We don't want to tangle all over again with the Zamboons."

Gingerly Mack picked his way over and around the bodies that littered the camp, trying to arrive at an accurate estimate of casualties. He strode along the top of the riverbank, grimly realizing what would have happened if they had come up the river. It would have been Selous Scouts providing the ravenous crocs with the gourmet dinner. Obviously this mission had been compromised. Somehow. It seemed impossible, yet their secrecy had been penetrated.

Mack explored the downstream end of the ambush site, walking out of the cleared area into the edge of the jungle where there was a trail that paralleled the river. This would be their withdrawal route to the assembly area where Adderley and his men were waiting. McCracken had already radioed for casevac choppers to come in for the wounded. Playing his flashlight on the path, Mack spotted the telltale black wires. Somewhere down the path there would be a sentry with a field telephone to warn the camp of approaching boats on the river.

He was just emerging from the jungle line, lowering his head to duck under the twisted tree branches that blocked his way along the riverbank, when he heard the unmistakable initial bang of a rocket leaving its launcher off to his left. An RPG-7 had been fired, the terrorists' favorite weapon. Theoretically it was an antitank, not an antipersonnel weapon. But the guerrillas loved the fact that it made two bursts of noise, one when it was fired and one when the projectile exploded.

Mack threw himself to the ground as the missile sailed over his position. A tremendous explosion just above and beyond him rocked the ground and the concussion of the rocket grenade knocked him senseless for a moment. He quickly came to with a sharp pain in his right shoulder. The unstable rocket had exploded on a branch of the tree. The terrs never learned that an RPG is not a bush weapon, that after the projectile has gone over fifty meters it takes merely a tree branch to explode it. Because of the shape of the charge, designed for destroying a vehicle, the shrapnel is intended to explode forwards. However, a certain amount of it sprays out, and Mack knew he had caught a steel shard.

It was the concussion that disabled him more than the pain in his shoulder. His head ached and he could not focus his eyes for a few moments. Then he heard a ferocious burst of automatic weapons fire, assuring him that *that* terrorist had fired his last RPG.

Groggily Mack rose to his knees, bleeding from his right arm and legs. Doc McCracken dove across him, forcing him back to a prone position. "Can't have you standing up wounded, sir. There are probably more of the bastards in the area," the senior medic said.

"For fuck's sake, I'm OK," Mack protested.

"Now that may be fact, sir," McCracken answered, "but let me be the judge."

"Goddamn it, I'm OK, just a little wobbly."

"With respect, sir, I'm going to casevac you and the other two wounded, just to be on the safe side." McCracken's voice was now businesslike. "Infection is a real problem out here and you know damn well I'm right, sir."

"Well, goddamn it, I'm leading these men back to the boats and that's that," Mack retorted evenly. "After that it's your show."

"OK, boss," the Rhodesian medic answered, "but as you Yanks say, let's put it in the wind and get the hell out of here." A tremendous explosion, followed by countless secondary detonations, rang out from the camp. Mack nodded in satisfaction.

He gave orders for three of the sticks to be deployed in a V formation, point foremost, while two sticks were to walk on each side of the main column for flank security. A long stick, designated rearguard, lagged slightly behind, making sure no enemy followed.

"Are you all right, *mon capitaine*?" shouted a familiar voice.

"I take it you blew the weapons bunker," Mack answered.

"*Oui, mon capitaine*. A twenty-five pound plastic charge and there's nothing left. It went poof!"

The Selous Scouts, carrying their dead and wounded, started the trek along the riverbank back to their boats. The security elements were alert although there could be few if any of the Camp Nkomo terrorists left to ambush them. It was always possible, however, that a reluctant Zambian Army expedition might have been hastily mounted to investigate. Individual Zambians had little sympathy for Nkomo's ill-disciplined cutthroats whose very presence invited attack from the Rhodesian Air Force and preemptive raids such as the one just carried out.

The Scouts hadn't gone far, walking more quickly and less stealthily now, when they were rewarded with the sound of another tremendous explosion. The boosted antivehicle mine had been detonated. Soon a series of smaller bangs indicated that any survivors of the main blast had stepped on the antipersonnel mines. An hour out of Camp

Nkomo the returning Scouts encountered the security guards from the boat detail.

Mack, looking as green as he felt, led his men on to the rally point. Adderley, in command of the boat security, had already alerted the helicopters. The choppers were now only fifteen minutes out.

"You OK, Mack?" Adderley called out. "You look pretty bad to me." As Mack didn't answer, he went on. "The Colonel has ordered all wounded to be flown out with the prisoners."

"Well, old chap, you won't be getting seasick," Doc McCracken said to his commander with a laugh.

"OK, OK, just make sure you guys get back to the mother ship with our bodies. The colonel would never forgive me if I were the sole survivor of this expedition."

"No problem," McCracken said. "We'll be miles inside Rhodesian waters by sunup."

As the Alouettes came in, Mack and the wounded watched the bound and blindfolded prisoners being roughly put aboard the first of them. Three of the wounded were helped in also. Seconds later, Mack and the other wounded men climbed or were placed aboard the second chopper while the third gunship circled protectively overhead.

Chapter 48

A subtle Jasmine fragrance accented the aura of sensuality that sheathed Carla Hudson as Ashley St. John held her in his arms. They were standing on the balcony of her bedroom at the luxuriously rustic Bumi Hills Lodge. That this exquisite creature could belong to a soldier of fortune with neither the breeding to be worthy of her nor the taste to truly appreciate such a prize exacerbated Ashley's frustration at coming short of possessing her body and spirit.

When they had arrived at the Bumi airstrip that evening in a private plane he had chartered, the consummation of an affair that had so far been no more that a succession of interrupted preliminaries seemed assured. Carla, to all intents and purposes deserted by her husband and resenting the unrelieved loneliness and boredom of her life, had welcomed the prospect of an exciting few days in exotic surroundings with a handsome and experienced lover.

But from the start, dark omens had distracted Carla. As they left Charles Prince Airport in Salisbury, Ashley had been obliged to pull rank in order to file a flight plan to Bumi, which was closed to civilian air traffic for twenty-four hours. Was a Selous Scouts operation taking place at Bumi? Carla questioned him anxiously.

Ashley had managed to alleviate her fears that Mack would be setting out on some dangerous assignment from the same place and perhaps at the very time she and Ashley were in the throes of illicit passion.

Then, when they arrived at the Bumi airstrip on the shore of Lake Kariba, there had been the helicopters and the Lynx aircraft which she knew to be an integral element of special operations. Once again Ashley had to assuage her fears. He did so with the aid of a forefinger traced lightly down her cheek.

Dinner on the veranda looking out over the lake restored the atmosphere they had sought for their tryst, but then more planes landed in the night. With wine and after-dinner drinks Carla once again regained her equanimity, holding his hand under the table, her eyes sultry and suggestive.

And then "Acorn," the three-man interrogation crew from Salis-bury, along with intelligence chief Ian Nicholson, took a table near them. Ashley could feel as he glanced from the grim newcomers to Carla that this latest portent of an extensive combat mission had once more driven the muses of love into the bushes.

"Why don't we take a bottle of champagne to your balcony?" Ashley suggested.

"Oh, Ashley, I think I've had enough," came the dampening reply.

Nevertheless, Ashley had firmly taken her in hand, ordered the bottle to be delivered and escorted her back to her room.

"Who were those people, Ashley?" she had asked nervously. "There is something happening, isn't there? Do you suppose the Scouts are—" Ashley quieted her with a kiss and then, as the cham-pagne arrived, poured them each a glass.

Now they stood on the balcony, gazing into a velvety blackness. "It's a dark night, isn't it," Carla murmured, setting his hopes on fire again. Then she added: "Just the kind they like for external opera-tions."

"Carla, can't you get your mind off the damned war for a while?" he chided with a hint of exasperation. "That's why we came out here."

Carla laughed self-deprecatingly, sipped her champagne, put the glass down and moved close to him. He put his own glass on the rail and held her in his arms, his lips finding hers. The inviting swell of her generous white breasts almost maddened him. She returned the kiss with sudden fervor, as though trying to lose herself in passions.

Then the unmistakable chuffing sound of a helicopter intruded upon them. Carla stiffened, the spell again broken. "Carla," Ashley pleaded softly, "let's go to bed and forget everything else." He kissed her neck, that delicate scent so suited to her femininity again heightening his desire. But Carla took a half step away from him. She turned and walked back to her bedroom. Ashley followed expectantly, rejecting the disquieting instinct that told him his tryst was ruined.

He tried to draw her down on the bed but Carla resisted. "I just can't make love tonight, Ashley," Carla said simply. "I want us to be together. I know it's hateful of me to raise expectations but—" Her eyes seemed to be searching the night sky beyond the French doors for the chopper. She faced him. "I can't help wondering if right out there somewhere the Scouts are in an operation and Mack is with them. How can I be making love to you wondering what's happening to him at the same moment? Can you understand?"

Ashley all but ground his teeth in anger that he had not been told an external mission was being launched from Bumi. Why hadn't he suggested Victoria Falls, or Kariba? Ordinarily, Bumi was the ideal spot for the first tender seduction of a desirable young lady. Yet now, when he was here with the woman he wanted to take most in the world, his little jungle paradise had failed him. No, that wasn't fair, it was Reid-Daley who had withheld from ComOps the plan for an operation to be staged out of Bumi. Damn Reid-Daley, he thought.

Carla sat down and patted the bed beside her. "Sit down with me for a minute, Ashley. Let's have one more glass of champagne. I'm sure that tomorrow we'll both be completely relaxed and ready to enjoy the scenery and each other."

They sat silently sipping champagne, exchanging occasional nothings. The evening was gone. Mortified but still the gentleman, Ashley finally gave her a chaste kiss and returned to his own room.

He slept fitfully and the first pale light of sunrise awoke him. He looked over the lake. How much longer would his patience last? he asked himself.

He experienced a glimmer of hope that today Carla might forget about her foreboding of the night before. A day with him, swimming, driving along the elephant trails with Peter Crockett as guide and a leisurely cocktail hour followed by a good dinner might do it. Should do it in fact.

Ashley St. John was not a man who gave up easily. But he resolved that if he had not bedded Carla by this time Sunday morning, he would give up on her. It just wasn't worth it, no matter how beautiful, how exciting this American woman was. Yes, she was more exotic, to put it bluntly a far greater trophy, than the Rhodesian beauties that he always found available to him. But the frustration was getting to be galling.

The sound of airplanes flying into the Bumi strip and the whirring of a helicopter suddenly decided him upon a course of action that would put him out of his teasing uncertainty. He would find out if Carla's husband were indeed in the vicinity. He would also find out what that confounded Reid-Daley was up to, which would have about it the sweet savor of revenge. He got out of bed, quickly shaved, put on the camouflage fatigues with his general's insignia on them and his leather bill hat with the red band. Then he buckled his boots, strode from the room, swagger stick in his right hand, and went down to the hotel's main entrance. The sun had not yet risen although dawn illuminated the hotel lobby. An African porter was sleeping on a chair beside the door, his head bent over. General St. John tapped him with his swagger stick and the man awoke with a start. "Get me a car and driver. Now-now," he added briskly.

"Yes, bass." The porter jumped to his feet and walked out into the driveway. Peter Crockett, the bluff Australian manager of the Bumi Hills Lodge, always had a Land Rover and a driver standing by. In moments the Land Rover's engine turned over and the driver backed up to the front door of the hotel.

The general climbed into the back. "Take me down to the airstrip."

"Yes, bass!" The Land Rover jerked out of the Bumi drive circle and headed down the hill toward the strip. In ten minutes they were driving onto the inland end of the strip used by civilian planes and the territorial air force. General St. John was well aware that the lake end of the Bumi airstrip was Selous Scouts land and off-limits to all other personnel, whether civilian or military, without specific authorization. He commanded his driver, nonetheless, to take him down the runway to the end.

Although the Bumi Hills Lodge driver protested, knowing that the area was prohibited, he was more afraid of the general's immediate wrath than of the prospect of being scolded by a guard. He braked the Land Rover in front of a barrier marked RESTRICTED AREA which was guarded by two Selous Scouts. The general frowned slightly but kept his emotions under control. Just seeing the fawn colored berets with their flashy ospreys irked him. As for Reid-Daley, the Scouts' commander, St. John considered him an upstart, a regimental sergeant major who had been promoted far above his station.

The general jumped out of the Land Rover, walked around to the guards, who saluted him, and tapped the barrier across the road with his swagger stick.

"Let my vehicle come through," he ordered.

"Sir, we have orders that nobody can pass this gate without instructions from the colonel." The harsh whirring and chuffing in the air caused the general to look up at the helicopter which was slowly settling down on the pad in the Selous Scouts encampment. Then he turned to one of the guards, a sergeant. "All right, sergeant, I'll leave my vehicle and driver outside. But you are commanded to let me through. I have to coordinate the final phase of this operation with ComOps. Do you understand me?"

The sergeant looked at the corporal standing on the other side of the gate. Both of them were perplexed.

"Now-now! We can't wait. I have to meet that helicopter." He tapped the gate impatiently with his stick. Finally the sergeant nodded to the corporal who pulled the gate back and let General St. John walk through.

He strode down the dirt road toward the helipad behind the Selous Scouts Headquarters building where the helicopter just settled. He wondered if this had been a duly authorized mission into Zambia. He suspected Reid-Daley of going off on his own at times and reporting back to the army later.

If Ashley St. John had one obsession where the Rhodesian Army was concerned, it was to preside over the disbanding of Reid-Daley's band of brigands.

Men in fawn berets and civilian interrogation experts were also going toward the chopper, but they said nothing to the general, even though he knew most of them personally. The sun was just rising, turning the thin ground mist to pink when St. John reached the helipad. As he watched, two Africans in the ragged camouflage outfits that the terrorists wore, were carried out of the helicopter. Both were wounded and one had what was obviously a serious gunshot wound in the chest. They were placed on stretchers and borne away to the HQ building, closely followed by the same "Acorn" interrogators and SB officers St. John had seen the night before at the Bumi Hills Lodge.

Several wounded Selous Scouts were assisted from the chopper just as a second one settled down beside it.

From the second machine several Africans were carried on stretchers and then, to his consternation, the general saw Captain Mack Hudson emerge. Hudson seemed dazed and his right shoulder and side were bandaged, with blood seeping through the gauze that had been wrapped around his bare chest. Disoriented though he appeared to be, he refused to be assisted out of the helicopter and walked unaided from the pad to a group of Selous Scouts and officers and men waiting for him.

"What in the hell are you doing here, General St. John?"

Ashley turned at the irate tone and found himself confronting Colonel Reid-Daley.

"Well, Colonel," he responded, trying to assume a casual air, "I just came down last night. As a representative of ComOps I felt it incumbent upon me to check on what was going on here. When I saw Ian Nicholson's crew last night at the Bumi Hills Lodge, plus a few of your own officers, I reckoned that something was up. Was the operation successful?" His eyes followed Mack's progress to the Land Rover. "I see you brought back some prisoners. They should prove productive, I would say."

Despite the fact that Reid-Daley was a lieutenant colonel and St. John a general attached to ComOps, it was the general who showed uneasiness.

"Did you finally take out Camp Nkomo?" he asked.

With great effort Reid-Daley kept his voice level. "I'll have you escorted back to the gate, General."

"I would appreciate a briefing first, Colonel," the general replied.

"I'm sure General Walls will brief his staff in due course," Reid-Daley said coolly. He turned to the RSM and the adjutant who were poised behind him. "RSM, will you and the adjutant escort General St. John out to the guard post?"

General St. John knew better than to pull rank in the midst of a Selous Scouts encampment. Haughtily he turned from Reid-Daley, thrust his head back and strutted toward the guard post from whence he had just come. At the gate the adjutant and the RSM saluted smartly, their eyes expressionless, and turned on their heels to go back to the staging area where a Lynx was now taxiing up.

With one hand on the roof of the waiting Land Rover, General St. John paused to gaze back at the brief scene that was unfolding in the staging area. A small van drew up beside the knot of Scout officers and Mack eased himself into the back. Then the van took off for the Lynx which had come to a stop some three hundred yards away. St. John heard the pilot shout something cheerful to Hudson in an American accent and saw him help the wounded man aboard. Clearly Hudson was on his way to the Andrew Fleming Hospital. St. John did not wait to see the Lynx become airborne.

Half an hour later Ashley St. John was back in his hotel room and changed into civilian clothes. It was still early in the morning when he knocked on Carla's door. "Come in, Ashley," she invited. "I'm ready for breakfast."

He walked into her room. Carla was wearing sandals and a tight-fitting blouse, which enticingly accented her full bosom and was tucked into a suede skirt. "What's the program for today?" she asked brightly.

"Leisure, my love. Total relaxation. I thought I'd commandeer some transport and we'd go track down some jumbos and photograph them."

"Sounds super, Ashley. And then maybe a swim and lunch at the pool?"

"Perhaps followed by a siesta," he added.

An inviting gleam in her eye and manner seemed to accept the suggestion. She smiled coquettishly. "I'm sorry I was such a stick-in-the-mud last night, Ashley. It won't happen again. Promise!" She took his arm and he led her from the hillside room up the wooden steps to the main level and from there down the long deck to the dining room beside the swimming pool.

"What a beautiful sight," Carla declared as Ashley seated her. "To think that big, beautiful lake was made by man."

"One of these holidays we must go to Kariba and see the dam and then maybe gamble a bit." Ashley was delighted that a good night's sleep had seemingly driven the Selous Scouts from her pretty head.

"It's really dreadful how little I've seen of Rhodesia outside of Salisbury," Carla suddenly blurted.

"Let me show you our country. Fort Victoria, the ruins of Zimbabwe which the Kaffirs have the temerity to proclaim was built by their forefathers. No houte's hands ever touched those stones."

Ashley reached across the table and took Carla's hand. Just then Peter Crockett appeared beside them. "Sorry to disturb you, General, but there's an urgent call for you from ComOps."

Ashely frowned. "I'll be right back, darling." He squeezed her hand and stood up.

At the desk he picked up the telephone. "General St. John," he barked.

"General, this is Major Banner, we have an Information Office problem."

"What is it then, Dick?" Ashley snapped.

"As soon as you get back from Bumi, hopefully no later than noon today, we have a meeting with the Minister of Information, Special Branch and the General Staff."

General St. John felt a sick, sinking sensation in his stomach but retained his bluster. "What is this all about, Richard? I just arrived here last evening."

"The World Press sent us pictures and a story filed by that reporter who disappeared a few weeks ago, Brigham. They are pretty damaging sir. The WP has asked us to comment on them before they release the story."

Shaken, General St. John stared at the phone a moment. Then: "I'll get there as quickly as possible. Can you get a plane to come pick me up at the Bumi strip?"

"There's a Dakota out there now that's been supporting some Selous Scouts exercise. We've already sent orders for it to bring you to New Sarum."

After a long pause, St. John rang off with a toneless, "Thank you, Dick. Have a staff car waiting for me when I land."

Slowly, in a state comparable to mild shock, Ashley proceeded back to the table. "What's the matter, Ashley?" Carla asked, alarmed at his drawn expression.

"ComOps needs me back now-now. There's a plane waiting on the strip."

"Oh Ashley, just when we had everything right," Carla moaned.

"I know, my dear. The damned war."

"Can you tell me what happened? Anything to do with the Selous Scouts?"

St. John shook his head. "No, it has to do with that bloody Yank reporter. Apparently the little bugger smuggled some photographs out of the country that can do us a lot of harm. That's all I know now."

"I'll go back with you then, Ashley."

"It's possible I could get back again this evening."

"No, I'll go with you."

Ashley waved down Peter Crockett. "Peter, we have to get back to Salisbury. Can you arrange a plane flight for Mrs. Hudson?"

"I was afraid of that when the call came through, General," Crockett said sympathetically. "I'll work something out."

Ashley turned back to Carla and took her hand. "I'm afraid I can't take you with me on a military flight." He smiled sadly. "Look, darling, I'll call you at your place when I'm through. I'm so sorry about Bumi having to be scrapped, just as we were ready to enjoy it. But— well, tonight maybe we can take up where we're leaving off. Even though it will be back in Salisbury."

He looked at her mournfully, but not without a certain glow in his eye. "I'll hope to see you tonight. Peter will look out for you and he'll put your plane flight on my account."

Chapter 49

If there was ever such a thing as a Selous Scouts convention, it was the wedding of Darryk Bullard and his faithful fiancée, Rose Gardner, at Kariba, Rhodesia's answer to the French Riveria. Colonel Reid-Daley gave all Scouts not actively engaged in operations against the terrorists a long Friday to Monday leave to attend the marriage ceremony and subsequent celebrations.

A few days before the wedding, a weeping President Kaunda of Zambia went on the air to launch a violent protest against the Camp Nkomo raid, which he described as the brutal murder of countless women and children in a refugee camp. Shortly after, Rhodesia announced its own version of the raid. It claimed that close to one thousand terrorists had been assembled at Camp Nkomo and were poised to strike across Lake Kariba in an effort to disrupt the coming Rhodesian elections by terrorizing the local populace. The camp had been destroyed and all the terrorists killed or dispersed.

Virtually every man, woman and child in Rhodesia, many with personal experience of the hideous atrocities visited on black and white civilians alike, cheered the raid. But while the morale of the little nation rose, the so-called free world outdid itself in condemnation of the raid. In the United Nations, the U.S. ambassador called for a resolution to castigate Rhodesia for the wanton murder of innocent civilians who had been fleeing the repressive white-supremacist regime of Prime Minister Ian Smith.

The U.S. Department of State issued statements supporting Rhodesia's national liberation movement and condemned the racist Smith regime for harsh repression.

In Britain, the Foreign Minister, Dr. David Owen, parroted his Bobbsey Twin of the African circuit, Andy Young, in decrying white violence against defenseless blacks and called for more aid to the Mugabe-Nkomo faction of the nationalist struggle.

Although it galled the Rhodesians on holiday that weekend to read about how little the Western world understood their struggle against Soviet- and Red-Chinese-inspired subversion, they took satisfaction in the knowledge that so many trained terrorists had been killed before they could run rampage through the Rhodesian countryside.

Thus it was indeed a time of celebration for everybody in Kariba that weekend. It was particularly so for the Selous Scouts and their friends, who were here to see one of their greatest living heroes, crippled and in a wheelchair though he was, marrying his long-time sweetheart. Just one fragment of a ricocheting bullet had, in a tragic freak of battle, cut into his spinal cord, permanently paralyzing him from the waist down.

The Lake Shore Hotel had been almost entirely booked by the wedding party for that Friday afternoon. Alvin Glenlord and Beryl Stoffel flew up from Salisbury with Roger and Jocelyn Masefield. Also on the plane was a radiant and excited Sarah Cobb Chase, her auburn hair switching in her excitement at being reunited with her British lover in Selous Scouts, Captain Colin Adderley. Beside her was Carla Hudson, on her way to meet Mack. Carla still shuddered inwardly at the thought of how close she had come to not being home when Mack called her from the hospital. She had literally just walked in the door, after her plane flight from Bumi, when the phone rang.

Carla still wondered if Ashley had known about the Selous Scouts' raid that morning and that Mack had been injured. She could only give him the benefit of the doubt. But supposing she had stayed with Ashley and Mack had been unable to find her? She repeatedly thanked the Lord that such a horror had been averted and swore to herself that never, no matter how lonely she felt, would she stray again.

Sarah sat across the aisle from Roger on the way to Kariba and regaled him and Jocelyn with the latest stories she was following up to send back to the newspapers and the broadcasting network for which she was now stringing.

Converging on Kariba by automobile, van and bus that Friday were numerous holidaymakers and at least one businessman in hopes of making a big sale. Mike Cleary borrowed a Mercedes and asked his friend, Cravenlow, to drive. It was early afternoon, and they had plenty of time to reach the resort before the ambush hour when the sun hung low on the horizon making visibility difficult and giving the terrorists a good chance of escaping the scene of their crime undetected. Lord Johnny drove with the gas pedal pressed to the floor. He had read about the raid on the terrorists.

"We can expect drastic retaliation," he said to Mike as his eyes searched both sides of the road, his Uzi submachine gun across his lap. "Now I can't promise to do more than introduce you to Colonel Reid-Daley and his procurement officer, Captain Paul Karl. I'll give you full marks and all that, but you'll have to make the sale. Theoretically I'm a journalist, you know. I don't get into politics or business."

"That's all I need, Johnny. I've heard through the grapevine that Captain Karl is the man to see on special deals." Mike replied contentedly. "By the way, will there be any loose birds about, do you suppose?"

"I would expect so. I've always found weddings fertile ground for immediate action. The unattached girls seem susceptible to getting a little of what the bride's enjoying that night."

Lord Johnny took a turn with a screeching of tire rubber that made Mike gasp. "Are we really in that much of a hurry?"

"The faster you go, the harder you are to shoot," Johnny replied airily. "I'm not going to write about it, of course, but what is your trouble in Salisbury?"

"Every weapon system I try to bring in, and I've got the American M-16 Armalites now, turns out to be unsalable here. Yet I discover that the buyers for the army are paying more for the same ordnance. I can tell you that there's a high-level purchasing ring that's making godawful big profits. I know Smitty is as honest as the day is long, and so is M.M. De Vries, but they're too busy saving the country politically. No, there's a consortium of business and political interests that don't want to see the likes of me come in and sell the Rhodesian

Army the materials they need without leaving room for their own payoff."

Lord Johnny shook his head. "It is rather discouraging, all that. But even in American history you read about members of Congress who made a fortune off their war against us. Greed. I reckon the honest man will always have to put up with it."

"I have some goodies in this car that will make the Selous Scouts want to do a unilateral deal with me all right," Mike chuckled.

"What do they do for foreign exchange, even assuming they have the money?"

"Oh come on, Johnny. You know what they're doing with ivory and skins. Ivory is one of the most valuable commodities in the world today. I'd even sell it for them, although I've heard that Paul Karl is one of the world's best traders in such items."

Lord Johnny checked the speedometer and his watch. "Won't be long before we're there."

Thanks to the efficiency of Air Rhodesia, the wedding guests who had flown up to Kariba were checked into their rooms exactly on time.

The sun was strong at three-thirty in the afternoon and Sarah decided to go to the swimming pool and deepen her tan. She was so busy in Salisbury tracking down story leads that she seldom had a chance to swim or play tennis.

Alvin Glenlord and Beryl checked into their respective rooms, then Al winked and for the benefit of the others and the check-in desk, said cheerily, "See you later, doll. I need to find the colonel."

Hearing this, Roger grinned at Jocelyn. They knew that M.M. De Vries would be up the following day and that, upon arrival, Beryl would be his. Whatever activity she and Al hoped to accomplish had to be wound up by then.

To his surprise Roger found a note waiting for him. "In the bar, Eddie."

As the porter carried their bags to the room, Roger peeked into the bar and saw Sergeant Eddie Wilson purposefully quaffing a tall glass of lager. He squeezed Jocelyn's elbow. "Go with this stuff to our room. I'll see you later."

Eddie bestowed a wide smile on his older fellow countryman. "Sit you down, Roger. Let me buy you a Castle."

Roger sat beside the short, rugged sergeant. "Don't mind if I do, Eddie." They were the only inhabitants of the dark taproom. "Looks like you're among the early arrivals."

"There's more around. Those with birds won't be off the nest for a while yet, I expect." The bartender put a foaming glass in front of Roger who took a long swallow. "Something special, Eddie? Or did you want a drinking companion."

Eddie kept his rusty head down, concentrating on his beer. Suddenly he fixed Rogers' eye with his. "A few of us had a talk a couple of days ago. I'm in Selous Scouts now, you know." Roger nodded. "And I was elected to tell you a few things on behalf of all us Yanks."

Roger attacked his beer again. Something made him think of Cary Donnelly. "I'm listening."

"First place, there isn't a man over here doesn't appreciate what you're doing for us. Making a club for us when we get into Salisbury means a lot. But I don't know as we're going to keep coming. I mean guys like Mack Hudson, Mike Wyatt, Joe Late, the rest of us who spend a lot of time slaying gooks."

"What's the trouble, Eddie?" Roger felt a surge of apprehension.

"You heard all about the external, the one our esteemed President is so exercised about. Where Rhodesia killed all those refugees?"

"Of course. What about it? I can't help it if President Carter is so afraid of the black vote at home he had to vote Communist over here." The agitation was apparent in Roger's voice.

"That mission was compromised." Eddie Wilson stared silently at Roger for a moment. "The colonel doesn't want it to get out. He hasn't told anyone but General Walls. They're hoping whoever is responsible will make a mistake and we'll get onto him."

Roger always made it a point never to ask leading questions and much as he would have liked more detail, he said nothing.

Wilson hunched over his dwindling beer, finished it and motioned to the bartender. A fresh beer mug slid in front of both men. "I'll get to the point, Roger. I drew this assignment because I know you and Jocelyn better than most. We know that Glenlord is CIA. He always has been and he always will be. Mack knew him when he ran CIA's CSG in the Nam. Remember Combined Studies Group?"

"Of course, Eddie. I worked with them but—"

WIlson held up a hand. "Glenlord was an upper five-percenter as a half-colonel. He said so himself and we know it's true. That means he was certain to make regular army full colonel and be top on the list for promotion to general officer. Now nobody turns that down just to become a press agent in Washington. If you think so, you don't know this military mentality you write about."

"He said he wanted to be his own man," Roger began lamely.

"Come on, we're trying to help you. He could get you into real trouble over here. He used you as his cover and now he doesn't need you any more. He's got one of the most influential women in the country behind him, or should I say under him." A frigid smile crossed Wilson's lips. "Let me just tell you, Roger, that we don't know how he did it but we think he found out about the Camp Nkomo raid and passed it on to the CIA. Naturally they passed it on to Carter who gave it to his man in the UN who shot it across to Nkomo."

Roger sat stunned. He found it hard to believe, but if all the Crippled Eagles believed this was fact, Glenlord was through as far as the Americans were concerned, and it was the Americans in whom Roger was most interested. He brooded over the beer in front of him.

As though reading his thoughts, Eddie said, "A good intelligence operator like Glenlord would have figured when Mack and the others were suddenly pulled from training and then isolated that something was up. And a fair guess would be that five or six days after their passing out parade at Andre Rabié the operation would go down."

"I get the message, Eddie," Roger said gloomily.

"Hey, Roger, you're the greatest with us, you 'numbah one GI,' as they used to say in the Nam. You're a writer. There are a lot of interesting stories we'll be able to tell you when this is all over." His brow darkened. "But if you want us, get rid of Glenlord. Can't you just fire him and tell him to get out of Rhodesia?"

"It's not as easy as that, Eddie. He's got a contract. Beryl's involved and you know they've got MM eating out of their hands. It would be a lot easier for them to have *me* PI'd."

"Do what you have to do. I wanted you to know how your friends feel."

"How come he's here at this wedding?" Roger asked.

"He and Beryl have been friends with Derryk. Besides, we haven't talked about this outside of ourselves. We can't prove anything, never will be able to get evidence that would stand up; the Agency is too tough. But think back: you made us all sign our names and units or addresses or something in your register so you could get in touch if you had to."

Roger grimaced. It was a sore recollection.

"You kept it under pretty tight security, yet it was stolen. Right?"

Eddie gave Roger a searching stare. "Think about it. We can help you. He's always wanting to go out on an operation with us or RLI or SAS. We could oblige and when we get him in the bush—take him out. Just give the word."

Appalled at the thought, Roger gulped half his second beer. These guys weren't kidding. They were ready, eager to do such a job.

"I'll let you know, Eddie." The reply sounded weak. "I think you guys are right not to let your suspicions go beyond the Americans."

"They ain't suspicions, they're convictions—Ambassador." A wide smile broke over Eddie's homely, honest face as he gave Roger the honorary title the Crippled Eagles had accorded him. "We feel bad enough that an American would come over here as a spy. And there's only one way you deal with a spy." The smile hardened and disappeared.

Wilson's eyes shifted to his empty beer stein then back to Roger. "Sorry about that, Roger. I didn't mean to lay it on you so heavy at the beginning of such a happy occasion, but you had to know. Forget it until these moments of merriment have passed. Then you can tell us what you want to do, and what you want us to do."

"All the way, Eddie." He tapped his empty stein against Eddie's. "One more before I go get Jocelyn and me settled?"

Sarah Cobb Chase, in as skimpy a bikini as she could wear without causing an outright scandal, was dozing in the warm sun beside the swimming pool and fantasizing about what she and Captain Adderley would be doing together in an hour or so. Her reverie was interrupted when she heard a familiar cultured drawl. "By George, we were looking for a bird and look what turns up. Did you ever see such tawny flesh stretched over so tantalizing a mold? And look at that long russet hair stirring in the zephers off the lake."

Sarah opened her eyes slightly and then sat up, a puckish smile coming across her freckled face. "Johnny, I didn't know you were a poet. And Mike? You never let me know you were in Rhodesia."

"Just made a fast trip up here from Joburg when I heard about the big event," Mike Cleary answered.

"Isn't she the answer to a birdless traveler's prayer?" Lord Cravenlow breathed, drawing up a deck chair and sitting beside Sarah's recumbent form.

"I'll flip a sovereign for her, Johnny," Mike offered. "Heads I win, tails you lose, old chap."

"You both lose; I'm spoken for," Sarah laughed.

"Oh, and where is the lucky chap?" Lord Johnny asked. "If it was me I'd be standing over my chattel with a shotgun to drive off interlopers."

"He'll be here."

"Since he isn't, what say we kidnap you?" Johnny suggested.

"Where were you when I was alone in Salisbury?" Sarah asked, pretending hurt. "Don't answer. Either you were out at Lord Argyle's farm in Chipinga with a visiting German beauty or you were escorting one of Rhodesia's most elegant and eligible queens to the parties we peasants of the press only hear about."

"Now, Sarah, don't be a critic. I was only after a story. If one doesn't mingle with the right people one doesn't get carte blanche to go out to the sharp end and file war stories and pictures."

"Well, I had to go after my stories without those advantages," Sarah retorted.

"Right, and scooped us all on at least one big one." Johnny chuckled and placed a hand on her bare shoulder. "You're hot. Let's take a dip in the pool, cool off, and I'll take you away for a marvelous drink and a super dinner."

"What about me?" squealed Mike. "I met her the same time you did."

"But I'll be here in Rhodesia to take care of her after you've made your little fortune and gone back to London or New York or Joburg or wherever," Johnny flashed back.

"Hey, hold it a damn minute," Sarah protested. "You gentlemen are moving too fast. In the next couple of hours Captain Adderley of the Selous Scouts will be here and I belong to him."

"You can't be serious, Sarah," Johnny said. "Here's our chance to get together again and you want to get all involved with a Selous Scout? He'll be away in the bush for a month or six weeks at a time. When I go out I'm usually back in less than a week."

"Hey girl, and I don't have to leave Salisbury and I never, hardly ever, go into the bush," Mike chimed in. "Better you settle down with a steady man."

"Have you already forgotten what we meant to each other in London?" Johnny pretended pain.

"I didn't until we were both in Salisbury for almost a month and I only saw you once," Sarah retorted.

"But that once was good, wasn't it?" Johnny quipped.

"Oh yes, but—" Then Sarah laughed. "Now look here, Colin and I are in love. We're going to get married as soon as the elections come and this situation is settled. Then we're going to have a good life together here in Zimbabwe." She looked at Johnny questioningly. "I sound crazy?"

"Yes, ma'am," Johnny answered.

"I was before, I'm not now. Maybe you don't know what it was like to be some third-class newsgirl, begging for the lowest paying assignments, trying to get my stories without lying on my back for them and even when I succeeded, being some kind of a laughing matter at the Overseas Press Club in New York, or at Costello's on 43rd Street or at the Press Club in London. You're a top international jour-nalist, Johnny. You don't know what it's like for the lowly stringer, particularly a girl. I hope someday you find one right girl and settle down with her. And you too Mike. I'm a happy lady for the first time in my life. I know where I'm coming from and where I'm going. I feel like a real, honest-to-God person now. Understand?"

She looked from Johnny to Mike. They both nodded somberly. "OK, if that's understood, I'd love a gin and tonic if one of you wants to buy. If you haven't met Colin I'll introduce you to him when he gets here. He's a Brit too, you know."

Lord Johnny stood up. "Let me have the honor of buying, Sarah. I'm glad it's all coming up good for you."

"Thanks, Johnny."

"Be right back, with doubles. Well, at least you can't go wrong with an Englishman."

Chapter 50

The Selous Scouts were beginning to check into the Lake Shore Hotel as the early evening winds off Lake Kariba turned chilly. Sergeant Major Princeloo was one of the first to arrive. He was accompanied by two African sergeants who had been on the operation with Captain Bullard when he sustained the crippling hit in the spine. They walked up to the registration desk and the middle-aged woman behind it gave them an apprehensive stare.

"Princeloo," the sergeant major announced. "I reserved two double rooms, one for me and one for these two gentlemen."

"I'll get the manager, sir." The shaken matron darted another glance at the Africans and began to hurry off.

"Wait!" Princeloo exploded. "Why do you need him? We made our reservations for the wedding."

"Right of admission is reserved, sir. I'll be right back!" Before the sergeant major could protest the woman had scuttled away, leaving him and the two African sergeants staring at each other blank-eyed.

"You leave this mess to me, blokes," Princeloo ordered. "I'll sort the manager out."

"We know a place we can get in," one of the Africans said.

"For Captain Bullard's wedding it best we make no trouble," the other agreed.

385

"The captain would never forgive me if I let this happen," Princeloo snapped. "Here comes the bugger now."

Briskly the manager approached the desk and faced Princeloo. "Yes now, sergeant major, what seems to be the problem?"

"None—*yet*." Princeloo shot a menacing look across the desk. "We made reservations for Captain Bullard's wedding weekend more than two weeks ago. We are here to check in."

The manager looked at the two Africans uneasily. "As I believe Mrs. Mundey told you, right of admission is reserved. This is not a commercial hotel in Salisbury. This is a family holiday resort. Our policy is different in some respects."

"Are you saying you will not register these two Africans?" Princeloo thundered in his best parade ground manner. "These two men have been Selous Scouts for more than a year. They were in Captain Bullard's stick when he was wounded. One of them actually pulled him out of the fire zone at enormous risk to his life. Captain Bullard will have your bleeding arse if you give us any more rubbish. Where do we sign in?"

"Captain Bullard is from South Africa; I'm sure he'll understand," the manager said smugly.

"Captain Bullard is one of Rhodesia's top war heroes, and one thing we're fighting for is an end to this sort of thing."

"I'm afraid we have to abide by the hotel's policy, sir."

"What a waste of white skin." Princeloo's beard bristled. He reached across the desk, grabbed the manager and pulled him half across the desk until his face was almost against his own angry countenance. "Now, you cunt, are you going to register the captain's men? And I can tell you there's going to be several more Africans in this party. Or do I jerk you over this counter, take you by the heels and pound your bloody head flat against the floor?"

The manager paused an instant too long and Princeloo yanked him from behind his refuge so only his knees rested on the registration counter.

"We'll register them," the manager gurgled. "But under protest."

"You can protest all the way to hell. Just give us our rooms." Princeloo shoved the limp form back across the counter. As the manager picked himself up, a shaking Mrs. Mundey pushed registration cards toward the men.

"That will be rooms 116 and 117," she gasped.

386

The two Africans had been careful to show no emotion over the scene.

"Will you want a porter?" she quavered, trying to regain her composure.

"We can manage." The burly sergeant major glared at the disheveled manager who was trying to slink away. "Oh, you can call the fuzz but it won't do you any good. This is Selous Scouts land until next Monday. Then we'll be out killing terrs for you until the last of those Communist terrorists are sorted out."

The manager beat a fast, wordless retreat and Princeloo took the keys and marched ahead of his Africans toward their assigned rooms.

The bearded Selous Scouts were now beginning to arrive in numbers. None of the Africans encountered a check-in problem.

The bar had been taken over for the reception and Roger Masefield, tired of the beer he had been quaffing with Eddie Wilson, was living up to his sobriquet, Bwana Martini, as he attempted to teach the bartender how to make a dry one. Colin Adderley had arrived, though too late to give immediate substance to his and Sarah's fantasies and still be present at the mandatory sundowners. They sat at a table near the bar, holding hands, hardly aware of their surroundings.

"Look at that bird," Lord Cravenlow snorted. "She and her Selousie don't know whether it's day or night. Well, not to worry, Mike, we'll drop by the casinos. There's a dozen or more sweethearts dealing cards and dice that like to take their recreation lying down."

"You just introduce me to the colonel and Paul Karl if you know him and I'll take it from there." Mike looked around the room. "Who's that tall drink of water?"

Johnny followed his gaze. "That's Peter Turneville. I think he's the adjutant. He gave me a briefing on Selous Scouts activities a few weeks ago. Matter of fact, he's the groom's best man. They were together when Derryk got it in the back." Johnny, looking about, patted Mike Cleary's arm. "There's the Yank from SAS who recently joined the Scouts. I believe he led that external into Zambia a week ago, although it's hard to get details from the Selousies, for obvious reasons."

"You sure made it around fast over here," Mike remarked admiringly.

"Well, I had the advantage of having been in the British SAS for a few years—good parachute training—and I had a couple of years sorting out the Irish. It all helped. I wish our bloody liberal Labor government had let us help the Americans in Vietnam; that's the experience I'd like to have behind me. Captain Hudson was four or five years in Special Forces during Vietnam. He'll appreciate the goodies you've got to show."

"And you'll appreciate the commission you get on my commission," Mike reminded his friend.

"I hope it will buy me that Tiger Moth I want to fly down here. If I had my own plane I could really cover some territory."

"You should be able to buy two, one for spare parts, if we can pull this off."

"Come with me, then." In the next ten minutes Lord Johnny introduced Mike Cleary to Colonel Reid-Daley, Paul Karl, Peter Turneville and Mack Hudson who formed a knot about this popular peer from England who was so sympathetic to their cause. Words from Mike about sensors, light intensifiers, laser beam sights and infrared sniper scopes held their total interest.

"Why hasn't Salisbury purchased this equipment and sent it to us?" Turneville asked indignantly.

Mike turned from the tall blond-bearded Scout to Paul Karl. "Why indeed? Perhaps you can shed some light on the matter, Captain Karl."

"I can, but discretion decrees that I do not," Karl replied with a grin.

"If we had the sensors we used in Vietnam we could really fuck up the gooks," Mack Hudson threw in excitedly.

"There are times when I can't help feeling that our friends in Salisbury do not always have our best interests in mind," the colonel remarked blandly. "Especially when I think of how the Swiss banking industry is being enriched by certain of our politicians and businessmen."

"Precisely what I've found," Mike agreed. "In any case, I have a car boot full of samples you might like to see."

Paul Karl looked from the Colonel and back to Mike. "How about ten o'clock in the colonel's suite tomorrow morning?"

"I'm at your disposal, gentlemen. I'm here to talk business with the ultimate consumers, yourselves, since your Salisbury representatives are not interested—unless, of course, satisfactory arrangements can be made on their behalf."

Suddenly a round of applause and loud cheers went up. Derryk Bullard wheeled himself into the room, dressed in civilian clothes, his radiant bride-to-be, Rose, walking behind him. Members of both families followed them in along with three young boys proudly wearing T-shirts proclaiming "Rhodesian Gook Killers." Standing beside Rose was a tall, stately young woman whose long raven tresses contrasted with the bride's blonde curls.

Forgetting about the arms sale, Mike Cleary nudged Johnny. "Who's that super-built beautiful bird—no, damn me—lady, with Derryk's bride?"

"I don't know but you can wager your entire commission I'll find out," Johnny replied. And in moments he did. Peter Turneville walked over and shook Derryk's hand.

"Everybody," Rose Gardner called out. "I want you all to meet Barbara Curzon, my maid of honor. Barbara is an air hostess and Air Rhodesia fixed it so she could work a flight up here today and go back on Sunday. As a publicity person for the Kariba Tourist Board, I ask you all to give a hand to Air Rhodesia." There were shouts and cheers from around the room, more for the maid of honor than the airline.

Peter Turneville took his eyes off his gorgeous counterpart at the marriage ceremony for a moment to pat the groom on his shoulder. "Hey, I didn't know you and Rose were going to take such good care of your old mate. Where's she been all this time?"

Rose explained before Derryk could. "Barbara and I were in school together at Umtali and then she went back to England for two years. But she's a Rhodesian and she's with us to stay now."

The last remark was greeted by a round of cheers from those who were standing nearby.

The bride and groom stayed at the cocktail reception for an hour while Turneville struggled to preserve Barbara Curzon for himself, despite stiff competition. Then the bride resolutely grasped the handles at the back of the groom's wheelchair and pushed him from the noisy bar. Those that had been invited to the special dinner for family and close friends followed them out. Turneville took Barbara firmly by the arm and followed in their wake.

"Well, I'm afraid we're euchred there," Johnny observed.

"Goddamn, I wish I didn't have that borrowed car here, I'd get on her flight to Salisbury. Say Johnny, would you—"

"No, I'm going to Wafa Wafa to observe a day's Selous Scouts training and do a story for my newspapers. I've also got to find a story with an American angle for *Time*. They're putting me on as a special Rhodesia correspondent."

"When do those casino girls you were mentioning start work?" Mike asked resignedly.

"Pretty soon, as a matter of fact. We'd better get our claim in early. We might even buy a couple of them dinner when they're on relief." He glanced over at Colin Adderley and Sarah Cobb Chase. "Damn, why didn't I do more for her when she first came to Salisbury. I can only say she was more than slightly sensational when I had her in London, once old Masefield got out of the way."

"Yes," Mike agreed slyly, "wasn't she?"

"You?" Johnny asked surprised.

"Why not. You could never stick with a bird more than two days at the most. That sort of neglect makes them irritable and peckish, you know. Oh, his lordship's leavings make the most exotic pickings."

A slight frown creased Lord Johnny's forehead; he didn't take joy in undue reference to his title. He considered himself strictly a journalist. They both smiled at Sarah Cobb Chase and her British captain.

"Sarah, look my darling," Adderley could be heard saying, "you simply are not going back to Salisbury. Reid-Daley has given us all until Monday. He even said we could trickle back Tuesday morning to headquarters."

"But my stories have to be filed."

"What's more important, your wretched stories or us having every minute together we can manage?"

"Us, Colin. But—"

"Forget it. Hey, what are we doing here with this lot? Let's stop wasting time now that the bride and groom have made their exit." Sarah needed no urging to stand up and follow her lover from the bar to a chorus of rude speculations from the Scouts left behind.

Mike Wyatt, reluctantly followed by Natalie, his attractive but sullen girl friend, made his way to where Roger and Jocelyn were sitting once he saw Al Glenlord and Beryl get up and leave the table. He and Natalie sat down. "I hear the Minister is coming for the wedding tomorrow," he remarked casually.

"Yes, the third side of the gleesome threesome," Roger responded, finishing off his martini. "Al ain't getting any more of that" — he gestured toward Beryl — "until after the new Minister of Information, on top of everything else, decides to leave. Mother! Have I got information for him!"

"Roger, you're awful," Jocelyn laughed. "And you're getting squiffed."

Roger glanced at his watch. "It's only six-thirty. Think what I'll be like at midnight."

"Seriously, you're supposed to be acting like an ambassador," she reprimanded.

"Goddamn, but you're right. I've got to give the bartender another lesson. There must be some way to overcome the lousy gin they make in Bulawayo."

"Why don't we go somewhere and have dinner," Mike suggested. "No point in hanging around this zoo."

"Good idea," Roger agreed. "This old missionary here might as well find a new convert to the ways of making an American mart."

At the Sombrero, where the ingenious Rhodesian cook made a gallant effort to simulate Spanish cooking, and Roger instructed another bartender in the art of constructing a drinkable American martini, Mike Wyatt changed the tenor of what had been light-hearted conversation. "I hate to lay another problem on you in one evening, but we've got one."

Roger seemed to come suddenly alert. "Let's have it."

"I've been temporarily relieved of my duties at Grey's Scouts."

"What the hell happened?"

"That little Fu Manchu of journalism, Brigham. Remember when you came out to Lupane?"

"Oh my God! What happened?"

"ComOps called me in, blamed me for letting the little bastard get pictures of my white troops brutally interrogating terrorist suspects, and said it was something you and I worked out together."

"Why haven't they called me in, I wonder?" Roger asked.

"Your buddy, Company man Al Glenlord, and Beryl might have something to do with that. They're probably waiting to spring it on you when the story comes out and they can really get you."

"Is World Press really going to run a faked-up story with posed pictures?" Roger mused aloud. "I'd better call my dear friend who sicked that hemorrhoid of yellow journalism on me in the first place."

"Give them a call if you think it will do any good. I understand the government is contemplating expelling WP from Rhodesia if they do put it out. The trouble is that with the elections coming up they want all the worldwide coverage they can get. They don't know what the hell to do."

Natalie made her first comment of the evening. "Mike, it's getting late."

Jocelyn, who had found Natalie as responsive as a mute squaw, backed her up. "You did want to get up early, Roger."

"Why?" Roger growled back. "If we don't take care of this problem I might as well go back to the U.S. of A."

"And they'll court-martial me," Mike joined in. "They can't let dear old General St. John, last of the English gentry in the Rhodesian Army, take the rap."

Mike sighed. "ComOps have asked WP to send Brigham back so he can press charges against any member of the Security Forces he saw abusing a suspect. Do you think he's stupid enough to come?"

"I'll call London and get my old Vietnam buddy Hans Foss on the phone. I was with him when he took the pictures that won him his Pulitzer Prize in 1965. I even went out and helped him buy many, many pairs of underpants at Korvettes in New York before he flew back to Saigon."

"Al and Beryl are out to get you anyway, Roger. But we don't have to go into that now."

"Well, we're off to the start of a great wedding party, I can see that," Roger philosophized.

"How about trying the casinos," Mike suggested.

"Mike." This petulant warning from Natalie effectively put the brakes on any more speculation about prolonging the evening.

"I guess I'm entitled to the check," Roger said, reaching for it.

"Let's split it."

"No way. You take Natalie back to the hotel while she's still speaking to us." Roger smiled graciously and bowed slightly to Mike's date.

Natalie stood up without a word and Mike Wyatt led her out of the Sombrero.

Roger took Jocelyn's hand. "At last we are alone. How about catching the casinos? Selous Scouts should be breaking them up pretty good about now."

"Whatever you say, Roger." She gave him a supportive smile. "Things aren't going too well for this party just now."

"An accurate appraisal of the situation in Rhodesia, sweetie," he replied wearily. "But no, I veto my own proposal. Let's go home."

At ten in the morning Lord Johnny, his eyes laying back in his head, a Bloody Mary in his hand, led a somewhat more vital weapons system salesman to Colonel Reid-Daley's suite. The colonel never looked more alert as Mike Cleary entered, followed by two porters carrying his trunks. Derryk Bullard, sitting in his wheelchair, a happy-looking Peter Turneville beside him, greeted the newcomers.

Mack Hudson, refreshed after an early evening and good night's sleep with Carla, was also waiting eagerly to see the contents of Mike's trunks. Paul Karl and Major Van Roolyan directed the placement of the trunks and tipped and dismissed the porters, after which Turneville, wrenching himself from more pleasant thoughts, walked around the suite locking the door, closing windows, pulling the curtain and shades and turning up the air conditioning.

"Before we get into this most interesting discussion that lies ahead of us," the colonel began, "are there any eye-witnesses to the events of last night? I have received one or two disturbing phone calls."

"I, as a journalist, was privy to certain actions inspired by certain Selous Scouts, sir," Johnny replied. "I'm sure the exuberance of the men, and in some cases their vented frustrations when some of the casino girls resisted their attentions, might come to you in an exaggerated form."

"It already has," Reid-Daley replied grumpily. "I just pray we can get through this wedding decorously. And never again will I allow this many Scouts to gather together in public premises again."

He turned to Mike Cleary. "Go on with the presentation. Since everyone in Salisbury from the Prime Minister and the new Minister of Information on down has complete confidence and trust in Lord Cravenlow, and since he brought you here, Mr. Cleary, we will permit him to sit in on this exercise."

"Can you get us the M-16 model of the old AR-15 Armalite?" Mack asked without waiting for Cleary to start.

"I can. I offered them in Salisbury at $155 U.S. but I got no takers. Then I discovered the government had put in an order at $170. I don't know why you didn't get them yet."

"It takes a long time for things we need to come our way," the colonel muttered. "I can't imagine where that extra fifteen dollars a weapon goes," he continued acidly.

"I can supply them, Colonel, at the price stated. $155. Delivered on the South African side of Beitbridge."

"With all the rounds we need?"

"Unlimited."

"It's the lightest assault weapon made, sir," Mack prompted.

"But if the Selous Scouts turned up with, say, three hundred Armalite rifles in the armory, complete with ammo, it would be virtually impossible to keep it a secret from the rest of the army. And then our little private procurement program would be compromised and General St. John might succeed in his fondest wish which is to tear us apart as a unit. No, I'm afraid we'll have to go with what they give us on internal missions and the AK-47 for externals, same as the terrorists use."

"Couldn't we capture three hundred Armalites on an external?" Mack asked. "The World Council of Churches gives the terrorists enough money to buy whatever they want."

"Not a bad idea, Mack. We'll keep our options open with Mr. Cleary on that one."

Mike opened his first trunk and brought out the latest model light intensifier which he handed to the colonel. "You can't beat this see-in-the-dark instrument, sir. Try it tonight. At one hundred yards you'll see a man picking his way through the bush as though you'd sent up flares."

"Jesus, that's what we need in Mozambique, sir!" Turneville exclaimed.

"And you shall have it," the colonel replied, examining the instrument.

"We also have an adapted sniper scope version. It attaches to any high power rifle and gives you two hundred meters range. Very useful at night, as you can imagine."

He reached into the trunk and took out a glossy wooden box lined in blue velvet. It contained the scope, which he handed to Paul Karl.

"Jeez!" Mack exclaimed. "Just the ticket when we start fucking up the Freddies. We'll knock them out of their posts one by one and scare the shit out of them."

"Right," Cleary agreed. "Now here's something you chaps should all have on extended external operations—a laser sight." He pulled the boxed object out of the trunk and handed it to Major Van Roolyan. "Just clamp it on a rifle, then look through and you'll see a little red dot. Lay the dot on the target and squeeze off. Funny thing, the target can see the dot on him but by then it's too late."

"I've been trying to get Salisbury to acquire those sights for a full bloody year!" Reid-Daley reached out for the laser sight and held it to his eye.

"Let me just switch on the power element, sir," Cleary said.

"Beautiful," Reid-Daley exclaimed, pointing it at the widest target in the room, Paul Karl. The dot slowly came to rest on his chest. "We'll give these all a test on Sunday at Wafa Wafa. It won't take us more than an hour to get there. I assume you're staying with us until we can strike a deal, Mr. Cleary."

"That's why I'm here, sir. And when I do go I'll leave these items with you to practice on until your order reaches you from South Africa."

"It's all there now?" the colonel asked.

"Depends what you decide to take. What isn't on hand we can get flown down from London and over from Atlanta, Georgia."

"It will be costly," Reid-Daley sighed.

"Yes, but I assure you I'm not making an inordinate profit. I'm sure Captain Karl will agree when we get down to prices and shipping costs. And my trading company has buyers in Hong Kong who will take large amounts of ivory at premium prices. Also we can sell your high quality animal skins. And of course I am aware you have access to certain gem quality stones. All that is in Captain Karl's province, I realize, but we will work together, and fast."

"That's of the utmost importance," Reid-Daley said emphatically. "We've already built up a fair amount of foreign exchange in Joburg and I believe we have a convoy ready to leave Wafa Wafa in a few days time. Yes, Karl?"

"We're about loaded now. You'll just have to get us the clearances all the way south and through Beitbridge."

"Mike, you said something about sensors," Mack Hudson probed.

"Indeed I did. I have a complete kit in this other trunk." He leaned over and opened the footlocker. "What we have here is about fifty sensor discs and two scopes that will tell you when any one of them

395

is disturbed. You chaps over in Vietnam learned to tell the difference between an animal, a man and a vehicle. This is the same instrument though improved and modified. If, for instance, you're over in Mozambique and you hit a target and have to move out fast, just drop a few of these behind you and you'll be able to monitor your pursuit. I'm surprised you haven't laid a string of these along the entire border. No terr could cross without your knowing it."

"And you couldn't sell this in Salisbury?" Van Roolyan asked in amazement.

"They won't give me an audience. They have their own sources and pay far more dearly than they would to my group. Also, I'm afraid, they're dealing with some unscrupulous traders who aren't giving them what they should get for Rhodesia's hard-earned foreign exchange. And the way these trader gents work things, in order to make a certain amount of cash stick to the side of the funnel, it takes much longer before delivery can be made in those great green-tailed sanctions-busting airplanes we see over at the far side of Salisbury Airport."

The colonel understood perfectly. "We'll take our supply needs into our own hands, Mr. Cleary. You and Captain Karl can work out the details. We'll use all our modest supply of foreign exchange to trade with you, assuming you can deliver, and at the fairest price possible."

"You can count on it, Colonel. Aside from my longstanding personal interest in Rhodesia, some family ties with substantial investments here, I plan to be a heavy trader when the new government is properly ensconced and sanctions have been lifted. I want you to defeat the Communists and even with a black government, if it's moderate, this nation can be the greatest economic entity in Africa next to our friends to the south."

"Sir," Turneville said, a sheepish smile on his face, "would it be all right if I reached Wafa Wafa first thing Monday? I'm expected to put the maid of honor on the five o'clock flight back to Salisbury."

The others laughed and the colonel gave his blessing to the arrangement. "She's quite a beauty, that one. You're a lucky bugger to be thrown in with such a find."

"That's what I thought, sir."

"As a matter of fact, why don't you go find her now. I'll join you all presently at the luncheon."

Turneville wasted no time in absenting himself from the meeting.

"Well, Johnny, looks like we go down to Wafa Wafa together," Mike remarked. "By the time young Turnie is through proposing to her, I suspect my flying with the girl would be a fool's errand anyway."

The Scouts laughed and Captain Karl said, "Mike, looks like we've got a lot of work to do. We might as well get started right here and now."

"I'll leave that to you business chaps," the colonel announced briskly. "I'll be on my way now. See you later, Mr. Cleary."

Mack, Van Roolyan, and the others broke up the meeting to join their women for lunch, leaving behind the two negotiators.

M.M. De Vries landed at Kariba at ten A.M. in his personal military transport plane and forty minutes later was in his suite at the hotel. Beryl was waiting for him and poured him a glass of cold champagne. "Ah, that tastes good," the Minister breathed appreciatively. "Damn awkward crisis this, I mean, the WP story. Could seriously damage us right on the heels of all the criticism of the Zambia raid. I think we ought to have a word with Al. Seems Roger Masefield was somehow involved in it all, along with that other American, Wyatt, out at Grey's Scouts. Fine officer that one; I can't understand how it all happened."

"Al is standing by in his room in case you want him, MM." Beryl lifted her glass. "To Rhodesia." She took a hearty sip of the bubbling liquid.

"In just a minute ask him to come by. You know, I sometimes wonder who he really is."

"What do you mean, MM?" Beryl looked at the Minister in surprise.

"I mean that if he is working for Roger Masefield he is not serving him well."

"He's using Roger in order to do a job for Rhodesia. Roger is just here on an expensive lark. He drinks too much, spends his time teaching our barmen how to make martinis—"

"And doing a capital job, I might add. I came to enjoy the American martini at graduate school in Boston," MM put in flippantly.

"He's got delusions of grandeur. He really thinks he's some kind of an ambassador, and I think Al is right in saying we should get him out of Rhodesia. Al has his power of attorney and could sign the house and car over to me at any time."

"Poor Mr. Masefield. He doesn't stand a chance," MM chuckled. "Yet he's tried to help us, you know. That WP story, as far as I can determine, was no fault of his. Anyway, call in Al."

Moments later Al bounded into MM's suite wearing his usual costume of safari jacket and shorts with high-quarter skin shoes and knee-length tan socks. "Good morning, MM. I hope you had a good trip up here."

"Uneventful," the Minister replied.

"What's on your mind? Anything I can help with?"

"I just wanted to talk a moment about this Brigham matter and see what light you can shed on it."

"Sure, MM. Here's what happened. Roger invited Brigham to the house or let him in or something and then introduced him around and put him with Mike Wyatt. As far as I know, it was Roger who suggested that Mike take Brigham to the bush. Brigham was able to get Roger coast to coast publicity in the States with WP stories and pictures. Roger showed his appreciation and hopes for continuing good publicity services by getting Brigham into the bush with Grey's Scouts."

"I've talked to the head of the WP London bureau and the photo editor, a friend of Mr. Masefield's," MM threw out.

"Are they going to run the story?"

"I think they realize it is inaccurate and the pictures posed. They indicated they would check it out with Mr. Brigham again. The trouble is the story and pictures are just what the world wants to believe."

"MM, if you leave it to Beryl and me, we'll get the monkey off General St. John's back. That's what's worrying you, isn't it?"

"He's a good officer, a good man. Like all of us he has his weakness, but it's a most understandable one. I would be distressed to see his career ruined over this affair."

"We'll work it out so if the story does hit the papers it will be Roger's fault," Al reassured the Minister. "Then you can PI him and perhaps court-martial Wyatt. That's all there is to it. Roger was out there in Lupane when the pictures were taken. He came back and told us about them."

"Why didn't you tell me?"

"We didn't want to bother you and of course we had no idea you were going to add Information to your other portfolios," Beryl replied.

MM looked at Beryl and then at Al, curiously. "If you wanted to get rid of Mr. Masefield, letting the pictures appear and blaming him was a good way to do it. Anyway, we'll talk about this later."

MM's phone rang. "Ah, maybe we'll have some late word from the Ministry regarding the World Press decision on running those alleged news pictures. I asked them to call me if anything develops."

MM picked up the phone and listened. His only comment, "So they have come to their senses," was uttered with a grunt of satisfaction. After more listening, he added, "Congratulate them for me and see what I can do in the future to be of assistance in their coverage here." He hung up, a smile on his face.

"Well, we can all relax and enjoy the wedding. World Press is not going with the story."

Glenlord barely concealed his disappointment as MM took a last sip of the champagne and stood up. He was in full ministerial regalia—striped pants, black coat and cream vest. He reached for his homburg and opened the door of his suite, clapping the hat on his head. Beryl and Al followed him out and Beryl shut the door behind them. Al watched MM take Beryl's arm and lead her down the corridor to the lobby. A government car was waiting at the hotel entrance to whisk them to the luncheon.

Alvin Glenlord's plan had just been destroyed. Maybe he would actually have to kill Roger now. He walked into the bar where a dozen Selous Scouts in civilian clothes were taking another hair of the dog that bit them and chortling about the events of the night before. Al took a seat and grinned at the others who included two Americans, Joe Late and Eddie Wilson. They virtually ignored him.

The marriage ceremony in the garden of the Lake Shore Hotel was conducted in the old British tradition. The groom, in full dress uniform and wearing his medals, was seated in his wheelchair at the altar, which had been set up in front of a green hedge. His best man, Peter Turneville, towered beside him. The statuesque brunette, Barbara Curzon, led the bride and her father to the altar as the guests looked on. To the rear of the rows of seats half a dozen suntanned, voluptuous, and in some cases rather blowsy, casino girls and their new

Selous Scouts boyfriends watched the proceedings through lachry-mose eyes.

Near the front Sarah Cobb Chase and Colin Adderley held hands as the ceremony began, dreaming of their own wedding after the war ended. Al Glenlord sat beside Beryl since MM was seated with the groom's family and Colonel Reid-Daley in the front row. He appeared stiff and slightly uncomfortable.

Many white handkerchiefs dabbed at eyes and served in delicate nose blowing as Peter Turneville pushed the wheelchair out beside the bride and the Anglican priest led the bride and groom in their vows.

Finally, in an emotional hush, the groom slid the ring onto the bride's finger and she leaned over the wheelchair so he could kiss her.

With the conclusion of the ceremony, a battery of photographers from the *Rhodesia Herald* and as far away as Durban and Johannesburg in South Africa snapped pictures of the couple and of the Minister Plenipotentiary, now Minister of Information too, who was standing behind them. Derryk called for his commanding officer, at the moment trying to escape the crowd gathering around the newly married cou-ple, and the publicity shy colonel posed for a few pictures with the Minister and happy pair. Beryl was photographed with MM, and finally as the sun was beginning to set, the guests trooped up to the hotel ballroom reserved for the reception.

An energetic band had been hired for the occasion and the first dance, by tradition, was reserved for the bride and groom. Derryk had removed his tunic and opened his shirt since a side effect of his wound had been a sensitizing of his skin which made clothing irritating. Then he and Rose took to the floor. Smiling up at his bride, Derryk tilted his wheelchair back and forth in time to the music and made it spin and turn so deftly around the girl's dancing form it seemed to be floating.

Handkerchiefs and kleenexes surreptitiously reappeared as the guests applauded and cheered the remarkable performance. Then Derryk called, "Turnie, come out here and join us."

Turneville led the maid of honor to the dance floor and they enthusiastically danced around the bride and groom, Derryk keeping his chair tilting and twisting to the music around Rose whose supple curves not even her billowing white bridal dress could hide.

"Everybody!" Derryk called.

M.M. De Vries escorted Beryl to the floor and they began an elegant dance step reminiscent of a slightly older generation which brought admiring comments from the families of the married couple.

"What are we waiting for, darling?" Colin Adderley whispered to Sarah, and the two of them took to the floor. Soon everyone was dancing.

"You are not going back tomorrow, by the way," Colin said into Sarah's ear. "We've got something better to do. We're all going to Wafa Wafa for lunch. The colonel has laid it on. Then the Scouts are going to have a meeting while you watch some of the training exercises the new recruits go through. You'll get a better story there than back in Salisbury."

Sarah's eyes lit up. "You know how to bribe a girl reporter, don't you?"

"If I can't do it with my body, the next best thing is a story, right?"

"Can I take pictures?"

"Sure. As a matter of fact, you should get some shots of Derryk and Rose dancing."

"My trusty Nikon is on our table, dear." They danced back and Sarah unlimbered that extension of her being, returning to flash pictures of the event.

Mike Cleary went up to Lord Johnny. "Well, I didn't even score with a casino girl but tomorrow will be what I came here for anyway. Apparently the Scouts are making an occasion of it, and while I'm selling them the equipment out in the bush, the girl friends and you journalists will see a training exercise."

"I can already see myself flying the new Tiger Moth down here," Cravenlow said happily. "As for the birds, we'll go back to the casino tonight and surely find you something."

Eddie Wilson sat down with Roger Masefield and Jocelyn who were talking animatedly with Mike Wyatt. Natalie was listening, expressionless and distant. "Are you coming out to Wafa Wafa tomorrow?"

"Damn right, wouldn't miss it," Roger replied. "I've always wanted to see where the Scouts train."

"Number one: just remember that Glenlord is not invited."

"Then I'll really enjoy it. I think he and Beryl are catching a ride back with MM in his plane tomorrow."

"We think you'd better watch your ass, Roger," Eddie said softly. "And like you said, we're keeping our opinions to ourself." The sergeant stood up. "See you all later."

In a moving salute to the newlyweds the Selous Scouts began to sing their traditional African songs. Then the band stopped and the buffet dinner was opened.

After dinner the party continued unabated, and the wedding cake was rolled in. Derryk wheeled himself up to it, grimacing as he pulled his bemedaled tunic back on for the inevitable pictures. Then, with his ceremonial sword, he and Rose cut their cake as flashbulbs popped. That done, Derryk removed both his tunic and his shirt in anticipation of further strenuous merrymaking.

"And now, sir, the Rhodesian song for the bride," Sergeant Major Princeloo proposed. After some good-natured protests from Derryk, the Scouts sang, in London Music Hall style, the taunt to the groom.

"What do they do on vacations?

"At 'ome it's all sixes and fives.

"But many a housewife's independent

"And they has the time of their lives."

Turneville looked longingly at Barbara Curzon and when Derryk and Rose finally said good night and went off in the specially adapted new car the Terrorist Victim's Relief Fund had given the Selous Scouts hero, he and Barbara likewise slipped away. The last anyone heard was Turnie trying to convince her that Air Rhodesia could do without her services the next day.

Chapter 51

A lovesick Captain Turneville drove his beautiful air hostess, Barbara Curzon, out to Kariba Airport late Sunday afternoon. No bride and groom had ever put a wedding night to better advantage than had this best man and maid of honor. They had known each other less than twenty-four hours when they first made love in Barbara's hotel room, but it wasn't until the last possible moment that they disentwined their bodies, having eschewed food all day.

It seemed a cruel twist of fate that Turneville could not go to Salisbury with Barbara any more than she could remain another night at Kariba. Sadly, yet at the same time savoring an exhilaration that he had never experienced before, Turneville embraced Barbara in one last hungry kiss and then watched her walk into the crew room at Kariba Airport to make ready for the flight to Salisbury. They had arranged that he would move into her apartment on Wednesday night, and each morning drive to the Selous Scouts main base, André Rabie Barracks within the Inkomo military complex.

For a few moments Turneville mingled with the passengers, a few of whom had been guests at the wedding, and then he decided to drive back to Kariba. The rest of the Scouts would be returning from Wafa Wafa for one more night on the town, a last revel with the casino girls they had commandeered, before reporting to base. After that they

403

would be engaged in ceaseless combat until the terrorists had been cleared out sufficiently so elections could be held.

About fifty miles west of Kariba Airport, on a direct line between the lake resort center and Salisbury, a gaggle of laughing, chattering ZIPRA infiltrators were lounging in the late afternoon shade afforded by the rocky foothills of the rugged Whamira Range, which provided excellent cover. Jobolingo sat with his back against a tree on top of a stony rise gazing back in the direction of Kariba and Zambia whence he and fifty highly-trained ZIPRA specialists had come just a few days before.

He could still see and hear Comrade Nkomo raging over the destruction of his staging area and the loss of over six hundred ZIPRA Freedom Fighters. Nkomo had shouted, banged his fists into walls and furniture and urinated on the floor of his office as Jobolingo, the last man known to have been in the camp, explained the camp commander's refusal to anticipate an attack from any quarter other than the river.

It was two days before Nkomo could think and speak rationally, and even some of the most sadistic murderers and white haters among his advisers took exception to the first orders he screamed out at his officers. In pursuance of those orders, nevertheless, here was Jobolingo, about to execute the terrible revenge that Nkomo was taking against the Rhodesians and then report his accomplishment to Mugabe.

Jobo had been given extensive training in the use of heat-seeking surface-to-air missiles, particularly the Russian model known as the SAM-7 which the Chinese had copied. Working with a technical adviser from the Soviet Embassy in Lusaka, Jobo and the more advanced ZIPRA technicians had plotted the take-off curve of the Air Rhodesia Viscount from Kariba airport which made the daily trip to Salisbury. The flight pattern was easily observable from within Zambia on the far side of the Kariba Dam. Thus the Russians were able to render full technical assistance in carrying out Nkomo's plan.

The Viscount climbed steep and straight at 160 knots on its way to a cruising altitude of 15,000 feet for the short, routine flight to Salisbury.

On this Sunday afternoon, as Peter Turneville was driving back to Kariba, Flight 825 turned at the end of the runway and exactly five minutes after five the captain fed full power to the four Rolls-Royce Dart Turboprop engines, each delivering 1600 horsepower, to start the plane on its take-off run.

Twenty miles down the line of flight, the Soviet-trained ZIPRA crew had primed one of their shoulder-launched SAM-7s. The aircraft would pass directly above the SAM crew who sat patiently waiting for it. While there was a strong probability that once the missile homed in on one of the Viscount's engines and exploded, the airliner's fuel supply would blow up destroying the plane in midair, the Soviet technicians had also predicted that the plane might only be severely damaged and able to glide down to earth for an emergency landing.

The most likely point for this landing was plotted in the Whamira Hills. Jobolingo had chortled to Comrade Nkomo that in the Shona language Whamira meant 'You can't go any further.' Nkomo's gross belly had shaken mightily as he laughed at the irony of it. Flight 825, with its white Rhodesian holiday-makers on board, would indeed go no further.

The Viscount was flying at between nine and ten thousand feet and still climbing when the Soviet-made warhead came streaking upwards on a cone of orange flame, homing in faster than the speed of sound on the heat of the aircraft's engine exhausts.

There was no escape, no evasive action the pilot could have taken, even had he known what was about to strike. Once the missile rocketed from the launch tube, Flight RH-825 was doomed.

With a blast that shook the entire aircraft the missile tore into the inner starboard motor, producing by almost simultaneous chain reaction an explosion in the outer engine as well.

Air Hostess Barbara Curzon was just walking down the aisle with a trolley of cocktails, the sundowners ordered before takeoff. She was not unaware of the men who ogled her shapely form up and down, but her thoughts were of Peter Turneville and lovemaking such as she had never known. Suddenly the plane lurched violently and the drinks spilled over the nearby passenger and into the aisle.

She had been trained to stay cool in any emergency and now tried to calm the passengers, who stared in dumbstruck horror as thick black smoke and long tongues of flame streamed past the cabin windows and chunks of debris spun away in the slipstream.

The aircraft shuddered like a mortally wounded bird and the flight captain and first officer, as well as most people on board, knew that they were about to die. Despite Barbara's efforts to calm the passengers at the tail end of the cabin, where she had started out with her drink cart, pandemonium broke loose. Men, women and children, knowing they were hurtling to their doom, shouted and screamed in a delirium of terror.

On the flight deck all was calm, but the pilot and first officer were bewildered by the suddenness with which disaster had struck. Years of constant training had equipped them to deal with any emergency likely to be encountered in the air, but no training manual yet devised lists the steps to be taken by an airline pilot when his aircraft is blasted by a heat-seeking ground-to-air missile. None of the crew had the slightest idea what had really happened. Impending catastrophe was heralded by the flashing of amber lights and the strident clamor of bells on the instrument panel, indicating that two engines were ablaze.

Fire in the air is a pilot's greatest nightmare, his constant overriding fear. The pilot of Flight 825 of course knew that a Viscount can, in certain circumstances, fly comfortably on only two engines, he also realized that to try to go back to Kariba would be fatal as the necessary turn would involve the loss of crucial airspeed.

Neither pilot panicked. They carried out the routine emergency drills with absolute professionalism: shutting down all systems on the engines afire; closing off high-pressure cocks and fuel lines; feathering both props; setting the stopwatch that would activate the first fire extinguisher; lowering the flaps to reduce airspeed during the descent—there was no time to drop the undercarriage to create more drag and slow the aircraft.

During the drill both pilots stared out the cockpit windows looking for somewhere, anywhere to put the plane down.

The pilot radioed distress signals and then, struggling to hold the plane on an even keel in its steep dive, called over the intercom to the passengers to fasten seat belts, keep calm and place their heads between their knees in the crash position.

"We are going in for an emergency landing." These were the last words he ever spoke.

On the ground, Jobolingo and Nkomo's ZIPRA guerrillas watched the Viscount, streaming smoke and flame, plunge toward them. The terrorists screamed and jumped in glee at the sight, pounding each other and brandishing their assault rifles. Below them lay a plowed field about the length of two football fields. As they watched, the fiery airliner streaked in, breaking off tops of the trees at the edge of the field; and then, with a screeching of metal against stone and earth, the Viscount dug into the field nose down and plowed along piling up a huge mound of earth and rubble ahead of it. For a moment Jobolingo thought the plane would make a safe landing and Nkomo's men would have the pleasure of obeying their leader's orders to have their way with the passengers as long as there were no survivors in the end.

But as he watched, the nose of the plane smashed into a ten-foot-high donga or earth wall across the field and instantly blew up with an explosion that almost knocked the guerrillas from their positions on the rocky promontory above the field.

The tail section of the plane separated from the rest of the burning fuselage at the moment of impact and a number of human forms came tumbling out onto the ground, to lie there inert. The guerrillas watched in awe as the plane seemed to split into pieces and out of the flames spewed luggage and other human possessions.

As the terrorists ran toward the flaming wreckage half a mile away, they soon felt the searing heat. They stopped, but only for moments. The sight of the people who had miraculously survived the holocaust and were wandering around the tail section spurred them irresistibly on again.

Dazed, most bleeding and all suffering from shock, eighteen men and women emerged from the tail section of the plane. Air Hostess Barbara Curzon, despite the pain from a broken right arm and from lacerations caused by flying metal, worked heroically to try to assist survivors. As the terrorists came closer, they could smell the stench of burning flesh from the crash site.

Before they reached the smoking ruins of the airplane, Jobolingo and the others observed a group of four survivors limping away into the bush as though seeking help. Of the rest, some were still lying in the dirt and some were gathered around them.

Shrieking "Chimarangaaaa!" Nkomo's men darted over the pitted field toward the survivors.

Barbara Curzon had gone into shock as the pain of her arm intensified. "Please give me some water," she begged.

One of the men who had gone looking for help had returned with a calabash of water from the village at the edge of the field, and as

Barbara sank to the ground he lifted her head and gently poured some water down her throat and then washed off her face.

"Don't move, you'll make the fracture worse," the passenger advised. "Just lie there until help comes. I'll go for more water." After some of the other survivors had finished the water, a small party went off to find more and also to bring back help.

Barbara, in considerable pain, looked after them; then, turning her head, she saw a sight that froze her to the marrow. A band of fifteen or twenty terrorists in rough civilian clothing and carrying rifles with bayonets on them were approaching the plane. Swaggering, with gloating grins of triumph on their faces, and crying slogans, they came up to the petrified survivors gathered around the broken-off tail section.

Shouting and motioning with their gun barrels, they herded the dozen survivors away from the burning Viscount toward the deserted village at the edge of the field. Barbara, moaning now and holding her broken arm, tried to keep up with the others, but as she lagged she felt the sharp pain of a bayonet point piercing her buttocks and back. A short distance in front of her, two sobbing and injured children, in the arms of passengers, brought up the rear of the departing group.

At the edge of the village the terrorists told the survivors to stop and then surrounded them. One young man among the survivors made a rapid assessment of the situation and ran for the bush as the terrorist leader was in the midst of crying out, "You have stolen our land!" A fusillade of shots cracked around him, but he managed to get away unwounded.

In a fury the terrorists turned their attention to the passengers who were standing before them or had sunk to the ground. A small boy whose leg was bleeding badly began weeping. In an instant, one of Nkomo's men plunged a three-sided bayonet through his chest. The child screamed and the terrorist worked his bayonet back and forth in the wound, laughing wildly. Soon the child was still.

Jobo knew what he was about to witness. Perhaps he could stop it, but he doubted it. Besides, Nkomo's orders were to let the boys have their way if anyone survived the crash. Jobo's interest focused on the girl in uniform who was holding her arm. She was tall with a generous bosom, and beautiful despite her smoke-blackened face and bloody, disheveled clothing, which seemed as though it might fall off her with a little help. A gold wristwatch gleamed from her left wrist. He thought of Sister McFarland and the lust for a white woman rose in him. Sister McFarland was not as fine a specimen of white womanhood as this one and anyway the nun had given herself to him willingly. How many other of the boys had felt her loins close on them, he frequently tortured himself by wondering. But this woman, she was of the highest class of Rhodesian white exploiters of Africans. He knew she had never seen an African man exposed, much less known the thrust of one inside her. As lascivious desire for the helpless white woman raged within him, he turned his attention from his fellow infiltrators.

"Please don't shoot us!" he heard one of the hated Rhodesians plead.

"We mean you no harm, we never have," an old woman begged.

With a shriek one of the boys let loose his AK-47 on full automatic, shooting off pieces of the bodies of the three survivors that lay crumpled on the ground.

Suddenly, with wild lunges of their pigstickers and bursts of automatic fire, the frenzied ZIPRA terrorists began slaughtering the rest of the survivors. Jobo took advantage of their blood-crazed spree to be the first to have the young white woman in the tattered uniform. She must have some official capacity with the government, he reflected.

Pulling his field knife, he knelt beside Barbara who screamed as she saw the savage, his eyes red with concupiscence, lower the knife toward her abdomen. Roughly he cut the remains of her tight stewardess skirt from her, pulled it away and ripped off the white half slip and then her panties, leaving her vulnerable and helpless. The pain in her broken arm seared through her as she tried to struggle, crying for help which could never come.

For a moment Jobo's eyes were distracted by the flash of the woman's gold wristwatch. Holding the blade of his heavy knife against her wrist as though to cut it off in order to get the watch, he applied pressure, cutting the skin. The woman screamed in horror and reached across with her right hand to unclasp the watch band. It fell from her wrist and the woman held it up to him, as though trying to trade it for her life. Jobo snatched it from her and thrust it into his trouser pocket.

To the stuttering beat of the assault rifles ripping into the bodies of the survivors, Jobo pulled off his own pants and in a fit of uncontrollable rut thrust his engorged member up and into the screaming white woman. Then he began to call obscenities to her, his fetid breath suffocating her like hot diesel exhaust. As she tried to struggle, his full length probing deep within her, Jobolingo's need for release became imperious and he barely had time to rip off her blouse and bury his woolly head in her breasts before he erupted inside her, with a more satisfying violence than he had known in his entire violent life.

He lay on her some moments before a blow sledged into the back of his neck, almost knocking him senseless. He felt himself being pulled away from the white woman. Painfully looking around, he saw that the other boys had decided he had taken more than his share and that, while the white woman was still conscious, they too wanted to vent their passions inside her.

The ZIPRA leader, cursing at Jobo for taking the white woman before himself, quickly dropped his own pants, roughly pulled Barbara's legs apart and giggling crazily, thrust himself into her. Barbara's agonized screams intensified as the ZIPRA leader drilled into her tortured body, expending himself in seconds.

The guerrillas raped the suffering airline hostess one by one until their feral lust was sated. Some of them, driven to the point of hysteria by the thrill of killing the white survivors and disfiguring their bodies, returned repeatedly to use the limp, by now deranged and babbling air hostess.

On their way back from the village, a small party of survivors who had gone to get help were at first too numbed by what they saw and heard in the near-distance even to run. But they would live to bear testimony to the subhuman savagery of Joshua Nkomo's self-described Freedom Fighters. Had not the terrorists been so crazed with their own depravity, they would have realized that some of their prey had got away, and remembered that Nkomo's orders had been to kill every man, woman and child who might possibly defy the laws of chance and escape the immediate scene.

With the coming of darkness and the realization that search parties would be dispatched to look for the downed airplane, the sated guerrillas knew they must disappear back into the bush so they could carry out their ongoing assignment which was to disrupt the elections.

The white woman was still alive and breathing fitfully, occasionally whimpering. She must be dispatched. Jobo was well aware of the final fate in store for her, and since he had been the first to take her and wished he could have kept her for himself, he walked away so as not to have to witness this particular enactment of the death penalty that had been decreed for white women.

The terrorists, still snorting and giggling, buttoned up their clothing. It was now the prerogative of the ZIPRA commissar and leader to administer the coup de grace to the white woman. With hyena-like sniggers, Nkomo's lieutenant slowly, mercilessly thrust the pigsticker into his convulsed victim's genitals and up into her body.

After almost an hour of low moaning and whimpering the survivors, hiding in the bush at the field's edge and still hoping to rescue the air hostess, heard a piercing scream: "Oh, my G-o-o-o-d!"

Then there was silence.

Chapter 52

Usually among the African representatives at the United Nations the United States Ambassador to the organization was genial and condescending. But today, in his penthouse office atop the Mission Building, he was anything but the jovial, self-satisfied diplomat that the black delegates expected to find when they came to visit Andrew Young.

Besides the Patriotic Front's clandestine advocate in America, Professor Eddison Zvobgo, the visitors included the regular representatives of Robert Mugabe's ZANU faction of the Patriotic Front and Joshua Nkomo's personal representative, the diminutive Dr. Callistus Ndlovu, an extremist so militant that even the U.S. Ambassador to the UN felt uncomfortable in his presence. A racist with a perpetually angry face, he openly advocated the death penalty for all Rhodesian whites who had in any way served the government.

Standing on his feet, the Ambassador addressed the group of black African militants seated around him. "At this moment I am too disgusted with you to trust myself to handle this meeting so I am turning it over to my Deputy Ambassador, Rocky Hills, whom all of you know." He turned to the younger black man wearing a bow tie and smiling broadly at the opportunity to speak for and represent the boss right in the Ambassador's office. Rocky, a basketball player like, tall skinny Negro, stood up stretching his lanky form.

"Rocky can speak for me, he knows my views, so I leave this important meeting for him to conduct." With that, the Ambassador stalked from the office leaving no doubt as to his present disposition toward the self-styled Zimbabwean Patriotic Front representatives in the United States.

"The Ambassador had Zimbabwe ready to hand you on a silver platter," the deputy ambassador railed. "We, the United States, we'll ensure Rhodesian independence no matter what happens at the elections. With great difficulty, the Ambassador forced the President to refuse any compromise with the senators who want the U.S. to lift sanctions against Rhodesia. This makes his work more difficult, but he goes along with the Ambassador. And what do you do?"

Rocky let the question hang a few moments and then plucked the answer out of the air. "You unnecessarily shoot down a civilian airplane and murder the survivors. This is what the Fascists have been waiting for. Fortunately, we've been able to get the press to downplay the incident.

"The Ambassador prevented the President from condemning it, or even mentioning it, even though my boss was able to get President Carter to condemn the Rhodesian attack on a ZAPU base. The United Nations has made no comment and no resolution has been introduced branding the killing of the survivors an atrocity. The World Council of Churches has not even acknowledged that the airliner was shot down. We've been lucky. Except for a few Americans, notably our nemesis, Mr. Masefield, little comment has been made. So then what happens?"

Again he let his question float above the chastened assemblage. "You, Callistus, openly take credit for the incident most Americans deplore. Even Nkomo had enough sense to say at first that he didn't order the death of the survivors. But you had to announce that the surviving passengers were gunned down to show that the Kariba sector is a war zone!"

Nkomo's representative at the UN gave the deputy ambassador a sullen look but didn't reply. "And then, on top of all that, the Ambassador just heard from his colleague, Dr. Owen in London, that Nkomo was interviewed by the BBC and that he laughed and boasted about his men shooting down the airliner. We have lost ground because of this. Mr. Young has been your only friend. If it were not for him the racists and Fascists would have succeeded in lifting sanctions against

Rhodesia by now. The white tribe's puppets would be in power. As it is, the President has lost his chance to defy the right-wing Fascist senators who want to invite Smith and his puppet Africans to visit the United States."

The Africans sat silent, their donut mouths turned down bearing their chastisement. "Do not misunderstand me"—the American diplomat knew his people well enough to realize that a scolding must be followed by a little levity—"what you do quietly out in the bush is your own affair and none of our business here. The more of the Uncle Toms, the sellouts, the white men you get the better." Chuckles and laughter broke out and the atmosphere lightened. "But don't rub it in our noses here. The President of the United States takes a stand against terrorism where it can be seen and proved. He was urged to make a statement about the Rhodesian airliner. If my boss didn't own him, he would have done it."

The deputy ambassador fixed the ZAPU representative with a steady gaze. "Callistus, we want you to inform Nkomo that he made a sick blunder and that if it weren't for my boss he wouldn't get away with it. Now enough of this; don't let it happen again."

Rocky Hills looked around his rapt audience and allowed a pause of some length for emphasis. Then: "Luckily, we do have a potential piece of propaganda that can be highly useful to us."

His listeners looked up hopefully and the deputy ambassador continued. "World Press is sitting on a picture story which vividly indicts the Smith regime for torturing nationalists in the fight for freedom. The president of WP has called the Ambassador about the story and solicited his opinion. Naturally, Mr. Young told him it was a free press and he should run it."

"Why didn't the Ambassador order him to print it?" Ndlovu cried out.

Rocky shook his head as though at a hopeless pupil. "We don't order the press in this country. You've been here long enough to know that. Furthermore, if the Ambassador used undue pressure it would appear that he was not the neutral American diplomat we know him to be."

Even Rocky couldn't suppress a grin and the statement was greeted with guffaws, which were silenced by an impatient gesture and frown. "Now, while you are all here I'll call Mr. Ranahan, president of WP, and see if we can't get the story released quickly. He's expecting the Ambassador to call. I'll put him on the speaker so you can all hear."

Moments later the ambassador's secretary had the chief executive of the world's most powerful news service on the line. "Hello, Bill, this is Rocky Hills for the Ambassador."

"Yes, Rocky," the news executive replied correctly. "Can I be of service?"

"What is the status of the Rhodesia atrocity story?"

"We've dropped all mention of the air disaster, partly at the Ambassador's insistence."

"I'm talking about the story filed by one of your reporters in Salisbury, Brigham," Rocky shot back.

"He's long gone from there," came the sardonic reply.

"When are you running the story?"

"We now seriously question its authenticity. The government of Rhodesia has asked us to send Brigham back so he can prefer charges against the offending men personally, but he refuses to return."

"But basically, you believe the story is authentic, don't you?" the deputy ambassador probed.

"To tell you the truth, we have grave doubts. And we wouldn't like to have our office closed in Salisbury just when so much really important news is coming out of there. As a matter of fact, we conveyed our decision to the Minister of Information, Mr. De Vries, not to release the story."

The deputy ambassador's voice rose in anxiety. "You can take our word, Ambassador Young's personal assurance that our commission on human rights turns up stories of atrocities and torture by the Rhodesian Security Forces every day."

"I'm sure you're right, Rocky, but we do try to achieve accuracy in all our news reporting. Our worldwide picture editor called me just this morning from London. He had heard from an American he knows well in Salisbury who claims to have been on the spot when the pictures were taken and is ready to swear in court that they were posed."

"You are probably talking about that renegade writer, Roger Masefield," Rocky snapped. "He is known to be a liar and paid propagandist for the Smith regime. The State Department is considering revoking his passport."

"Perhaps, but when our picture editor himself has reservations, we must proceed cautiously."

"Bill, the Ambassador will personally vouch for the authenticity of the story and pictures," Rocky said urgently. "Furthermore, you can rest assured that he will nominate the World Press and the reporter for a Pulitzer Prize the day the story is published."

There was a lengthy pause as the president of WP considered this last statement. "Your boss is that convinced the reporting is accurate?"

"He is. After talking to two gentlemen who have recently returned from Rhodesia, we can tell you that the United Nations will back up the World Press if there is any controversy over the story."

"That's a pretty strong argument for changing our mind and going ahead. All right, Rocky, tell the Ambassador we'll consider running it the end of the week."

"You will be doing the world a service," the deputy ambassador answered heartily. "And by the way, that exclusive interview you requested with Mr. Young? As you know, since the last time he was misquoted and statements were taken out of context he has been granting no press meetings. However, if you will have your assigned writer call my office I will be glad to make an appointment with the Ambassador for him."

"Thank you, Rocky. He'll call in an hour."

"I'll be expecting to hear from him. And we'll be looking for the story."

Rocky Hills hung up and grinned triumphantly at the group of African representatives. "So, as you see, we took care of the problem this time. Don't let it happen again."

"We're with you, Rocky," they chorused raggedly, giving the clenched fist black power salute.

"You better be. Just remember who got all the damn power around here. It's Andy and don't you forget!"

Chapter 53

Briskly the Selous Scouts boarded the two Dakotas on the Chiredzi airstrip and, heavily encumbered with parachutes and equipment, lowered themselves into the bucket seats that lined the two sides of the interiors. The pilots wasted no time in revving up the engines and taxiing out into takeoff position. Mack's plane would take to the cool night air first; the second would follow ten minutes later.

It was a ten-minute flight from Chiredzi to the pre-positioned blinking light on the Rhodesian side of the Mozambique border. This was the first navigation point, and looking out the door through which he would soon be exiting, Mack could see it clearly. Thirty minutes later the Dakota would fly over the road between Jorge de Limpopo and Machalia. Although this mission had been hastily mounted, Colonel Reid-Daley had for several weeks been preparing for it.

Mack well recalled walking into the colonel's office just three days previously and waiting for him to finish a telephone call. From the conversation Mack realized how carefully Reid-Daley had been planning this operation. "See here, Wing Commander Stoffel," Reid-Daley was saying, "you will in fact keep up those dummy flights and dummy para drops until further notice. Yes, yes, I'm aware of your aircrews being overworked over Mozambique but frankly, old boy, I don't give a damn. Be a good lad, do as you're told and don't make me go over your head, or the air marshal's head, for that matter."

There was a pause during which Reid-Daley looked up and winked at Mack. Into the phone he said, "No, you most certainly may not know the reason for this activity. Just put it down once again to my madness and peculiar ways. I expect the flights to begin again tonight and continue until first light in the morning in the areas I designated. Any questions? No? Well that's good. Then I'll bid you goodbye, Wing Commander."

Reid-Daley placed the phone in its cradle and faced Mack. "Major, I know you'll be ready to go across in two days time. We put in a lot of pre-planning on this caper, as you Yanks might call it. You undoubtedly gathered from my phone conversation that the Blues are committing considerable flying hours to this effort. They're bitching like hell and I can't really blame them. They're supplying maximum effort without really knowing what the full story is."

"I understand, sir. Only essential personnel among my men know where we're going." Mack paused in a double take. "By the way, sir, what was it you just called me?"

"Oh yes—Major." The colonel reached into his desk drawer and pulled out a box. "Here are your crowns. You might as well not waste any time putting them on your shoulder straps. I had a bit of a time with ComOps promoting a Yank to major, but in the end, after reviewing your record, they agreed with my recommendation. Congratulations, Major Hudson. And while I was at it I secured a commission for Sergeant Late. He's Lieutenant Late as of today. Now where were we? Oh yes, the Blues. For the past two days they've increased air traffic all over southwestern Mozambique. At first the FRELIMOS were alarmed but now they've settled down and accepted this air traffic as routine night patrolling. In two nights you jump in. With any luck your transport aircraft won't be taken for anything special by the Freds."

Again Mack looked out the door of the aircraft and in the light of the full moon he could watch the countryside slide by below. Mack had great faith in the Blues, and on this occasion Wing Commander Christian Stoffel himself was the pilot. It was to be a very precise mission. They had estimated it would take thirty minutes on a magnetic heading of 180 degrees from the first beacon until they reached the point where the road between Jorge de Limpopo and Machalia intersected the Pinto River.

Mack thought of Carla back at André Rabie. It would be boring for her, he knew. But he much preferred having her there than in Salisbury. He never asked about her social life but suspected that General St. John was seeing her when he was away. Now it looked as though Mack wouldn't see her again for twenty, perhaps even thirty days; yet he couldn't tell her how long he'd be away. She would just have to wait from one day to the next, each day living on hope.

From Carla back at base camp his mind turned to the surprise that had awaited him in Chiredzi. He had hardly settled into the Selous Scouts advance base in this southeast sector when who should appear but Lord Cravenlow and Roger Masefield. Both had passes to travel pretty much at will throughout Rhodesia.

Apparently the Prime Minister and the commander of ComOps, General Peter Walls, had approved of and been impressed by Roger Masefield's recently published book on Rhodesia. Lord Cravenlow, of course, was recognized as perhaps the foremost journalistic advocate of the current political scene in southern Africa. His stories, photos and motion picture documentaries were extremely influential in the United Kingdom and recently even in the United States. Both Masefield and Lord Cravenlow were having a perceptible influence on the United States and British governments' attitude toward moderate black majority rule in Rhodesia.

Mack Hudson was a soldier, not a politician, and he tried to steer clear of controversy. Nevertheless, having these two internationally famous writers appear at the Selous Scouts secret forward operating base disturbed him. He considered them both friends, Roger Masefield in particular since he was a fellow American, and Roger had perhaps the best understanding of the war Mack had fought in Vietnam of any newsman currently serving in southern Africa.

And this morning there had been a new complication, the arrival of Alvin Glenlord, complete with authorization from the Minister of Information, M. M. De Vries, virtually commissioning him to observe Selous Scouts operations and report back to the Minister with suggestions on dealing with the press with regard to military actions.

Glenlord's presence had pleased neither Colonel Reid-Daley nor Mack Hudson. To Mack it was like reliving his own part in the clandestine war he had fought on the borders of Vietnam. The CIA officer,

Lieutenant Colonel Alvin Glenlord, had inevitably been looking over his shoulder then. Now, incredibly, in a different army, in a different war on a different continent, he was on the scene again.

Sergeant Eddie Wilson had needed no urging from Mack to keep his eye on Glenlord at all times. If this shadowy American whom all the Crippled Eagles violently mistrusted accompanied a Selous Scouts patrol, tracing down terrorists within the borders of Rhodesia, it was Wilson's duty to watch him unobtrusively.

Right on schedule thirty minutes later, the Jorge de Limpopo road to Machalia came into view below the Dakota, the river, shimmering in the moonlight, intersecting it. The number one dispatcher, who had been searching the terrain for this navigational guide, clicked on his stopwatch. Mack glanced at his Rolex. Twenty more minutes to the DZ, he thought. The number two dispatcher held up a small blackboard with the number twenty chalked on it for all of the stick to see. The paratroopers nodded comprehension of the message.

Mack reached over, patted Captain Colin Adderley on the knee and gave him a thumbs up gesture and a big smile. The former British officer was the key to the upcoming operation.

Mack thought back to the colonel's briefing on this mission. Pointing toward a large map of the southeastern operational area, Reid-Daley had traced a line from the Indian Ocean through Mozambique right to the Rhodesian border. "Mack," he had said, "as you know, this bloody railroad runs from the Maputo docks straight to our border. When the Portuguese were in power it was a great boost for trade, but now that the Communist FRELIMO are running things, the railroad is like a dagger at our throat."

The colonel's voice hardened. "Mack, if we don't cut that rail line in the next seven days there's going to be hell to pay in the southeastern operational area."

Then Reid-Daley traced another route down the map. "Intelligence reports that at this moment a large Russian freighter is taking on several thousand Tanzanian-trained terrorists here at Dar es Salaam." He stabbed at the capital of Tanzania.

"From here they will sail to Maputo." Another stab. "They will board trains at the dock and proceed by rail to Malvernia right here on our border. From there they will infiltrate us. The train will have to make several trips due to the large number of terrorists involved

422

and the limited rolling stock that the FRELIMO have to work with. Obviously these multiple trips make our terrorist friends very vulnerable to attack."

Although Reid-Daley had not given any orders thus far in the conversation, Mack felt the old excitement and thrill coursing within him. Christ, he thought to himself, Carla is right. I'm worse than an old goddamn warhorse responding to the bugle. Just mention combat and I'm revved up to go.

"Mack." Reid-Daley's voice broke into his thoughts. "I want this goddamn rail line cut. I want maximum casualties and confusion inflicted. I want you to go in there and raise merry hell with the bastards." The colonel's fist pounded the map in the operational area. When he looked at Mack again a low smile was breaking over his face.

"Demolitions is the answer to our plan of attack on the rail line. So I'm attaching Captain Adderley to you for the operation. He's a specialist in that field."

Mack took another look out of the Dakota from the door through which he would soon be hurtling.

Ten minutes from the drop zone the dispatcher ordered the twenty-five men to stand, hook up and check equipment as the plane descended to the drop altitude of one thousand feet. Mack's stick would go first, secure the drop zone and then await the arrival of the second Dakota, now fifteen minutes behind.

"Stand in the door!" the dispatcher shouted. Mack shuffled forward, welcoming the cooling rush of air as he looked down and saw the edge of the drop zone below. He just had time to think that the DZ looked good, with no big trees, when the dispatcher's second shout, "Go!" roared above the engines.

Mack leaped out into the moonlight. The aircraft slip-stream caught him immediately and hurled him down and under the Dakota's tail. He felt the static line jerk the parachute free from the pack on his back, and then felt the reassuring jolt of the canopy which had opened perfectly. Glancing down at the ground coming up at him, he activated the quick release hooks securing his equipment container to his waist.

The container fell away cleanly, and was towed ten feet below his feet by the nylon rope attached to his waist. Mack was relieved there was no wind blowing.

In the eerie silence of his descent he surveyed the landscape he was entering and saw nothing but sparse vegetation. Other parachutes were drifting slightly above him. His twenty-four paratroopers had exited quickly, forming a tight stick. Dispersion on the ground would be minimal.

Hearing his container hit, he braced himself for what was a smooth, gentle landing. Quickly disengaging himself from his parachute harness, Mack chambered a round as quietly as he could into his AK assault rifle. Then, placing his weapon close by, he pulled the container to him by the suspension rope.

He extracted his pack and gathered in his parachute, stuffing it into the carrying bag. There were to be no parachutes left on the drop zone to compromise the mission.

The rest of the stick began assembling at Mack's position. The first man to reach him was Sergeant Major Princeloo. A quick check showed all men present with no injuries just as the second Dakota could be heard in the distance.

Vectoring the plane to a correct run-in heading with his radio, Mack ordered blinking strobe lights activated and moments later a stick of paratroopers blossomed from the Dakota. The first several men landed not more than twenty meters from Mack's position with the others landing in a roughly straight line that ended no more than three hundred meters away.

"Nice job, Blues!" Mack whispered into the radio.

"Glad to do it, Yank," came the reply.

"See you in SBY for a drink."

The night drop had gone so well that within one hour after jumping from their aircraft the paratroopers were proceeding toward their objective, the rail line. The moon was bright, the vegetation relatively sparse, so progress was rapid. Most important, Mack felt sure their entry into Mozambique had been undetected.

The railroad line and a road paralleling it came into view a full forty-five minutes ahead of schedule.

Silently, efficiently, the fifty men set up an ambush on a small embankment overlooking the railroad. Now the show belonged to Colin Adderley, the demolitions wizard.

Mack, at the center of the ambush party with his medic, Horst Houk, beside him, watched Colin walk into the moonlight followed by LeClair's stick of four men for immediate security.

As Colin began to work his explosive wonders on the rail line out in front of the ambush, Mack recalled their discussions just two days ago as they planned their mission.

"Colin," Mack had said to the demolitions expert, "have you figured out how you're going to blow the train?"

"I most certainly have," Adderley replied positively. "There's a fundamental precept here—less is more."

"Explain please to a retarded soldier?" Mack had replied.

Adderley nodded confidently. "To derail a speeding train, the book says one must blow twenty to thirty feet of rail. Although this is a good method, it creates certain problems. Lots of explosives have to be carried in on the jump, and much rail line must be tampered with. In other words, a large section of track must be prepared. And in our case that would increase the chances of the explosives being detected by FRELIMO's Shangaan tribesmen, who I'm told are the world's finest trackers, should they be patrolling the rail line." Adderley bestowed a self-satisfied smile on Mack. "I've devised a method whereby the train will destroy itself. I can accomplish this mission with just ten pounds of C-4."

"How?" Mack had hardly believed his British friend.

"I place five pounds of C-4 on each side of the track where two rail sections come together. Hooked into the explosive charges that I place will be a small radio beam sensor device. When I send out a correct coded beam the charges detonate." Adderley smiled like one explaining a tricky concept to a child.

"The charges detonate when the train is three to five feet from them. The blown rails are forced up under the speeding locomotive, they become entangled in the wheels, ripping up more rails as the fouled train, still going at high speed, eventually runs off the rails, dragging the passenger cars with it, and overturns. So you see, the train has destroyed itself with its own momentum."

Mack had been impressed by the ingenuity of the plan. "So all we've got to do is estimate where the train will finally come to rest and set up our ambush killing ground there?"

"Precisely, my dear Yank," Adderley exclaimed.

"By the way, my dear Brit, has this ever been done before?"

"Certainly not," replied the Englishman with exaggerated complacency. "Do you think that I, a member of the officer corps, would plagiarize? My God, what do you take me for?"

Now as Mack watched Adderley place his charges on the tracks, he silently prayed that the theory would in fact work. Everything depended upon it. As Adderley had observed, the mission would have been infinitely more difficult if, instead of the ten pounds of highly stable C-4 plastic explosive they were using, the group had been forced to carry in fifty pounds or more of the unstable gelignite, which was the only explosive available to them in quantity. Hopefully that problem would be rectified soon when the ivory and wild-animal-skin party from Wafa Wafa arrived in South Africa to meet Mike Cleary.

Finally, after what seemed like hours to Mack but in fact was only about fifteen minutes, Colin Adderley stood up, rubbed the small of his back, wiped his brow with a grunt of satisfaction and, gesturing to his security patrol, started back toward Mack and the ambush site. It was set up thirty meters down the track from where the detonation would take place.

Noticing the puzzled look on LeClair's face, Adderley leaned over and said softly, "I say, old boy, the train will blow here and stop down there in front of your mates. Right?"

LeClair's answering smile showed that he at least understood the intention. He signaled his two men, who had been observing the rail line and its adjacent dirt road through night vision scopes, to rejoin him and start back in the direction of the ambush. Carefully anti-tracking by stepping on the railroad ties and pushing trampled grass back into an upright position after they left the tracks, they finally reported to Mack.

Having assured Mack that all was well, Adderley assumed a position on the left flank of the ambush line where he could clearly observe the demolition charges he had so painstakingly placed.

Mack settled down into his firing position, then suddenly rose to his knees, straining to identify a distant sound. Herr Doktor Houk, in the position next to him, crawled over to confer.

A muffled voice came over Mack's radio. "This is Zero Foxtrot One. Two ten-ton trucks, twenty troops on each, coming your way. No scout vehicles evident. Troops are FRELIMO. Over."

"Roger, Sierra Foxtrot One," Mack acknowledged. The trucks were clearly audible now. Everyone's weapon was at his shoulder ready to fire. Quickly Mack whispered, "No go," to Houk on his right and Adderley on his left. Then he spoke urgently into his radio.

"All call signs, all call signs, no go. I repeat, no go!" Mack growled into the set. The trucks were now visible. Like all FRELIMO vehicles they were loud, rattling and poorly maintained. Looking up and down the ambush line Mack saw that all his men were crouching down behind the embankment. Jeez, what a pity, he thought to himself. But we've got bigger fish to fry.

He glanced down the line again toward the approaching vehicles and almost cried out. Creeping back into firing position was Trooper Van Heredon, one of the few youngsters in the Selous Scouts unit. "*Mein Got*," Mack heard Houk growl, "if that little bastard blows this operation I kill him!"

Mack and Houk both heard the muffled thud and saw Van Heredon slump down behind the embankment. Startled, they observed the grinning presence of Sergeant Major Princeloo crouched over the young trooper. The trucks sped up the road and through the ambush killing zone, the FRELIMO soldiers in their green fatigue pants and shirts with matching soft hats laughing and jabbering like a truckload of baboons, unaware of the certain death from which they had been spared by Princeloo's quick thinking.

Mack nudged the German. "Herr Doktor, let's go see if the sergeant major killed the silly fucker." Crouching below the rim of the embankment, Mack and the medic proceeded down the line. "Is he OK, Sergeant Major?" Mack queried.

"Oh not to worry, sir," the bearded Sergeant Major replied. "He's a bloody Dutchman. Hitting him on the head with a rifle is a compliment. Right, Van?"

Propping himself up on one elbow, the young soldier looked at them ruefully, rubbing his slightly cut head. Mack crawled closer and fixed him with a glowering eye. "Van Heredon, everyone makes mistakes. The trick in combat is not to repeat your mistakes. What the fuck were you doing preparing to fire without my command?"

"Sir, I wasn't going to fire, I was . . ."

A crashing right fist from sergeant major Princeloo almost knocked the hapless trooper senseless again. Looking at the man he had just struck, the sergeant major continued, still smiling. "Boyo, we don't lie to officers. As a matter of fact, in Scouts we don't lie at all. Now do we?"

Van Heredon rose weakly to his knees and peered at Mack anxiously. "I'm sorry, sir. I guess I got excited. It won't happen again, sir."

"It better not, trooper. We're a long way from home." To the German he said, "Take a look at his head, Houk. Then come back to our position."

With sunrise, the chill of the night disappeared and by mid-morning the heat, accompanied by hordes of insects, made the ambush site almost unbearable. Despite these adverse conditions the Selous Scouts displayed impeccable discipline. Movement within the ambush position was minimal. The men remained silent and alert. The heat killed any appetite for rations they might have had, but their great temptation, to be resisted at all costs, was to empty their water canteens all at once. Even if static, the body perspires heavily under a blazing sun and sends screaming signals to the brain for water.

As they lay there in the ambush position with only the objective to watch, thoughts of water became maddening. "Shit, I wonder what's worse, having water and being tempted to drink it or not having it at all," Mack muttered.

"Ja," the German medic agreed. "I've seen French officers put men in the hole for three days without food or water when they drank from their canteens without permission."

"What the hell did a smart Kraut like you think he was doing, joining the French Foreign Legion?"

"I told you I got how you say fed up with NATO so I joined the Foreign Legion and went to Indo-China and then Algeria. You should be glad. They, the French, made a paratrooper medic out of me."

"And the Rhodesians sent you to school for higher medical learning." To take his mind off the thirst that was plaguing all of them, Mack encouraged the German to talk more about himself.

"Ja, and now Colonel Reid-Daley is having me to give classes on first aid and train some African Selous Scouts as troop medics."

"How did they take to medicine?" Mack asked out of curiosity.

"Damn good. My Kaffir medics will after the war no doubt be opening abortion clinics and make for themselves a bloody fortune."

Mack chuckled. Houk was about forty, he knew. A first-rate soldier. If ever a foreign enlisted man should have been an officer, it was the Herr Doktor, Mack thought. He had come to know the German quite well in their torturous weeks in the Selous Scouts selection course.

A Berliner, Houk was well aware of what it meant to live in an island of democracy surrounded by communism. That was why, after getting out of the French Foreign Legion and going back to Berlin for a while, he had joined Rhodesia's struggle against the Soviet and Red Chinese Communists who had succeeded in subverting all of the sub-Saharan countries except for South Africa and Rhodesia.

The day wore on, with no further activity on the road or along the rails. No natives were seen, no foot patrols observed. The sun beat down and the heat continued. The men's faces were streaked with grime from wiping away insects. The thought of water dominated everyone's thoughts.

Toward late afternoon Mack turned to Colin Adderley on his left. He too was obviously suffering from thirst. "Carla and I like your girl," Mack commented.

"Yes, Sarah is one of the greatest birds I've ever met. Journalism is no place for a lady like her. I expect to take her out of it as soon as the war is over here."

"You mean you're going all the way, Colin?" Mack asked, surprised.

"As soon as I can get a divorce from my old witch, Stella. I believe Sarah's already written to her parents. Her father is the headmaster of some boys' school in Connecticut, you know."

"No, I didn't know."

"We've decided to live in Rhodesia, maybe even become Rhodesians. That is, of course, if we stop the Communists. It's up to us, out here, to do it."

"You won't mind fighting for a black prime minister, a black cabinet, a black parliament?" Mack queried.

"I'm convinced that Prime Minister Smith has worked out the most viable solution possible. I'd be proud to serve under Bishop Muzorewa or whatever moderate African is elected. I think Sarah and I will make good Rhodesians in the new era."

Conversation lapsed as the two men once more fought off their craving for water.

Mack started a game in his mind. He began naming every large body of fresh water he could think of. The major lakes of North and South America, the major lakes of Europe and Russia. When he started on the world's major rivers he abruptly stopped, feeling that this self-imposed torture had gone far enough. A while later, Colin Adderley, apparently deciding that rasping words through a throat of sandpaper was less painful than fighting off the urge to consume his precious water supply, leaned over toward Mack and observed, "Captain Turneville should see plenty of action according to the sensor scopes he was monitoring last night before we left."

"Yes, we pulled a real screen pass on them," Mack chuckled hoarsely.

"Afraid I don't understand you."

"A screen pass. American football. That's where we let the other side come in on us and then throw a pass over them. That's just what we've done. We've let a whole forward line of terrorists come over the border; as they poured in our group made the forward pass against them, and here we are about ready to fuck them up where they live."

"I just hope Turneville and the others can take care of them."

"God help any terrorist that Turneville gets his hands on," Mack said grimly. "We had a terrible time keeping him from taking off for Zambia to kill Nkomo personally." Mack struck the ground with his fist violently and squeezed his eyes shut. For a moment all thoughts of water were expelled from his mind.

A few Selous Scouts had been helicoptered into the wreckage site of the Rhodesian airlines plane and had been the first to find the massacred survivors and blackened, unrecognizable bodies of those burned to death in the crash. It had taken only a cursory examination of Barbara Curzon's body to see what had happened to her and the inhumanly cruel manner in which she had been finally murdered when the terrorists had finished with her body.

The government, on being informed of what had happened, immediately clamped total censorship on the story, allowing none of the details told by the survivors to be published in Rhodesia. It was felt, and rightly so, that the horror inflicted on the survivors, if known, could have sparked wholesale anarchy within Rhodesia with the whites howling for revenge and urging bombing raids on Lusaka, Maputo and Dar es Salaam, all of which were within easy range of Rhodesian aircraft. Violent reprisals against all Africans even suspected of being terrorists would have surely followed. Only the survivors, those few Selous Scouts and the investigative police teams knew exactly what had happened and they were sworn to temporary secrecy.

"Yes, Turnie is going to get plenty of action these next few days mopping up the terrorists we let in," Mack commented. "It was damn smart of the colonel to excuse him from his duties as adjutant and give him a chance to work off his feelings killing gooks." Silence again came over the men as their thoughts drifted back to water.

Some twenty minutes later Adderley remarked, "You don't seem to have much time for your fellow American, Colonel Glenlord. I couldn't help hearing you tell Sergeant Wilson to watch him like he would a cobra poised to strike."

Mack's lower lip curled. "Maybe he's a general for all we know. Whatever he is, he's not one of us Crippled Eagles. Salisbury is making one godawful mistake letting him wander around the operational areas."

"What about Masefield? And for that matter His Lordship," Adderley asked.

"They're both accredited. And I feel they have our best interests at heart. There's no way they would compromise what we are doing out here."

Finally, mercifully, darkness fell. With one man at each stick on guard, the exhausted Scouts slept for the first time in almost two days. One hour before first light Mack was shaken awake by Houk. "Stand to," the German sergeant said softly.

"Thanks, Horst. This green motherfucker is OK."

"Major?" the German asked, perplexed.

"The green motherfucker, doc. You know, the army. I've been saying that every morning for fifteen years," the American commander explained with a grin.

Checking by radio to assure that his flank security elements were standing by, Mack slowly and quietly inspected the ambush line. Crouched over behind the embankment he half crawled, half scrambled from one position to the next, pleased to see everyone alert and scrutinizing his own individual field of fire. He smiled here, gave a pat on the shoulder there.

As he came up to Sergeant Major Princeloo's position, the Rhodesian NCO touched his arm. Wordlessly Princeloo motioned Mack to follow him. The two men moved slightly back from the ambush. It still amused Mack to reflect on how their positions had reversed since Princeloo had been dedicated to making his life miserable during the selection course at Wafa Wafa only a few weeks ago.

"Sir," whispered the assault force's senior NCO, "about Van Heredon yesterday. I just wanted to explain."

431

Mack held up his hands. "Lester"—he had never addressed the sergeant major by his Christian name before—"There's nothing to explain. I'm relatively new to this army but one thing is universal. A man fucks up in combat and the book goes out the window. You probably saved the operation from being compromised. Are you worried that Van Heredon will make a big deal out of it, when and if we get back?"

"Not at all, sir. He's a good lad. Just a little young and inexperienced. He knows he fucked up; he'll come right."

"That's good Lester. I want you to know one thing. I back my NCOs one hundred percent. Loyalty is a two-way street."

"Thank you, sir. I can tell you this operation is going to be a genuine pleasure." Shaking hands, both men, once bitter adversaries, returned to their positions.

They heard the train ten minutes before it came into view, its whistle tooting at frequent intervals. Mack glanced at Adderley interrogatively. "Bloody Kaffir driving that engine," Adderley observed. "They do the same thing in a card, you know. Blow the horn all the time."

Mack's radio crackled to life. "This is Sierra Foxtrot One to Sunray," the words came from the Scout posted a quarter mile down the tracks. "Boss, it's a steam engine pulling three passenger coaches with a flatcar full of Freds. The flatcar is mounting a heavy machine gun and a couple of light machine guns. Over."

"Roger D," Mack acknowledged.

Soon the train became visible. Decrepit as it was, the steam engine was making about 50 mph. Colin Adderley watched the oncoming train, an alert, anticipatory smile on his face. This was his moment and he was savoring it to the fullest. Mack stared at his demo officer, praying that his theory, which sounded so good, would in fact prove practical. If only ten pounds of C-4 plastic explosive could really make this train destroy itself, Adderley had hit on a whole new method for lightly encumbered airborne assault teams to destroy an enemy's rail system.

Adderley held the radio detonator in his right hand, his eyes concentrated on the oncoming engine. "This is for Barbara Curzon and the rest of the people on that plane, you bastards!" he cried. The plastic explosives detonated sharply just in front of the engine. The detonation was the signal for the Rhodesians to open fire.

The din of automatic weapons blending with the screech of the steel rails as they entwined with the wheels of the locomotive puncturing and twisting the engine's undercarriage, made a sound like a giant gasoline-driven chain saw chewing through solid iron. As the train careened toward Mack in the center of the ambush line, throwing up clouds of dust and steam, it appeared to be still on the tracks and about to speed through their position. But suddenly it crashed over on its side, reminding Mack of the many elephants he had seen killed since coming to Rhodesia.

The locomotive was now a mass of twisted junk, lying precisely in the killing ground. Two of the passenger coaches had tumbled over onto their sides. However, one coach, plus a flatcar containing the FRELIMO troops remained upright. The terrorists in the overturned coaches attempted to crawl to safety through the windows of what was now inverted, tangled wreckage. As Mack watched, heads appeared through the windows in front of him only to be exploded like rotten melons by the concentrated machine gun fire of the Scouts.

Confused as to where the fire was coming from, many terrorists ran toward the ambush position. At a range of less than twenty meters their bodies were literally gouged to pieces by a curtain of small arms fire.

Frantically trying to bring their own weaponry to bear on the ambushers, the FRELIMO troops on the flatcar caught the fleeing terrorists in a deadly crossfire. The 50-caliber bullets from their heavy machine guns cut many of them in half.

The legs of one man who had been struck at the waist continued running several more paces without the torso before crumpling to the ground. One 50-caliber FRELIMO round sliced through several running terrorists before cutting off a large tree branch just above the Rhodesian ambush. From his position Mack could see that the left side of the ambush line was coming under increasingly accurate fire from the enemy on the flatcar.

Moving off to his right, Mack located an RPG-7 crew; then, motioning with his hands, he indicated what he wanted them to do. The first RPG projectile crashed into the flatcar, silencing the heavy machine gun. The concussion from the next two tossed the FRELIMO troopers and their equipment onto the ground. The few terrorists able to stagger to their feet were swiftly killed by the unrelenting small arms fire.

Renewed enemy fire was now coming from the far side of the overturned train. Obviously some terrorists had escaped to the tree line across the tracks, from which they were directing a stream of bullets against the Rhodesians. Quickly conferring with Princeloo, Mack ordered an attack on that section of the tree line. Princeloo would outflank the enemy while Mack established a base of fire from the ambush site.

Directing his 60mm mortars to rake the tree line and concentrating the fire of his automatic weapons on where the enemy lay hidden, Mack signaled Princeloo to go.

In bounding leaps the flanking force was across the tracks, over the road beyond and into the trees. When Princeloo was in position Mack directed his men to shift their fire to the extreme right of the hastily formed enemy line. Then, as Princeloo's assault force became visible, sweeping into the enemy position from the left, Mack ordered his men to cease fire. Heavy firing could be heard as Princeloo's men closed with the so recently Rhodesia-bound guerrillas, and screams and shouts rose above the din. Mack distinctly heard African voices pleading, then bursts of automatic fire.

"He is one hard bugger, that Princeloo," volunteered Adderley.

"Ja, hard, but with good reason," Houk interjected.

"How's that, Doktor?" Mack asked.

"Have you wondered ever why Sergeant Major Princeloo has two little girls living in his house at André Rabie and no wife?"

"I just assumed he was divorced."

The German shook his head. "The terrorists killed her. It was very bad. The little girls and their mother were visiting their grandparents. Somehow the terrorists did not find the girls but they did dreadful things to the mother. One little girl still cannot talk to anyone. The doctors don't know if she will ever come right."

"Christ!" Mack breathed.

"Sierra Foxtrot Sunray," the words crackled over the radio. "This is Sierra Foxtrot Sunray Minor."

"Go, Lester," Mack answered over the radio.

"All clear this side, sir. I'm posting pickets. I'll rejoin you in figures five. Over."

The radio conversation was interrupted as heavy firing came from the flank security elements along the railroad line. "Sierra Foxtrot One and Two, this is Sierra Foxtrot Sunray. You guys OK?"

"Sierra Foxtrot One here. That's affirmative. Just a few stragglers trying to run up the road."

"This is Sierra Foxtrot Two. Same deal here, sir."

"OK, stay in position. We're going to search bodies. Over."

At that moment Princeloo crossed the tracks followed by three men. Walking up to Mack, he was obviously happy.

"Any prisoners, Lester?" Mack asked.

"About a dozen thought they were, sir, but you know how those cunts lie."

Mack gave a tight smile. "OK, Lester. If the far side of the tracks is secure I want you and a search team to start going through the train and bodies for intelligence items. I'm going to get back to the boss on the big means and give him a quick sitrep."

Sergeant Major Princeloo led his men to their gory task.

Instructing his signaler to set up the powerful HF radio, Mack was soon in contact with headquarters. Using code, he gave Colonel Reid-Daley a succinct report of the action.

Reid-Daley's clipt, distinctive voice was soon on the air. "Tell all concerned very well done, bloody well done. I'm very pleased, very well pleased." He spoke with an unmistakable note of pride.

As Mack finished his radio traffic, a young trooper approached him. "Sir?"

"What is it, Van Heredon?"

"Sir, Sergeant Major Princeloo wants you to know that a precise body count will be impossible."

"Why is that, lad?"

"Some of the bodies, sir, are just pieces of meat. Some of them aren't even bodies at all. We've just got a bunch of goo out there."

"That's OK. What's his rough estimate?"

"About two hundred, sir."

Pleased, Mack patted the young trooper on the shoulder. "You see, Van Heredon, how well things go when you follow orders. Tell Sergeant Major Princeloo I'll join him in a minute."

"Yes, sir," the smiling youth answered.

It was about a two-hour job inspecting what was left of the bodies and collecting intelligence information but finally the task was completed. The terrorists had obligingly carried a large tank of drinking water in one of the passenger cars and the Scouts, after drinking their fill from the canteens, refilled them from the tank. Refreshed and exhilarated, having sustained no casualties, they listened to Major Hudson as he gave them their next orders.

"From here we will proceed back toward the Rhodesian border, doing as much damage and killing as many Freddies as we can. The purpose of our exercise now is to convince Samora Machel in Maputo that it is not profitable for him to support Mugabe and his gooks. We've got open season from Salisbury to pop anything that moves."

As the Selous Scouts prepared to move out and start back toward the border, Mack held a conference with Captain Adderley, Sergeant Houk and Sergeant Major Princeloo.

"It is our job to devise ingenious ways to frighten, to terrorize, to paralyze the FRELIMO initiative. Nothing is too extreme to make them understand that supporting the terrorists who come into Rhodesia and murder our people can only bring them extreme grief. You understand me?"

"I think I do, sir," Princeloo smiled.

"OK, I've done a little studying about these Freds we're up against and the terrorists they're supporting. I've noticed that when they come into a Rhodesian Kraal their favorite method of killing is to blow the heads off the village chiefs. There is something about fucking up a human head, separating it from its body, that seems to strike inordinate terror into most villagers. Am I making myself clear?"

"I think so, Mack," Adderley replied.

"Do you think we could find a few volunteers, perhaps some of our Africans, to cut the heads off the bodies left intact and pile them up in a nice neat stack, like cannonballs in front of antique cannons?"

"No problem, sir. Leave it to me," Princeloo replied stoutly.

"Excellent. When the decapitation detail has finished its task, we'll move out."

Princeloo's only problem was that everybody wanted to volunteer and he wanted to do the job in an orderly, disciplined fashion. He picked the six Africans whom he felt most deserved this special privilege and instructed them to employ their bush knives to best advantage.

One hour later Princeloo reported back to Mack. "When the next train comes through they'll find three neat piles of gooks' heads."

"Let's have a look at your handiwork." Mack strode down the rail line to where the African Scouts were proudly finishing their task. The grinning, bloody heads were stacked in symmetric pyramids, at the top of each a single head staring down the rail line toward Maputo whence the ill-fated mission of death had originated. Mack picked up a blood-soaked cloth FRELIMO hat from the ground and dropped it on the head that formed the apex of the foremost grisly pyramid.

"A nice touch, sir," Princeloo approved. "Should tend to discourage them, I'd say."

"Yes, I'd say so too," Mack agreed. "Maybe they won't be so enthusiastic about disrupting our elections when they see what happened to their buddies. OK, let's start moving back toward home. It's a long way to walk and the Freddies won't waste much time putting their Shangaan tribe trackers on our spoor. We should have a nice opportunity to try out our sensors, though."

Once again the fifty-man assault force broke into two files of twenty-five men each, and even though it was daylight they set out for the Rhodesian border one hundred and twenty five miles away.

Chapter 54

The Captain Peter Turneville who was briefing his Selous Scouts' officers and NCOs was a far cry from the genial bantering adjutant they had known prior to the Air Rhodesia tragedy. Hollow-eyed, and with new lines cutting into his lean young face, his appearance boded ill for any terrorist that crossed his path.

"And now, going into phase two of Screen Pass, the operation named in honor of our Yank major, it's our job to kill all the gooks we let come through. Thanks to the goodies our friend Mr. Cleary left for us, we've been able to rather thoroughly salt the infiltration route with sensor discs and thus have been able to track the progress of our friends from across the border electronically. All of whom we hope to make very dead very soon.

"From our base here at Chiredzi we will go by truck up to the forward operating base fifteen kilometers from the FRELIMO railhead across the border in Malvernia. We're getting some very interesting reports regarding these sensor operations. The gooks that came in last night, perhaps a hundred judging from the sensor signals, have gathered in a main body on a rather large kopje right here."

Turneville tapped a spot on the map and laughed hollowly. "At least one of the stupid buggers actually saw a sensor disc and picked it up. Apparently he slipped it in his pocket thinking it might have some value. As a result we've been able to get a much more accurate fix on them than we might otherwise have. From the forward base, located about seven thousand meters from the main terr force, we'll split into companies of forty men each and branch out into a pincer movement on the kopje where the terrs are currently encamped. We'll be in constant radio contact with the base. Our sensor scope there will tell us about any large-scale movements the gooks may make. Meantime, they're comfortably perched on their little rocky bush-covered mountain where they think they're safe. We'll call this little sub-exercise within Screen Pass, Operation Sensor in honor of the new, sophisticated electronic equipment we have finally been able to acquire.

"Since this is an entirely internal operation, we have allowed three civilian observers to join us. They're cleared by ComOps and we know them intimately. All three have been on Selous Scouts and SAS internal operations before. Lord Cravenlow was partially responsible for us acquiring this equipment. Both Roger Masefield and Colonel Glenlord have had experience with sensors in Vietnam."

Slowly, deliberately, Eddie Wilson pushed his chair back and stood up.

"Yes, Sergeant Wilson?"

"Sir, I think we're making a mistake taking the civilians along. I've never said it before but there is not a Crippled Eagle in Rhodesia that trusts Glenlord. Furthermore, we're just going to get Roger Masefield and Lord Cravenlow killed on this operation. There'll be ambush parties out waiting for us. Nothing we can't take care of, but if the gooks got Roger or Lord Cravenlow instead of Glenlord, it could sure spoil our day."

Turneville laughed mirthlessly. "But it they get Glenlord, no sweat, to use your expression. Correct?"

"I would say that is pretty much the substance of my feelings, sir."

"As you know, Wilson," Turneville explained patiently, "Cravenlow and Masefield have blanket permission to get themselves killed any time, any place, in the operational area. It rather surprises me that neither of them has succeeded in so doing. As for Glenlord, he arrived here with a special letter from the Minister of Information giving him permission to observe our operations in order to assist the Minister in devising new ways to deal with the press, who are complaining that they are not allowed to see anything of this war. We have no choice. Any further questions, Sergeant Wilson?"

"No, sir. You've answered them all." Eddie Wilson sat down.

"Now, all stick leaders synchronize watches." The men in the room pulled back the leather flaps over the faces of their watches and prepared for the time check. "In exactly two minutes it will be 0800 hours. Major Hudson and his Screen Pass infiltration group are by now in place along the railroad line. The gooks up on that kopje are waiting for reinforcements which I trust will never arrive."

At nine A.M. the trucks filled with Selous Scouts trackers were just leaving the Chiredzi camp for the forward base. The area commander had extended the curfew until twelve noon which meant that any civilian seen in the bush or on the road was automatically a terrorist and liable to be shot. Even so, the Scouts were well aware the *mujibas* would be lurking in the deep bush watching for military traffic and then run through the undergrowth to warn terrorist sentinels. These young boys ranging in age from seven or eight to thirteen, at which point they could become full-fledged terrorists, were the core of the terrorist intelligence-gathering operation as well as its communications capability. The *mujibas* could be as dangerous as the terrorists themselves, if not more so. It generally took several bloody operations that had been compromised before the white Rhodesians could bring themselves to shoot African children. The black troops were far more philosophical about the need for instant dispatch of *mujibas* and killed them without hesitation.

By ten in the morning the Selous Scouts had reached the forward base and Captain Turneville, accompanied by Captain Spence and Sergeant Wilson, went inside the headquarters. There another Yank, Lieutenant Joe Late, was waiting for them. Because of his experience with sensors in Vietnam he was temporarily assigned to evaluating the information gathered from the sensitive green scopes, plotting the signals from the small discs which had been spread along the Mozambique border in this operational area.

Outside the headquarters building, trying to hide from the blazing sun in what shade was available beside the scrub trees and other ramshackle wooden buildings, Lord Cravenlow and Roger Masefield discussed the coming operation. Alvin Glenlord walked up. Roger had been surprised, shocked would have been a better word, when Glenlord arrived at Chiredzi. By now Roger was convinced that even if his chief of staff was not a CIA agent, at best he could not be trusted.

441

At least Roger now derived a sense of security from having sent Jocelyn down to Johannesburg until further notice.

"What weapons are you going to carry, Johnny?" Al asked jovially.

Lord Cravenlow looked at Al in a way only a British aristocrat can when he wants to make his interlocutor feel inferior. After a moment, however, Johnny realized that his vintage hauteur was lost on this brash American. "I have my trusty super-eight Sony movie camera here, Al," he said distantly. "What more could I want? All by myself I can take excellent quality sound film and then transfer it to videotape, edit it and have my documentary, a one-man operation all the way."

"No terrorist is going to drop dead when you take his picture," was Al's jocular rejoinder.

"I made a discovery that you can be either a good gunman or a good cameraman but you can't be both at the same time," Cravenlow replied. "I've been both and I prefer the camera."

"Suppose you get separated from your stick?" Al asked, genuinely curious. "The time could come when a weapon will save your life."

"Well, as you can see, right here on my left hip I have a very fine .44 magnum I bought off a Yank a couple of years ago. If I really get stuck, quarters will be so close that my handgun will be as effective as one of their AK-47s. But, as I've always said, if the enemy does get the drop on you, there really isn't all that much you can do, you know."

Al focused on Roger, looking him up and down. "And what about you?"

"In some ways I agree with Johnny but I'm not a cameraman. I think maybe I'll accept the loan of an FN."

"Too bad we haven't got AR-15s," Al observed. "Honey of a weapon. I fell in love with it in Vietnam and it's been my sweetheart ever since."

The Selous Scouts officers and noncoms filed out of the headquarters building and began gathering their men waiting outside.

"Well, so long chaps, see you later, I hope," Lord Cravenlow said to Roger and Al cheerfully. "Looks like Turnie and I are off, he to get the gooks in his sights, I to get them in mine." He lifted his compact 8mm camera to his eyes, squinted through it and then put it back in its case. Turneville's Delta party started out for the north face of the kopje, and Captain Spence's Tango group, stretched out behind its point man, Luthu, in two files, began walking through the bush toward the south base. The terrain alternated between heavy bush and open brown veldt. They sensed eyes watching them as they proceeded but there was no turning back now. Operation Sensor was committed.

Roger and Al Glenlord were wearing identical camouflage suits and soft hats, both carrying FN rifles and five magazines of twenty rounds each. At first they exchanged some conversation. "So you sent Jocelyn home," Al opened.

"Just to Joburg," Roger said tersely.

"There's not going to be widespread urban insurgency in Salisbury."

"Maybe not. But I plan to be in the bush for a while. She's better off away."

"When are you going home?" Al asked pointedly.

"When I figure my job here is done," Roger snapped. "Not before."

After the first hour of trudging through the dense jungle and skirting the edges of the open tundra, Roger wished he had claimed the journalist's prerogative of not carrying a weapon. With the heat and the rough terrain the rifle's weight was fast becoming oppressive.

Al strode briskly along beside Roger, a mustache of sweat dribbling down both sides of his mouth. They were walking close to the front of the formation where Captain Spence could drop back at a moment's notice and confer with them if need be, or add his own firepower to theirs in case of an ambush. As they approached the south base of the kopje, Luthu held an arm up and stopped in his tracks. The two files halted. Luthu motioned for everybody to get down close to the ground. Roger needed no second bidding. At any moment he expected the crackling of AK-47 rifle shots to ring out from the jungle. Surely the terrorists in the kopje would have sent out sentinels. According to intelligence, these were a well-trained group in the tactics and techniques of guerrilla warfare.

Roger tried to take note of everything occurring around him. A sudden flight of birds could mean the presence of a terrorist ambush nearby. Methodically Captain Spence's Tango group pushed its way forward again after Luthu had furtively scanned the growth about them and alone had ventured off into the jungle and then returned.

Roger would have been apprehensive, he knew, had his mind not been meticulously storing every detail for future use in his writings.

It all happened so fast that Roger could hardly comprehend the sequence of events. Luthu had instinctively sensed the presence of a terrorist ambush party, whirled around, held his arm up and cried out in warning; then hit the ground just as a fusillade of sharp cracks, unmistakable AK-47 fire, sounded from the bush beside them. The unnerving zing of bullets traveling close by the head drove Roger and Al Glenlord to the ground, but the automatic weapons fire continued to probe for them.

Roger turned his face sideways in the dirt, pressing his heels downwards, remembering the old expression "inspecting the ants." Then Captain Spence shouted, "Let's go!" and everybody in the stick assumed a crouching position and started running toward the incoming fire, letting go with their own weapons on full automatic.

The Scouts carrying rifle grenades fired them at the ambush and charged directly into the terrorists. By luck they dispersed the terrorists with no casualties. The rifle grenades had accounted for two of the ambushers whose torn bodies they quickly came across. The rest of the terrorists had run from the onslaught, disappearing back into the deep bush.

Al Glenlord bent over one of the terrorist bodies and picked up the AK-47 the dead guerrilla had been firing moments before. Captain Spence and Sergeant Eddie Wilson directed their men to pick up the expended Communist cartridges for the ballistics lab back at police headquarters in Salisbury.

Three other AK-47s were policed up and then Spence regrouped his men and they continued toward their objective, the kopje which loomed ahead of them.

Al Glenlord strode through the bush, FN in his left hand, the AK in his right, and the operation continued. Sergeant Wilson was never far away from Glenlord and Roger.

"The bush is probably full of gooks with AK-47s aimed at us," Glenlord remarked. "I think we discouraged them just now, but it's getting like Vietnam. You never know when the odd terr will have some guts and take one of us out, knowing he's going to get it himself anyway."

"I've seen it happen more than once over here," Wilson agreed.

The action, the firing, the counterattack had dried Roger's mouth into crackling parchment and he longed to reach for his canteen and drink some water. However, he forced himself to abstain until the others went for their canteens. Water discipline was one of the most important features of Selous Scouts training.

As if to reinforce Glenlord's warning, occasional shots rang out, heralding the presence in the bush of terrorist sentinels. There was no mistaking the sharp stinging crack of the AK-47.

In a firefight it was always possible to tell who was hostile and who friendly inside the Rhodesian border. Much as they might have preferred the AK-47, Rhodesian Security Forces only used that weapon when they were in Communist territory.

Spence gave the signal for his men to spread out and prepare for the assault and then contacted base on his radio.

"Tango Sunray in position at south base of objective. Is Delta in place?"

"That's a negative, Tango Sunray."

"We'll report back in figures ten. Are we getting K car and gunship support?"

"Roger dodger, Tango Sunray. The Hueys have already departed Chiredzi." Captain Spence grinned broadly at the Americanisms coming over the radio from base. Sometimes Spence thought he was surrounded by Yanks. He looked around for Roger Masefield, Al Glenlord and Sergeant Wilson, none of whom was to be seen.

Colonel Alvin Glenlord, already on the army secret list for promotion to brigadier general, unobtrusively moved away from Roger Masefield and the Selous Scouts elements with whom he had been marching through the bush. It was not difficult to slip away unseen since everybody's attention was focused on the kopje where at least a hundred of the best trained and best armed guerrillas recently infiltrated from Mozambique were anxiously awaiting nightfall to slip away and begin terrorist operations.

By now, of course, the Communists would know that security forces were pushing toward them. The sounds of the ambush would have clearly carried to the rocky terrorist bastion. Furtively Glenlord picked his way through the bush, straightening up spears of vegetation he had disturbed. There was a slight promontory he had noticed about a hundred meters behind the Selous Scouts positions. Bit by bit he made his way toward it. From this position he would have a clear view of the assault force.

In a few minutes he had reached his objective and lying prone, concealed by the foliage atop the ledge, he observed the activity before him. He scanned the camouflage-suited figures until finally he spotted Roger Masefield standing apart from the others.

Al grinned, watching Roger sneak a long swig of water from his canteen when he thought he was not being observed by the others.

With great care Glenlord adjusted the sights on the AK-47. It was a weapon he had learned to use with deadly precision in the last days of the Vietnam War. The cross-border raids he ran into North Vietnam and Cambodia were all conducted with so-called sanitized weaponry, guns that were not made in the United States.

He estimated that he was approximately a hundred meters from where Roger was standing, thirstily guzzling from his water.

Sorry about this, Roger, Al said to himself. A soldier may not like his assignment but by God he carries it out.

He would just have time to squeeze off the shot that would kill Masefield and get himself out of his position, abandoning the AK-47. Then he would charge the site from which he had killed Masefield, firing off his own FN at the imagined terrorist who had fired the sniper shot. There was no reason for anybody to suspect Glenlord of taking out his friend and employer. But back in Langley another citation would be added to the top secret file on Colonel Alvin Glenlord.

Laying his cheek against the wooden stock and taking deadly aim through the familiar AK-47 sights, he curled his finger around the trigger and stared through the V at the end of the barrel. He drew a deep breath, held it and began the slow, gentle squeeze on the stock and trigger that would detonate the single round.

A sudden explosion from the rear and the zing of a bullet that almost creased his ear before plowing into the ground beside him, disrupted his aim. Disciplined soldier that he was, Al managed not to fire off a wild round but merely to drop the AK-47 and whirl around to face whoever had fired at him with the FN rifle. He found himself staring directly into the hard features and steely eyes of Sergeant Eddie Wilson. Al managed a grin. "What the hell are you trying to do, Eddie? Shoot a friendly Yank."

"Give me that AK," Wilson answered hoarsely. "Be goddamn careful how you hand it to me."

"Why sure, Eddie. If I'd known you wanted a souvenir so much I would have let you carry it." Sergeant Wilson took the butt end of the AK-47, the barrel pointing at Al.

"What's this all about?" Glenlord asked.

"You may be a colonel, even a general in the United States. But out here you're a spy, pure and simple."

"Come on, Eddie, you know better than that." Al started to take a step toward the sergeant who quickly backed one pace and trained the FN directly on Glenlord's chest. "I wouldn't hesitate, Colonel. You know that." Wilson's eyes glinted savagely.

A crashing and crackling of bush could be heard as four Scouts headed from the assault line to the rear position whence had come the crack of a friendly rifle. "It's OK, it's me, Wilson. I just took a shot at an enemy. He dropped his AK and took off." Out of the bush broke two Scouts. They saw Wilson and Glenlord standing together.

"If the gooks didn't know we were coming before, they sure as hell know now," a corporal complained.

"Do me a big favor, Randy," Wilson said to the lead scout. "Go back and find Mr. Masefield. Tell him I want to see him right away."

"Yes, sergeant," the corporal affirmed briskly. "I'll get him for you."

"Now why in the hell do you want to get Roger Masefield in this?" Glenlord asked.

"I think he'd like to know that he came within a split second of taking an AK round between the shoulder blades from his old Vietnam buddy. Maybe it will teach him a lesson that will save his life if he's going to continue the sort of thing he's been doing the past fifteen years. I don't know why you felt you had to take him out. I assume you had orders from Langley."

Al shrugged his shoulders, holding his palms out. "I've told you guys a hundred times I'm not with the Agency anymore. I've been out of the army for three years."

"Maybe Roger Masefield believed that but none of us did." Wilson's voice was ice-cold. Moments later Roger Masefield, following the corporal, appeared at the vantage point from which Al had aimed his AK-47.

"Yes, Eddie, you wanted me?" Roger asked. He looked around at Al and, in a flash, understood.

"That's right, Roger. Remember our talk at the wedding? Well, you came about as close to buying the farm as you ever will until it happens."

"What do you mean?" Roger asked, although he already knew the answer.

"Colonel Glenlord here had a bead on your back, his finger was already tightening on the trigger when I happened to let off an FN round in his direction."

Roger looked straight at Glenlord. "I'm doing my job that well, am I, Al?" He turned to Sergeant Wilson. "Thanks for saving my life, Eddie. I guess I was pretty goddamn careless. Seems like you never learn, doesn't it?"

"That's right, Roger. I thought I'd let you have the pleasure of taking him out yourself." Sergeant Wilson handed Roger the AK-47. "Do it with a gook weapon the way he was going to do it to you. That way it makes it easy for us if we get his body back to show that the terrs did him in."

Roger took the proffered AK-47 and held it in his hands. "You really were going to take me out, weren't you?"

"No I wasn't, Roger. Eddie Wilson's got it all wrong." Al's voice took on an edge of desperation; a sweaty film glistened on his face. "Listen, Roger, I know it looks bad but I can explain when we get back to Salisbury."

"And you wonder why I sent Jocelyn away," Roger rasped. "My God, I thought this terminating with extreme prejudice was a thing of the past. How many congressional committees OK'd this little plan?"

"Get it over with, Roger," Eddie Wilson commanded. "We haven't much time. Go on, shoot him." Roger hesitated. "If you don't, I'll handle it," Wilson prodded. "Give me back the AK-47."

Roger started to hand the weapon over to Eddie and then stopped. "Hold it, Eddie. We can't kill him. He was doing his job as an agent of the United States, our country. I don't believe he decided on his own to take me out."

"What's the difference. He was going to do just that. Now get it over with." Eddie's tone was urgent. "For chrissake, every second counts!"

"We can't kill a fellow American for doing his duty."

"Whose side are you on, Roger?" Eddie cried in exasperation. "Rhodesia or that fuckin' nigger in the United Nations that's trying to give all of southern Africa to the Communists?"

"Damn it, Eddie, we're Americans first. It's one thing for us Crippled Eagles to be out here fighting for what we know is right. But that does not give us leave to kill a fellow American carrying out orders from his government. Sure, he was about to kill me. I can feel the bullet stab in my back looking at him."

Roger stared into Wilson's burning eyes which looked like two portholes into hell. Slowly the fires seemed to subside and then Wilson sighed. "OK, Mr. Masefield. You're older than me, you've seen more of the world, I will have to respect your judgment." He shot a look of disgust at Glenlord who stood without moving as his fate was being decided.

Wilson sucked in his breath as if at some inner thought. "All right, Colonel Glenlord, let me tell you one thing. Every Crippled Eagle in Rhodesia knows what you really are and they'll hear about this assassination attempt, I'll see to that. If you ever leave Salisbury again to go out into the field you can be sure that an American will kill you, and there are a couple of hundred of us around here, in every unit. You understand?"

Glenlord nodded sullenly.

"If you don't get yourself out of the operational area and back to Salisbury before dark tonight, you won't see another sunrise. Now let's move!"

Captain Spence glared angrily at Roger, Sergeant Wilson and Al Glenlord as they entered the assault line. "Where, if I might ask, have you bloody Yanks been? All bloody hell has been breaking between Salisbury, Colonel Reid-Daley, Chiredzi and then the forward base where another Yank has been relaying it all out here to me."

"What's the flap, sir?" Wilson asked.

"They want Mr. Masefield back in Salisbury faster than a croc can take a pickanin."

"Colonel Glenlord is on his way back right now, sir. He feels he's seen enough of this operation."

"Good." Spence sounded relieved at getting rid of the civilians. "I hope you two can find your way back to the forward base," the captain snapped. "I can't send any of my men with you."

"No problem, Captain," Glenlord assured the Rhodesian officer.

"What's so pressing in Salisbury?" Roger asked.

"I don't bloody know, Mr. Masefield. Something about a big news story that came out in the international press."

Roger glanced at Glenlord and saw the suspicion of a satisfied smile on his face which was quickly suppressed. Roger felt a metallic knot of apprehension in the pit of his stomach but said nothing more.

"I'll see them on their way, sir," Wilson volunteered.

"Right. And get back here," Spence ordered. "Something has slowed down Delta group, but when they're in place and the gunships come over we're going up that kopje to kill the gooks."

Sergeant Wilson marched Roger and Al Glenlord away from the assault line toward the Scouts' forward base. Out of sight of Spence and the Scouts, he handed Roger the AK-47 and the FN.

"Sling the FN over your shoulder and carry that gook gun pointed at your buddy," Wilson advised. "Don't be afraid to shoot if he acts funny or he'll be showing up at the base alone."

"We wouldn't want that," Roger replied. "Let's go, Al. I sure as hell never expected to see the day when you and I would be in this position."

"Nothing to sweat, Roger," Glenlord replied pleasantly. "Even if I had wanted to take you out, as Wilson claims and I deny, the need has passed now. With the Brigham story going around the world, they'll take care of you in Salisbury."

Chapter 55

Captain Turneville led his Delta assault group through the bush, Lord Cravenlow walking beside him. The tall, grim-faced Selous Scouts officer was pushing his assault force as rapidly as possible toward the north base of the kopje since they planned to launch the assault and mop up the terrorists before dark.

Lord Cravenlow kept his movie camera cradled in his arms for instant shooting if any action occurred. It was the first time that a movie cameraman had been allowed out on an actual mission where contact with the enemy was virtually certain. In the present situation, there was no way the terrorists could leave the kopje in broad daylight with the Scouts closing in on them from the north and south.

The African point man signaled from ahead to slow down while he looked for signs of terrorist ambushes.

"Intelligence indicates we're coming up against real hardcore commies," Turneville remarked. "Trained in Tanzania, probably led by Tanzanian officers. We've been finding more and more of that lately. The Tanzanians are getting a year's training in the Canadian Army. Last time we hit a terr camp over in Mozambique we found bodies of about six Tanzanian officers all with names and addresses of people in Canada. Looked like some of those Canadian girls were getting it on with the Kaffirs," he added in disgust.

The hike through the bush continued; then suddenly the distant sound of firing could be heard. "For chrissake," Turneville exclaimed. "Sounds like Tango ran into an ambush. The terrs must have this area salted with ambush parties. Keep an eye out on the point," he called. The adrenalin flowed through the assault group as they pushed toward the guerrilla-occupied kopje.

"What are you going to do with the film you get today?" Turneville asked.

"Produce a television documentary for the BBC. They've been trying to get some good combat footage out of Rhodesia for a year now."

"We should be able to oblige you today, my lord," Turneville replied.

"Turnie, you would oblige me greatly if you would forget the lordship rubbish. I'm a combat journalist, and before that I was a British SAS officer. In neither case is there room for this peer of the realm business. Understood, old chap?"

"Indeed, Johnny. Now watch yourself from here on in. I've got three men covering you at all times, but we're up against a higher grade of gook out here than we've seen before."

Lord Cravenlow raised his camera to the ready position as they broke their way through the heavy trailless bush.

The crackling hail of AK-47 bullets poured in on them without warning. Even the point man, an experienced tracker, was caught by surprise. Cravenlow was sighting through his camera when the burst of rounds caught him in the chest. He was dead before he hit the ground.

Turneville, who had been standing close to him, was appalled by the suddenness with which the lethal fire had torn through their positions. He threw himself down, firing as he fell. The well-drilled Scouts let loose with their full firepower and in moments had come up to a crouching position and then begun charging the ambushers, keeping a withering fusillade of bullets and grenades. In moments they had dispersed the ambushers and raked their positions. The terrorists retreated into the bush, leaving five of their dead behind.

It was with deep sorrow that Captain Turneville walked back from the ambush position and, after giving orders to police up the weapons and the cartridge cases, knelt beside the body of Lord Cravenlow, the only man in his group killed in the ambush. His camera, still attached by a cord to his right wrist, lay in the dirt beside him.

Why? Why? he asked himself. Why Johnny? It could have been any of us. Why shoot a man with a camera when you could get a man with a gun? But then Johnny had perhaps made the best target, searching as he was for something to photograph.

Two of his Africans had been wounded and would have to be taken back to the base camp. The medic patched them up as best he could while Turneville called into base.

"Delta Sunray to base," he intoned hollowly over his radio.

An American voice returned the call. "Come in Delta Sunray."

"We just sustained an ambush. One dead, two wounded. We need every man for the assault. We'll have to leave the wounded and the body here and pick them up on the way back."

"Who is the KIA?" Joe Late asked over the base radio.

"I regret to say it is Lord Cravenlow," Turneville replied.

"Oh Jesus! I will notify the colonel immediately. We were all afraid something like this would happen," the American replied, forgetting normal radio procedure in the shock of hearing of Lord Johnny's death. "How far are you from the assault position?"

"We're almost there. Ten minutes and we'll be ready to attack."

"Roger, Delta Sunray. The gunships and K car will be overhead in figures ten."

"It appears that Screen Pass is already a costly operation," Turneville remarked dryly into his radio.

Chapter 56

The fifth Earl of Cravenlow had helped build the Protestant church in Salisbury where a funeral service was to be held for his great grandson, the last of the Cravenlow line, after his tragic death at the hands of the Communist terrorists. It was a mournful occasion for those of Johnny's friends who were able to be present. Most of them, however, were out in the sharp end or in Mozambique, desperately trying to scotch the terrorists plans for disrupting the elections due to be held a month hence.

The Minister Plenipotentiary was to deliver the eulogy. Sitting somberly in the front pew of the church were Alvin Glenlord and Beryl Stoffel; Roger Masefield, Mike Wyatt and Sarah Cobb Chase sat together near the back. The press corps had turned out en masse to honor a fallen colleague whom they had both liked and respected.

His hands gripping the edge of the pulpit, his voice tense with emotion, M.M. De Vries brought his eyes down from the church's magnificent high-arched ceiling and addressed his listeners. "Lord John Cravenlow was one of the best friends Rhodesia ever had. He was also one of the best friends I ever had. His bravery was matched by his integrity. He came to us not seeking personal aggrandizement, but to serve a cause he believed in, that of laying the foundations for a genuine multiracial society here in Rhodesia which might set an example to the world." The Minister paused. His last words lingered in the air a moment, and then there was total silence in the spacious church.

"Johnny was succeeding, he was helping us to succeed, when he was struck down—by the bullets of those who do not want to see a peaceful multiracial settlement in Rhodesia, and have no respect for those of us that do; who want instead to establish a uniracial dictatorship, and choose terror as their means.

"With his clear, objective reporting and, sadly for us, his determination to go where the danger was greatest, Johnny was our ambassador to the world, perhaps the most effective we've had since 1965 when, like the American colonies in 1776, and for the same good reasons, we declared our independence from Great Britain.

"Johnny's preferred weapons were not the sword and the gun, but the pen and the camera, weapons which, when used in the right hands, are the weapons of truth."

Whether MM intended to say more his audience would never know. He seemed to struggle with himself for a few moments and then stepped briskly down from the pulpit. The organ crashed out a final anthem, the bishop officiating at the service gave his blessing and the mourners filed out into the bright sunshine, following Lord Johnny's bier which was borne by six smartly attired troopers of the RLI.

Roger, Mike and Sarah watched Al Glenlord and Beryl intercept De Vries and walk away with him. "I guess we're in the shit up to our necks, Mike," Roger said, "I'll sure miss Johnny. He was the only person that could have told MM that I had nothing to do with little friggam Brigham and his fake pictures."

"They sure got me out of the army and on my way out of this country fast," Mike added ruefully.

"How can they blame either of you?" Sarah cried, vexed. "Everybody knows you had nothing to do with Jeff Brigham's story."

"We make convenient scapegoats," Roger observed. "If the whole story of General St. John chasing that blonde skirt from South Africa and being made a fool of by Jeff ever got up to Peter Walls and the Prime Minister, he'd be out of the army himself."

"As long as Ashley St. John has De Vries behind him," Mike said bitterly, "nothing's going to happen to him."

"When are you leaving, Mike?" Roger asked.

"I'm going down to Joburg tomorrow. I've got to check on my passport anyway. The Communists in our State Department have some unpleasant things in mind for me, I'm afraid. All of us Crippled Eagles are going to be up the creek when we go home."

"I may go with you, Mike. Jocelyn's down in Joburg and I guess we'll both head home. I got a nice friendly advisory from our new Minister of Information that if I should decide to leave Rhodesia now, without any urging on their part, it might be possible for me to return someday."

"They threatened to PI you?" Mike was surprised.

"Let's just say I got the message. And if I do go back I might be able to counteract Brigham's story."

"We heard it has already been nominated for a Pulitzer Prize!" Sarah Cobb Chase exploded. "Can you imagine, the Pulitzer Prize committee giving an award to a fake story?"

"It's what they want to see coming out of this war," Roger replied. "They don't want stories showing whites and blacks getting along together, that's for sure. That would spoil everything that Andy Young is trying to sell the American public. No, I think my place is back in the U.S. for a while, not here. I don't want any eulogies for me, at least until after I finish my book about this place."

"My God, that story of Glenlord trying to zap you is scary," Mike said lugubriously. "Not that it's surprising. Ol' Al better not shown himself out in the bush ever again. I guarantee you he'll be taken out. I just wish I was around to do it."

"Can you imagine M.M. De Vries being so dumb," Roger exclaimed as a chauffeur opened the doors to the Minister's limousine and he and Beryl climbed in the back, letting Glenlord sit by the driver. Bemused, they watched the government sedan drive off. It seemed almost incredible to them that the most powerful minister in the cabinet was letting himself be duped by a CIA agent whose cover, as they saw it, had pretty well been blown.

"Did you see Colin when you were down south?" Sarah asked anxiously.

"I saw him just briefly with Mack Hudson. They're across the border," Roger answered.

"I worry about him," Sarah said plaintively. "I couldn't take it, I mean I really couldn't, if anything happened to him."

Roger put a hand on her shoulder. "Nobody's indispensable, Sarah, though it's a hard concept to live with. But this isn't your first war, either. You know better than to get emotionally involved. Kills your objectivity." Roger wished be believed his own kindly meant little lecture.

"I know, but I can't help myself. Without Colin I don't feel I'm complete as a human being."

"For chrissake, Sarah, don't go soft on me," Roger cried. "We all loved Johnny. It seems impossible that he's dead. It can happen to any of us, all of us, if we keep chasing trouble, and there's a good chance it will. So do yourself a favor, go write a nice story, a real grabber about Johnny, and send it off. Maybe it's time you went home anyway."

"I'll never go anywhere until Colin is out of the army and free of his dreadful wife."

"And another good reporter goes off the deep end," Roger joked hollowly. "Say, why don't you all come around to the Embassy and we'll have a drink to Johnny."

"You're on, Roger," Mike replied, some of his old jauntiness back. "Maybe we can fly down to Joburg together."

"Just what I was thinking. Maybe I can be of some help to you at the American embassy in South Africa. You know, one ambassador to another," Roger chuckled.

Mike Wyatt guffawed. "If either of us is more unpopular than the other, you're sure *numero uno*. I understand from some of the guys that had to go down and renew their passports that they're about to put your picture up: wanted dead or alive. Preferably the former, I imagine."

Roger looked somber. "One agent sure tried to oblige them."

"I think it's shocking what Al Glenlord tried to do," Sarah declared. "Everybody knows it, nobody says anything about it, nobody does anything about it, nobody will say anything about it. Have you got your car somewhere nearby?"

"Sure. I'll give you all a ride up to the Embassy. I somehow get the feeling that my tenure as self-appointed ambassador has been terminated."

"It's not fair," Sarah stormed. "You've done so much for so many people."

Al Glenlord and Beryl Stoffel ate a subdued lunch with M.M. De Vries at his house. MM had maintained particularly close ties with Lord Johnny Cravenlow. Perhaps it was the snobbish streak in MM that drew him to the dashing young earl. At any rate, MM was visibly diminished by his friend's death perhaps partly because, ironically, it was his own brand of favoritism and special privilege bestowal that put Johnny in the way of the bullets.

Over an after-luncheon cordial Al finally asked in a tone edged with spite, "Has the Ministry actually notified Roger that he is being declared a prohibited immigrant?"

"We didn't have to go that far. I understand he's leaving anyway. He thinks he can do something about that story, perhaps get it declared spurious, if he goes back. I greatly dislike putting the PI label on anyone who has sincerely tried to help us here."

"Well, they say that the streets of hell are paved with good intentions," Beryl snapped.

"You've heard Roger's latest story, I suppose, MM," Glenlord said tentatively.

"Which one?"

"He's saying now that I am a CIA agent and using him for my cover." Al put indignation into his voice.

"Are you?" MM asked with a frosty smile.

"You don't believe that, MM, do you?" Al asked, an icy claw hooking into his gut.

"We happen to think you have value. God knows, if the United States had sent some sort of official envoy to Rhodesia a few years ago they'd have a much greater respect for what we're trying to do here. I've always hoped that your Central Intelligence Agency does have high-level agents implanted in Rhodesia. If they report the truth and the CIA has any influence at all with your good president, he'll stop trying to feed this country to the Communists."

His brow clouded. "Of course, with the press of the world screaming that we are torturing blacks, and that bloody Brigham's spurious pictures everywhere, God knows what his attitude toward us will be, not that it could be much more hostile than it is. We can only hope that with free and fair elections and an African prime minister we'll make the world see things differently. Assuming, of course, that Monsieur Mugabe and his pals let us *have* free and fair elections."

"Well, from what I saw, your people are doing a fine job on the military front, MM," Al said cheerfully. "And I've written up a four-page report on how I think the Ministry should deal with the press these days. I think it's important, obviously, to keep them away from the men in the field. You never know what lies they're going to tell after some bloody punch-up. I think it's particularly important you should keep the press away from the foreigners in the army, the Americans especially." As though the Minister of Information hadn't quite got the point, he added, "And the quicker you get Roger Masefield out of here, the better."

"What Roger Masefield says is true." MM jabbed a finger at him.

"Yes, but Masefield typifies the right-wing, ultra conservative nut. In the United States they expect people like him to be over here, and if he's supporting you that's enough to convince most Americans who think of themselves as responsible that they're against you."

"Well, in any case he'll be leaving shortly, I imagine. I had my top chap go over and have a word with him yesterday."

"Good, MM," Beryl cut in. "We're taking over that place tomorrow or the next day. Roger doesn't know it but Al has already used his power of attorney to transfer title to me."

"What are you going to do with the place, my dear?"

"After elections, when the sanctions against us are lifted, it will become a center for businessmen who want help in getting established here in Rhodesia. We'll put it to good use," she beamed.

"I'm sure you will." He smiled wanly. "Well, I think it's time for me to get back to the office. I've called the international journalists in for a little discussion. I want to point out to them that they mustn't try our patience again; and, of course, I still have to make a decision whether or not to PI the entire WP staff."

"If you want my advice, that's just what you should do," Al interjected. "Half the journalists over here are looking to make a name for themselves the way Brigham did. At least Roger Masefield won't be around helping them."

"My lord and master at Government House does not share your opinion on that matter, nor mine either, since I happen to concur with you. The press are not to be trusted, except for those very few journalists like Johnny who are truly honest and objective and publish the truth about us." MM let a soft gaze fall on Beryl. "Will you accompany me for sundowners at Government House at five-thirty?"

"Of course I will, MM," Beryl chirped.

"Meet me here, then, about five o'clock and we'll go over together." He turned to Al. "If it seems appropriate we can always PI Mr. Masefield after he's left, thus preventing his return."

"Good idea, MM," Glenlord approved. "Beryl, you want to ride to the office with me?"

"Yes, indeed. I guess now we can start planning alterations. This should be the last time we have to go back there and see Roger Masefield around." She sounded as merry as a new bride about to enter her dream home.

"He has been convenient as somebody we could blame that story on," MM reminded her. "We couldn't really let Ashley carry the burden of responsibility on his shoulders, now could we?" He flashed a craggy smile. "The P.M. now subscribes to the theory that Roger Masefield is responsible for Brigham's World Press story." The Minister stood up and escorted Al and Beryl to the door.

Chapter 57

Colonel Reid-Daley himself came down to Chiredzi to brief the Selous Scouts on their final series of missions prior to the elections. The Scouts were spread up and down the Mozambique border at forward operating bases from which they penetrated enemy territory and did as much psychological and physical damage as they could. The infiltration of terrorists into Rhodesia was noticeably declining as a result.

In Chiredzi, Captains Turneville and Spence, along with their American counterparts Sergeant Wilson, Lieutenant Joe Late and others, were listening attentively to the colonel.

"And, let me express my appreciation to Captain Turneville and Captain Spence for managing to preserve a few terrorists alive for us in Operation Screenpass. It was one of our great internal victories and the P.M. himself called to congratulate the Scouts on a job well done.

"After a touch of persuasion on our part, the prisoners confirmed our suspicions on two interesting points. First, there were several Tanzanian officers among the terrorists. Second, now that construction has been completed on the bridges along the road from the railhead at Mapai to Espungabera just inside Mozambique, this will be the new route for bringing the terrs to southern Rhodesia. We also learned that many of Mugabe's terrorists would like to come back to Rhodesia and vote in the elections for the new African government here and become reunited with their families. Indeed these Africans are more terrified of their own people than they are of the security forces, to whom they would like to surrender.

"This further emphasizes the need for us to produce a fair election and put one of the African politicians into the prime minister's office. It was also reaffirmed by several of the prisoners that Mugabe knew he could not be elected in a fair election without coercion and that's why he would not accept the government's invitation to run for prime minister."

Reid-Daley looked about the room. Opposite him was the glowing green scope of the sensor. His eye kindled. "Now that little gadget has been of great use to us. Captain Paul Karl reports that he will be bringing us a dozen scopes and the sensor discs to go with them. It seems very strange that we were not provided with these instruments much sooner. Our unconventional methods of procurement were obviously required."

"That's because the only payoff we wanted was dead terrorists, sir," Turneville piped up.

"You may be right, Turnie."

Reid-Daley moved to the map behind him and traced the route of the Espungabera Road. "There are four bridges on this side of the mountain range and one on the other side. Our mission is to blow all five of these bridges as soon as possible and wipe out the joint FRELIMO-Tanzanian garrison in Espungabera. If we do this it will be at least two months, well after the elections, before the hard-core commies trained in Tanzania can be shipped into this part of Rhodesia. Further to the north, Major Van Roolyan is marauding across the Mozambique border just as Major Hudson is doing in this southern sector. The RLI and the SAS are concentrating on external raids against terrorist camps even further to the north.

"I have been in radio contact with Major Hudson. His hoods are moving through the mountain range and have twice ambushed their own spoor and killed quite a number of Freddies along with their Shangaan trackers. They report their portable sensor is the neatest piece of equipment they've used since the radar scopes on the boats up in Kariba. Matter of fact, they had the same experience you did here. One of the trackers picked up a sensor disc and put it in his pocket. That made counter-tracking easy."

"Maybe we should make the discs look like big coins. Then they'd be sure to pick them up," Captain Spence suggested jovially.

"Good idea," Reid-Daley agreed. "I'll get that Aussie armorer onto it. He can do anything with metal."

The colonel tapped the map in several places. "Each of these bridges is between one hundred fifty and two hundred meters long. Captain Adderley estimates we'll need seven tons of gelignite to blow them. We'll start with the bridge furthest from the border on the other side of the mountain range and blow the bridges one by one on our way back."

"Won't that give a pretty clear indication of where we're going to be at any given time?" Captain Turneville asked.

"Yes, I suppose it will. But there is no other reliable exit out of this area of Mozambique. The rains have washed away the dirt roads. You'll come back into Rhodesia up here at Chipinga, a hundred miles north of us."

Reid-Daley surveyed the men gathered around him. "We need somebody to drive a lorry full of gelignite into Mozambique and rendezvous with Captain Hudson. I must tell you that the gelignite we have managed to acquire from the Ministry of Mines has unfortunately been around a while. I looked at some of it this morning and was a bit disturbed to see that it is weeping nitroglycerin. As you know, on a scale of one to ten the stability of gelignite is about seven. But in this case I'm afraid the stability may have decreased drastically. However, it's all we have."

"I'll drive it in, sir," Sergeant Wilson volunteered. "I've driven high explosives before. As long as we can avoid a firefight I think we'll be all right."

"It will take you the better part of a day after you cross the border to drive up to the mountain range where Major Hudson will intercept you and get on about the business of blowing those bridges. Our air reconnaissance indicates a huge construction camp just beyond the range which is the base for the road work underway. It has bulldozers, cranes, big trucks and other assorted equipment, all of which we want back here. With our shortage of foreign exchange, heavy equipment is very hard to come by. So after you've taken the construction site we will helicopter in engineering personnel to drive the equipment back to Chipinga. Any questions?"

There were none.

The expedition set out after midnight from the Selous Scouts' forward base camp on the Mozambique border. Sergeant Eddie Wilson, his face covered with black camouflage grease, drove a captured Mozambique army truck with a seven-ton cargo of gelignite. He followed the main body of the convoy at a respectful distance. Leading the column was a Mozambique bus which, complete with poultry tied to the roof, appeared to be an ordinary passenger vehicle of the type that transported people about the countryside. Actually it was a deadly combat machine. The Selous Scouts had captured the bus in Mozambique a few weeks before and driven it home. Its walls had been reinforced with steel plates and a .50-caliber machine gun had been cunningly mounted on each side so that they were invisible to a casual observer.

On the roof of the bus, hidden under a wood case, was a third heavy machine gun. Inside, African Selous Scouts, wearing either FRELIMO uniforms or the ordinary working man's denims, concealed their weapons below the windows. Some of the Scouts were even disguised with wigs to look like nannies. With three more trucks full of fighting men trailing the bus, it was a formidable force that made its way under cover of darkness into Mozambique.

Eddie Wilson maintained one hundred meters between his cargo of explosives and the last troop carrier but even so, had it blown up, most of the convoy would have been destroyed along with it.

By the time the sun rose, the vehicles were peacefully rattling along the road between Espungabera and Mapai. Approaching the first bridge, the bus was a good hundred meters ahead of the truck following it. The driver pulled the bus onto the bridge where it was stopped by a squad of FRELIMO sentries.

Several of the "nannies" were able to speak the Portuguese and Shona dialect of the FRELIMO sentries, and some of the latter, seeing what they thought were chattering young women on the bus, stepped up to it eager for some banter. Two others challenged the driver in an unaggressive manner, since buses like this one came down the road every day.

Two of the Scouts in civilian garb got out of the bus, ostensibly to urinate. Suddenly, with knives and handguns, the whole Selous party ripped into the sentries, killing all of them in a matter of seconds. Other FRELIMO troops at the end of the bridge, hearing the shots, started toward the bus to investigate but were cut down by the AK-47s of several Scouts who had climbed onto the bus's roof. The convoy began rolling over the bridge. By the time Eddie Wilson was gingerly driving his truckload of explosives over the first span, Lieutenant Joe Late and a squad of Scouts had already set up two heavy machine guns and two 60mm mortars on a nearby hill that over-looked the bridge and the stretch of road leading to the FRELIMO-Tanzanian garrison on the border with Rhodesia that the assault group had bypassed but would try to eliminate on their way back.

As Eddie brought his truck to a gentle halt beyond the bridge, Scouts from the truck in front began swiftly unloading the half-ton of gelignite that would be used to blow up the bridge. Lieutenant Late and his squad set themselves to placing the charges in a line across the bridge and against the pylon in the middle which supported it.

"I wish we had Captain Adderley here," Late grumbled to Eddie. "He's the expert at this sort of thing."

"Hell, you ought to be able to blow a bridge like this, Joe," the sergeant admonished. "We all had the bridge-blowing course at Fort Bragg and we've all done our share of demolitions in the Nam."

Joe Late studied the massive pile of gelignite bricks in awe. "I hope we don't get into a firefight with the Freddies before we get the job finished."

"We'll leave it all in your capable hands, Joe," Eddie said cheerfully, swinging himself up into the truck. He waited for the truck in front of him to move ahead and then followed it at a distance of one hundred meters.

Joe Late and his Scouts watched the bus and trucks head deeper into Mozambique before continuing their task of laying down the gelignite blocks. They found eight FRELIMO bodies, dragged them onto the bridge and laid them over the gelignite charges, thus providing tamping that would direct the force of the charges downward when they were detonated.

"Only eight bodies," Joe muttered to the Rhodesian sergeant. "Now we'll have to fill up these bags with sand to finish the job. Too bad there weren't a few more Freds around."

"We'll blow the bridge good enough when the time comes, sir," the Rhodesian replied. "It's the bridges up ahead that may be difficult. I hope the Freds and their Tanzanian friends *do* come up this road from their garrison and try to cross the bridge—we'll have a nice little surprise for them."

467

"We will at that," Late grinned.

In an hour the bridge was ready to be blown, the detonating cord stretching to the machine gun positions commanding it.

With the security elements of the American lieutenant's squad ready to hold off any attacks there might be on the rear of the demolition column, the bus and the captured FRELIMO trucks proceeded along the road toward the rendezvous with Major Hudson. An hour after they had left Joe Late and his group behind, Turneville, Spence and their men approached the next bridge which was guarded by a considerably larger garrison.

The bus was waved onto the bridge and once again two sentries came up to check the papers of the driver and look the passengers over. The FRELIMO troops lounging by the roadside, convinced that the heavily armed two-and-half-ton Unimog Mercedes-Benz trucks were theirs, paid them scant attention.

As the two sentries stepped up into the bus, they were abruptly jerked inside and stabbed through the throat, a favorite form of sentry elimination. Machine gun and automatic rifle fire suddenly sputtered from the sides of the bus and the dummy carton on the roof fell aside as the .50-caliber machine gun there also got to work.

The trucks in the rear added their firepower to that of the bus and in moments the Communist guard company was wiped out. Laughing, shouting, singing FRELIMO songs, the convoy continued to move ahead, Eddie Wilson following in the distance, praying nothing would happen to test the volatility of his cargo.

Again the regulation dark-green vehicles of the Mozambique Army moved on toward the third bridge, leaving FRELIMO bodies sprawled behind them.

The bus was now a quarter of a mile ahead of the armed trucks, the driver having been spurred to greater speed by his passengers who were thoroughly caught up in the spirit of the deadly game they were playing. Once again the brutally efficient process was repeated: the FRELIMO guards were tricked and mowed down, and the bus barreled on over the bridge, heading further into the interior of Mozambique. This time when the three armed trucks appeared on the scene, there was nothing for them to do but cross the bridge, to the chagrin of the men.

As they approached the third bridge, this presumption was confirmed by the absence of visible guards. Subterfuge now being useless, the new tactic was "Overwhelm with Speed and Firepower."

Some two hundred meters from the next objective, the trucks stopped and two 80mm mortars were placed on each side of the road. Then, precisely as the mortars began to hurl their bombs toward the bridge and to lay down a sheath of fire on both sides of the road, the trucks and the bus roared forward, all their machine guns blazing. The mortar rounds sweeping the roadside walked forward of the careening vehicles. The appearance of the bearded, screaming, laughing Selous Scouts frightened the FRELIMO even more than did their firepower and those not killed or wounded by the mortar barrage and the machine guns broke and ran.

At the fourth and final bridge before the mountain range, where a garrisoned village fell away from both sides of the road, the entire force of Selous Scouts dismounted from their vehicles and launched a conventional infantry attack. Again the resistance was soon quelled and the FRELIMO troops ran, leaving their dead and wounded behind. The Scouts had yet to sustain their first casualty.

By midday the column had reached the mountain range. It pushed along the rutted road, firing on and dispersing the terrified construction crews who were enlarging the mountain pass so as to improve the Communist assault route that ran across Mozambique to the Rhodesian border.

Chapter 58

From their vantage point above the pass cutting through the range, Mack Hudson and his men watched the approaching convoy. "Looks like they're having a lot of fun," Mack commented to Colin Adderley who was peering through his field glasses.

Eddie Wilson drove his volatile load of explosives along the rough road, nearly getting a stroke each time a pothole shook the truck. As the lead vehicle, with Captain Turneville up beside the driver, rolled under Mack's position he fired a green flare. The trucks and bus came to a stop and Mack and his troops ran down to greet them.

Mack squeezed in beside Turneville and his men clambered into the other trucks and the bus.

Turneville grinned at Colin Adderley who had sprung onto his running board. "Why don't you wait until Sergeant Wilson catches up with us? Wouldn't you like to ride with your explosive package?"

"As a matter of fact, you're right. We're not going to have much time. I'd like to check out the explosives as we drive along."

"Be my guest, Colin," Mack said. "I kind of figured Eddie Wilson would be driving the demo truck. Let's move out sharply. We're late. And we're going to have one big fight at that last bridge. The construction camp is crawling with Freddies. They must have a hundred men on guard. There's at least ten million dollars' worth of equipment out there. They'll be expecting us. Christ, I could hear you coming ten miles away."

"We couldn't help it, Mack," Turneville said in mock apology. "Those Freddies just didn't seem to want us here."

"You can be damn sure they won't want us occupying the construction camp either. What a beauty that bridge is. They just finished it. It even has aluminum guardrails. The commies will be driving a hundred trucks a day over this road when it's finished. Or that's what they think," he chuckled.

The convoy started off again. "We'll be out of the mountain range around that next corner," Mack warned, "and heading right into the construction camp. The bridge is behind it and Freddie is ready."

"So are we," Turneville growled.

The Selous Scouts assault force suddenly broke from the hills into the open terrain beyond. There, interspersed among the heavy construction equipment and the workers, were FRELIMO troops waiting for them. The workshops and storage sheds stretched out for a mile in either direction.

Screaming like banshees, their guns blazing, their vehicles roaring, the Selous Scouts were a fearsome sight as they raced toward the bridge. In moments the FRELIMO troops had been killed or wounded, or had fled from the stuttering fusillade of death, and the Scouts occupied both ends of the bridge. Hastily they set up mortars to discourage further Communist attacks while Eddie Wilson and Colin Adderley drove up onto the bridge with their truckload of demolitions.

"Well, you got the load here, Sergeant," Adderley congratulated the Yank driver. "Let's hope we make a clean job of this." Sporadic fire from two pockets of FRELIMO resistance beyond the bridge was quickly silenced by a few well-placed mortar rounds. While Mack Hudson, Turneville and Spence led detachments away from the bridge and set up protective positions around the demolition party, Adderley began the biggest demolition job of his career.

The bridge was 150 meters long with three pylons supporting it. Tying a rope to the guardrail of the bridge above the first pylon, Adderley slid down the rope and stood on the base of the support motioning for the demolitions to be lowered to him. He packed three 200-pound charges of gelignite on one side of the pylon, then repeated the process on the other side so that the charges were facing each other through the four-foot thickness of concrete. As he placed his charges, Sergeant Wilson duplicated his efforts on a second pylon and Sergeant Major Princeloo on the third.

With the charges placed and detonating cord run through the charges and out to a fuse that would set them all off at the same moment, the demolition men climbed back up on top of the bridge and placed lines of gelignite charges across the center of each span, the extremities of which rested on the pylons. Other Scouts had been filling bags with sand to be used for tamping down the charges. All the available FRELIMO bodies had also been dragged onto the bridge to provide further tamping.

Mack Hudson's first act when the two forces had linked up and taken the construction camp had been to radio the Selous Scouts base and report they were ready to receive helicopters. Adderley was still placing his gelignite charges on the bridge when the choppers appeared over the mountain range and dropped in to deposit a squad of engineers who would pick out the best equipment and drive it back to Rhodesia. The engineers had been given no clue as to their destination and were horrified to find themselves in the middle of a combat operation deep in enemy territory. However, they fell to their task, letting out whoops and whistles as they saw the superb heavy construction equipment that was to be their prize.

In short order they picked out a crane, several bulldozers, six new Swedish trucks and the finest earth-moving equipment that misguided American and European aid missions had sent to Mozambique and began organizing a convoy to transfer it all home.

Such equipment as the engineers didn't have the manpower to drive away was pushed or driven into a massive multimillion dollar heap of hardware which Princeloo, Adderley and Wilson strode over to inspect.

Mack Hudson anxiously consulted his watch as the demolitions men did their work. Finally they pronounced the bridge ready to be blown. It was four in the afternoon. All the trucks were backed off the bridge, turned around and readied for the trip back to the Rhodesian border. They'd blow each bridge as they came to it.

The engineers had by this time cranked up the motors of the new equipment and were preparing to drive it back into Rhodesia where it was badly needed.

With the bridge ready to blow and the commandeered heavy equipment already rumbling slowly through the mountain pass, Adderley carefully placed charges in the pile of abandoned machinery and detailed some Scouts to lay a trail of gelignite blocks connected by det cord the full length of the machine shops and storage sheds.

Over a ton and a half of gelignite had now been set and the entire Selous Scout mission, with the exception of Adderley, retreated from the bridge and the construction camp and climbed into their vehicles which began winding into the mountains. Eddie Wilson had long since driven the truckload of explosives away from what would be a blast almost nuclear in intensity.

In front of Adderley were a series of plunger-type detonators, a console of destruction. He gave a last look at the bridge and the construction camp and, one by one, activated the detonators. He had built a five-minute delay into the detonators which would give him time to run to the last truck of the convoy which Spence had halted a short way off.

The blast, when it came, sent shock waves reverberating through the mountains and the concussion could even be felt by an understandably nervous Eddie Wilson who had reached the other side of the mountain range.

"Jesus Christ!" Adderley exclaimed. "That's the biggest bang I've ever heard in my life." As he looked back, a cloud of dust and debris could be seen sifting down over the construction camp and the bridge. "Stop the truck on that rise there, driver," he ordered. "I want to get a good mental shot of all this for the colonel."

"Look at what's left of that bridge!" Adderley exclaimed, happily gazing at the crumbled concrete slabs jutting from the ravine the bridge had traversed.

"Should take them over a year to build a new one." The store-houses and workshops had been reduced to twisted shards of metal and the equipment was a writhing mass of blackened steel spears.

"I'd love to see Samora Machel's face when he hears about this," Spence laughed. "And if he doesn't get Mugabe out of his country pretty quick, he knows it'll happen again. And again and again and again."

"OK, one down, three more to go," Adderley said cheerfully. "Looks like we'll be working all night. We should still have daylight for the next job and after that we'll have to feel our way."

On the other side of the mountain range Eddie Wilson pulled his truck over and allowed the three armored trucks and the bus to pass him and lead the way to the next bridge. So thorough a job had the Selous Scouts made of blasting the village and fortifications around this objective on their way through to the construction camp that Adderley was able to place his charges without interruption. The trucks, bus and construction equipment ground on toward the next bridge.

Wilson breathed a little easier now that he had four tons less of gelignite blocks stacked behind him in the truck as he drove on westward. It was a false sense of security, of course, and he grinned wryly at Adderley who now sat beside him. One pound of the stuff would have blown them up and there were three tons still back there. It was dark by the time they reached the third bridge.

An hour later two green flares drifted across the black sky above it, the signal from Colin Adderley that he was ready to detonate the explosives.

The convoy was well on its way again when Adderley detonated a ton of gelignite. In a thunderous display of pyrotechnics the bridge split apart and fell into the river below. Shock waves tore through the surrounding hills.

"Three down, one to go!" Adderley exclaimed as he and Eddie Wilson ground out the mileage behind the bulldozers, the huge earth-moving trucks and the crane, which swung menacingly as it was driven over the badly pitted road to Espungabera.

Looking more like Ace Construction Company than a military formation, the Selous Scouts assault force arrived at the last bridge. The engineers drove their equipment over the bridge and made for the Rhodesian border while the Scouts set about the destruction of the bridge.

It was a job requiring technical skill of the highest order. Each charge of gelignite had to be placed in mathematical proportion to the thickness and height of the supporting pylons. The secret of the destruction of these concrete structures lay in the shock waves from the gelignite ricocheting off each other deep inside the supports, crumbling the concrete. Let the charges be placed a foot out of place and the destruction would be minimal and perhaps fail to drop the bridge.

Adderley threw the rope over the side of the bridge, lowered himself down the first pillar and began setting the charges lowered to him. A hail of machine gun, RPG and mortar fire suddenly split the night. FRELIMOs and Tanzanians who had bypassed Joe Late's blocking positions had joined with other guerrilla forces. This time, undoubtedly, they were led by Cuban or Russian advisers who had stiffened the black revolutionaries' resolve to interdict the demolition party before it could blow up this last strategic bridge. Mack Hudson, Turneville, Spence and their men fired back with their own mortars and heavy machine guns.

Colin Adderley, meticulously placing the charges, knew that it would only take one round, one mortar bomb blast to detonate the volatile gelignite charges prematurely, saving the bridge from major damage and blowing the Scouts to pulpy bits.

Trying to ignore the fire streaking through the air, he coolly went about the job of setting the gelignite charges around the base of the pillars as other members of his demolition party placed the less technical pressure charges across the bridge itself.

The occasional spatter of bullets and shrapnel striking against concrete and steel shook the English officer as he hung from the rope above the turbulent river, but it didn't deter him. Tempted though he was to leave the charges as they were, and thus only partially destroy the bridge, he hauled himself up the rope onto the bridge and then in a crouch raced to the second pylon.

With the firefight raging about him and the glow in the eastern sky signaling the imminent advent of dawn, he threw his rope once again over the side of the bridge and, attaching the D-ring of his harness to it, lowered himself down to the base of the last pylon of the last bridge of this mission. His feet hung just above the raging torrent caused by the rains that had been falling for the past week. He looked up and signaled Eddie Wilson to lower the charges. Could his luck hold out just one more time? He would allow nobody to assist him in this exposed and dangerous position. Amazingly the casualties had been light considering the amount of action the Scouts were now encountering.

Sergeant Houk was kept busy working on casualties in the back of one of the trucks. The construction equipment, shepherded from the front by two armed trucks whose firepower was too much for the ragged FRELIMO opposition that tried to block its way, moved inexorably toward the Rhodesian border.

476

Joe Late's squad was now virtually surrounded by FRELIMO and Tanzanian troops who were ferrying themselves across the river by boats. For every craft that made it, two were destroyed by Late's 60mm and 80mm mortars and the RPGs. Late radioed to Captain Turneville that he was unsure of how many troops were getting around him but to be wary. Turneville and Mack with only two platoons of Scouts were guarding the bridge as they had sent the main body of their force back with the invaluable construction equipment.

It was hard to estimate which was more important to the Rhodesian government, the destruction of the last of the bridges or the delivery of the badly needed heavy-duty construction equipment.

But now the fire directed at the demolition party on the bridge was increasing in intensity and accuracy. Eddie Wilson leaned over and screamed down at Adderley: "Sir, for shit's sake forget it. Come on up. We'll blow the bridge with what we've got on it now. So what if it doesn't get totaled?"

"I've almost got her rigged!" Adderley shouted back.

His voice was accompanied by the moans of several wounded Scouts who were being helped back to the now-empty explosives truck which was standing beside the bridge ready to make a dash for Rhodesia.

"OK, det cord set. Pull me up, Sergeant!" Adderley shouted. Wilson leaned over and began hauling on the rope as Adderley pushed against the pillar with his feet and once more gave his aching arms the task of helping the sergeant take his weight. Finally he and the sergeant were standing together on the bridge, the end of the det cord in the captain's hand.

"Pressure charges set and ready to blow!" Wilson shouted. "Come on, let's get out of here." Both men, unreeling det cord behind them, ran from the bridge as a mortar bomb screamed in and enveloped them in a shower of shrapnel. Wilson had heard the familiar whine of the incoming round and fallen to the road at the end of the bridge shouting, "Incoming, get down!"

But Adderley, intent on attaching the fuse to his detonator, either didn't hear the warning or ignored it. Pieces of metal tore into him and he fell bleeding from multiple wounds.

"Blow it, sergeant," he cried weakly. "Take the detonator. Blow it, goddamit!" he cried again as Eddie Wilson went to him and started to pull his rent body from the edge of the bridge. "You can't help me now," Adderley gasped.

Wilson grabbed Adderley under both arms, lifted him off the ground and carried him over his shoulder to the truck where he lay him on the truckbed. Then the American dashed back through incoming rounds to the bridge and, finding the detonator Adderley had just connected to the fuse, pressed the plunger. With a shattering blast the last bridge blew asunder in several places and almost simultaneously, its supports gone, collapsed into the torrent below. The concussion lifted Wilson off the ground and blew him ten feet from where he had activated the detonator. For several moments he lay stunned. Then he picked himself up and staggered for the truck.

Gasping for wind, he pulled himself into the cab, started up the engine and drove off across country, the rising sun directly behind him. The Selous Scouts in the back of the truck would do the best they could for Adderley, he knew, but there was no counteracting the shaking and rattling of the vehicle. He knew how agonizing the jouncing would be to a wounded man but there was nothing he could do now except keep going.

As soon as they heard the explosion, Lieutenant Joe Late and his rearguard unit pulled out of their positions above the blown bridge on the Espungabera Road and moved overland to join up with Major Mack Hudson and the rest of the assault force.

Jolting over the fields and through the bush in their truck, they soon caught up with the armored bus and the last truck in the convoy and joined the column heading homeward. They passed through several lightly fortified village garrisons which they quickly wiped out with mortars and heavy machine gun fire.

Mack Hudson sent a patrol ahead to radio back information on enemy installations they would pass enroute to the border. As they entered the final Mozambique village before reaching the border, the heavy construction equipment was moving well ahead of them. To his amazement Mack saw one of the Selous Scouts sergeants of the advance party standing legs apart, arms outstretched in front of the door of one of the buildings, a store, as though begging for its life. The Scouts had burned or otherwise destroyed every structure they came upon and this village close to the border was to be no exception.

Mack tapped his driver on the shoulder, told him to pull to a halt in front of the store and jumped from the cab.

"Not this one, sir," the sergeant cried. "Take a look inside." Mack pushed the sergeant aside, walked through the door and found himself in a building full of multishaped and multihued bottles. It was a large liquor store, he quickly recognized, one that no doubt served the FRELIMO and other troops in the area.

On Mack's orders dozens of cases of Manica beer, various types of local liquor and even some imported Portuguese brandy and wine were liberated and stashed aboard the trucks. The store was then torched.

As they crossed back into Rhodesia in the area around Chipinga, they met dozens of Rhodesian Africans going to work in the fields, their eyes rolling in amazement at the mechanized force coming out of Mozambique. The Africans cheered and applauded, swiftly deducing what the construction equipment signified.

Well inside Rhodesia Mack gave the order to circle up and all the vehicles formed a perimeter in which the Selous Scouts and engineers took stock of themselves and their booty.

"Sergeant Wilson and Captain Adderley have not arrived with their truck, sir," Sergeant Major Princeloo reported. "Sergeant Houk was with them tending the wounded."

"What were our casualties, Sergeant Major?" Mack asked.

"We were lucky, sir. So far two dead, eight wounded, and six missing. But as I said, sir, they're probably all with Captain Adderley and Sergeant Wilson."

"Well, we'll wait right here for them to join us. In the meantime let's have a look at that last bit of loot we captured."

The Selous Scouts needed no urging to break open the evil-tasting local whiskey and beer. In short order the entire contingent, including the engineers, were gurgling down the contents of the late lamented liquor store across the border.

On the HF radio Mack raised Colonel Reid-Daley, who was back at the André Rabie headquarters and he and his officers made their reports.

The air force had already taken pictures of the destroyed construction camp and ComOps had congratulated Reid-Daley once again on the job his men had accomplished.

As Turneville was reporting the details of the mission to Reid-Daley, the last truck of the convoy with Sergeant Eddie Wilson at the wheel bounced into the circle of Selous Scouts vehicles and construction equipment. Several of the Scouts ran up to the truck carrying bottles which they offered to Wilson. Eddie took a bottle of beer, twisted off the cap and guzzled half of it at a gulp. Then he walked around to the rear of the truck and looked in. Horst Houk was still ministering to wounded Scouts and when Eddie Wilson pointed at Colin Adderley's inert form, the German medic sadly shook his head.

The bottle of beer dropped from Eddie's hand as he turned and strode into the circle where the officers were in radio contact with the colonel.

"We've been looking for you, Sergeant," Mack boomed out. "I saved a little of the real stuff, the imported brandy for you."

"Thank you, sir," Wilson replied. "I have one KIA in the truck."

Mack, Turneville and Spence stared at Wilson, none of them wanting to ask the inevitable question.

"Captain Adderley, sir," Wilson reported in a subdued tone.

"How," Mack asked.

"He was standing on the bridge when a mortar round came in. He had just finished placing the charges when it happened. I took the detonator and blew it up."

A pall of gloom descended on the Selous Scouts so recently jubilant over their highly successful mission. "I will have a pull of the brandy, sir," Wilson said. Silently Mack handed him the bottle. Then he walked over to the radio. To Joe Late he said, "Report Colin Adderley KIA. See if the colonel can get a plane down here to pick up the body and the casualties."

Chapter 59

"So you were Colin's little Yankee Doodle doodad?"

Sarah Cobb Chase winced at Stella Adderley's derisive laugh and harsh tone. The jarred mourners gathered at the Selous Scouts parade ground glanced uneasily at the two women in Colin Adderley's life.

Sarah had always been aware that Colin was married, and they had frequently discussed the divorce he would get on his next long leave from duty; but the last thing she expected was that Colin's estranged wife would appear in Salisbury for the funeral. Yet after Stella had been informed of Colin's death she had been on the next flight from London to Johannesburg and thence to Salisbury.

Colin had told Sarah of his income from a family trust, most of which would have to be paid out to Stella in alimony to get rid of her so they could get married. "Look at it this way, darling," he had so often pointed out; "if Stella wasn't so hateful I probably wouldn't have fled to Rhodesia and we never would have found each other."

Stella's hard mouth, pointed features and vinegary expression made her seem more like a bitter spinster aunt than a fitting consort for the youthful-looking Colin. "If you think Colin's will leaving you his trust will stand up in a British court, you're mad, you know. *I'm* his wife—no judge would give his little colonial concubine any of his money," she spat.

"I—I didn't know about such a will," Sarah stammered. "Colin never mentioned it to me."

"Likely story," Stella sniffed. "Tonight I'm taking Colin back to England and he'll be buried in his family plot. I promised his mother," she added self-righteously.

"But he always said that if anything happened to him he wanted to be buried with his friends who died here," Sarah protested.

"You have nothing to say in the matter. You're no more than another one of Colin's toys," Stella snapped contemptuously.

Sarah shrank back from this acidic shrew, wondering how Colin had ever loved her. Actually he hadn't. He was twenty-one, just graduated from Sandhurst, when the marriage had virtually been arranged between the parents.

"Furthermore you have no right to be here at Colin's funeral services." Stella's strident tones carried across the assembly of mourners waiting for the ceremony to commence. "I specifically gave the colonel instructions to bar you—I'll see that he is severely reprimanded for allowing you to be present."

"Please, Mrs. Adderley, the parade is about to start," Captain Turneville, back in his role as adjutant, quietly admonished.

"Why is this woman here?" Stella demanded.

Turneville, without answering, took a stricken Sarah by the arm and led her away to join Carla Hudson.

It wasn't necessary to understand the African words to the song being sung by the Selous Scouts as they appeared from the trees following their colors, mounted on a staff from whose top sprouted the horns of a water buffalo, and slow-marched onto the paved parade ground. The dirge rang out from three hundred voices, African and European, mourning their fallen comrades. The men halted in front of the visitors and turned to face them.

Sarah Cobb Chase, her auburn hair blowing in the breeze, her thin dress clinging about her knees and thighs, held herself erect, her face beautiful despite the grief devastating her and the humiliating situation she was in.

Carla Hudson stood beside her and Mike Cleary provided the arm that she clutched with her right hand.

Little groups of Africans and Europeans lined the parade ground or sat in the reviewing stand. Colonel Reid-Daley and the chaplain,

both in full uniform and wearing medals, stood in front of the spectators facing the parade.

The chaplain conducted a short, dignified service in English and
in Shona, and then Reid-Daley took the salute as the men marched
past the reviewing stand and continued toward the trees from which
they had emerged, once more breaking into their eerie lament for the
dead.

When the column had disappeared, the colonel went directly to
Sarah Cobb Chase, put both his hands on her shoulders and looked
into her eyes. "I'm sorry about that Mrs. Adderley, Sarah. We all know
how much Colin loved you. Nobody contributed more toward the
possibility of a free and fair election than he did."

Sarah tried to hold back the tears she knew Stella Adderley would
ridicule. "He wouldn't want to be taken from Rhodesia back to England," she said forlornly.

"We can't do anything about it, Sarah." Reid-Daley nodded to
Mike Cleary. "Take care of her, Mike. She's a Selous Scout's woman."

"I'll watch out for her, Ron," Mike said somberly. "Do you need
me anymore today?"

"No, Mike." The colonel sighed deeply. "Now to take care of Mrs.
Adderley. Please don't leave Salisbury without contacting me, Mike.
We may need some more goodies."

"You have my word on it, Colonel." Then, putting a brotherly arm
around Sarah Cobb Chase's shoulder, he said, "Come on, Sarah. Let's
go back to town."

Later, after escorting a complaining Stella Adderley from the parade to the Mercedes he had provided for her, Colonel Reid-Daley met
in his office with Major Hudson, Major Van Roolyan and his other
officers.

"Gentlemen, were it not for the loss of Captain Adderley, I would
pronounce this the most productive week in the short history of Selous
Scouts. Mack, the figures we got from your operations brought rejoic-
ing at ComOps, I can tell you. The railroad line will certainly be out
for at least three months. That heavy construction equipment you
captured and brought back is worth more than three million dollars.
They estimate that the equipment you destroyed on the ground cost
the enemy over five million dollars. The replacement cost of the bridges alone we estimate at twenty million. That, of course, is assuming

they can replace them." Then he turned to Major Conrad Van Roolyan. "Van, as far as we can see, there is nothing left moving in your area of operations. No camps, nothing. Of course, the United Nations is screaming at the bloodthirsty Rhodesians for not permitting the terrorists to come in and slaughter us as they promised they would during the elections. I believe that at the United Nations"—he glanced at Mack Hudson with an ironic smile—"your Mr. Young has condemned us as barbarians."

"He's not my Mr. Young, sir," Mack spoke up. "He's not a real American, he's a Communist and a traitor."

Reid-Daley let the comment hang in the air a moment, and then briskly returned to the business at hand. "The final objective is the destruction of Mugabe's camp. One of our Scouts, actually your friend Luthu, Mack, was in Camp Mugabe just a week ago. He successfully posed as one of the thousands of displaced persons, victims of Samora Machel's destruction of the tribal system in Mozambique and was taken in for training. Mugabe's best fighting men are in that compound. They've been coming down from their training camps in Tanzania with Tanzanian officers and Cuban and Russian advisers for a month or more now. ComOps is mounting the largest assault of the war so far. All three commando units of the RLI will jump in on the camp. RAR troops, over a thousand of them, will be transported by trucks to a site near the battle and will go in by helicopter. Our mission is to act as a blocking force to track down and kill any terrs who escape from the camp. I'm on my way to ComOps now to get a briefing from General Walls, and when I come back we'll go over the Selous Scouts contribution to this engagement in detail. Any questions?"

"Just one, sir," Van Roolyan boomed. "Out of curiosity, are the three African leaders of the interim government being briefed on this attack?"

"I'm afraid so. I've been able to resist giving them any information on Selous Scouts activities but on a raid as extensive as this I should very much doubt if the Prime Minister would fail to make the African leaders of the interim government aware of what we're planning."

A bleak expression crossed Van Roolyan's face.

"I know what you're thinking, Van. But don't say it. If we can successfully disperse the Communists in Camp Mugabe, we will be assured of elections without Communist coercion. Mugabe and Nkomo will not have the men available on the spot to carry out their bloodbath threat. It's to the advantage of these black politicians that the army successfully accomplish this mission. One of them will become the prime minister."

"All I can say, sir," Turneville announced, "is that those Afs, I don't care if you call them political leaders or what, are about as closemouthed as a hungry hippo."

Reid-Daley shrugged expressively but left the remark unanswered. "All right gentlemen, you've got the rest of the day and tonight to yourselves. We'll meet for a briefing tomorrow at six A.M." He looked at his chagrined men. "Change that to eleven A.M.," he amended, enjoying the smiles on his officers' faces.

Chapter 60

Samuel Jobolingo walked through the largest ZANLA staging area in Mozambique with the two Chinese advisers assigned to the camp commander. They spoke no Shona, just mangled English which he could hardly understand, and communication was difficult.

Another five hundred men had arrived this morning and camp strength was now about five thousand. The Freedom Fighters were arranged in squads, platoons, companies and battalions, their tents in neat rows throughout the square-mile area. The logistics of keeping this many men housed, armed and disciplined were beyond the scope of Mugabe's officers, but with the aid of the Chinese, the Tanzanians and more recently the Cubans and Russians they had managed to whip these men from training camps in Mozambique, Tanzania and eastern Zambia into something resembling a military division. They would, at any rate, be the vanguard of the ZANLA force.

Jobolingo had been appointed political commissar of the entire staging camp and for several days had been supervising the arming and equipping of the troops. Within a week, well before the elections, the entire camp would cross the border into Rhodesia and disrupt the elections as Comrade Mugabe had promised. The news from the southern areas was bad, but for some reason the Boers had never come near Mugabe's Camp.

487

The Chinese advisers complimented Jobolingo on the orderly manner in which the Freedom Fighters comported themselves as they waited to carry the class struggle back to Zimbabwe.

Two sentries slapped the stocks of their assault rifles in salute as Jobolingo and the Chinese comrades walked into the camp commander's headquarters. Although the military commander out-ranked Jobo, the commissar, the political tactician, Jobo wielded more actual power than he. They were expecting momentarily a visit from General Josiah Tongogara, the most powerful man in the ZANU po-litical party after Comrade Mugabe himself.

Jobo was afraid of very few men but one of them was Tongogara. He knew about the number of rising young ZANU men who, when they reached a certain level of power, had been assassinated by Tongogara's political action squads. Jobo himself had risen so fast in the ZANU power structure that he was never quite sure when his status would be resented by the general. The only other man on the general's level in ZANU was Rex Nhongo and of course there was a bitter rivalry between Nhongo and Tongogara.

Tongogara tried to assassinate Nhongo when they were both in Geneva, Switzerland at an abortive all-parties conference aimed at solving the Rhodesian situation. There was no doubt in Jobo's mind that either Tongogara or Nhongo would be murdered, one by the other, before the final takeover of Zimbabwe. In the meantime the two leaders had tacitly agreed to refrain from trying to assassinate each other.

Jobolingo, followed by the Chinese advisers, walked into the camp commander's office without having himself announced. The com-mander looked up from behind a wide, document-strewn desk. Jobolingo pulled a chair up for himself uninvited and gestured to the two Chinese advisers to be seated. The two Africans stared at each other warily.

"General Tongogara will be here soon," Jobolingo announced un-necessarily. The camp commander frowned but made no comment.

"I was disappointed in the sanitary facilities, Comrade Com-mander," Jobo began. "If the men are sick they can't fight."

"Then why don't you go out and teach them to dig and use slit trenches, Comrade Commissar," the camp commander sneered.

"My job is to observe and make suggestions to you, and to General Tongogara and even to Comrade Mugabe if necessary. It is not my job to go out and dig slit trenches."

The camp commander frowned again.

There was the sound of an automobile driving up to the headquarters building. Since only the general and highest ranking ZANU members had automobiles, it was apparent that General Tongogara had arrived. They heard the car door slam and moments later the sharp clatter of booted heels on a wooden floor. Jobolingo got to his feet and stood at some semblance of attention as Tongogara swaggered into the commander's office. The general affected Idi Amin type field marshal's regalia and his heavy form and pockmarked face filled the door.

His appearance had an electrifying effect on the camp commander who jumped to rigid attention, saluted and offered his seat to the general. Tongogara took it and sat down, grunting his acknowledgment of the other men's presence. He was known to dislike the Chinese advisers but they were a necessity if he was to get the weaponry required to fight the battle for national liberation.

Tongogara fixed the camp commander with glowering eyes. "Now, I want a report on the troops. Are they ready to go into Zimbabwe?"

"General Tongogara, we are waiting for you to give the order. The weapons are in the armory ready to be issued; every man is equipped and knows his targets."

Tongogara nodded in satisfaction. "The puppet elections are scheduled for three weeks from now. We have decided that infiltration should start ten days before the people go to the polls. If we start any earlier the security forces may track our Freedom Fighters down before they can finish their job. We have suffered serious losses in the south. The rail lines and roads going to the Zimbabwe border have been destroyed. Now Comrade Samora Machel is complaining about our presence in Mozambique. ZANLA will cross the border one week from today," Tongogara declared. "Until that time see that the men are not idle." He turned to Jobolingo. "Are you keeping the indoctrination sessions operating?"

"Yes, Comrade General. We have four hours of political meetings every afternoon."

"Which takes too much time away from training," the camp commander got in. "In one week, one week from today, we make a massive crossover!" Tongogara was not listening, being wrapped in a vision of his own. His eyes bulged with excitement.

Suddenly the general looked up, a surprised scowl on his face. He stood, facing the door, and leaned his knuckles on the desk. "What are you doing here, Rex?" he queried sharply.

Jobolingo shifted his gaze from the general to the doorway and to his surprise saw Comrade Rex Nhongo standing there. This was totally unexpected. Nhongo walked into the office and greeted Jobolingo affably. Jobo shot to his feet and offered the top political officer of the movement his chair.

Nhongo shook his head. "I'll stand." Nhongo was a leaner, cleaner-looking African leader than Tongogara of the swelling girth. Without further comment he broke into the meeting. "We have just received word at Comrade Mugabe's headquarters in Maputo that the Boers plan a massive attack on this camp within the next day or two. Comrade Mugabe and I have discussed this new intelligence information at length."

"Why was I not informed?" Tongogara growled.

"You're being informed now, Comrade General," Nhongo replied levelly. "You left before our people in Salisbury were able to send us this information."

"We thought they didn't know we were here," Tongogara cried. "They are fighting most in the south."

"They know this place. Their code name for it is Camp Mugabe," Nhongo chuckled.

Tongogara addressed the camp commander. "Alert all your officers to have their men ready for the Boers when they arrive. We'll wipe them out on our own ground."

"We must be more realistic, Comrade General," Nhongo said authoritatively. "Neither Comrade Mugabe nor I have fooled ourselves as to the quality of even our best trained men when it comes to fighting the security forces. We need to save our trained men in this camp for infiltration and indoctrination. We cannot afford to have any of them killed. And remember, Comrade Tongogara, the real enemy is in Zambia. When ZANLA and ZIPRA meet, we must be the stronger of the two."

Tongogara and the camp commander looked at Nhongo question-ingly but Jobolingo nodded, "You are right, Comrade Nhongo. We will move our troops out of here now!"

"I say we stay and fight!" Tongogara shouted. "For too long we have been running from the enemy. Now we have our best men and we outnumber the security forces. We'll shoot their paratroopers in the air. We'll blast the helicopters! It will be the worst military defeat the Boers have ever suffered."

"It has been decided already, Comrade General," Nhongo interjected firmly. "The Boers have been roaming at will throughout the southern part of Mozambique. It will be months before we can reestablish communications. We are at a disadvantage for the moment and we will put ourselves at a worse disadvantage if we lose half of the men in this camp, no matter how many Boers we kill."

"The elections mean nothing," Nhongo continued his lecture, soft-ening his tone as though explaining a simple concept to a backward student. "The man who owns the American President, our brother Ambassador Young, has told Comrade Mugabe that we will win po-litically. Just as the Americans lost the war in Vietnam, we will take over Zimbabwe. The real fight will be against that fat pig Nkomo and his army. America and Britain will not recognize these elections next month. They will condemn them in the United Nations. Yes, if we could turn the balloting booths into bloodbaths that would be fine, but not at the cost of losing maybe half of our best fighting men. The orders from Maputo are to disperse the men in this camp. Order them to retreat into the mountains. We have assurances from Comrade Samora Machel that FRELIMO will fight beside us if the Boers try to pursue our troops into the countryside." Nhongo laughed merrily. "Let General Walls stage his exercise here. He will find an empty camp."

Tongogara shot a thunderous look at Rex Nhongo, but Jobolingo cut in before he could make another protest.

"Comrade Nhongo, there's a problem we must face. I take the blame. Some of the Freedom Fighters in this camp, men we have not had time to indoctrinate, are questioning why we continue to fight when a true man of Zimbabwe will be the prime minister after the elections. The propaganda leaflets the security forces are dropping along the border are infecting some of our men. We've had defections already. We've had to shoot some of our troops who have talked

491

treason or tried to go back home to their families before the class struggle is won. When we let everybody out of here we'll have many defectors."

"We've got to get our troops out so they can fight another day," Nhongo replied. "Since the responsibility is yours, Comrade Jobolingo, you will form a network of political action squads to shoot defectors as we evacuate the camp. When you have eliminated all of them, and only then, pull back yourself. We do not like to take a chance of having a political commissar captured but in this case, as you said, the responsibility is yours."

"Yes, Comrade Nhongo." Jobolingo started for the door. "I'll form the political action squads now. There's no time to lose."

"Comrade Mugabe will be pleased to hear how quickly you can respond to an emergency, Comrade Jobolingo." Nhongo then turned to Tongogara. "As for you, Comrade General, it wouldn't do for you to be caught in the middle of an attack. You would be a prize captive, wouldn't you? We'll leave the evacuation of the camp in the hands of our commander here and I will see you back in Maputo."

General Tongogara glared at Rex Nhongo, his chief rival in the ZANU party, his only equal under Mugabe. When the ZANU faction of the Patriotic Front finally captured Zimbabwe, either he or Nhongo would succeed Mugabe who could only be used as a figurehead until the political battle was won and power consolidated. No man without all his parts could be a *permanent* leader of Africans.

Chapter 61

Stella Adderley worked in Sarah Cobb Chase's much larger grief like a painful piece of grit.

To take her mind off their abrasive encounter at the funeral, Sarah tried to file one of those sentimental feature stories, the death of a soldier on foreign soil sort of thing. But she could not even strike out a lead on her typewriter. Almost desperately she decided to leave her lonely hotel room and go over to the Quill Club where there would be other journalists to talk to.

She walked to the Ambassador Hotel three blocks away. Climbing the stairs to the mezzanine, she headed into the Club and found a coterie of journalists in their usual state of frustration at being prevented by government regulations from seeing the war at first hand.

The journalists, to be effective, had to develop their own contacts and prevail upon military personnel to give them choice tidbits about what was happening out in the sharp end. With Colin's help Sarah had been able to file two or three exclusive stories a month whose contents were later picked up on the wire services. Although she had prided herself on being as tough as the next reporter, the first remark that greeted her jabbed into her feelings like a spear.

"Hello, Sarah," a brash young free-lancer from New York greeted. "Hey, I was really sorry to read about your source getting killed. Can I buy you a drink?"

She stared at the callow young would-be war reporter a moment, almost in disbelief. Is that all they thought Colin Adderley was to her? A source? Sarah shook her head and moved down the bar to find an empty stool. She ordered a drink and a girl from one of the South African television stations asked her what her plans were.

"This is my last war," Sarah replied. "I don't know what I'm going to do. I guess I'll head back for New York, maybe go home and spend some time with my parents."

"And miss the elections? That's going to be a big story. Hey, I heard Roger Masefield was coming back as an observer with a delegation of big shots from New York and Washington. He was a pretty good friend of yours, wasn't he?"

"I worked for him once."

"I understand Bullethead and the Dragon Lady really put it to old Roger," the woman reporter went on. "Real dirty trick. Roger trusted Glenlord, gave him a power of attorney I hear, and Glenlord used it to take over the Embassy. Too bad. You could always dig up a story there when you needed it. And Roger was always good for a newsworthy interview. It will be good to have him back. Even if only for a week or two."

Suddenly Sarah realized she was not in a mood to talk to anyone. She left the Quill Club, resisting the cheery suggestions of several of the male reporters that she hang in and have a drink with them. Sarah couldn't really blame them. She had never flaunted her relationship with Colin Adderley, in fact had tried to keep him away from her press colleagues; and usually she could respond to, even enjoy, the suggestive but harmless bantering of which the male reporters made her the object. Everybody said she was the best looking woman in the Salisbury press corps. Now it meant nothing to her, whether or not it was true. There was only one man she wanted to be attractive to, and he was gone.

Sarah slowly descended the stairs to the lobby of the Ambassador and walked out on the street. She paid no attention to the calls from troopies on leave whose eyes were caught by the long legs, swishing hair and the sheer lightweight dress she wore. When she first came to Salisbury, before she had met and fallen in love with Colin Adderley, she used to smile back at the soldiers and enjoyed their attention. How she wished back in those days that Johnny Cravenlow would pay more attention to her. But then Roger Masefield had introduced her to Colin and that was it.

Listlessly she retraced her steps to the Jamison Hotel and took the elevator up to her room. She opened it with her key, locked it behind her and proceeded to her suitcase which she opened. Inside was the nickel-plated .38 she had brought over from the United States. Told that everyone in Rhodesia had a revolver, she had purchased one in a Connecticut sport shop along with a box of .38-caliber rounds.

No, a note was not necessary. There was nothing to say anyway.

It was funny, she thought, she had gone to such lengths to buy the handgun and the only time she'd used it was when Colin Adderley took her out to a firing range and taught her how to shoot.

The only real use it had been to her was the sense of financial security it gave her. She could sell it in Salisbury for at least five times what she paid for it back in Connecticut.

Just as Colin had taught her, she loaded the cylinder with six bullets and snapped it back into place. Irrelevantly, the thought came to her that she only needed one bullet. Then, with the same controlled impetuosity with which she used to throw herself into the cold waters of Long Island Sound early in the summer, she cocked the weapon by pulling the hammer back, put the barrel to her temple and evenly squeezed the handle and trigger.

The following day a worried Mike Cleary, who had been trying to find her, called her room in vain, then tried knocking on her door. Finally he persuaded the hotel authorities to open up her room to see if she was all right.

Mike looked over the hotel manager's shoulder as he turned the key and pushed the door open. What he saw wasn't completely unexpected. Sarah lay on the floor face down as she had fallen, her auburn hair matted in blood.

Chapter 62

Jobolingo had picked four two-man teams of the most thoroughly indoctrinated Freedom Fighters in camp to act as his political action squads. As the main body of ZANLA guerrillas left the staging area, some seven thousand strong and not too badly out of step, Jobo's men fanned out over a three mile area in order to intercept any defectors from the retreating army. It was distressing to see these troops who had been scheduled to go into Zimbabwe and disrupt the elections heading instead in the opposite direction, though Jobolingo was convinced of Rex Nhongo's wisdom in ordering the withdrawal. It angered him, however, that the propaganda of the Salisbury regime was having such a disastrous effect on many of the guerrillas.

How could they fail to see that Bishop Muzorewa, Senator Chief Chirau and the Reverend Ndabaningi Sithole, a defector from the Patriotic Front, were all merely pawns of the white man? Only Comrade Mugabe and his Marxist ideals would bring the new nation of Zimbabwe to greatness for its own native people. He would throw out and kill off the hated white tribe which had come in, built glass and concrete cities and cleared vast tracts of land for farms. The white man lived in the lap of luxury exploiting the African in his own land.

Mercilessly Jobolingo and his action teams had already gunned down those in the camp who in the confusion of the withdrawal had attempted to walk westward toward the Rhodesian border instead of east to the new camp deeper in Mozambique. Undoubtedly during the night some defectors had escaped back to Zimbabwe but they would be taken care of later when ZANLA finally triumphed and Mugabe was in power.

Now, anxiously looking skyward as the sun rose, Jobo was one of the few occupants of what had been the teeming staging area. He wondered how the information about the raid had come from Salisbury but assumed it must be accurate or Comrade Mugabe would not have abandoned his plan to send the Freedom Fighters swarming into Zimbabwe.

As he stood on the tower at the corner of the camp training his binoculars on the bush to the east, Jobo suddenly caught sight of a string of tiny figures, two of them seemingly women. They must have spotted their chance to defect just before the main party left. But they would not reach their Tribal Trust Land in Zimbabwe, Jobo reflected with grim satisfaction; and even as he nursed this thought he heard soothing bursts of distant AK-47 fire which told him that the political action squads were doing their work. Then, to his surprise, he observed what looked like an entire company of men with their dependents coming out of the rising sun back toward the camp. Obviously it was their intention to surrender to the Rhodesian troops as the latter came in. Anyone caught in possession of one of the leaflets that the Rhodesian government had showered along the Mozambique border—leaflets offering amnesty, land, money and security in the new African-controlled Zimbabwe—was shot. Yet somehow they circulated inside the camp.

Jobolingo watched the defecting troops straggle back to the staging area and congratulated himself on having had the foresight to persuade the camp commander not to give the men arms until the moment they actually set out for Zimbabwe. As he counted the defectors he realized how seriously he had miscalculated the true feelings of many of the men in the staging area. His confidence in the exhaustive political indoctrination sessions by which he had set such store was severely shaken. If Rex Nhongo or General Tongogara were here to observe this large-scale defection of the people they had been counting on to fight for Comrade Mugabe's Marxist principles, Jobo would himself be executed. But it was too late for self-criticism now. He would have to act decisively and mercilessly. A few defectors had been anticipated, of course. But in such numbers—he felt sickened to his very core. He watched as the deserters came closer and then, laying down his AK-47, positioned himself behind the tower's RPD machine gun which was mounted on its tripod and ready to fire. Carefully he swung the weapon until the deserters were in his sights. He noted that they had already discarded their uniforms for the denim civilian clothing only to be worn during actual infiltration.

Trembling despite his firm resolve, he waited until the entire group was well within range and could not escape. They were clustered together as if giving each other mutual encouragement. Encouragement to commit this appalling act of treachery.

Gently Jobo depressed the trigger of the machine gun and a hail of deadly fire spewed forth. The victims screamed as he cut them down in precisely timed short bursts, their bodies jumping and twisting grotesquely. Not until he had expended the entire 200-round belt of heavy bullets did he cease firing.

There must have been close to a hundred of the turncoats, not counting their women, who now lay bloody and broken near the eastern fringe of the camp. Some had tried to take refuge in flimsy shacks and tents but the bullets had pitilessly ripped the structures apart, killing all within.

His deed accomplished, Jobo looked up from the scene of carnage and was shocked to see even more of the subversives straggling into the camp. Slinging his AK-47 over his shoulder and picking up a lighter machine gun intended as a supplement to the one on the tripod, he climbed down the tower's ladder and headed out toward the east boundary of the camp.

Out of the seven thousand men in the staging area, he concluded that at least ten percent had been waiting their chance to cross over and join the new, multiracially-ruled Zimbabwe.

Jobo left the camp and pushed on as rapidly as he could, encumbered by his two weapons and the belt of ammunition hanging in loops over his shoulders.

The bush was sparse but he found a rocky hillock, conveniently dotted with prickly shrubs, that overlooked the terrain over which the deserters must come. He set the light machine gun on its bipod and locked the belt into place. Then he waited. And watched. It seemed incredible that the Boers' propaganda about the elections could have been so effective, yet here was the proof of the tenuous hold Comrade

Mugabe had on so many of the Freedom Fighters. Obviously a great deal more indoctrination was needed. But not for these traitors, Jobo told himself in a spasm of vindictiveness. For them it was too late.

The stragglers were coming into plain view, beginning to walk across a patch of open ground directly below Jobolingo's position. He steadied himself behind the gun, pulled the stock firmly into his shoulder, sighted carefully along the barrel—and fired.

Many of the defectors fell at once; others turned to run but were caught in the deadly fire, which shredded their bodies. Jobo didn't stop firing until he had wiped out every last man, woman and child. Then he felt strangely at peace.

So intent was he on his one-man mass execution that he failed to hear the airplanes overhead. It wasn't until he raised his eyes from the satisfying sea of corpses that he saw the parachutes blossoming out of the sky above him. The Boers were coming in.

Jobolingo stood up. Then, abandoning the machine gun and cradling his AK-47 in his arms, he began to run toward the east.

As he loped along he was seized with fits of hysterical laughter at the thought of the attackers' frustration when they realized they'd gone to all this trouble only to capture an empty camp.

Chapter 63

Mack Hudson was the first man out of the lead Dakota as the planes passed over the drop zone three kilometers to the east of Camp Mugabe. Three sticks, comprising seventy-five Selous Scouts, made up this stop group of which Mack was the overall commander. Its purpose was to intercept survivors of the attack on the camp who might be fleeing to the protection of FRELIMO forces in the mountains. The stop group would be the anvil and the attackers from the west would be the hammer. By the time the scouts were in place the helicopters would be bringing in the commandos from the RLI, and further para drops of SAS and Rhodesian African Rifle troops would follow. The mission was considered vital to the success of the upcoming elections.

The sun was beginning to climb over the mountain range just to the east of Camp Mugabe as Mack hit the ground. He disengaged himself from his parachute and stuffed it in the canopy bag which he left to be picked up later. Equipment and ammunition, para-dropped from the plane, lay on the ground nearby and now the rest of Mack's stick, which included Eddie Wilson and Luthu, were gliding down. In minutes they had stowed their chutes and formed up on their commander.

The second stick, led by Captain Turneville, was floating groundward and the third stick was just exiting its Dakota. So far everything was routine and on schedule.

Within twenty minutes from the time Mack landed, the entire stop group was in position. All the Scouts were strung out in one long line, Mack's stick in the middle and his command post in the center of that. Sergeant Horst Houk now walked rapidly down the row of heavily-armed men to determine whether any of them had been injured in the drop. They had not.

"Seems strange, everything's so quiet in there," Mack observed. "They must have seen us come down. You'd think they'd at least be firing a few mortar rounds at us." With binoculars he swept the area between the Selous Scouts' positions and the eastern perimeter of the camp. Then he focused in on one spot and, after a moment, handed the glasses to Turneville. "Turnie, take a look. See if you can make out that rubble on the ground. I can't say for sure but it looks like freshly killed gooks. We were the first in; we haven't killed any terrs. What do you make of it?"

Captain Turneville peered through the binoculars. "You're right, Mack. No doubt about it. Those are bodies. Now what in the hell do you suppose happened?"

"Damned if I know." He looked skyward. "Here comes the rest of the assault force."

"Drive 'em into us, guys!" Eddie Wilson called out. He patted the RPD he had set up on its bipod pointing at Camp Mugabe. "We're ready for 'em!"

Luthu's attention had been caught by some movement in the bush a kilometer or so away and he patted Mack on the shoulder. "Major, I see man out there."

Mack, who frequently marveled at Africans' acuteness of vision, looked in the direction Luthu was pointing but failed to see a human figure. With his binoculars, however, he did—there was a man moving stealthily through the clumps of scrub brush that grew abundantly on this high veldt. Adjusting the focus of the binoculars, he clearly made out an African in camouflage outfit, a rifle in his arms.

"I see him, Luthu. Now what the fuck is one lone terrorist doing crawling away from the camp at sunrise. If he is one of the dissatisfied guerrillas you mentioned, I should think he'd be going in the opposite direction."

"He is not deserter, sir. See, he still wear the camouflage."

"He's probably some kind of courier with a message. Let's see if we can capture him alive."

Over to the west the chuffing of helicopters grew louder, then the ominous whop-whop of the blades could be heard distinctly. The figure in the bush seemed to quicken his pace. Another string of parachute canopies materialized in the sky above Camp Mugabe and the helicopters began settling on the ground. "There hasn't been a shot fired from Camp Mugabe yet. Something's up!" Mack commented.

"Sir, let me go with Luthu to take that man. Maybe we'll find something out from him in interrogation," Eddie Wilson suggested.

"Good idea, Sergeant. You, Luthu and two Scouts go out and bring him back alive. I know it's tough to bring a hardcore terr in alive but I'm sure with your ingenuity you'll figure a way."

"Yes, sir." The four men set off as Mack radioed to all call signs that friendly forces were out in front and fire should be held until further orders. Through his binoculars he watched Wilson's party heading toward the mysterious moving form which appeared to be the only living thing between the line of Scouts and the camp.

Eddie Wilson kept abreast of Luthu as they half crawled, half ran through the open bush keeping a constant eye on their quarry. Obviously the guerrilla cadre, whoever he was, had to be aware of the paratroopers who had landed between him and sanctuary. He seemed to be paralleling the stop group line in an effort to get around it.

Luthu and Wilson were moving at about the same pace as the terrorist, perhaps a little faster. They were well within range of him with their assault rifles but feared that an unlucky shot might kill him. Their target turned, measured the distance between him and his pursuers and then obviously decided to run for it.

Luthu jumped to his feet and began running, followed by the two Scouts, both Africans, and Eddie Wilson. Suddenly their man whirled, dropped to his knees and fired a burst from his AK-47. Wilson threw himself down as the rounds cracked over his head and shouted to Luthu: "I'll try to get around to the other side of him."

Luthu fired a burst from his AK-47, deliberately aiming above the fugitive, who returned fire; then he continued to distract the now prone guerrilla with sporadic rounds as Eddie moved around him in a wide arc, hoping the laser beam sniper scope with which his modified FN rifle was equipped would enable him to squeeze off an accurate shot.

Hudson watched the pursuit through his binoculars, giving a running commentary to Turneville who related it to the call signs up and down the line.

Luthu and the fugitive were still firing at each other when Eddie finally got the latter in his laser sight. He could clearly make out the features of the African and even see the colored spots on his camouflage fatigues which were almost exactly like the jungle uniform of the Rhodesian African Rifles. With intense concentration Eddie sighted on the guerrilla's right shoulder against which he was holding his AK-47. Through the telescopic sight he could see the little red dot which indicated the exact spot where the bullet would hit. He moved the spot fractionally to make it settle in the middle of the upper right chest. Then he squeezed the stock and trigger simultaneously and the bullet sang out of his sniper rifle.

Still looking through the telescopic sight, he saw the weapon suddenly torn from the guerrilla's grasp as a red splotch stained his camouflage suit. At that point he jumped to his feet and started to sprint toward the guerrilla, though he didn't expect to reach him before Luthu and the two other African Scouts who were racing like springboks in the same direction. The wounded man was trying to reach his rifle but his right arm was paralyzed.

Half-dazed from pain and shock as he was, the guerrilla was also tough and evidently in no mood to be captured. He now made a desperate groping plunge with his left arm toward his AK-47, no doubt hoping to fire it from the hip at his attackers. Just as his fingers curled around the weapon, Luthu crashed down upon him, after a flying leap that would have been the envy of a rugby star, and plunged his knife into the outstretched arm. The guerrilla screamed, and in the same instant a wild burst of rounds from his weapon went skimming harmlessly across the veldt.

By the time Eddie Wilson raced up, the man he had shot lay pinned to the ground by the three black Scouts, only his eyes registering resistance. Eddie enjoyed a moment of self-congratulation as he noted the perfection of his shot. Luthu put a noose around the captive's neck and another of the Scouts tied his wrists behind his back. He was bleeding profusely from the wound just below his neck. Eddie's bullet had torn through the clavicle and right shoulder but fortunately had missed an artery and the blood, though flowing steadily, was not pumping out.

Luthu looked up at Eddie Wilson triumphantly. "He is the camp political commissar! I never think we get him." There was a fast exchange of Shona between Luthu and the terr and Eddie could see the shock on the latter's face at being recognized. Luthu grinned broadly. "He very unhappy I know him from time I am in his camp. I listen to him talk all one afternoon."

"Outstanding!" Wilson exclaimed. "We'll get the whole story from him."

They hauled their prisoner to his feet, a knife in the small of his back, and marched him back toward the Selous Scouts, Luthu questioning his prize as they went. Eddie couldn't understand what was being said but looked at Luthu curiously when the captive began to laugh wildly.

"He say everybody go from the camp. He say the Boers make the biggest operation of the year and nobody in the camp." The prisoner continued to laugh as he was marched toward the command post Mack had set up in the middle of the skirmish line.

"Our prisoner tells us there's nobody in Camp Mugabe," Eddie explained to Mack.

Again the prisoner laughed raucously. Luthu pulled his 9mm handgun from its holster and gave his captive a crack across the skull which sent him reeling, effectively silencing him.

"Hey, don't hurt him too bad, Luthu," Mack warned. "He's a valuable prisoner. Special Branch will definitely want to question him."

"His name is Samuel Jobolingo," Luthu continued excitedly.

"Search him, let's see what identification he's got."

One of Luthu's men went through Jobolingo's pockets and fished out a glassine folder containing documents from his inside jacket pocket and a leather wallet from his trousers. Hanging around Jobo's neck on a chain was a gold woman's wrist-watch. Mack took all the items and looked through them.

"This is the same commissar you told us about in the briefing?" Mack asked with a grimace. "The man who boasted about being at Kariba when the plane was shot down?"

"Yes, sir. This him."

Mack turned to Eddie Wilson. "Beautiful shot, Sergeant. Now find Herr Doktor. Have him patch this man up." To Jobolingo he said: "All right, let's talk English. Don't try to hide behind shona language with me."

Jobolingo shook his head and started talking in Shona. Mack looked at Luthu. "Give him another shot on the head, Luthu," he cried. Instinctively Jobo ducked the blow he expected and Mack laughed. "You understand English just fine. Now who are all those dead people out there?"

"Sellouts!" Jobo suddenly cried. "Sellouts going back to the Boers. Death to the Boers!"

Mack's cursory interrogation was interrupted by the crackling of the radio and the arrival of Sergeant Major Princeloo. "The camp is deserted, sir. Not one damn terr inside. They say there are over a hundred bodies they can't account for."

"We can tell them all about it, Sergeant. Any orders for us?"

"None yet, sir. Captain Turneville is coming up from his stick to talk to you."

"Right, Sergeant. Stay by the radio. When we get further orders relay them to me." Mack turned back to Jobolingo. "So you killed all those people trying to get back to their families and Tribal Trust Lands?"

"Yes, sir!" Luthu answered for the prisoner.

"Well, that should be good enough to get him the big drop at Salisbury Central prison," Mack commented. He glanced down at the documents, the wallet and the gold wristwatch he had taken from the prisoner. At that moment Captain Turneville approached him. "Mack, what's the situation out there? We hit an empty camp?"

"Just about empty. Believe it or not, we got the P.C. Never happened before. Apparently he stayed behind to kill any defectors with ideas of going back to Rhodesia. Special Branch should find a lot of interesting information from him before they hang him." Mack sensed the tension in Turneville and noticed he was staring at the items that had been taken from Jobolingo.

"Yeah, we found this stuff on the fucker," he observed uneasily.

Trembling, Turneville reached out and took the gold wristwatch from Mack. He looked at it carefully and then opened the clasp and looked at the inscription on the inside of the gold bracelet. His face suddenly turned white.

"Turnie, what the hell's the matter with you?" Mack cried. "Get a grip on yourself. What is it, man?"

Before any of the startled Scouts could make a move, Turneville had reached out a huge hand and grabbed Jobolingo by the neck. Although Jobolingo was tall and strongly built, Turneville at six foot five was an exceptionally powerful young man and Jobolingo's eyes started to bulge from their sockets, while his knees buckled so that Turneville was almost holding him off the ground by the neck. "Where did you get that watch!" he shouted.

"There's no way he's going to be able to answer if you don't let go of his throat," Mack Hudson put in calmly.

With an added shake for encouragement Turneville released his grip on the guerrilla leader's throat and Jobolingo sagged to the ground.

"Where the hell is Houk before the motherfucker bleeds to death on us," Mack shouted. Then to Turneville: "What is it, Turnie?"

"This was Barbara Curzon's watch."

"Are you sure?" Mack frowned at the unexpected crisis.

"Of course I'm sure. I helped her take it off. It was beside our bed. Her father and mother gave it to her when she graduated from school in England." He thrust the gold watch into Mack's hands. "Look at it, for God's sake. It's got her initials on it and the date of graduation—June 1976."

Mack stared at the watch in silence, turning it over in his hands.

"He couldn't have been involved in that crash. It was done by Nkomo's people. This is a Mugabe commissar."

"He's got her watch. He must have taken it from her after she died."

"He could have bought it from someone," Mack suggested.

"He say he help shoot the plane," Luthu insisted.

Princeloo, who had been looking through the documents Jobolingo was carrying, let out a shout. "Look, right here, he's carrying some sort of dossier on himself. I expect the murdering bugger uses this to show who he is. It's his record of accomplishment, so to speak. Now look here if you will, sir," Princeloo slapped the document. "Right in plain English. He was a liaison officer between Mugabe and Nkomo. He was in Lusaka just before the Rhodesia airline flight was shot down. He's a smart bugger. Look at all the courses he's taken. Maybe he *was* with the terrs who shot the plane down."

"Well, SB will find interrogating this man a rewarding experience," Mack grunted.

A strangled sob came from Turneville's throat. "Look, Yank. This is our affair, not yours. If we take him back, by the time SB finishes with him and he goes on trial, the elections will be over, some black bastard will be running Zimbabwe, he'll be pardoned and out, and for all we know they'll end up giving him a big job in government. I'm going to kill him right now." Turneville turned his AK-47 onto Jobolingo who was still sprawled on the ground.

"You're really going to make it easy on him, aren't you?" Mack said acidly. "If he was one of the gooks who raped and murdered Barbara, he's getting off easy with a couple of bullets through his heart, isn't he?"

A look of terror came into Jobolingo's face as he squinted up at the American major.

"Shit, Major, you're right," Turneville acknowledged. "Just plain shooting is too good for the hout." He glared down at Jobolingo. "How did you get this watch, you munt bastard?"

Jobolingo, weak from loss of blood, nearly out of his head with pain and despair, experienced a surge of defiance and momentary strength. He was going to die, he knew. He wanted to die fast, not as the victim of the Boers' torture which he had been told many times was horrible beyond belief. He looked into the barrel of the AK-47 from whence an honorable and sudden death would be the best thing that could happen to him now. "Death to the Boers!" he screamed. "You will all die when Comrade Mugabe takes over. I fuck your women. I fuck your nuns. I fucked your woman from the plane crash. I fucked her, the boys all fucked her, then killed her with a bayonet. She liked my fuck better than any she got from the white man!"

Mack Hudson leaped at the AK-47 in Turneville's hand as it spit a burst of fire, the bullets narrowly missing the shrieking guerrilla and pounding harmlessly into the earth.

Turneville glared at his commanding officer and seemed on the verge of turning the gun on him, but Mack steadily fixed the towering Rhodesian's eyes with his own. His chest heaving, Turneville slowly regained control of himself. After what seemed like a struggle to find words, he sobbed out, "Thanks, Mack. He tried to buy a quick death."

"Look, I'm for killing the fucker just as much as you are. But judging by his papers he could be a valuable source of information."

"And then go free after what he did?"

"I doubt if even the new African prime minister, whoever is elected, would pardon him," Mack remarked. "In any case, there's going to be a lot of fighting left after the elections. Mugabe isn't going to give up. SB will crack this Kaffir and what they get out of him could change the war. They can probably find out who compromised this operation."

Turneville stared at the small gold watch in his huge palm, tears in his eyes. Mack was deeply touched. Yes, the man *should* get his justice. He put an arm around Turneville's shoulder and gripped him tightly in understanding and sympathy.

"You're right, Turnie, I'm a Yank. The decision is up to you as the ranking Rhodesian officer here. There's plenty of time to give him a slow death in as imaginative a way as you can conceive. He's all yours. I'm going over to the big means radio to raise Brigadier MacIntyre's headquarters. I'll report one terrorist captured but dying."

Jobolingo's head turned, his eyes following Mack as he walked away from the group of Boers who now were free to inflict the horrifying death he had been taught to expect.

Mack walked down the line of disappointed Selous Scouts who had been anticipating the destruction of Camp Mugabe and its terrs with relish. The VHF radio operator saw him coming. "Major Hudson, Brigadier MacIntyre is trying to raise you."

Mack reported in on the radio: "Tango Foxtrot Sunray to Op Mugabe Sunray."

The voice of the commanding officer of the operation crackled back. "Operation Mugabe Sunray here. The enemy withdrew before we arrived." The disgust and disappointment in his Scotch burr came through strongly. "Anything to report?"

"No, sir. We captured one Charlie Tango in very bad condition, not expected to live."

"Tango Foxtrot Sunray, listen to me! Try to keep him alive. Have you learned anything from him?"

"Apparently he executed the defectors whose bodies are in the camp," Mack reported. A shrill, wailing scream from behind him pierced the air. Mack hoped it hadn't gone over the radio.

The operation commander's voice continued. "If you can possibly keep the C.T. alive, it would be very useful to interrogate him."

Mack waited until a second quavering shriek of agony died down before pressing the transmitter button on the microphone. "I'm sorry, sir, I don't think that's possible now."

"Tango Foxtrot Sunray," the voice came urgently over the radio. "I'm sending a helicopter to your position instantly. An Op Starlight will be on board—" A doctor was coming, but the agonized screeches Mack had just heard left little hope that he'd find a live prisoner. "I'm dispatching the casevac chopper this instant," MacIntyre continued anxiously. "Tell your medic to do his best."

"Roger Op Mugabe Sunray. Foxtrot Tango Sunray out." Mack Hudson shrugged hopelessly and walked back to observe Jobolingo's death throes. At least this grisly revenge would have the effect of exorcising the trauma which had been torturing Turneville's psyche since that ghastly morning when the Scouts had been helicoptered to the scene of the crash as a prelude to tracking the terrorists who had murdered the survivors.

To his surprise Jobolingo was alive when he returned. He was lying spread-eagled, naked from the waist down, his clothes having been slashed from him. Houk was performing some extensive medical service to the terrorist in the groin area. The man's eyes were wide open, his eyeballs were rolling in his head and in his mouth was stuffed an outsized black penis and a large set of testicles. He was barely able to breathe enough air through his nose to sustain life.

"Major," a grinning Turneville greeted him, "we discovered a means by which we could have our cake and eat it too, so to speak."

Mack looked down grimly at the writhing terrorist. "So I see."

"If they don't hang him, at least he won't be producing any more bloody murdering little Kaffir bastards," Turneville breathed hoarsely.

"Oh he'll be able to sing when he's questioned, sir," Princeloo added. "In a bright loud soprano."

"Ja, if I can keep him from bleeding to death," Houk threw in. "I wish I had some plasma now."

"You'll have everything you need in about two minutes," Mack assured the medic, noting out of the corner of his eye that the casevac chopper was already hovering close by. Mack faced Turneville. "Turnie, if I might make a suggestion, perhaps you could remove the fucker's cock and balls from his mouth before we send him back. It's perfectly legitimate that we shot them off when he resisted capture but explaining how they ended up in his mouth might prove dicey."

The chopper's huge rotor blades were now beating the air above them.

"I guess you're right, sir," Turneville agreed, deftly obliging with the point of his knife.

Jobolingo's eyes were glazed with agony, but Turneville felt no pity. "Now, you lucky Communist bloody bastard, you and your bossman, Comrade Mugabe, have something in common that you can talk together about if you ever live to see him again."

The helicopter had settled down close to the command post and already two corpsmen with a stretcher were running toward the wounded guerrilla, followed by a brisk-stepping military doctor carrying a black bag. The doctor looked at Jobolingo in surprise as he was lifted onto the stretcher. "He's in much better shape than I was led to believe."

"We have the finest medic in the army here," Mack said. "You can thank Herr Doktor Houk for keeping this terr alive for the benefit of SB."

"Just pump a couple of pints of plasma into him, sir," Houk suggested. "He'll be in good enough shape to answer any questions they want to ask." The doctor looked suspiciously at the bandages about the groin. "What happened there?"

"Doctor," Mack chided, "we were lucky to take this terr alive without suffering casualties of our own. Just so happens we have a superb sniper."

"I understand," the doctor replied dubiously. "Congratulations, Doctor Houk."

"Doctor Houk is what I hope to be, sir, after I've gone to the University of Salisbury."

"Good luck, then."

As the doctor prepared to follow the stretcher-bearers to the helicopter Mack reminded him, "This man is a terrorist, doctor. I would like to send one of my men back with him. He might be strong enough to cause trouble on the chopper. I've seen it happen with the fuckers."

"Good idea, Major," the doctor assented.

"Princeloo, go with them. Make sure that gook doesn't suddenly get enough strength back to start any tricks."

"Don't worry, sir," Princeloo answered with a broad smile. "I think I know how to handle him. And I'll take him over to SB personally."

Mack Hudson watched the helicopter lift off and remarked to Turneville, "Well, I guess we can now look forward to a reasonably peaceful election. It'll take the terrs a while to replace *that* fellow."

"I guess so, sir. God knows what's going to come up, but we'll learn to live with Zimbabwe-Rhodesia all right. As for the three candidates, they all seem like pretty decent blokes and for my part I don't care who gets elected even though one of them probably compromised this mission. At least we won't be living under the goddamn commies."

Chapter 64

On April 18, 1979, Rhodesia became the setting for the first non-coercive, multiracial, universal-franchise elections in the history of Africa.

The populace were given a five-day period in which to find a convenient time to register their preference for one of the three prime-ministerial candidates, Abel Muzorewa, Ndabaningi Sithole and Senator Chief Chirau, the winner to bear the title of Prime Minister Designate until such time as he and his cabinet could smoothly take over the reigns of government from Ian Smith and be legally sworn in.

During the five days a spirit of carnival prevailed throughout the country, a spirit in large measure due to the ceaseless vigilance and fighting prowess of the Rhodesian armed forces, and in particular to the activities of the Selous Scouts whose lightning strikes against the terrorists' staging areas in Mozambique had seriously damaged their assault capability and knocked their strategy into disarray. Where necessary the government laid on special buses to get the voters to the polling booths in outlying areas; many of the larger white farmers did the same for their workers and their workers' families, or, more commonly, used their own trucks for the purpose. The vast majority of Africans streamed along by bicycle or on foot. Far from being bloodbaths, the polling booths were scenes of festive orderliness as chattering villagers and townsfolk lined up to cast their vote and in many cases were entertained by bands of dancers and singers who, in typically African fashion, seemed to spring out of the occasion itself.

Seventy-six observers from free-world nations plus hordes of newsmen flew into the country by the planeload, straining to the utmost the Rhodesian government's capacity to fly them to whatever distant polling area they chose to visit. They even came from Britain and the United States, countries whose leaders took a jaundiced view of the elections and, certainly in the latter case, had tried to ensure that they never took place.

Among these visitors, though he came more to carp than to observe, was Lord Banglish, accompanied by an English girl of somewhat washed-out beauty called Margot whom the acidulous peer described as his secretary. While Banglish watched the electoral process, Margot watched "Bangie"; she was notably silent as she followed him around, perhaps because she had nothing to say, and it was clear that her principal function was to act as a decorative sounding board.

Unlike most of the observers, Lord Banglish confined his attention to the Salisbury area. To M. M. De Vries and other Rhodesian officials, who extended a courteous greeting to the sharp-nosed little peer even though they detested the British Laborite views he represented, he seemed snappish and, for some reason that they couldn't fathom, out-of-sorts. The fact was that since the death of his genuine friend Johnny Cravenlow, Lord Banglish had been finding fewer and fewer people ready to listen to him. Indeed he was now somewhat in the position of a court jester without a court, not that his political comments had ever contained much humor. After two days of seeing what he wanted to see and ignoring the rest, he flew back to London, Margot in tow, muttering things like "rigged elections" and "monumental confidence game" to anyone within hearing. Not too many people had come to the airport to see him off.

Another observer, though of a very different kind, was Roger Masefield whose PI order was temporarily rescinded by the Minister Plenipotentiary when he announced his intention of traveling in the company of an influential and independent-minded Republican ex-senator whom MM was particularly anxious not to offend.

"Do you see who I see, Al?" Beryl whispered to the bullet-headed CIA man at her side as they stood among a knot of foreign dignitaries in the crowded waiting room at New Sarum Air Force Base. These VIPs were about to emplane for Chipinga near the Mozambique border, site of the "hottest" polling booth in the elections and therefore the one with the most showcase value for the Rhodesian government.

"Christ, Masefield," Glenlord responded, almost without moving his lips. "Quick, let's go get some coffee. And let's hope to God he isn't going to Chipinga."

But they were a fraction too late.

"Hi, you two," Roger cried in his breeziest voice. "Off to watch the polling? Or you got something other than watching in mind, Al?" Roger gave Glenlord a slow music-hall wink that made the CIA colonel wish he were back at Langley, while the muscles along his cheek tightened and his eyes darted nervously to the people nearby.

"Good to see you," Glenlord said unconvincingly. "By the way, Roger, about the—"

"Good to see you too, Al," Roger cut in, before turning away abruptly and lavishing a beaming smile on Beryl. "How's the Embassy, Beryl, if I can still call it that? You must be having quite a lot of fun there, I should think. Though I don't suppose you have too many Crippled Eagles coming around, right? Oh well, they always were a bit noisy, those guys."

Beryl was searching in her mind for some suitably caustic rejoinder, but the circumstances made the task too difficult. She forced her lips into a bleak grin.

Just then, striding toward them, the very acme of elegance in a navy blue pin-striped suit topped with a white carnation, was M. M. De Vries. As the Minister caught sight of Roger, he seemed to make a slight swerve and his smile flickered, but he bore on toward Al and Beryl with whom he had arranged to fly to Chipinga.

"MM," Roger greeted him affably. "Nice of you to let me come back and see the show. This is a great day for Rhodesia."

"Ah, Mr. Masefield," MM returned. "You're here. Yes, this is a great day for Rhodesia. And a bad day for the Communists—I hope."

"The observers' flight for Chipinga is now boarding," fluted a female announcer's voice over the loudspeaker. "Will all passengers have their passes ready."

Beryl hoped desperately that Roger would sit well away from them on the Dakota, a plane that until the previous week had been ferrying paratroopers to their drop zones, but this was not to be. Roger seated himself in a bucket seat directly across the aisle from the Minister and his two friends and frequently grinned at them throughout the noisy flight, to their acute discomfort.

After the briefing that night at the Meikels Hotel, where the election results for the day were posted, together with encouraging military reports indicating that terrorist activity was minimal, Roger Masefield threw a party in his spacious suite at the Monomotopa for all the Crippled Eagles that were still in Rhodesia and could get to Salisbury. He had sent out the invitations before leaving the States.

Carla Hudson seemed to be the happiest person at the party, which turned out to be the last gathering of the Crippled Eagles in Rhodesia.

"We're going home, we really are, Roger. Mack's three years are up; he served out his contract. He was going to sign up again but for once I was able to convince him to go home first and think it over. Once we get back to the States I think he'll stay."

"Don't count on it, Carla," Roger said. "And don't forget when you and Mack get back you're to come and stay with Jocelyn and me in New York."

"We're looking forward to it," Carla answered. "You know, it's funny. Look at Mack over there with the other Americans. He won't admit it to himself but in another month we'll be on our way to the U.S. Huey McCall is staying . . . Oh! There he is. I'll bring him over and stop him from trying to talk Mack into renewing his contract."

"You know Mack, he'll do what he's got to do."

"He wants to go get his Ph.D. and be a teacher of political science," Carla said.

"They should give him a Ph.D. in military science just for what he's been through here in the last three years," Roger called after her as she moved cheerfully off to get Huey.

Eddie Wilson and Joe Late were drinking beer and discussing their future when Roger came up to them.

"Tomorrow we'll get the election results," Roger said. "There'll be an African Prime Minister Designate, and more of the guerrillas will stop fighting and come over to the new black government. Are you all staying on?"

"I'm beginning to think I found a home in Rhodesia," said Huey McCall who had just joined the group. "I've got a Rhodesian wife, Josie. I've got a Rhodesian son almost a year old. I haven't anything to go back to in the United States except a government that gives our money away to welfare and to supporting half-ass little Marxist dictatorship countries all over the world. No, I'm going to become a Rhodesian. When this war is over I'm going to buy a farm and become rich growing tobacco or tea or coffee or some other money crop."

"What are you going to do, Eddie?" Roger asked.

"Well, I've still got one year to go on my contract."

"That doesn't mean anything," an American voice chipped in. "Didn't you go to the meeting at army headquarters? Any American, any foreigner who wants to get out of the army can put through an application and he'll be out in one month. Doesn't make any difference who wins the election, the Africans don't want us here in the army."

"Well, I think I'll stay around until my contract is up anyway," Eddie Wilson declared.

"The Selous Scouts are putting up a safe house down in South Africa near Joburg," Joe Late commented. "If this newly elected government doesn't hold together and the Communists take over we'll all have to get out of here. You know what Mugabe and Nkomo say. All Selous Scouts will be executed. Do you think the United States is going to let whoever is elected tomorrow form a government and run this country peacefully? If you do you don't remember Vietnam. We blew it. We gave it to the Communists. And what about Taiwan? We kicked them out of the United Nations and brought the commies in. You think President Carter, you think Andy Young, you think those Communists are going to let Rhodesia exist in peace? Hell no. We'll fight, but we've learned that no matter how well we fight, no matter how many good men die, in the end we can count on the good old State Department of the United States to sell us down the river."

"So why don't you give up then, Joe?" one of the Crippled Eagles called out across the room.

"Why don't *you* give up?" Joe called back.

Eddie Wilson summed it up for all of them. "As long as we keep fighting the Mugabes, the Nkomos, the Idi Amins, all the Marxist revolutionaries who are nibbling away the free world country by country, as long as we keep *fighting*, maybe some day America will get its guts back and save what's left of the free world." He took a moody gulp of his beer. "Before it's too late."

"Eddie's right," said Mack Hudson who had been listening to the conversation for the past few moments. "As long as some of us keep fighting, others will join and it may not be too late."

"Sure, we'll keep fighting, Mack," another Yank avowed. "We'll think of you back there becoming a professor at some liberal college in the United States."

"Oh you're going to love it!" Eddie Wilson said with jovial sarcasm.

"Sergeant! At ease."

"Civilian! Fuck off!" There was a wide grin on Eddie Wilson's face as he delivered this coup de grace.

"Touché, Eddie," Mack replied. "I don't think I'm going to last as a civilian. But I'll give it my best shot."

"What do you think, Carla?" Roger asked quietly.

"He'll never make it. We'll be back somewhere. He's already talking to that South African major in the Scouts, Conrad Van Roolyan, about a commission in a South African airborne reconnaissance unit."

Roger lifted his drink and called out, "Gentlemen. May the white tribe and all the tribes here in Rhodesia-Zimbabwe learn to live and work in harmony as a result of the fair elections you fought so hard to bring about."

Epilogue

The Rhodesian elections of April 1979, pronounced democratic and fair by observers from the western world including the American civil rights leader Bayard Rustin resulted in a multiracial government led by Prime Minister Abel Muzorewa. This "Uncle Tom" was unacceptable to Andrew Young and therefore to President Jimmy Carter even though duly elected by the entire population of Rhodesia.

Within a year another election was decreed by the United States and the United Kingdom. In this British-supervised election rife with gun-barrel coercion on the part of the Soviet- and Red-Chinese-supported Patriotic Front, Robert Mugabe easily overcame his undisciplined rival Joshua Nkomo in bloody factional warfare and the Marxist guerrilla leader swept into power. Mugabe wasted little time consolidating his hold on the government of Zimbabwe, bringing the North Korean Fifth Brigade into his country to train his military and police in the fine art of political repression.

President Jimmy Carter announced that the visit of Robert Mugabe to Washington D.C. was the most "emotional day" he had known in the White House. Eleven years after the "one-man one-vote one-time" election of Mugabe, the Marxist dictator is still in the process of confiscating white-tribe-owned farm lands with an order to strip former Prime Minister Ian Smith of his farm in southern Zimbabwe. Immediately after Mugabe became Prime Minister of Zimbabwe the Selous Scouts and many other black and white Rhodesians who had supported moderate African leaders for Prime Minister, such as Bishop Abel Muzorewa, and resisted Mugabe's Marxist encroachment were forced into exile in South Africa.

Mugabe's longevity has been a surprise to observers of the Zimbabwe political scene since an operation for cancer of the penis brought on by syphilis resulted in the loss of vital parts without which Africans believe no man can be an accepted leader. For this reason the men around Mugabe considered the post of Deputy Prime Minister the stepping stone to the number one spot.

General Josiah Tongogara died in an "automobile accident" in Mozambique just days before his arch rival for the number two spot under Mugabe, Rex Nhongo, arrived in Salisbury which became Harare in the New Zimbabwe. Nhongo played a prominent role in the 1980 installation of Robert Mugabe as the communist dictator of the new one party government which has lasted eleven years and shows no signs of becoming less repressive.

And now the Rhodesia-Zimbabwe scene is replaying itself in South Africa. The moderate leadership of Zulu Chief Mangosuthu Buthelezi is being challenged and opposed by the Marxist oriented African National Congress (ANC) led by Nelson Mandela, its provisional president. Mandela and the ANC continue the armed struggle and it is appropriate that its most militant wing's group leader is named Terror Lekota.

The battle against moderation in taking control of the South African government when the White Tribe relinquishes power has been firmly joined by Mugabe. In a direct political attack on Buthelezi and his Zulu Inkatha movement, Mugabe invited Mandela and the ANC leaders to meet in the capital city of Zimbabwe where the Harare Declaration was drawn up.

This document clearly spells out the ANC's intention not to negotiate with the present South African Government in the presence of any other political party. It also calls for the present South African government to relinquish power and turn it over wholesale directly to the ANC thus establishing Mandela as President-for-life in a Zimbabwe model one-man one-vote one-time election.

It should have come as no surprise that when Ethiopia's Marxist dictator, Mengistu Haile Mariam, fled his country just ahead of the rebel armies in May of 1991, he pitched up in Harare to seek the protection of his friend and fellow Marxist dictator Robert Mugabe. Mengistu was responsible for the violent death of untold hundreds of thousands of his countrymen by violence and famine.

Mugabe went to his old allies, such as Andrew Young, who had forced the handover of Rhodesia to him. With their help he began to "sell" the Harare Declaration. First, The Organization of African Unity endorsed it, and then the Non-Aligned Countries followed suit. Finally it was taken to the United Nations where its substance was endorsed with minor reservations.

In an effort to promulgate the spirit of the Harare Document, Nelson Mandela visited the United States. After a tumultuous welcome in Washington, New York, Boston and other American cities Mandela visited his true hero, Fidel Castro in Cuba. The African National Congress president is being hailed as the true leader of black nationalism in South Africa by those Americans who consider moderation among black leaders as betrayal of their race.

There will almost certainly be burgeoning armed conflict between the ANC and Chief Buthelezi's Inkatha Freedom Party. The ANC is using the Harare Declaration to establish its "rightful" accension to power even though it is not a people's document, endorsed by the people of South Africa.

Buthelezi is not abandoning his principles of moderation and peaceful negotiation with the existing government even though the ANC refused to even sit in on discussions with Prime Minister F.W. DeClerk's government if any representatives of any party other than the ANC were present.

In his book *South Africa, My Vision of the Future,* Buthelezi writes, probably for Nelson Mandela to read and heed, as follows. "I warn now of troubled times ahead. I warn in the sense of the old Zulu folk tale of a herdboy who tells a passing stranger that there is a deadly snake around the next bend and to be careful that it does not rise up and strike him. The fact that the herdboy knew of the danger did not mean that he put the snake there."

Meanwhile, even as the Nkomo and Mugabe factions in Rhodesia battled each other as well as the white led government in the late 1970s, we can expect to see continued bloody factional fighting between Buthelezi's Zulu Inkatha brigades and Mandela's mostly Xosha ANC hordes until, when the White Tribe relinquishes power, one or the other prevails.

It is also interesting to consider that many veterans of the Rhodesian war against the Nkomo-Mugabe terrorists, including Selous Scouts, have been living in South Africa since 1980 and support the moderate stance of Buthelezi against the one-party political system the ANC is trying to establish.

As of this writing Buthelezi is reportedly prepared to utilize the discipline and experience of some of the old Rhodesian hands if the ANC declared armed struggle compromises his political position. His offering of peace and understanding between the black and white tribes, as opposed to the ANC's oft stated intention to inflict Mugabe style punishment on the former ruling White Tribe, could bring many capable people, black and white, to Buthelezi's banner.